366

**A Leap Year of
Great Stories from History**

366

A Leap Year of
Great Stories from History

W.B. Marsh and Bruce Carrick

ICON BOOKS UK   TOTEM BOOKS USA

Published in the UK in 2007 by
Icon Books Ltd, The Old Dairy,
Brook Road, Thriplow,
Cambridge SG8 7RG
email: info@iconbooks.co.uk
www.iconbooks.co.uk

Reprinted 2007

Sold in the UK, Europe, South Africa and Asia
by Faber & Faber Ltd, 3 Queen Square,
London WC1N 3AU
or their agents

Distributed in the UK, Europe, South Africa and Asia
by TBS Ltd, TBS Distribution Centre, Colchester Road
Frating Green, Colchester CO7 7DW

This edition published in Australia in 2007
by Allen & Unwin Pty Ltd,
PO Box 8500, 83 Alexander Street,
Crows Nest, NSW 2065

This edition published in the USA
in 2008 by Totem Books
Inquiries to Icon Books Ltd.,
The Old Dairy, Brook Road,
Thriplow, Cambridge
SG8 7RG, UK

Distributed to the trade in the USA by
National Book Network Inc.,
4501 Forbes Boulevard, Suite 200,
Lanham, Maryland 20706

Distributed in Canada by
Penguin Books Canada,
90 Eglinton Avenue East, Suite 700,
Toronto, Ontario M4P 2YE

ISBN 978-1840468-27-4

Typesetting by Hands Fotoset

Printed and bound in the UK by
J.H. Haynes & Co. Ltd

Contents

CONTENTS

CONTENTS

CONTENTS

Preface

FOR MOST of us, some dates have an instant connection to great historical events. For example, 11 November signifies the end of the First World War and 4 July is America's declaration of independence. For those with a greater interest in history, 21 October may mean Horatio Nelson's victory and death at Trafalgar. But most days in the calendar no longer conjure up images of events gone by – even most of the French have forgotten that Joan of Arc was born on Epiphany. It is our belief, however, that something exciting and memorable happened on every day of the year.

We put this idea to the test in 2005 when we published *365 – Great Stories from History for Every Day of the Year*. Its popularity showed that a great many readers shared our love of history and enjoyed the historical accounts that the book contained. When our publishers at Icon Books asked us to do another volume, we were happy to agree.

As in our first book, on each day we have tried to tell a full story in a brief space, with as much colour and anecdotal background as we could pack in. We have also attempted to bring to life the individuals involved, with arresting details and entertaining quotations that we hope enliven the stories.

The selection of what we cover is inevitably arbitrary owing to the vast array of history from which to pick. We include births, deaths, marriages, funerals, coronations, assassinations, scandals, executions, battles, publication dates, duels, and treaties. Often the stories involve famous figures, like Augustus Caesar, Galileo, Richard the Lionheart, Benjamin Franklin, the Marquis de Sade, Napoleon and Dostoyevsky. There is even a story about Robin Hood. We've also tried to include interesting historical minutiae, like the tale of Britain's last-ever cavalry charge – with Winston Churchill in the saddle.

Many of the stories cover truly momentous occasions, such as the fall of Rome to barbarians (24 August AD 410), French King Philip the Fair's suppression of the Templars (3 April 1312), Mehmet's the Conqueror's taking of Constantinople (29 May 1453) and the start of the Spanish Civil War (18 July 1936).

Other events recounted in this book may not be so earth-shattering but are, we hope, equally entertaining. Examples include the origins of Valentine's Day (14 February 270), the death in the Bastille of the Man in the Iron Mask (19 Nov 1703), Howard Carter's discovery of the tomb of Tutankhamen (4 November 1922) and the début of the bikini on a catwalk in Paris (5 July 1946).

In all, our stories cover some six thousand years, the earliest one dated 23 October 4004 BC – the Beginning of the World (for those Creationists among our audience). The most recent is the building of the Berlin Wall (12 August 1961). We have not included more recent seismic occurrences such as Richard Nixon's resignation in 1974 because we regard them as current events rather than history.

We have tried to be as historically accurate as possible, sometimes a difficult task when historians disagree even about facts, let alone interpretations. But, in the spirit of offering an entertaining narrative, we have on occasion included reported historical detail that today may not seem altogether credible, such as the 'fact' that the monks in Winchester were forced to move Alfred the Great's remains from the church where they were originally buried when the King's ghost took to wandering in the cloister at night.

Many great men have rather disapproved of history. George Santayana called it 'a pack of lies about events that never happened told by people who weren't there,' while Henry Ford famously declared that 'history is more or less bunk.' Perhaps the most damning definition comes from the American writer Ambrose Bierce, who wrote in *The Devil's Dictionary* in 1911: 'HISTORY, n. An account mostly false, of events mostly unimportant, which are brought about by rulers mostly knaves, and soldiers mostly fools.'

While not denying the opinions of our betters, we suggest that history, for us at least, above all is entertainment, an endlessly shifting kaleidoscope of fascinating people doing their best (or sometimes their worst) to shape their lives and the world they lived in. To us, history's only drawback is that there is so much of it. Having crammed 366 historical stories into a single book, we can only agree with Henry James's comment that 'it takes a great deal of history to produce a little literature.'

For those readers who might be entertained by some of the historical events covered in our first volume, *365: Great Stories from History for Every Day of the Year*, we have marked them in **boldface** in the sections entitled *Also on this day* that appear at the end of each day's story. *365: Great Stories from History for Every Day of the Year* is available in most good bookstores and through Icon Books – www.iconbooks.co.uk.

1 January

Lincoln frees America's slaves

1863 On this day Abraham Lincoln's Emancipation Proclamation became law, freeing the 4 million slaves living in the Confederate states. Most of these remained in bondage for another two years, until the North had finally won the Civil War.

Slavery in the Americas was neither unique to the United States nor new. Since time immemorial, many of the indigenous Indian tribes such as the Comanche, Yurok, Pawnee and Creek owned slaves, and by the time Lincoln freed America's, an estimated 7–10 million blacks had been shipped from Africa. Many were brought to the American states but far more went to the Caribbean and South America, especially to Brazil.

Although there had been slaves in the American colonies almost since the first arrival of the British (slavery was abolished in Great Britain only in 1772), the number of slaves grew dramatically after American independence, increasing from 650,000 to 3,838,765 in 1860, according to the census that year.

Ripped out of Africa with no hope of ever returning, America's slaves were generally docile and accepting of their bleak fate, but there were occasional rebellions such as the 1739 Stono uprising in South Carolina, the Gabriel plot in Virginia in 1800; the Denmark Vesey conspiracy in South Carolina in 1822; and, in particular, Nat Turner's two-day revolt in 1831 in rural Virginia, in which about 75 black slaves ruthlessly slaughtered 60 whites before being killed or hanged. None of the rebellions had even the remotest chance of actually freeing any slaves, let alone bringing to an end the institution.

The ending of slavery was an extended process in America. The Vermont constitution of 1777 outlawed slavery (although Vermont did not become a state until 1791). Pennsylvania abolished it in 1780, and other northern states followed suit. In 1808 all importation of slaves was outlawed. The southern states, however, dependent on slave labour for house servants and particularly to pick their extensive cotton fields, came to see slavery not only as an economic imperative but also as part of God's Great Plan, with the black man forever subordinate.

By the time of Lincoln's election to president in 1860, many northerners were demanding vociferously that all slaves be freed. But, with the advent of the Civil War the next year, abolition was not Lincoln's foremost goal. Holding the United States together as a single nation was his primary reason for leading his country into war. 'If I could save the Union without freeing *any* slaves, I would do it', Lincoln wrote, 'and if I could save it by freeing *all* the slaves I would do it; and if I could save it by freeing some and leaving others alone, I would also do that'.

By 1862, however, Lincoln had come to realise that the only way to save the Union was through military victory, and he knew that Emancipation would not only weaken the South economically but would also give the North a higher moral posture. What he wanted was to strike a double blow, one against the enemy's army, the other against his economy, and both with a background of high moral purpose. He therefore delayed announcing the Proclamation until he had a major victory in hand. On 17 September, the Battle of Antietam provided him with that (although history rates it as a draw rather than a Union victory), and five days later he issued the Emancipation Proclamation, which came into effect on 1 January the next year.

Also on this day

1431: Roderigo Borgia (Pope Alexander VI) is born * 1449: Florentine leader Lorenzo de' Medici (the Magnificent) is born * 1515: François I becomes King of France on the death of Louis XII * **1660: Samuel Pepys starts his diary** * 1729: British statesman Edmund Burke is born * 1735: American revolutionary Paul Revere is born * 1901: The Australian Commonwealth is established

> Events written in **boldface** are covered in full in
> *365: Great Stories from History for Every Day of the Year*,
> the first volume in this series.

2 January

A Welsh buccaneer loses his treasure

1669 The Welsh pirate captain Henry Morgan was violent, cruel and so successful that he was occasionally sent on missions against the Spanish with secret backing from the English government.

One of Morgan's more infamous exploits was the sacking of Porto Bello on the coast of Panama in 1668. Rather than his usual thunderous assault, under cover of darkness the captain and his crew boarded canoes and paddled noiselessly into the harbour. They quickly overpowered two of the surprised forts, but one more remained, now alerted and staunchly defended. Morgan then rounded up several captured priests and nuns and used them as human shields as his crew attacked the fort. The appalled and dispirited Spaniards soon surrendered and were forced to ransom their city with 200,000 pieces of eight and several hundred slaves.

At the beginning of following year Morgan was sailing off the coast of Haiti on the 150-foot *Oxford*, heavily laden with treasure – the pieces of eight from Porto Bello plus his own fabulous personal collection of jewels, gold and silver.

But Captain Morgan was not to enjoy his treasure. While the *Oxford* was anchored near the Ile à Vache, he decided to throw a victory banquet to celebrate the capture of two French ships and unwisely ordered a pig to be barbecued on deck. Sparks from the fire flew into the powderhold, triggering a mammoth explosion that blew off the front of the ship. Morgan was propelled through a window in his cabin and escaped to raid another day, but most of his 250 sailors – and all the treasure – sank to the bottom.

Six years later Morgan returned to Haiti but failed to find his sunken booty. For over three centuries countless treasure hunters have had no more success, but in April 2004 a team of professional divers finally located the wreck in only twelve feet of water. To date they have found cannon, powder barrels and musket balls, but so far the fabulous treasure has continued to elude them.

Also on this day

AD 17: (By tradition) Roman poet Ovid and Roman historian Livy die * **1492: Spanish monarchs Ferdinand and Isabella capture Granada, the last Moorish stronghold in Spain** * 1635: Cardinal Richelieu establishes the Académie Française

3 January

Nietzsche goes insane

1889: Today Friedrich Nietzsche suffered a mental collapse in the streets of Turin, an event that put him in the care of his sister, who paradoxically ensured both his eventual deification by Germany's Nazis and his posthumous fame as a great thinker.

Nietzsche had been born near Leipzig in 1844. He was a brilliant but sickly child, plagued by migraines and severe stomach problems. While a student at the University of Leipzig, he took time off to serve in the Prussian artillery, where he was seriously injured while mounting a horse. He became a professor at Basel, but in 1870 his poor health was permanently shattered when he caught diphtheria and dysentery as a medical orderly during the Franco-Prussian War. Nonetheless, in 1872 he published his first book, *The Birth of Tragedy from the Spirit of Music*, but sickness soon forced him to relinquish most of his professorial duties.

Finally, in 1879, Nietzsche's illnesses compelled him to search for a more salubrious climate, and for the next eleven years he wandered between Genoa, Rapallo, Turin and Nice in the winters and St Moritz and Sils Maria in the summers. According to the historian Bernd Magnus: 'Seriously ill, half-blind, in virtually unrelenting pain, he lived ... with only limited human contact.' But, despite his condition, these were his most productive years; his work included *Thus Spoke Zarathustra, Beyond Good and Evil, On the Genealogy of Morals* and *The Antichrist*. Although his output was huge, few appreciated it; he even had to finance the printing of two of these works himself.

Then came his breakdown in Turin. As he walked through the Piazza Carlo Alberto, he saw a horse being whipped. Running across the square, he threw his arms around the horse's neck to shield it and collapsed to the ground. From this moment he spoke incoherently, screamed repeatedly and was often delirious, unaware of where he was.

Brought to a psychiatric clinic in Basel, Nietzsche showed no improvement (he thought an orderly was Prince Bismarck), so he was put in the care of his mother in Naumburg. But his insanity was permanent, probably the result of tertiary syphilis; it looked as if he might die, largely unknown, in his mother's care. But in 1893, Nietzsche's sister Elisabeth returned from Paraguay after the suicide of her rabidly anti-Semitic husband, where the 'pure Aryan' colony they had founded had collapsed. Within four years she had taken her demented brother into her own household, where he died in 1900, probably from pneumonia.

Nietzsche once wrote that some men are born posthumously, a perfect description of himself.

On his death, Elisabeth determined to use his writings to support her own proto-Nazi views. She gained control of his manuscripts, renamed her family home the Nietzsche-Archiv and transformed her dead brother's image into that of her dead husband. Taking some of his notes, she cobbled together *The Will to Power* while editing his work to suit her prejudices and even forging a few letters in his name.

Although Nietzsche had been neither chauvinist nor anti-Semite, parts of his writing, if taken out of context, seemed to make a perfect fit to Nazi thought three decades after his death.

He created the concept of the *Übermensch* (Superman), whose superiority allows him to act towards the lower ranks (whom Nietzsche termed 'the herd') in any way he sees fit, for he is 'beyond good and evil', in a world where '*Gott ist tot*' ('God is dead'). The very title *The Will to Power* seemed to embody Adolf Hitler. Foreshadowing the spirit of the Third Reich's '*Kinder, Küche, Kirche*' ('Children, Kitchen, Church'), on the role of women he wrote: '*Du gehst zu Frauen? Vergiss die Peitsche nicht!*' ('You are going to women? Don't forget the whip!'). He also accused Jews of having a 'slave morality' based on envy.

Elisabeth corrupted Nietzsche's work to reflect her own belief in Teutonic supremacy, but she also gave his writings more prominence than they had achieved while he was still alive. Inadvertently she helped him to be seen eventually as one of the great philosophers; among those he influenced are Paul Tillich, Karl Jaspers, Martin Heidegger, Martin Buber, Sigmund Freud, Carl Jung and Alfred Adler. Those who wrote about him include Thomas Mann, André Malraux, André Gide, Albert Camus, Rainer Maria Rilke and George Bernard Shaw.

A basic Nietzschean concept was perspectivism, the belief that 'facts are precisely what there is not, only interpretations.' His own posthumous reputation became a startling demonstration of the truth of his thesis.

Also on this day

106 BC: Roman statesman Marcus Tullius Cicero is born * **1463: French poet François Villon vanishes from Paris and is never seen again** * 1777: George

Washington defeats General Cornwallis's forces at the Battle of Princeton * 1833: Britain seizes control of the Falkland Islands

4 January

A Napoleonic marriage with unforeseen results

1802 Today France's First Consul Napoleon Bonaparte made his first move in consolidating a Napoleonic dynasty when he coerced his 23-year-old younger brother Louis into marrying his stepdaughter Hortense de Beauharnais, who now became his sister-in-law as well. It was an unhappy union with surprising consequences.

Hortense was the daughter of Napoleon's wife Joséphine, whose first husband had been guillotined during the Revolution when Hortense was only eleven. She may well have inherited some of her mother's hot Creole blood, for within two years of her marriage, when she was still only 21, she had fallen for Napoleon's grand marshal Geraud Duroc, which made her husband violently jealous. This affair, such as it was, faded away, as Duroc was also commanding at the front, most famously at the Battle of Austerlitz in 1805, but Hortense's relationship with Louis, already rocky, could hardly have been helped by his own philandering, which infected him with venereal disease.

Louis and Hortense stayed together to produce two sons, although after Napoleon made him King of Holland in 1806 they largely lived apart. Back in Paris, Hortense gave birth again in April 1808, and Louis initially refused to accept the child as his own. However, the couple had been together in Toulouse the previous August, so Louis may well have been the father of this son, who would one day become Emperor Napoleon III.

The next year Napoleon divorced Joséphine but refused Louis's pleas to be allowed to divorce Hortense, although he permitted them to separate in 1810, the same year he annexed Holland to France, chasing Louis out of the country to settle in Germany.

Now Hortense returned to Paris without her husband and in October 1811 secretly gave birth to yet another son, although this time there was no dispute about his parentage; his father was the French general Charles-Joseph, comte de Flahaut, who himself was the illegitimate son of Talleyrand. Hortense's and Flahaut's son was whisked off to be raised by his grandmother, eventually to reach manhood as the duc de Morny.

At Napoleon's fall in 1814, Hortense was still only 31, an attractive, unattached mother of three. When the allies occupied Paris, she was rumoured to have enjoyed a fling with Tsar Alexander I. But, although unfaithful to her husband, she remained loyal to his brother, avidly supporting Napoleon during his Hundred Days, for which she was banished from France. She spent most of the rest of her life in Switzerland, where she died at the age of 54.

5

Louis lived out his days in Leghorn, expiring on 25 July 1846 at 68. Neither he nor his wayward wife lived to see their son Louis become French emperor by his *coup d'état* in 1851 – with the help of his half-brother, the duc de Morny.

Also on this day

1797: Napoleon defeats the Austrians at the Battle of Rivoli * **1785: German fairy-tale collector Jacob Grimm is born in Hanau** * 1809: Birth of Louis Braille, the French deviser of an alphabet for the blind, who himself was blinded at three * 1951: North Korean and Communist Chinese forces capture the city of Seoul during the Korean War

5 January

Charles the Bold perishes on the snowy fields at Nancy

1477 Perhaps because he challenged the French, in English we call him Charles the Bold. But the French have always called him Charles le Téméraire, more properly translated as Charles the Rash. The French were closer to the mark.

Charles was a strange and moody man, with dark brown hair cut pageboy style and expressive eyes that could be soft or gay or with *une dureté métallique* (a metallic hardness). Intelligent and hardworking, he spoke French, Dutch, English, Latin and Italian. He was also a fine musician who both composed and played the harp and may have invented counterpoint. A thoughtful man, he felt keenly the sadness and transience of life. According to his contemporary Lorenzo the Magnificent, he had '*un animo inquieto*' ('a troubled spirit'). But most of all he was ambitious. It was a family tradition.

Just 115 years earlier, Charles's great-grandfather, Duke Philip the Bold, had made Burgundy virtually independent, with only spasmodic and fiercely resisted control from France. During the intervening years the duchy had been ruled by the same talented, determined and ruthless family, father to son: Jean Sans Peur, Philip the Good and now Charles. But Charles was even more ambitious than his forefathers, for he dreamed of resurrecting the ancient kingdom of Lotharingia, one of the three parts of Charlemagne's empire. The greatest obstacle in his path was his wily enemy, King Louis XI of France. Although King Louis could hardly match Charles on the battlefield, he was so adroit at political manoeuvring that he was known as the Universal Spider for the deceitful webs he wove. After years of inconclusive (if sometimes bloody) sparring with Charles, Louis concluded a treaty with Charles's English brother-in-law and erstwhile ally, Edward IV. Then in August 1471 he signed another with René of Lorraine, who hired scores of feared Swiss pikemen to bolster his forces.

In 1476 Charles was twice defeated by René and his Swiss auxiliaries, and by early the next year even he must have known he stood little chance, obliged to fight in the bitter cold of winter. But somehow his moody sense of destiny and his famed obstinacy prevented him from retreat.

The two forces met outside Nancy on Sunday, 5 January 1477. Charles's Burgundian troops were badly routed, and for two days no one knew what had become of the great duke. But then a captured Burgundian page was led to the barren and frozen battlefield, where he identified Charles's naked body lying near the pond of St Jean. Charles's face had been opened from ear to jaw by the blow of an axe and his body was pierced by two lance thrusts. Wolves had gnawed the bloody remains.

And so died the Burgundian dream of power and with it the 43-year-old ruler, Charles by the Grace of God Duke of Burgundy, Lorraine and Brabant, of Limbourg and Luxembourg, Count of Flanders, Artois and Burgundy, Palatine of Hainault, Holland, Zealand and Namur, Margrave of the Holy Roman Empire, Lord of Frisia, Salins and Malines.

Also on this day

1066: Edward the Confessor, England's only king to be declared a saint, dies in London * 1585: Walter Raleigh is knighted * 1589: French queen Catherine de' Medici dies * 1592: Shah Jahan, the man who built the Taj Mahal, is born

6 January

Joan of Arc is born

1412 Epiphany would seem to be a suitable day for a saint to enter the world, and in the year 1412 one did, in the tiny French village of Domrémy, a hamlet some 170 miles south-east of Paris.

The saint-to-be was named Jeanne (Joan in English), the daughter of humble tenant farmers Isabelle and Jacques d'Arc. Sixteen years later she achieved the inconceivable – persuading the French king to let her, a teenage girl, lead an army against the perfidious English and their Burgundian allies.

Believing she was commanded by the 'voices' of St Michael, St Catherine, and St Margaret, Joan recognised a disguised king (Charles VI) at his fortress at Chinon, was given a small army and routed the enemy at Orléans and Patay.

Although already king for four years, Charles had not been crowned because his enemies held Reims, the traditional place for the coronations of French kings. This was of major importance in the medieval world when an unconsecrated monarch could still be challenged. But now Reims was under Charles's control, and Joan persuaded him to hold his coronation there and attended it herself.

After more minor battles against the English/Burgundian alliance – and against French towns which had sided with it – she was captured by the Burgundians at Compiègne and sold to the English for 16,000 francs in one of the most sordid deals in history. Condemned as a heretic, she was burned at the stake at Rouen.

Today her birthplace honours her with its name of Domrémy-la-Pucelle (Domrémy-the-Maiden) and the French have proclaimed the second Sunday in May a civic holiday in her honour. The Church was less certain, as Joan of Arc's sainthood was a long time coming. She was not canonised until 1920, some 508 years after her birth.

Also on this day

1017: Canute is crowned at St Paul's, making him king of England, Denmark and Norway * 1286: Phillip IV (the Fair) of France is crowned at Reims * 1838: Samuel Morse gives the first public demonstration of his invention, the telegraph * 1919: American president Theodore Roosevelt dies in Oyster Bay, Long Island

7 January

Wasted hope and sure defeat

1942 The defence of the Philippines took a new turn today as American and Filipino forces contesting the Japanese invasion of Luzon Island were gathered to form a last-ditch defensive line on the Bataan peninsula. For their com-mander, General Douglas MacArthur, it was the only course left open.

MacArthur's command included the Philippine army, some 100,000-strong, much of it barely trained and inadequately armed. In addition, he had some 13,000 American regular military personnel: soldiers, Marines and an assort-ment of what one historian described as 'aviators without planes, coast artillerymen without guns, cooks without stoves'. Lacking any air or naval support for its efforts on the ground, this force proved unable to contain the advance of the invaders, who had landed in Lingayen Gulf just sixteen days earlier with two reinforced divisions of the Japanese Fourteenth Army totalling nearly 50,000 veteran troops.

A Marine officer on the scene described the attempt to stem the Japanese advance. 'The Filipino Scouts held them off for the first eleven days and eleven nights after the Lingayen invasion. It was continuous attacking, retreating to new positions, stopping long enough to slaughter a few hundred more, then being driven back by the sheer force of overwhelming numbers. There weren't enough guns to stop them.'

So MacArthur declared Manila an open city and drew his forces behind a defensive line at the head of the Bataan peninsula, stretching across twenty miles of rugged jungle terrain from the South China Sea to Manila Bay. From the beginning, the defenders of Bataan, known as Luzon Force, were critically low on supplies, ammunition and medicine, a situation greatly aggravated by the presence within their lines of thousands of Filipino civilians fleeing the invaders.

Despite MacArthur's brave (and often misleading) words about the condition of his command, conveyed in frequent radio broadcasts to the outside world from his headquarters on the island of Corregidor, the ultimate outcome was never in doubt, only the timing. The Japanese had expected to take the Philippines within fifty days; even as the defensive line at Bataan was formed against them, they released troops for service in Java. But the resistance of Luzon Force was so fierce that on 8 February General Homma, with losses of 7,000 troops, was forced to suspend the initial Japanese offensive and bring in reinforcements. But the siege continued, and the attacks were renewed, slowly pushing the defenders southward towards the tip of the peninsula. Now they were surviving on less than 1,000 calories a day.

Meanwhile, on 12 March, under President Roosevelt's personal orders, General MacArthur left Corregidor to make his way through enemy-held waters to Australia where he would become overall ground commander of the Allied effort against Japan. His deputy, General Wainwright, took command in the Philippines and General King took over Luzon Force on the peninsula.

In early April, aided by heavy air and artillery bombardment, the Japanese broke through the line on Bataan. On 9 April 1942, 108 days from start of the invasion, General King surrendered his battered command to the Japanese, the biggest surrender of American troops since General Lee handed over the Army of Northern Virginia at Appomattox, exactly 77 years earlier.

Corregidor itself, the 'concrete battleship' off the tip of the peninsula, would fall on 6 May, thus adding the Philippines to the long list of Japanese war trophies that already included Guam, Wake Island, Rabaul, Hong Kong, Malaya, and Singapore.

As soon as the surrender document was signed, Japanese soldiers began herding their captives into long columns for the march to prison camps. On this 65-mile journey, known ever after as the Bataan Death March, an estimated 750 Americans and 5,000 Filipinos died of starvation, exhaustion, disease, mistreatment or execution. About their long and gruelling experience on Bataan, an American lieutenant, Harry G. Lee, wrote these lines.

> Saved for another day
> Saved for hunger and wounds and retreat
> For slow exhaustion and grim retreat
> For a wasted hope and sure defeat.

Also on this day

1558: The French recapture Calais, the last English possession on mainland France * 1619: English miniaturist painter Nicholas Hilliard dies * 1768: Napoleon's brother Joseph Bonaparte, future King of Naples, is born

8 January

The Grimaldis take over Monaco

1297 Lying 'between snow-white summits and a glittering sea', the walled fortress of Monaco lay quiet this night, when a Franciscan monk appeared at the gates. Allowed to enter by careless guards, the monk drew a sword from beneath his habit and attacked, while his troops, who had been waiting outside hidden by darkness, charged through the gates before the guards could slam them shut. In a few moments the fortress was overrun; Monaco had a new proprietor, whose family would rule it for most of the next seven centuries.

The monk, of course, was no monk at all, but François Grimaldi (now to be called François Malizia (the Cunning) – for his exploit), leader of the Guelphs (supporters of the Pope) who were fighting against the Ghibellines, supporters of the Holy Roman Emperor, who had held the fortress. From this time on, the Grimaldi family escutcheon included the image of two armed Franciscan monks – a playful and fortuitous symbol in that 'Monaco' in Italian means 'monk'.

François's triumph was rather short-lived, as he stayed in power for just over four years. When the Grimaldis were in control again a few years later, a merchant-turned-pirate called Lanfranco Grimaldi became the first Lord of Monaco. On his death in 1309 his cousin Rainier I inherited the throne. It is from Rainier that all subsequent Monegasque monarchs are descended, even though Grimaldi dominance was alternately lost and regained several times during the centuries ahead, most notably during the French Revolution when Monaco was taken over by France until the fall of Napoleon 22 years later.

The Grimaldis were once masters not only of Monaco but also of many of the jewels of today's Côte d'Azur, including Antibes, Juan-les-Pins, Menton and Roquebrune. Eventually they lost these territories, ceding the last two in 1848, but at the same time the family set the stage for the glittery popularity of today's Monaco; the Belle Epoque Casino de Monte Carlo was built in 1863, followed in 1869 by the abolition of all direct taxes. Aristocratic playboys, louche business moguls and glamorous women on the make have flocked there ever since.

But, as much as anything, the Grimaldis owe their continuing power to a 15th-century Lord of Monaco, one Jean Grimaldi, who set up the formal Rules of Succession that, by their flexible nature, have kept Monaco in the family's hands over the last five hundred years. He ruled that, in the absence of legitimate heirs, illegitimate ones could inherit the principality. This included illegitimate females, provided they marry *'unum hominem seu virum natum legitime de progenie seu albergo Grimaldorum'* – a man born legitimately of the Grimaldi family. Even these elastic regulations were broken at times to keep the Grimaldis in control.

The most recent example came after the First World War, when Monaco found itself without a legitimate heir. Eventually it was discovered that in 1898 Prince Louis II of Monaco had fathered a bastard daughter by a cabaret singer (or possibly a laundress or a dressmaker) named Juliette Louvet. The daughter, Charlotte, took the Grimaldi family name and married the French nobleman Pierre de Polignac. They became the Prince and Princess of Monaco. From this union was born Prince Rainier III, who also became a Grimaldi (i.e. took his mother's name rather than his father's) and married the American movie star Grace Kelly. Their son is the currently reigning Prince Albert, Monaco's 32nd hereditary ruler.

Also on this day

1337: Italian painter Giotto dies ∗ 1499: Louis XII marries Anne de Bretagne, putting Brittany under the control of the French crown ∗ 1642: Astronomer and physicist Galileo Galilei dies in Arcetri, Tuscany ∗ 1713: Italian composer Arcangelo Corelli dies ∗ **1815: In the War of 1812, American general and future president Andrew Jackson defeats the British at the Battle of New Orleans, fifteen days after a peace treaty had been signed**

9 January

Death of earthy Victor Emmanuel

1878 '*On me dit que les danseuses françaises ne portent pas des caleçons. Si c'est comme cela, ce sera pour moi le paradis terrestre.*' ('They tell me that French dancers don't wear underwear. If it is really like that, for me it would be heaven on Earth.') A ribald remark by a French travelling salesman? No, a casual comment by the first King of Italy, Victor Emmanuel, to the beautiful but rigid and frigid French Empress Eugénie, wife of Napoleon III.

Victor Emmanuel was squat, strong and athletic and bore an immense upturning moustache. According to an English nobleman who met him, he was 'as vulgar and coarse as possible'. He preferred peasant stews to fine cooking and pursued game and women with equal enthusiasm.

Beneath Victor Emmanuel's boorishness, however, were determination and a certain shrewdness. As the King of Sardinia-Piedmont, he recognised in Camillo di Cavour a man of political genius whose will towards a united Italy surpassed his own. During the struggle against Austrian hegemony he took command of his own armies, leading them in person at the decisive battles of Magenta and Solferino. Although a conservative monarchist, he later covertly backed the revolutionary Garibaldi in his efforts to bring together the various Italian kingdoms into a single nation.

In 1860 Victor Emmanuel became the first king of a united Italy and then transferred the capital from Turin first briefly to Florence and finally, in 1871, to the nation's ancient heart, Rome. It was there that he died on this day in

1878 at the age of 57, five years to the day after the demise of his ally at Solferino, Napoleon III.

Also on this day

1522: Adrian of Utrecht is elected Pope Adrian VI, the last non-Italian pope until John Paul II from Poland in 1978 * 1799: British prime minister William Pitt the Younger introduces income tax, at two shillings in the pound, to raise funds for the Napoleonic Wars * 1828: The Duke of Wellington becomes Prime Minister * 1873: French emperor Napoleon III dies in exile in England * 1896: French poet Paul Verlaine dies * **1916: The last British soldiers abandon Gallipoli, bringing to a close the failed invasion**

10 January

A pugnacious revolutionary is born

1738 Today in Litchfield, Connecticut, was born one of colonial America's most pugnacious, irascible and determined leaders, Ethan Allen. Although he fought in the American Revolution against Great Britain, he gained his greatest fame for his political battles against other American states.

At nineteen Allen joined the American militia that aided the British army to fight in the French and Indian War, but saw no action. At its close he moved to Salisbury, Connecticut, where he and his brother built a blast furnace. This was the cause of his first contretemps with the law.

Allen wanted to sell the furnace, but in an argument over the sale he assaulted the would-be purchaser and ended up on trial. According to the court record: 'Ethan Allen did, in a tumultuous and offensive manner, with threatening words and angry looks, strip himself even to his naked body, and with force and arms, without law or right, did assail and actually strike the person of George Caldwell of Salisbury, aforesaid, in the presence and to the disturbance of His Majesty's good subjects.' Allen was fined ten shillings and soon moved to what, largely through his efforts, would one day become the state of Vermont.

Before the Revolution, land in Vermont was variously controlled by New York and New Hampshire, but Allen was determined that Vermont should have independent status. He led the patriot militia called the Green Mountain Boys that confronted a group of sheriffs from New York, sent to toss out Vermont residents who had received their land grants from New Hampshire. At one stage the bellicose Allen captured two of the sheriffs and jailed them in adjoining cells. One night he hanged a human-sized dummy outside the jail, close enough so that the sheriffs would see it but far enough away so that they would think it was human, and in the morning he informed each sheriff that the other had been hanged the previous night. Then, one by one, he released his terrified captives.

During the Revolution, Allen led a group of 83 Green Mountain Boys in a joint attack with the American general Benedict Arnold on the British-held Fort Ticonderoga. The Americans attacked at dawn, catching the surprised commander still in bed. Allen demanded immediate surrender, and when the British commander asked on whose authority he acted, the forceful American thundered: 'In the name of the great Jehovah and the Continental Congress!' Only four months later, however, Allen led a reckless attack on Montreal and was captured. He was imprisoned for a time in England and then paroled in New York City. In 1778 he was exchanged for a British officer and then joined Washington, who made him a colonel in the Continental army.

After the Revolution, Allen returned to his favourite cause, the gaining of statehood for Vermont, arguing that people who had fought for independence deserved recognition by the national government. Infuriated by the reluctance of the Continental Congress, at one point he started to negotiate with Canada to absorb Vermont if the Americans wouldn't make it a state, but this was probably just a bluff to force the issue.

In spite of all his efforts, Allen must have believed he had failed, as the Continental Congress continued to deny Vermont statehood. Then in February 1789, when he was still only 51, he fell ill while returning with hay from a neighbouring farm. It was soon clear that he was dying, and the local minister was summoned to his bedside.

'The angels are waiting for you, General Allen', whispered the minister, hoping for a few last words of piety.

'They are, are they?' growled the dying man, belligerent to the end. 'Well, God damn 'em, let 'em wait!' But a few minutes later he was dead.

Two years after Allen's death, on 4 March 1791, Vermont was at last admitted into the Union as the fourteenth state.

Also on this day

49 BC: Caesar crosses the Rubicon to start a Roman civil war * 1645: William Laud, Archbishop of Canterbury, is executed * 1769: French marshal Michel Ney is born in Saarlouis in Lorraine * 1776: Thomas Paine publishes *Common Sense* * 1941: President Franklin Roosevelt proposes the Lend Lease programme that gives the president the power to sell or lease military equipment to other countries as a stopgap against German aggression in Europe * 1946: The United Nations holds its first meeting

11 January

An unexpectedly rough outing in Zululand

1879 Reveille blew well before first light this morning at Rorke's Drift. By 6 am troops were crossing the Buffalo River from Natal into Zululand, mounted units splashing across first, followed by British infantry in punts and native infantry wading through the chest-high water, arms linked against the force of the current. By day's end, with the entire column across – 4,500 soldiers, 300 wagons, 1,600 transport animals – and a base camp established, the Zulu War had begun.

The column, accompanied by the overall invasion commander, Lord Chelmsford, was one of three widely separated British forces entering Zululand that day. Their common objective was Ulundi, the royal kraal of the Zulu king Cetshwayo, some 70 miles away. The war took barely six months from start to finish – Ulundi was captured and burned to the ground on 4 July in the last big battle – and resulted in the complete destruction of the Zulus (both as a fighting force and as a nation) and the incorporation of their lands into the British Empire.

The war was not especially memorable for its ultimate success for the British. But if the outcome seemed preordained in a conflict that pitted the Martini-Henry rifle against the assegai, there occurred in the course of the campaign a setback for the British so severe and spectacular that for a while the entire enterprise was cast in doubt. It was perhaps the greatest defeat of a British army in the entire Victorian era.

The setback occurred in the shadow of Isandlwana, a huge rock outcrop dominating the landscape, some ten miles by winding road from the border crossing at Rorke's Drift. On 22 January a force of 1,700 British soldiers and native auxiliaries was engulfed and destroyed by 20,000 Zulus attacking in their classic formation, the 'horns of the beast', in which the 'chest' attacks the centre while the two 'horns' sweep around the sides, often hidden by terrain, to encircle the enemy, and the 'loins' stand in reserve to join the attack where needed. The Zulus struck just before noon. The fighting was over by 2.30 pm, leaving 1,300 British dead and the rest fleeing to Rorke's Drift, where a heroic defence took place against further Zulu attacks.

The Zulus attacked all three invading columns that day. Their success against the centre column at Isandlwana left the flanking columns unsupported – the southernmost falling under siege for three months. The invasion came to a sudden halt, leaving the Natal border virtually undefended and vulnerable to counter-attack. But against British rifle fire, the Zulus had suffered heavy losses in all three attacks – 2,000 alone slain at Isandlwana – and were not ready to seize the opportunity to carry the war into enemy territory. Back in Natal, Lord Chelmsford asked London for reinforcements, and with British prestige on the line, the government of Benjamin Disraeli gave Chelmsford everything he asked for and a good deal more.

In late March, with some 23,000 British and native troops in the field, Chelmsford began a second invasion against a weakened enemy. Reaching Ulundi, British battalions went into a classic formation of their own, forming a huge hollow square, with artillery pieces at the corners that fought off repeated attacks and destroyed what was left of the Zulu army. The second invasion was a success, marred only by the death in Zululand of a highly popular figure in

14

England, 22-year-old Louis Napoleon, Prince Imperial of France, son of the former French emperor Napoleon III. Serving with the British army in a voluntary and unofficial capacity, he was killed on 1 June by Zulus ambushing a patrol. His death, one historian reported, 'horrified the population of England as Isandlwana had never done'.

The price of empire was high. In six months of war, an estimated 8,000 Zulus were killed in battle, with perhaps twice that many wounded. The British lost some 2,100 European and native troops. They captured the Zulu king Cetshwayo and sent him into exile near Cape Town for four years, while his country, with its traditional structure broken up into thirteen separate kingdoms under a British Resident, fell into decades of turmoil.

Also on this day

1449: Italian painter Domenico Ghirlandaio is born * **1755: American statesman Alexander Hamilton is born illegitimate in Charlestown, British West Indies** * 1891: French city designer Georges Haussman dies in Paris * 1928: British novelist Thomas Hardy dies * 1935: Amelia Earhart becomes the first woman to fly solo across the Pacific

12 January

The chef of kings and the king of chefs

1833 This should be a day of mourning for gastronomes everywhere, for today died Antonin Carême, the Parisian chef who created *haute cuisine*.

French cooking had been characterised by rich food with little or no thought given to the compatibility of flavours and textures. Carême changed all that by emphasising fresh ingredients, refining and simplifying (although he did upon occasion present a dinner of 48 courses). He was the first and greatest 'celebrity chef', in demand in the grandest courts and houses in Europe. He made French *haute cuisine* the standard of excellence, a legacy still with us today. He also invented the chef's hat, the toque.

Folklore has it that at the beginning of the 16th century Carême's ancestor Jean had been chef to that aristocratic trencherman, the Medici pope Leo X. One year during Lent he presented the pontiff with an especially tempting soup, so good that Leo gave him the name of Jean de Carême (Jean of Lent), and his family bore the name from then on.

Two centuries later, however, the family's fortunes had fallen; Carême's father was a stonemason who barely eked out a living, unable to support his 25 children (of whom Antonin was the sixteenth). When Carême was only eleven his destitute father took him to Paris, bought him a cheap meal and abandoned him in the street.

Somehow Carême managed to find a job in the kitchen of a chophouse, where he first learned to cook. Five years later he moved to a pâtisserie near the Palais-Royal, working under the famous pâtissier Sylvain Bailly, and it was here that he first began to make his mark.

Carême spent his spare time wandering the streets of Paris admiring its exquisite buildings and visiting the Bibliothèque Royale, where he immersed himself in illustrations of architectural masterpieces. This inspired him to create elaborate pastry constructions, sometimes several feet high, which Sylvain Bailly would display in his pâtisserie window. Soon smart Paris was talking about Carême's fabulous *pièces montées* and buying them for centrepieces for their grand tables. Shortly he began working freelance, and it is said that Napoleon Bonaparte hired him to design his wedding cake for his marriage to Joséphine.

One of the aristocrats who appreciated Carême's work was the French foreign minister, Charles-Maurice de Talleyrand, who engaged him as *chef de cuisine* at his Château Valençay, where Carême remained for twelve years.

After Napoleon's fall, Carême went with Talleyrand to the Congress of Vienna, where he astonished more of Europe's nobility with his skills. He then embarked for England in the service of the Prince Regent, the future George IV. Once George reproached Carême: 'You will kill me from eating too much; I want everything you prepare and the temptations are too much.' The great chef testily replied: '*Monseigneur*, my most important duty is to whet your appetite through the variety of what I serve; it is not my job to control it.' But after two years Carême found the English fog too depressing and returned to France.

Next came Russia, when Tsar Alexander I brought him to St Petersburg for a series of banquets, and then Paris again, where he continued to serve the high and mighty, including Baroness Rothschild, the richest woman in Europe. No wonder he was known as *le cuisinier des rois et le roi des cuisiniers* (the chef of kings and the king of chefs).

Carême also wrote the definitive cookbooks of his time. In one, *L'Art de la cuisine au dix-neuvième siècle*, he gives recipes for 289 different sauces.

Still only 48, Carême died today tasting food in his own kitchen in Paris. His last known words were to one of his assistants: 'The quenelles are good, only they were prepared too hastily. You must shake the saucepan lightly.' The cause of his death is uncertain, although the French 19th-century poet Laurent Taihade wrote that he was '*brûlé par la flamme de son génie et le charbon des rôtissoires*' ('burnt out by the flame of his genius and the charcoal of the roasting pit'). If you care to lay a wreath on the great chef's tomb, you will find it in the cemetery in Montmartre.

Also on this day

1519: 'The man who married Austria into a great power', Holy Roman Emperor Maximilian I, dies in Wels, Upper Austria * 1519: In Acla, Panama, Spanish conquistador Vasco Núñez de Balboa is beheaded on trumped-up charges of treason and rebellion * 1729: British statesman and political thinker Edmund Burke is born in

Dublin * 1882: German composer Richard Wagner completes *Parsifal* in Palermo, Sicily * 1856: American painter John Singer Sargent is born in Florence

13 January

The death of Gaius Marius, the general who saved Rome from the barbarians

86 BC Today the Roman general Gaius Marius died of a stroke in his 70th year, just three months after he had been elected consul for the seventh time. His death came none too soon because he had suffered some sort of mental collapse and was hardly sane during his final months, unleashing a reign of terror against any he felt had opposed him. Surrounded by a guard of slaves, he walked through Rome ordering instant executions.

Yet Marius had been one of Rome's very greatest generals. He had saved his country from almost certain invasion and changed the very nature of the Roman army.

Marius had been born a *novus homo* or new man, someone without senatorial forebears, in Arpinum, a provincial town 60 miles south-east of Rome. According to Plutarch, when he was a young boy Marius caught an eagle's nest falling from a tree. In it he found seven eaglets that he brought home to his parents, who consulted the augurs to find the meaning of this omen. The augurs foretold that Marius 'should become the greatest man in the world, and that the fates had decreed he should seven times be possessed of the supreme power and authority'.

As a soldier, Marius became both respected and rich through his victories in Spain and North Africa, and when he was about 45 he married into the patrician Julii Caesar family. His wife Julia was Julius Caesar's aunt. Three years later he was elected consul for the first time, an enormous honour for a *novus homo*. He was subsequently elected six more times, fulfilling the augurs' prophecy.

During Marius's first consulship in 107 BC Rome found itself threatened by the Cimbri and Teutones, two fierce tribes that had descended from Germany en masse with 300,000 fighting men plus an even greater number of women and children, determined to conquer Italy. After the tribes had destroyed two Roman armies near Lake Geneva, Marius led his army against them at Aquae Sextiae (now Aix-en-Provence) and Vercellae (between Turin and Milan). He utterly routed the invaders, killing tens of thousands and selling the prisoners and their families into slavery, saving the Roman Republic.

Marius vastly improved the fighting ability of the army. He made the cohort of 600 men the standard unit, and equipped each legionnaire with the same armament, a pilum (a sort of javelin) and a sword. He trained his men ferociously, using techniques from gladiatorial schools, and had them carry their own supplies and shovels, thus eliminating slow-moving baggage trains.

From this his soldiers earned the proud sobriquet 'Marius's mules'.

Even more important in the longer term was Marius's change in the way new soldiers were recruited. Previously only Romans who owned land could join, but Marius dropped all property qualifications and instead offered land as reward for faithful soldiers. The result was an influx of poorer citizens who stayed in service even after battle, thus for the first time creating something like a professional standing army. It was Marius who gave each legion a standard in the form of an eagle. Critically, the legions' first loyalty now was to their commander, who alone could reward them, rather than to the Roman state, a change exploited to the full first by Sulla and then by Pompey and ultimately by Julius Caesar.

Although a military genius, Marius was a clumsy politician who made enemies both in the Senate and among rival commanders, especially his one-time subordinate Sulla. Consequently, at one point he had to flee for his life, but was captured and imprisoned in a dark cell. Then a Gallic soldier was ordered in to decapitate him. According to Plutarch: 'The room itself was not very light, that part of it especially where he then lay was dark, from whence Marius's eyes, they say, seemed to [the soldier] to dart out flames at him, and a loud voice to say, out of the dark, "Fellow, darest thou kill Gaius Marius?" The barbarian hereupon immediately fled, and leaving his sword in the place, rushed out of doors, crying only this, "I cannot kill Gaius Marius."'

Marius escaped and eventually returned to Rome where he was elected consul for the final time, when he wreaked havoc among his enemies. By now he was clearly becoming unhinged, drinking heavily, suffering hallucinations and running 'into an extravagant frenzy fancying himself to be a general at war … throwing himself into such postures and motions of his body as he had formerly used when he was in battle, with frequent shouts and loud cries'. Despondent and afraid, he fell ill and died seven days later.

Also on this day

1599: English poet Edmund Spenser dies in London * 1625: Flemish painter Jan Bruegel the Elder dies in Antwerp * 1628: Charles Perrault, French author of *Mother Goose*, is born in Paris * **1898: French author Emile Zola publishes '*J'accuse*' in *L'Aurore*, igniting the Dreyfus Affair** * 1898: Writer of *Alice's Adventures in Wonderland* Lewis Carroll (Charles Dodgson) dies

14 January

Attentat *against Emperor Napoleon III*

1858 Napoleon III and Eugénie, Emperor and Empress of France, were relaxing in their closed carriage as it neared the Opera House on rue Lepelletier in Paris when suddenly an explosion shattered the calm. Then came a second explosion and then a third. Four Italian revolutionaries, led by a deranged terrorist named Felice Orsini, had hurled three bombs, hoping for a revolution in France that would spread to Italy.

Immediately there was chaos. Gas lamps went out, shards of glass rained down from broken windows, and horses and people bolted in panic. The Emperor and Empress nursed superficial cuts on their faces, but they nonetheless left their carriage to enter the opera. Eugénie was so intensely shocked that when Napoleon wished to stop to speak to the wounded she cut him short with: *'Pas si bête. Assez de farces comme ça.'* ('Don't be stupid. There have been enough jokes like that already.')

The opera audience went into frenzied cheering at the sight of their courageous monarchs. They had survived what King Alfonso XIII of Spain would later term *'la risque du métier'* ('the risk of the trade').

In the street outside, 144 people were wounded and twelve lay dead. As for Felice Orsini and his fellow conspirators, they were condemned and brought to the guillotine.

Also on this day

1208: Pope Innocent III's representative is murdered near Toulouse, triggering the Albigensian Crusade against Cathar heretics in Provence * 1742: Astronomer Edmond Halley dies in Greenwich * 1867: French painter Jean-Auguste Ingres dies in Paris * 1875: Alsatian–German theologian, philosopher, organist and mission doctor Albert Schweitzer is born in Kaysersberg, Upper Alsace (then in Germany, now in France)

15 January

Elizabeth is crowned

1559 When Elizabeth Tudor had been told of her half-sister Mary's death in mid-November 1558, she had piously quoted her psalter in Latin: 'This is the Lord's doing; it is marvellous in our eyes.' But when she set a date for her coronation, she turned not to the Church but to John Dee, a renowned astrologer, who revealed that the stars and planets favoured 15 January.

And so it was that on this Sunday 25-year-old Elizabeth slipped on a dress of embroidered silk over which she wore a cloak lined with ermine, for she not only would have to stand for long hours in draughty Westminster Abbey but would also ride from the Tower of London through the city so that the crowds could see her.

When she finally arrived at the Abbey, she entered across a blue carpet, which the crowd instantly shredded for souvenirs the moment she had passed within the church doors.

The ceremony was the traditional Latin service used since medieval times, for Protestant England had not yet created its own service. At its climax the Bishop of Carlisle placed on Elizabeth's head the gold- and jewel-encrusted Crown of St Edward, said to have belonged to Edward the Confessor in the 11th century and first used in Edward I's coronation in 1272. Then, to the deafening sounds of trumpets and drums, the new Queen presented herself to the congregation.

When at last the ceremony was over, Elizabeth moved on to Westminster Hall for her coronation banquet, where 800 guests sat at four long tables, each stretching the full length of the hall. The banquet, which lasted from three in the afternoon until one the following morning, was enlivened by a knight in full armour riding among the tables symbolically throwing down his gauntlet and daring anyone to challenge Elizabeth's right to the crown. Then, fatigued but exhilarated, she could finally go off to bed, an anointed queen who would reign for 44 years, two months and nine days.

Also on this day

1622: French playwright Molière (Jean-Baptiste Poquelin) is born in Paris * 1759: The British Museum is opened at Montague House, Bloomsbury * **1815: Nelson's mistress Lady Emma Hamilton dies penniless in Calais** * 1902: Tribal and Muslim religious leader Ibn Sa'ud ambushes and kills the Rashidi governor at Riyadh to become the ruler of Saudi Arabia * 1929: American civil rights campaigner Martin Luther King is born in Atlanta

> Events written in **boldface** are covered in full in
> *365: Great Stories from History for Every Day of the Year*,
> the first volume in this series.

16 January

America goes dry

1920 Today, Prohibition became law in the United States, appropriately at the very start of the decade known as the Roaring Twenties, an era celebrated for its flappers, speakeasies, bootleggers and stock-market speculation. It seemed like an unending party – much of it due to the unintended effects of Prohibition.

Nowadays we have the impression of bemused citizens caught unawares by a puritanical law denying them the right to drink. But in truth, Prohibition had been a long time coming.

Back in 1846 Maine had become the first state to prohibit the sale of alcohol, and soon other states followed; by 1855 thirteen of the 31 states were 'dry'. By the time the 18th Amendment to the Constitution was ratified in 1919,

Prohibition was already in force in 33 states, covering 63 per cent of the nation's population.

America had had a long history of fighting demon drink, much of it stemming from religious revivalism, usually led by worthy women from the Middle West. The Women's Christian Temperance Union was founded in 1874 and the Anti-Saloon League in 1895, both in Ohio. The Anti-Saloon League's feisty Carrie Nation assaulted bars and taverns armed with a hatchet to smash the bottles and trash the furniture. The League pronounced that saloons '[led] astray 60,000 girls each year into lives of immorality' and claimed that 'liquor is responsible for 19% of the divorces, 25% of the poverty, 25% of the insanity, 37% of the pauperism, 45% of child desertion, and 50% of the crime in this country'. Across the nation virtuous women simpered:

> Lips that touch wine
> Shall never touch mine.

The move towards nationwide Prohibition snowballed after the First World War, when American soldiers returning from Europe shocked those who had stayed at home with their more sophisticated ways, including a fondness for alcohol. As vaudeville star Eddie Cantor sang:

> How're you going to keep 'em
> Down on the farm,
> After they've seen Paree?

In December 1917 Congress submitted the 18th Amendment to the states; the next month Mississippi became the first state to ratify, and on 16 January 1919 Nebraska completed the job, since now the necessary three-quarters of the states had ratified.

Almost as soon as the ink was dry on the new Amendment, bootleggers began bringing alcohol in from Canada, and speakeasies (so called because to gain entrance you had to 'speak easy' to the doorman) flourished. Soon there were tens of thousands of them in New York City alone.

Otherwise law-abiding citizens also set up home stills to produce 'bathtub gin', from which a number were blinded, while others used car radiators to distil liquor, a process that sometimes led to fatal lead poisoning. Unscrupulous doctors had a field day prescribing 'medicinal' whiskey for their thirsty patients.

But the most malevolent transformation was in organised crime, for now legendary gangsters such as Lucky Luciano, Dutch Shultz, Albert Anastasia, Bugs Moran, Frank Nitti and Bugsy Siegel battled with Tommy guns and bribed policemen for control of the illegal trade in alcohol, garnering enormous profits. Al Capone is supposed to have earned $60 million a year. In response came illustrious lawmen like Izzy Einstein and Moe Smith from New York and the FBI's Eliot Ness and his Untouchables.

America lived with Prohibition for thirteen long years, but gradually a more sophisticated population and the tidal wave of crime turned the nation against it. (The homicide rate increased by almost two-thirds during the Prohibition years.)

When accepting the Democratic nomination to run for president, Franklin Roosevelt delighted most (if infuriating hard-line dries) with his speech. 'This convention wants repeal. Your candidate wants repeal. And I am confident that the United States of America wants repeal.' With Roosevelt safely in office, on 14 February 1933 a Wisconsin senator introduced a repeal amendment. Within six days both the Senate and the House had voted to put the amendment to the states, and repeal came on 5 December 1933, a joyous process that had required only 8 months and 22 days. Back to the top of the hit parade came a 1929 song by Jack Yellen and Milton Ager.

> Happy days are here again
> The skies above are clear again
> So let's sing a song of cheer again
> Happy days are here again

Also on this day

1547: Ivan the Terrible is crowned first Tsar of Russia * 1794: English historian Edward Gibbon dies * **1809: British General Sir John Moore is killed at the Battle of La Coruña** * 1891: French composer Leo Delibes dies

17 January

Benjamin Franklin is born

1706 It was a quiet Sunday in the Massachusetts Bay Colony town of Boston (population 6,000) when Josiah Franklin's seventeenth and last child was born in the family house on Milk Street. Perhaps Josiah thought of the famous Biblical youngest son as he named the child Benjamin.

Although his formal schooling stopped at the age of ten, Benjamin Franklin would display a profound intellect and a dazzling versatility of achievement.

Most of us know Franklin as a printer, postmaster, diplomat and of course one of his nation's Founding Fathers. But he was also an inventor (of the Franklin stove, the lightning rod and bifocals), a musician (he played the harp, guitar and violin and invented a type of harmonica), a linguist (French, Italian and Spanish) and a philosopher. During his long life he raised a militia, organised a fire department and was a director of the first American fire insurance company.

Finally, of course, he was his country's great aphorist. 'Keep your eyes open before marriage, half shut afterwards', he advised, along with: 'It's as plain as

Euclid, that whoever was constant to several persons was more constant than he who was constant only to one.' He also believed that 'three may keep a secret, if two of them are dead'.

Three of his more famous lines are 'Fish and visitors smell after three days', 'Time is money', and 'Snug as a bug in a rug'. And as for the motto *'E Pluribus Unum'* ('Out of many, one') on every piece of American money, well, Franklin, er, coined that too.

Also on this day

38 BC: Octavian (the future Emperor Augustus Caesar) marries Livia * **532: Empress Theodora inspires her husband Justinian to crush the Nika revolt in Constantinople** * 1377: The 'Babylonian Captivity' comes to an end, as the papacy returns to Rome from Avignon * 1751: Italian composer Tomaso Giovanni Albinoni dies * 1861: Irish adventuress and 'Spanish' dancer Lola Montez (Marie Dolores Eliza Rosanna Gilbert) dies in New York of pneumonia * 1863: English Prime Minister David Lloyd George is born

18 January

Red rose marries the white

1486 For thirty years the houses of Lancaster and York had torn England apart during the bloody Wars of the Roses, and only five months earlier Henry Tudor, the last representative of the Lancaster faction, had invaded England and killed the usurper King Richard III at Bosworth Field, seizing the throne as Henry VII. The English Parliament immediately recognised him as king, but, in their first face-to-face encounter, the Parliament petitioned Henry to unite the two warring families by marrying Elizabeth of York, eldest daughter of Edward IV and as such heiress to the Yorkist claims.

Being a shrewd politician, Henry agreed, and was perhaps pleasantly surprised to find that Elizabeth was young (21), blonde and beautiful. The wedding took place on this day in 1486, only 79 days after Henry's coronation.

Although a love match in no sense of the word, the royal couple produced two sons and five daughters. Elizabeth died in 1503 at just 37, but Henry ruled England until his death at 52 in 1509. In all, the Tudors would wear the crown of England for 118 years, until the death of Henry's and Elizabeth's granddaughter Queen Elizabeth I in 1603.

Although largely forgotten except by lovers of history, Elizabeth plays a more prevalent role today than you might imagine, as you see her face every time you play cards. She is said to be the model for the Queen of Hearts.

Also on this day

1778: James Cook discovers Hawaii * **1871: Prussian King Wilhelm I is proclaimed**

German Emperor at Versailles, during the siege of Paris * 1919: The Versailles Peace Conference opens * 1936: British author Rudyard Kipling dies in London

19 January

A mad empress finally expires

1927 Today Carlota, wife of the ill-fated Mexican emperor Maximilian, died in the 12th-century Bouchot Castle on the outskirts of Brussels. She had lived 86 years, mad for the last 60 of them.

Carlota had been born Marie Charlotte Amélie Augustine Victoire Clémentine Léopoldine, the only daughter of the Belgian King, Leopold I. At seventeen she had married Maximilian von Habsburg, the younger brother of Austrian Emperor Franz Joseph, a weak and amiable man of neither talent nor ambition. But Carlota (as she would be known when her husband became Emperor of Mexico) more than made up for her spouse's lack of drive. When reactionary Mexican aristocrats, backed by France's Napoleon III, offered Maximilian the crown of Mexico, Carlota endlessly and enthusiastically urged him to accept.

Carlota proudly accompanied her husband to Mexico in 1864, but only two years later her dream started to collapse. Pressure mounted from the United States, which was proclaiming the Monroe Doctrine, a policy that made it a hostile act against the United States for a European power to attempt to control any nation in the Western hemisphere. Napoleon III withdrew his army from Mexico, and Maximilian's regime was doomed as forces of the pre-imperial republican government of Benito Juárez smashed what remained of the Emperor's army.

On 9 July 1866 Carlota set out from Mexico City for Europe to rally support for her beleaguered husband. She was never to see him again. It was then that she showed the first signs of insanity. Stopping at the town of Puebla, she rose from bed at midnight and ordered her entourage to take her to the house where the local prefect had entertained her months before. Although the house now held only servants, she insisted on revisiting the rooms where she had once been royally fêted.

The next day she moved on to Veracruz to sail for Europe. Her first stop was Paris, where she failed to persuade Napoleon to restore his army in Mexico. In desperation, she travelled on to Rome to enlist the support of that dogmatic reactionary, Pope Pius IX. To His Holiness she begged to be allowed to spend the night in the Vatican (although no woman had ever been granted that privilege) because she feared for her life: Napoleon III, she said, was trying to poison her.

The Pope granted her wish, but the next day sent her back to her hotel. There she refused all food and drink except live chickens that she kept in her hotel suite and had slaughtered and cooked by her own servants, and water that she collected herself from the Trevi Fountain. She busied herself with writing letters to the court in Mexico accusing Napoleon of ordering her murder.

News of Carlota's paranoia soon reached her brother, now King Leopold II of Belgium. He brought her to Brussels and placed her in the care of an Austrian doctor who directed a lunatic asylum. Here she remained for the rest of her pitiful life, continuing to ask until she was in her 70s why Maximilian was not there. In the spring of every year she would board a tiny skiff afloat in the moat of her castle and inform her companions: 'Today we are leaving for Mexico.'

Why Carlota fell into insanity is still a mystery, although there is no lack of conjectures. Some say she was driven mad by feelings of guilt at having left Maximilian in Mexico, emotions greatly exacerbated when he was executed by firing squad less than a year after her departure; Queen Victoria blamed it on Napoleon III for having talked Maximilian into his imperial adventure and then removing his support; and modern psychiatrists see possible cause in her failure to produce an heir to the Mexican throne; but the most bizarre theory was that Benito Juárez had had a secret Indian drug administered to her during her trip to Europe.

One final mystery has outlived the deranged empress. In January of 1867, six months after Carlota had left Mexico for Europe, a baby boy was born in Brussels. For unexplained reasons he was reared in Carlota's household. He was said to be the illegitimate son of a Polish aristocrat, but rumours have continued ever since that he was in fact the lovechild of Carlota and one of Maximilian's officers. Whatever the truth of his parentage, this baby boy grew up to be Maxime Weygand, the French general who in the Second World War, as commander-in-chief of the Allied armies in France, advised the French government to capitulate to the Germans in 1940.

Also on this day

1568: Philip II locks up his mad son, Don Carlos, who is never seen in public again * 1788: The first British convicts reach Botany Bay, Australia * 1807: Confederate general Robert E. Lee is born in Stratford, Virginia * 1839: French painter Paul Cézanne is born in Aix-en-Provence

20 January

Nice at last becomes French

1860 On this day at last, after centuries of dispute, attack, besiegement, defeat, pillage and changes of ownership, the great city of Nice finally became a permanent part of France.

Today's Nice is an idyllic sweep of coastline along the Baie des Anges on the Côte d'Azur. Its most famous street, the wonderfully named Promenade des

Anglais, runs for two and a half miles along the shore, embellished with palm trees and flowers. Originally built by English residents in 1822, it follows the long pebble beach where bikinied temptations loll in the sun and the chicest hotels like the pink-roofed Négresco face the sea.

It was not always so. Archaeological remains indicate that some 40 millennia ago early man settled here, but the first true city was founded in about 350 BC by Greeks from the colony of Marseille, who called it Nikaia, a name derived from the word 'victory' (*nike* in Greek).

About four centuries later Nice was taken over by the Romans, but with the fall of the empire, barbarians and Saracens sacked it in turn, obliterating the Roman city. By the 10th century, however, Nice had recovered its prosperity and was appropriated by the Counts of Provence. Then, in the 14th century, greed and murder led to its annexation by the House of Savoy. At that time Nice was ruled by the beautiful and kind Queen Jeanne of Provence, who had earlier made the fatal error of adopting Charles de Durazzo, Prince of Naples. Hungry to inherit the city, in 1382 Durazzo ordered his stepmother smothered. Into the ensuing chaos stepped Amadeus VII, Count of Savoy, who in 1388 fomented a rebellion and annexed the city, to the joy of the population.

For the next four centuries Nice remained part of the House of Savoy, although it was occasionally besieged, most famously in 1543 by the combined forces of France and Turkey under the generalship of that famous corsair Barbarossa.

During one assault, an earthy Niçoise named Catherine Ségurane was bringing food to soldiers manning a rampart when suddenly the Turks started swarming over the walls. Grabbing her carving knife, Catherine threw several attackers into the moat, grabbed their banner and inspired her fellow defenders. As the Turks fled in panic, Catherine mounted the walls and, turning her back on the enemy with scorn, lifted her skirt in one of the first recorded incidents of mooning.

In the late 18th century during the Revolution, French troops marched into Nice, and in 1793 it was incorporated into France. But when Napoleon fell in 1814, Nice once again reverted to the House of Savoy.

Finally, in 1859, French Emperor Napoleon III entered an alliance with the House of Savoy to kick the Austrians out of the north of Italy. As reward for his help he received Nice on this day in 1860 on the signing of the Treaty of Turin, an exchange confirmed by the Niçois in a plebiscite by 25,743 to 260.

Also on this day

1265: The Earl of Leicester Simon de Montfort convenes the first English parliament in Westminster Hall * **1936: George V dies with the 'help' of his doctors** * 1942: Reinhard Heydrich and fourteen other top Nazis meet at the Berlin suburb of Wannsee to set in motion the 'Final Solution'

21 January

Lenin is felled by a stroke

1924 Already partially paralysed, bedridden and unable to speak, this morning at his villa in the village of Gorky, Communist Russia's ruthless and implacable leader Vladimir Ilich Lenin suffered his fourth stroke in twenty months. At 5.50 that evening he died at the age of 53. No horny-handed son of toil, Lenin was born to an inspector of schools and was an inspired intellectual who spoke four languages. But he focused his brilliance on what he saw as the intolerable inequities of tsarist Russia. More than any other man, he established what he called 'the great experiment, the dictatorship of the proletariat'.

Ironically, Lenin's early death may have been brought on by the attack not of a tsarist counter-revolutionary but of a fellow radical. In November 1917 the Congress of Soviets had elected Lenin chairman of the Council of People's Commissars, in effect the most powerful man in Russia. Only months later he had peremptorily ordered the dissolution of the democratically elected Constituent Assembly in order to guarantee Bolshevik supremacy. The following August a disgruntled Socialist Revolutionary named Fanya Kaplan fired three shots at him as he headed for his car after a meeting, hitting him in the lung and at the base of his neck.

Fearing another assassination attempt, Lenin insisted on being taken to his own apartment rather than the hospital. There his doctors decided that it was too dangerous to remove the bullets, as one was lodged too close to his spine. In the meantime Kaplan was arrested, interrogated and, four days later, shot.

Lenin seemed to recover from his wounds, but from that time his health, already under the intolerable strains of revolution and war, started to deteriorate. Four years later he became so ill that in April 1922 the bullet from his neck finally had to be removed. Only a month later he suffered his first stroke, which left him paralysed on his right side.

A second stroke followed in December, leaving him bedridden, and in March a third stroke deprived him of speech. Ten months later his fourth and final stroke finished him off.

Three days after his death Petrograd was renamed Leningrad, and at his funeral, Lenin's corpse was swathed in a red flag saved from the Paris Commune of 1871. Four days after that, his mummified body went on display in the Lenin Mausoleum in Moscow's Red Square, but before his embalmment, his brain was removed so that it could be studied to identify the precise location of the cells responsible for his revolutionary genius.

Despite the adulatory theatrics of a grieving Communist Party, only weeks after Lenin's death rumours began to circulate that the real cause of his demise was not a stroke at all but syphilis. It was thought that he had contracted the disease as early as 1895, and in 1923 he had been treated with potassium iodide and a drug called Salvarsan, which were used at the time against syphilis. It was also said that the pathologist in charge of his autopsy had been ordered not to mention syphilis, and any syphilis-related indications were expunged from his report.

In all probability, however, the rumours of syphilis were simply malicious gossip fostered by Lenin's numerous enemies. His body bore none of the syphilitic lesions that normally occur in the last stages of the disease, and most historians concur that it was the stroke that killed him. So died the man who replaced one form of Russian tyranny with another that would keep his people oppressed until the end of the century. As Lenin had said: 'Liberty is precious – so precious that it must be rationed.'

Also on this day
1793: Louis XVI is guillotined * 1932: English critic and biographer Lytton Strachey dies * 1950: English writer George Orwell dies

22 January

'Mysterious little Victoria is dead and fat vulgar Edward is King'

1901 After 63 years, eight months and two days on the throne of England, Queen Victoria died on this day at the age of 81. 'We all feel a bit motherless today', wrote the American expatriate writer Henry James, 'mysterious little Victoria is dead and fat vulgar Edward is King'.

For most of her long life Victoria had enjoyed robust health, but in her last years, stricken by rheumatism, she had first used a stick and later needed a wheelchair. Nonetheless she continued to work until five days before the end. Then, in the words of British historian Lytton Strachey, 'as she lay blind and silent, [she] seemed to those who watched her to be divested of all thinking – to have glided already, unawares, into oblivion'. She died painlessly in her bedroom at Osborne House on the Isle of Wight, the royal residence designed by her husband.

Queen at eighteen on the death of her uncle, William IV, Victoria had the good fortune to marry her handsome cousin Prince Albert of Saxe-Coburg-Gotha, whom she adored, and the misfortune to lose him to typhoid fever after 21 years of marriage. Not an intellectual woman herself, for the remainder of her life she based her decisions on what she believed he would have thought. Essentially conservative, she had a particular dislike of women's suffrage, writing (in the third person, as was her wont): 'The Queen is most anxious to enlist everyone who can speak or write to join in checking this mad, wicked folly of "Woman's Rights", with all its attendant horrors on which her poor feeble sex is bent, forgetting every sense of womanly feeling and propriety.'

By the time of her death Victoria had become a sort of Queen Mother of

Europe. She and Albert had nine children, from whom many of Europe's royal houses were descended. Her grandsons George V of England and Kaiser Wilhelm II of Germany fought each other in the First World War, and 37 of her great-grandchildren were still living when she died.

Ironically, although Victoria spent 60 years fighting to retain the political power of the throne, during her long reign the British monarchy was gradually transformed into a predominantly ceremonial institution.

Also on this day

1561: English writer Francis Bacon is born * **1666: Taj Mahal builder Shah Jahan dies imprisoned in Agra** * 1788: English poet Lord Byron is born * 1879: Zulus massacre British troops at Isandlwana * 1924: Ramsay MacDonald takes office as Britain's first Labour Prime Minister

23 January

Birth of the painter who gave birth to Impressionism

1832 A Parisian newspaper once described him: 'Yellow gloves, a crisp cravat, superb shoes, light-coloured trousers and a flower in his buttonhole, he can be found striding along the Boulevard des Italiens with the hurried step of a man who is meeting a pretty woman; or one sees him at ease, smoking a good cigar, on the terrace of the Café Riche or the Café Tortoni.' Actor? Politician? Confidence man? None of these but one of Europe's greatest painters, Edouard Manet, who was born this day in Paris in 1832.

Born to wealth, Manet was expected to follow his father into law, but he was determined to become an artist. His first real fame came in 1863 when Napoleon III established the famous 'Salon of the Rejected' for paintings turned down by the prestigious but hidebound 'official' salon at the Louvre. It was there that Manet first displayed *Le Déjeuner sur l'Herbe*, a painting that both shocked and titillated the public by showing a nude woman casually enjoying a picnic in the woods with two unconcerned but fully dressed men.

Manet rejected the idea of painting classical allusions, claiming to paint only the commonplace, showing life as it was lived. 'There is only one true thing', he said, 'to paint spontaneously what one sees' – a comment that might have made some people wonder where he saw *Le Déjeuner sur l'Herbe*.

Although not truly an Impressionist himself, Manet is widely considered the father of Impressionism and one of the most influential painters of his century.

By the time he was in his late forties, Manet was suffering from the symptoms of syphilis. In constant pain and partially paralysed, he was forced to have his gangrened left foot amputated, but, further weakened by the operation, he died eleven days later on 30 April 1883 at the age of 51.

Also on this day
1783: French writer Stendhal (Marie Henri Beyle) is born * **1806: British prime minister William Pitt the Younger dies in London** * 1944: Norwegian painter Edvard Munch dies * 1947: French painter Pierre Bonnard dies in Le Cannet on the Côte d'Azur * 1989: Spanish painter and sculptor Salvador Dalí dies

24 January

The California Gold Rush

1848 It all started in the small Caloma Valley in California on this day in 1848 when a young carpenter named James Marshall was building a sawmill for his friend John Sutter. Glancing in the millrace of the new sawmill, he spied a golden pebble. 'I reached my hand down and picked it up', he wrote. 'It made my heart thump, for I was certain it was gold. The piece was about half the size and shape of a pea. Then I saw another …'

Marshall and Sutter quickly became partners, trying simultaneously to gather up the gold and keep their find a secret, but word slipped out. Thousands of prospectors were soon camped out nearby, searching for the precious metal; the California Gold Rush was on.

By the next year over 80,000 'forty-niners' (as the prospectors were called) had stampeded to the California goldfields, a number that had swelled to a quarter of a million within four years. The area became famous for its squalor, violence and lawlessness as brawling miners fought for their claims (and indeed for the claims of others).

Within ten years of Marshall's find, almost a million miners gouged and scraped the California landscape for over $500 million in gold, and the California Gold Rush forever left its legends of wild no-holds-barred frontier America, where prospectors could make a million or die in a gunfight.

Also on this day
AD 41: Roman emperor Caligula is assassinated * AD 76: Roman emperor Hadrian is born * **1712: Prussian king Frederick the Great is born in Berlin** * 1893: Randolph Churchill dies of syphilis & 1965 his son Winston Churchill dies of old age * 1920: Italian painter Amadeo Modigliani dies of TB in a Paris hospital

25 January

A marriage made in hell

1533 The bride was two months pregnant, and her elder sister had once been the bridegroom's mistress. The bridegroom, on the other hand, was still married to his first wife (who previously had been married to his elder brother). No wonder today's wedding ceremony was held in secret, in the western turret of what was then the old cardinal's palace, now called Whitehall.

And no wonder the marriage didn't work. It ended dramatically three years later when the bride lost her head for another man – and then lost it for her husband.

The bride of course was Anne Boleyn, at 26 not beautiful but dark-eyed and alluring. The bridegroom was Henry VIII, already 41, suffering from gout and running to fat. Anne's sister Mary was a previous mistress of Henry's, although he was still married to Catherine of Aragon, whom he had wed 24 years before. Before this, Catherine had been married at sixteen to his elder brother Arthur, who had died in less than a year, before the marriage had been consummated, or so claimed Catherine. Her marriage to Henry was finally annulled by Henry's own Archbishop of Canterbury, Thomas Cranmer, five months after Henry and Anne tied the knot.

The 'other man' to whom Anne lost her head was, according to the patently false charges against her, in fact several other men, including her own brother. And of course it was her loving husband Henry who finally made her lose her head forever so that he could marry once again.

The only success from the wedding was the two-month-old foetus that Anne was carrying in her womb. It turned out to be the future Queen Elizabeth I.

Also on this day

1515: French king François I is crowned at Reims * 1759: Scottish poet Robert Burns is born in Alloway, Scotland * **1947: Slow of mind from the ravages of syphilis, American gangster Al Capone dies in Florida**

26 January

Birth of a Romanian tyrant

1918 One of thirteen children from a peasant family, Nicolae Ceauşescu was born today in Oltenia, Romania. The hard life he lived created a hard man, one who joined the Communist Party's youth organisation at fifteen, later served a prison sentence for 'agitation' and finally rose to the top Party rank at the age of 47, in effect the Romanian dictator.

Ceauşescu followed three basic principles throughout his long dictatorship: independence from Russia (while still firmly in the Communist bloc), brutal repression of the Romanian people and extravagant self-aggrandisement. He razed great parts of Bucharest to build a massive presidential palace and destroyed countless villages for reconstruction along collectivist lines. His wife Elena virtually shared power with him, so great was her influence, and 38 other family members had important government posts.

The price Romania would pay for his rule was enormous in both human and economic terms. And finally, at the very close of 1989, the Romanian people decided they would no longer pay it.

In late December civil demonstrations against the government were met with gunfire and thousands were killed. But finally Ceauşescu and his wife were forced to flee Bucharest by helicopter, only to be captured almost immediately by his own army, which had joined the revolt.

Quickly put on secret trial by the insurgent army, the man who had ruled with an iron hand for 25 years was condemned to die along with his wife. Unrepentant to the end, he claimed: 'The people had everything they needed.' Still rock hard, the couple's last words were: 'We want to die together.' They faced a firing squad in an army barracks courtyard, refusing to be blindfolded. At four o'clock in the darkening afternoon a volley rang out. It was Christmas Day.

Also on this day

1823: French painter Théodore Géricault dies in Paris and British scientist Edward Jenner dies in Berkeley, Gloucestershire * 1880: American general Douglas Mac-Arthur is born * **1885: British general 'Chinese' Gordon is killed in the fall of Khartoum** * 1905: The Cullinan diamond, weighing 3,106 carats, is found near Pretoria, South Africa

27 January

Pushkin is killed in a duel

1837 On this winter afternoon a duel was fought, pistols at ten paces, in a lonely spot on the outskirts of St Petersburg. The Frenchman fired first, and Aleksandr Pushkin fell to the ground. Helped to his feet by a second, the poet aimed, then fired off a shot, hitting his adversary in the arm. It would have been a draw if both men had survived their wounds. But Pushkin, Russia's greatest poet, did not survive, dying two days later at the age of 37.

Imperial Russia was never a congenial place for free spirits, especially if the Tsar's government suspected them of harbouring dangerous political views, such as liberalism. Pushkin, however, was no longer the free spirit of his youthful days, his genius increasingly tethered to his desire for social standing in the capital. This desire led not only to ruinous debt but also to a dependence on the Tsar's favour for income and privileges, for which he gave up the right to travel and write as he pleased. The poet turned courtier knew that in court circles he was mocked for his pretensions. He also knew that his correspondence was regularly opened by the police.

Pushkin chose to fight a duel over an anonymous letter alleging that he was a cuckold, owing to his wife's affair with a Frenchman serving in the Russian

Horse Guards. He issued the challenge more to protect his position in society than because of the truth of the charge, which, knowing his wife's narcissistic nature, he doubted.

Upon his death, the government ordered his room sealed so police agents could inspect his papers. Troops were posted around the house in case of an outburst from the crowd of mourners gathering in the street. Only the briefest, most formal death notices were allowed in newspapers. Fearing public demonstrations at the scheduled cathedral service, the government secretly transferred the body to a smaller church in a futile attempt to limit attendance.

The public outcry at the loss of Pushkin was widespread among the middle classes and the intelligentsia, who blamed court aristocrats and the Tsar's repressive regime for his death. He became a symbol of liberalism destroyed by autocracy. When a young hussar officer circulated a bitter poem about Pushkin's aristocratic enemies, he was arrested for it and banished to the Caucasus. The officer's name was Mikhail Lermontov, and in time he would be the genius of the next generation, a successor to the great Pushkin.

On 6 February Pushkin's body was buried at Mikhaylovskoe, his country estate, a police spy in attendance to the end. The Tsar forbade the erection of a monument.

In *Eugene Onegin*, composed some years earlier, Pushkin foretold his own fate when he described the poet Lenski's death by duel.

> And Lenski, closing his left eye,
> Also began to aim – just then
> Onegin fired his fatal shot …
> The poet's destined hour had struck.
> Silent he let his pistol fall.

Also on this day

AD **98: Trajan becomes Roman Emperor when Nerva dies of apoplexy** * 1756: Wolfgang Amadeus Mozart is born in Salzburg * 1859: Kaiser Wilhelm II of Germany is born in Potsdam * 1901: Opera composer Giuseppe Verdi dies in Milan

28 January

Henry VIII dies in St James's Palace

1547 When Henry Tudor had mounted the throne of England in 1509 as King Henry VIII, he had been young, handsome, dashing, athletic, musical – in a word, glorious, all that a king should be. But now, prostrate and close to death, he had become at the age of 57 a megalomaniac – a callous, brutal and self-glorifying tyrant. A giant of a man for his time, he was 6 feet 2 inches tall and weighed over twenty stone, with a 54-inch waist. Partially crippled by a festering ulcer on his thigh caused by a jousting accident a decade before, his body was so bloated he could not mount the stairs on his own.

At the end, Henry lay dying in St James's Palace in London, surrounded by his counsellors, including the Archbishop of Canterbury Thomas Cranmer.

Legend has it that this great and terrible king died defiant, calling for a bowl of white wine, cursing monks and clerics and abruptly dying with the agonised shout: 'All is lost!'

In truth, however, Henry died as he had lived, refusing to believe that any power, even death, would dare approach him. During the night of 27 January he was asked if he wanted a priest. 'I will first take a little sleep', he replied, 'and then, as I feel myself, I will advise upon the matter'. So, confident that there was more time – that there would always be more time – Henry slipped off into a coma. At about 2 am on Friday, 28 January 1547 bluff King Henry passed from this earth.

Also on this day

814: Charlemagne dies at Aachen (Aix-la-Chapelle) * 1457: Henry Tudor, the future King Henry VII of England and first Tudor king, is born * 1521: The Diet of Worms opens, at which Martin Luther is outlawed by the Church * 1596: British admiral and freebooter Francis Drake dies off Porto Bello, Panama * 1935: Iceland becomes the first European country to legalise abortion

29 January

A tale of two cardinals

1630 Two men, who between them would control the destiny of France – and of Europe – for 38 years, met today for the first time, and quite by chance, at Lyon. There, papal envoys parlayed with King Louis XIII and his first minister, Cardinal Richelieu, in hopes of bringing to an end the War of the Mantuan Succession that had pitted France against Spain for the domination of northern Italy. Among the papal party was the son of a 29-year-old Roman steward with a reputation for brilliance and courage. His name was Giulio Mazzarino. On the cardinal's death he would take over his role as de facto ruler of France.

Even at this first meeting, Richelieu was impressed by Mazzarino, who had gained renown the previous year when he had galloped between the opposing armies at Casale shouting 'Peace, peace!' as if a truce had been signed. The armies fell back, and Mazzarino was marked as someone who would put his life on the line to stop a war. Richelieu invited him to dinner, later recalling: 'I took to him by instinct.' As for the young Mazzarino, he was captivated by the powerful cardinal. 'I resolved', he wrote, 'to devote myself to him entirely'.

Born in the Abruzzi and raised in Rome, Mazzarino had gone to university in Madrid and then entered the papal service, first as a captain in the papal army, then as a diplomat. After the Mantuan War he returned to Rome but was shortly sent to the French court as extraordinary nuncio. During the next few years he served both in France and back in Rome, always becoming ever closer to Richelieu.

During one of his sojourns in Paris, Mazzarino found himself at the gaming table, where his winnings were so great that a crowd gathered to watch him wagering stacks of gold écus. Among the onlookers was the French Queen, Anne of Austria. In a daring move, Mazzarino placed all his winnings on a single bet, and won. Claiming that the Queen's presence had brought him luck, he gallantly offered her 50,000 écus. He thus created a bond with the Queen that would serve him well only a few years hence.

In 1639 Mazzarino left the Pope's service and moved permanently to Paris, Frenchifying his name to Mazarin. (Contrary to some reports, Mazarin did not become a French citizen.) Richelieu, who had now been France's first minister for fifteen years, came increasingly to appreciate his dedication and perception, especially since his own health was failing. At the end of 1641, at Richelieu's urging, Pope Urban VIII made Mazarin a cardinal.

On 4 December just a year later, Richelieu finally succumbed to pneumonia compounded by pleurisy. On his deathbed he implored King Louis to appoint Mazarin as his successor. Louis named Mazarin first minister the next day. It was not a moment too soon, for Louis himself died of tuberculosis a mere five months later, leaving his wife Anne of Austria as regent for the four-year-old Louis XIV.

Despite her title, Anne of Austria was Spanish, and Mazarin's fluency in the language, acquired while studying in Madrid, had enabled him to form such solid bonds with her that she kept him on as first minister. According to Voltaire, he exercised 'that control that a shrewd man could have over a woman born with enough weakness to be ruled and enough firmness to persist in her choice'. Some historians maintain that the handsome, elegant cardinal entered into a loving affair with the Queen, and a few insist they actually married.

Whatever the relationship, Mazarin continued to guide the French ship of state, becoming the peacemaker of Europe. Helped by the victories of Turenne and Condé, he was largely responsible for the end of the bloody Thirty Years War in 1648. By 1659 he at last brought to a close the conflict with Spain. He also moved France even more towards the absolute monarchy that would reach its peak under Louis XIV. (This latter policy caused some of France's noblity to join in a revolt called the Fronde, which Mazarin eventually overcame, after having been twice forced to flee abroad.)

While serving his adopted country, Mazarin also managed to serve himself. He became a great art collector, with works by Titian and Raphael, and patronised Molière. He amassed a fortune of 40–50 million livres, worth at least £25 million in today's terms, and his mansion in Paris was so grand that it is now the Bibliothèque Nationale.

Mazarin died on 9 March 1661 at the age of 59. A cardinal who had never been ordained a priest, an Italian who had governed France for nineteen years without being a Frenchman, he was a worthy successor to his hero Richelieu, who had put him in a position of power.

Also on this day

1327: Edward III is crowned * 1737: Political essayist Thomas Paine is born * 1813: Jane Austen publishes *Pride and Prejudice* * 1820: George III dies after 60 years as king * **1853: Napoleon III marries the beautiful Spanish countess, Eugénie de Montigo** * 1856: Britain's highest decoration for valour, the Victoria Cross, is established

30 January

The scaffold built by a saint

1278 Wandering through Paris in the tenth arrondissement near the Gare de l'Est, you will come upon the historic Hôpital St Louis, built for plague victims in 1605. Ironically, it was next to the hospital's site, on the present rue de la Grange-aux-Belles, that St Louis himself had a more sinister edifice constructed during the first half of the 13th century. The saintly king's construction was the infamous gallows of Montfaucon.

Montfaucon was built like a great hall without a roof. It featured sixteen pillars attached to one another by chains of iron, standing on great stone blocks. Here the criminals and traitors of France were hanged – and left hanging until their corpses disintegrated.

On 30 January 1278 an unfortunate victim named Pierre de la Brosse was brought to the scaffold. De la Brosse had started life as a surgeon and valet to King Louis himself and had risen to become finance minister under Louis's son Philip III, the Hardy. Sadly, court intrigue eventually brought de la Brosse down, but in his death he started something of a tradition for French ministers of finance.

For after de la Brosse, Pierre Rémy (minister to Charles IV), René de Siran (to Philip the Fair), Euguerrand de Marigny (to Louis X), Olivier la Daim (to Louis XI) and Beaune de Samblançay (successively minister to Charles VIII, Louis XII and François I) all met their ends on the gallows of St Louis's Montfaucon. In fact, the dreaded platform endured until 1627 as a place of execution and was finally pulled down only in 1761.

Also on this day

1649: British King Charles I is beheaded * 1882: American President Franklin Delano Roosevelt is born at Hyde Park, New York * **1889: Rudolph, Crown Prince of Austria, shoots his seventeen-year-old mistress Maria von Vetsera and himself at his hunting lodge at Mayerling** * 1933: German dictator Adolf Hitler assumes power * 1948: A disgruntled fellow Hindu who blamed him for the partition of India and Pakistan shoots Indian leader Mohandas Gandhi to death at a prayer meeting

31 January

Shogun

1543 Japan in the 16th century was much like England in the 15th – a country nominally ruled by the emperor but in fact divided by warring *daimyos* (feudal barons) who constantly fought and schemed for power in a kaleidoscope of ever-shifting alliances. Born today near modern Nagoya was the great *shogun* (hereditary military dictator) Tokugawa Ieyasu, the man who would unite his country and give it 250 years of peace and stability.

Ieyasu's first permanent impact on Japanese history came when he was 46, even before he become *shogun*, when he transformed the small fishing port of Edo into his headquarters, bringing in thousands of his vassals and their families and building the largest fortress in the world. This was the real beginning of the city that today is called Tokyo, and now the Japanese emperor lives in Ieyasu's fortress, known as the Imperial Palace.

In 1600 Ieyasu took almost full control of Japan by annihilating a force of enemy *daimyos* at the Battle of Sekigahara, executing or banishing those who fought against him. In 1603 the powerless Japanese emperor awarded him the title of *shogun*. Fifteen years later Ieyasu subjugated the last remaining independent stronghold when he conquered Osaka. He ordered the beheading of every soldier who had defended it, lining the road from Kyoto to Fushimi with the heads of tens of thousands of samurai. But Japan was now united, truly under one government for the first time. It would remain so under the control of Tokugawa *shoguns* until 1857.

Ieyasu believed that another threat to Japan was Christianity, convinced that Catholic missionaries had spearheaded Spanish and Portuguese colonisation in Asia. (In Japan itself, the arrival of Francis Xavier in 1549 had been followed by the conversion of about 300,000 Japanese.) Therefore Ieyasu sanctioned official persecution of Christians, a precedent his Tokugawa successors expanded by banning all Christians shortly after his death.

What Ieyasu valued above all else was stability – in government and for the stratified Japanese social order. He laid down new laws to control the *daimyos* and their clans and discouraged foreign trade, thus starting the policy of 'national seclusion' that his successors would take to the extreme of forbidding Japanese to travel abroad or to return from overseas. (Foreign sailors who were shipwrecked on the coast of Japan were summarily executed.) Except for a handful of Dutch and Chinese merchants allowed to do business through the port of Nagasaki, Japan remained closed to foreigners until American warships under Commodore Matthew Perry forced the country to open for foreign trade in 1854.

Ieyasu died on 1 June 1615 at age 73. Recognised as the country's greatest leader, he was enshrined at Nikko as an aspect of the Buddha.

Also on this day

1606: English terrorist Guy Fawkes and three others are hanged, drawn and quartered * 1797: Austrian composer Franz Schubert is born * 1882: French republican statesman Léon Gambetta dies in Ville-d'Avray, near Paris * **1943: The Germans surrender at Stalingrad**

1 February

A king's assassination leads to the end of the Portuguese monarchy

1908 Cultured, multi-lingual, sophisticated and an expert in oceanography, King Carlos I of Portugal was better known to his subjects for the less inspiring aspects of his personality, namely his extraordinary extravagance and licentiousness. Perhaps his main distinction is that he is Portugal's only monarch ever to be assassinated.

Carlos had become King in 1889, but his country was beset by severe political and economic problems, including the metastasis of a rabid republican opposition. As problem led towards crisis, in 1906 the King, impatient with politics and popular demands, appointed João Franco as Prime Minister and virtual dictator. Despite Franco's attempts to reform the government's finances, rumours grew that he was illegally siphoning off money from the treasury to help Carlos pay for his profligate lifestyle.

Finally the combined pressure of Franco's stifling dictatorship and a faltering economy brought open revolt, and on 1 February 1908 King Carlos and his son Luís Filipe were gunned down in an open carriage riding through the Terreiro do Paço square in Lisbon. The two assassins were immediately shot by Carlos's bodyguard, and although they were later identified as members of the Republican Party, no one has ever proved whether they were anti-monarchical fanatics acting alone or agents of the Carbonária, a republican secret society. Carlos's eighteen-year-old son Manuel had also been riding in the carriage and was wounded in the arm. He was immediately acclaimed as King but, less than two years later, the Carbonária ignited another uprising in October 1910. This chased Manuel into permanent exile in England and brought an end to the rule of the House of Bragança, which had first gained the throne of Portugal on 15 December 1640.

Also on this day

1328: King Charles IV of France dies, ending the Capetian dynasty after 341 years, and Philip VI takes the throne, starting the Valois dynasty * 1793: Britain declares war on France, to last for 22 years * **1896: In Turin, Puccini's *La Bohème* is performed for the first time**

> Events written in **boldface** are covered in full in
> *365: Great Stories from History for Every Day of the Year,*
> the first volume in this series.

2 February

Of Candlemas and Groundhog Day

AD 1 Called Candlemas because of the custom of lighting candles during the festival, today commemorates the day in the year 1 when the Virgin Mary went to be purified in the Temple of Jerusalem 40 days after the birth of her son and to present Jesus to God, as described in the second chapter of Luke. Today this religious remembrance bears another name in Britain, and in America it has been transformed into something surprisingly different.

The earliest record of Candlemas comes from 4th-century Jerusalem, when it was celebrated on 14 February, forty days after the Eve of Epiphany, which was then celebrated as Jesus' birthday. But there was another, pagan, holiday on 15 February called Lupercalia, the Roman fertility festival honouring the god Pan. To wean good Christians away from heathen rituals, in AD 492 the canny (and saintly) Pope Gelasius I abolished Lupercalia and replaced it with Candlemas. (Good Pope Gelasius is also said to have replaced Lupercalia with Valentine's Day, so you'll have to take your pick which tale to credit.) In any event, fifty years later, Byzantine Emperor Justinian set Candlemas's date on 2 February, 40 days after Christmas Eve, but the holiday was celebrated only in the Eastern Empire, where Justinian held sway.

In the 7th century Pope Sergius I introduced Candlemas to his Catholic subjects in Rome, and over the centuries it made its way across Europe to the cold and remote outposts of Great Britain. There small children would celebrate the holiday with this song.

> If Candlemas be fair and bright,
> Come, Winter, have another flight;
> If Candlemas brings clouds and rain,
> Go, Winter, and come not again.

Although the verse is English, it will have a familiar ring to Americans, who need look no further than to America's Groundhog Day, also celebrated on 2 February. American tradition decrees that this is when the hibernating groundhog (really a woodchuck) comes out of his burrow to see if he can see his shadow. All is well if the day is cloudy, for this forecasts an early spring, but if his shadow can be seen, the groundhog returns to his hole for another six weeks' sleep.

Although the basic tradition of predicting the weather originated in Britain, German settlers in Pennsylvania brought with them the tradition of the beaver, transmogrified over time to the groundhog.

Sadly, while Groundhog Day reigns supreme in North America, the evocative name of Candlemas is no longer used in Britain, replaced by the more pious term the 'Presentation of Christ in the Temple'.

40

Also on this day

1594: Italian composer Giovanni di Palestrina dies on his 69th birthday * 1626: Charles I is crowned King of England * **1650: Charles II's mistress Nell Gwyn is born in London** * 1848: After the Mexican War, Mexico and the United States sign the Treaty of Guadalupe Hidalgo, setting the boundary at the Rio Grande and giving the United States 525,000 square miles of land (now most of Arizona, California, western Colorado, Nevada, New Mexico, Texas, and Utah) * 1882: Irish writer James Joyce is born in Dublin

3 February

Emperor Charles V lays aside his burdens

1557 On this day began the most celebrated retirement since Diocletian had resigned as Roman Emperor, 1,252 years before. This time it was a Holy Roman Emperor who was laying aside the burden of office, Emperor Charles V, who today at last reached his chosen sanctuary at the monastery of San Jeronimo at Yuste.

Once the ruler of more land than even Charlemagne, Charles had relinquished his titles one by one – Spain, the Lowlands and Spain's gigantic holdings in the Americas to his cold-eyed son Philip II, and Austria, Italy and the German provinces to his brother Ferdinand. He retained only a small but luxurious villa next to the monastery in the hard country of Spain's Extremadura. There he slept in a room from which, when the door was open, he could see the altar in the chapel from his bed and smell the incense carried in by the breeze.

For Charles was sick both physically and at heart. Ridden by gout (the disease from which his son Philip was later to die), he arrived at Yuste carried in a litter, too ill to mount a horse. And in his great task of reuniting the Christian world from the cleavage caused by Martin Luther, he knew he had failed. 'I have done what I could and am sorry that I could not do better. I have always recognised my insufficiency and incapacity', he mourned.

Charles installed himself in comfort with religion to support him and courtiers and his collection of clocks to while away the hours. Humble, saddened and sick, the great emperor prepared himself for a *buen morir*, a good death. He died eighteen months later at the age of 58, probably from malaria.

Also on this day

1377: A future pope butchers the citizens of Cesena, which leads to the Great Papal Schism * 1809: German composer Felix Mendelssohn is born * 1913: The 16th Amendment to the US Constitution is ratified, authorising the collection of income tax * 1924: 28th US president Woodrow Wilson dies

4 February

The Big Three meet at Yalta

1945 Today allied leaders Franklin Roosevelt, Winston Churchill and Joseph Stalin met at Yalta for a week of meetings that would determine the future and structure of post-war Europe.

Yalta is in the Ukraine facing the Black Sea. Once a chic resort where tsars built summer palaces and Russian nobility flocked, because of its beauty and mild climate, now it was battered and forlorn after the depredations of the Nazis and Stalin's deportation of the Tartars. Churchill called it the 'Riviera of Hades'.

By the time of the conference, the war in Europe had almost been won. In the East, Russia was crossing the Elbe, while in the West, American and British troops were racing for the Rhine, Paris liberated six months before. In total, the Allies had about 25,000 tanks and the same number of aircraft against fewer than 4,000 tanks and aircraft that Nazi Germany could still field.

Plans put forth at Teheran, the previous Big Three meeting of December 1943, to split post-war Germany into four occupied zones were confirmed at Yalta, and further progress was made in defining the functions of the United Nations, the founding conference of which was to be held in San Francisco only two months later. Trials for major war criminals were agreed, and the subject of German reparations was assigned to a commission when it became clear that Russia was determined to beggar Germany, stripping it bare of all heavy industry, including the steel, electrical power and chemical industries. As a sop to Roosevelt, Stalin promised to enter the war against Japan.

The most contentious question was Eastern Europe, where Stalin was determined to establish Soviet satellites, in direct contradiction to Roosevelt's and Churchill's vision of free democratic states. When Churchill pointed out 'You know, we have two parties in England', Stalin replied: 'One is much better.' To proposals that Allied observers should monitor elections, Russian Foreign Minister Molotov protested that it would be insulting to the self-respect and sovereignty of newly liberated countries.

Poland was a particularly acrimonious issue, especially for Churchill, whose country had gone to war to defend Polish independence in 1939. Stalin insisted that the Communist-backed Lublin government should run the country, while Roosevelt and Churchill demanded that members of Poland's London government-in-exile be included and free elections be held.

Eventually Stalin agreed to British-American demands for the establishment of 'interim governmental authorities [in Eastern Europe] broadly representative of all democratic elements in the population ... and ... free elections of governments responsive to the will of the people.'

And so, on 11 February the three leaders headed home, Churchill and Roosevelt hoping for the best, Stalin planning the worst. Two months later the exhausted Roosevelt died of a stroke.

In May Germany capitulated after Hitler's suicide, and in August, after the destruction and shock of two atom bombs, Japan surrendered unconditionally. And now Stalin broke all the promises he had made: there would be no free elections in Poland, Hungary, Czechoslovakia, Romania or Bulgaria. Russia would set up puppet Communist governments that would suppress other parties and rule by force, backed by Soviet tanks. As Churchill so memorably stated the following year: 'From Stettin in the Baltic to Trieste in the Adriatic an iron curtain has descended across the continent.' The Cold War had begun.

When the Yalta agreements were made public in 1946, the American right reacted with fury, aimed equally at perfidious Russia and at Roosevelt, who, they claimed, debilitated by his final illness, had 'given away' Eastern Europe.

The idea of Roosevelt's 'giving away' Eastern Europe was of course patently absurd. At the time of Yalta Russian troops already occupied most of Eastern Europe, including virtually all of Poland and parts of Germany. The only way to evict them would have been by force, something the Americans and British never contemplated – and could almost certainly not have achieved.

Always suspicious of Stalin, even before the conference Churchill had wondered whether 'the end of this war may well prove to be more disappointing than was the last'. And only a month after the conference closed, when the Russians declared the 'free' Poles ineligible for government, Roosevelt came fully to understand Stalin's duplicity. 'We can't do business with Stalin', he said. 'He has broken every one of the promises he made at Yalta.' When challenged on Yalta's outcome, he answered: 'I didn't say the result was good; I said it was the best I could do.'

Although Stalin died in 1953, the execrable system he instituted kept millions in totalitarian oppression until the collapse of the Communist system 44 years after his deceit at Yalta.

Also on this day

211: Caracalla becomes Roman Emperor * **1716: James Francis Edward, the Pretender, flees Scotland for France, never to return** * 1789: George Washington is elected President of the United States * 1794: In France, the Convention adopts the blue, white and red flag; blue and red were the colours of Paris, white the symbol of the monarchy * 1861: In Montgomery, Alabama, seven secessionist southern states form the Confederate States of America

5 February

The madness of King George brings on the Regency

1811 Today Parliament declared one of Britain's most unfortunate monarchs, King George III, insane – after 51 years on the throne. This act made regent one of the nation's most contemptible monarchs, George's son, the fat and indolent future George IV.

The elder George had succeeded to the throne in 1760 at the age of 22. Less than a year later he married Charlotte of Mecklenburg-Strelitz, who bore him fifteen children and probably provided some contentment for a king whose reign was beset by intractable problems such as Catholic emancipation in Ireland, revolution in North America and war with Napoleonic France.

For the first 28 years of his reign, George seemed entirely normal and was fondly referred to by his subjects as 'Farmer George' due to his love of agriculture. But some noticed his obsessive need to control his children and his rage when he failed. By the autumn of 1788, however, he began to show the first real symptoms of the madness that would eventually overwhelm him. In one famous incident, he mistook an ancient oak in Windsor Park for the King of Prussia, doffed his hat and engaged the tree in polite conversation.

Later George's madness became more virulent. He would ramble incoherently and foam at the mouth, occasionally turning violent, once trying to smash his son George's head against a wall. He let his beard grow, and then permitted only one side to be shaven. He also issued bizarre orders and suffered delusions, on one occasion claiming he could see his kingdom of Hanover through a telescope.

Today we know that George suffered from an excruciatingly painful metabolic defect known as porphyria that can bring on frenetic over-activity and delirium. But 18th-century medicine could see only insanity, and George was placed in the care of Dr Francis Willis, who proposed to cure his patient using methods 'for breaking in wild horses'. The King was often confined by a straitjacket or tied to his bed or his chair. When he babbled nonsense he was gagged, and Willis constantly threatened him to force him to behave. When Willis's methods failed to cure, other royal physicians tried to draw out the king's 'ill humour' by wrapping his feet and legs with cloths impregnated with blister powder.

In spite of this barbarous treatment, over the next twenty years George recovered intermittently and was mostly well enough to perform his role as king. But in November 1810, now seventy-three, he once again lapsed into incoherence and was manifestly unable to rule. Then, on this day the following year, under the terms of the Regency Act his son George was sworn in at the Privy Council in Carlton House, taking on all the functions of king.

Regent until George III's death in 1820 and then king until his own death in 1830, young George (IV) became one of his country's shabbiest monarchs. Addicted to laudanum, he was also an alcoholic whose favourite drink was cherry brandy. He wore corsets to disguise his corpulence and was so fat that he could not mount his horse. Repeatedly importuning Parliament for more money, he followed a sybaritic lifestyle surrounded by sycophants and eventually spent most of his time at the domed Royal Pavilion at Brighton, a farmhouse he had converted in Indian style with fanciful Chinese interior decorations. One Whig MP maintained that his lifestyle 'resembled more the pomp and magnificence of a Persian satrap seated in all the splendour of Oriental state, than the sober dignity of a British prince, seated in the bosom of his subjects'.

George III died on 29 January 1820, deaf, blind, and mad, at the age of 82. His son carried on in the same vein, also something of a fantasist, occasionally claiming to have been present at Napoleon's catastrophic defeat at the battle of Leipzig. Once he proudly announced that an attempt had been made on his life when someone fired an air pistol at his carriage as he was riding down the Mall. He spent his final years mainly in bed, weighing in at 350 pounds, with a 58-inch waist. Afflicted by high blood pressure and cirrhosis, he was finally felled by a stroke at 67 in June 1830. In reporting his death the *Times* summed up: 'There never was an individual less regretted by his fellow creatures than this deceased king. What eye has wept for him?'

Also on this day

1788: British statesman Robert Peel is born, Bury, Lancashire * 1881: Scottish historian Thomas Carlyle dies in London * 1897: French novelist Marcel Proust fights a duel with fellow writer Jean Lorrain for insinuating he was homosexual * 1937: President Franklin Roosevelt proposes increasing the number of Supreme Court justices and is accused of trying to 'pack' the Court

6 February

Philip the Fair becomes King of France

1286 When Philip the Fair was crowned in Reims today, it was the start of a 28-year reign that would change French history. (Some Anglophone historians have assumed that Philip was called 'The Fair' because he was blonde – which he was. But in French he is 'Philippe Le Bel' – the handsome.)

But handsome as he may have been, Philip was also silent, cold-blooded and moralistic, worshipping the memory of his grandfather Louis IX, whom Pope Boniface cannonised in 1297 as a favour to Philip. (Despite the pope's gesture, Philip refused all his attempts to increase his temporal power, even leaving posthumous curses on any of his sons who dared to subordinate France to any authority other than God's. In 1303 he sent his agent Guillaume de Nogaret to beard the pope at Anagni, a confrontation that led to Boniface's death two months later 'of shame and rage'.)

Apart from his quarrels with Boniface, Philip is best remembered for three acts that demonstrated his great and malevolent power.

In 1305 he manipulated the papal election, ensuring that a Gascon named Bertrand de Got would gain the papal throne. Got, assuming the name of Clement V, caused the papacy to enter into what is known as its Babylonian Captivity, moving its seat from Rome to Avignon, largely as a political reward for Philip.

A year later, in an act of anti-Semitic Christian piety combined with royal greed, he expelled all Jews from France, confiscating their property.

Then, a year after that, he suppressed the Order of the Templars, seizing the order's riches and eventually causing their innocent leader Jacques de Molay to be burnt at the stake for heresy.

Tradition has it that Molay, as he was being tied to the stake, called down a curse on all those involved. Whatever the reason, Philip, Pope Clement, who acquiesced in this judicial murder, and Philip's Prime Minister Nogaret (the same who had confronted Pope Boniface) all died within a year of Molay's immolation. Then Philip's three sons each died in turn without male heirs, bringing to an end the Capetian line of kings after 341 years of power.

Also on this day

1508: Maximilian I becomes Holy Roman Emperor * 1564: English poet and dramatist Christopher Marlowe is born * **1685: British King Charles II dies of kidney failure** * 1911: Fortieth US President Ronald Reagan is born * 1918: Women receive the vote in Great Britain * 1939: American detective story writer Raymond Chandler publishes his first novel, *The Big Sleep*

7 February

France votes for dictatorship

1800 Along with a new century, France had a new leader, Napoleon Bonaparte, the glamorous 23-year-old general who had triumphed first in Italy and then in Egypt.

Napoleon had staged a virtual *coup d'état* only a couple of months earlier, his celebrated *19 Brumaire*. (This was the date according to France's republican calendar that had been instituted in 1793. The rest of the Western world called it 9 November.) On that day he had sent his troops into the government chambers in the Orangerie, forcing the members of the Council of the Five Hundred to flee through the windows. That evening he was declared First Consul. But today was a peaceful affair, as the French electorate overwhelmingly confirmed him in that position and approved a new constitution by 3,011,007 votes in favour to 1,562 against. (Property laws and other restrictions meant that only a fraction of France's 30 million citizens could cast a vote.)

No doubt the French believed they were electing a strong leader for a democratic republic. But the new constitution for which they had voted gave the First Consul responsibility for initiating all new laws, appointing all ministers and declaring war and peace. He would also choose half the members of the Senate. The other two consuls could only advise and consult.

Only ten days after the results were in, Napoleon moved himself and his wife into the Tuileries, traditional home of the French monarch. It proved a portent for things to come.

Also on this day
1478: English statesman and Catholic martyr Thomas More is born * 1807: Napoleon defeats the Russians and Prussians at the Battle of Eylau * **1812: Charles Dickens is born in Portsmouth** * 1950: The United States recognises Emperor Bao Dai of Vietnam rather than Ho Chi Minh, who is recognised by Russia

8 February

Peter the Great dies at 52

1725 At 5 o'clock this morning Peter the Great, Tsar of all the Russias, suffered his last terrible convulsion, and death released him from agony.

Two years earlier Peter had put considerable strain on his health by his long campaign against Persia along the Caspian Sea. Then, in late 1724, he had heroically leaped into the frigid waters of the Gulf of Finland to save some soldiers whose ship was foundering on a sandbank. He had caught some sort of chill or flu but foolishly continued to work. But, although Peter was severely weakened by his exertions, modern analysis suggests that what actually killed him was acute cirrhosis, a condition doubtless caused by his frequent bouts of brutish drunkenness, bouts that he delighted in forcing his whole court to join.

Peter's ruthlessness and cruelty are well documented. To his enemies he gave no quarter, and after the Streltsy rebellion in 1698 he beheaded 80 conspirators with his own hand. But he denied that he was cruel, his perverse logic leading him to punish those who claimed that he was by having their tongues cut out. He also had his own son tortured to death.

In spite of it all, Peter was great indeed, as he virtually single-handedly turned Russia from an Asiatic nation into a Western one in just 35 years of dictatorial rule.

He reformed government at every level, introduced secular education and sponsored the Russian Academy of Sciences. In 1703 he permitted publication of the first Russian newspaper, *Vedomosti* (*Records*).

But most of all, he changed the outlook of his people, making Western dress mandatory and prohibiting beards. Strongly resisted by the *boyars* (landed aristocracy), he personally cut off their beards. Those who insisted on keeping them were forced to pay a 'beard tax'.

He also introduced scores of European industries to Russia and was responsible for his country's first navy – and first secret police.

When he died at 52, this giant of a man (he was about 6' 6") left his Swedish-born wife Catherine to succeed him as Russia's first woman ruler.

Also on this day
1587: Mary, Queen of Scots, is beheaded * 1828: French writer Jules Verne, author of *Twenty Thousand Leagues Under the Sea* and *Around the World in Eighty Days*, is born in

Nantes, France * 1820: US general William Tecumseh Sherman ('War is hell') is born * 1825: The House of Representatives elects John Quincy Adams as the sixth US president * 1904: The Russo-Japanese War begins

9 February

The mysterious death of a beautiful royal mistress

1450 The *maîtresse en titre* is a peculiarly French institution – the king's official mistress, recognised at court and usually wielding more influence than the queen. Many of France's most glamorously famous women have proudly borne this title – Diane de Poitiers, Gabrielle d'Estrées and Madame de Pompadour come to mind. Today the very first *maîtresse en titre*, Agnès Sorel, the dazzling 28-year-old mistress of King Charles VII, died suddenly at the Manoir de Mesnil near Rouen, igniting rumours that she had been murdered, perhaps even by the King's son.

Charles had first met Agnès when the court celebrated a festival at Nancy in 1444 when he was 41 and she was 22. Perhaps Charles was bored by his wife, Marie d'Anjou, whom he had married when he was ten and she only nine. Plain with a rather sharp nose, Marie had given Charles thirteen children but now, at 40, offered none of Agnès's vibrant sexuality.

Marie's remonstrances notwithstanding, Charles installed Agnès by his side, showering her with jewellery and giving her the beautiful château at Loches on the Loire and a grand estate called Beauté-sur-Marne, from which she gained the sobriquet *la Demoiselle de Beauté* (the Lady of Beauty).

Soon Agnès became the best client of the famed merchant and silversmith Jacques Coeur and was setting the fashion for bare shoulders and a deep décolletage. The court was intrigued but scandalised. One contemporary deplored her '*ribaudise et dissolution*' ('lewdness and dissoluteness'), and accused her of debauching the King, previously content with his wife. The court painter Jean Fouquet painted her as the Virgin – but with her left breast bared.

In less than five years as Charles's mistress, Agnès gave him three daughters, whom he legitimised. She also was a celebrated cook whose dishes were so renowned that today, over 500 years later, several are still included in the French 'cooking bible', *Larousse Gastronomique*. But all was not smooth sailing, as she made an enemy of Charles's son Louis (the future Louis XI), who hated her for displacing and, he thought, humiliating his mother the Queen. On one occasion he even slapped her across the face and chased her through the royal palace, sword in hand. She escaped only by running to the King's bedroom.

At the time of Agnès's ascendancy, King Charles was completing the rout of the English, begun by Joan of Arc fifteen years before. After retaking Guyenne and Normandy, at the beginning of 1450 he was pursuing the enemy near Rouen. Pining for her lover, Agnès, some six months pregnant, left Paris to meet him at Jumièges, but before she could join him she was struck down by a severe and bloody *flux de ventre* (stomach flux, i.e. dysentery). In two days she was dead. In her last words she lamented the human condition. *'C'est peu de chose, et orde et fétide, de nostre fragilité.'* ('It's a trifling thing, just filth, foulness and frailty.')

Agnès's death had been so quick that rumours immediately swept the court that she had been poisoned, probably on orders of the King's son Louis, but no proof could be found. Her heart was buried in Jumièges abbey while her body was interred at Loches.

So the cause of Agnès's death remained a mystery until, in 2004, her tomb at Loches was opened for forensic examination of her corpse. Tests confirmed that she had indeed died of poison – mercury found in a hair from her armpit was 10,000 times the normal amount. But also found in her body were eggs from worms, opening the possibility that she had overdosed herself with mercury in an attempt to cure herself. According to the forensic archaeologist: 'It is quite clearly an overdose administered by accident or deliberately. But which – we cannot say.'

Also on this day

1408: Henry IV defeats and kills Henry Percy, Earl of Northumberland, at Bramham Moor * **1567: Mary, Queen of Scots' husband Lord Darnley is murdered** * 1881: Fyodor Dostoyevsky dies in St Petersburg

10 February

The 18th century's greatest general runs from his first battle

1741 Frederick II had inherited the throne of Prussia only six months before, and now he decided to snatch the province of Silesia from the Austrians, who he supposed would be weak since Maria Theresa had been in power three months less than he had. Marshalling the formidable army left to him by his father, Frederick marched into Silesia, where on this day he met the Austrians in the snows of Mollwitz. Although Frederick had served under the great Austrian commander Eugene of Savoy in the Rhineland in 1734, this was his first real battle, and he had never before commanded an army in the field.

Shortly after noon on a day blindingly white with snow, the two armies formed up lines of battle, the Prussians outnumbering the enemy 21,000 to 19,000. But as the Prussian infantry advanced, Austrian cavalry smashed into its right wing, leaving the Prussian flank dangerously exposed. The battle looked so desperate that the young Prussian king, terrified he would be captured, galloped from the field, leaving command in the hands of his experienced field marshal, Phillip von Neipperg, who quickly rallied the Prussians. Asked if his men should fall back, Neipperg told his soldiers: 'We'll retreat over the bodies of our enemies.' Ordering a general advance, he soon had the Austrians on the run.

Although Prussia won the battle, it was an inauspicious beginning for the King, but it was the last time he would leave the field early. As he later recalled: 'Mollwitz was my school.'

During the next 45 years Frederick made Prussia the foremost military power in Europe and firmly established himself as the greatest commander of his age. If he had run from his first battle, he aggressively attacked in most of the rest, once chiding his Guards when they hesitated to charge the Austrians at Kolin: '*Ihr Racker, wollt ihr ewig leben?*' ('You rascals, would you live forever?') We know him as Frederick the Great.

Also on this day

1258: The Mongols destroy Baghdad * 1482: Florentine sculptor Luca della Robbia dies * 1763: The French and Indian War ends with the Peace of Paris * 1775: English essayist Charles Lamb is born in London * **1840: Queen Victoria marries Prince Albert Saxe-Coburg-Gotha in the Chapel Royal, St James's Palace, London**

11 February

The legend of Japan's first emperor

660 BC According to a 14th-century Shinto monk, in the Age of the Gods Japan was known by the snappy name of 'ever-abundant land of reed-covered plains and bountiful rice fields'. Later, at the time of the sun goddess Amaterasu, another name was used, Yamato (meaning 'footprints on the mountains'), in remembrance of the time when the soil was still soft and men trekked across the mountains for food.

Amaterasu sent her celestial grandson Ninigi to govern the Earth, giving him the sacred sword and mirror, which became imperial emblems. Ninigi in turn had a great-grandson named Jimmu, who hopped from island to island conquering Japan's early tribes and ending in Yamato, where he became Japan's first emperor, consecrated at Kashihara on Unebi Mountain this day in 660 BC.

From that day forward the same imperial line has ruled Japan. In 1890 the Japanese government built a Shinto shrine at Unebi where Jimmu is believed to be buried, and even now, every 11 February is a holiday called Kenkoku Kinen no hi (National Foundation Day), and large crowds gather at the Kashihara Shrine to celebrate that first royal enthronement over two and a half millennia ago.

Also on this day
1650: French philosopher René Descartes dies in Stockholm * 1732: George Washington is born (when the Gregorian Calendar is introduced in Britain and its colonies in 1752, 11 February becomes 22 February) * **1847: Inventor Thomas Edison is born in Milan, Ohio** * 1879: French caricaturist Honoré Daumier dies

12 February

A simple beginning

1809 The American legend of men making good on their own merits, without money, connections or influence, is given substance in the life of a man who was born today in the humblest of circumstances.

A photograph still exists of the small log cabin on Sinking Spring Farm in the backwoods three miles south of Hodgenville, Kentucky where he was born. With only one room, a dirt floor and a plain clay chimney to carry out the smoke, it was just eighteen feet wide by sixteen feet long.

The child's grandfather had been scalped and killed by Indians, so his father grew up a wandering boy labourer, without education and functionally illiterate, and eventually became a farmer and carpenter. His fervently religious mother, who was probably illegitimate, was stoop-shouldered and flat-chested, worn away with the effort of raising a family in primitive settler conditions. Unable to write, she was reduced to 'making her mark' instead of signing her name.

When the child was seven the family moved to Indiana, where he helped clear fields and harvest crops. Then his mother died when he was nine and he went only sporadically to school, attending five of them but receiving in all only eighteen months of formal education. An early schoolmate described his haphazard appearance: 'His shoes, when he had any, were low. He wore buckskin breeches, linsey-woolsey shirt and a cap made of the skin of a squirrel or a coon. His breeches were baggy and lacked by several inches meeting the tops of his shoes, thereby exposing his shin-bone, sharp, blue and narrow.'

As a teenager he split rails to fence his father's farm and later crewed on a flatboat on the Mississippi. Meanwhile he taught himself with borrowed books despite his father's complaint that he was 'still fooling hisself with eddication; I tried to stop it, but he had got that fool idea in his head and it can't be got out.'

Now a young man, he worked as a storekeeper, postmaster and surveyor until at 23 he took up the study of law in his spare time and eventually entered politics.

Such were the humble beginnings of Abraham Lincoln, America's greatest president, who freed 4 million black slaves and preserved the United States by his leadership during the Civil War. Always self-effacing about his early life and never self-important about what he had achieved, he once observed: 'Tis better to be silent and be thought a fool, than to speak and remove all doubt.'

Also on this day
1554: Lady Jane Grey and her husband are beheaded for treason * 1804: Prussian philosopher Immanuel Kant dies * 1809: British naturalist Charles Darwin is born

13 February

The long, adventurous life of Benvenuto Cellini

1571 Sculptor, author and perhaps history's greatest goldsmith, Benvenuto Cellini was also a notorious adventurer who at fifteen had been banished from his native Florence for brawling, at 23 condemned to death for fighting, and at 35 pardoned by the Pope for killing a rival goldsmith.

He was a true Renaissance man. His exquisite jewellery was as famous in his own time as it is today, and his greatest piece of sculpture, the bronze Perseus holding the Gorgon's head, still stands in Florence's Loggia dei Lanzi. (Cellini was so sure of his own genius that when Duke Cosimo de' Medici wanted to buy the statue for a nominal price, the sculptor angrily told him that 'his Excellency would find any number of men who knew how to build cities and palaces, but for making statues like my Perseus, I doubted whether he would find a single one in the whole world.')

This immensely talented artist was also a fierce soldier. He played a critical role in defending Pope Clement VII in the Castel' Sant'Angelo against the rampaging troops of Emperor Charles V when they sacked Rome in 1527. Cellini claimed to have shot the attacking commander, the constable of Bourbon.

Later Cellini became court goldsmith to François I of France and, while creating masterpieces, scandalised Paris by using prostitutes for models, whom he would occasionally beat. His own mistress publicly accused him of sodomising her, and he was constantly involved in fighting in the streets.

Yet in the Renaissance talent was all. When asked why he had not had Cellini punished, Pope Paul III replied: 'Men unique in their professions, like Benvenuto, were not subject to the laws.'

Cellini died on this day in his native Florence at the age of 70.

Also on this day
1542: English Queen Catherine Howard is beheaded at age 22 * 1867: Johann Strauss the Younger's waltz the 'Blue Danube' is played publicly for the first time in Vienna * 1883: German composer Richard Wagner dies * **1945: British aircraft firebomb Dresden**

14 February

The martyrdom of St Valentine leads to a romantic tradition

AD 270 Today in Rome, Bishop Valentine of Interamna (now Terni in Umbria) was stoned to death and then beheaded on the orders of Emperor Claudius II Gothicus, but the reasons for the Emperor's brutal command have become clouded with the passing of the centuries. (Indeed, there are even stories of two other Valentines, both improbably executed on 14 February.)

One story maintains that Claudius had outlawed marriage for young men, believing that bachelors without the encumbrance of families made better soldiers, but Bishop Valentine had continued secretly to perform weddings. Another account insists that Valentine had been arrested for converting Romans to Christianity (Claudius was a pagan). Whatever the true reason, Claudius ordered his execution.

But while Valentine was in prison he fell in love with the blind daughter of the jailer. Through his love for her and his Christian faith he restored her sight, and just before he was led away for execution he sent her a last letter signed 'from your Valentine'. And so the romantic legend of Valentine began.

Over two centuries later, in 496, another saint, Pope Gelasius I, declared 14 February a Christian feast day to honour him. But canny Gelasius was doing more than simply commemorating the martyrdom of a saint. At the end of the 5th century many people stubbornly hung on to a pagan celebration called Lupercalia, an ancient Roman fertility festival that took place each year on 15 February.

During Lupercalia the priests, called *Luperci*, sacrificed a goat and a dog and then smeared the animals' blood on the foreheads of two naked young men. The young men then put on loincloths and ran about the city gently striking young women with strips of hide from the sacrificed goats, thus ensuring the women's fertility. Another feature of the Lupercalia was a lottery in which the names of nubile young girls were placed. Then each young man of the town drew lots to find the name of his lover for the duration of the festival.

Over the centuries Roman soldiers spread this festival throughout Europe, and even when Pope Gelasius substituted St Valentine's Day for the Lupercalia, some of Lupercalia's sexual celebration continued to be associated with the holiday.

By happy coincidence, during the Middle Ages the tradition of finding a partner at Lupercalia/St Valentine's Day was reinforced by an old folk belief that halfway through February birds find their mates. Some claim that Geoffrey Chaucer was the first to make this connection explicitly in his 1381 poem 'Parliament of Foules' honouring the engagement between England's King Richard II and Anne of Bohemia:

For this was sent on Seynt Valentyne's day
Whan every foul cometh ther to choose his mate

At about the same time it became the fashion for young men to give the women who attracted them *billets doux* mentioning St Valentine. It is said that in 1415 Charles, duc d'Orléans, who had been captured at the Battle of Agincourt and sent to the Tower of London, sent the first true Valentine card to his wife.

The tradition of sending Valentines took a big step forward in 1797 when an English publisher brought out *The Young Man's Valentine Writer*, a self-help manual for the lovelorn. Valentine's cards became widespread in the United States only in the 1840s, when Esther Howland, a romantic Mount Holyoke graduate from Worcester, Massachusetts began mass-producing them.

Today millions of Valentines are sent each year, 85 per cent of them by women. Sadly, in 1969 Pope Paul VI dropped the Feast of St Valentine from the Catholic calendar, maintaining that the saint's historical origins were highly suspect.

Also on this day

1400: Richard II is murdered at Pontrefact Castle * 1776: English economist Thomas Malthus is born * 1779: Natives on Hawaii kill Captain James Cook * 1929: The St Valentine's Day Massacre: Al Capone's gang machine guns seven members of Bugsy Moran's gang in a warehouse in Chicago

15 February

Galileo is born in Pisa

1564 Pisa: the home of the Leaning Tower and of course its most famous resident, Galileo Galilei, who was born there today.

When Galileo was about ten, his family moved to Florence, but in 1581 he returned to Pisa to enter the university there, intending to study medicine, but soon switching to Aristotelian philosophy and mathematics. It was then that his genius began to blossom.

Galileo's first great discovery took place in the Pisa cathedral, next to the leaning campanile. There at the age of nineteen he timed the oscillations of a swinging lamp against the pace of his own pulse to find that each swing took exactly the same time no matter what its width. Thus the pendulum was born. Later he used the Leaning Tower itself to demonstrate that two objects of different weights fall at the same speed and acceleration.

At 28 Galileo moved to Padua and later to Florence where, having invented the refracting telescope, he discovered that the Sun has spots, the Moon is cratered and mountainous instead of smooth, Jupiter has satellites and the Milky Way is composed of stars.

But what launched Galileo into controversy was his confirmation of the heretical theories of Copernicus that the Earth revolves around the Sun. To make matters worse, his unorthodox book, *Dialogo Sopra i Due Massimi Sistemi del Mondo, Tolemaico e Copernicano* (*Dialogue on the Two Great Systems of the World, Ptolemaic and Copernican*), was written not in scholarly Latin but in Italian that any educated man could understand. Horrified, the Jesuits thought his teachings were in direct contradiction to the Scriptures and more dangerous 'than Luther and Calvin together'. Summoned to Rome by the Inquisition in 1633, Galileo recanted his views, but as he rose from his knees at the end of the trial he muttered the famous: '*E pur si muove.*' ('But it *does* move.')

Condemned by Pope Urban VIII, Galileo never returned to his natal Pisa, spending the remaining eight years of his life under house arrest in Arcetri on the outskirts of Florence, seeing only those visitors permitted by a watching Church.

When Galileo died on 8 January 1642 in his 78th year, Rome forbade the construction of any memorial, but the Medici family, which had long supported him, arranged for him to be buried in Santa Croce. Always cautious, the Vatican waited 350 years until finally absolving him of his sins in 1992.

Also on this day

1710: Louis XV is born * **1898: The battleship *Maine* explodes in Havana harbour, touching off the Spanish-American War** * 1944: Allied planes destroy the ancient monastery at Monte Cassino in Italy

> Events written in **boldface** are covered in full in
> *365: Great Stories from History for Every Day of the Year*,
> the first volume in this series.

16 February

The unscrupulous king who unified Portugal

1279 In spite of having a language distinctively its own, Portugal had great difficulty in becoming a single nation, but its final unification owed much to King Alfonso III, who died on this day.

The country's name stems from Portus Cale, an ancient community established in pre-Roman times on the Douro river. From the 3rd century BC the Romans were in control – Julius Caesar governed the territory for a period before his Gallic conquests. The Romans called it Lusitania, after a local tribe that lived there. Centuries later, as Rome collapsed, the Germanic Suebi took over, only to be conquered by the Visigoths who in turn were brought down by Moors invading from North Africa in the 8th century.

In the centuries that followed, the Portuguese themselves gradually reconquered much of their own country, and the nation finally became independent in 1139, but some of what is today's Portugal was still under Moorish control. At the beginning of the 13th century Muslims in Portuguese Portugal were theoretically allowed to become citizens, although large numbers were captured and sold into slavery.

Born in about 1225, Alfonso was the son of King Alfonso II. On his father's death the kingdom went to his elder brother Sancho, leaving poor young Alfonso no way forward except to usurp the throne. Aided by a Church enraged by Sancho's confiscation of Church property, he won a two-year civil war, exiled his brother to Toledo and took the title of Alfonso III.

Once in power, however, Alfonso showed little gratitude, first entering a bigamous marriage and then suffering excommunication for commandeering yet more Church property.

In the meantime he was slowly occupying the last remaining Muslim enclaves in the Algarve, completing the reconquest of the country and transferring the capital from Coimbra to Lisbon, where it has remained to this day. When he died, he had ruled his nation for 34 years.

Also on this day

1822: English scientist and founder of eugenics Francis Galton is born * 1862: General Ulysses S. Grant wins the first major Union victory of the American Civil War when Fort Donelson in Tennessee surrenders with 15,000 troops * **1940: The Royal Navy captures the *Altmark*, freeing 300 British sailors but triggering Hitler's invasion of Norway** * 1959: Fidel Castro takes over the Cuban government, with the support of the United States

17 February

'Peccavi!'

1843 In London's Trafalgar Square stands a bronze statue of General Sir Charles Napier, the intrepid British soldier whose fame today is based more on his way with words than on his military exploits.

While soldiering in British-controlled India, Napier was admonished by local Hindus for maintaining the British prohibition of *suttee*, the practice of burning widows alive on the funeral pyres of their husbands. 'You say that it is your custom to burn widows', Napier told a delegation of Hindus. 'Very well. We also have a custom: when men burn a woman alive, we tie a rope around their necks and we hang them. Build your funeral pyre; beside it, my carpenters will build a gallows. You may follow your custom. And then we will follow ours.'

Perhaps even more famous was Napier's earlier report on his accomplishments in the province of Sindh (now in Pakistan).

On the morning of this day he entered in his diary: 'It is my first battle as a commander: it may be my last. At sixty, that makes little difference; but my feelings are, it shall be do or die.' He then led his small force of 400 British and 2,200 Sepoys to a crushing victory over 30,000 Baluchis in the battle of Miani. Napier hurled himself into the midst of the conflict, fighting hand-to-hand. At the end of the battle he finished off the enemy by personally leading a devastating cavalry charge.

Five weeks later he scored a second major victory at Dabo, near Hyderabad, gaining full control of the entire province of Sindh. Entering Hyderabad, he ensconced himself in the Emir's palace and reported his triumphs to headquarters with one of the most remarkable military communications of all time, consisting of a single word: '*Peccavi!*' (Latin for 'I have sinned [Sindh]').

Also on this day

1653: Italian composer Arcangelo Corelli is born * **1673: At the Palais Royale theatre in Paris, French playwright Molière collapses on stage and dies** * 1776: Edward Gibbon publishes *The History of the Decline and Fall of the Roman Empire* * 1821: Irish femme fatale Lola Montez (Marie Dolores Eliza Rosanna Gilbert) is born in Limerick * 1909: Apache leader Geronimo dies of pneumonia at Fort Sill, Oklahoma

18 February

Martin Luther is happy to die

1546 Perhaps the strain of all the years of defying the Pope and most of the Christian world became unbearable for Martin Luther, because once when the Dowager Electress of Saxony wished him many years of long life, he replied: 'Madame, rather than live another forty years I would give up my chance of Paradise.'

So felt Martin Luther, who was first an Augustinian monk, and then had become, in order, a priest, a university teacher and a celebrity and condemned heretic.

In the midst of a snowy winter in early 1546 Luther travelled to Eisleben to effect a reconciliation between two young princes to whom he owed obedience. Already elderly and somewhat frail, he contracted a chill, and now, at the age of 62 years, three months and eight days, he died of a heart attack in the town where he was born. He was buried in Wittenberg, where he had famously nailed his 95 theses to a church door 29 years before.

Through his protestations and strength of belief, Luther gave the world Protestantism, as well as several centuries of religious war. But perhaps Luther was a less solemn character than his monkish dedication might suggest. He is thought to have written this cheerful doggerel:

Wer nicht liebt Wein, Weib und Gesang,
Der bleibt ein Narr sein Leben lang.
(Who loves not woman, wine and song,
Remains a fool his whole life long.)

According to legend, he also gave us a most joyful tradition, the Christmas tree. The story goes that one Christmas Eve he took a walk in a nearby forest where he was profoundly moved by the snowy fir trees shimmering in the starlight. To remind local children of the beauty of God's creation, he brought a tree indoors and decorated it with candles to simulate the stars.

Also on this day

1455: Florentine painter Fra Angelico (Guido di Pietro) dies in Rome * **1478: Edward IV's brother George, Duke of Clarence, is executed by being drowned in a butt of Malmsey** * 1564: Michelangelo Buonarroti dies * 1678: John Bunyan's *Pilgrim's Progress* is published

19 February

John Wycliffe is tried for heresy

1377 John Wycliffe considered himself a great reformer. He saw the Church and its masters waxing ever fatter and richer and moving ever further from the spiritual needs of mankind. Indeed, he bitterly attacked everyone from the Pope and his cardinals to monks and friars for their greed and worldliness. He also carried on a somewhat arcane debate about transubstantiation, a subject of interest so typical of the medieval world.

Not surprisingly, the Church struck back. On this day a somewhat frail (he was only 47), white-bearded Wycliffe was brought to trial for heresy in the Lady Chapel of St Paul's Cathedral in London. The presiding Bishop of London, William Courtenay, demanded that he 'explain the wonderful things which had streamed forth from his mouth'. Surely Wycliffe would have been condemned and probably put to death if not for the armed intervention of Duke John of Gaunt, son of the King, who threatened that he 'would humble the pride of the English clergy'. With the Duke's guard intimidating the prosecuting churchmen, Wycliffe went free, able to return to his greatest work, the first English translation of the entire Bible.

But the mighty Church was not to be denied. At the Council of Constance some 31 years after Wycliffe's death, he was at last condemned of heresy. His corpse was disinterred, burned and thrown into the River Swift.

By then, of course, it was far too late to prevent the spread of his teachings. Church reform became inevitable, and Wycliffe has become known in English history as the Morning Star of the Reformation.

Also on this day
1405: Mongol conqueror Tamerlane the Great (Timur) dies at 68 in Kesh, near Samarkand, Transoxania (now in Uzbekistan) * 1473: Astronomer Nicholas Copernicus is born in Torun, Poland * 1717: English actor David Garrick is born * 1743: Italian composer Luigi Boccherini is born in Lucca * **1945: US Marines land on Iwo Jima**

20 February

'Here lies Josef II, who failed in all his undertakings'

1790 Today died one of history's most infuriating and contradictory monarchs, Josef II of Austria.

Josef was a man fired by a mission – to better his people and modernise his country. Unfortunately his lofty aims were matched by his stubborn insistence that only he knew how to achieve these aims and his dogged determination to involve himself in the smallest details.

On the death of his father, at the age of 24 Josef became co-regent with his remarkable mother, the Empress Maria Theresa, but, realising her son's shortcomings, she took all the important decisions herself. But when Maria Theresa died in 1780, Josef was on his own.

A man of boundless energy, Josef formulated innumerable decrees to improve the lives of his subjects but never thought to consult those very subjects themselves. He infuriated the richer ones by his own simple lifestyle, putting an end to imperial extravagance, and alarmed those lower down the social scale by his insistence on continual change from traditional ways of doing things.

Josef fought two unnecessary wars with mixed results, but his most contentious acts were domestic. He abolished serfdom, no doubt to the joy of those freed but to the rage of many landowners. Much more controversial, he broke the power of the Church in a highly religious country, dissolving any monasteries he felt were not 'useful' – not involved with teaching or tending the sick. Some 700 were shut down, forcing 36,000 monks to leave their orders. He also established freedom of religion in a highly Catholic country and further infuriated the Church by freeing the Jews from many of their legal constraints, but with this act greatly enriched Austria's cultural life.

All the while Josef's subjects disliked and resisted most of his reforms, largely because they were imposed from above by this arrogant, opinionated monarch. Meanwhile Josef himself became increasingly bitter and self-pitying as he came to realise how little thanks he got for what he saw as vast improvements in the lives of his people. Just before he died he wrote his own epitaph with instructions for it to be carved on his tomb. 'Here lies Josef II, who failed in all his undertakings.'

As the historian Friedrich Schreyvogl has written: 'When Josef died, deserted by all his friends, his efforts to achieve freedom and general welfare for his subjects seemed to have been in vain. Today, however, … he is considered the benefactor of his subjects, the people's emperor, who by his many voyages and inspections devoted himself to all matters of greater or lesser importance. In his century he had predicted there would be a time when general welfare took precedence over individual prosperity. But he was born one century too soon.'

Also on this day

1437: Sir Robert Graham and a band of Highlanders stab James I of Scotland to death at a Dominican monastery at Perth * **1810: Austrian patriot Andreas Hofer is executed on orders from Napoleon** * 1872: The Metropolitan Museum of Art opens in New York

21 February

Борúс Годунóв

1598 Were it not for the power of art, today only historians might remember Boris Godunov, an anomaly in the long, bloody history of Russian tsars. Today the *Zemsky Sobor* (national assembly) elected him Tsar of Muskovy, confirming his de facto seizure of power six weeks before.

Of Tatar extraction, Godunov had served in the court of Ivan IV (the Terrible) and saw combat as an archer in Ivan's guard. When he was 29 he was promoted to the rank of *boyar* (roughly, nobleman) when Ivan married his son the tsarevich Feodor to Godunov's sister Irene. Four years later Ivan died, and Feodor now became Tsar. But, fortunately for Godunov (if unhappily for Irene), Feodor was severely mentally retarded, so Feodor's uncle Nikita Ramanovich and Godunov were appointed joint regents. Then, only three months after Feodor's coronation, Ramanovich died, leaving Godunov as the most powerful man in Russia.

For fourteen years Godunov ruled Muskovy through the weak-minded Tsar, and generally governed wisely, in spite of political attacks from other *boyars*, who tried to destroy his power by divorcing Feodor from Godunov's sister. Godunov's solution was to banish or tonsure the chief conspirators.

Godunov's next major challenge came in May 1591 when the Tsar's younger brother Dmitry suddenly died. Fingers pointed at Godunov, who was suspected of arranging the death so that he could put himself in line for the throne after Feodor. Some historians still argue that Godunov was guilty, although there is no compelling proof.

Once again Godunov survived the threat, but six years later, on 7 January 1598, Feodor died, leaving the country both without a tsar and without an heir. Recognising that rival *boyars* would depose if not execute him, Godunov convened the *Zemsky Sobor*, which unanimously elected him Tsar on this day in 1598.

Tsar Boris ruled well, importing foreign teachers and sending young Russians abroad in an effort to modernise his backward country. But he was increasingly hated for the coldness of his demeanour and his unending suspicion about the motives of all around him. He sought out informers and convicted suspects on unproven accusations, even forbidding the most powerful *boyars* to marry for fear that they might raise families with royal ambitions. One of the families he banished would be heard from again – the Romanovs.

But in 1603 a pretender claiming to be Prince Dmitry started to raise an army in Lithuania while declaring that he, not Boris, was the real Tsar. In fact, he was a deluded but convincing nobleman-turned-monk named Yury Bogdanovich, who probably sincerely believed he was Dmitry. Leading a force of Cossacks reinforced by adventurous Lithuanian and Polish nobles, False Dmitry invaded Russia in the autumn of 1604. As his forces neared Moscow the following April, Boris died of a heart attack. Then the Russian army switched their allegiance to False Dmitry, who jubilantly entered Moscow in June and was proclaimed Tsar. Rid of Boris at last, Russian *boyars* put his infant son to death. But False Dmitry's reign was short; only eleven months later a disgruntled *boyar* murdered him during a *coup d'état*.

Although a competent ruler, Godunov's most noted accomplishment was usurping rather than inheriting the throne like almost all the other Russian tsars. Like Macbeth in Scotland and Don Carlos in Spain, his most enduring fame comes less through his achievements than through works of art. In 1831 Aleksandr Pushkin published his great drama *Boris Godunov*, in which an insatiably ambitious Godunov murders the real Dmitry to clear his own path to the throne, and False Dmitry is portrayed as a liberator. At the close, a guilt-stricken Godunov, haunted by hallucinations, descends into madness and expires. Then in 1874 the Russian composer Modest Mussorgsky staged his opera *Boris Godunov* based on Pushkin's play. Today Mussorgsky's work is still enthusiastically performed, having thrice been re-orchestrated, twice by Mussorgsky's great friend Nikolai Rimsky-Korsakov and half a century later in 1959 by Dmitri Shostakovich.

Also on this day

1431: Joan of Arc's trial begins in Rouen * 1613: The Romanov dynasty begins: Michael Romanov, son of the Patriarch of Moscow, is elected Russian Tsar * 1893: Spanish classical guitarist Andés Segovia is born in Linares * **1916: German artillery opens fire to start the Battle of Verdun** * 1940: The Germans begin construction of a concentration camp at Auschwitz

22 February

Scandale *at the court of Louis XIV*

1680 It was the greatest scandal of the entire 72-year reign of Louis XIV. First there were ever-increasing rumours circulating at court, and then little by little hard evidence had started to come in: certain members of the French nobility were practising witchcraft. Worse, the evil art extended all the way to murder by poison and blasphemous black masses. Worse yet, there was proof that the leading practitioner was the notorious Catherine Monvoisin, known as Madame La Voisin, and that one of her chief clients for love potions was none other than the King's *maîtresse en titre*, Françoise-Athénaïs de Montespan.

Luckily hearty King Louis survived the love potions with no worse effects than recurring headaches and an upset stomach. But he realised that the only way to end the scandal was to close forever the mouths of those who knew about it, a sad collection of supposed witches and philtre-suppliers.

Some hundreds of poor wretches were locked anonymously in prisons all over France, never to emerge. And on this day the chief culprit, Madame La Voisin, was led to the stake in the place de Grève (now the place de l'Hôtel de Ville), where she died in agony.

But the ripples didn't end there. One of Louis's former mistresses, Olympia Mancini, had been suspected of poisoning her husband and had fled to Brussels. As a consequence her son was rejected for a military career and he in turn fled to Austria. That son was Prince Eugene of Savoy, destined to battle Louis to a standstill as Austria's greatest general.

Also on this day
1358: Étienne Marcel terrifies the French Dauphin * 1788: German philosopher Arthur Schopenhauer is born * 1819: Spain cedes Florida to the United States * 1857: English soldier and founder of the Boy Scout movement Robert Baden-Powell is born

23 February

Fair Kate is crowned Queen

1421 Catherine de Valois, Queen of England's Henry V, was supposed to have been a beauty, the Fair Kate of legend and Shakespearean renown, so no doubt she looked her handsomest on this February Sunday when she was crowned Queen of England in Westminster Abbey.

Catherine was the daughter of mad King Charles VI of France and his concupiscent wife Isabeau. The previous June she had been married off to Henry virtually as a trophy of war after he had whipped the French at Agincourt.

Still just nineteen at her coronation, within eighteen months she would bear a child and lose her husband, who was carried off by dysentery. That child would become Henry VI of England, who would reign 40 years but rule for few, a gentle, pious, not quite sane monarch in the midst of the Wars of the Roses. He would also be anointed King of France but never rule. But the more lasting significance of Catherine's queenship was that she would stay in England even after her husband was dead.

Given Wallingford Castle but cut off from the court and her son by English barons who distrusted her for being French, Catherine turned for solace (and much else) to a dashing Welsh squire at her court named Owen Tudor. Whether they ever married is much debated, but, single or wed, she bore him five children before dying in childbirth at 35. Owen lived another 24 years but was beheaded for backing the wrong side (the Lancastrians) during the Wars of the Roses. Legend says his last words, spoken as he faced the axe, were 'the head that used to lie in Queen Catherine's lap would now lie in the executioner's basket'.

But Catherine and Owen's true impact on the English throne was still to come. In 1485 their grandson Henry would invade England, defeat Richard III at Bosworth Field and found the Tudor dynasty as Henry VII.

Also on this day

AD 303: **Roman emperor Diocletian begins his persecution of the Christians** * 1455: Johannes Gutenberg publishes a Latin Vulgate translation of the Bible, the first Western book printed from movable type * 1633: English diarist Samuel Pepys is born * 1792: English portrait painter Sir Joshua Reynolds dies * 1820: British police arrest the Cato Street conspirators who planned to blow up the British Cabinet * 1821: English poet John Keats dies in Rome of tuberculosis

24 February

The fall of the last king of France

1848 Louis-Philippe had gained the crown of France in 1830 when his fellow citizens had driven the reactionary Charles X to abdication and exile. The new monarch tried to rule in a simple and unpretentious fashion, and his subjects were soon calling him the 'Citizen King'. But by 1848 he had been on the throne for eighteen years, and now the French public was stirring once again; he had refused to extend the vote to the country's lower bourgeoisie, and the economy was in disarray. In February 1848 the unhappy citizens exploded into revolt.

On the 22nd, protesters demanding political reform were denied permission to march and reacted by burning park benches and overturning buses. The next day Louis-Philippe sacked his prime minister, but still the demonstrators mobbed the streets. When they advanced down the rue des Capucines towards the Ministry of Foreign Affairs, the King's troops opened fire, killing 52. The following day the tired and defeated 72-year-old monarch and his Queen fled to England disguised as 'Mr and Mrs Smith', the King wearing a tradesman's hat and goggles.

Thus on 24 February 1848 ended the Bourbon monarchy in France that had commenced 259 years earlier under Louis XIII. So, too, ended the role of kings in France, who, except for the Revolutionary and Napoleonic years of 1793 to 1815, had ruled the country for 1,347 years, since the fifteen-year-old Clovis became the first French king in 481.

Also on this day

1500, 1525, 1530: Charles V is born, wins the Battle of Pavia (capturing the French king, François I) and is crowned Holy Roman Emperor * 1786: Fairy-tale writer Wilhelm Grimm is born * 1836: American painter Winslow Homer is born

25 February

Essex is executed

1601 Robert Devereux, Earl of Essex, was a classic Elizabethan adolescent: handsome, courageous, witty, dashing – vain, egotistical, foolhardy, fatuous. He had once been Queen Elizabeth's favourite – he was her first cousin, once removed, since his grandmother had been sister to Elizabeth's mother, Anne Boleyn. Although the Queen was 33 years his senior, they enjoyed a flirtatious relationship.

Essex was a fearless soldier, particularly distinguishing himself in the capture of Cádiz, but in general his childish pride and ambition for glory led him to one foolish adventure after another, culminating in his failure to overcome rebels in Ireland when he was Lord Lieutenant there. To make matters worse, he continued his practice of knighting his own officers, to such a degree that the Irish rebels claimed 'he never drew sword but to make knights'. His handing out of knighthoods was particularly galling to Elizabeth's chief minister, Robert Cecil, since through it Essex seemed to be building up a party that could challenge Cecil's supremacy.

On Essex's return from Ireland, Cecil brought charges against him for his Irish failure and had him tried by a commission of eighteen men. Convicted, Essex lost his monopoly on sweet wines, which ensured his financial collapse, and Elizabeth banished him from court.

It was then that Essex determined to revolt. On the morning of Sunday 8 February, he rode through the city of London with some 200 supporters shouting 'For the Queen!' with the hope of inciting the populace into rebellion against Cecil and his government. But as the mob rushed down the Strand a royal messenger appeared, who informed them that Elizabeth had declared Essex a traitor. Immediately the crowd started to melt away, and Essex, realising that he had failed, desperately returned home, only to find the Queen's soldiers there waiting for him, with a cannon trained on his mansion. The Essex revolt was over in just a few hours, and Elizabeth's one-time favourite was taken to the Tower.

During his last days the once-proud earl wildly confessed to his treasons, trying to implicate as many of his own friends and family as he could. He hoped for Elizabeth's mercy, but had forgotten her warning: 'Those who touch the sceptres of princes deserve no pity.'

On this day, seventeen days after his revolt, Essex paid for his treachery. Taken to the scaffold in the Tower yard, he knelt and prayed, then shed his dark coat to expose a scarlet waistcoat and placed his head on the block. It required three blows of the axe to sever his head. He was still only 34.

Also on this day

1309: Edward II is crowned * 1634: On orders from Emperor Ferdinand II, English captain Walter Devereux wakes the traitorous Bohemian general Albrecht von Wallenstein and, disregarding his pleas for mercy, runs him through with his sword * 1723: English architect Christopher Wren dies in London * **1841: French Impressionist painter Pierre-Auguste Renoir is born in Limoges**

26 February

Come the Revolution

1848 Today in London a portly, bearded German gentleman of 29 and his urbane young friend of only nineteen published a pamphlet that would lead to three-quarters of a century of global conflict, with the people of half the developed world living in oppressed conditions in totalitarian states. It was entitled *Manifest der kommunistischen Partei*, better known to most of us by its English name, *The Communist Manifesto*. The authors were Karl Marx and Friedrich Engels, two middle-class German revolutionaries who had fled to London on the failure of Germany's workers to seize power during the uprisings of 1848.

The *Manifesto* opens dramatically with the words: 'A spectre is haunting Europe – the spectre of communism.' This was no threat but a promise, as the young authors claimed that 'the history of all hitherto existing society is the history of class struggles', and that united Communists would abolish all private property and 'raise the proletarian to the position of the ruling class'. The pamphlet's closing rhetoric became world-famous: 'The proletarians have nothing to lose but their chains. They have a world to win. Working men of all countries, unite.'

Happily for the authors, Marx died in 1883 and Engels in 1895, far too early to see the revolution they had so hoped for and the appalling consequences it brought for millions of Russians, East Europeans and other states swallowed by Communism. But the monster they had given birth to strangled itself with its own inner contradictions. Had he lived to see the slow implosion of Communism and the peaceful fall of the Berlin Wall on 9 November 1989, Engels might have been bemused by the irony of his accurate prediction that: *'Der Staat wird nicht "abgeschafft", er stirbt ab.'* ('The State is not "abolished", it withers away.')

Also on this day

1781: British prime minister William Pitt the Younger makes his maiden speech in the House of Commons * 1802: Victor Hugo is born in Besançon * **1815: Napoleon escapes from Elba** * 1871: Prussia and France sign a peace treaty at Versailles, ending the Franco-Prussian War * 1901: Boxer Rebellion leaders Chi-Hsin and Hsu-Cheng-Yu are publicly executed in Peking

27 February

Americans defeat the Scots

1776 Today, to the sounds of drums and bagpipes, a Highland army of 1,000 soldiers, kilted, wielding muskets and claymores and yelling Gaelic war cries, met disaster at a bridge in North Carolina. A force of patriot militiamen holding a strategic crossing of Moore's Creek met the Scottish charge with musketry, then routed the survivors. The timely American success had the strategic effect of preventing the loyalist force from linking up with redcoats to retake the region for King George.

It is an irony of history that the Highlanders who fought at Moore's Creek Bridge, most of them recent immigrants to North Carolina, chose to fight as loyalists of the British crown rather than remain neutral or join the rebels of their adopted country. But it was not for love of King George that they fought. Many of them had tasted the fruits of rebellion against England before – in the Stuart uprising of 1745 – and found it bitter. Forced then to take oaths of loyalty in the savage aftermath of the Battle of Culloden, they were not prepared, even 30 years later and in another land, to break their word and once more risk defiance of the crown.

So, when their clan leaders seconded the call of the royal governor for His Majesty's subjects to put down the patriot rising, the Highlanders rallied to the King's colours. For despite their new surroundings, they remained what they had always been: clansmen of strong but narrow loyalties, many still speaking only Gaelic, resolute in their historic enmity towards Lowlanders and Ulstermen, so many of whom had joined the rebel camp.

Some 850 Scots were captured at Moore's Creek. The soldiers were disarmed and ordered to their homes. Officers were sent prisoner to Philadelphia and eventually paroled or exchanged, their properties confiscated. Among these last were the husband, son and son-in-law of one Flora MacDonald, who had achieved everlasting renown after Culloden by leading the defeated Bonnie Prince Charlie to the Isle of Skye and safety from his pursuers, a deed that landed her in a British prison ship. Impoverished like so many of her countrymen after the failed uprising, she and her husband, a leader of the MacDonald clan, sailed for the New World. Now once again they were on the losing side.

If Moore's Creek proved a disaster for the Highlanders, it was heady news for Carolina patriots already inspired by the previous year's events at Lexington, Concord and Bunker Hill. Only six weeks after the battle, South Carolina instructed its delegates to the Continental Congress sitting in Philadelphia to declare their support for the complete independence of the American colonies from Britain. It was the first such declaration by a colony and would lead to the Continental Congress's Declaration of Independence on the following 4 July.

Also on this day

AD 274: Roman emperor Constantine the Great is born * 1594: French King Henri IV is crowned in Chartres Cathedral * 1807: American poet Henry Wadsworth Longfellow is born in Portland, Maine * 1854: German composer Robert Schumann throws himself in the Rhine and is rescued by fishermen; six days later he is sent to an insane asylum for the rest of his life * 1873: Italian tenor Enrico Caruso is born in Naples * **1933: In Berlin, an anarchist burns down the German Reichstag**

28 February

Birth of the inventor of the essay

1533 Today was born literature's most famous essayist, Michel Eyquem, Seigneur de Montaigne, in his family's château near Bordeaux.

Montaigne's aristocratic father brought him up according to a carefully worked-out plan. Almost as soon as he was born he was shipped off to live with a local peasant family in one of his own villages to acquaint him with *la plus basse et commune façon de vivre* (the lowest and most common way of life). Montaigne returned to the family château when he was three years old.

Subsequently, his father had him brought up entirely in Latin until he was six and then trained him in law. Although he became a judge and later mayor of Bordeaux, Montaigne 'retired' at the tender age of 38 to devote the rest of his life to writing. Living in the château (which he had by now inherited from his father), Montaigne worked daily in his book-lined library in one of the château's towers. His most famous work is simply entitled *Essays*; Montaigne actually invented the term for short philosophical pieces.

Although Montaigne married and fathered six children, his heart was always in his work. But when he reached his late 50s he was plagued by ill health, perhaps prompting his famous perception: *'Le continuel ouvrage de votre vie, c'est bâtir la mort'*, he wrote. (The constant work of your life is to build the house of death.)

When he was 59 he was struck by a severe inflammation of the tonsils, leaving him literally speechless. He finally died while hearing Mass on 13 September 1592 in the château where he was born.

Also on this day

1066: Westminster Abbey is opened * 1820: John Tenniel, illustrator of *Alice's Adventures in Wonderland*, is born * **1854: The Republican Party is founded in the United States** * 1916: American/British writer Henry James dies in London

29 February

The pope who started the Counter-Reformation

1468 Today in the small town of Canino in the Papal States was born an Italian aristocrat who would become the first pope to lead the Catholic response to Protestantism, the Counter-Reformation.

Alessandro Farnese came from a family that had already served the papacy for three centuries. Studious and intelligent, as a young man he was educated in Florence, coming under the influence of Lorenzo the Magnificent. During this period he first met Lorenzo's son Giovanni, seven years his junior.

Although the success of Farnese's career in the Church was never in doubt, his prospects took a quantum leap when his sister Giulia became the mistress of the notorious Borgia Pope Alexander VI. Alexander created young Farnese a cardinal deacon when he was just 25. In the corridors of the Vatican young prelates referred to him as the 'petticoat cardinal'.

While serving the Church, Farnese also managed to service his aristocratic mistress, who bore him four children. Even after Alexander died, he continued to progress, as his old friend Giovanni de' Medici kept his career on track when he became Pope as Leo X in 1513.

Finally, on 13 October 1534, when he was already 66, Farnese was elected Pope, taking the name of Paul III. Although sincerely religious, he was always one of Catholicism's more worldly pontiffs, with a strong interest in the arts. He built the magnificent Farnese Palace in Rome, persuaded Michelangelo to finish *The Last Judgement* on the wall of the Sistine Chapel and commissioned him to build St Peter's dome.

Oddly, this sophisticated Italian also had a lasting effect on the Church itself. He is remembered for excommunicating England's Henry VIII and for approving a fledgling monastic order called the Society of Jesus (the Jesuits), naming Ignatius Loyola as its first general. But his greatest achievement came in 1545 when he convened the Council of Trent, Catholicism's first attempt to reform itself in the face of Protestant revolt.

In the autumn of 1549 the 81-year-old Pope Paul was stricken with a raging fever and died in his bed in the Vatican.

Also on this day

45 BC: The Western world celebrates its first Leap Year, created by Julius Caesar's new calendar, in effect since 1 January * 1792: Italian composer Gioacchino Rossini is born * 1868: Benjamin Disraeli becomes British Prime Minister for the first time * 1880: The St Gotthard railway tunnel through the Alps is completed, linking Italy with Switzerland

1 March

Ethiopians crush the Italian army at Adwa

1896 At the end of the 19th century, colonialism was every European nation's favourite sport. In what is known as The Scramble for Africa, Great Britain, France, Germany, Portugal, Spain and Italy manoeuvred with each other and suppressed the natives to colonise an entire continent, until only Ethiopia and Liberia remained independent. (In the midst of this Great Power carve-up, King Leopold II of Belgium, acting as a private citizen leading a group of European investors, wolfed down the Congo, treated the natives like slaves and with appalling irony called the territory the Congo Free State.)

Now, as the century drew to its close, the Italians, who for the most part had stopped being someone else's colony only 30 years before, felt that honour obliged them to carry on the game. This time their target was Ethiopia.

Italy had already been at war with the Ethiopian King Yohannes IV, and Italian forces had tasted the future when they were defeated at Bogali on 25 January 1887. But during the next nine years Italy at least nominally controlled much of the country, while armed conflict alternated with diplomacy.

By 1895, however, Ethiopia's new king Menelek II, whom the Italians had helped to gain the throne six years before, was now intent on pushing them out. Italian Prime Minister Francesco Crispi felt that national honour was at stake and ordered General Baratieri to advance against the King's apparently primitive army at Adwa.

On 1 March 1896, some 17,000 foolhardy Italians, with about 50 artillery pieces and reinforced by a brigade of *askari* (native infantry from Eritrea, then a province of Ethiopia), advanced on Menelek's army of over 100,000 riflemen supported by a significant number of cavalry. First caught in a crossfire and then overwhelmed by sheer numbers, the Italians were annihilated.

Surviving Italian soldiers attempted to escape through difficult terrain while under constant attack. When the battle was over, more than 10,000 had been killed, wounded or captured and held to ransom. Most of the 3,000 Italian prisoners endured their captivity and were eventually released, but 800 captured *askari*, considered traitors by the Ethiopians, had their right hands and left feet cut off.

Adwa was one of the worst colonial defeats ever recorded, putting an abrupt halt to Italy's efforts to build an African empire. The battle also forced Italy to recognise the independence of Ethiopia – until 1935.

Also on this day

1780: Pennsylvania becomes the first US state to abolish slavery * **1810: Frédéric Chopin is born in Zelazorawola, Poland** * 1815: Napoleon lands at Golfe-Juan on the Côte d'Azur after escaping from Elba * 1845: The USA annexes Texas

2 March

Death of the last Holy Roman Emperor

1835 Today died Emperor Franz II, a dry old stick of a man of 64. He had been the 66th Holy Roman Emperor since Charlemagne, and was the last one.

Franz had inherited the imperial crown in 1792 when he was only 24, just three years after France had exploded into revolution. His aunt, Marie Antoinette, was guillotined the following year, and Franz, a fervent believer in absolute monarchy, took his country into the first coalition war against revolutionary France, occasionally leading his army in person. Unfortunately, his opponent was a young general named Bonaparte, and Austria was soon asking for terms.

In 1798 Franz once more joined a coalition against France, but Napoleon overwhelmed him at the Battle of Marengo and forced him to sign the Treaty of Lunéville, which required him to renounce all claims to the Holy Roman Empire. Franz demoted himself to Emperor of Austria and brought to an end the Holy Roman Empire after 844 years.

Never a man to give up, in 1809 Franz once again went to war with France and was once again defeated. Having lost his imperial crown, Franz now saved his Austrian one by agreeing to marry his daughter Marie-Louise to Napoleon (whom he privately despised as a parvenu).

In the end, however, Franz had the last laugh. In 1813, for the fourth and last time, he attacked France, but this time, largely thanks to his coalition partners Prussia, Russia and Sweden, he won at the Battle of Leipzig. Then, after Napoleon's final defeat at Waterloo, he hosted the Congress of Vienna, where his brilliant minister Klemens Metternich set the reactionary agenda that determined the future of Europe for most of the century to come.

Also on this day

1476: Swiss mercenaries defeat Charles the Bold at Granson and steal his treasure * 1791: British preacher John Wesley dies in London * 1882: Deranged poet Roderick McClean tries to shoot Queen Victoria with a pistol for having snubbed a poem he sent her * 1904: American bandleader Glen Miller is born * 1917: Nicholas II abdicates, bringing to an end the Romanov dynasty and the monarchy in Russia

> Events written in **boldface** are covered in full in
> *365: Great Stories from History for Every Day of the Year*,
> the first volume in this series.

3 March

Alexander II frees Russia's serfs

1861 At the beginning of this year there were only two 'civilised' nations that still permitted slavery of a sort: the United States with its black slaves and Russia with its serfs. The serfs were technically better off than the slaves, but in the 18th century Peter the Great had bound them to landowners rather than to the land, so in effect they had little or no control over their own lives. Unlike a slave, a serf could not be bought and sold, but traditionally he could not marry or even leave his village without his lord's permission. (Fortunately for the Russian serf at this time, the lord could not exercise *droit de seigneur* over the nubile young women of the serf's household.)

Russia's 42 million serfs accounted for almost half of the rural population, and many Russian aristocrats believed serfdom was not only a blot on the honour of Mother Russia but also a block to the sort of industrial development they wanted. On the other hand, landowners across the country bitterly resisted any move towards emancipation. The chief emancipator of the serfs was, surprisingly, that supreme autocrat, Tsar Alexander II. Shocked by Russia's mauling during the Crimean War in 1856, Alexander urgently wanted Russia to progress and thought that a free peasantry would be a more productive one.

But even an absolute ruler like the Tsar could not simply free the serfs with the stroke of a pen. Instead, Alexander, who had first announced his intentions in 1856, ordered provincial committees of noblemen to recommend the steps to be followed. These recommendations eventually wound their way to a Chief Committee and then the State Council, as landowners did all in their power to mitigate the impact of emancipation. Eventually, on 3 March (19 February by the Russian calendar) 1861, Alexander published the *Emancipation Manifesto* with its seventeen accompanying legislative acts. In addition to their personal freedom, the serfs received allotments of land for which they had to repay the government over the next 49 years.

From that time the United States remained the only advanced country with legal slavery – until Abraham Lincoln issued the Emancipation Proclamation 22 months later.

Also on this day

1513: Ponce de León sets sail to seek the fountain of youth * 1847: Telephone inventor Alexander Graham Bell is born in Edinburgh * 1875: The first performance of Bizet's *Carmen* is staged at the Opéra Comique in Paris * 1878: The Treaty of San Stefano frees Bulgaria from Turkish rule after almost five centuries * 1931: 'The Star-Spangled Banner' is officially adopted as the US national anthem

4 March

Edward of York grabs the English throne

1461 Today blonde, handsome Edward of York, still only eighteen years old, strode into the English Parliament in London's Westminster Hall, sat down on the marble throne and proclaimed himself King Edward IV, even though the reigning king, Henry VI, was still alive.

Henry had been king for the past 39 years, but first because of his youth and then because of his weak intellect and monkish inclinations, chaos had ruled the land, as warring barons defended their turf with private armies.

For the past six years England's two greatest families had vied for power in a period known as the Wars of the Roses. The House of Lancaster was nominally headed by the King but now in fact controlled by his French Queen, the indomitable Margaret of Anjou, and her courtiers. Edward commanded the House of York, determined to defend its interests in the face of what he saw as unbridled queenly ambition. He was backed (or, some say, manipulated) by his cousin, that unscrupulous opportunist Richard Neville, the Earl of Warwick, soon to be called the Kingmaker.

On 17 February Henry's army, led by Queen Margaret, badly mauled Warwick's forces at the Second Battle of St Albans, and the Earl fled to the Cotswolds. There he met Edward and put forward a daring proposal: that Edward should do more than just protect the interests of his house; he should claim the throne of England for himself, based on his descent from Edward III, who had died almost a century before.

Ten days later the two men rode into London, a city already fervently opposed to Queen Margaret because of the depredations of her greedy courtiers. The canny Warwick summoned an assembly of nobles, soldiers and the odd friendly bishop to St John's Fields and orchestrated a 'spontaneous' acclamation of Edward as king. Then, at 9 o'clock today, Wednesday 4 March, he called together the people of London to the old St Paul's Cathedral, where once again Edward was enthusiastically acclaimed as king. With the public so obviously behind him, Edward then crossed town for Westminster Hall to claim the crown before Parliament.

Edward remained king until 1470 when the weak-minded Henry was momentarily restored to power, backed by the turncoat Warwick. But only five months later he defeated and killed Warwick at the Battle of Barnet, and three weeks later he routed the indefatigable Queen Margaret, captured poor Henry once again and had him put to death in the Tower of London.

During his reign Edward proved to be an exemplary medieval king. In 1475 he invaded France with a huge army and extorted an annual subsidy of 50,000 crowns. In general he brought prosperity to his kingdom and pacified a lawless Wales. He also took an interest in the arts and was a patron of England's first printer, William Caxton.

Edward was noted for his passion for fighting, drinking, pageantry and women, possibly in reverse order. He claimed that he 'had three concubines which in diverse properties diversely excelled, one the merriest, the other the wiliest, the third the holiest, harlot in the realm'. He secretly married a stunning divorcée named Elizabeth Woodville, an act that infuriated his barons because of her low birth. The clandestine wedding lent substance to his brother Richard's claim after his death that Edward had not been properly married and that his sons (those famously murdered in the Tower) were illegitimate.

Edward died of pneumonia (and possibly high living) in 1483, seventeen days short of his 41st birthday.

Also on this day

1193: The great Saracen leader Saladin dies in Damascus * 1394: Portuguese patron of explorers Prince Henry the Navigator is born * 1678: Composer and violinist Antonio Vivaldi is born in Venice * 1789: The first US Congress under the Constitution convenes in New York * 1861: Abraham Lincoln is sworn in as the 16th president of the United States * 1877: The Russian Imperial Ballet stages the first performance of *Swan Lake* in Moscow

5 March

Stalin solves his own problem

1953 On the last day of February, ensconced in his dacha outside Moscow, Joseph Stalin ate and drank with his top Politburo cronies Georgy Malenkov, Nikolay Bulganin, Nikita Krushchev, and the terrifying NKGB (secret police) boss, Levrenty Beria. The ageing dictator finally let his toadying guests depart at 4 o'clock the next morning.

Noon came and went, and then afternoon, but Stalin had yet to arise. At six he turned on his lights but still failed to emerge. His nervous guards became increasingly anxious but were too intimidated by their boss to enter his rooms. Finally, at ten in the evening, one of his attendants ventured inside, bringing the Central Committee mail. There he found the tyrant, conscious but helpless and unable to speak, stretched out on the floor, dressed in an undershirt and pyjama bottoms. Stalin's watch had been broken as he collapsed, stopping at 6.30 pm, the moment he had been felled by a massive stroke.

The Politburo members were immediately called – and immediately began to panic. For twelve hours no one had the courage even to send for a doctor because of the so-called Doctors' Plot, an alleged (and false) conspiracy of prominent Russian physicians to murder leading party officials. Should the paranoid Stalin suddenly recover, he might interpret a call for medical help as attempted murder. When doctors were finally summoned, they hardly dared examine the stricken despot as the brutal Beria lurked at the back of the room, noting their every move.

For three days Stalin lay between life and death, as high-ranking party members like Voroshilov, Mikoyan and Molotov came to visit. Who knows what thoughts passed through Molotov's mind as he eyed the dying dictator who had forced him to divorce his wife and then imprisoned her on fabricated charges? Beria, who had come to loathe Stalin, alternated between spewing out his hatred of the comatose dictator and fawningly kissing his hand whenever Stalin showed signs of life. As Stalin's life ebbed away, orders were given to ask medical advice from the doctors imprisoned and tortured as 'conspirators' in the Doctors' Plot.

On Friday 5 March, Stalin's breathing slowed, then almost stopped. At noon he vomited blood as his stomach started to haemorrhage. Later his daughter Svetlana recorded how, at nine in the evening, her father 'literally choked to death as we watched. The death agony was terrible ... At the last minute, he opened his eyes. It was a terrible look, either mad or angry and full of the fear of death.'

Now that Stalin was no more, his fellow Politburo thugs lined up to give the corpse a ritual farewell kiss and then, led by Beria, raced back to the Kremlin to search Stalin's papers and destroy anything that might incriminate them in the catalogue of Stalin's crimes.

So died the cobbler's son who had tyrannised his own country for 31 years. He once summed up his approach to life: 'Death solves all problems ... No man, no problem.' He meant it: he sent 18 million people, mostly innocent, to the Gulags and, through firing squads and mass starvation, killed perhaps 20 million others.

Also on this day

752: St Boniface crowns Pépin the Short King of France at Soisson * 1696: Italian painter Giovanni Battista Tiepolo is born in Venice * 1770: British soldiers kill five Americans during the Boston Massacre * **1776: American rebels drive the British out of Boston** * 1933: Hitler and Nationalist allies win the Reichstag majority, the last free election in Germany until after the Second World War

6 March

Joan of Arc recognises her king

1429 The castle of Chinon still rises rugged and formidable near the Loire, as it did nearly six centuries ago when France's uncrowned king, Charles VII, held pitiful court there while the English ruled much of his country. Although Charles's father had died five years before, the cathedral at Reims, the traditional venue for the investiture of French kings, was in the hands of Charles's English and Burgundian enemies. In addition, since October 1428 the English had been besieging Orléans, where a French garrison was growing progressively desperate.

But in May of 1428 sixteen-year-old Joan of Arc had travelled to Vaucouleurs, one of Charles's few loyal strongholds, to persuade the captain of the garrison that she was on a mission from God to deliver her king. At first rebuffed, she returned at the beginning of 1429, and now, with the siege of Orléans daily becoming more threatening, there was one more reason to serve her sovereign. This time her piety and obvious sincerity won over the captain, who sent her with a guard of six men-at-arms on an eleven-day march, much through enemy territory, to Chinon.

Joan arrived at the King's castle on 4 March, to be greeted with scepticism by his bemused courtiers. When asked why she had come, she replied: 'I have been commanded to do two things for the King of Heaven: one, to raise the siege of Orléans, the other, to conduct the King to Reims for his sacrament and coronation.'

For two days Charles refused to see her, doubting her purpose, but on this day, according to legend, he orchestrated a simple test. He stood among his courtiers, clad in simple dress, and then had Joan brought into the room. Although she had never seen him before, she instantly picked him out and made reverence to him. 'After leaving her', an eyewitness said, 'the King appeared joyful'.

And so he should have been. Within four months Joan had fulfilled both her commissions. After passing examinations for virginity and for possible heresy, she was given armour and a horse and sent to join a French force stationed at nearby Blois. Then she marched on Orléans. By 8 May the English had abandoned their siege, and on 17 July Charles was duly crowned at Reims.

Also on this day

1204: French cunning captures Richard the Lionheart's impregnable Château Gaillard * 1447: Tommaso Parentucelli is elected Pope as Nicholas V, ending the Great Schism * 1475: Michelangelo Buonarroti is born in Florence * 1836: In Texas, the twelve-day siege of the Alamo ends, with only six survivors out of the original force of 155

7 March

Napoleon confronts the King's army

1815 Today the ex-emperor Napoleon added another celebrated chapter to his own legend by facing down royalist soldiers with the dramatic words: '*S'il est parmi vous un soldat qui veuille tuer son empereur, me voilà.*' ('If there is among you a soldier who wants to kill his emperor, here I am.')

On 26 February Napoleon had escaped from Elba after 9 months and 22 days of regal confinement. After a night in Cannes, he started his advance towards Paris, almost 600 miles away, with a small corps of 1,200 soldiers.

Knowing that troops loyal to Louis XVIII were to the west in Marseilles and the Rhone Valley, he headed straight north through Grasse and, following small trails and mule tracks, climbed into the foothills of the Alps, past Séranon and through the Clue de Taulanne in heavy snow. By nightfall on 4 March he was at the château de Malijai.

The next day, while Napoleon was lunching in Sisteron, in the royal palace in the Tuileries King Louis received the news of his escape. Frantically, he summoned his generals and sent word to block Napoleon's progress. (Not all royalists were as concerned as the King; the optimistic newspaper *Moniteur* called Napoleon's escape 'an act of madness which can be dealt with by a few rural policemen'.)

When Napoleon reached the hamlet of Laffrey on 7 March, he found that the 5th battalion of the Royal French Army was waiting there, ready to capture or kill him. On a meadow at the south end of the Lac de Laffrey, the ex-emperor's soldiers nervously faced the royalist troops, all with rifles at the ready. But Napoleon had already seen (and caused) enough French blood spilt. Dismounting from his horse, he directed his guard to raise the Tricolore flag and play the *Marseillaise*, which had been outlawed by the monarchy.

Now he sent 100 of his Polish lancers forward in a slow advance. When the opposing soldiers pulled back, he ordered the lancers to wheel and return. He then stepped forward alone, a proud figure in his grey battle coat and black bicorn hat, and moved within pistol range of the enemy line.

'Fire!' cried out a royalist officer, but there was only silence. 'Fire!' he cried again, but still with no result. Then Napoleon called out : '*Soldats du Cinquième, je suis votre empereur. Reconnaissez-moi.*' ('Soldiers of the 5th, I am your emperor. Recognise me.')

Another moment of hush, and then Napoleon dramatically opened his coat to expose his breast and issued his famous invitation for the troops to open fire. The response was an immediate roar of '*Vive l'Empereur!*', as the royalist ranks broke and men ran towards him, acclaiming and touching him. Their desperate commander broke into tears and offered his sword to Napoleon, who embraced him.

The same day Napoleon trekked a further seventeen miles to Grenoble, his force now doubled in size, joined by the royalist soldiers from Laffrey. Then north through Lyon and on to Paris, picking up more reinforcements in every town he passed. He reached Paris on 20 March, the day after Louis XVIII had scuttled off to Belgium. Arriving at the Tuileries at nine in the evening, Napoleon found himself cheered by 20,000 Parisians. He was emperor once more.

Napoleon had covered a 40-day journey in twenty days, converted opposing troops through a magnificent display of personal courage and regained his throne without a trace of violence or a single shot being fired.

Also on this day

322 BC: Aristotle dies * AD **161: Marcus Aurelius becomes Roman Emperor on the death of Antoninus Pius** * 1274: Italian Christian philosopher St Thomas

Aquinas dies * 1875: French composer Maurice Ravel is born * 1876: Alexander Graham Bell patents the telephone * 1945: American troops seize the Ludendorff Bridge over the Rhine at Remagen and cross into Germany

8 March

Death of a self-made duke

1466 Francesco Sforza had been born illegitimate in 1401. His father was a peasant from Romagna named Muzio Attendolo, who had risen to become commander of a band of mercenary soldiers that had once kidnapped him. Such leaders were called *condottieri* because they signed a contract (*condotta* in Italian) with the city for which they agreed to fight. Always ambitious, often brutal and sometimes capable, *condottieri* preferred armed cavalry for their mercenaries.

Perhaps to enhance his status as a leader and fighter, Muzio Attendolo changed his name to Sforza (*sforzo*: Italian for effort or will) and gave it to his son Francesco, although declining to marry Francesco's mother.

At the age of 22, the younger Sforza took over the band of mercenaries when his father was drowned during a battle, and became one of Italy's most renowned *condottieri*. Tall, strong (he could bend metal bars with his bare hands), direct, honest and shrewdly intelligent, he managed to marry another bastard offspring, Bianca Maria, illegitimate daughter of Filippo Maria Visconti, the last Visconti duke of Milan.

In 1447 Milan was attacked by Venice, and Sforza's father-in-law called on him for help. But before Sforza arrived, Duke Filippo Maria died, unexpectedly leaving his city to the King of Naples. Egged on by Sforza, the disgruntled Milanese proclaimed Milan a republic and appointed him captain general. Shortly thereafter he forced Milan to recognise him as Visconti's heir and the new duke.

Sforza proved to be an able and energetic ruler as well as a patron of the arts in the blossoming Renaissance. When not fighting wars or commissioning paintings, he sired eight children by Bianca Maria, while producing a further eleven illegitimate ones on the side. When he died today at 65 of gout and oedema, he left behind the dynasty that bears his name and that ruled Milan until 1535.

Also on this day

1265: Simon de Montfort forms the first Commons in Westminster Hall * 1702: Anne becomes Queen of England after William III dies in a riding accident * 1855: Charles XIV of Sweden (the former Napoleonic marshal, Jean-Baptiste Bernadotte) dies * 1869: French composer Maurice Ravel dies in Paris

9 March

The first battle of ironclad ships

1862 The Union ship *Monitor* looked rather like a hatbox on top of a raft, while the Confederate *Merrimac* was shaped like a bar of Toblerone chocolate with a smokestack in the middle. Yet when these two peculiar warships met in combat in Hampton Roads, Virginia, they changed forever the nature of naval warfare. For on this day took place the first battle ever between ironclad ships.

At first blush the ships seemed very different. The *Merrimac*, at over 100 yards long, was twice the length of the *Monitor*, and her crew of 300 was more than five times as large. Further, she was armed with ten guns to her rival's two. The *Monitor*, on the other hand, sported the first naval gun turret in history, so her guns could be aimed in any direction without turning the ship.

Prior to the meeting of these metal monsters, the *Merrimac* had destroyed several wooden ships while remaining impervious to cannon fire.

The Battle of Hampton Roads started about eight in the morning. Both ships fired unceasingly at each other, at so close a range that the vessels actually touched five times during the engagement. The *Merrimac* even tried to batter the *Monitor* with its cast-iron ram.

After several hours of fighting the Confederate ship withdrew unharmed. Neither ship had been able to inflict significant damage on the other.

The two ironclads never fought again. The Confederate sailors scuttled the *Merrimac* when the South pulled out of Norfolk, Virginia, while the *Monitor* was lost in a storm off Cape Hatteras on the last day of the year. But naval warfare would never be the same. The wooden warship was relegated to history.

Also on this day

1074: Pope Gregory VII excommunicates all married priests * 1451: Italian navigator Amerigo Vespucci is born * 1661: French Cardinal Jules Mazarin (Giulio Mazzarino) dies at Vincennes * **1796: Napoleon Bonaparte marries Joséphine de Beauharnais** * 1932: Eamon De Valera is elected President of the Irish Free State, promising to abolish all loyalty to the British Crown

10 March

Death of the 'most dangerous man in Europe'

1872 Today in Pisa, Giuseppe Mazzini – the man whom the reactionary Prince Metternich once called the 'most dangerous man in Europe', died of pleurisy at the age of 67.

To a large degree, the unification of Italy was the work of three very different men: Cavour, the brilliant politician, Garibaldi, the soldier and leader, and Mazzini, the republican and social reformer.

Born in Genoa and son of a doctor, Mazzini was slender and swarthy, with black hair and beard. Intelligent and intense, he was committed to Italian independence and unity all his life. He was an outstanding propagandist but also an activist in the cause he loved. So great was his moral influence that he was forced to flee abroad and was condemned to death *in absentia*. At different times he lived in France, Switzerland and England, and, like Karl Marx, who arrived in London a year after he left, Mazzini wrote and studied at the British Museum.

Mazzini was considered a dangerous revolutionary by every conservative and status-quoer in Europe, most particularly by the Austrians who controlled most of northern Italy. He seemed to be a threat not just because he worked for a united Italy but also because he was seen as a visionary who could elevate his cause. His views had a moral and religious basis, and he passionately believed that justice and individual liberty would be the true fruits of the revolution he preached. (Reactionary fear of Mazzini was not totally unfounded; one of his disciples, Felice Orsini, had tried to assassinate Napoleon III in 1858.)

When he died, the reunification he had devoted his life to had been completed just two years earlier, with the annexation of Rome completing the task. But in some ways Mazzini was bitterly disappointed, since the united Italy he had fought so hard for was not a republic but a monarchy. 'I thought I was awakening the soul of Italy', he said, 'and I see only the corpse before me'. But perhaps he found some solace at the end, as his last recorded words were: 'Yes, yes, I believe in God!'

Also on this day

515 BC: The building of the great Jewish temple in Jerusalem is completed * 241 BC: The Romans sink the Carthaginian fleet near the Aegates Islands, ending the first Punic War * **1831: The French Foreign Legion is formed** * 1876: Alexander Graham Bell makes the first telephone call

11 March

The end of Cesare Borgia

1507 Today died one of history's most infamous characters, Cesare Borgia, the ambitious, energetic, murderous and totally unscrupulous son of Pope Alexander VI.

During his lifetime – and since – there have been numerous accusations of Cesare's foul crimes, most of them true. Through his father he became captain general of the papal forces and later was created a duke by Louis XII of France. He was a brilliant general who reduced many an enemy fortress, but he also conquered by guile and treachery. Once he invited four enemy captains to truce talks, disarmed them and then had them publicly garrotted.

Cesare was also not beyond individual assassination to further his ambitions. Historians still debate whether he arranged the murder of his elder brother Juan, although he gained much by his brother's death, inheriting many of his titles and estates. Regarding the murder of his brother-in-law, however, there is no doubt that Cesare organised it. In 1498 his sister Lucrezia had married Alfonso de Bisceglie, bastard son of the King of Naples and heir to the throne. Two years later, however, it became apparent that instead of a help, Naples was becoming a hindrance to Cesare's plan to make himself ruler of the Romagna in middle Italy.

In July 1500, assassins set upon Alfonso as he left the Vatican. Alfonso escaped, badly wounded, and no one as yet suspected Cesare. But as Alfonso refused to die of his wounds, on 18 August, Cesare sent his notorious hench-man Michelotto to the room in the Vatican where he lay recovering. After shooing Lucrezia and Alfonso's sister away with threats, Michelotto proceeded to strangle the wounded man, demonstrating Cesare's single-minded determin-ation to succeed at all costs, as suggested by his motto: '*Aut Caesar, aut nihil.*' ('Either Caesar or nothing.')

Although Lucrezia grieved at the loss of her husband, Cesare and his father the Pope were very content. Cesare's plans of conquest moved forward. Aided by French troops (his other brother-in-law was the King of Navarre) and the papal army, he captured large swathes of Romagna, including the key cities of Pesaro, Rimini, Faenza and Urbino.

Although Cesare became a duke, he never achieved his ambition to carve out an independent Borgia state and make himself a prince. When Alexander VI died in 1503 he found himself without political support in an area where he was both feared and detested because of his vicious military campaigns. Imprisoned in Spain by Pope Julius II, he escaped two years later and enlisted in the services of his brother-in-law, Jean d'Albret, King of Navarre. Leading a force of 5,000 troops against the Castilians, today Cesare was ambushed near Viana and hacked to death, his body pierced by 25 wounds. Perhaps reflecting on the evils he had perpetrated, just as he died he lamented: 'I die unprepared.' He was only 31.

It was an unusually bloody career for a man who had been a cathedral canon at seven, a bishop at fifteen, an archbishop at sixteen and a cardinal at eighteen.

Also on this day

1513: Giovanni de' Medici is elected Pope Leo X * 1851: Verdi's *Rigoletto* is performed for the first time, at La Fenice in Venice * 1905: The Parisian métro is officially opened * **1942: General MacArthur leaves the Philippines, vowing: 'I shall return'**

12 March

Belisarius' magnificent defence of Rome

537 Today the beleaguered troops of the great Byzantine general Belisarius cheered and jeered from the walls of Rome as the Ostrogoth King Witigis and his downhearted men burned their camps and withdrew towards their capital in Ravenna. In one of the most astonishing defences in history, an army of only 5,000 men had held the city against enemy forces of over 100,000 for a year and nine days.

With its capital in Constantinople, the Byzantine Empire controlled the eastern half of the old Roman world. In the west, the Ostrogoths had ruled Italy since AD 493, when their legendary King Theodoric had completed his conquest. But now the Byzantine Emperor Justinian was determined to wrest back the old western part of the Roman Empire and dispatched his greatest general to do it.

During the previous seven years Belisarius had defeated the Sasanian Persians in Mesopotamia and the Vandals in North Africa. He had also saved Justinian's throne by massacring the rebels during the Nika insurrection in Constantinople. He was about 30 when he advanced on Italy.

His first major operation came in the summer of 536 when he besieged and occupied Naples. Then, on 9 December of the same year, he entered Rome virtually unopposed. The city had been in decline for over a century, ever since the Visigoths had sacked it in 410. Many inhabitants had abandoned it, many buildings and monuments lay in ruins, and cows grazed in the old Roman forum. But Rome was still the largest city in Western Europe, and Belisarius knew that the Ostrogoths would soon counter-attack. Less than three months later, King Witigis arrived with a massive army.

Belisarius' exiguous force had to defend circuit walls twelve miles in circumference against an encircling enemy. To strengthen his defences he placed catapults on the city walls and ordered a deep ditch dug beneath the walls. To prevent the Ostrogoths from using boats to row up the Tiber he had a chain drawn across the river, and he garrisoned Hadrian's tomb, the fortress known today as the Castel' Sant'Angelo.

Stymied by Belisarius' defensive tactics, Witigis attempted to force surrender by diverting the city's aqueducts, but his plan backfired when his own camps were turned into malaria-breeding swamps.

Witigis then ordered four siege towers with battering rams to be drawn up by teams of oxen against the Roman walls. As Belisarius watched the enemy's approach, he borrowed a bow from one of his soldiers and killed an Ostrogoth officer at a great distance. He then ordered his bowmen to fire, not at the enemy soldiers but at the oxen. As the oxen fell pierced by arrows, the siege towers were left standing in the open, never having reached the walls.

The Byzantine army's greatest strength was its cavalry of armoured archers.

According to the historian Procopius, who was there: 'Their bows are strong and weighty; they shoot in every possible direction, advancing, retreating, to the front, to the rear, or to either flank.' Infantry armed with axes, spears and swords supported the cavalry.

Unable to man all points along the walls, Belisarius mounted a series of surprise sorties. First the horse archers would put the enemy cavalry to flight and then Byzantine infantry would close in to slaughter the unprotected Ostrogoth infantry. In spite of the numerical odds, such attacks were almost invariably successful.

While battling the enemy outside the city, Belisarius also had to guard against treachery from within. At first he feared that the Roman citizens, foreseeing eventual Ostrogoth victory, might throw open the city gates, but with continued Byzantine success, the Romans gained confidence in Belisarius and even volunteered to join the fight. One surprise betrayal, however, was that of Pope Silverius, who wrote to Witigis offering to surrender the city. Belisarius dressed the Pope as a monk and sent him into exile.

Eventually some 4,000 reinforcements reached Rome and entered the city during a truce, bringing with them a large quantity of supplies. Having already lost some 30,000 men, Witigis saw the situation was hopeless and abandoned the siege.

Also on this day

1881: Turkish leader Kemal Atatürk is born * 1925: The 'father of modern China' Sun Yat Sen dies, Peking * 1933: President Paul von Hindenburg drops the flag of the German Republic in favour of the swastika and empire banner * **1938: Hitler's troops march into Austria; he declares the Anschluss the next day**

13 March

Metternich is gone at last

1848 Only three weeks earlier, while imperial Vienna swirled in the celebration of Fasching before the start of Lent, King Louis-Philippe had been unceremoniously chased from the throne of France, soon to be replaced by Napoleon III. Now the revolution was spreading to Austria, where its focus was on that sardonic old embodiment of frozen conservatism, the arbiter of Europe, Prince Klemens Metternich, now 74 years old and in power since the days of the first Napoleon.

As excitement grew in the streets, exhilarated Viennese students marched towards the Hofburg imperial palace, armed with a copy of the Hungarian patriot Lajos Kossuth's speech demanding the end to Habsburg absolutism and guarantees of liberty for the people. Imperial grenadiers shot a few dead, but the Austrian imperial family came increasingly to realise that the price of salvation was Metternich's ruin, and so he was figuratively tossed to the wolves. On this day he resigned from office and fled into exile in England.

Although detested by the liberal intelligentsia, Metternich had been a genius in his own way, preserving the peace across Europe since Napoleon's defeat at Waterloo. He was hated for his arch-conservatism, his determination to retain the status quo and his ubiquitous secret police. (Metternich himself had once boasted: 'You see in me the chief minister of Police in Europe. I keep an eye on everything. My contacts are such that nothing escapes me.') But his downfall may also have been hastened by his vanity: only weeks before he was driven from Austria he had pronounced to a French diplomat: '*L'erreur n'a jamais approché de mon esprit.*' ('Error has never approached my mind.')

Also on this day

565: Byzantine general Belisarius dies in Constantinople * 1519: Conquistador Hernán Cortés lands in what will become Mexico * 1881: Tsar Alexander II is assassinated by a terrorist bomb * **1905: The spy Mata Hari springs fully grown into the world on stage in a Parisian cabaret**

14 March

The villain who wrote an English classic

1471 An inveterate criminal died today in London's Newgate Prison. This was his eighth incarceration; he had spent much of his life in jail on charges ranging from horse stealing to extortion to attempted murder to rape. Who would have guessed that the manuscript he left behind unpublished would hold chivalry, knightly honour and courtly love as the highest virtues and would soon be viewed as one of the greatest and most enduring pieces of English literature? The criminal was Sir Thomas Malory, his work *Le Morte d'Arthur*.

Born in Warwickshire in about 1410–15, Malory's first recorded brush with the law came in 1443, when he was charged with wounding and imprisoning a certain Thomas Smith in order to rob him, but the charges were dropped. Seven years later he seduced and attempted to elope with a married woman, an act that by the laws of the time constituted rape, and three months later seduced her again, this time stealing 40 pounds' worth of goods from her husband. But his greater crimes may have been partly political.

Malory lived in that chaotic period leading up to the Wars of the Roses. Inevitably he became embroiled in the murderous politics of the day, sometimes supporting the Yorkists, occasionally the House of Lancaster. In January 1450, he and 26 armed men unsuccessfully ambushed the Duke of Buckingham in the Abbot of Combe's woods near Newbold Revel. We do not know the reason for his attack, but Buckingham was a fervent Lancastrian.

Shortly afterwards Malory organised a band 100 strong to steal cattle and sheep and on one raid they targeted the Duke once again, wrecking his hunting lodge and slaughtering his deer.

An enraged Buckingham gathered a posse of 60 men to pursue Malory. Caught and imprisoned in a castle in Coleshill, Malory escaped after only two days by swimming the moat at night. He then led his band back to Combe Abbey, breaking down the doors to steal the abbey's funds while contemptously insulting the monks.

At the beginning of 1452 Malory was jailed again, this time in London, where he spent much of the next eight years. At one point he was bailed out, only to ride with his band on a horse-stealing expedition in East Anglia. Recaptured, he was incarcerated in Colchester but broke out, subduing the guards with a sword and halberd (a five-foot axe with a pike at the top of the staff). Despite his daring getaway, he was recaptured and brought back to prison in London.

Now, however, the Wars of the Roses began in earnest with the Battle of St Albans on 22 May 1455. Perhaps because both sides wanted his support, Malory was several times pardoned, at least once by Henry VI and later by the Yorkists after their leader Edward of York had seized the throne as Edward IV. After his release, Malory joined Edward's attacks on the three Lancastrian-held castles.

But nothing could stop Malory's intriguing, and in 1468 he was flung into Newgate Prison once more, after having been involved in yet another conspiracy, this one against King Edward. Perhaps hoping that somehow it might secure his release, he now turned to writing his great epic. At the end he addresses the reader: 'I pray you all, gentlemen and gentlewomen that readeth this book of Arthur and his knights … pray for me while I am alive, that God send me good deliverance, and when I am dead, I pray you all pray for my soul.' But he died confined, without ever having been tried.

We don't know Malory's original title for his work, but it has since been known as *Le Morte d'Arthur*, taken from the printer William Caxton's 1485 edition. Here in eight tales Malory recounts the saga of King Arthur and the Knights of the Round Table, the heroic but ultimately tragic tale of the King, his queen Guinevere, and knights like Lancelot and Sir Galahad.

Malory was not the first to write of Arthur or his knights – back in the 12th century Geoffrey of Monmouth had published *Historia regum Britanniae* (*History of the Kings of Britain*) and a few years later Chrétien de Troyes had written romances featuring Lancelot and the pursuit of the Holy Grail, but Malory's was the first prose account in the English language. He not only made King Arthur accessible to English readers but also changed the episodic character of Geoffrey of Monmouth's work into a more cohesive narrative while empha-sising knightly ideals of chivalry.

Le Morte d'Arthur was avidly read on publication and forms the basis for most modern versions of King Arthur, including Tennyson's 'Idylls of the King', T.H. White's *The Once and Future King* and even the musical *Camelot*. Through the epic he wrote in prison, the lawless and violent Malory created the legend of noble King Arthur that has entranced the English-speaking world for the past five and a half centuries.

1492: The Catholic Monarchs Ferdinand and Isabella of Castile order the expulsion of 150,000 Jews from Spain * **1757: British admiral John Byng is court-martialled and shot for having failed to relieve Menorca from the French fleet** * 1804: Johann Strauss the Elder is born in Vienna * 1879: Albert Einstein is born in Ulm * 1883: Karl Marx dies in London

15 March

Catherine de' Medici attends an execution

1560 For an example of pragmatic brutality and logical cruelty, it is hard to beat today's mass execution of Huguenots sanctioned by one of the Renaissance's most vicious characters, Catherine de' Medici, Queen Mother (and de facto ruler) of France.

The Protestant Huguenots had made the fatal error of attacking the castle at Amboise on the Loire, where the French royal family was in residence. Defeated, the Huguenot leaders were rounded up, and 15 March was set for the execution of 57 of them in the castle courtyard.

Chief among the spectators was Catherine herself. In order to demonstrate how the traitorous are punished, she had placed her son, the sixteen-year-old King François II, beside her with his equally impressionable wife, young Mary of Guise, better known to us as Mary, Queen of Scots. Feeling that few were too young to benefit from the occasion, Catherine also brought along her second son, Charles d'Orléans, age ten.

As the 57 were beheaded or hanged in turn, so the younger generation learned. Even when the crowd called for mercy for the final condemned man, Catherine refused. These were the lessons that helped set the tone for the following years of destruction, barbarism and murder during the French religious wars. Twelve years after this edifying slaughter, the ten-year-old son, now King Charles IX, ordered another Huguenot bloodbath, the Massacre of St Bartholomew.

44 BC: The Ides of March: Julius Caesar is assassinated in the Roman Senate * 1767: American president Andrew Jackson is born * 1807: The first performance of Beethoven's Fourth Symphony takes place at the palace of Prince Lobkowitz in Vienna * 1842: Italian composer Luigi Cherubini dies

> Events written in **boldface** are covered in full in
> *365: Great Stories from History for Every Day of the Year,*
> the first volume in this series.

16 March

Creating America's army officers

1802 Fifty miles north of New York, the high ground at West Point overlooks the Hudson River. Should it fall to the British, they would control the river valley and could split the American colonies in two. Recognising its strategic importance, in 1778 American rebels fortified the point, and a year later General George Washington established his headquarters there.

The US Army has never relinquished this base (although the treasonous general Benedict Arnold tried to sell it to the British in 1780), and West Point therefore remains the oldest continuously occupied military post in the United States. In 1802, however, it took on a special new purpose – turning young Americans into army officers.

In 1783 Washington had been one of the first to propose an American military academy, but newly independent Americans had rejected his call, fearing that a such a training school might lead to a military aristocracy.

Two decades later, however, Congress had seen the wisdom of Washington's idea and drew up a bill that President Thomas Jefferson signed on this day, establishing the United States Military Academy at West Point. Appropriately, the Academy opened for business on Independence Day.

Surprisingly, except for the British Royal Military Academy at Woolwich founded in 1741, America was among the first countries to establish a formal training school for officers. The current British officer training school at Sandhurst opened to train staff officers in 1800 but first admitted cadets in 1802, the French École Spéciale Militaire de Saint-Cyr was set up by Napoleon in 1803, and the Prussian Kriegs Akademie (War Academy) in Berlin was established in 1810.

As one would expect, West Point has produced the preponderance of the country's most illustrious soldiers, but never more so than during the Civil War, when Southern graduates agonised over whether to stay loyal to the Union or to join the forces of their home states. In the end, 638 West Pointers fought for the North, compared to 259 joining the Confederacy. The most famous northern generals were Ulysses S. Grant and William Tecumseh Sherman, although another Union general and West Point graduate, George Armstrong Custer, gained rather less glorious renown after the war at his Last Stand at Little Bighorn.

The Confederacy's two greatest generals, Robert E. Lee and Stonewall Jackson, were both West Point graduates, as was the president of the Confederacy, Jefferson Davis.

According to one historian: 'The Civil War became a West Pointers' war, with 151 Confederate and 294 Union generals. West Pointers commanded both sides in 55 of the war's 60 major battles, and one side in the other five.'

Other famous West Point graduates include Black Jack Pershing, who commanded the American Expeditionary Force during the First World War, and Second World War generals Douglas MacArthur, Omar Bradley, George Patton, and future president Dwight D. Eisenhower. (Among America's most senior Second World War army generals, only George Marshall did not attend West Point, receiving his degree from Virginia Military Institute.)

West Point has also produced three heads of state other than American presidents: Fidel Ramos of the Philippines, José Maria Figueres of Costa Rica and Anastasio Somoza Debayle of Nicaragua, who was forced to resign and was assassinated in exile in Paraguay.

Finally, some fascinating dropouts have also gone to West Point. Edgar Allan Poe was in the class of 1834, but he hated the Academy and was expelled during his first year for missing his classes and drills for a week, and the artist James McNeill Whistler withdrew from the class of 1855. Perhaps the most unlikely of all was the psychedelic Timothy Leary, who dropped out of the class of 1943 and later made a virtue of it with his famous catchphrase: 'Turn on, tune in, drop out.'

Also on this day

AD 37: **Roman emperor Tiberius dies, perhaps murdered** * 1521: Ferdinand Magellan discovers the Philippines * 1792: King Gustav III of Sweden is shot in the back at a masquerade ball in Stockholm and dies twelve days later * 1850: American novelist Nathaniel Hawthorne publishes *The Scarlet Letter* * 1898: English illustrator Aubrey Beardsley dies

17 March

The start of the greatest career

1787 Today a young man not quite eighteen years of age joined the British Army as an ensign in the 73rd Highland Regiment. He was shy, of indifferent health, and played the violin. Born in Dublin into an old family of the Anglo-Irish nobility now in reduced circumstances, he was a product of Eton and the Royal Academy of Equitation in France, where he had received a year's instruction in riding, swordplay and mathematics.

The young man wasn't looking forward to service in the army – it was a derelict time for that institution after the defeat in North America and before the coming war against republican France – but it was not in his character to protest his fate. To the contrary, he would make the best of it.

The commission came via the head of the family, his older brother Richard, who had importuned the Lord Lieutenant of Ireland for it. He persevered in the soldier's trade. In 1794, as a lieutenant-colonel, he got his first taste of combat leading an infantry regiment in the Duke of York's failed campaign to take the Low Countries from the forces of revolutionary France. The ensign signed his name A. Wesley. It was not until 1798, when the older brother was to be made a marquess, that the family name was realigned for heraldic purposes to Wellesley. In that year he was Colonel Arthur Wellesley. By this time he was in India, where he would in time attain the rank of major general.

But it was in Portugal and Spain, in the period 1808–13, fighting against the French, that Wellesley's remarkable string of battlefield successes laid the basis for his enduring fame and won him the recognition of his countrymen. In 1809, for his victory at Talavera, he was made a viscount. In 1812, after his successful siege of Ciudad Rodrigo, he became an earl, and later the same year, following his triumph at Salamanca, he was raised to a marquess. And for chasing Joseph Bonaparte out of Madrid, he had his portrait painted by Francisco Goya.

Finally, on 3 May 1814, with the Peninsular War won, Napoleon gone to Elba, and King Louis XVIII on the throne of France, Lieutenant-General Arthur Wellesley, hailed affectionately as 'Nosey' by his veterans and 'El Liberador' by a grateful Spain, received the title by which the world would know him for all time: duke – the Duke of Wellington. To a letter that he wrote to his brother Henry the next month he added: 'I believe I forgot to tell you that I was made a Duke.' No one else forgot. To his countrymen, as one biographer noted, 'he was henceforth *the* Duke'.

Also on this day

AD 180: Roman emperor Marcus Aurelius dies of plague in Vindobona (now Vienna) * *c.* AD 389: St Patrick (original name, Maewyn Succat), the patron saint of Ireland, is born at Kilpatrick, near Dumbarton, Scotland * **1680: French aphorist François, duc de La Rochefoucauld dies in Paris** * 1861: The Kingdom of Italy is proclaimed and Victor Emmanuel becomes its first king

18 March

Insurrection in Paris

1871 The people of Montmartre were fed up with their new government, the newly formed Third Republic, for they thought that too many concessions were being made to the victorious Prussians who still occupied large parts of France in the aftermath of the Franco-Prussian War. Worse, they believed that the National Assembly favoured the rich and feared that it might move to restore the monarchy. Sullenly, they collected on street corners, whispered conspiratorially to each other and eyed the paving stones as possible missiles.

In an attempt to stabilise the situation in Paris, Adolphe Thiers, the head of the national government, decided to impound the cannon held by the National Guard, which was thought to be sympathetic to the republican mob. But instead of establishing calm, Thiers's move triggered insurrection; on 18 March

Montmartre's doughty citizens commandeered 171 cannons, and when French forces appeared to reclaim them, the crowd dragged one general from his horse and shot him, and shortly seized and shot another. The National Guard quickly joined the insurgents, and the uprising known as the Paris Commune had begun.

In panic, Thiers fled to Versailles, and within ten days the Paris Commune was officially proclaimed, its Council ordering revolutionary changes such as giving women the right to vote and decreeing the separation of church and state, while confiscating all church property and banning religion in schools. The Tricolore of France was replaced with the socialist red flag symbolising 'the blood of angry workers'.

In response to the Commune's usurpation of state powers and the slaughter of the generals, French troops began a siege of Paris that lasted two months. By the end of May, forces under General Mac-Mahon had breached one of Paris's city walls and entered the city, summarily executing any National Guardsmen or civilians caught with weapons. In retaliation, the Communards murdered more than fifty hostages, while setting up barricades in the streets and torching the Hôtel de Ville and the Tuileries Palace.

The government's revenge was swift and terrible; during *la semaine sanglante* (the bloody week) that followed the entry of the French army, 20,000 civilians were killed, among them 17,000 who were executed, including women and children. About 750 soldiers also lost their lives. Crushed by the forces of the Third Republic, the Commune collapsed, but the government's reprisals continued. Almost 40,000 more Parisians were arrested, a fifth of whom were deported to New Caledonia.

Also on this day

1229: Emperor Frederick II crowns himself King of Jerusalem * **1584: Russian Tsar Ivan IV (the Terrible) dies, probably poisoned** * 1745: Robert Walpole, first prime minister of Great Britain, dies * 1890: Germany's Kaiser Wilhelm II forces Otto von Bismarck to resign as Chancellor

19 March

La Salle orders one exploration too many

1687 On this day René-Robert Cavelier, Sieur de La Salle, one of the great explorers of North America, was murdered at the age of 44. A Frenchman ennobled by Louis XIV for his exploits in North America, this Jesuit-trained adventurer had once wanted to become a priest, but instead became a fur trader and would-be empire builder for France. He was the first white man ever to 'sail' the Mississippi from top to bottom (he did it in a canoe) and in 1682 he claimed the Louisiana Territory for his country, naming it after his sovereign.

(For this latter deed, La Salle received scant thanks from King Louis, who wrote to the governor of Canada: 'I am convinced … that the discovery of the Sieur de La Salle is useless and that such enterprises ought to be prevented in the future.')

Determined to start a French colony at the mouth of the Mississippi, La Salle returned to France for approval (and money) from King Louis and then in 1684 set sail with four ships and 400 men. His plans extended to conquering part of Mexico, then owned by Spain. But misfortune plagued him. First the Spanish captured one of his ships. Then he missed the mouth of the Mississippi by some 500 miles, and two more ships were wrecked on the coast of what is now Texas.

Desperate, La Salle went ashore at Matagorda Bay. Only 45 of his men remained alive. Unable to locate the Mississippi, he ordered a march north to Canada, then a French colony, the one destination he knew where they would find safety, Frenchmen, and a ship to take them back to France. But Canada was some 2,500 miles away through uncharted wilderness, and his men thought their chances were better if they waited for a rescue vessel. When the headstrong La Salle insisted, his men rebelled, and several ambushed their leader and killed him.

Like many adventurers, La Salle's strong personality was the reason for his success and ultimately the cause for his failure. As one of his subordinates on his last voyage later wrote: 'His firmness, his courage, his great knowledge of the arts and sciences, which made him equal to every undertaking, and his untiring energy, which enabled him to surmount every obstacle, would have won at last a glorious success for his grand enterprise, had not all his fine qualities been counterbalanced by a haughtiness of manner which often made him unsupportable, and by a harshness toward those under his command, which drew upon him an implacable hatred, and was the cause of his death.'

Also on this day

1314: Jacques de Molay, last Grand Master of the Templars, is burned at the stake in Paris on orders from France's King Philip IV (the Fair) * 1452: Frederick III is crowned in Rome, to reign for 53 years, longer than any other Holy Roman Emperor * 1943: Gangster Frank Nitti shoots himself in the head twice (the second time successfully) at Chicago's Illinois Central railyard

20 March

Napoleon's return to Paris

1815 To the consternation of Europeans everywhere but to the joy of Frenchmen, Napoleon entered Paris today in triumph, borne shoulder-high to the Tuileries by a huge crowd crying 'Vive l'Empereur!' Only three weeks earlier he had escaped his exile on Elba to land near Cannes and take the Continent by surprise. As he travelled north through a France war-weary but discontented under the restored Bourbon regime, peasants hailed him as their champion, and his veterans, forgetting the realities of recent campaigns, cheerfully disobeyed orders and flocked to his side.

Napoleon's cause seemed to gather strength with every mile of his progress. In Vienna the Congress pronounced him an outlaw. In Paris King Louis XVIII and the royal court decamped for the safety of Ghent.

A handbill caught the spirit of the day.

> The Tiger has broken out of his den.
> The Ogre has been three days at sea.
> The Wretch has landed at Fréjus.
> The Buzzard has reached Antibes.
> The Invader has arrived in Grenoble.
> The General has entered Lyon.
> Napoleon slept at Fontainebleau last night.
> The Emperor will proceed to the Tuileries today.
> His Imperial Majesty will address his loyal subjects tomorrow.

The Hundred Days had begun.

Also on this day

43 BC: Roman poet Ovid is born * **1413: English usurper King Henry IV dies in the Jerusalem Chamber of Westminster Abbey** * 1727: Sir Isaac Newton dies in London * 1815: Switzerland becomes permanently neutral

21 March

The best and worst of Napoleon

1804 History knows few characters as controversial as Napoleon Bonaparte, and today saw him at his best and worst.

The most dramatic event of the day was the execution by firing squad of the duc d'Enghien at the Château de Vincennes east of Paris.

Louis de Bourbon-Condé, duc d'Enghien was an attractive and well-meaning 31-year-old prince who lived in the German castle of Ettenheim in Baden, idly plotting with other aristocratic émigrés the overthrow of the government, of which Napoleon was First Consul. But d'Enghien came from one of France's greatest aristocratic families and thus could be a candidate for the throne should the monarchy be restored. Then Napoleon received intelligence (false, as it turned out) that linked d'Enghien with a serious conspiracy of several generals. Incensed, he sent three brigades of infantry plus 300 dragoons across the Rhine into Germany to seize the poor prince as he lay sleeping peacefully in his undefended house.

Forcibly brought back across the border, d'Enghien was imprisoned at Vincennes. Although Napoleon's wife Joséphine begged her husband to be lenient with the aristocratic prisoner, the First Consul accused him of plotting against France and sent him to a mock trial juried by eighteen generals. Quickly convicted and sentenced to death, he was refused a priest and led into the château's moat, to be summarily shot beside a freshly dug grave. Most of Europe was horrified by this brutal kidnap and murder, while the sardonic Talleyrand quipped: '*C'est plus qu'un crime; c'est une faute.*' ('It's more than a crime; it's a blunder.')

On the very same day of the execution Napoleon published a new civil code, the Code Napoléon. This immense body of law was a dramatic improvement over the hodgepodge of existing and sometimes conflicting laws, and its intrinsic fairness was so great that even today it remains the basic law of France, Belgium and Luxembourg.

Also on this day

1556: Archbishop Thomas Cranmer is burnt at the stake for heresy and treason * 1646: Roundheads defeat Royalists at Stow-on-the-Wold in the last battle of the English Civil War * 1685: Johann Sebastian Bach is born in Eisenach, Saxony * 1806: Mexican president Benito Juárez is born

22 March

Stephen Decatur is killed in a duel

1820 Today one of America's most celebrated naval heroes, Stephen Decatur, was mortally wounded in a duel with a fellow officer as a result of bitter acrimony between the two men that had lasted for thirteen years.

Decatur had first gained national renown in 1804 during America's war with Tripoli, a conflict triggered by the piratical pasha's demand for increased tribute in return for not attacking American merchant ships in the Mediterranean. During a night raid Decatur led 74 volunteers into Tripoli harbour and burned the captured American frigate *Philadelphia* without losing a man. The great British admiral Horatio Nelson called it 'the most daring act of the age'. Decatur's reward for his derring-do was to be promoted to the rank of captain at the age of 25, the youngest captain ever in the American navy.

Eleven years later Decatur, by now a commodore, took on the pirates once again during the Second Barbary War. Leading a fleet of nine ships, he riddled and captured the Algerian frigate *Meshouda*, killing the admiral on board and taking over 400 prisoners. Then, with his guns trained on the harbour of Algiers, he delivered an ultimatum to Omar, the Dey of Algiers. When Omar begged for an annual tribute of 'a little gunpowder' from the United States in order to save face with his people, Decatur replied: 'If you insist upon receiving powder as tribute, you must expect to receive balls with it.' The Dey capitulated in two days, putting a stop forever to American payment of tribute to pirate states.

Back in 1807 an American officer named James Barron had allowed a British warship to board and search his frigate and carry off four supposed British deserters, one of whom was hanged. A year later Decatur served on the court martial that had expelled Barron from the Navy for five years. From that moment on the two men, who had previously been friends, continued to wrangle and exchange heated letters, a situation made worse when Decatur accused Barron of malingering abroad instead of returning home to fight in the war against Great Britain of 1812. By 1820 the hostility had become so fierce that Barron challenged Decatur to fight.

The two men met at Bladensburg Duelling Field at what is now Colmar Manor, Maryland, five miles outside Washington, DC. During the preliminaries Decatur remarked to his second: 'I do not desire his life. I mean to shoot him in the hip.' They were to fire at eight paces, but the gentlemanly Decatur did not back up the full distance for safety because of his opponent's poor eyesight.

Both men fired; Decatur wounded his opponent in the hip as planned, but Barron's shot caught Decatur in the stomach. As they lay on the field together, Decatur said that he had never been Barron's enemy, to which Barron replied: 'Would to God you had said that yesterday.'

Taken back in agony to his home on Lafayette Square, Decatur cried out just before he died: 'I did not know that any man could suffer such pain!'

President James Monroe led the mourners at Decatur's funeral, which drew a crowd of 10,000 people and included the entire Supreme Court and most of the Cabinet. Secretary of State John Quincy Adams later described Decatur as 'kind, warm-hearted, unassuming, gentle and hospitable, beloved in social life and with a soul totally and utterly devoted to his country.' Even now there are still eleven American cities named after him, and five Navy warships have been called USS *Decatur*.

Also on this day

1459: Holy Roman Emperor Maximilian I is born at Wiener Neustadt * 1599: Flemish portraitist Anthony van Dyke is born * 1765: The British Parliament passes the Stamp Act to tax the American colonies * **1832: Johann Wolfgang von Goethe dies in Weimar at 82**

23 March

Pope Innocent bests King John

1208 Pope Innocent III was an Italian from Aragni whose primary objective was to increase the temporal power of the papacy. In both Italy and Germany he played one prince off against another to the benefit of Rome, and he liked to show his strength by challenging the marriages of kings. He forced Philip Augustus of France to take back his Danish wife Ingeborg, made Alfonso IX of León give up his wife Berengaria on grounds of consanguinity, and caused Peter of Aragon to break off his intended marriage to Bianca of Navarre.

Innocent's greatest victory came against King John of England. Each had put forward a candidate for Archbishop of Canterbury, and when John refused to yield, the Pope placed all of England under ban of interdict on this day in 1208. Interdict was a potent weapon in the religious 13th century. It meant not only that no church services could be held but also no marriages, baptisms or funerals.

But still John insisted, so Innocent excommunicated him. Even that produced no result, so Innocent used his final weapon: he declared John deposed as King of England and nominated Philip Augustus as his successor, suggesting that Philip might invade with papal blessings.

This last move finally brought John to his knees (or, as Innocent no doubt would have termed it, to his senses). Not only did he accept the Pope's candidate as archbishop, he declared England a fief of Rome and Innocent his temporal overlord. Innocent had in effect conquered the nation, something that no one had done since William the Conqueror a century and a half before, and that no one would ever do again.

At last Pope Innocent was appeased. He lifted his interdict in May 1213. It had lasted over five years.

Also on this day

1801: Tsar Paul I is assassinated * 1842: French novelist Stendhal (Marie-Henri Beyle) dies * 1887: Spanish Cubist painter Juan Gris is born * 1919: Mussolini founds his own party in Italy, the Fasci di Combattimento (Fascists) * 1953: French painter Raoul Dufy dies

24 March

Wingate crashes in the jungle

1944 Sometime in the early evening a Mitchell bomber on a flight from Imphal, India, to Lalaghat crashed on a jungle hillside, killing all nine on board. Among them was a British officer recently described by Prime Minister Winston Churchill as 'a man of genius and audacity'. The officer in question was Major-General Orde Wingate, a brilliant but controversial military leader, a Bible-quoting mystic, an apostle of irregular warfare, an eccentric man whose successes in the field won him admirers in high places but whose arrogant behaviour brought him enemies on many levels.

Despite his off-putting eccentricities – he sometimes received visitors while nude after a bath; and he often wore an alarm clock on his wrist with which to signal the end of an interview – Wingate, a graduate of the Royal Military Academy, showed a special ability to organise and lead small-scale military operations behind enemy lines. In Palestine in the 1930s his Special Night Squads – British-led Jewish commandos – successfully fought against Arab gangs threatening not only the Jewish settlements and oil pipelines of the region but also the security of the British Mandate itself. In the Sudan in 1940 he organised Gideon Force, a mixed unit of Britons, Ethiopians and Sudanese, with which he raised a rebellion that helped liberate Ethiopia from Italian occupation and restore Haile Selassie to the throne.

In 1942 he was called to India, where he set to work devising a way to combat the Japanese forces that had seized Burma and now threatened India. He took a brigade-sized unit of British and Gurkha battalions and trained it as a long-range penetration group. In the spring of 1943 he led his Chindits, as they became known, into Burma's rugged terrain. In the course of three months, organised into separate columns but connected by radios and supplied by air, they blew up bridges, destroyed railway lines, and played havoc with the Japanese line of communications, penetrating some 200 miles. But the getting back proved difficult, and when the columns returned to India they had lost a third of their strength, and only 600 of those who made it back were considered fit for active duty.

Whether the expedition was a success – 'worth the loss of many brigades' as Wingate put it, or 'an expensive failure' as General Slim, 14th British Army commander and Wingate's boss, wrote – is still a matter of debate. But the feat was unquestionably a great morale-booster, capturing the imagination of the press, which dubbed him 'Clive of Burma', and of Allied leaders starved for some sign of success on the South-East Asia front. 'Whatever the actual facts', Slim himself conceded, 'to the troops in Burma it seemed the first ripple showing the turn of the tide'.

Now the man of the hour, even though his unorthodox views of warfare seemed dubious or even threatening to certain quarters of the British military establishment, Wingate was sent for by Winston Churchill, who brought him to the 1943 Quadrant Conference in Quebec, where the Prime Minister and President Roosevelt were to meet with their combined chiefs of staff. At the conference, it was agreed to send in a second and larger Chindit force to Burma the following year, bolstered by American air support.

But as the second Chindit expedition got underway in the spring of 1944, with some 20,000 men entering North Burma on foot and by air, Wingate met his fate in the crash of the Mitchell bomber. The operation continued with some success, but without their leader the days of the Chindits as a separate enterprise were numbered, and the unit soon fell under other commands, including that of US General Stilwell, whose celebrated Merrill's Marauders were modelled after them. The early Chindit experiences in the field had at the very least demonstrated that even an enemy as skilled in jungle fighting techniques as the Japanese was vulnerable to the kind of warfare Wingate preached. Ultimately, the combined operations of which they were a part were successful in the 1945 reconquest of Burma, in part because the Allied forces had become, in the words of the theatre commander, Lord Mountbatten: 'Chindit-minded'.

Also on this day

1401: Mongol leader Tamerlane the Great captures Damascus * **1603: Queen Elizabeth I dies and the crowns of England and Scotland are united when James VI of Scotland succeeds to the English throne** * 1721: Johann Sebastian Bach publishes the six Brandenburg Concertos * 1874: Magician Harry Houdini (Erich Weiss) is born in Budapest

25 March

Trial by Jury *opens in London*

1875 On this date *Trial by Jury* opened at London's Royalty Theatre. It was not the first joint enterprise of William S. Gilbert and Arthur Sullivan – four years earlier they had collaborated on *Thespis*, which ran 64 performances – but it was the first of their operettas that are still performed today. It was also the first to be produced with the theatre impresario Richard D'Oyly Carte. *Trial by Jury* was an immediate success, and in its first two years ran for some 300 performances. Critics and audiences were delighted by the close partnership of Gilbert's words and Sullivan's music, one reviewer noting that they seemed to have 'proceeded simultaneously from one and the same brain'. Only 45 minutes in length, much shorter than any other G&S operetta, *Trial by Jury* was usually performed as part of a double bill with *HMS Pinafore* or *The Pirates of Penzance*.

Over the next 21 years, Gilbert and Sullivan would collaborate on twelve more of the works that have come to be known as the Savoy Operas, after the Savoy Theatre which D'Oyly Carte opened for his theatre company in 1881 and in which all the operas after *Patience* had their first English performances. Mostly satirical in manner and with 'topsy-turvy' plots, the Savoy Operas poked fun at many prominent features of the late Victorian age.

The object of *Trial by Jury*'s gentle satire is the British legal system. The plot involves a breach of promise of marriage in which the Defendant (Edwin) is being sued for breaking off his engagement to the Plaintiff (Angelina). The trial is complicated when both the Judge and the jury fall in love with Angelina.

'Never, never, never, since I joined the human race', sings the Judge, 'Saw I so exquisitely fair a face'. 'We love you fondly and would make you ours', intone the jurymen. Faced with an unsympathetic courtroom, Edwin makes an offer: 'I'll marry this lady today, and I'll marry the other tomorrow.' Plaintiff's Counsel, however, balks at this solution on the precedent that: 'In the reign of James the Second, it was generally reckoned as a rather serious crime to marry two wives at one time.' Exasperated by the parties' inability to reach a settlement, the Judge finally interrupts the proceedings with a notable decision: 'Put your briefs upon the shelf, I shall marry her myself', at which the entire courtroom bursts into a finale of song and celebration. Curtain.

Also on this day

1133: England's first Plantagenet king Henry II is born in Le Mans * 1347: St Catherine of Siena is born * 1436: Brunelleschi's dome in the Duomo in Florence is consecrated * 1821: Greece declares independence from Turkey

26 March

Raymond Chandler sleeps the big sleep

1959 Raymond Chandler, the master of the hard-boiled detective story, known worldwide for his best-selling novels and the movies made from them, died today in La Jolla, California. Only seventeen people showed up for his funeral.

Born in Chicago in 1888, Chandler moved back and forth to England with his English mother until, after the First World War, he settled in Los Angeles. There, at 36, he fell in love with and married a woman of 54. Nine years later, in 1933, he lost his job at an oil company because of his drinking, and only then decided to write. In December he published his first story, 'Blackmailers Don't Shoot', in the pulp magazine *Black Mask*, and he continued producing detective stories for the next five years. Then, in the spring of 1938, in only three months he wrote his first full-length novel, *The Big Sleep*, featuring his world-weary private eye, Philip Marlowe.

Chandler conceived Marlowe as a tired latter-day knight-errant, both sceptical and irreverent. In his 1944 essay, 'The Simple Art of Murder', the author defined his operative:

> Down these mean streets a man must go who is not himself mean, who is neither tarnished nor afraid ... He talks as the man of his age talks, that is, with rude wit, a lively sense of the grotesque, a disgust for sham, and a contempt for pettiness ... He is neither a eunuch nor a satyr; I think he might seduce a duchess and I am quite sure he would not spoil a virgin ...

The Big Sleep was an instant success and was twice turned into a movie. The 1946 version, with a shooting script co-written by William Faulkner, starred Humphrey Bogart and Lauren Bacall, and the 1978 adaptation featured Robert Mitchum and Sarah Miles.

Chandler wrote seven more Philip Marlowe novels, *Farewell, My Lovely, The High Window, The Lady in the Lake, The Little Sister, The Long Goodbye, Playback* and *Poodle Springs*, which was incomplete at Chandler's death but was finished by Robert B. Parker in 1989. All were adapted for film.

Chandler placed his novels in Los Angeles, memorably writing in his story 'Red Wind' that when the hot winds blow there: 'Meek little wives feel the edge of the carving knife and study their husbands' necks.' His breezy, sardonic style perfectly complements his private detective. A typical Chandleresque paragraph in *The Little Sister* begins:

> The pebbled glass door pane is lettered in flaked black paint: 'Philip Marlowe … Investigations.' It is a reasonably shabby door at the end of a reasonably shabby corridor in the sort of building that was new about the year the all-tile bathroom became the basis of civilization …

Chandler is now venerated for his witty, ironic descriptions, none better than his famous lines in *Farewell, My Lovely*: 'It was a blonde. A blonde to make a bishop kick a hole in a stained glass window.' Not everyone, however, appreciated his syntax. He was once taken to task for his use of split infinitives, to which he responded to his editor: 'Would you convey my compliments to the purist who reads your proofs and tell him or her that I write a sort of broken-down patois which is something like the way a Swiss waiter talks, and that when I split an infinitive, God damn it, I split it so it will stay split.'

Chandler was a heavy drinker all his life. In an early story he has a character say: 'I'm an occasional drinker, the kind of guy who goes out for a beer and wakes up in Singapore with a full beard.' Later, after several stays in drying-out clinics, he wrote: 'Alcohol is like love. The first kiss is magic, the second is intimate, the third is routine. After that you take the girl's clothes off.'

In 1946 Chandler moved to La Jolla, but his wife died in 1954, leaving him inconsolable, and he turned once more to alcohol and even attempted suicide. Five years later, now 70, almost without friends and debilitated by drink, he died of pneumonia in the Scripps Clinic. In *The Big Sleep* he had expressed his own jaded views about death.

> What did it matter where you lay once you were dead? In a dirty sump or in a marble tower on top of a high hill? … You were not bothered by things like that. You just slept the big sleep, not caring about the nastiness of how you died or where you fell …

Also on this day

1726: British architect Sir John Vanbrugh dies, London * **1827: Ludwig van Beethoven dies in Vienna** * 1859: English poet A.E. Housman is born * 1874: American poet Robert Frost is born * 1892: American poet Walt Whitman dies, Camden, New Jersey * 1902: Cecil Rhodes dies, Muizenberg, Cape Colony * 1953: American doctor and researcher Jonas Salk announces his new polio vaccine

27 March

Robert the Bruce is King

1306 Today at the abbey of Scone, the ancient crowning place of Scottish kings, a ten-year interregnum ended with the coronation of Robert Bruce, Earl of Carrick, as King of Scotland.

Scotland had lived without a monarch since 1296, when Edward Plantagenet, King of England, dethroned and exiled to France the very Scottish king he had placed upon the throne four years earlier. From that date on, Edward ruled Scotland as he did Wales, not through a vassal king but through an English governor.

Robert Bruce was not a hero born. While he joined the resistance to English rule that followed the dethroning, he later withdrew, then vacillated, and for a time even served Edward against his fellow Scots. All the while, his hope was that with Edward's support he could realise his family's claim to the throne of Scotland, a claim unsuccessfully pursued by his father and grandfather before him. But in time, Bruce came to see that his only path to the throne lay not through the pleasure of Edward, the 'Hammer of the Scots', but in leading an armed struggle for Scottish independence. Still, his hand needed forcing.

What forced it was his arch-rival for power in Scotland, John Comyn, nephew of the exiled king. Former enemies for dynastic and political reasons, Comyn and Bruce now put aside their differences to plot a way in which one or the other might secure the empty throne. But Comyn betrayed the plot to Edward, and in January 1306 Bruce was forced to flee the London court for Scotland. Crossing the border at Dumfries, he arranged a meeting with Comyn in the church of the Greyfriars. There, in a fiery confrontation before the altar, Bruce accused Comyn of treachery, then slew him with his sword. From such a deed there was no turning back. So, Bruce proclaimed himself King of the Scots and summoned the great and powerful of the land to gather at Scone for his coronation.

With an English army assembling on the border, few of the great and powerful answered the call: only three bishops, three earls, and an abbot were present this day to cry 'God save the King'. Of symbolic importance to the occasion, however, was the attendance of Isabel, Countess of Buchan. Though married to a Comyn, she defied her husband and made her way to Scone, where she fulfilled her family's ancient privilege at Scottish coronations by placing a gold circlet on the new king's head. For this act she would go to prison.

Three days after the coronation, Bruce, his wife, his brothers and a handful of knights headed north to rally the country. It was just the beginning of the struggle for which there was no end in sight. He and many of those loyal to him endured frustrations, betrayals, narrow escapes, false hopes, defeats, imprisonments, and death. But the tide finally turned – slowly at first, then with gathering force – and in the year 1314 came the great victory at Bannockburn and the accomplishment of Scottish independence.

Scotland remained separate and independent for almost three hundred years – until 1603 when, by inheritance upon the death of Queen Elizabeth I, King James VI of Scotland became as well King James I of England.

Also on this day

1204: French and then English queen Eleanor of Aquitaine dies at the abbey of Fontevrault * 1615 : French queen Margot (Marguerite de Valois) dies * 1625: James I dies in his hunting lodge at Theobalds, Essex * 1770: Italian Baroque painter Giovanni Battista Tiepolo dies in Madrid * 1809: Georges Eugène, Baron Haussman, the man who redesigned Paris, is born

28 March

Death of a fat pope

1285 Fat Pope Martin IV, who died today in Perugia, had only two major objectives during his five-year reign, and he failed at both of them.

Born of noble birth as Simon de Brie in the town now so famous for its cheese, he was short and corpulent, known for his prodigious appetite. Stories abounded of his feats as trencherman, as he spent lavishly for the latest culinary delicacies.

Martin was an adviser to France's saintly King Louis IX and later his chancellor, but his real patron was Louis's brother, Charles of Anjou, King of Naples and Sicily. It was largely thanks to Charles's influence that he was elected Pope in February 1281.

During the 13th century, Christianity was split into two halves, with competing Churches in Rome and Constantinople. Martin's first ambition was to bring all Christians back under the aegis of Rome. In this his powerful ally was King Charles who, according to a contemporary report, 'hoped to become ruler of the world, rejoining east and west to recreate the great empire of Julius Caesar'. The answer for both Pope and King was to conquer the Byzantine Empire.

While Charles would look after the fighting, Martin would use spiritual weapons. In pursuit of his goal he excommunicated the Byzantine emperor Michael VIII Palaeologus, while elevating Charles's planned invasion of Byzantium to the level of a 'Holy Crusade' – even though the Byzantines were Christian. But Charles made only one serious (and unsuccessful) attack, and the only result of Martin's excommunication was to split the churches of Rome and Constantinople irrevocably.

For King Charles, things then went from bad to worse. Having failed to conquer the Byzantine Empire, he then lost his Kingdom of Sicily during the

War of the Sicilian Vespers. So Martin decided to help him get it back in the same manner that he had helped against Michael Palaeologus. This time he excommunicated Peter III of Aragon, who had taken control of Sicily.

The result was predictable: another failure, as Peter stayed firmly in control.

Worn out and disheartened, King Charles died in January 1285 at the age of 59. Not three months later, the obese Pope Martin ingested yet another gargantuan meal and died of dyspepsia, an end that was immortalised by Dante when he included the gluttonous pope in his *Inferno*.

Also on this day

1515: St Teresa (Teresa de Cepeda y Ahumada) is born in Avila * 1854: France and Britain declare war on Russia to join the Crimean War * **1930: The Turkish government changes the name of its capital from Constantinople to Istanbul** * 1939: The Spanish Civil War ends as Madrid surrenders to Francisco Franco * 1941: English novelist Virginia Woolf throws herself into the River Ouse * 1946: Juan Perón is elected President of Argentina

29 March

Birth of a man who would inherit the presidency

1790 Today in the Tidewater region of Virginia south-east of Richmond was born John Tyler, who 51 years later would become President of the United States.

The America in which Tyler was born was a small nation of fewer than 4 million people, of whom almost 700,000 were slaves. There were just sixteen states, of which the most populous was Virginia. Only eleven months earlier George Washington had become its first president.

Coming from a powerful Virginian political family, Tyler was elected to the state legislature at 21, the US Congress at 27, the governorship of Virginia at 35 and the US Senate at 37. Finally, in 1840, he made it to the White House, as Vice President to William Henry Harrison, who had been elected on the alliterative campaign slogan of 'Tippecanoe and Tyler too!' (Tippecanoe was a battle against Indians that Harrison had won almost 30 years before.)

Then suddenly, only weeks into office, Harrison died of pneumonia and Tyler became the first American vice president ever to assume the presidency. He was the country's tenth president, the sixth born in Virginia (and the last one born there until Woodrow Wilson).

A devoted believer in states' rights, Tyler was undistinguished at best as leader of the nation. He achieved another presidential first when the House of Representatives, led by former president John Quincy Adams, passed a resolution of impeachment because he had vetoed so many bills. The impeachment failed, but at one point his entire cabinet resigned except for his

Secretary of State Daniel Webster, and his own party, the Whigs, repudiated him for his views on states' rights. Not surprisingly, when his term ended he declined to run for re-election.

Settling back in Virginia, Tyler continued to work for states' rights and the prolongation of slavery, although he initially opposed the secession of the Southern states. On the eve of the Civil War the American population had mushroomed to 31 million, almost ten times its total at Tyler's birth, and included some 3.5 million black slaves. When the Confederacy was established, the slave-owning Tyler, now 70, became a member of the Confederate House of Representatives, but he died in less than a year, just seven months before Abraham Lincoln issued his historic Emancipation Proclamation freeing all the slaves.

Also on this day

1461: The Yorkists defeat the Lancastrians under Henry VI at the Battle of Towton in the Wars of the Roses * 1848: American fur and property tycoon John Jacob Astor dies in New York * 1891: French pointillist painter Georges-Pierre Seurat dies * **1951: American communists Julius and Ethel Rosenberg are found guilty of treason for passing atomic secrets to Russia**

30 March

The United States buys land seven times the size of Great Britain

1867 On this date Russia sold Alaska to the United States for $7.2 million. Alaska was formally transferred on 18 October the same year, the result of brilliant negotiations by American Secretary of State William Seward. Although now the intelligence of Seward's purchase is plain to all, at the time so many doubted the sense of buying this enormous area of frigid wilderness that it was colloquially called 'Seward's Folly'.

Alaska remained an American territory for almost a century but finally became the country's 49th state on 3 January 1959. The largest American state, it covers 591,004 square miles (1,530,700 square kilometres), twice as big as Texas and almost seven times the size of Great Britain. When it became a state, it increased the size of the nation by almost 20 per cent. But with only 600,000 inhabitants, it has the lowest population of any state.

Seward's purchase was one of the shrewdest in history. Alaska boasts a huge fishing industry, specialising in salmon, herring, cod and halibut as well as several types of crab. It also has mammoth timber resources and, to the fury of animal rights activists, a thriving business harvesting pelts from baby seals. But perhaps the state's biggest treasure is oil. Had the $7.2 million that Seward spent been invested instead at 5 per cent interest for all the years since 1867, it would be worth about $6.7 billion today. But the value of the oil alone beneath

Alaska's surface is an estimated $600 billion, $1 million per inhabitant. No wonder the official state motto is 'North to the Future'.

Also on this day

1282: Palermo's citizens butcher French occupying soldiers during the bloody 'Sicilian Vespers' * 1746: Francisco de Goya is born in Fuendetodos, Spain * 1842: American doctor Crawford Long uses ether for the first time as an anaesthetic during surgery * 1853: Vincent van Gogh is born in Zundert, the Netherlands * 1856: The Treaty of Paris ends the Crimean War

31 March

Le grand roi François *passes on*

1547 According to the court chronicle, the last words of King François I of France were 'Jesus, Jesus', and when he could no longer speak 'he clasped his hands, lifted his eyes toward heaven and tried to cross himself'. He died at 2 o'clock this Thursday morning at his château at Rambouillet.

François was the 24th king of France in an unbroken line since 987 when Hugh Capet founded the Capetian dynasty. He reigned for 32 years, during which he fought four pointless wars with Emperor Charles V (and lost the last three of them) and vied in fatuous and costly kingly splendour with Henry VIII. But it was François more than anyone who brought the Renaissance to France, even enticing Leonardo to spend his last years near him on the Loire.

François built or reconstructed a large number of châteaux in the Loire Valley, including those at Amboise and Blois, and he created the magnificent château at Chambord, which Leonardo may have helped design. He also financed the Hôtel de Ville in Paris, but perhaps the building most associated with him is the royal château at Fontainebleau, which he completely rebuilt and expanded. In keeping with his love of luxury, one of its courtyard fountains gushed with a mixture of water and wine. To his countrymen then and still today he was *le grand roi François*.

Although François had a passion for hunting, loved his food and wine, and had earned an enviable reputation as a seducer, his last years had been sombre. Plagued by illness and perhaps syphilis, he suffered from bouts of melancholy and remorse. His courtiers noticed that he often lacked focus, his mind wandering. Now he was wearing his beard long, his hair was thinning and he had lost most of his teeth, making him look much older than his 52 years. His depression only deepened when he learned that his old friend, enemy and rival Henry VIII had died in January.

During his last weeks he moved incessantly from château to château, from Saint-Germain, to Limours to Rochefort and finally to Rambouillet, so ill that he had to be carried in a litter. There he died, apparently penitent, refusing to see his distraught mistress during his final hours. Bizarrely, three days after his death, as part of his funeral ceremonies a painted wooden statue of him, dressed in his clothes and wearing the royal crown, was placed on his throne, where it remained for eleven days with meals set before it, each carefully tasted by the Grand Master as if François were still alive. Finally, on 22 May, the old king's corpse was interred in the royal chapel at Saint-Denis.

Pious as he may have been in his final hours, François is better remembered today for his love of women, a reputation enhanced three centuries after his death with Victor Hugo's drama *Le roi s'amuse*, which in turn inspired Verdi's *Rigoletto*.

Also on this day

1596: French philosopher René Descartes is born * 1631: The bell tolls for John Donne in London * 1732: Austro-Hungarian composer Joseph Haydn is born * 1837: English novelist Charlotte Brontë dies * 1837: English landscapist John Constable dies * **1854: Under the guns of American Admiral Perry, Japan signs the Treaty of Kanagawa, opening Japan to trade with the West** * 1889: The Eiffel Tower is inaugurated

1 April

Napoleon marries Marie-Louise

1810 Today at age 40 the Emperor Napoleon married Austrian archduchess Marie-Louise, twenty-one years his junior and daughter of the Austrian Emperor Franz I.

Desperate to found a dynasty but unable to produce a child with the Empress Joséphine, the previous August Napoleon had impregnated his mistress Marie Walewska, giving him hope that a new wife might provide an heir. In January 1810 he dissolved his sixteen-year marriage and began the hunt for a bride, preferably one with royal blood. Then the shrewd Austrian statesman Klemens von Metternich suggested Marie-Louise, winning over Franz by pointing out that it would consolidate his hold on the Austrian throne at a time when Napoleon was virtually master of Europe. Napoleon was heartened by the news that Marie-Louise's mother had borne thirteen children, her grandmother seventeen and her great-grandmother 26; surely the buxom Marie-Louise would produce the desperately desired successor.

Napoleon was enthusiastic, Marie-Louise was easily persuaded, and the couple were wed by proxy on 11 March.

Two weeks later Marie-Louise and her entourage left for Paris for the formal marriage ceremonies. Knowing her route, Napoleon intercepted her carriage at Courcelles and rode with her to Compiègne, where he whisked her off to consummate the marriage. Years later, when imprisoned at St Helena, Napoleon wistfully recalled: 'She liked it so much she asked me to do it again.'

The proxy-weds reached St Cloud on the last day of March, welcomed by a 100-gun salute. The next morning was a day of intense cold and heavy rain, but hundreds of onlookers waited outside the palace at St Cloud, where two thrones had been placed side by side in the grand gallery. There, observed by civil and ecclesiastical dignitaries and a pride of foreign ambassadors, the Archchancellor pronounced Napoleon and Marie-Louise man and wife.

Just six weeks after the wedding Napoleon received news that he had a child at last – Marie Walewska had given birth to a healthy son at her husband's estate in Walewice, near Warsaw. But Marie-Louise proved equally fertile and gave Napoleon a second son on 20 March 1811.

Although the marriage was manifestly a political and dynastic one rather than a love match, at first all went smoothly, and Marie-Louise even served as regent while Napoleon was campaigning in Russia. But when Napoleon abdicated in 1814, she returned to Vienna with her son. Ignoring Napoleon's pleas to join him on Elba, she soon entered an entrenched affair with Adam Adalbert, Count von Neipperg. She never saw her husband again, refusing to come to him even during his brief Hundred Days ascendancy after he escaped from Elba.

A few years later, when incarcerated on St Helena, Napoleon bitterly remembered Marie-Louise with the comment: 'With her I stepped onto an abyss covered with flowers.' But perhaps in the end he forgave her. Just before he died in 1821 he directed that his heart be offered to her – a gift she declined, perhaps because by that time she was living openly with Neipperg and had already borne him two children.

Four months after Napoleon's death Marie-Louise married Neipperg, and together they governed the duchies of Parma, Piacenza, and Guastalla until his death eight years later. Napoleon's son, known as the Duke of Reichstadt, fell victim to tuberculosis in 1832. After a third marriage Marie-Louise died in Parma at the age of 56.

Also on this day

1815: Germany's Iron Chancellor Otto von Bismarck is born in Schönhausen, Prussia * 1920: The Germany's Workers' Party changes its name to the National Socialist German Workers' Party (Nationalsozialistische Deutsche Arbeiterpartei), or, for short, Nazi * 1924: Adolf Hitler is sentenced to five years in prison for the 'Beer Hall Putsch'

Events written in **boldface** are covered in full in
365: Great Stories from History for Every Day of the Year,
the first volume in this series.

---

2 April

Did Richard the Lionheart really meet Robin Hood?

1194   King Richard hearing of the pranks
          Of Robin Hood and his men,
          He much admired, and more desired
          To see both him and them.

So goes an ancient English ballad, and most of us would like to think that Richard the Lionheart did in fact encounter history's most famous outlaw, Robin Hood.

Most historians believe Robin Hood is a sort of composite figure of several different medieval outlaws, while some believe he is complete fiction. But maybe – just maybe – the old ballad is right.

What we know for sure is that on 2 April 1194, King Richard stopped overnight in Clipston Palace, on the edge of Sherwood Forest. This fact and Richard's known love of high and noble drama give some underpinning to the legend that he met Robin here. As every schoolboy knows, Richard went into the forest disguised as an abbot, met Robin and his men and engaged them in sports, outwrestling Little John but yielding to Friar Tuck's superior prowess with the sword. The King then revealed his true identity and, after much swearing of loyalty, king and outlaw dined together in the forest.

> Venison and fowls were plenty there,
> With fish out of the river;
> King Richard swore, on sea and shore,
> He ne'er was feasted better.

Also on this day

742: Charlemagne is born * 1725: Italian seducer Giovanni Giacomo Casanova is born * 1800: In Vienna, Beethoven's First Symphony is performed for the first time * 1801: Horatio Nelson leads the main attack against the Danish fleet in the British victory at the Battle of Copenhagen * 1840: Emile Zola is born in Paris

3 April

Philip the Fair suppresses the Templars

1312 The Order of the Temple had been founded in the early 12th century to guard routes to the Holy Land travelled by devout pilgrims. Its original members were dedicated and selfless knights whose conduct resembled that of warrior monks. Over the years, however, the Templars became secretive and introverted, confused by their own rituals and initiations. With the fall of Acre in 1291, Christianity lost its last toehold in the Holy Land and the Templars their very *raison d'être*. But by then the Order was rich – very rich – and a tempting target for Philip the Fair, King of France, who resolved to destroy it.

At first Philip spread harmful rumours about the Order, lies cleverly blended with truth. Then came more outrageous condemnations: the Templars were heretics and idolaters who spat on the Cross; they practised human sacrifice; they were renegades and sodomites. Then, in a single day on Friday, 13 October 1307, Philip arrested every Templar knight throughout France. (Some believe the superstition of unlucky Friday the thirteenth stems from this day.) So began Philip's campaign to convince his pet Pope Clement V to suppress the Order entirely. (French by birth and elected Pope through Philip's manipulation in 1305, this was the same pope who had moved the papacy from Rome to Avignon.)

The main evidence of the evils of the Temple was admissions of guilt by imprisoned knights. Torture was used to enrich these confessions, the severity of which can be judged by the fact that 36 knights did not survive their inquisition. When some 500 Templars tried to recant their confessions, five were beheaded and nine burnt at the stake for 'relapsing'. The remainder quickly recanted their recantations.

Philip the Fair finally met in council with the Pope at Vienne on 3 April 1312. Clement and he sat side by side, the pontiff on a slightly higher throne, as befitted his spiritual seniority. The Pope pronounced judgement. The Temple was formally suppressed; after 184 years it no longer existed. Those knights who confessed and repented were released. The few who continued to proclaim their innocence were imprisoned for life.

Also on this day

1203: King John murders his nephew Arthur * 1721: Robert Walpole becomes the first prime minister of Great Britain * 1794: French revolutionary Camille Desmoulins is guillotined * 1882: American outlaw Jesse James is shot in the back by one of his own gang * 1897: German composer Johannes Brahms dies of cancer in Vienna

4 April

A saint dies on Good Friday

AD 397 This was Good Friday and so perhaps a fitting date for the death of a saint.

St Ambrose had been born 57 years earlier of a noble Roman family. Raised a pagan, he achieved the rank of governor in the empire's civil service and was sent to Milan. There he converted to Christianity, the religion given official status only a few years earlier by Constantine the Great's Edict of Milan in 313. Entering the Church, Ambrose eventually attained the rank of bishop, determined to help the Church 'rise like a waxing moon' to become the spiritual force behind the Roman Empire.

Ambrose influenced four separate emperors and had no fear of imperial power. He once personally prevented Emperor Theodosius from entering Milan cathedral, and kept him out for eight months until he had purged himself for having 7,000 Greeks put to death for murdering their tyrannical governor. He created the medieval idea of emperors as sons of the Church 'serving under orders from Christ' and hence subordinate to the Pope – a concept that often led to bitter conflict between emperor and pope for centuries to come.

Ambrose was a powerful voice in making pagan worship illegal, but perhaps his best-remembered achievement was the double baptism of two pagans, a father and his illegitimate son. The father was eventually canonised as St Augustine of Hippo, who considered Ambrose the model bishop and adopted some of his Neo-Platonist ideas in his philosophy, which would eventually transfigure Catholic theology.

Ambrose died of unknown causes. Today, in the Milanese church that bears his name, his bones reside still clothed in bishop's raiment.

Also on this day

AD 188: Emperor Caracalla is born in Lugdunum (Lyon) * 527: Byzantine emperor Justinian is crowned * 1648: Dutch-born woodcarver and sculptor Grinling Gibbons is born * **1774: English playwright Oliver Goldsmith dies in London**

5 April

Pocahontas gets married

1614 'Little Wanton' or 'playful, spirited little girl' she was called, better known to us by the Indian word '*Pocahontas*'. Today, at the age of about nineteen, she was married for the second time – bigamously by our standards but not by those of the time, for her first husband, who was still alive, was a heathen Indian.

Pocahontas was an Algonquian, daughter of the mighty chief Powhatan in the Tidewater region of Virginia, and as a young girl she had come to know the English settlers in Jamestown. At fifteen she married an Indian brave named Kokoum, but about two years later an unscrupulous English captain, named Samuel Argall, lured her onto his ship and then held her for ransom. By the time her father Powhatan had agreed to the terms of payment, Argall had taken her back to Jamestown and then moved to the nearby town of Henrico, where she fell in love with the widower John Rolfe, a leading Virginia planter ten years her senior. In 1613 Pocahontas was briefly reunited with her father and he agreed with her wish to marry Rolfe.

Rolfe, too, wanted to marry, but he insisted that Pocahontas first become a Christian. After a brief introduction to the faith she was christened with the new name of Rebecca, and on this day the couple married, her first husband Kokoum apparently forgotten. They soon had a baby son.

Two years later John, Pocahontas and their son travelled to England as part of the colony's campaign to raise more funds. There she became an instant celebrity. Still only 21, she was strikingly handsome, dressed in the height of European fashion with her black hair and Indian complexion. She and her husband were presented to the highest members of English society, including King James I.

In March 1617 the Rolfes set sail for Virginia, but Pocahontas was so ill that the ship returned to harbour at Gravesend. There she died of smallpox, just 22 years old. After her funeral her husband John went back to Jamestown and remarried. In 1622 he perished in an Indian massacre at his farm.

Under normal circumstances the tale of Pocahontas's short life and minor celebrity would long since have vanished into the lists of historical trivia, but five years after her death the founder of Jamestown, a dashing English adventurer named John Smith, published his *Generall Historie of Virginia*, in which he included his now-famous tale of Pocahontas.

According to Smith, in December 1607, when Pocahontas was still only about twelve, Algonquian warriors captured him while he was exploring the Chickahominy river. In triumph they brought him before Chief Powhatan. Here, in Smith's own words, is what happened next:

'Having feasted him [i.e. Smith] after their best barbarous manner they could, a long consultation was held, but the conclusion was, two great stones

110

were brought before Powhattan; then as many [braves] as could layd hands on him, dragged him to them, and thereon laid his head, and being ready with their clubs, to beate out his braines, Pochahontas, the Kings dearest daughter, when no intreaty could prevaile, got his head in her armes, and laid her owne upon his to save him from death.'

John Smith's tale immortalised Pocahontas in American folk history. Sadly, today, historians conclude that the story was a fabrication, as Smith published it years after the event and it is not mentioned in his diaries. At best, this mock execution and salvation was part of a stock Indian ritual of welcome and friendship.

Also on this day

1794: French revolutionary Georges Danton is guillotined * 1803: Beethoven's Second Symphony is performed for the first time, in the Theater an der Wien, Vienna * 1837: English poet Algernon Charles Swinburne is born in London * 1955: Winston Churchill resigns as British Prime Minister

6 April

The Declaration of Arbroath

1320 If 4 July 1776 is remembered for the momentous statement that begins, 'When in the course of human events . . .', then 6 April should be noted for an equally stirring declaration of independence, written some four and a half centuries earlier, when another nation struggled for freedom from English rule. It read in part:

'For as long as one hundred of us shall remain alive we shall never in any wise consent to submit to the rule of the English, for it is not for glory we fight, for riches, or for honours, but for freedom alone, which no good man loses but with his life.'

These brave words were set down in Latin today at the abbey of Arbroath, where Scottish earls, barons, freeholders and clergymen – representing 'the whole community of the realm' – had gathered for the purpose of sending a message to the Pope in Rome. Known thereafter as the Declaration of Arbroath, the document asserted Scotland's independence, militarily confirmed by the great victory at Bannockburn six years earlier, and the assemblage's choice of Robert the Bruce as their king.

In the course of the long and complicated struggle for his nation's independence, Bruce had slain his rival for the Scottish throne, John Comyn, and subsequently had himself crowned King – deeds that won him excommunication by Pope John XXII and an oath by King Edward of England never to rest until Scotland was thoroughly restored to English rule. Against all odds, Bruce and the Scots were victorious in the war that followed. But in the aftermath

Edward's son, ruling as Edward II, would not recognise the independence of Scotland or Bruce as its rightful monarch: a position buttressed by Bruce's excommunication, which, while it remained in force, cast in doubt the legitimacy of his kingship.

The Declaration of Arbroath, encapsulating as it did the determination of a united people, had effect. The Pope issued a temporary waiver of the excommunication and in 1324 recognised Bruce as the King of the Scots. Border raids and broken truces continued to mark Scotland's relations with England, but in 1328 Edward III signed the Treaty of Southampton, recognising Bruce as the king of an independent realm.

Also on this day

1199: Richard the Lionheart dies of gangrene resulting from a crossbow wound at the siege of Châlus * 1529: Raphael dies in Rome on his 37th birthday * 1528: German painter Albrecht Dürer dies * 1909: American explorer Robert Peary becomes the first to reach the North Pole * 1917: The United States declares war on Germany

7 April

A French king's fatal accident

1498 The beautiful château of Amboise, on the south bank of the Loire, is strongly connected to one of France's least beautiful kings, Charles VIII. Born and raised at Amboise, Charles had a long, drooping nose and mumbled through flabby, wet lips. His oversize head sat atop a small, crippled body. Although called Charles l'Affable for his agreeable nature, he lacked both education and intelligence. (His unappetising appearance may have been why his bride, Anne de Bretagne, arrived for her wedding with her entourage carrying two beds. But perhaps his affability won her over – they produced four children.)

Despite his shortcomings, Charles was a well-meaning man with some real sensitivity to beauty. It was he who built much of Amboise, and he introduced France to much of the Renaissance, as he had been strongly influenced by Italian art and civilisation during his invasion of Italy in 1494. (This absurd adventure gained for Charles the crown of Naples, which he fervently believed was his by right of his Angevin inheritance, but by the time he returned to France the following year he had lost all that he had won.)

In 1498 Charles was back in his beloved Amboise, planning another Italian incursion. On 7 April he was watching a game of tennis being played in the moat of the château. Leaving the court, he hit his head on the low lintel of a doorway. Laughing off the accident, the King returned to the game, but suddenly he collapsed, falling to the ground barely conscious. That evening he died, not yet 28 years old. Amboise, where he had been given life, had taken it back.

Also on this day
331 BC: Alexander the Great founds Alexandria * 1300: The start date of Dante's *Divine Comedy* * 1614: Greek/Spanish painter El Greco (Domenikos Theotokopoulos) dies in Toledo * 1770: William Wordsworth is born * 1795: Talleyrand's proposal of a metric system is adopted in France; 1 metre is set as 1/10,000,000 of the distance between the North Pole and the Equator * **1862: 20,000 are killed or wounded at the Battle of Shiloh during the American Civil War**

8 April

Emperor Caracalla is murdered

AD 217 Suffering from dysentery while leading his army to Carrhae in Parthia (modern Iran), Emperor Caracalla stepped behind some shrubs to relieve himself. As he lowered his breeches, Julius Martialis, an officer in the imperial bodyguard, killed him with a single thrust of his sword. At last Rome was free of one of its most bloodthirsty emperors, a tyrant who had commanded mass slaughter in Germany and Alexandria, as well as murdering his own wife and brother.

The son of Emperor Septimius Severus, Caracalla had been born in Lugdunum (today's Lyon) in AD 188 with the original name of Septimius Bassianus. According to the Roman historian Cassius Dio, his nickname came from a costume he invented – an ankle-length version of the Gallic *caracallus,* a short, close-fitting cloak with a hood.

When Caracalla was only ten, Septimius Severus made him and his younger brother Geta joint emperors, to prepare them for shared authority when he should die. But, as Gibbon puts it, 'The fond hopes of the father, and of the Roman world, were soon disappointed by these vain youths, who displayed the indolent security of hereditary princes and a presumption that fortune would supply the place of merit and application.' The brothers hated each other, and over the next thirteen years each was committed to the other's destruction. So bitter was their rivalry that each tried, unsuccessfully, to poison the other.

When Septimius Severus lay dying in 211, he counselled his sons: 'Be united, enrich the soldiers, despise all others.' Caracalla followed the last two of these directives but energetically rejected the first, immediately starting to plan Geta's demise. The next year he killed his brother with his own hands, while Geta was cowering in their mother's arms in the imperial palace. Caracalla then threw himself under the protection of the Praetorian Guard and informed a powerless Senate that he had murdered in self-defence.

Now sole dictator, Caracalla melted down the coinage that displayed his brother's features and then ordered the massacre of some 20,000 Romans whom he suspected of having supported him. People were killed in the streets, at the public baths and even in their own homes. Included in the slaughter was his own wife Publia Fulvia Plautilla, whom he had previously exiled.

Caracalla now became obsessed with Alexander the Great. He adopted what he thought were Alexander's dress and weapons and added a corps of elephants to his army. Appending the descriptor 'Magnus' (Great) to his own name, in 216 he set out to conquer Parthia as Alexander had done half a millennium before.

All the while Caracalla was becoming increasingly megalomaniacal. He issued new coins that portrayed himself as a god, claiming to be the son of the Egyptian deity Sarapis. He was the only Roman emperor to commission a statue of himself dressed as a pharaoh. But Caracalla's delusions of grandeur were matched by his growing paranoia. He suffered from threatening nightmares in which his dead father and brother pursued him, armed with swords, and, a few days before his murder, he dreamt that his father came to him, saying: 'As you killed your brother, so will I slay you.'

The reasons why Caracalla was murdered remain debated. Some maintain that his assassin, Julius Martialis, acted in revenge, as the emperor had ordered the execution of his brother a few days before. Cassius Dio, however, insists that Martialis's motive was more mundane: Caracalla had refused to promote him to centurion. Finally, Herodian makes the more likely claim that the commander of the Praetorian Guard, Marcus Opellius Macrinus, instigated the killing in order to take over the empire. (Macrinus did, in fact, become the next emperor, and, perhaps as a belated apology, agreed to Caracalla's deification, but only fifteen months later he was overthrown and executed.)

In spite of the evil that Caracalla wrought in his lifetime, he left us one immense and beautiful memorial, the Baths of Caracalla in Rome, originally designed to accommodate 1,600 bathers, but now where, on a summer evening, you can hear the triumphant arias of Verdi and Puccini during spectacular performances of open-air opera.

Also on this day

c. 563 BC: By tradition, the founder of Buddhism, Siddartha Gautama, is born in Lumbini in today's Nepal * 1336: Tamerlane (Timur) is born in Kesh, near Samarkand * **1795: George, the Prince of Wales (the future George IV) makes a calamitous marriage to Caroline of Brunswick** * 1973: Pablo Picasso dies in Mougins in the south of France

9 April

The American Civil War comes to an end

1865 Palm Sunday at Appomattox Courthouse, a small village in Virginia, the final scene of the American Civil War. In the morning the Southern rebels had launched one last attack – and failed. Outnumbered, outgunned, worn out, the rebel army was near collapse. The great southern general Robert E. Lee was making a last desperate attempt to reach Lynchburg, where he could head for the mountains and take up guerrilla warfare, but the huge Union army under the command of General Ulysses Grant dogged their every step.

Suddenly the Southern vanguard ran into a concentrated troop of Union cavalry. Refusing to attack, the cavalry simply opened their lines so that the Confederates could see a solid wall of Union infantry backed by cannon blocking the Confederate path. There was nowhere left to go.

Now Lee knew the end had come. 'There is nothing left for me to do but go and see General Grant, and I would rather die a thousand deaths,' he said.

The two generals met in the parlour of a local farmer, Lee immaculate in his best uniform and gold-mounted sword, Grant rumpled and scruffy in a second-hand private's jacket, on which he had pinned his general's stars. Grant offered the terms of surrender under which Lee's men were allowed to keep their horses and Southern officers their side-arms. Lee signed his acceptance, shook the hand offered by Grant and stepped out the door. The war was over.

In all, some 620,000 American soldiers died during the Civil War, almost 60 per cent of whom were from the victorious North. The total is more than the American dead from all other wars combined, from the Revolution through the two World Wars to Korea, Vietnam and the two Gulf Wars.

Also on this day

1492: Lorenzo the Magnificent dies at Careggi, near Florence * 1553: French writer and priest François Rabelais (Alcofribas Nasier) dies in Paris * 1821: French poet Charles Beaudelaire is born in Paris * 1940: Germany invades Denmark and Norway * 1945: German admiral and former head of the *Abwehr* (military Intelligence) Wilhelm Canaris is executed by slow strangulation for his involvement in the plot to kill Hitler in the dying days of Nazi Germany

10 April

The greatest explosion in the recorded history of man

1815 At dawn today on the coast of the Indonesian island of Sumbawa a huge volcano named Mount Tambora stood facing the sea, rising to a height of 13,500 feet, just shorter than Mont Blanc. But in a few hours three gigantic columns of fire would rise from its crater and an apocalyptic explosion would decapitate the mountain, blasting almost 4,500 feet from its summit. This gigantic eruption, which lasted two days, would kill 12,000 people outright and leave another 50,000 to starve to death as volcanic ash stifled their crops. It was the greatest explosion in the recorded history of man, equivalent to about 60,000 Hiroshima-type atom bombs.

For about three years prior to this cataclysmic blast, natives could observe steam and minor eruptions coming from Tambora, and these intensified during the seven months immediately prior to 10 April. When the full eruption came, the volcano spewed out some twelve cubic miles of ash – more than twice the amount from the more famous eruption of Krakatoa 68 years later. Near the volcano, ash deposits accumulated to a depth of 90 feet, and about 200,000 square miles of sea and land (about the size of France) were covered to a depth of half an inch.

The outside world first heard of the Tambora explosion literally. The sound could be detected as far as 1,000 miles away. Gradually the colossal cloud of dust and ash made its way around the world, and by late June Londoners began to observe prolonged and brilliantly coloured sunsets, orange or red on the horizon, purple or pink above it. Today you can still see what the English saw two centuries ago, as these spectacular sunsets were captured in the works of the great English painter J.M.W. Turner. Lord Byron, on the other hand, ignored the beauty and wrote a poem called 'Darkness' about the ash cloud's effect in dimming the sun.

A year after the eruption both North America and Europe experienced what was called 'the year without a summer', as cold and rain gripped the land, leading to disastrous harvests. In Paris the rainfall was three times normal.

Today a vast and tranquil lake occupies Tambora's crater, and the volcano seems to sleep. But those unwary enough to live too close should remember that Tambora erupted again in 1819, 1880 and 1967.

Also on this day

1585: The pope who gave us our modern calendar, Gregory XIII, dies in Rome * 1829: Founder of the Salvation Army William Booth is born * 1864: Austrian Archduke Maximilian is made Emperor of Mexico * 1919: Mexican revolutionary leader Emiliano Zapata is shot by Mexican government troops * 1925: F. Scott Fitzgerald publishes *The Great Gatsby*

11 April

Napoleon abdicates (the first time)

1814 Napoleon had been the master of some 70 million people, including 30 million French, and his empire extended to Belgium, Holland, Spain, Portugal, most of Italy and Germany and parts of Poland and Yugoslavia. But then, in 1812, he made the fatal blunder of invading Russia, occupying Moscow but finally making a humiliating retreat, with most of his *Grande Armée* left dead on the Russian steppes.

The next hammer blow came in June 1813 when the Duke of Wellington liberated Spain, defeating Spain's nominal king, Napoleon's brother Joseph, at

Vitoria, and forcing the French to retreat over the Pyrenees and back into France. At the same time the Emperor's former general, Joachim Murat, whom he had made King of Naples, betrayed him by entering into negotiations with the Viennese court.

Then, in October the following year, Napoleon led a reconstituted army of 185,000 unseasoned troops to Leipzig, where it was crushed by a massive force of 320,000 Austrians, Prussians, Russians and Swedes.

Emboldened by their success and unified by their hunger to rid themselves of this turbulent dictator, in March 1814 Russia, Prussia, Austria and Great Britain bound themselves by the Treaty of Chaumont to continue the war until he was overthrown. Now, 300,000 strong, they marched on Paris, entering the city on 31 March as Napoleon hunkered down 40 miles south in the château of Fontainebleau, his far-flung territories reduced to a single grand building.

The Emperor wavered, hoping to save his throne, but his marshals Ney and MacDonald implored him to abdicate in favour of his three-year-old son. His former Foreign Secretary, Talleyrand, was already hosting the Russian Tsar in his Paris *hôtel particulaire*, and then one of his closest comrades-in arms, Marshal Marmont, surrendered his VI Corps of 12,000 men to the Austrians.

And so, on this Monday, Napoleon's ten-year reign came to a close, as he abdicated as Emperor, declaring grandly in the third person that 'There is no personal sacrifice, even life itself, which he is not ready to make for the good of France.'

As if to prove his point, the next day Napoleon attempted to poison himself with a mixture of opium, belladonna and hellebore, but after some painful vomiting he recovered. Following a tearful farewell to his Old Guard, seventeen days later he was en route to exile in Elba, there to wait and plot his brief return.

Also on this day

1599: Henri IV's beautiful mistress Gabrielle d'Estrées dies in agony * 1713: The War of the Spanish Succession ends by the Treaty of Utrecht * 1945: American troops liberate the Buchenwald concentration camp near Weimar in Germany

12 April

FDR *dies in office*

1945 Elegant as usual in a double-breasted grey suit and a bright red tie, President Franklin D. Roosevelt was sitting for a portrait while waiting for lunch at his retreat in Warm Springs, Georgia. Suddenly his head nodded forward and his hands trembled. 'I have a terrific pain in the back of my head,' he whispered to his secretary. He then seemed to sink into semi-consciousness. While his doctor was summoned, his valet and his butler carried him to his bed in the next room. In spite of the doctor's ministrations, at 3.35 in the afternoon Roosevelt's breathing stopped. America's 32nd president, one of its very greatest, was dead of a cerebral haemorrhage at the age of 63.

Fifth cousin to President Theodore Roosevelt, Franklin Roosevelt was brought up to wealth and privilege on his family's estate in the Hudson River Valley of New York state. After being educated privately at home until he was fourteen, he attended one of America's most elite boarding schools at Groton, Massachusetts and then spent four academically undistinguished years at Harvard. During his last year there he became engaged to Theodore Roosevelt's niece Eleanor, whom he married in 1905.

Roosevelt entered political life with election to the New York state Senate and progressed within the Democratic Party to such an extent that by 1920 he was chosen as the vice-presidential candidate (running with the now forgotten James M. Cox), only to be soundly thrashed by the Republican ticket of future presidents Warren Harding and Calvin Coolidge.

Then came the event that would have destroyed a lesser man. While vacationing at Campobello Island in Canada in August of the following year, Roosevelt was stricken with polio and almost completely paralysed. He never regained the use of his legs, spending the rest of his life in a wheelchair.

Undaunted by his infirmity, Roosevelt ran successfully for governor of New York in 1928, and when the Democrats nominated him for president in the midst of the Depression in 1932, he addressed the Convention with his famous promise: 'I pledge you, I pledge myself, to a new deal for the American people.' He defeated the incumbent Herbert Hoover with almost 57 per cent of the vote. Re-elected in 1936, 1940 and 1944, he was the only American president to serve more than two terms.

During his thirteen years in office Roosevelt largely brought the country out of the Depression and led the nation from isolationism to acceptance of war against tyranny, urging Americans during a radio broadcast in 1940: 'We have the men – the skill – the wealth – and above all, the will [. . .] We must be the great arsenal of democracy.' After Japan devastated the American fleet at Pearl Harbor (which Roosevelt described as 'a date which will live in infamy') he successfully waged a two-front war against Germany and their Italian allies in Europe and Japan in the Pacific.

When Roosevelt died at Warm Springs, his country was on the brink of victory – Hitler committed suicide just eighteen days later, and the Germans formally surrendered on 8 May. (Japan would follow suit in August, after being devastated by the atomic bombs for which Roosevelt had authorised development.) As the nation mourned their president and celebrated success in Europe, few knew that at Roosevelt's side during his final hours was Lucy Mercer Rutherford, once his mistress 27 years before. Eleanor, his wife of 40 years, to whom he had promised never to see Lucy again, was away on a speaking tour.

Also on this day

1204: Soldiers from the Fourth Crusade sack the Christian city of Constantinople *
**1861: Southern troops fire on Fort Sumpter, the first shot of the American Civil
War** * 1945: Harry Truman becomes the 33rd president of the United States on the
death of Franklin Delano Roosevelt * 1961: Soviet cosmonaut Yuri A. Gargarin
becomes the first man in space

13 April

The story of Queen Crazy Joan

1555 Her parents were the great Catholic monarchs of Spain, Ferdinand and
Isabella, and she married Philip the Handsome of Burgundy, son of Holy
Roman Emperor Maximilian I. Her name was Juana (in English, Joan).

Juana's husband apparently was handsome indeed, and his affairs were
numerous and unconcealed. But Juana loved him passionately and frantically.
Only fifteen when she married, she was widowed ten years later, when he
suddenly died of typhus in Burgos on 25 September 1506, and her passion
turned to mania.

At first she brooded in her darkened room for almost two months,
exclaiming: 'A widow who has lost the sun of her own soul should never expose
herself to the light of day.' Juana then set out around Spain with her husband's
body. For almost two years she took Philip's coffin with her wherever she went
and periodically prised off the lid for a loving look at his corpse. She ordered an
armed guard around the coffin at all times to prevent the approach of any other
woman. Eventually the entourage arrived in Granada, where Philip at last was
laid to rest.

Finally her son, the Emperor Charles V, had Juana restricted to a castle in
Tordesillas, and here she remained year after year, often lucid, sometimes not.
In 1520, however, she was briefly liberated during the Revolt of the Comuneros
(an uprising against Charles), and after her reincarceration she was locked away
in a windowless room until death came to her on 13 April 1555.

When Juana died she was 76, already known as Juana la Loca – Crazy Joan.
But the family that had sprung from her womb was in power everywhere. In
the Holy Roman Empire, Italy, Spain, Portugal, France, Hungary, England,
Denmark and Poland, the reigning monarchs were her children or grandchildren
or their husbands.

Also on this day

1598: Henri IV of France issues the Edict of Nantes, giving religious freedom to
France's Protestants * **1743: Author of the Declaration of Independence and
third American president Thomas Jefferson is born** * 1829: The British
Parliament passes the Catholic Emancipation Act, lifting restrictions on Catholics *

1605: Russian Tsar Boris Godunov dies * 1655: Louis XIV tells the French Parliament that '*L'État, c'est moi.*' * 1946: *Maisons closes* (brothels) are declared illegal in France

14 April

The Kingmaker meets his maker

1471 No likeness has survived to reveal to us his no doubt shrewd and forceful face, but his name alone stirs the imagination: Richard Neville, the Earl of Warwick – Warwick the Kingmaker. Today, Easter Sunday, this man – who had put two men on the throne of England – died on the field of battle during the Wars of the Roses.

The Wars of the Roses were a series of dynastic conflicts fought for the crown between the Houses of Lancaster and York amid the anarchy of 15th-century England. The Lancastrians had ruled since the usurpation of Henry IV in 1399, but now the king was the pious and weak-minded Henry VI, who in a half-century on the throne had never had effective control of the country since inheriting the crown at the age of nine months in 1422. Now great barons ruled their territories with private armies, and chaos reigned.

Born in 1428, Richard Neville had come into this world both titled and wealthy, but his marriage at 21 to the daughter of the Earl of Warwick made him the richest man in England, including the King. He was also the most dynamic and capable – and the most ambitious.

Allied with the House of York, in 1455 Warwick had played a major role at the first battle of the Wars of the Roses at St Albans. Six years later he had provided the armed muscle to help Yorkist Edward IV usurp the throne from Henry VI. But three years after that, Edward married Elizabeth Woodville, and soon her Woodville relations were displacing Warwick in the king's councils. Unable to dominate Edward, in 1470 Warwick pushed him off the throne into exile and restored Henry. Behind it all lay no loyalty to any king but Warwick's determination to be the country's most powerful man, perhaps, with luck, even to become king himself.

Only a year after fleeing to the Netherlands Edward returned to England at the head of an army. On this day the armies of Edward and his former supporter clashed at Barnet, now incorporated into London but then a hamlet just to the north.

Both armies had reached the field of battle on the previous evening and had spent the night within earshot of each other. Then, on the morning of 14 April, Warwick rose at 4 am to brief his soldiers and ordered his cannon to open fire. But the day was still dark and the field shrouded in fog, so the stones fired by his primitive cast iron artillery carried over the heads of the enemy he could not yet see.

Then, in the words of historian Paul Murray Kendall, 'Warwick signalled his trumpeters. Archers and gunners fired into the blankness of the fog. Close ahead, the trumpets of the Yorkists rang out. A great shout gave notice that they were coming on the run [. . .] With a crash the two hosts came together out of the murk.'

In order to buoy up his men, Warwick was fighting on foot like his soldiers, rather than from horseback, having ordered his war steeds taken to the rear. At first the battle seemed to turn in his favour, but then, in a mix-up in the fog, his ally Oxford's cavalry accidentally fell on his brother Montagu's flank. Amid cries of 'Treason!' Warwick's line, under severe attack from Edward, began to collapse.

Seeing that the situation was hopeless, Warwick turned to regain his warhorse behind the lines, but, encumbered by heavy armour, he was soon surrounded by Edward's soldiers. One forced open his visor with an axe, another plunged in his sword.

The next day Edward had Warwick's body, naked except for a loincloth, displayed at St Paul's in London, there for all to see that the Kingmaker was actually dead. Warwick was then buried in Bisham Abbey, but during the reign of Henry VIII the abbey was destroyed and his tomb and bones obliterated. Such was the end of the man who put two kings on the throne and died still hoping to occupy it himself.

Also on this day

978: Ethelred the Unready is crowned at Kingston-upon-Thames * 1759: German composer George Handel dies in London * **1865: Abraham Lincoln is assassinated while attending the theatre**

15 April

Suleiman the Magnificent's disastrous Russian bride

1558 Throughout history Russia and Turkey have often been at each other's throats, but Russia's greatest success came by accident, through a woman who died today.

For almost 40 years Suleiman the Magnificent had been Sultan of Turkey, undoubtedly the greatest leader in the history of the Ottoman Turks. During most of that time his favourite concubine had been a woman known as Roxelana. Roxelana was not a Turk but a Russian, the daughter of an Orthodox priest. She had been captured during a Turkish raid and was promptly sent to Suleiman's harem.

Over the years Roxelana gained increasing influence over her master, while bearing him three sons. Sadly for Turkey, her favourite was Selim, a man of little ability but a great thirst for alcohol.

But Roxelana was blind to Selim's faults, while contriving to make Suleiman blind to the virtues of his brothers. First the older brother was framed for treason and ordered strangled by his own father. In 1558 Roxelana died, but by then the poison against Selim's younger brother was deep in Suleiman's system. Eventually this brother too was executed, leaving the path to the throne clear for Selim, who became Sultan on Suleiman's death in 1566.

Selim, called Sari (the Blonde, for the colouring he inherited from his mother), was a weak and indolent ruler, dominated by the women of his harem and his Janissary guards. Although Turkey under Selim managed to regain Cyprus, the act prompted the formation of an anti-Ottoman alliance of Spain, the Pope and the Italian states that eventually routed the Turkish fleet at the Battle of Lepanto.

Turkey never recovered its former power, all because of the myopia of a Russian mother.

Also on this day

AD 73: Over 1,000 Jewish zealots commit suicide at Masada just before Roman legions breach the walls of the fortress * 1452: Leonardo is born in Vinci in Tuscany * 1755: Dr Johnson publishes his dictionary * 1764: Louis XV's mistress, Madame de Pompadour, dies of lung cancer * 1912: The British ocean liner *Titanic* sinks after hitting an iceberg * 1947: Jackie Robinson plays his first game for the Brooklyn Dodgers, becoming the first black ever to play major league baseball

> Events written in **boldface** are covered in full in
> *365: Great Stories from History for Every Day of the Year*,
> the first volume in this series.

16 April

St Francis renounces his worldly goods

1207 Born to a rich cloth merchant father from Assisi, named Pietro di Bernardone, he had been baptised Giovanni, but his father called him Francesco (meaning 'French one') in honour of his French mother, and the name stuck. Francesco spent much of his youth squandering his father's money in a conspicuous and lordly fashion, and his exuberant spirit made him one of Assisi's most popular young men.

When he was about 22 Francesco joined Assisi's forces in a war with Perugia, but instead of finding glory he was captured and held for a year. Three years later he offered his services to the papal army in the conflict with Holy Roman Emperor Frederick II, but before he could join he experienced a vision, commanding him to return home and wait for a sign from God. Back in Assisi he started a regimen of prayer and gave up his former extravagance.

Outside Assisi's gates stood the derelict chapel of San Damiano, served by an indigent priest. There Francesco heard the crucifix above the altar command him: 'Go, Francesco, and repair my house which, as you see, is nearly in ruins.' Rushing home, he gathered his own fine clothes and some magnificent cloth from his father's shop, which he sold in a neighbouring town. But when he offered the money, San Damiano's priest refused it, so Francesco threw it out the window.

Infuriated by his son's theft of cloth and alarmed by his transformation to militant piety, Francesco's father had him brought up before an ecclesiastical court in order to disinherit him.

The hearing took place on this day in 1207. The presiding bishop ruled that Francesco must give up all his property, since it all came from his father, and the young man, now 24, promptly stripped to the skin in the courtroom, declaring that from now on the only father he would recognise would be God. So touching was the scene that the bishop was brought to tears. Rising, he wrapped Francesco in his own cloak.

From that time on Francesco forswore property altogether, entirely devoting himself to God. During the next twenty years he founded two of the great religious orders, the Friars Minor, commonly called Franciscans, and the Poor Clares. He is also credited with the introduction of the first ever Christmas nativity scene.

Francesco died on 3 October 1226. Two years later he was declared a saint, whom we know as St Francis of Assisi.

Also on this day

AD 69: Roman emperor Otho commits suicide after defeat at Cremona * **1746: English soldiers crush Bonnie Prince Charlie's troops at Culloden Moor** * 1828: Spanish painter Francisco de Goya dies in Bordeaux * 1867: American aeroplane inventor Wilbur Wright is born * 1889: Film icon Charlie Chaplin is born in London

17 April

The telling of The Canterbury Tales

1397 It probably seemed like just another dreary day at the court of Richard II. The nation was at peace and, at least temporarily, the country's troublesome barons were docile. In the stultifying atmosphere of the rigid royal protocol that Richard insisted on, it must have been a relief when part of the day's entertainment was announced to be a reading by a 54-year-old courtier named Geoffrey Chaucer. What's more, Chaucer's work would be in English, an innovation to ears accustomed to Anglo-Norman French as a literary language.

No records remain to tell us of the court's response, but we assume it must have been enthusiastic, for on this day, for the first time, Chaucer read publicly from *The Canterbury Tales,* now universally recognised as the finest work by the first great vernacular writer in English.

Although known nowadays almost exclusively for his writing, Chaucer was no coddled court poet. He was a soldier and a high-ranking government official who led a life of high adventure and service to his king: writing was just his passionate hobby. He twice fought with the English army in France, first at 17, when he was taken prisoner at Reims and ransomed by Edward III for £16, and again at 26. He also went on diplomatic assignments for the king to Flanders, Spain, France and Italy, where he learned Italian and met Petrarch and Boccaccio. (Chaucer may have taken the framework of *The Canterbury Tales* from Boccaccio's *Decameron*.)

Despite his success in diplomacy, Chaucer must have been a fiery, quick-tempered man, for he was once accused of rape (he was acquitted) and later fined for beating a Franciscan friar in a London street.

The Canterbury Tales is Chaucer's last and most famous work. He laboured on it for some thirteen years but never completed it. It is the story of a mixed group of 30 pilgrims, including a miller, a knight, a nun, a parson, a merchant, a physician and most famously the so-called Wife of Bath. During April they set off on horseback from the Tabard Inn in Southwark to the shrine of St Thomas Becket in Canterbury Cathedral, amusing themselves with storytelling along the way. Two of the tales are in prose, and the rest are in poetry.

The prologue to this great work starts with the famous lines:

> Whan that aprill with his shoures soote
> The droghte of march hath perced to the roote

In the 19th century an assiduous study of the text suggested that the first day of the tales was 17 April 1387, ten years to the day before Chaucer introduced his monumental poem to the court.

Chaucer died three years after his first presentation of *The Canterbury Tales*, on 25 October 1400, possibly of the plague. One bizarre theory, however, maintains that he was murdered on orders from Thomas Arundel, the Archbishop of Canterbury, because the parson in 'The Parson's Tale' quotes the Bible in English, while the Archbishop was fanatically opposed to anything but Latin. Whatever the cause of his death, Chaucer was buried in Westminster Abbey, a signal mark of honour for a commoner, but perhaps one he would have seen with a certain irony. As he wrote in 'The Knight's Tale',

> What is this world? what asketh men to have?
> Now with his love, now in his colde grave,
> Allone, with-outen any companye.

Also on this day

1607: Armand-Jean du Plessis (the future Cardinal Richelieu) is ordained a priest * **1790: American revolutionary, statesman and polymath Benjamin Franklin dies in Philadelphia** * 1895: The Sino-Japanese War ends with the Treaty of Shimonoseki

18 April

Paul Revere's ride

1775 It was at ten o'clock on a Tuesday evening filled with bright moonlight when Paul Revere set out on the most celebrated ride in American history, in order to alert his countrymen that British troops were marching.

The British were to leave Boston for nearby Lexington, where two dangerous radicals, Sam Adams and John Hancock, were in hiding. Then the soldiers would fall on Concord, only a few miles further, to seize rebel arms and supplies.

'One if by land, two if by sea', Revere is traditionally supposed to have said, referring to the lanterns he would place in a church steeple. Indeed, his first move was to light two lanterns in Boston's North Church, as a signal that the British troops were leaving Boston by boat across the Back Bay to Cambridge. Then he set off for Lexington on a borrowed horse called Brown Beauty to warn Adams and Hancock. Revere then galloped off on his historic 12-mile run to Concord, waking every household and warning every Minuteman (members of the local militia who promised 'to be ready in a minute') on the way.

Revere's ride was more than effective. Adams and Hancock both escaped, and about 3,700 American patriots came to defend against the British.

The next day the undisciplined Americans, many hunters and Indian fighters, used every trick of concealment and stealth to rout a British force at Lexington and Concord during the first battles of the American Revolution. At day's end some 73 British lay dead with a further 200 missing or wounded. Forty-nine Americans were killed plus 46 more wounded.

Although Paul Revere is remembered mainly because of his famous ride, his real talent was as an artisan. He was the greatest silversmith America has yet produced.

Also on this day

1480: Lucrezia Borgia, illegitimate daughter of the future Pope Alexander VI, is born * 1506: The first cornerstone of a new St Peter's Cathedral in Rome is laid * **1521: Martin Luther refuses to recant at the Diet of Worms** * 1593: Shakespeare's poem *Venus and Adonis* is entered for publication * 1942: American General Jimmy Doolittle leads a bombing raid on Tokyo, Osaka, Kobe and Nagoya, the first American attack on mainland Japan in the Second World War * 1955: Albert Einstein dies at 76 in the Princeton Hospital of a ruptured arteriosclerotic aneurysm of the abdominal aorta, having opposed any surgery to prolong his life

19 April

The first battle of the American Revolution

1775 Determined to crush a nascent rebellion, British General Thomas Gage today led some 700 soldiers on a pre-dawn raid towards the small Massachusetts town of Concord, where the American colonists' military supplies were stored. En route he captured Paul Revere, one of America's staunchest patriots, who only the previous day had ridden to warn his compatriots that the British were coming. Here is Revere's eyewitness account of the start of the first battle of the American Revolution:

'I [took] to the right, toward a Wood, at the bottom of the Pasture, intending when I gained that, to jump my Horse & run afoot; just as I reached it, out started six [British] officers, siesed my bridle, put their pistols to my Breast, ordered me to dismount, which I did. One of them, who appeared to have the command there, and much of a Gentleman, asked me where I came from; I told him, he asked me what time I left it; I told him. He seemed surprised, said Sr, may I crave your name. I answered my name is Revere, what said he, Paul Revere; I answered yes; the others abused me much; but he told me not to be afraid, no one should hurt me. I told him they would miss their aim. He said they should not, they were only waiting for some Deserters they expected down the Road. I told him I knew better, I knew what they were after; that I had alarmed the country all the way up [. . .] and I should have 500 men there soon [. . .] one of them [. . .] clapd his Pistol to my head, and said he was going to ask me some questions, if I did not tell the truth, he would blow my brains out [. . .] he then ordered me to mount my horse [. . .] He said to me "We are now going toward your friends, and if you attempt to run, or we are insulted, we will blow your Brains . . ."

'We rid toward Lexington, a quick pace; they very often insulted me calling me Rebel, &c &c. after we had got about a mile, I was given to the Serjant to lead, he was Ordered to take out his pistol [. . .] and if I run, to execute the Major's sentence. When we got within about half a Mile of the Meeting house, we heard a gun fired; the Major asked me what it was for, I told him to alarm the country [. . .] when we got within sight of the Meeting House, we heard a Volley of guns fired, as I supposed at the tavern, as an Alarm; the major ordered us to halt [. . .] he then asked the Serjant if his horse was tired, he said yes; he Ordered him to take my horse; I dismounted, the Sarjant mounted my horse [. . .] & rode off down the road. I then went to the house where I left [Sam] Adams & [John] Hancock, and told them what had happened; their friends advised them to go out of the way; I went with them, about two miles a cross road; after resting myself, I sett off with another man to go back to the Tavern [at Lexington], to enquire the news; when we got there, we were told the troops were within two miles. We went to the Tavern to git a Trunk of papers belonging to Col. Hancock, before we left the house, I saw the [British] troops from the Chamber window. We made haste & had to pass thro' our Militia, who were on the green behind the Meeting house, to the number as I supposed, about 50 or 60. I went thro' them; as I passed I heard the commanding officer speake to his men to this purpose. "Lett the troops passby, & don't molest them, without they begin first." I had to go a cross Road, but had not got half Gun shot off when the [British] Troops appeared in sight behinde the Meeting House; they made a short halt, when a gun was fired. I heard the report, turned my head, and saw the smoake in front of the Troops, they imeaditly gave a great shout, ran a few paces, and then the whole fired . . .'

Of the Lexington militiamen who had assembled on the green at daylight, seven lay dead; nine more were wounded. Now the British column marched west towards Concord.

But when the British finally reached Concord, a force of about 3,700 armed Americans compelled them to withdraw to Boston some fifteen miles away. This ignominious retreat was a disaster for the British, as Americans sniped at them from behind trees and stone walls along the roadside. By the time the British reached safety they had suffered 273 casualties against only 95 for the rebels and the American Revolution was well under way.

Also on this day

1587: Sir Francis Drake leads sixteen warships into Cádiz and sinks 24 Spanish ships * 1739: English highwayman Dick Turpin is executed for horse stealing * 1824: George Gordon, Lord Byron, dies of malaria in Missolonghi on his way to fight for Greek independence * 1881: British statesman Benjamin Disraeli (Lord Beaconsfield) dies * 1882: British naturalist Charles Darwin dies

20 April

Napoleon III is born

1808 Born this date was one of history's few dreamers who actually accomplished most of his dreams – Louis Napoleon Bonaparte. Forty-five years later he was to become Emperor Napoleon III of France, having staged a *coup d'état* the previous year because the French constitution prohibited him from seeking a second term as president. He managed to retain that glorious position for eighteen years, some eight years longer than his famous uncle Napoleon I had done. (Despite his greater longevity in power, Napoleon III's opponents derisively called him Napoléon le Petit, in reference not only to his physical stature but also to his tepid accomplishments compared to his uncle's.)

Napoleon III was a curious mixture of tyrant and liberal. Fearing a challenge from French republicans, he strongly curtailed individual liberty, resorting to the methods of a police state. Until late in his reign he dictated to all government departments, ensuring that his will – and his alone – would prevail. He capitalised on false crises (like a non-existent revolution in 1851) and was a master of propaganda.

On the other hand, Napoleon sometimes referred to himself as a socialist, restored universal suffrage and promoted public works, industry and agriculture. He backed the building of the Suez Canal and the construction of railways in France. He was deeply involved in the renewal of Paris and empowered his prefect of the Seine, Baron Haussmann, to rebuild great swathes of the city.

Louis was the son of the first Napoleon's brother Louis (erstwhile King of Holland) and Hortense de Beauharnais, the daughter of Napoleon's first wife Joséphine by a previous marriage. Therefore, Napoleon I was both Louis's uncle and his step-grandfather.

Also on this day

1314: Death of Pope Clement V, who moved the papacy to Avignon and suppressed the Templars * 1768: Venetian topographical painter Canaletto (Giovanni Antonio Canal) dies in Venice * 1770: Captain James Cook discovers Australia * 1792: The French Assembly declares war on Great Britain, to last until 1815 * **1889: German dictator Adolf Hitler is born in Braunau, Upper Austria**

21 April

Rome – the beginning

753 BC On this day, according to Plutarch, the city of Rome was founded.

The tale starts at Alba Longa, a town about twelve miles south-west of Rome. Virgil tells us that Aeneas, a Trojan who escaped from Troy after its fall, established the tribe that lived there.

Years later, Alba Longa's King Numitor was betrayed by his brother Amulius, who seized the throne and forced Numitor's daughter Rhea Silvia to become a Vestal Virgin to preclude her producing a child to threaten his rule.

But Rhea Silvia was less virginal than her order. Seduced by the god Mars, she produced twin sons, Romulus and Remus.

When Amulius learned of the birth he imprisoned poor Rhea Silvia and ordered her twins to be drowned in the Tiber. But the man who should have drowned them took pity instead and left them in a shallow trough that floated down the river until they reached the spot where Rome now stands.

Here Romulus and Remus were suckled by a she-wolf until they were found by a farmer, who raised them. In time they returned to Alba Longa thirsting for revenge. They succeeded in killing their uncle Amulius and restored their grandfather to the throne.

Having satisfied family honour, they returned to the exact place on the Tiber where the she-wolf had found them, and founded Rome on 21 April 753 BC.

Romulus's career did not end there, although Remus's shortly did, as his brother killed him in a dispute over a city wall. Romulus became King of Rome and later organised the rape of the Sabine women. But he never died. One day he mysteriously disappeared in a storm, and Romans believed he had been turned into a god.

Also on this day

1142: French theologian and philosopher Pierre Abélard dies in the Priory of Saint-Marcel, near Chalon-sur-Saône, his mistress Héloïse outliving him by 22 years * 1574: The first Medici duke, Cosimo de' Medici, dies of an apoplectic fit in the Medici Palace, Florence * 1699: French playwright Jean-Baptiste Racine dies in Paris * 1910: American author Mark Twain (Samuel Clemens) dies in Redding, Connecticut * 1918: German fighter ace Manfred von Richthofen (the 'Red Baron') is killed in combat near Amiens, either hit by Australian ground fire or shot down by a Canadian air force fighter * 1944: Charles de Gaulle gives Frenchwomen the right to vote

22 April

Birth of a great *salonière*

1766 Although born today in Paris, Germaine de Staël was actually a Swiss, daughter of Jacques Necker, a banker from Geneva who would be Louis XIV's director-general of finance for fifteen years. At twenty she made a marriage of convenience to the Swedish ambassador in Paris, Baron Erik de Staël-Holstein, which formally ended after eleven years and three children (of whom the third was probably the child of her lover Benjamin Constant).

Even though both her parents and her husband were firm monarchists, Madame de Staël became a rabid republican, whose theatrical antics amused many but infuriated a few, including Napoleon, who eventually forbade her to reside within 40 leagues of Paris. She was also, by any standards, an accomplished intellectual, and invitations to her Parisian salon were prized.

Most of Madame de Staël's life was spent intriguing, writing now-forgotten books, moving from lover to lover and overdramatising herself. '*Jamais, jamais, je ne serai jamais aimée comme j'aime!*' ('Never, never, never shall I be loved as I love!') she once famously lamented.

She took many lovers but typically considered her relationships as noble womanly sentiments, writing: '*L'amour est l'histoire de la vie des femmes; c'est un épisode dans celle des hommes.*' ('Love is the story of a woman's life; it is an episode in a man's.')

The lover with whom she was most associated was another Swiss, the novelist Benjamin Constant, with whom she spent a see-saw fourteen years, but an earlier one, Talleyrand, by whom she had a child, probably knew her best. 'She is such a true friend', he said, 'that she would throw all her friends into the water for the pleasure of pulling them out again.'

Germaine de Staël had a romantic fear of death as well as her share of sexual conceit. 'When I look on these arms, these breasts at the sight of which every eye is filled with lust,' she confided to a friend, 'and when I think that this splendour must one day be food for repulsive reptiles, a cold shudder passes through me, a combination of horror and pity.' That day arrived in Paris on Bastille Day in 1817 when she was 51.

Also on this day

1370: The first stone is laid in the Bastille in Paris * 1500: Portuguese explorer Pedro Cabral lands on the coast of Brazil, claiming it for Portugal * 1566: French King Henri II's mistress Diane de Poitiers dies * 1707: English writer Henry Fielding is born * 1724: Prussian philosopher Immanuel Kant is born * **1787: Catherine the Great sails down the Dnieper with her ex-lover/minister Grigory Potemkin to see the 'Potemkin villages'** * 1870: Russian revolutionary and dictator Vladimir Lenin (Vladimir Ilich Ulyanov) is born in Simbirsk, Russia

23 April

St George loses his head

AD 303 Today in Nicomedia (near today's Istanbul), St George of dragon fame was beheaded on the orders of the Roman emperor Diocletian.

George was born to a Christian family in about 270 in Cappadocia, where his father was an officer in the Roman army. When his father died, his mother moved back to her native Lydda in Palestine (now Lod, near Tel Aviv). There George grew up, joined the army and rose to the rank of *comes* (count). A member of Diocletian's personal bodyguard, he was stationed in Nicomedia, then the capital of the empire.

In 303 Diocletian issued his first edict against Christianity, which the army was commanded to enforce. When George confessed to being a Christian and refused to obey, Diocletian had him tortured and beheaded in front of Nicomedia's walls. His body was taken back to Lydda, where his tomb quickly became a shrine. You can still see it there today.

Soon wonderful tales about George began to spread. He was said to have been put to death three times, chopped into small bits and buried or burned to ashes, only to be resuscitated by the power of God. The most famous story is his battle with the dragon, first recorded by the German bishop Arculf in the 7th century, but probably in circulation much earlier.

A fearsome dragon lived in a lake near Silena (now in Libya). In order to draw the lake's water, villagers each day fed it two sheep, but when they ran out of sheep, they substituted beautiful maidens, selected by lot. One day the king's daughter drew the fatal lot, but before the dragon could devour her, George rode in. Crossing himself, he charged the dragon and skewered it with one thrust of his lance. Having saved the princess, he then converted the king and his villagers to Christianity and rode away into the sunset.

The story may be a Christian allegory of Diocletian's persecution, with the emperor as dragon, or perhaps a Christianised version of the Greek myth of Perseus, who saved Andromeda from a sea monster, but no matter its origin, many a good Christian believed it. Pope Gelasius proclaimed George a saint in 496, but hedged his bets on the miracles by describing him as among the saints 'whose names are rightly reverenced among us, but whose actions are known only to God'.

Some say that in the 6th century St George came to England to visit the abbey at Glastonbury and became the patron saint of the knights at King Arthur's Round Table, although sceptics would have it that St Adamnan introduced his legend at the beginning of the 8th century. What is certain is that in around 1000 the Anglo-Saxon writer Aelfric included him in his *Lives of the Saints*, and in 1061 a church at Doncaster became the first in England dedicated to him.

St George is said to have led crusaders to victory at Antioch during the First Crusade in 1098. In all likelihood, soldiers returning to England from the Crusades reinforced his legend, and during the Middle Ages he became a special favourite of English kings.

Richard the Lionheart adopted the banner of St George (the red cross of a martyr on a white background) for his soldiers during the Third Crusade, and in 1344 Edward III made St George patron saint of England. Four years later he named him patron of the Order of the Garter.

When Richard II invaded Scotland in 1385, his troops wore the badge of St George, and he swore to execute any Scottish soldiers 'who do bear the same crosse or token of St George, even if they be prisoners'. Thirty years later Henry V called on St George before the Battle of Agincourt (or at least so says Shakespeare):

> 'Follow your spirit; and, upon this charge
> Cry God for Harry, England and St George!'

Other famous writers who have included St George in their works include Edmund Spenser in *The Faerie Queene* and John Bunyan in *Pilgrim's Progress*.

In 1908 Robert Baden-Powell chose St George as patron of the Boy Scouts because 'he is the patron saint of cavalry, from which the word chivalry is derived'. (Clearly Baden-Powell had forgotten that St George is also the patron of lepers, plague sufferers and syphilitics.) And as recently as 1940 King George VI established the George Cross (named for the saint, not for himself) for 'acts of the greatest heroism or of the most conspicuous courage in circumstances of extreme danger'.

While not busy promoting English causes, St George also managed to become patron saint of Greece, Portugal, Serbia, Canada and Tsarist Russia. He was once a full-fledged saint, but in 1969 the Church downgraded him to the lowest category, commemoration. In 2000, however, Pope John Paul II elevated him once again and awarded him his 'day of solemnity'.

Also on this day

1605: Russian usurper and tsar Boris Godunov dies * 1616: William Shakespeare and Miguel Cervantes die on the same day, Shakespeare's 52nd birthday * **1661: Charles II of England is crowned, starting the Restoration** * 1775: British painter J.M.W. Turner is born * 1850: British poet William Wordsworth dies at Grasmere

24 April

Emperor Charles V wins the Battle of Mühlberg

1547 The 47-year-old Holy Roman Emperor Charles V was at the height of his powers. Over two decades earlier he had seen the heretic Martin Luther outlawed; later he had held the King of France in captivity in Madrid for a year; still later he had chased Suleiman the Magnificent and his vast army from the gates of Vienna; and now he was on the verge of crushing the rebellious Protestant princes of Germany, who dared challenge the authority of their emperor.

Charles's army was like its master – of no fixed nationality. There were Netherlanders and Italians, good German Catholics and those prime shock troops, the Spanish *tercios*. Reaching the Elbe near Leipzig early on a misty morning, some valiant Spaniards under the command of the Duke of Alba took their swords between their teeth and swam the frigid river. Soon the rest of the army was across, and the enemy, caught completely by surprise, was shortly scattered in defeat. Of their force of 10,000 men, the Protestant princes suffered 2,500 killed, 4,000 wounded and 1,000 captured. Two of the Protestant leaders, the Elector of Saxony and the Duke of Brunswick, were among the prisoners.

This was the famous Battle of Mühlberg, which gave Charles control of all of Germany. He was then at the pinnacle of his power, master of much of Europe, without challenger. Today, Titian's great equestrian portrait of Charles celebrating the victory hangs in the Prado in Madrid. The armoured emperor rides a prancing horse of unnerving black, the skies overhead are somehow full of menace, and Charles's sad eyes seem to reflect the disillusions of a lifetime rather than triumph. Indeed, within eight years, the great emperor would retire to the Spanish monastery of San Jerónimo de Yuste, defeated by the knowledge that his aim to unite his empire in the religion of Rome could never be accomplished.

Also on this day

1731: English novelist Daniel Defoe dies * 1770: English writer Thomas Chatterton kills himself by taking arsenic * **1854: Emperor Franz Joseph marries the beautiful Elisabeth of Bavaria (Sisi) in the Augustinerkirche, Vienna** * 1898: Spain declares war on the US to start the Spanish–American War

25 April

Joseph Conrad publishes his first book

1895 In London this day the firm of T. Fisher Unwin published a first novel by an unknown author. It was a romance set in an exotic locale, East Borneo, with a plot that involved an obscure Dutch trader who presided over a derelict trading post, his very large but unfinished house, his Malay wife, their beautiful daughter, and his dreams of wealth, now all but crumbled.

The title of the novel was *Almayer's Folly* and the author, a Polish-born ship's officer in the British maritime service, the former Józef Konrad Korzeniowski, who some years earlier had taken the name of Joseph Conrad. He had begun writing the novel in 1889, and it took him five years to complete, during which he had been at sea for considerable periods. He had nearly lost the manuscript twice, once in a Berlin railway station, later in the rapids of the Congo.

Before a typescript was delivered by messenger to the publisher, only one other person had read the novel. In 1893 Mr W.H. Jacques, a young Cambridge graduate suffering from tuberculosis, was travelling for his health aboard the full-rigged clipper *Torrens* on its Adelaide–London run (126 days). In the course of the voyage he had struck up an acquaintance with the ship's first mate, who on an impulse asked if the passenger would care to read nine handwritten chapters of an unfinished novel. Jacques took the manuscript to his cabin. The next day Conrad asked him whether the book was worth finishing. Jacques said, 'Distinctly.' Then Conrad asked if the tale had caught his interest: 'Very much', replied Jacques.

The two house readers for T. Fisher Unwin must have agreed with Jacques' opinion, for the novel was quickly accepted for publication. When it came out, reviews were generally favourable, romances set in exotic places then being very much in fashion, thanks to the works of Rudyard Kipling, Robert Louis Stevenson and others. One reviewer wrote that Conrad might well become the 'Kipling of the Malay Archipelago'.

A better indication of Conrad's future was the fact that by the time *Almayer's Folly* was published he was at work on a second novel, which would appear in print the following year as *An Outcast of the Islands*.

Also on this day

1214: Louis IX (St Louis) is born at Poissy near Paris * 1284: English king Edward II is born at Caernarfon, Wales, becoming the first Prince of Wales * 1599: English dictator Oliver Cromwell is born at Huntingdon * 1945: American and Soviet troops meet on the Elbe river during the Second World War

26 April

The Pazzi Conspiracy: murder in the cathedral, Italian style

1478 Lorenzo the Magnificent was only 28 years old, but he was already senior among the Medici and as such de facto ruler of republican Florence. Athletic, fun-loving, shrewd and intelligent, he had a dark, masculine face of no beauty but strong appeal. But as the greatest man in Italy's grandest family, he also had his enemies, and in early 1478 Florence's other leading family, the Pazzi, were conspiring to take over the state.

The chief conspirator was young Francesco de' Pazzi, who schemed with Francesco Salviati, Archbishop-designate of Pisa, whom Lorenzo had prevented from taking over his bishopric. The two plotters worked with the tacit approval of conniving Pope Innocent VIII.

The plot was simple. Lorenzo and his brother Giuliano had to die, and the most convenient time and place would be in church, when they would be together, unsuspecting, and with luck, unarmed. So the murder was planned for Sunday 26 April, in the red-domed cathedral of Florence. The signal for attack was to be the ringing of the sanctuary bell for the Elevation of the Host. In such a setting, it seemed appropriate that those enlisted to stab Lorenzo in the back were two priests in disguise.

As the bell sounded the priests struck, but so ham-handedly that only one even wounded Lorenzo, slashing him across the back of his neck. Pouring blood, Lorenzo spun to avoid his attackers and escaped through a side door of the cathedral. His brother Giuliano was not so lucky: in a frenzy of blood lust, Francesco de' Pazzi and an accomplice stabbed him nineteen times and left him dead on the cathedral floor.

Still trying to carry out the coup, the conspirators rushed to the Palazzo della Signoria, Florence's town hall, to seize control of the city, but there Medici supporters surrounded and cornered them. Seizing Archbishop Salviati, Lorenzo's allies tied a rope to his neck and lowered him out of the window.

Francesco de' Pazzi was stripped naked and then hanged from another window to dangle alongside the archbishop. Rioting citizens in the piazza below saw the archbishop fix his teeth into Pazzi's naked body as they swung choking and goggle-eyed at the end of their ropes.

Some 80 conspirators were hunted down and executed, including the two priests, who were first castrated, then hanged. When all was over the Medici were more powerful than ever, thanks to the crushing of what has become known as the Pazzi conspiracy. To this day *pazzo* in Italian means 'crazy'.

Also on this day

AD 121: Sixteenth Roman emperor and sometime philosopher Marcus Aurelius is born * 1765: Nelson's mistress, Emma Hamilton, is born * 1933: Nazi minister Hermann Göring establishes the Geheime Staatspolizei (Secret State Police, i.e. the Gestapo)

* **1937: The Spanish town of Guernica is attacked by German bombers supporting Franco's Nationalists in the Spanish Civil War**

27 April

Edward Gibbon, the man who called the collapse of the Roman Empire 'the triumph of barbarism and religion'

1737 Today we celebrate the birth of Edward Gibbon, the great historian who gloomily concluded that 'history is little more than the register of the crimes, follies and misfortunes of mankind'.

Born into an affluent family in Putney, Gibbon entered Oxford at fifteen but left after fourteen months, later describing them as 'the most idle and unprofitable of my whole life'.

At sixteen he converted to Catholicism, which, under the laws of the time, disqualified him for all public office. His outraged father sent him to Lausanne under the care of a Calvinist minister. Eighteen months later Gibbon returned to Protestantism, but he remained a religious sceptic. 'Many a sober Christian,' he later wrote, 'would rather admit that a wafer is God than that God is a cruel and capricious tyrant.'

During his five years in Lausanne Gibbon perfected his French (his first books were written in it), met Voltaire, and fell in love with a pastor's daughter named Suzanne Curchod. But his father opposed the match and called him home to England. Gibbon obeyed, later remembering: 'I sighed as a lover, I obeyed as a son.' He never again came close to marriage. (Gibbon's loss was history's gain, because Suzanne married Jacques Necker, to become French finance minister under Louis XVI, and was the mother of Madame de Staël.)

In 1763 Gibbon left for Paris and later moved on to Rome. Then, 'It was at Rome on the fifteenth of October, 1764, as I sat musing amidst the ruins of the Capitol, while barefoot friars were singing vespers in the Temple of Jupiter, that the idea of writing the decline and fall of the city first started to my mind.'

Gibbon shortly returned to London. A lonely and sombre figure – small, ugly, and corpulent – he washed so seldom that one contemporary complained that he could not bear to stand close to him. Nonetheless, he was elected to Parliament and joined the famous Club of Samuel Johnson, Joshua Reynolds, David Garrick and other luminaries. More importantly, now he started his great work, *The History of the Decline and Fall of the Roman Empire*.

This magnificent account covers more than thirteen centuries, ending with the fall of Constantinople in 1453. Because of its elegant prose, compelling narrative and persuasive arguments, it is widely considered the greatest work of history ever written in English.

The first volume was published in 1776, to tumultuous applause from the public but condemnation from the Church of England, offended by the

135

author's depiction of Christianity as a primary cause for Rome's collapse. Instead of eulogising the early Christian martyrs, Gibbon claimed that 'the persecuted sects became the secret enemies of their country'. He was even more disparaging about Christianity's role after it became the empire's official religion:

> The clergy successfully preached the doctrines of patience and pusillanimity [. . .] A large portion of public and private wealth was concentrated to the specious demands of charity and devotion; and the soldiers' pay was lavished on the useless multitudes of both sexes, who could only plead the merits of abstinence and chastity.

Five years later Gibbon published the second and third volumes and then returned to Lausanne to finish his masterwork, summarising: 'I have described the triumph of barbarism and religion.' He wrote the last lines on 27 June 1787 and published the final three volumes on his 51st birthday.

Once more back in England, Gibbon was widely lionised for his achievement, although during the next century the art critic John Ruskin declared that: 'Gibbon's is the worst English that was ever written by an educated Englishman.' But most have agreed with Winston Churchill: 'I devoured Gibbon. I rode triumphantly through it from end to end and enjoyed it all.'

Gibbon returned to Lausanne for his final years, writing: 'The abbreviation of time, and the failure of hope will always tinge with a browner shade the evening of life.' Overweight and suffering from an enlarged scrotum, he travelled to London in 1793 for surgery but died there the following January, possibly from infection caused by the surgery.

Also on this day

1521: Portuguese explorer Ferdinand Magellan is killed in a skirmish with islanders in the Philippines * 1791: Telegraph inventor Samuel Morse is born * 1805: The US Marines capture Derna, on the shores of Tripoli * 1822: American president and general Ulysses S. Grant is born * 1840: American writer Ralph Waldo Emerson dies

28 April

Mutiny on the Bounty

1789 Humiliated and harassed beyond endurance, master's mate Fletcher Christian of HMS *Bounty* on this day forced tyrannical Captain William Bligh into an open boat at sword-point and took command of the ship.

Bligh and eighteen men loyal to him sailed 3,600 miles in 41 days before reaching Timor and safety, a remarkable feat of seamanship and leadership.

Only 24 at the time, Christian fled in the *Bounty* with 25 other crewmen and first tried to establish a colony in Tubuai (in French Polynesia), but conflict between the mutineers and the local natives forced them to abandon the island. Sailing on to Tahiti, Christian married the daughter of a local chieftain and left behind fifteen of his crew, all of whom claimed not to have actively participated in the mutiny. Nonetheless, three of these were eventually taken back to England and hanged.

Christian and eight other mutineers then sailed to the isolated, volcanic Pitcairn Island, 1,350 miles south-east of Tahiti, where they stripped and burned the ship and settled down with some Tahitian men and women who had accompanied them.

The whereabouts and fate of Christian and his fellows remained a mystery until 1808, when an American sealer anchored off the island and found a single survivor and the crew's descendants. According to their story, a year or two after settling on Pitcairn Island, the Tahitian men had rebelled against the English crewmembers, who had treated them as slaves, and during the fight Christian, four other mutineers and all the Tahitian men were killed. Later, another mutineer fell from a cliff while drunk, and then two of the remaining three mutineers killed the third. Some eleven years after the original mutiny, one more mutineer perished from an attack of asthma, leaving only one of the original band to be found by the American sealer.

Despite the last mutineer's tale, over the years a legend grew that Christian had found passage on another English ship and secretly returned to England, where he was sighted on the streets of Plymouth.

Also on this day

1758: Birth of the fifth US president James Monroe, whose doctrine warned European countries against interfering in the Western hemisphere * 1798: French painter Eugène Delacroix is born at Charenton-Saint-Maurice * **1945: Italian partisans lynch Italian Fascist dictator Benito Mussolini and his mistress near Lake Como**

29 April

Hirohito – Japan's longest reigning emperor

1901 The Japanese empire was founded in 660 BC by the emperor Jimmu, who was (according to tradition and official Japanese history until 1945) the descendant of the sun goddess Amaterasu and direct forebear of every emperor since. And in all these two and a half millennia, no emperor reigned as long as Hirohito, born this day in Tokyo, and none shattered imperial tradition as much as he.

When he was only twenty, Hirohito set a precedent by becoming the first Japanese crown prince ever to travel abroad. But by the time he returned home, it had become clear that his father, the emperor Taisho, was sinking into depression and Hirohito became prince regent. In December 1926 Taisho died, making Hirohito the 124th ruling descendant of the Japanese imperial family. With exquisite historical irony, his reign was designated *Showa* (Enlightened Peace).

Although Hirohito was invested by the Japanese constitution with supreme authority and still officially (and popularly) considered a god, historians hotly debate his exact role during the next fifteen years. Some maintain that he encouraged Japanese aggression in China and South-East Asia and backed Japan's ambitions for territorial and trade domination called the 'Greater East Asia Co-Prosperity Sphere' that eventually led to the attack on Pearl Harbor. Others claim that he was just a figurehead, a pawn controlled by his belligerent ministers. What is certain is that, in the dying days of the Second World War, he resisted the die-hards in his government and pushed for peace. He broke another precedent on 15 August 1945, six days after Americans dropped an atomic bomb on Nagasaki, by broadcasting Japan's surrender to the nation. Five months later he once more went to the airwaves, this time to repudiate his own divinity. As defined by the new Japanese constitution, drafted by the occupying Americans, he was now a constitutional monarch.

In 1959 Hirohito broke tradition once more by allowing his son to marry a commoner, the first crown prince ever to do so. Then, in 1971, he travelled to Europe, thus becoming the first Japanese emperor ever to leave the country.

A mild, bespectacled man, whose real interest was marine biology, Hirohito died in 1989, just two months before his 88th birthday, after a reign of 62 years. His son Akhito succeeded him, taking the (this time appropriate) reign name *Heisei* (Achieving Peace).

Hirohito's funeral was attended by the largest collection of world dignitaries ever assembled, with representation from 163 countries, including 54 heads of state.

Also on this day

1380: St Catherine of Siena, who persuaded the pope to move back to Rome from Avignon, dies in Rome * 1429: Joan of Arc enters Orléans after relieving the English siege * 1945: US soldiers liberate the Dachau concentration camp in Germany

30 April

Thomas Jefferson doubles the size of the country for 2 cents an acre

1803 Thomas Jefferson's greatest contribution to the United States was his understanding of, and commitment to, liberty. But he also doubled the size of the country.

From the start of his presidency in 1801 Jefferson had been looking for ways the United States might expand west beyond the land of the original thirteen states. West of the Mississippi, running from the Canadian border all the way south to the Gulf of Mexico, lay the vast Louisiana Territory, but it was owned by Napoleonic France. Worse, France had regained the Territory from Spain in 1800 only with the promise that it would not be given or sold to a third power. Not only did this seem to block American hopes of expansion, it also raised fears in Washington that Napoleon might even deny Americans use of the Mississippi river.

Nonetheless, on instructions from Jefferson, the US minister to France, Robert R. Livingston, opened negotiations with the French to buy New Orleans, the key port in the Territory on the Gulf of Mexico. During this time Napoleon had been looking for cash and an ally against Great Britain. While making his offer, Livingston had subtly suggested that, if America were stymied in its desire for enlargement, it might consider a rapprochement with France's great enemy. With this added incentive, when Livingston offered to buy simply New Orleans, Napoleon offered the entire Louisiana Territory.

Just at this moment future president James Monroe arrived in Paris as Jefferson's minister plenipotentiary. Neither he nor Livingston had the authority to buy the whole Territory, but nonetheless on 2 May 1803 the deal was finally struck, antedated to 30 April. Later the American Senate heatedly debated the need for a constitutional amendment but then voted 24 to 7 to approve the purchase.

The United States paid a mere $11,250,000 and at a stroke gained some 833,000 square miles of territory. The Louisiana Purchase included most of the land for twelve future states: Montana, Wyoming, North Dakota, South Dakota, Minnesota, Nebraska, Iowa, Kansas, Missouri, Oklahoma, Colorado and Louisiana. It was perhaps the best real estate bargain in history, at 2.1 cents an acre.

The US at this time had a population of little more than 4 million but the Louisiana Purchase hardly added to that. Apart from several thousand indigenous Indians, the only people to come with the deal were some 40,000 Creoles.

Also on this day

1396: The last crusade leaves from Dijon under the command of Burgundian Jean de Nevers (Jean Sans Peur) * 1789: George Washington is inaugurated first president of the United States * 1883: French painter Edouard Manet dies in Paris * 1936: A.E. Housman dies in the Evelyn Nursing Home in Cambridge * **1945: Adolf Hitler shoots himself in his bunker in Berlin after giving poison to his wife of one day, Eva Braun**

1 May

La Serenissima *comes to an end after 1,100 years*

1797 When Lodovico Manin became Doge of Venice, he hoped to preside over the great republic's regeneration. Instead, he found himself in charge of its dissolution.

Manin's family had moved east from the Veneto to neighbouring Friuli in 1312 but had returned in 1651, soon becoming one of the richest in Venice. As the republic was traditionally led by its most prominent citizens, in 1791 the Greater Council nominated Manin as the new Doge, the 120th since it had installed its first, Paolo Lucio Anafesto, in the year 697. When the Council's decision was announced to the waiting crowd, one onlooker, referring to Manin's family's stay in Friuli a century and a half before, cried out: '*Ga fato doxe un furlan, la republica xe morta!*' ('They've elected a Friulian, the republic is dead!') The danger, however, came not from Friuli but from France, where the Revolution was now entering its third year.

For five years Manin ruled well, but in 1796 he could only watch nervously as General Napoleon Bonaparte, commander-in-chief of the French army of Italy, marched on Turin. Despite Austria's attempts to stop him, Bonaparte soon merged Modena, Emilia and Bologna into the Cisalpine Republic. Then, in January 1797, he flattened the Austrians at Rivoli and Mantua surrendered. When would it be the turn of Venice?

Her turn came three months later. On 30 April, 4,000 French troops arrived on the shore of the Venetian lagoon, causing Manin to declare in despair to the Greater Council: '*Sta notte no semo sicuri neanche nel nostro letto.*' ('Tonight we're not safe even in our own bed.') It was the first time in the republic's history that enemy soldiers had trod on Venetian soil.

On the following day, 1 May 1797, Bonaparte presented his demands: the Doge was to abdicate and the republic to cease to exist. He had offered Venice to the Austrians if they would give up their claims to Bologna, Ferrara and Romagna.

Outmanoeuvred and outgunned, Manin was forced to agree to Bonaparte's ultimatum and the Republic of Venice, *La Serenissima,* came to an end after a glorious history of 1,100 years. Along with the republic, the office of doge also vanished, although a strange echo of the name would resonate in the 20th century. 'Doge' is the Venetian for the Latin *dux,* or leader, a title to be revived by Benito Mussolini as '*Il Duce*'.

After his abdication Manin refused to become governor of the once-proud state and turned into a gloomy recluse. He abandoned good society, refused visitors at home, and never again set foot in Piazza San Marco or the Doges' Palace. On the few occasions when he ventured forth, he was taunted and jeered at in the streets. Five years later he died of dropsy and pulmonary congestion, leaving in his will 110,000 ducats for the insane, abandoned children and poor girls without dowries.

Also on this day

1274: Dante meets his muse Beatrice for the first time * 1769: Arthur Wesley, later Duke of Wellington, is born in Dublin * 1803: Napoleon opens the French officer training academy; two years later it moves to St Cyr * 1851: The Great Exhibition opens at the Crystal Palace in London

> Events written in **boldface** are covered in full in
> *365: Great Stories from History for Every Day of the Year*,
> the first volume in this series.

2 May

Sophia von Anhalt-Zerbst (aka Catherine the Great) is born

1729 Today is the birthday of Catherine the Great of Russia. Her name was not Catherine, she was not Russian and her greatness is open to debate.

She was born Sophia von Anhalt-Zerbst in Stettin, Germany, daughter of a minor prince. She became Catherine (or, more properly, Ekaterina) and Russian when, at the age of sixteen, she married the heir to the Russian throne, the future Tsar Peter III. From the beginning she was resolved to do everything in her power to gain public favour and perhaps royal power. She converted to the Russian Orthodox Church and was so determined to learn Russian that at night she walked around her bedroom barefoot practising her lessons.

The first obstacle in Catherine's path was her husband Peter, a weak and shallow man who generally ignored her. In 1762, seventeen years after her marriage, she and her lover Grigory Orlov staged a *coup d'état,* and the hapless Peter was easily captured, imprisoned and murdered. Catherine was quickly proclaimed empress.

Catherine ruled Russia for 34 years and expanded the country by some 200,000 square miles – equivalent in size to California and New York state combined, and more than twice as large as Great Britain. She snatched the Crimea from Turkey and dismembered Poland (having installed a former lover as king), and during her reign more than 100 new towns were built. But perhaps her greatest contributions were in the arts.

Diderot spent some months at her court, and she corresponded with Voltaire for over fifteen years, although she never met him. (Somewhat obsequiously, he christened her 'The Star of the North'.) She founded the Imperial Ballet School (the school of the Kirov Ballet), and her art collection became the basis for the Hermitage Museum. (She called her art gallery 'my hermitage', since she allowed so few people to visit it.)

In spite of her enormous contributions, Catherine's regime became progressively reactionary. She freed all nobles from both taxes and service to the state, while making their positions – like those of the serfs – hereditary and permanent.

In her private life, Catherine had a ferocious appetite for men, taking a series of progressively younger lovers as she grew older and fatter. (Frederick the Great called her the Messalina of the North.) But the most famous story about her love life is surely apocryphal – that she was also serviced by her horse.

Also on this day

1519: Leonardo da Vinci dies with King François I at his bedside at Amboise on the Loire * 1611: The Authorised Version of the Bible (King James Version) is first published * 1660: Composer Alessandro Scarlatti is born in Palermo, Sicily * 1808: The population of Madrid rises against Napoleon, starting the Spanish War of Independence (Peninsular War) and inspiring Goya's painting, *Dos de Mayo* * 1869: The Folies-Bergère opens in Paris

3 May

The sad story of Europe's first modern constitution

1791 Inspired by the creation of the United States and frightened by the chaos in France, today Poland's King Stanisław Augustus and the Polish Sejm (parliament) agreed the first modern written constitution in Europe, creating a constitutional monarchy.

Although the new constitution retained many Polish traditions, it established fundamental democratic reforms. Henceforward the King's decrees had to be countersigned by his ministers, who in turn were responsible to the Sejm. The Sejm itself was elected by Polish citizens, although there were some property qualifications. There were even some new civic freedoms, as religious discrimination was abolished.

Sadly, there was still a strong reactionary force among the Polish aristocracy, and Poland's watchful neighbours, Russia and Prussia, looked with alarm on the fledgling democracy and the possibility of a strengthened Poland.

The following year, Russia's Catherine the Great came to the aid of the reactionaries and sent in her soldiers to crush both the small Polish army and Stanisław's democratic reforms. (The fact that Stanisław Augustus had once been her lover and that she had manoeuvred him onto the Polish throne counted for nothing in affairs of state.) After a series of defeats, the King and government realised their cause was hopeless and agreed to abolish the new constitution.

Even a return to the past was not enough for Catherine and her Prussian allies. In 1795 they partitioned Poland for the third time since 1768, including Austria in the spoils. Russia took 62 per cent of Poland's territory, Prussia 20 per cent and Austria 18 per cent. King Stanisław abdicated, to live out his years under quasi-house arrest in St Petersburg. He was the last King of Poland, and Poland as a nation ceased to exist, except as a partitioned country, until after the First World War.

Also on this day

1469: Niccolò Machiavelli is born in Florence * **1481: Conqueror of Constantinople Mehmed II the Conqueror dies, poisoned by his own son** * 1493: Pope Alexander VI publishes the first Bull Inter Caetera, dividing the New World between Spain and Portugal * 1814: Arthur Wellesley is created Duke of Wellington

4 May

The Battle of the Coral Sea begins

1942 At 6 am today, carrier-launched American aircraft made a surprise bombing raid on Japanese shipping at Tulagi in the Solomon Islands, doing only minor damage but beginning a five-day naval battle that would be the first check to Japan's bid for supremacy in the Pacific.

In the spring of 1942, flushed with their recent successes against the British, the Dutch, and the Americans in South-East Asia and the Pacific, the Japanese decided to extend their reach by capturing bases from which they could sever the vital supply line from the United States to isolated Australia. In April they gathered strong naval and invasion forces at their great base at Rabaul, then sent them south-eastward, supported by a striking force of two big aircraft-carriers, towards the Coral Sea.

By this time, however, Allied cryptographers had broken the Japanese naval code. Learning that the enemy's first moves would be to take Port Moresby in New Guinea and Tulagi in the Solomons, Admiral Nimitz, the US Pacific Commander-in-Chief, dispatched a task force with the carriers *Yorktown* and *Lexington* to spoil the game. The United States drew first blood when the *Yorktown* launched its surprise attack this morning on Tulagi, seized by the Japanese only the day before.

What followed over the next four days in the Coral Sea was the first naval battle in history in which no ship on either side ever sighted the enemy. It was also an engagement of air attacks and counter-attacks that Samuel Eliot Morison described as 'full of mistakes, both humorous and tragic, wrong estimates and assumptions, bombing the wrong ships, missing great opportunities, and cashing in accidentally on minor ones'. Battle ended on 8 May and both forces withdrew, the US having lost more tonnage sunk, including the *Lexington,* the Japanese more aircraft.

In other circumstances the Battle of the Coral Sea might have been judged a tactical draw. The outcome, however, was a strategic American victory because it forced the Japanese to halt their expansion around the perimeter of Australia. Moreover, ship damage and aeroplane losses sustained in the battle prevented both of the big Japanese carriers from joining their fleet the next month at Midway, where the US Navy achieved an even greater and more decisive victory.

Also on this day

1643: Louis XIII dies * 1814: Napoleon arrives on the Island of Elba * **1891: Sherlock Holmes and the villain Moriarty fall off the Reichenbach Falls** * 1926: In Great Britain, the General Strike begins, during which 3 million workers down tools for ten days * 1932: American gangster Al Capone enters the penitentiary at Atlanta, Georgia, convicted of tax evasion

5 May

Garibaldi launches the Risorgimento

1860 Today began the greatest military adventure of the Italian Risorgimento (literally 'rising again' – the resurgence of nationalism that resulted in the reunification of Italy), the conquest of Sicily by Giuseppe Garibaldi and his Thousand.

In 1860 Sicily and southern Italy still formed the Kingdom of the Two Sicilies, an economic backwater ruled by a reactionary and repressive king.

On this day Garibaldi and his Thousand irregulars set sail from Genoa to free Sicily from its sovereign and his 30,000-man army. The irregulars had no proper uniforms, but to identify themselves all wore red shirts, and it was as Red Shirts that subsequently they were known. The actual count was 1,089, consisting of lawyers, brigands, middle-aged clerks, teenage boys, doctors, vagrants and one woman. (Some sources insist that Garibaldi introduced the red shirts so that soldiers who ran from battle would be instantly noticed.)

Astonishingly, the Thousand outmanoeuvred and outfought Sicily's demoralised troops, gathering local peasant reinforcements as they went. The bearded Garibaldi, who brilliantly planned the campaign, led continually from the front, risking himself for his cause. By June the island had been liberated and Garibaldi proclaimed dictator. It was the first truly significant step towards the reunification of Italy, which would finally be completed with the taking of Rome some ten years later.

Also on this day

1818: Karl Marx is born in Trier, Prussia * **1821: On St Helena, Napoleon dies of stomach cancer (or possibly poisoned)** * 1835: The first passenger railway line in Continental Europe opens at Allée Verte in France, eleven years after the first British line

6 May

The French government moves to Versailles

1682 Today Versailles became the seat of the French monarchy and government, even though, 21 years after work had first begun, a force of 36,000 labourers and 6,000 horses was still toiling on its construction. The great château would not be completed until well into the next century.

Versailles was originally a hunting lodge built by Louis XIII, but his son Louis XIV started to transform it in 1661, when he was still just 23. He was determined to create a palace that would surpass Vaux-Le-Vicomte, the château built by the disgraced (and soon to be imprisoned) finance minister, Nicholas Fouquet. Versailles would be far more grandiose – a fitting monument to glorify a king. To emphasise the point, Louis hired Louis Le Vau as architect, André Le Nôtre as garden designer and Charles Le Brun as decorator, all of whom had been working for Fouquet.

Versailles's grandest room was the 225-foot long Galerie des Glaces, pierced by seventeen huge windows, each reflected by an equal-sized wall mirror. The immense formal gardens (they extend over 250 acres) surrounding the palace were dotted with 1,400 ornate fountains and 100 statues. Louis ordered planted 3,000 orange, pomegranate, laurel and myrtle trees, which had to be transplanted annually into the orangery, while 150,000 new bedding plants were required every year. It was said that Le Nôtre had designed the gardens to symbolise the power of the King over nature.

Despite its splendour, however, Versailles was draughty and uncomfortable, built to house not only Louis and his family and mistresses but also a court of over 1,000 nobles with their 4,000 servants. Five thousand of Louis's own servants lived in the palace annexes, while the royal stables housed 2,500 horses and 200 carriages.

Even at the time, Versailles was attacked for its vainglorious ostentation. One contemporary bishop wrote: 'This city of riches would have great splendour and pomp but it would be without strength or solid foundation [. . .] and this pompous city, without needing other enemies, will finally collapse by itself, ruined by its own opulence.'

The bishop's direful prediction proved correct. Versailles removed the French king from daily contact with his people, and its very richness and arrogance helped set the stage for the destruction of the monarchy a century later.

Also on this day

1527: Troops of Emperor Charles V sack Rome, killing 4,000 inhabitants * 1758: French revolutionary Maximilien Robespierre is born * 1856: Sigmund Freud is born in Freiberg, Austria (now Pribor, Czech Republic) * 1910: King Edward VII dies in London, ending the Edwardian era * 1932: Russian émigré anarchist Pavel Gorgoulov

shoots French president Paul Doumer at a book fair in Paris; he dies the next day *
1937: The German Zeppelin *Hindenburg* catches fire in New Jersey, killing 36
passengers * 1954: English neurologist Roger Bannister runs a mile in 3 minutes, 59.4
seconds, the first to break the four-minute barrier

7 May

The fall of Dien Bien Phu

1954 Gabrielle, Huguette, Claudine, Isabelle, Dominique, Béatrice, Eliane,
Marcelle. What charming names. So Gallic, so feminine. You can almost smell
their perfumes, hear the soft tones of their voices. But today Gabrielle and all
her sisters had fallen. And so, most tragically, had the very centre of their
existence, what they were meant to surround and protect: the French base at
Dien Bien Phu, in Vietnam, overrun this afternoon by Communist troops after
a siege of four and a half months.

And Gabrielle, Claudine, and the others? They were the outlying strongpoints and artillery bases protecting the main position, all named, so it was
believed, for the current and former mistresses of the garrison commander, a
dashing cavalryman with a fine record in the Second World War, and – it hardly
needs saying – irresistible to women.

Dien Bien Phu, scarcely more than a place name on a map, lies in a remote
valley some 220 miles west of Hanoi, near the Laotian border. Its strategic
value for the French army was as a launching point for operations against the
Communist Viet Minh forces, led by General Giap, fighting for the
independence of Vietnam from French control. In November 1953, the French
sent in paratroopers to occupy the place, built a fortified position, constructed
an airstrip, and airlifted in the first of what would eventually be 16,000 men.
But the strategy was faulty in several key respects: the French were outnumbered
and outgunned, the position could be resupplied only by air, and the French
lacked the air power that might change an adverse outcome on the ground.

So General Giap brought up his men, 40,000 of them, and his guns, and
Dien Bien Phu turned into a trap for the French. As the weeks went by, the
perimeter, entrenched and protected by barbed wire, shrank under heavy
Communist artillery fire, tunnelling tactics, and savage infantry assaults. It was
Vicksburg, or Stalingrad. The airfield fell to the attackers on 27 March. Now
the defenders were forced to rely on airdrops from low-flying planes that
proved all too vulnerable to anti-aircraft fire. The strongpoints fell one by one,
faithful Isabelle holding out to the very last. Dien Bien Phu now became, in
Bernard Fall's phrase, 'Hell in a very small place'.

And so today, 7 May, with the Communist lines only yards away, the French
prepared for the end by destroying everything of military value: artillery pieces,
engines, rifles, optical equipment, radios. At 17.50 hours the last radio message

went out to French headquarters in Hanoi: 'We're blowing up everything. Adieu.' The firing slackened, then ceased. There was no white flag of surrender. Instead, three Viet Minh soldiers hoisted a red flag with a gold star over the command bunker.

Of the 16,000 French soldiers who fought at Dien Bien Phu, only 73 were able to escape. Some 10,000 were captured, many of them wounded, and marched away to prison camps. The rest were dead. Communist losses were estimated at 25,000. The debacle of Dien Bien Phu marked the effective end of French control in South-East Asia, and the beginning of an increasing role in the region for the United States, which within a decade would be drawn into a much-expanded conflict, the Vietnam War.

Also on this day

1824: In Vienna, Beethoven's Ninth Symphony is performed for the first time, with Beethoven conducting * 1833: Johannes Brahms is born in Hamburg * 1840: Russian composer Pyotr Tchaikovsky is born in Kamsko-Votkinsk * 1892: Yugoslav dictator Josip Broz Tito is born in Zagreb * **1915: German U-boats sink the British liner *Lusitania*** * 1945: In Reims, German colonel general Alfred Jodl signs the terms of unconditional surrender, to take effect the following day, ending the Second World War in Europe

8 May

Gauguin expires in Polynesia

1903 Today, in the sultry heat of the Marquesas Islands, just north-east of Tahiti, Paul Gauguin finally passed away a month before his 55th birthday. His death was no surprise, as he had suffered a series of heart attacks and was frequently afflicted by fever, faintness and vertigo, his body severely marked by syphilitic lesions.

Gauguin spent twelve years living in grass-roofed huts in the South Pacific, and during that time he helped transform the world's idea of painting. Traditionally, a painting had been an attempt to represent a three-dimensional world on a two-dimensional canvas, but Gauguin helped to redefine it as a flat surface covered with colours – important not for what it represented but for what it was. He wanted his pictures to provoke a feeling in the viewer, not just represent a scene.

Gauguin has long enjoyed the reputation of being the man of commerce who gave up his family and his business for his art and a life of adventure. The truth is more pedestrian. He had been painting since his early teens but earned his living as a stockbroker. In his spare time he developed his artistic talent and was good enough to be invited to display a landscape at the Paris Salon in 1876 – about the same time that he came under the influence of the Impressionist

147

Camille Pissarro. In 1880 Gauguin was asked to show his works at the fifth Impressionist exhibition, an invitation repeated in 1881 and 1882.

In 1882, however, a financial crash cost him his broker's job, and he fled to Copenhagen with his Danish wife and four children. There his marriage collapsed, and he returned to Paris to devote himself to painting while living in penury, despite the admiration of fellow artists like Cézanne and Van Gogh.

In 1887 Gauguin travelled to Martinique, where he developed his taste for exotic backgrounds and flamboyant colours. Fed up with city life, he first moved to Brittany and then in 1891 decamped to Tahiti to paint 'primitive' men and women living, he thought, as nature intended. In exchange for a small gift to her parents, he set up house with a thirteen-year-old girl named Teha'amana.

It was in Tahiti that Gauguin painted the first of his many boldly coloured visions of bare-breasted Polynesian women and developed the art that would lead the way to post-Impressionism. It was here, too, that he contracted the syphilis that would eventually kill him.

In 1901 Gauguin moved to the Marquesas Islands, in part because his syphilitic sores repelled the girls from Tahiti. Setting up house in Hiva Oa, he found a fourteen-year-old girlfriend who agreed to move in with him. There he continued to paint until his death two years later.

It seems fitting that the South Pacific should be the place of Gauguin's demise, as it was there that he created his greatest works. Perhaps this day Gauguin found the answers to the three stark questions that he had written on the face of his greatest painting: *'D'où venons nous? Que sommes nous? Où allons nous?'* ('Where do we come from? What are we? Where are we going?')

Also on this day

44 BC: Julius Caesar adopts his great-nephew Octavian (the future Emperor Augustus) * 1660: Charles II of England is proclaimed King by Parliament * 1794: French chemist Antoine Laurent Lavoisier is guillotined * 1873: English philosopher John Stuart Mill dies * 1880: French novelist Gustave Flaubert dies * **1884: American President Harry Truman (the *'reductio ad absurdum* of the common man') is born**

9 May

The oldest peace treaty in Europe

1386 The ancient sheepskin document lies at Windsor Castle, yellowed and wrinkled with age. Written in Latin, it affirms an alliance 'forever' between England and Portugal, as young King Richard II and João I pledged 'an inviolable, eternal, solid, perpetual and true league of friendship'. The so-called Treaty of Windsor is the oldest unbroken alliance in European history – it has now been actively in force for over 600 years and invoked as recently as 1982.

In the spring of 1385 the Portuguese Cortes (assembly) had elected João king, and three months after that he had devastated an invading Spanish army at the Battle of Aljubarrota with the help of a small force of English archers, safeguarding Portugal's independence and greatly enhancing João's value as an ally. Already enjoying warm relations with England, João now agreed the Treaty of Windsor with Richard, which came into force on this day.

Two months after the signing of the Treaty, King Richard's uncle John of Gaunt travelled to Portugal and reinforced João in his invasion of Castile. Although the offensive was not successful, the British–Portuguese alliance was further strengthened, and João married John of Gaunt's daughter Philippa the following year. (One of their children was the famous Henry the Navigator, who paved the way for Portugal's Golden Age with his sea voyages of discovery.) João and Philippa are buried side by side in the Abbey of Batalha, their hands clasped in a symbolic expression of the 'harmonious relations between Portugal and England'.

In 1661, almost three centuries after the Treaty was enacted, Portugal once again turned to Britain for help, this time against threats from France. The two nations signed a military treaty, and Charles II married the Portuguese Infanta, Catherine of Braganza.

Once more, during the War of the Spanish Succession at the beginning of the 18th century, the Treaty of Windsor was put to the test. France declared war on Great Britain and asked Portugal to close its ports to British ships, but instead Portugal joined Britain and the Netherlands in the 'Grand Alliance'. Then, a century later, when Napoleon invaded Portugal in 1807, the Portuguese invoked the Treaty and Britain sent troops during the Peninsular War.

During the Second World War Portugal was neutral, but the Treaty was the basis for the Allies setting up bases on the Azores. Finally, England invoked it yet again in 1982 when asking Portugal for airbases during the Falkland Islands War with Argentina.

Also on this day

1805: German poet Friedrich von Schiller dies in Weimar * **1892: Zita, the last Habsburg empress, is born near Viareggio** * 1936: Italian troops capture Addis Ababa in Ethiopia and annex the country * 1941: British ships capture the German submarine U-110 along with its Enigma encoding machine

10 May

Hitler invades the West as the seeds of his own destruction are sown

1940 Smug with his achievements and supremely confident of future success, Adolf Hitler stood poised to obliterate all opposition to his plans to dominate Europe. With 122 infantry and twelve Panzer divisions, 3,500 tanks and 5,200

warplanes on the Western front, he was ready to invade the preposterous French and any other nation that opposed his plans for expansion.

And why not? Four years earlier Hitler had called Europe's bluff in remilitarising the Rhineland. Two years after that he had absorbed Austria without firing a shot. Then he had seized the Sudetenland in Czechoslovakia, while Continental and British leaders had only wrung their hands in alarm. Then came the non-aggression pact with Russia, effectively ending any Soviet threat, and finally, after manufacturing a spurious border incident, the German army swept into Poland on the morning of 1 September 1939. The German blitzkrieg destroyed the Polish air force in 48 hours, and the last resistance in Warsaw surrendered in only 27 days, after the Soviet Union had joined Germany in invading the country.

Since the invasion of Poland, Germany had, in theory, been at war with France and England, but typically the European powers' words were louder than their actions, as no battles were fought during a period sardonically known as the 'Phoney War' or 'Sitzkrieg'. But while the Allies were dawdling, on 9 April 1940 Hitler sent his armies to occupy Denmark and Norway.

Now the time had come to put Western Europe in its place. Following the brilliant plan of German general Erich von Manstein for a Panzer attack through the Ardennes forest, at dawn today the Wehrmacht began its invasion of Luxembourg, Belgium, Holland and France. By afternoon, German forces had penetrated as far west as Maastricht and Liège.

Now an icily self-assured Hitler knew that Europe soon would be his. Who could resist the mighty German onslaught? He was probably only vaguely aware of a change across the English Channel and discounted its importance, but it would be the first nail in his coffin.

In Great Britain the frail and ageing prime minister Neville Chamberlain, following the advice of his friends in the Conservative Party and the Opposition of the Labour Party, resigned. His successor was a dark horse candidate, Winston Churchill, First Lord of the Admiralty, whose 40 years in politics had convinced many in his party that he was unreliable, mercurial, and a lone wolf not to be trusted with supreme political power. Moreover, he had been in charge of the Royal Navy during its recent failure to prevent the German invasion of Norway. But the younger Conservatives, like the nation at large, were behind Churchill, for they saw that he – virtually alone among the senior leadership of the nation – had been outspokenly right on the great issues of the decade: Hitler, rearmament, and appeasement.

And so it was that at 6 pm on the same day that Hitler charged into Western Europe, Winston Churchill, the man who would do most to destroy him and his Third Reich, took over the leadership of Great Britain. 'We cannot yet see how deliverance will come, or when it will come,' growled the new prime minister, 'but nothing is more certain than that every stain of his infected and corroding fingers will be sponged and purged and, if need be, blasted from the surface of the earth.'

It was not a moment too soon. The preliminaries were over and the main bout had begun.

Also on this day

1508: Michelangelo begins work on the ceiling of the Sistine Chapel * 1774: Louis XV dies of smallpox at Versailles * 1775: Ethan Allen, Benedict Arnold and 83 Green Mountain Boys take Fort Ticonderoga during the French and Indian War * 1857: The Sepoy revolt at Meerut triggers the Indian Mutiny * 1863: Confederate general Stonewall Jackson dies five days after being accidentally shot by his own men at the Battle of Chancellorsville during the American Civil War

11 May

Birth of a balladeer

1888   I'm dreaming of a white Christmas
Just like the ones I used to know
Where the treetops glisten
and children listen
To hear sleigh-bells in the snow.

Today was born the man who wrote the words and music to this perennial favourite, 'White Christmas', a song that has sold more than 50 million records since its publication in 1942 and is still going strong, the biggest selling record of all time.

Strangely enough, the author of this Christmas classic was Jewish, born Israel Baline, originally from Temur in Siberia. When he was four his cantor father moved the family to New York, where young Israel grew up with only two years of formal education but a talent for music. Settled in New York's tough Lower East Side, he became a singing waiter and started writing songs, even though he couldn't read or write music. At nineteen he published his first song, entitled 'Marie from Sunny Italy'. Eventually he would become America's greatest composer of popular ballads, writing both music and lyrics for more than 800 songs, many that in themselves would form an all-time hit parade. His list includes favourites like 'There's No Business Like Show Business':

There's no business like show business
Like no business I know
Everything about it is appealing
Everything the traffic will allow
Nowhere could you get that happy feeling
When you are stealing that extra bow

– and other notable tunes such as 'Alexander's Rag Time Band', 'A Pretty Girl is Like a Melody', 'Easter Parade', 'Let's Face the Music and Dance', 'Always', 'Blue Skies', 'Puttin' on the Ritz', 'What'll I Do?', 'God Bless America', and 'Cheek to Cheek':

> Heaven, I'm in heaven
> And my heart beats so that I can hardly speak.
> And I seem to find the happiness I seek
> When we're out together dancing cheek to cheek.

Israel Baline of course was Irving Berlin – a name adopted after a printer's error on an early piece of sheet music.

Berlin defined four themes for popular songs: home, love, happiness, and self-pity. As fellow composer Jerome Kern said of him: 'Irving Berlin has no *place* in American music. He *is* American music.'

Berlin wrote until he was in his 90s and died on 22 September 1989 at 101 years old.

Also on this day

AD 330: Emperor Constantine dedicates Constantinople as the capital of the Roman Empire * 1647: Peter Stuyvesant arrives in New Amsterdam * 1778: William Pitt the Elder (First Earl of Chatham) dies at Hayes, Kent * **1812: The deranged John Bellingham shoots dead British prime minister Spencer Perceval in the House of Commons** * 1904: Spanish Surrealist painter Salvador Dalí is born

12 May

Richard the Lionheart marries his queen

1191 It is a mark of the esteem in which the English hold their king Richard the Lionheart that even today a statue of him stands near Westminster Abbey, eight centuries after his death. Richard was one of history's most storied kings, and contemporary chroniclers extol his manliness, courage and chivalry. It seems they never talked to his wife.

In the 12th century the English still controlled great expanses of France – their huge Norman inheritance and the even larger territories of Richard's mother, Eleanor of Aquitaine, the richest woman in France, who was married to the English king, Henry II. Therefore the political realities of this feudal age dictated that Richard should have a French bride, and his first choice was Princess Alys, the sister of France's King Philip II (later called Augustus).

Inconveniently, however, Alys had been the mistress of Richard's father, King Henry, and everyone understood that the Pope would never sanction her union with Richard. Hence Richard put off all thoughts of marriage until after he succeeded to the English throne at age 31, on Henry's death in 1189. Even then, Richard had priorities other than matrimony, for in 1190 he set off for the Holy Land on crusade, eager to confront the mighty Saladin, who had reconquered Jerusalem three years before.

Although he had not taken a bride at a time when most princes married in their teens, Richard understood the dynastic necessity of producing a Plantagenet heir, and his mother Eleanor settled upon King Sancho VI of Navarre's daughter Berenguela (anglicised to Berengaria), whose huge dowry would defray much of the ruinous cost of crusading.

By this time, however, Richard was in Sicily preparing for his invasion of the Middle East, so Eleanor, now nearly 70, scooped up Berengaria and brought her to Messina. But Richard refused to marry, on the grounds that it would be a sacrilege because it was Lent. He then immediately embarked for the Holy Land with a fleet of 200 ships, while another ship carrying Berengaria meekly trailed behind. Eleanor returned to France.

But as the convoy passed near Cyprus, a great storm grounded three of the ships, including Berengaria's. Learning of the royal refugee, the bloodthirsty Cypriot tyrant Isaac Comnenus took her prisoner to hold for ransom. As soon as Richard heard the news, he returned with part of his army to liberate his bride-to-be. He quickly subdued Isaac, freed Berengaria and then incarcerated the tyrant in the castle of Markab on the Syrian coast. Now, as tongues wagged about what Berengaria may have been subjected to while in Isaac's custody, Richard insisted upon an immediate wedding.

And so it was that on this day in 1191 the royal couple were joined in the Chapel of St George at Limassol. Immediately after the ceremony, however, Richard once more set out for the Holy Land, even, according to some accounts, avoiding the wedding night with his new bride. Berengaria was not to see her husband again for the next three years.

Richard scored some notable triumphs in Palestine, but failed to retake Jerusalem. After concluding a peace treaty with Saladin, he sailed for home in December 1192, only to be captured in Austria. After fourteen months in captivity he was ransomed for the colossal sum of 150,000 marks and headed for England. There, in April 1194, he celebrated a second coronation, although he failed to invite Berengaria, who by this time was living in Richard's French territory in Poitou. Even when he returned to France he rarely visited her, spending most of his time fighting his great rival, the French king Philip Augustus.

So what accounts for Richard's total indifference to Berengaria? Most historians believe Richard was homosexual (although he is thought to have sired at least one bastard). Some report that earlier he had even formed a liaison with Berengaria's brother Sancho, when he had visited Navarre as a sixteen-year-old. Another tale, highly unlikely, is that he entered into an affair with Philip Augustus (which would have made the ferocious battling between the two over the last six years of Richard's life nothing more than a lovers' spat writ large). More famously and believably, however, in 1195 a religious hermit warned Richard: 'Be thou mindful of the destruction of Sodom and abstain from what is unlawful.' The issue of Richard's sexuality will never be definitively determined, but, whatever the cause, he and Berengaria had no children.

In 1199 Richard succumbed to gangrene after being wounded with a crossbow bolt in a minor siege. On his death Berengaria retired near Le Mans, where she spent 30 cloistered years at Pietas Dei, a Cistercian convent she had founded at L'Epau. There she died in 1230, the only English queen in history who never set foot in England.

Also on this day

1812: English painter and author of the *Book of Nonsense* Edward Lear is born in London * **1820: English nurse and heroine of the Crimean War Florence Nightingale is born in Florence** * 1943: Axis forces in North Africa surrender to the Allies * 1949: The Russians call an end to the Berlin Blockade

13 May

Churchill offers blood, toil, tears, and sweat

1940 Today, with German armour advancing invincibly across the Continent towards the English Channel, Winston Churchill entered the House of Commons for the first time since becoming Prime Minister of Great Britain three days earlier. In this moment of military crisis, he had come to present his administration's policies and ask for a vote of confidence. We remember the great words he spoke on this occasion and through them we imagine his voice already to be that of a nation united behind him. It was not so. Instead, the new prime minister faced an uncertain, almost hostile political atmosphere in the Commons. As he strode into the chamber, the Opposition Labour benches greeted him with loud cheers, but across the aisle the Conservatives – his party – remained silent. Their hearts were still with his predecessor, Neville Chamberlain, brought down by the fiasco in Norway that many thought should have been laid at Churchill's door.

This first speech was a test. Here are the words he gave them: 'I have nothing to offer but blood, toil, tears, and sweat [. . .] You ask, what is our policy? I will say: it is to wage war, by sea, land, and air, with all our might and with all the strength that God can give us; to wage war against a monstrous tyranny, never surpassed in the dark, lamentable catalogue of human crime. That is our policy.

'You ask, what is our aim? I can answer in one word: Victory – victory at all costs, victory in spite of all terror; victory, however long and hard the road may be; for without victory there is no survival. Let that be realised: no survival for the British Empire; no survival for all that the British Empire has stood for; no survival for the urge and impulse of the ages, that mankind will move forward towards its goal.

'But I take up my task with buoyancy and hope. I feel sure that our cause will not be suffered to fail among men. At this time I feel entitled to claim the aid of all, and I say "Come, then, let us go forward together with our united strength."'

It was a good beginning. Churchill got a unanimous vote from the House that afternoon, and if some members grumbled that showy rhetoric might be all he had to offer, and others predicted a short life for his administration, he soon proved the doubters wrong on both counts.

Also on this day

1717: Austrian empress Maria Theresa is born in Vienna * 1787: British ships with 778 prisoners leave Portsmouth to found Sydney * **1793: In Paris the Terror begins, with the first of 1,343 decapitations** * 1846: The United States declares war against Mexico * 1882: French Cubist painter Georges Braque is born at Argenteuil

14 May

Edward Jenner gives the first smallpox vaccination

1796 Today, at a farm in Gloucestershire, an English doctor made history when he inoculated an eight-year-old boy with cowpox pus, drawn from lesions on the hand of an infected dairymaid. The boy suffered a fever for a week but recovered. Then the doctor reinoculated him, this time with deadly smallpox – but the boy remained immune.

So it was that Edward Jenner, a surgeon with a rural practice, took a giant step towards the eradication of this centuries-old scourge, which in its frequent outbreaks around the world has killed hundreds of millions of people – among them England's William and Mary (ten years apart), Louis XV, and Pocahontas – while leaving countless others badly scarred, including George Washington, Louis XIV, Mirabeau and Joseph Stalin.

In the 18th century the only defence against the virus was the ancient Chinese practice of variolation, in which a healthy person was infected using pus from someone with a slight case of the disease. This system, however, had two major drawbacks. In about 1 per cent of cases the recipient caught a full-blown case of smallpox and died, and even if he survived, he could still transmit it.

But Jenner had seen that local farmers often contracted cowpox, a relatively mild illness picked up from cows, and noticed that they subsequently became immune to smallpox. He reasoned that it might be possible deliberately to infect people with cowpox as protection against the deadlier disease. Following this theory, he conducted his groundbreaking experiment.

Jenner named his process vaccination, based on the Latin *vacca* (cow). Fully aware of the possibilities of what he had accomplished, he wrote: 'The

155

annihilation of the Small Pox, the most dreadful scourge of the human species, must be the final result of this practice.'

But smallpox turned out to be tougher to stamp out than Jenner had imagined. Although it exists only in humans and is transmitted primarily by human contact, it can also lurk in clothing, bed linen and even in dust for as long as eighteen months. In the 20th century some 300 million people are thought to have died of it.

Since Jenner's first experiment, major improvements have been made to his system of vaccination, as now the vaccine is no longer taken from cowpox victims but from the deadliest smallpox virus, variola major. After the Second World War the World Health Organisation conducted an immense effort to stamp out smallpox, following up every reported case worldwide and inoculating all contacts. In Somalia in October 1977, a 23-year-old hospital cook named Ali Maow Maalin came down with the disease, but no one else was infected. There has never been another natural case.

But even though smallpox has now been vanquished, we still have reason to fear it. In the middle of the 18th century, during the French and Indian War in North America, the British army set a despicable precedent by deliberately giving smallpox-contaminated blankets to troublesome Indian tribes, killing about half their number. Two centuries later, according to the BBC, 'In the late 1990s [. . .] [w]hile the rest of the planet had celebrated the elimination of this horrendous disease, the Russians had embarked on an ambitious smallpox programme of their own; to turn it into an effective weapon.'

Also on this day

1264: King Henry III is captured by his brother-in-law, Simon de Montfort, at the Battle of Lewes * 1607: On the Chesapeake Bay, John Smith and other colonists disembark at what was to become Jamestown, founding the first permanent English settlement in North America * **1610: French king Henri IV is murdered** * 1643: Henri IV's son Louis XIII dies * 1727: English landscape painter Thomas Gainsborough is born * 1948: Israel declares itself an independent state

15 May

Semmelweiss introduces hygiene in the hospital

1847 This morning made medical history, but no one knew it, when the following notice appeared on the door of the obstetrical clinic of the Vienna General Hospital: 'every doctor or student who comes from the dissecting room is required, before entering the maternity ward, to wash his hands thoroughly in a basin of chlorine water which is being placed at the entrance. This order applies to all without exception.'

The hospital staff were outraged. Surgeons and obstetricians resented the washing up and sterilisation order as scientifically senseless and an affront to Viennese medical tradition; medical students and nurses took their cue from the senior staff. But the notice was the result of a truly great scientific discovery – and of one young doctor's zeal.

Ignaz Semmelweiss, a 28-year-old Hungarian doctor and the author of the new regulation, had concluded on the basis of his own observation that infection – in this case, puerperal fever – could be transmitted to the mothers in the obstetrical clinic by the hands and instruments of doctors who had just come from conducting autopsies on corpses. Semmelweiss also found that in the same manner diseases could be passed from a sick patient to a healthy one. And he was soon to discover that unclean bed linens were yet another source of infection in patients.

The facts were incontrovertible: in the spring of 1847, before Semmelweiss put his regulations into effect, the mortality rate in the obstetrical unit was 11.4 per cent of mothers admitted; in 1848 the rate dropped to 1.33 per cent.

For his troubles, the Vienna General Hospital refused to renew his two-year medical contract and his successor promptly cancelled his orders. Semmelweiss then went to Budapest, where, in 1851, at St Roch's Hospital, he initiated the same regulations, encountered the same institutional opposition and resentment, and duplicated his Viennese success. His ideas became accepted in Hungary but Vienna remained hostile to them.

Through lectures and writing, Semmelweiss tried to persuade doctors and medical professors of the efficacy of his discoveries, but he found his doctrine ignored and himself ostracised. The effect on him was tragic: as time went on he became increasingly erratic in his behaviour, and in 1865 he was confined to an insane asylum in Vienna. He died there on 14 August – of septicaemia, the very disease he had been fighting for twenty years, contracted in one of his last operations in Budapest.

Semmelweiss died forgotten, but the principle he discovered would soon be rediscovered – and eventually introduced as scientific truth in the practice of medicine – by medical scientists like Joseph Lister in England and Robert Koch in Germany.

Also on this day

1682: During the Streltsy Revolt, musketeers murder two government ministers in front of ten-year-old Peter the Great * 1702: The War of the Spanish Succession begins * 1768: France's Louis XV buys Corsica from Genoa * 1773: Austrian chancellor Klemens Metternich is born in Koblenz, Germany * 1911: Under the Sherman Antitrust Act, the US Supreme Court dissolves John D. Rockefeller's Standard Oil Company

Events written in **boldface** are covered in full in
365: Great Stories from History for Every Day of the Year,
the first volume in this series.

16 May

Prince Louis's troubles with Marie Antoinette

1770 Young Louis the groom was only fifteen, slim, shy, ignorant and, unknown to himself, just four years from becoming King of France, as he would when his grandfather Louis XV would die of smallpox. The bride was Marie Antoinette, christened Maria Antonia, ninth child of Austrian empress Maria Theresa. She was only fourteen when she married at Versailles on this day in 1770.

A few weeks earlier Marie Antoinette had set out from Vienna in a cavalcade of 48 six-horse carriages to make a symbolic exchange in a tent on an island in the Rhine near Kehl. Here she was literally stripped naked of her Austrian garments under the watchful eye of the comtesse de Noailles, to be reclothed in French finery. Now she had become French.

On the afternoon of 14 May in the forest of Compiègne she met her husband-to-be for the first time, accompanied by his grandfather, the King. Young Louis chastely kissed her on the cheek.

Two days later the couple were joined in the chapel of Versailles, but according to witnesses, Louis 'was more timid than his wife. He seemed to shiver during the ceremony and blushed up to his eyes when he gave the ring.'

In perhaps a metaphor for the relationship, rain fell during the afternoon and the fireworks had to be postponed. After a light supper King Louis and the Queen escorted the young couple to Marie Antoinette's bedchamber. Finally the two were alone, but the wedding night saw no pyrotechnics either, as Louis found himself unable to perform. In fact, the marriage was not consummated for another three years, when Louis reportedly underwent an operation on his foreskin.

Marie Antoinette's continuing failure to produce a child alarmed the courts of both France and Austria. Her brother Joseph, now the Holy Roman Emperor, even visited Paris to investigate the problem. He sent his brother a detailed report of his astounding findings: 'Louis has fine erections, introduces his member, and then stays there without moving for a minute or two and then pulls out without climaxing.' Joseph's solution was direct: 'He should be beaten to make him ejaculate as you beat a donkey.'

Eventually Louis somehow learned to perform, and the marriage produced two children.

Also on this day

1703: Author of the *Mother Goose* fairytales Charles Perrault dies in Paris * 1763: James Boswell meets Dr Samuel Johnson for the first time and in 1791 Boswell publishes *The Life of Samuel Johnson, LL.D.* * 1804: Napoleon is declared Emperor * 1928: The first Academy Awards ceremonies take place in Hollywood

17 May

History's greatest diplomat dies

1838 He had been a Catholic bishop and had married a woman of easy virtue. He had brilliantly advised four kings, an emperor and a republican government, while amassing a huge fortune by soliciting bribes. His many mistresses included his own nephew's wife – and her mother. His private *hôtel* in Paris was in the rue de Rivoli, his country residence the breathtaking Château de Valençay, and for twelve years his personal chef was the fabled Antonin Carême.

Such a man was Charles-Maurice, Prince de Talleyrand, a small French aristocrat (he was just 5 feet 5 inches) who walked with a limp due to a foot crushed by a nurse when he was an infant.

This extraordinary man served as Foreign Minister to the Directory, the Consulat, the Empire and the Restoration. In 1814 he was President of the provisional government, and he was twice made a prince, once by Napoleon and once by Louis XVIII. His final post was ambassador to England, where he served until he was 80.

Talleyrand's immense abilities were surpassed only by the cynicism by which he lived. 'You must guard yourself against your first impulse,' he warned; 'It is almost always honest.'

The great diplomat died today at 3.35 in the afternoon at the ripe old age of 84, surrounded by mourning nobles, including King Louis-Philippe. According to one tale, the dying man murmured, 'Sire, I am suffering like a soul in hell', to which the King replied: 'Already!'

Told that the Archbishop of Paris had said he would sacrifice his own life if it would save Talleyrand's, the dying man laconically commented: 'He can find a better use for it.'

On the morning of his death Talleyrand had signed his last treaty – an agreement between himself and the Church, which in essence renounced much of his life (including a wife of 35 years) and which, presumably, he hoped might gain for him an influential post in heaven. But popular opinion saw him going in the other direction. The *tout Paris* joked that when he entered hell, the Devil welcomed him with praise: 'Prince, you have even surpassed my instructions.'

Also on this day

1510: Sandro Botticelli (Alessandro Di Mariano Filipepi) dies in Florence * 1792: The New York Stock Exchange is established at 70 Wall Street in New York * **1900: The British relieve Mafeking during the Boer War**.

18 May

Lee stymies Grant at Spotsylvania Court House

1864 Planned for 4 am, launched at 8 am, and called off by 10 am – that was the fate of the Union army's final assault at Spotsylvania Court House this morning, shattered well short of the Confederate trench line by a deadly hail of artillery fire, and bringing to an end ten days of horrific warfare in the rain-sodden terrain of central Virginia.

The fighting around Spotsylvania was like that on the Somme in 1916. The historian Bruce Catton described it this way: 'Here men fought with bayonets and clubbed muskets, dead and wounded men were trodden out of sight in the sticky mud, batteries would come floundering up into close-range action and then fall silent because gun crews had been killed; and after a day of it the Union army gained a square mile of useless ground, thousands upon thousands of men had been killed, and the end of the war seemed no nearer than it had been before.'

General Ulysses Grant's Union Army of the Potomac had crossed the Rapidan two weeks earlier to begin its advance on the Confederate capital at Richmond. It was to prove a costly road. In the first confrontation with Robert E. Lee's Confederates, fought in early May in the murky nightmare of the Wilderness, the Union army lost some 18,000 men. Despite that, Grant resumed his advance, hoping to catch Lee's Army of Northern Virginia in the open, where it could be destroyed. But Lee fell back and dug in at Spotsylvania, where, in ten days of hard fighting – including this morning's failed assault – Grant suffered another 18,000 killed, wounded or missing.

Spotsylvania was a testing ground, not only for Grant but also for a new style of warfare. A commander of an army so repulsed might have admitted defeat and withdrawn his battered forces to rethink both tactics and strategy. Fredericksburg and Gettysburg were precedents for such a move. But Grant was a different sort of commander, who realised that to end the war, now in its fourth year, you had to keep pushing ahead, no matter the cost, always keeping your enemy on the defensive, never allowing him the initiative. So it was that before dawn on 21 May the Union army was on the march once again, its divisions pulled out of line and sent around the enemy flank. The next stops on the road to Richmond would be North Anna and Cold Harbor: engagements that would add yet another 18,000 to Grant's losses.

By mid-June, Grant would give Lee the slip a final time, taking positions around Petersburg, some eighteen miles south of the capital. But by then the Army of the Potomac's appetite for frontal attacks would be more than sated. Exhausted, both armies built trench lines from which they would face each other until almost the end of the war, which was finally in sight. Richmond itself remained elusive, falling only on 4 April 1865, after the Confederate army had left on its final campaign, which ended in surrender at Appomattox.

Also on this day
1152: The future Henry II of England marries Eleanor of Aquitaine, former Queen of France * 1525: Flemish painter Pieter Bruegel the Elder is born * 1803: England declares war on Napoleon's France * 1846: Russian jeweller Peter Carl Fabergé is born * 1868: The last Russian tsar, Nicholas II, is born * 1920: Pope John Paul II is born near Kraków, Poland

19 May

Anne Boleyn is beheaded

1536 'Madame Anne is not one of the handsomest women in the world,' reported a Venetian ambassador about Henry VIII's second wife, Anne Boleyn. 'She in fact has nothing but the English king's great appetite and her eyes, which are black and beautiful.' After three years of marriage, however, Henry's appetite for Anne had dulled, while his taste for Anne's lady-in-waiting Jane Seymour had sharpened. Furthermore, Anne's pregnancies had resulted in one daughter (the future Queen Elizabeth) and one miscarriage, but no son.

Henry's interest in Anne now vanished entirely, and she soon found herself charged with adultery, an indictment that most historians consider a convenient fiction to release the King from his marriage. No sooner had the charge been laid than Henry's chief minister, Thomas Cromwell, assured Henry that it was equivalent to treason, for which the only penalty was death.

To commit adultery one requires a partner, but in a divorce case five would be even better than one. Francis Weston and William Brere were members of Anne's Privy chamber. Henry Norris was a courtier, and Mark Smeaton a court musician. All were friends of Anne. The fifth accused, astonishingly, was Anne's brother George, thus enabling the courts to add incest to the charges against the Queen.

On 2 May Anne was imprisoned in the Tower of London, and on the 15th the five accused paramours were brought to trial. Although only Smeaton admitted adultery with the Queen (under torture), all were condemned and two days later went to the block, perhaps a merciful punishment for treason, which usually was rewarded with hanging, drawing and quartering. Possibly Henry had taken into account the fact that they were innocent. On the same day Anne was tried, convicted and condemned to death.

On the morning of 19 May Anne was taken to the Tower Green for execution. As a special kindness to his wife, instead of turning her over to the public axeman, Henry had imported an expert executioner from Calais, who employed a sharp French sword instead of a common axe, which often required several chops to decapitate the victim. When told of this signal favour, Anne commented bitterly: 'He shall not have much trouble, for I have a little neck.'

Wearing a dark gown trimmed in fur, her mahogany hair bound up under her headdress, Anne knelt upright before her executioner, not required to place her neck on the block. One of her ladies-in-waiting removed the headdress and blindfolded her. Then, in a small act of kindness intended to make her think she still had a few moments left to live, the executioner said, with feigned confusion, 'Where is my sword?' He then deftly decapitated her with one sideways blow.

The next day Henry became betrothed to Jane Seymour and married her ten days later.

Also on this day

1879: Mary Langhorne, the future Viscountess Astor and first female member of the British Parliament, is born in Danville, Virginia * 1890: Vietnamese leader Ho Chi Minh is born * **1935: Lawrence of Arabia is killed in a motorcycle accident** * 1898: British politician William Gladstone dies in Hawarden

20 May

Death of a revolutionary aristocrat

1834 Guess who died today. He:

- was an American major general at the age of nineteen.
- once wrote to George Washington that 'I always consider myself, my dear General, as one of your lieutenants on a detached command.'
- was present at the British defeat at Yorktown.
- was spirited, energetic and enthusiastic, but, according to James Madison, had 'a strong thirst of praise and popularity'.
- arrived in America for the Revolution in his own private brig.

If you haven't guessed yet, he also:

- had Louis XVI brought back from his flight to Varennes.
- drafted the Rights of Man and presented it to the French National Assembly.
- ordered the final demolition of the Bastille after 14 July.
- created the modern French flag by combining the blue and red of Paris with the Bourbon royal white.
- commanded the National Guard that helped oust King Charles X and bring Louis-Philippe to the throne.

The answer is Marie-Joseph-Paul-Yves-Roch-Gilbert du Motier, the marquis de Lafayette, revolutionary aristocrat in both France and America, who died today in Paris at the age of 76.

Although he was laid to rest in the Cimetière de Picpus in Paris, Lafayette was, literally, buried in American soil. When he left the United States after the American Revolution, he had become such a fervent Americanophile that he carried with him enough earth to fill a grave. As he had wished, he was buried in it.

Also on this day

1444: Sandro Botticelli (Alessandro Di Mariano Filipepi) is born in Florence * 1506: Christopher Columbus dies in Vallodolid * 1688: English poet and satirist Alexander Pope is born in London * 1799: Novelist Honoré de Balzac is born in Tours * **1802: Napoleon creates the *Légion d'Honneur*** * 1902: The US ends the occupation of Cuba and it becomes a sovereign, independent nation

21 May

About the sad life of dismal Henry VI

1420, 1471 At the beginning of the 15th century, King Charles VI of France had become incapable of ruling his country due to frequent fits of madness. Into this power vacuum stepped two competing dukes, Bernard VII of Armagnac and Jean Sans Peur (John the Fearless) of Burgundy. In 1415 came a threat from across the Channel, as the English King Henry V launched an invasion. Jean Sans Peur quickly allied himself with the invader.

Thinking it would help her retain her own position, Charles's wife Queen Isabeau sided with Burgundy and his English allies. Abandoning Paris to the Armagnacs, the Queen chose Troyes for her capital.

On 21 May 1420 Isabeau signed a treaty with the English called the Treaty of Troyes. This dishonourable pact disinherited Isabeau's own son and delivered France to the invaders. The treaty was sealed by the marriage of the Queen's daughter, Catherine de Valois, to the English king. Henry was named Regent of France, with the solemn pledge that the French throne would descend to Henry's and Catherine's male heir, should they have one. On 6 December of the following year the couple celebrated the birth of a healthy boy and christened him after his father.

Then, in August 1422, King Henry died, only to be followed within two months by mad King Charles, leaving the thrones of both France and England to a baby boy of less than a year. Thus an infant became Henry VI of England and Henri I of France, the only monarch ever to be crowned king of both countries, although he never ruled France for a day.

Unfortunately, young Henry succeeded to more than two thrones. He also inherited a streak of insanity from his grandfather, which progressively incapacitated him as he grew older. To make matters worse, he was caught up in that great baronial struggle, the Wars of the Roses, and after 40 years on the

English throne he was abruptly deposed by Edward of York and his mentor, the Earl of Warwick. York then proclaimed himself Edward IV.

Poor Henry spent the next ten years alternately imprisoned or in hiding in various monasteries, of which the latter may at least have been pleasing to this pious and simple-minded man.

In 1470, however, the innocent Henry was dramatically returned to the throne (if not to power), as Warwick changed sides and unhorsed his former protégé – an act for which he earned the sobriquet of 'Kingmaker'. But this momentary return to glory in fact spelled the end for Henry. Edward IV defeated and killed the Kingmaker at the Battle of Barnet on Easter Sunday 1471, and quickly had old Henry clapped back into the Wakefield Tower of the Tower of London.

On the morning of 22 May 1471, word was given out that the ageing Henry had died the previous night of 'pure displeasure and melancholy', and his body was laid out in St Paul's for all the citizens to view. But in all likelihood Edward had simply realised that England could not hold two living kings and had put Henry to death during the night of 21 May. Proof of this royal murder surfaced over 400 years later when Henry's remains were analysed in 1910. A blunt instrument had caved in the back of his skull, and his tangled hair still bore traces of blood.

The old king died exactly 51 years to the day since he had become heir to the throne of France.

Today Henry VI is largely forgotten, considered a pious pawn among the unscrupulous barons. But he has one lasting memorial: he founded the world's most famous boys' school at Eton.

Also on this day

427 BC: Plato is born * 1471: German painter Albrecht Dürer is born in Nürnberg * 1542: Spanish explorer Hernando de Soto dies on the Mississippi River (in modern Louisiana) * 1881: Clara Barton founds the American Red Cross * **1927: American aviator Charles Lindbergh becomes the first to solo across the Atlantic, landing in Paris, and in 1932 Amelia Earhart completes the first transatlantic flight by a woman pilot**

22 May

The first battle of the Wars of the Roses

1455 Today the English royal army met that of the rebellious Richard, Duke of York, at St Albans, just north of London, in the first battle of that bloody internecine slaughter picturesquely called the Wars of the Roses.

Leading the royal army of perhaps 2,000 men was King Henry VI, son of the great warrior Henry V, who had died without ever seeing his infant son.

But Henry VI was the very opposite of his cold and belligerent father. A studious and pious loner, who just five months earlier had suffered a nervous breakdown, he was dominated by his wife, the ambitious Margaret of Anjou.

At the head of an enemy force some 6,000 strong was Richard, Duke of York, supported by the Earls of Salisbury and Warwick, the latter known to history as Warwick the Kingmaker.

There was a legitimate question whether Henry or Richard had the better right to the throne, for both men claimed it through descent from Edward III. The House of Lancaster now held it only because Henry's grandfather Henry IV had usurped it from the hapless Richard II.

But Richard of York had no real desire to make himself king. The conflict stemmed from the anarchy caused during Henry VI's long minority, when every baron maintained a private army in a lawless country. During one of Henry's fits of insanity Richard had become protector of the realm, but had been forced out by Henry's wife Margaret when Henry regained his senses. Hated by Margaret, Richard feared for his position, his wealth and his head, and took up arms in self-defence.

As the armies jockeyed for position around St Albans, Richard sent word offering to negotiate, swearing fealty to the king. Perhaps enraged by his subject's refusal to submit instantly, Henry sent back a message vowing to hang, draw and quarter any who questioned his authority. Now battle became inevitable.

The first Battle of St Albans lasted less than an hour, as Henry's troops wilted before the rebel charge, especially when Warwick got round behind them. About 60 were killed, and King Henry, grazed by an arrow in the neck, was captured. Now in full command, Richard allowed Henry to remain king, subject to his control, but the uncertain peace lasted only until 1458. The terrible dynastic brawl continued to drench England in blood for 30 years, until the pivotal Battle of Bosworth Field ended the struggle of rival Plantagenets and Henry VII, the last representative of the House of Lancaster, founded the Tudor dynasty.

According to Shakespeare, the Wars of the Roses gained its name one day when Richard of York was walking in the garden of the Inns of Temple in London, where he encountered one of King Henry's advisers, the Duke of Somerset. During an argument, Somerset picked a red rose from a bush, saying: 'Let all of my party wear this flower!' In retort, Richard simply plucked a white rose to represent the House of York.

Although Shakespeare's version is apocryphal, the white rose was certainly one of the symbols of the House of York. Historians disagree, however, on the red rose. Some say it was originally a symbol of Henry's great-grandfather John of Gaunt, while others insist that it was assumed by the House of Lancaster by Henry VII only after the wars were over. In any case, the actual nomenclature – the 'Wars of the Roses' – was coined only in 1829 when Sir Walter Scott used it in his novel *Anne of Geierstein*.

Also on this day
AD **337: Roman emperor Constantine the Great dies** * 1813: German composer Richard Wagner is born in Leipzig * 1859: Sir Arthur Conan Doyle is born in Edinburgh * 1885: Victor Hugo dies in Paris * 1939: Adolf Hitler and Benito Mussolini create the Axis by signing the 'Pact of Steel'

23 May

Captain Kidd goes to the gallows

1701 Today the notorious pirate Captain William Kidd was hanged on the mudflats of the Thames at Execution Dock in Wapping.

In the morning Kidd's jailors plied him with rum until he could only stagger and then loaded him onto an open cart with three other pirates. Hands tied behind their backs, the four men were drawn through the streets of London to the gallows, where an enormous crowd waited to cheer on their final moments.

As the rope was placed around his neck, Kidd slurred out a last bitter comment about the rich and powerful men who he thought had betrayed him: 'This is a very false and faithless generation.' Then the executioner slapped the horse's side and the cart moved forward, leaving the condemned men strangling in space. But suddenly the rope around Kidd's neck snapped and he was dropped into the mud below as the other three pirates kicked and struggled for a last gasp of air.

The executioner and his assistant immediately bundled the mud-encased and drink-befuddled Kidd back onto the cart and slipped a new rope around his neck. Once more the horse pulled away the cart, and, to the delight of the roaring crowd, this time the rope held fast. Captain Kidd was dead at the age of 47.

Kidd had followed a profitable piratical career since the age of 25, preying largely on merchants and traders in the Indian Ocean. The plan that eventually brought him to the gallows, however, was hatched when he was based in New York in 1694. Backed by a syndicate of rich and powerful men from New York and London, and blessed by King William III, Kidd fitted out his 34-gun galley and hired a crew of 150. His orders were to capture 'pirates, free-booters and sea-rovers' and to attack all French shipping. Kidd and his backers greedily anticipated that he would seize a fortune in prizes. The only forbidden targets were British and allied ships.

But after almost two years of paltry success, Kidd's contract was running out, and his crew, impatient for booty, neared mutiny. When his gunner William Moore accused him of cowardice and betrayal, Kidd responded by braining him with a wooden bucket. Moore died the next day.

Then, in January 1698, off the southern tip of India, Kidd captured the *Quedagh Merchant,* stuffed with a cargo of silk, sugar, silver and saltpetre, which alone was worth some £7,000. But although she flew a French flag, the *Quedagh Merchant* had an English captain and was owned by the Indian prince Muklis Khan, who adamantly demanded reparations from the East India Company, the trading monopoly that in effect represented the British government in India. They responded by declaring Kidd a pirate. Back in London, tales of torture in Kidd's earlier adventures began to circulate and his backers discreetly started to disown him.

Meanwhile, Kidd had sailed the *Quedagh Merchant* to Hispaniola, where he left her, bought another ship and made full sail for New York, passing by Long Island and Gardiner's Island en route, possibly burying his treasure there. He tried to persuade one of his original backers, the colonial governor of New York, of his innocence, but instead of helping him, the governor had him sent to London to stand trial for piracy and the murder of his gunner William Moore.

After just two days Kidd was found guilty on both counts, and when sentenced to death he made one last desperate attempt to buy off his execution by writing to the judge that he had hidden 'goods and Tresure [*sic*] to the value of one hundred thousand pounds', which he would help the government find if he could escape the gallows. Although his offer failed to save his life, it further inflamed the rumours that he had secreted a vast fortune.

After Kidd's barbarous execution, according to the custom of the times, his corpse was left hanging on the gallows while the tide ebbed and flowed three times. Then it was cut down and tarred and gibbeted by the Thames so that sailors coming into London could see the punishment meted out to pirates. There he stayed for two years, a feast for the birds and insects.

Captain Kidd has now been dead for over three centuries, but tales of his buried plunder inspired writers like Edgar Allan Poe and Robert Louis Stevenson, and treasure hunters still search in the Caribbean, Nova Scotia, and islands near New York for his fabulous fortune.

Also on this day

1498: Fanatical Dominican friar Girolamo Savonarola is burned at the stake in the Piazza della Signoria in Florence * 1533: Henry VIII divorces Catherine of Aragon * 1706: The Duke of Marlborough defeats the French at the Battle of Ramillies * 1945: Hitler's second-in-command Heinrich Himmler commits suicide by swallowing potassium cyanide

24 May

The sun sets on Nicholas Copernicus

1543 No less an authority than Martin Luther said of him: 'The fool will over-turn the whole art of astronomy.' Luther was referring to Nicholas Copernicus, the Polish astronomer who would change forever our way of seeing the universe, and whose work would eventually destroy much of the underpinning of the medieval world.

Copernicus (Mikołaj Kopérnik in the original Polish) was born in the small town of Torun in 1473. He was a canon who practised medicine, but his great contribution of course was in astronomy. He was the first to postulate a heliocentric view of the universe in which the Sun, not the Earth, is at the centre.

Copernicus spent much of his life in East Prussia, and it was there that he wrote his immortal work, *De revolutionibus orbium coelestium* (On the Revolutions of the Celestial Spheres), which laid out his theory. Earlier he had summarised his main points, among which were: 'The centre of the Earth is not the centre of the world. All the planetary orbits circle around the Sun at the centre of them all.' In the 16th century such a theory was not only psychologically threatening but heretical. If it was true, the Earth was no longer the constant, unmoving centre of the universe but just a planet like any other. Copernicus was challenging head-on Ptolemy's geocentric theory, which had been accepted for 1,400 years. His theory was also directly counter to the teachings of the Catholic Church.

The great astronomer finished *De revolutionibus* when he was 57 but, due to its contentious subject matter, he was unable to publish. Finally, in 1543, a Lutheran printer in Nürnberg, free from the pressures of the Church in Rome, brought out the great work. This same year, when he was 70, Copernicus was living in Frauenberg (now Frombork), Poland. Before even seeing his book in print, he suffered a stroke and soon lapsed into unconsciousness. Then one of his colleagues placed a copy of the work, printed at last, in his unfeeling hands. Immediately before he died he regained consciousness just long enough to realise that his theories had at last been published.

His tombstone is said to have been graven with the words: *Stand, Sun, move not.*

Also on this day

1626: Dutch colonist Peter Minuit buys Manhattan from the Lenape Indians for 60 guilders' worth of trinkets * 1685: Physicist Gabriel Fahrenheit is born in Danzig, Poland * 1743: French revolutionary Jean-Paul Marat is born in Geneva * 1819: Queen Victoria is born in Kensington Palace * 1844: Samuel Morse sends the first telegraph message, from Washington to Baltimore

25 May

Louis Napoleon escapes from prison

1846 In September 1840, Prince Louis Napoleon Bonaparte had been sentenced to life imprisonment for having the temerity to invade France with a force of 56 men. He had been imprisoned in the 13th-century fortress at Ham, in the north of France, near Amiens.

Although the prison was grim and dark, conditions were not insupportable. Louis spent his time penning pamphlets of a mildly socialistic bent, including his most important work, *De l'extinction du paupérisme*. His cell and laundry were looked after by his parlour maid Alexandrine, whom he taught how to read. She also enlivened his imprisonment in other ways, bearing him two sons.

By 1846, Louis had decided that he had had enough. On 20 May he sent his maid/mistress away, and early on the morning five days later he disguised himself as a prison mason (or, as some legends have it, as a washerwoman), having shaved off his moustache and dyed his hair. Throwing a plank over his shoulder, he simply walked out of the guarded but open door and then through the main prison gate to freedom.

Within 24 hours Louis was in London, where he was to wait only four more years before returning to France to win an overwhelming victory for the presidency. Three years after that, the ex-prisoner staged a *coup d'état* and made himself emperor of the French.

Also on this day

735: Anglo-Saxon historian the Venerable Bede dies * 1521: The Edict of Worms declares Martin Luther an outlaw * 1681: Spanish playwright Pedro Calderón de la Barca dies in Madrid * 1703: English diarist Samuel Pepys dies * 1803: American philosopher Ralph Waldo Emerson is born in Boston * **1895: Oscar Wilde is convicted of 'the love that dare not speak its name'**

26 May

The mystery boy of Nürnberg

1828 It was Whit Monday afternoon in Nürnberg, the streets quiet, the stores closed, when a cobbler noticed a teenage boy dressed like a peasant wandering aimlessly, clearly confused. Asked where he was going, the boy could only repeat '*Weiß nicht*' ('Don't know'), but he handed the cobbler a letter. So began a tale brief in duration but long in mystery, one that remains unsolved two centuries later.

The letter was addressed to a captain in the Sixth Cavalry Regiment, stationed nearby, but when the boy was taken to him, the captain knew nothing. Now the boy began repeating another phrase: 'I want to be a rider, like my father.' Taken to the police station for questioning, he broke down in tears, babbling like a six-year-old, but when given pen and paper managed to write a name: Kaspar Hauser. The police examined the letter.

'Honoured Captain,' it began. 'I send you a boy who wishes to serve the king in the Army. He was brought to me on 7 October 1812. I am only a poor labourer with children of my own. His mother asked me to bring the boy up, and so I thought I would raise him as my own son. Since then, I have never let him go one step outside the house, so no one knows where he was raised. He, himself, does not know the name of the place or where it is . . . '

The police found a second letter on the boy, apparently written to the author of the first. It read in part: 'This child has been baptised. His name is Kaspar; you must give him his second name yourself. I ask you to take care of him [. . .] When he is seventeen, take him to Nürnberg, to the Sixth Cavalry Regiment; his father belonged to it [. . .] He was born 30 April 1812. I am a poor girl; I can't take care of him. His father is dead.'

Sixteen years old, Kaspar acted like a toddler, stumbled when he walked, was clumsy with his hands, and ate only bread and water. Put in the care of a school teacher, who taught him how to speak, read, and write, he slowly responded, and at last began to reveal his story.

All his life he had lived in a small cage, some six feet long, four feet wide, and five feet high, with a dirt floor, boarded-up windows, and virtually no light. The door was always locked and he was never allowed out; he slept on a straw bed, with only a bucket for his needs. He never once saw his jailer, who made him turn his back when bread and water were brought. Sometimes the water tasted bitter and sent him into a deep sleep. When he awoke, he found that his hair and nails had been cut.

One day his jailor entered the cell and taught him to write 'Kaspar Hauser' and to recite 'I want to be a rider, like my father.' When the man changed Kaspar's clothes and released him from his tiny prison, the boy fainted, unaccustomed to the light. When he awoke he was on the streets of Nürnberg, where the shoemaker found him.

Some thought Kaspar a con artist, others that he was deluded. But some saw in him a strong resemblance to Karl, Grand Duke of Baden. Furthermore, it was known that in September 1812, Karl's wife Stéphanie de Beauharnais (a cousin of Napoleon's wife Joséphine) had given birth to a boy who supposedly died just fifteen days later. But the mother had not been allowed to see her dead son's body. Could Kaspar somehow be Stéphanie's son?

Kaspar continued to make progress in speaking and writing. Then, seventeen months after his appearance in Nürnberg, a hooded stranger dressed in black slipped into the house and slashed his forehead with a butcher's knife, narrowly missing his throat. The would-be assassin fled, but his assault further fuelled rumours about Kaspar's possible connection with the house of Baden – who else might wish him dead?

A year later, in March 1830, Grand Duke Karl died and, with no male heir, was succeeded by his uncle Leopold. The same year Kaspar was taken to live in Ansbach. There, on 14 December 1833, another stranger lured him to a park, promising information about his birth. The stranger drew a knife from beneath his cloak and stabbed the boy in the chest. Kaspar was able to stagger home but died three days later, unable to identify his assailant.

Despite two centuries of investigation, Kaspar's true identity has never been discovered. In 2002 scientists found a strong DNA link between a descendant of Stéphanie de Beauharnais and a sample of the boy's hair. Was Kaspar the son of Karl and Stéphanie? So her husband would succeed to the throne of Baden, had Leopold's wife somehow arranged to steal the baby and substitute the body of a dead peasant child? Then passed the boy on to someone else with instructions to keep him entirely sequestered until a certain date – that May day in Nürnberg – when he would be transferred to the care of a cavalry officer?

We will probably never know the truth about Kaspar Hauser beyond the words on a small monument erected in Ansbach in the park where he was stabbed: *Hic occultus occulto occisus est.* (Here an unknown was killed by an unknown.)

Also on this day

604: St Augustine dies in Canterbury * **1234: Louis XI (St Louis) marries Marguerite of Provence** * 1650: John Churchill, the Duke of Marlborough, is born near Axminster in Devon * 1799: Poet Aleksandr Pushkin is born in Moscow * 1868: Michael Barrett is hanged at Clerkenwell for trying to free two Irish revolutionaries, the last public hanging at Newgate * 1896: Charles Dow publishes the first edition of the Dow Jones Industrial Average based on twelve stocks, closing at 40.94 * 1907: Screen cowboy John Wayne (Marion Morrison) is born in Iowa

27 May

St Petersburg/Petrograd/Leningrad/St Petersburg is born

1703 Today Tsar Peter the Great laid the foundation stone of the Peter and Paul Fortress in what was to become St Petersburg as a first step in creating a new capital for Russia.

In the spring of 1700 Peter had allied himself with Denmark and Saxony/Poland in attacking Sweden, then the dominant power in northern Europe. Sweden's redoubtable King Charles XII quickly forced Denmark out of the war and then focused his attentions on Saxony/Poland. With Charles occupied elsewhere, on the last day of April in 1703 Peter's troops, under the command of General Sheremetev, started the first bombardment of a small Swedish fortress at Nyenskans, which was located on an island at the mouth of the Neva river.

The Swedes soon surrendered to the superior Russian force, and Peter became the owner of a grim, swampy, clammy and cold piece of real estate. But to Russia this conquest was of great importance: it at last gave the country true access to the Baltic Sea.

So enamoured was Peter with his new island that he resolved to build a city there, naming it after his own patron saint and therefore in a way after himself. So Swedish Nyenskans became St Petersburg. In 1712 he transferred the Russian capital there from Moscow.

Two centuries later, however, at the outbreak of the First World War in 1914, Tsar Nicholas II decided that St Petersburg sounded too German and rechristened it Petrograd. (This same Germanophobe spirit caused Britain's George V to change the name of the royal family from Saxe-Coburg-Gotha to Windsor and his cousin Louis of Battenberg to translate his to Louis Mountbatten.)

But four years after that Tsar Nicholas was gone, murdered by Russian Bolsheviks, and Lenin, hating Petrograd for its aristocratic pedigree and fearing that it was too vulnerable to German attack, moved the capital back to Moscow. When Lenin died in 1924, the Communist Party renamed the city that he distrusted in his honour, now calling it Leningrad. Finally, in post-Communist 1991 the city's citizens voted to revert to St Petersburg, which it remains (at least for the moment).

Also on this day

1199: King John of England is crowned * 1332: Dante Alighieri is born in Florence * **1564: Preacher John Calvin dies in Geneva** * 1840: Genoese violin virtuoso and composer Niccolò Paganini dies in Nice * 1941: The British navy sinks the German battleship *Bismarck*

28 May

Cantigny – America's first major battle in the First World War

1918 At 0545 today elements of the US 1st Infantry Division – the Big Red One – launched a surprise attack against the German line, cutting out a salient and seizing the town of Cantigny. Supported by French tanks and artillery, three battalions of the 28th Infantry Regiment advanced a mile into what had been German-held territory, taking some 240 prisoners and suffering only light casualties. Later in the day, with two more regiments brought forward to strengthen the position, the division withstood five determined counter-attacks, losing almost 1,000 men in the process but inflicting almost double that number on the attackers.

The action at Cantigny was the first major combat operation conducted by American troops in the First World War. For the Americans fighting in France, whose leadership and battle-readiness had been questioned by their French and British allies, Cantigny was a major test of military prowess. Trumpeting the victory, General John J. Pershing, Commander-in-Chief of the American Expeditionary Force, said that it proved 'our troops are the best in Europe'.

Not everyone among the Allied war-planners agreed with Pershing's assessment. And yet, however one rated it, Cantigny became the first step towards the realisation of an important American war goal: the establishment of an independent fighting force. 'In military operations against the Imperial

German Government,' Pershing's orders read, 'you are directed to co-operate with the forces of the other countries employed against that enemy; but in so doing the underlying idea must be kept in view that the forces of the United States are a separate and distinct component of the combined forces, the identity of which must be preserved.'

The first American troops – infantry units – began arriving in France in June 1917, just two months after the United States declared war on the Central Powers. By the end of the year, there were nearly 200,000 'doughboys' on the Western Front. As the divisions arrived, they were quickly amalgamated into French and British corps for training. The newcomers lacked almost everything – from artillery to transport to aircraft – wrote the British historian John Terraine, 'except enthusiasm and numbers'.

But it was their enthusiasm and numbers that counted most at this critical juncture of the war. The Central Powers, suffering badly under the Allied naval blockade of Europe, needed a decisive victory in 1918 to win the war. With Russia fallen from the Allied ranks since the end of 1917, Germany began transferring divisions from the Eastern Front to France, in order to launch a new series of spring offensives ahead of the American build-up. But it was the Allies who won the manpower race, for by the summer of 1918, some 250,000 American troops were arriving in France each month.

Following the Big Red One's success at Cantigny came favourable actions by other American divisions at Château Thierry, Belleau Wood, and the Marne. Then, in the big Aisne-Marne offensive of July, which blunted the last of the German offensives, eight US divisions totalling 270,000 men fought as parts of three French armies, contributing almost 25 per cent of the troops involved. Meanwhile, Pershing never forgot his orders. So it was that in August, after acrimonious wrangling at the highest levels, Pershing won the reluctant agreement of his fellow Allied commanders – General Haig of Great Britain and Marshals Foch and Pétain of France – to gather fourteen of the 25 American divisions in France and form the First United States Army. It was an achievement that Premier Clemenceau of France sourly ascribed to Pershing's 'invincible obstinacy'.

Now the tide of war had turned. In September this new army took a major role in the Allied advances in the St Mihiel and Meuse-Argonne sectors. In October, the Second United States Army was formed, and Pershing became an army group commander, joining Pétain and Haig in that elevated status. By this time, there were over 1,200,000 American troops in France.

In early November, with final victory almost assured, the Supreme Allied Commander Marshal Foch paid tribute to the Americans: 'Certainly the American Army is a young army, but it is full of idealism and strength and ardour. It has already won victories and is now on the eve of another victory; and nothing gives wings to an army like victory.'

As to whether the first American victory at Cantigny measured up to Pershing's fevered description, the man who planned the assault, the 1st Infantry Division's operations officer, Lieutenant-Colonel George C. Marshall,

Jr, who would one day become the US Army's chief of staff and later American secretary of state, had a different view. He described the action that day as a 'small incident'.

1358: In France, peasants revolt in the bloody Jacquerie uprising * 1738: French doctor and inventor Joseph Guillotin is born in Saintes * 1759: British statesman William Pitt the Younger is born in Hayes, Kent * 1779: English furniture-maker Thomas Chippendale dies

29 May

Constantinople falls to the Turk – the end of the Middle Ages

1453 Tradition says that today marked the end of the Middle Ages, as Constantinople finally fell to the Turkish forces of Sultan Mehmed II, the Conqueror.

The siege had started in February, when the Byzantine emperor Constantine XI Palaeologus tried to defend the city with only 10,000 troops against a Turkish army of 150,000 men.

In spite of their numbers, the Turks made little headway during the first months of the siege. Constantinople's massive stone walls, 25 feet high and studded with square towers, seemed unbreachable and a great iron chain shut the Turkish fleet out of the Golden Horn, the narrow body of water forming the north boundary of the old city. Finally, however, Mehmed had 70 of his ships dragged overland from the Bosphorus to the Golden Horn, forcing Constantine to fight on two fronts. Even then the defenders held firm, despite Mehmed's intimidating practice of impaling the occasional prisoner.

But then nature came to the aid of the attackers. Back in the 15th century, all believed in signs and portents, and during the preceding months exceptionally explosive thunderstorms had pummelled the city. By their abstruse calculations Byzantine astrologers took this to signify that Constantinople would hold out against attack. But on 22 May came a very different omen: the Moon entered an eclipse so that all that was visible was a thin crimson sickle – the very image of the Turkish crescent moon emblazoned on Mehmed's banners.

Four days later another ominous sign appeared. A dense fog enveloped the city, and when it started to lift, the refracted evening sunlight was reflected in the city's windows and on the great copper dome of the Hagia Sophia church, making it appear to be wreathed in flame. As the Byzantines began to lose heart, Mehmed's men gained confidence. The Turkish sultan ordered three days of massive cannon bombardment, and on 29 May his inspired troops stormed the Romanos Gate to enter the city.

In despair at his plight, Emperor Constantine cried out: 'Is there no Christian to cut off my head?' His own men refused, but shortly Turkish soldiers dispatched him. Mehmed ordered his head to be severed from his corpse and displayed to those few Greeks who had survived the slaughter. He subsequently gave Constantine an honourable burial. The Byzantine Empire was no more, and Constantinople was lost forever to Christendom just 1,123 years after the first Emperor Constantine – the man who legalised Christianity across the Roman Empire – had made it his capital.

Also on this day

1415: Antipope John XXIII is stripped of his title * **1431: At her trial in Rouen, Joan of Arc is judged a heretic and condemned to the stake** * 1630: Charles II of Great Britain is born in London * 1814: Napoleon's first wife, Joséphine de Beauharnais, dies of pneumonia at Malmaison * 1953: New Zealander Edmund Hillary and Sherpa mountaineer Tenzing Norgay become the first men to climb Mount Everest

30 May

The mysterious death of France's Charles IX

1574 France's King Charles IX died today at only 24, but bloody and contradictory legends surround his final hours.

Intelligent, sensitive, unstable and totally dominated by his darkly scheming mother, Catherine de' Medici, Charles had inherited the throne when he was just ten. Twelve years later he remained under Catherine's thumb, hysterically agreeing to her urging to butcher France's troublesome Protestants, unleashing the Massacre of St Bartholomew's Day on 24 August 1572.

Riven by guilt, Charles became even more erratic when, eight days later, a flock of crows perched on the Louvre. In his mind their cawing became the sound of dying Huguenots. Ill with intermittent fevers and haunted by nightmares, he began to look like an old man, and within two years it became clear that his life was draining away.

One unlikely tale concerning Charles's death is that his mother Catherine accidentally poisoned him. Hating her son-in-law Henri de Navarre (the future King Henri IV) for his Protestantism, she gave him a book on falconry, with the pages sprinkled with arsenic. Somehow, before the book could be delivered to Henri, Charles inadvertently picked it up and touched a finger to his lips. Gripped by nausea and a terrible burning in the mouth and throat, he collapsed and died within hours. Few credit this story, considering it calumny spread by Catherine-hating Huguenots.

An even more implausible yarn suggests that Charles died of fear. Tormented by fever and dreading what was to come, he lay in bed, exhausted, his breathing increasingly laboured. Turning to his old nurse, he whispered, 'Nurse, how much blood there is around me! Isn't it that which I have shed?'

Knowing her son close to death, the Queen Mother saw only one way to save him, through the appalling black magic rite, the Oracle of the Bleeding Head.

As the clock struck midnight, Catherine and her apostate chaplain began the celebration of the Black Mass before the dying king. A young child was brought in, given communion and then beheaded at an improvised altar. The chaplain then beseeched the Devil to speak through the dead child's mouth.

The severed head was heard to murmur, *'Vim Patior'*. ('I suffer violence.') Seized with terror, the King shrieked: 'Take the head away! Take the head away!' Shivering in horror and loathing, and desperately repenting of the St Bartholomew's Day massacre, he then cried out: 'What streams of blood, how many murders! What wicked counsel I have had!' He continued to scream until a few hours later he gave a last terrible groan and died.

What we do know is that Charles's final years were sombre, and he was distraught by his role in slaughtering France's Huguenots. But in all likelihood he succumbed neither to poison nor to fear but to tuberculosis. Whatever the true cause of his death, however, it did not break his mother's grip on the throne of France. The new king was Charles's brother, Henri III, through whom Catherine continued to rule.

Also on this day

1431: Joan of Arc is burned at the stake * 1593: English poet and dramatist Christopher Marlowe is killed in a tavern brawl near London * 1640: Flemish painter Peter Paul Rubens dies * 1672: Peter the Great of Russia is born in Moscow * **1778: Voltaire (François-Marie Arouet) dies in Paris**

31 May

Of Prussian kings

1740 Frederick William of Prussia was one of history's oddball kings. Ruler of a smallish nation of 5 million people, he restored economic stability and laid the foundations for the powerful and professional Prussian armies of the future.

Yet Frederick William also had a peculiar side. He established a corps of guards of the tallest men in Europe – most were over 6 feet 6 inches tall. To get recruits he sent agents across the Continent who didn't hesitate to kidnap unwilling candidates. It was also Frederick William who instilled the most ferocious discipline among his troops, believing that his soldiers should fear their officers more than the enemy.

Although intelligent, Frederick William was also violent and totally insensitive to others, even to his own son. He suffered from a metabolic derangement called porphyria (the same illness that plagued England's George III) that afflicted him with gout, piles, boils and unendurable pains in the stomach. Such suffering triggered insane rages, when the maddened king would assault his courtiers with his cane.

None suffered more than the King's son, the future Frederick II, the Great. His father beat him, spit in his food to keep him from eating too much, and once imprisoned him. He had his son's best friend beheaded before his very eyes for plotting to 'escape' with young Frederick (and possibly for suspected homosexual behaviour). Voltaire called Frederick William 'a crowned ogre'.

Frederick William died today at the age of 51. His son Frederick the Great inherited his kingdom and his disciplined army. He ruled from this day for over 46 years, making Prussia one of the great powers in Europe.

Also on this day

1594: Italian painter Jacobo Tintoretto dies in Venice * **1785: Cardinal de Rohan is tried for stealing a diamond necklace for Marie Antoinette** * 1809: In Vienna 77-year-old Austro-Hungarian composer Joseph Haydn dies of shock and humiliation at Napoleon's occupation of his beloved city * 1902: The Peace of Vereeniging ends the Boer War in South Africa

1 June

'Don't give up the ship!'

1813 Today a mortally wounded American naval captain earned immortality for himself by commanding his crew, 'Don't give up the ship!'

James Lawrence had been an unruly youth brought up in Burlington, New Jersey. At seventeen he joined the American navy and soon saw action against Barbary pirates. But it was in the War of 1812 against Great Britain that he gave his life and gained his fame.

When the war started the 31-year-old Lawrence was given command of the USS *Hornet* and sank the British ship HMS *Peacock*. Promoted to captain, he then took over the 49-gun frigate USS *Chesapeake* with a new and untrained crew.

On this day Lawrence was refitting the *Chesapeake* in Boston harbour when the British 38-gun HMS *Shannon,* commanded by the experienced Captain Philip Bowes Vere Broke, hove into view. Broke, whose crew was one of the best trained in the Royal Navy, issued a challenge to the American, to meet 'ship to ship, to try the fortune of our respective flags'. Unwisely, Lawrence sailed out to fight.

The battle was over almost before it began, as the *Shannon* battered the *Chesapeake* into a helpless hulk in less than fifteen minutes and fatally wounded her captain. 'Tell the men to fire faster and not to give up the ship,' Lawrence cried, 'fight her till she sinks!' Inspired by their captain's bravery, every officer aboard the *Chesapeake* fought until killed or wounded. Nonetheless the American ship was captured in less than an hour, and taken to Halifax in Nova Scotia under a prize crew. Lawrence died en route four days later.

To pay tribute to the gallant captain a group of women stitched 'Don't Give Up The Ship!' into a flag that was given to the American commander Oliver Hazard Perry, whose flagship was renamed the USS *Lawrence* in honour of Captain Lawrence. Only three months after the capture of the *Chesapeake* Perry avenged Lawrence's death by defeating an entire British squadron in the Battle of Lake Erie, although the *Lawrence* was so badly damaged that Perry had to transfer his flag to another ship.

After the war Lawrence's famous exhortation became the motto of the US Navy, and Perry's flag emblazoned 'Don't Give Up The Ship!' is now proudly displayed in the United States Naval Academy. Little mention is usually made of Captain Lawrence's final order on the *Chesapeake*. Seeing the situation was hopeless, he commanded, 'Burn her!'

Also on this day

836: Viking raiders sack London * 987: Founder of the Capetian dynasty Hugues Capet is crowned King of France at Senlis * 1794: During the Battle of Ushant, the first great naval engagement of the French Revolutionary Wars, a British fleet captures or sinks seven French warships but allows a convoy of 130 merchantmen to escape to France ＊ **1879: Napoleon III's son, Louis (the so-called Napoleon IV) is killed in a skirmish against the Zulus**

> Events written in **boldface** are covered in full in
> *365: Great Stories from History for Every Day of the Year,*
> the first volume in this series.

2 June

The man who gave pornography a bad name

1740 Today in Paris was born the most infamous writer in history, Donatien Alphonse François, Marquis de Sade. Son of a nobleman, he was partially raised by his dissolute uncle, the Abbé de Sade, and early showed signs of the fascination with sexual perversion for which he became famous.

At the age of fifteen, however, de Sade seemed to be headed for the normal life of any French aristocrat when he joined the King's light cavalry regiment as a sous-lieutenant. A year later he was in combat in the Seven Years War, in which he showed himself to be a courageous soldier, personally leading a successful attack against the British at Port Mahon. He stayed in the army for twelve years.

But in 1768 de Sade left the army and suffered the first of many arrests after he incarcerated a young prostitute named Rose Keller in his house in Arcueil. She managed to escape and went straight to the police, claiming that de Sade had cut her with a knife, whipped her with a knotted rope and poured molten wax into her lacerations. De Sade was sent to prison.

The next half-century of de Sade's life was a sordid story of repeated sexual perversion and imprisonment. Once the Parlement at Aix even sentenced him to death *in absentia* and executed him in effigy. His marriage had mixed results: for a while his wife helped de Sade arrange his orgies, but eventually she divorced him.

On 13 February 1777 de Sade was jailed once again, this time in the gloomy Château de Vincennes. It was here that he started to write, as a defence against the intolerable boredom of prison. In 1784 he was transferred to the infamous Bastille, where on a continuous 13-yard roll of paper he wrote the explicit and perverted novel *Les 120 Journées de Sodome* (120 Days of Sodom).

Apprehensive that the discovery of such a corrupt work would only ensure he stayed in prison, he concealed the scroll in a hollow bed frame.

Suddenly, on 14 July 1789 the Paris mob stormed the Bastille, but de Sade, instead of being freed, was transferred to the insane asylum at Charenton for another nine months. Believing that his scroll of *Les 120 Journées* had gone down with the Bastille, he started writing his most notorious work, *Justine*. (By a quirk of fate, in 1904 the original *Les 120 Journées* manuscript was discovered still in the bed frame.) *Justine* was published anonymously in 1791, when de Sade was 51.

Now de Sade was once more at liberty, while all around him France fell into revolutionary chaos. He had the wit to pretend to be a republican, even advocating the abolition of all personal property, but with exquisite irony he was charged with *modérantisme* – being too moderate – and escaped the guillotine only by the fortunate fall of Robespierre.

Then, in 1801, came his final prison spell when he was seized at his publisher's, along with several copies of *Justine*. Once again he was consigned to the lunatic asylum at Charenton, where Napoleon personally intervened to make sure he remained confined. There de Sade died on 2 December 1814. His elder son burned all copies of any work in progress.

So notorious was de Sade that by 1834 the word 'sadisme' was already included in French dictionaries. At the beginning of the 20th century the French bohemian poet, Guillaume Apollinaire, attempted to rehabilitate his reputation, claiming that, although a pornographer, he was also a philosopher and artist, the human embodiment of *plaisir à tout prix* (pleasure at any price). Now the subject of serious intellectual discussion, de Sade would have been delighted when, in his last film, the Italian director Pier Paolo Pasolini produced *Salo o le 120 giornate di Sodoma* (*Salo, or the 120 Days of Sodom*), which linked de Sade with Mussolini.

Also on this day

1420: Henry V marries Catherine de Valois (Shakespeare's 'Fair Kate') * 1840: English writer Thomas Hardy is born at Higher Bockhampton, Dorset * **1882: Italian unifier Giuseppe Garibaldi dies on the island of Caprera near Sardinia**

3 June

ULTRA wins the Battle of Midway

1942 On this day, in the middle of the vast Pacific Ocean, David met Goliath. Goliath was, of course, by far the stronger of the two and very confident of his ability to prevail. David, however, came to the contest armed, not with a sling and five smooth stones, but with ULTRA.

In the spring of 1942 Allied cryptographers managed to break the Japanese navy's operational code. The ability to read the enemy's coded messages, one of the war's most closely guarded secrets, was known as ULTRA. From decrypts of the radio traffic, US naval intelligence pieced together what appeared to be the Japanese strategy for achieving total victory in the Pacific. Under the cover of a diversionary attack in the Aleutians, the first step was to be the capture of Midway Island, scheduled for 4 June. Forewarned by ULTRA, Admiral Chester B. Nimitz, commander of the US Pacific Fleet, gathered his carriers under Admiral Jack Fletcher to counter the enemy's main thrust.

Seizing Midway Island, now the westernmost American base in the Pacific, looked to be a pushover for the huge Japanese Combined Fleet, 163 vessels strong and steaming eastward in several groups spread across the ocean. Shortly before sunrise this day, Japanese bombers left their carriers for the initial strike on Midway. Admiral Nagumo, who had led the great raid on Pearl Harbor six months before, had no suspicion that just over the horizon three US carriers – *Yorktown, Enterprise* and *Hornet* – carrying 233 planes, were closing in. When he found out, it was too late.

Shortly before 10 am, while the flight decks of Nagumo's four carriers were jammed with returning aircraft refuelling and rearming for a second strike against the island, the first American attack came in. Three waves of low-flying torpedo bombers were almost entirely destroyed by Japanese anti-aircraft fire and fighter planes. 'For about one hundred seconds,' wrote Samuel Eliot Morison, 'the Japanese were certain they had won the Battle of Midway, and the war.' But on the heels of the first attack, swarming down from 14,000 feet, came 36 Dauntless dive-bombers. Within six minutes three of the Japanese carriers lay in flames, sinking. Later in the day the fourth carrier was so badly bombed that it had to be scuttled. During the evening Nagumo withdrew his invasion force from around Midway to avoid further losses, but hoping the American carriers would follow in the night and encounter the destructive power of Japanese battleships and cruisers converging on the scene. Admiral Fletcher, with his flagship the *Yorktown* fatally damaged and heavy losses in aircraft, declined pursuit.

Thus David, armed with ULTRA, prevailed over Goliath: Midway remained in American hands and the Japanese Combined Fleet withdrew westward, its vital carrier strength crippled. The defeat was so momentous for Japan, which until now had enjoyed almost unbroken success against the Allies in the Pacific, that the Imperial Navy did not inform Prime Minister Tojo of the outcome for over a month. Later, Admiral Nimitz acknowledged ULTRA's crucial role in the victory, concluding: 'Had we lacked early information of the Japanese movements, and had we been caught with carrier forces dispersed [. . .] the Battle of Midway would have ended differently.'

Also on this day

1162: Thomas Becket is consecrated as Archbishop of Canterbury * 1843: American/English writer Henry James is born in New York * 1864: 7,000 Union troops are killed during the first half-hour of the Battle of Cold Harbor in Virginia * 1875: French composer Georges Bizet (*Carmen*) dies of heart failure at 36 * 1877: French Fauvist painter Raoul Dufy is born in Le Havre * **1924: Czech writer Franz Kafka dies of tuberculosis in a sanatorium in Kierling, near Vienna, his major works still unpublished**

4 June

The first hot-air balloon

1783 America may be the mother of the aeroplane, but France is the mother of flight. On this day, before an astonished crowd in Annonay, just a few miles from Lyon, Joseph and Étienne Montgolfier made the first public demonstration of a hot-air balloon. It was man's first step towards the stars.

It was the elder brother Joseph who first dreamt of flying. In 1777, when he was 37, he was nodding by the fire while his laundry was drying and saw that hot air caught beneath it caused it to billow upwards. Five years later he began to apply the principle he had observed.

At the time France was once again enmeshed in war with England but had failed to take Gibraltar. Joseph imagined that soldiers could assault the fortress if the same force that had caused the laundry to billow up could carry them into the attack. Now experimenting with his idea, he built a 3 x 3 x 4 foot wooden frame covered on the sides and top with taffeta. When he lit some paper beneath it, it flew up and hit the ceiling.

Excited by his discovery, Joseph asked his brother Étienne to work with him. Together they constructed an even larger cube and tested it in December 1782, but the lift produced by the fire was so great that the cube floated away and was destroyed on landing.

After more experiments, the brothers were now ready to go public with their earth-shaking invention. On 4 June 1783 in their hometown of Annonay, a large crowd gathered in the marketplace to witness the first public demonstration of flight. Beneath a huge cotton and paper balloon almost 40 feet in diameter the brothers placed a fire of wool and straw. Gently the balloon rose from the ground, eventually attaining an altitude of about 3,000 feet. After staying aloft for more than ten minutes, it drifted to earth more than a mile away.

The next quantum leap came the following September when Joseph and Étienne mounted a demonstration at Versailles before Louis XVI and Marie Antoinette, as well as a large crowd of spectators. Now they enclosed a rooster, a duck and a sheep in a round wicker basket hung under a balloon. It reached a height of 1,500 feet, stayed aloft for eight minutes and floated two miles before landing safely. King Louis added the sheep to his royal menagerie.

Before the end of the year, man's first ascent had been accomplished. That, too, was in a Montgolfier-designed balloon. The age of flight had been born.

Also on this day

1798: Italian seducer Giovanni Giacomo Casanova dies in Dux, Bohemia * 1831: The Belgians elect Queen Victoria's uncle Leopold of Saxe-Coburg as their first king * **1940: The British complete the evacuation of Dunkirk, withdrawing 340,000 British and French troops from the encircling German army** * 1941: Ex-Kaiser Wilhelm II dies in exile in the Netherlands

5 June

'A lawless shepherd, of ugly deeds' becomes Pope

1305 Bertrand de Got was born in Gascony and practically from birth was destined for a high career in the Church. Since the lord of Gascony at the time happened also to be the King of England, Bertrand grew up adept at balancing three masters: the King of England, the Pope and the King of France, who was the English king's suzerain for his Gascon territories.

Bertrand's talent for fair compromise led him ever higher in the Church until, on 5 June 1305, when he was still only 41, he was chosen as Pope in an election manipulated by King Philip the Fair of France. Bertrand took the name of Clement V.

Although the papacy was situated in Rome, Clement was a true Frenchman. Even after becoming Pope he remained in France, choosing Lyon for his coronation, which was attended by King Philip. He never once set foot in the Eternal City, and one of his first acts as Pope was the creation of nine French cardinals.

Clement's motives were mixed. He feared that the frightful political conflict convulsing Italy between Guelphs, who supported the papacy, and Ghibellines, who backed the Holy Roman Emperor, might endanger the Church government, and he desperately wanted to please King Philip, who had engineered his election. In March 1309 he formally settled in Avignon, bringing the whole papal court with him. There he led the Church and did Philip's bidding, most notoriously in helping the French king to outlaw and condemn the Templars. He also followed common lay practice of offering high office to his relatives, and those places not filled by family were often sold to the highest bidder.

Clement died in Provence in April 1314. Those who considered him a disgrace to the Church (and there were many) saw God's hand behind the lightning bolt that struck the church where his body lay in state, destroying the building and virtually cremating the papal remains.

Today Bertrand/Clement is largely forgotten, even though his move to Avignon started the 70-year Babylonian Captivity before the papacy returned to Rome. Perhaps scholars of classical literature remember him best, for he earned a mention in Dante's *Inferno,* where the great poet called him 'a lawless shepherd, of ugly deeds' and placed him in the eighth circle of Hell.

Also on this day

1594: French painter Nicolas Poussin is born in Villiers * **1916: British Field Marshal Herbert Horatio Kitchener dies when the ship carrying him sinks after hitting a mine in the North Sea** * 1947: US Secretary of State George Marshall calls for a European Recovery Programme (the Marshall Plan)

6 June

Sergeant Dan Daly creates a Marine Corps legend

1918 German armies were stretched out along an endless front anchored in the English Channel east of Calais and extending east and south across northern France. Nowhere was the pressure greater than in Belleau Wood, a small wooded tract just 40 miles from Paris. Should the Boche break through the crumbling French defence there, the capital was theirs for the taking – and perhaps the war.

In early June the French received long-awaited reinforcements – two battalions of United States Marines. Today a legend was born, based on the heroism of one man, a 49-year-old Marine gunnery sergeant named Dan Daly.

The Marines attacked early in the morning, but the attack faltered when it was met by murderous machine gun fire from the entrenched Germans. Daly and his men were pinned down in a wheat field as casualties mounted. A newspaperman present at the battle reported what happened next:

'[Daly] stood up and made a forward motion to his men. There was slight hesitation. Who in the hell could blame them? Machine-gun and rifle bullets were kicking up dirt, closer and closer. The sergeant ran out to the centre of his platoon – he swung his bayoneted rifle over his head with a forward sweep. He yelled at his men: "Come on, you sons of bitches! Do you want to live forever?"'

Daly's men charged and the Germans fell back, their momentum towards Paris broken, never to be regained. Although the Marines did not capture the wood, it fell nineteen days later to American army reinforcements. But the Marines had made the difference. One hyperbolic US Army general even claimed: 'They saved the Allies from defeat [. . .] France could not have stood the loss of Paris.' Later the grateful French renamed Belleau Wood the *Bois de la Brigade Marine*. And to this day every new Marine recruit hears the tale of Sergeant Dan Daly.

Also on this day

1599: Spanish painter Diego Rodríguez da Silva y Velázquez is born in Seville * 1606: French playwright Pierre Corneille is born in Rouen * 1808: Napoleon's brother Joseph becomes King of Spain * **1861: Italian unifier Camillo Benso, conte di Cavour, dies in Turin, his last words 'Italy is made – all is safe'** * 1944: The Allies land in Normandy during the Second World War

7 June

Two vain monarchs meet at the Field of the Cloth of Gold

1520 Henry VIII of England and François I of France were two of the vainest of history's monarchs, and nothing vainer can be imagined than their first meeting, which took place today, a Thursday, in the Val d'Or near Calais in France. It has come to be known as the Field of the Cloth of Gold.

To symbolise their immortal friendship, the two kings erected two virtually entire towns of nearly 400 luxurious tents festooned with gold and silver cloths. Henry's headquarters was at the village of Guînes, where he ordered built a sumptuously decorated castle of wood and canvas that covered 2½ acres, with a chapel and great reception hall. Outside was a gilt fountain with three runlets spewing out red wine, spiced wine, and water. François set himself up in nearly equal splendour at nearby Ardres, and the two kings met in the Val d'Or, halfway between the two royal camps.

Some 10,000 French and English courtiers joined this eighteen-day festival of jousting, dancing, drinking and singing. On 24 June the two kings bid each other farewell after a solemn outdoor mass conducted by Cardinal Wolsey. The mass had been spectacularly interrupted when a dragon flew over the crowd, which was seen as a sure sign of God's favour (modern historians suspect the 'dragon' was probably a firework set off to create a miraculous effect).

The total cost of the Field of the Cloth of Gold was immense, nearly bankrupting both monarchies, especially the English, with a population of only 3 million at the time, compared with some 15 million in France. And in the end, of course, it changed nothing. François went back to seducing women, Henry to beheading them. Shortly they were at war.

Also on this day

1494: By the Treaty of Tordesillas, Spain and Portugal agree to divide the New World between themselves * 1654: Louis XIV is crowned King of France * 1778: English dandy Beau Brummell is born in London * 1848: French Post-impressionist painter Paul Gauguin is born in Paris * **1914: The first ship passes through the Panama Canal, 32 years after construction began**

8 June

Death of the Black Prince

1376 On this mild Sunday in June died Edward, the Black Prince, in his palace south of the Thames in London.

Son of Edward III (who was still alive when the younger Edward died), the

Black Prince was the most notable fighting man of his age. He distinguished himself at the famous English victory at Crécy. (As his father said, 'Also say to them, that they suffre hym this day to wynne his spurres, for if God be pleased, I woll this journey be his, and the honoure therof.' – commonly quoted as 'Let the boy win his spurs.')

It was at Crécy that Edward won his famous nickname, which came not from his colouring (he was blonde and blue-eyed) but from the black armour he wore. It was also after Crécy that he established two royal traditions. During the battle the blind King John of Bohemia had charged into the action against the English, only to be instantly cut down. Edward picked up his helmet and found it lined with ostrich feathers. Admiring the King's courage, he adopted both the feathers and his motto *homout; ich dene (courage; I serve,* later shortened to *ich dien).* All subsequent Princes of Wales have retained the feathers as their emblem and used *ich dien* as their motto.

Later, Edward commanded at the victory of Poitiers, where the French king Jean II was captured. Because of his conspicuous gallantry, he was the first member of the Order of the Garter, created by his father.

When the Black Prince died just seven days short of his 46th birthday, he succumbed to a lingering and painful disease, probably dropsy (oedema). He left behind a blonde-haired son of nine, who would one day gain the throne as the tragic Richard II.

Also on this day

AD 68: The Roman Senate declares Galba emperor * 1042: Hardicanute dies, bringing Edward the Confessor to the English throne * 1290: Dante's heroine Beatrice Polinari dies at the age of 24 * **1795: The ten-year-old French Dauphin (Louis XVII) dies imprisoned in the Temple Tower in Paris** * 1784: Fabled French chef Antonin Carême is born in Paris * 1804: Revolutionary pamphleteer Thomas Paine dies

9 June

Louis XIV's unfortunate bride

1660 Today at Saint-Jean-de-Luz the Infanta of Spain, Princess María Teresa, entered the church wearing a dress of silver brocade under a lavender velvet cape 40 feet long stitched with fleurs-de-lys. She was here to marry the biggest catch in Europe, her 21-year-old cousin, Louis XIV of France, himself an imposing figure in gold brocade with touches of black. As the Bishop of Bayonne performed the wedding rites, she had no idea she was about to become the most pathetic of royal wives.

Poor Marie-Thérèse (the Frenchified version of her name) started with the handicaps of a submissive and shallow personality and a total lack of French, while Louis spoke no Spanish. Furthermore, he was still enamoured with Marie

Mancini, the niece of Cardinal Mazarin, whom he had given up only under pressure from his mother and the Cardinal himself. But Marie-Thérèse was unfazed by her husband's previous amour, certain that royalty could truly love only royalty. Indeed, so proud was she of what she convinced herself was Louis's passion for her that whenever he made love to her, she would clap her hands at her *lever* the next morning so that the entire court would know. How little did she understand her husband.

Within a year of the wedding Louis had established his first *maîtresse en titre* (official mistress), Louise de la Vallière, a court beauty of seventeen. When Marie-Thérèse objected, Louis responded: 'What are you whining about, Madame, don't I sleep with you every night?'

La Vallière bore Louis four children during the eight years of her 'reign' before being supplanted by the exquisite and fascinating Athénaïs de Montespan, who gave him eight more. The King had started this second affair while Louise was pregnant, and to her dismay, forced her to share an apartment with her rival.

Next came the intelligent but humourlessly religious Françoise de Maintenon, who had been born in prison while her father was incarcerated for debt and forced at sixteen to marry the crippled poet Scarron. Widowed at 25, she lived quietly on her wits until, at 33, through her friendship with Athénaïs, she became governess of the royal bastards – and then replaced Athénaïs as Louis's mistress. (She married Louis in secret after Marie-Thérèse's death and stayed with him for the rest of his life.)

Marie-Thérèse remained unhappily married to the lusty Louis for 22 years, forced publicly to accept his mistresses and even to share a carriage with them on royal outings. When she died in 1683, Louis shrugged: 'Poor woman. It's the only time she ever gave me any trouble.'

Also on this day

AD **68: Abandoned by his court and pursued by his own army, Roman emperor Nero commits suicide** * 1672: Russian Tsar Peter the Great is born * 1815: The final act of the Congress of Vienna settles Europe's boundaries until 1870 * 1866: Bismarck's Prussian troops invade Holstein * 1870: Charles Dickens dies at Gad's Hill, Kent * 1934: Donald Duck first appears, in the cartoon *The Wise Little Hen*

10 June

Marlborough meets Eugene of Savoy

1704 Today began one of the most productive partnerships in military history, when England's greatest general, John Churchill, the Duke of Marlborough, first met Prince Eugene of Savoy, the greatest general ever to serve the Holy Roman Empire.

Marlborough had first received his commission in the foot guards in 1667, when Eugene was only four years old. During the next four decades he had fought both for and against the French and was made a duke by King William III for his victory at Kaiserswerth two years before his historic meeting with Eugene. His rise to fame and fortune – he was also awarded the Order of the Garter and made commander-in-chief of the Allied armies in Europe – was also furthered by his wife's close connections to Queen Anne, William's successor as monarch when, in 1702, William was killed from being thrown from a horse.

Eugene had been born in the highest aristocracy, a prince of the House of Savoy, and was rumoured (almost certainly falsely) to be the illegitimate son of Louis XIV, who indeed had had an affair with his mother. Slight, ungainly and somewhat horse-faced, at 40 he hardly looked like a seasoned warrior, but, even though he was thirteen years younger than Marlborough, he was at the time a more celebrated general; he had fought in his first battle at the Siege of Vienna in 1683, had routed the Turks at Zenta in 1687 and had become a field marshal five years later, still only 29.

Now England and the Holy Roman Empire were allied to halt the expansion of Europe's largest and most powerful nation: the France of Louis XIV. At about five in the evening on this day Eugene rode into Marlborough's camp at Mundelsheim, south-east of Stuttgart. The two generals took to each other instantly; their partnership was to last for almost ten years.

The first fruits of their friendship came just two months later when their combined forces destroyed the French at the Battle of Blenheim, securing Bavaria and all of Germany for the Empire and forcing Louis XIV to pull back behind the Rhine, never again to threaten Germany. Subsequent triumphs included French defeats at Oudenaarde, which eventually led to the recapture of Ghent and Bruges, and Malplaquet, the last great battle of the war. Between the two of them, Eugene and Marlborough demolished forever Louis XIV's hope of hegemony over Europe.

Also on this day

1190: HRE Frederick I (Barbarossa) drowns crossing a river while on crusade in Turkey * 1540: Henry VIII arrests Thomas Cromwell as a heretic and traitor * 1688: James Francis Stuart, the Old Pretender, is born in London * 1819: French painter Gustave Courbet is born in Ornans * 1926: Spanish architect Antonio Gaudí dies in Barcelona

11 June

The start of the Second Crusade

1147 The First Crusade had ended triumphantly in 1099 with Antioch and Jerusalem conquered and a Frenchman proclaimed King of Jerusalem. Half a century later, however, the Christians of Jerusalem were living precariously, as the Saracens continually threatened to reconquer all that the First Crusade had gained. In 1144 Zangi, the Muslim ruler of Aleppo, had captured Edessa and overrun the northernmost crusader state.

In response, Pope Eugenius III called for another onslaught in the Holy Land, and the Cistercian monk St Bernard of Clairvaux took up the call, exhorting French and German knights to enlist in the service of God.

Therefore, mindful of both the heavenly glories and the earthly riches to be gained, Louis VII of France and Holy Roman Emperor Conrad III determined to lead the new crusade.

On this day Louis and his French force set out on the feast of their patron saint, St Denis. Trudging through Constantinople and then Nicaea, they were joined there by Conrad's Germans – or what was left of them, for on 25 October they had been virtually annihilated en route by the Turks at Dorylaeum in Anatolia. Nonetheless, the crusaders could now field an army approaching 50,000 men. Onwards they marched, to Ephesus, Antioch and then Jerusalem, short on supplies but eager to attack.

After much internal bickering, the crusaders chose Damascus for their first target. But, having reached the city on 23 July, five days later they were forced into a humiliating retreat by the arrival of a large Muslim force under Nureddin, Zangi's son and successor. Conrad left immediately for Constantinople and Louis sailed home to France.

The Second Crusade lasted less than two years and was as much a failure as the First Crusade had been a success. No great cities were taken, and nothing remained of the huge treasure collected to finance the adventure. Of the host that left Europe in 1147, few returned.

Nonetheless, the Second Crusade may have helped change history, as one of its saltier features was an illicit romance between the French queen Eleanor of Aquitaine and her uncle by marriage, Robert of Antioch, both of whom had joined the crusade. It is likely that Eleanor's adventure was a prime reason why her husband Louis sought an annulment of their marriage on his return to France.

Eventually, their marriage was dissolved (1152) and the spirited Eleanor went on to marry the future Henry II of England and to be mother of the Plantagenet dynasty, which would rule for over 300 years.

Also on this day

1292: English philosopher and father of the empirical approach to science Roger Bacon ('Doctor Mirabilis') dies in Oxford * 1572: English dramatist Ben Jonson is born in London * 1776: English painter John Constable is born in East Bergholt, Suffolk

12 June

Jeb Stuart rides around McClellan

1862 This morning began a military adventure right out of the pages of *Ivanhoe*, as Brigadier General J.E.B. Stuart led 1,200 Confederate cavalrymen out of Richmond on a reconnaissance mission that would become famous as the 'ride around McClellan'.

With General George McClellan's 100,000-strong Union army threatening the Confederate capital at Richmond – so close now the city's residents could glimpse the Yankee campfires – the newly appointed commander of the Southern forces, General Robert E. Lee, badly needed to know the exact location of the enemy's right flank so he could plan a spoiling attack. 'Make a scout movement to the rear of the enemy on the Chickahominy . . . ' his orders to Stuart read, and be sure 'not to hazard unnecessarily your command . . . '

As they left the city behind and rode north past Yellow Tavern, 'Jeb' Stuart's troopers guessed they were going to join Stonewall Jackson's army now making life difficult for the Union forces in the Shenandoah Valley. But on reaching Ashland Station, the long grey column turned east and soon halted for the night, setting no campfires to alert the Union pickets to their presence.

Assembling quietly at dawn, they resumed their eastward ride, now clearing the Union's right flank. At Old Church they burned and looted an enemy camp, taking some prisoners. Now, Federal pursuit began to gather. But as night fell, Stuart's men had the advantage, for they knew the terrain better than the invaders, 'an obscure country of woods and swamps, where all roads were crooked and narrow and looked exactly alike, especially in the dark'.

By the morning of the 14th, Stuart and his command were well around the enemy's right flank and far behind his lines. With the mission essentially accomplished, he must decide whether to turn back or ride on. Ever the showman, he chose the latter, a course the Yankees never expected. Over three days of hard riding, intermittent clashes, and much destruction of the Union supply line, Stuart thoroughly buffaloed McClellan's commanders, one of whom was his own father-in-law. Finally, on the morning of the 15th, the weary column rode full circle into Richmond from the south, cheering crowds lining the streets. Southern morale soared. Stuart had made his name.

But for all the glamour of Stuart's 'ride around McClellan' it had one unintended effect. By exposing the vulnerability of the Union supply lines so dramatically, it prompted a slow-thinking McClellan to change his supply base from the York river to the James, thereby avoiding the fate that an attack behind his right might have brought. 'Still,' wrote the historian John W. Thomason of Stuart's exploit, 'military history would be poorer by a fine and daring thing.'

Also on this day
1931: Gangster Al Capone and 68 of his henchmen are indicted for violating Prohibition laws * **1937: Stalin executes Marshal Mikhail Tukhachevsky to start his purge of the Russian army** * 1964: Nelson Mandela is sentenced to life in prison in South Africa

13 June

Nazi Germany fires the first guided missile

1944 Today the world moved into a new and more terrifying age of offensive weaponry as Hitler's Germany fired the first jet-powered guided missile. Launched against London from the Pas-de-Calais on the northern coast of France, it killed six civilians. The missile was called the V-1, short for Vergeltungswaffe 1 (Vengeance Weapon 1), a designation coined by Joseph Goebbels, the German Minister for Propaganda.

The V-1 looked like a small plane, 25 feet long with a wingspan of seventeen feet. It could carry a 1,900-pound warhead a maximum distance of 250 miles.

In all some 8,000 of these 'doodlebugs' were launched, and about a third successfully reached their targets, killing or wounding an estimated 24,000 people. Flying at only 360 miles an hour, the buzz bombs became increasingly vulnerable targets for British anti-aircraft and fighter pilots.

Less than four months after the launch of the first V-1, on 6 September, Germany launched the more formidable V-2: a 47-foot ballistic missile with a 2,200-pound explosive payload, which flew at 3,000 miles an hour and was thus invulnerable to both anti-aircraft and fighter plane attack. The first V-2 was aimed at Paris, but two days later the first of 1,100 of these sophisticated rockets started to rain down on Great Britain. Belgium was attacked almost as vigorously.

V-2s were developed and launched from Peenemünde, a village on the Baltic coast of north-east Germany. They were largely the brainchild of the brilliant German scientist Wernher von Braun, who was Peenemünde's technical director. Captured by American troops in the closing days of the war, von Braun and his colleagues were quickly moved to White Sands, New Mexico, to continue their work on rockets under different masters. Later, von Braun became chief of the American ballistic weapons programme at Huntsville, Alabama, which developed the Redstone, Jupiter-C, Juno and Pershing missiles.

Von Braun always maintained that scientific research is inherently impartial and that governments, not scientists, must bear the responsibility for the use that scientific developments are put to. Or, as satirised by the American composer and lyricist Tom Lehrer:

'Once the rockets are up, who cares where they come down? That's not my department', says Wernher von Braun.

Also on this day

323 BC: Alexander the Great dies in Babylon, probably of malaria * 1865: Irish poet William Butler Yeats is born * 1886: Mad King Ludwig (II) of Bavaria drowns himself in the Starnberger See * 1900: The Boxer Rebellion begins in China

14 June

France's most victorious day

1658, 1800, 1807 The 14th of June was perhaps the most victorious day for French arms in the nation's history.

In 1658 the pre-eminent French general of the 17th century, vicomte Henri de Turenne, defeated a Spanish force reinforced by a contingent of English royalists commanded by the Duke of York, the future James II. (It was after this victory that Turenne summed up the results in his famously terse report to King Louis XIV: 'The enemy came, was beaten, I am tired, good night.') Fought near Dunkirk, the conflict is called the Battle of the Dunes.

In 1800 the greatest French general of the 19th century (and probably of all centuries), Napoleon Bonaparte, grasped victory from the jaws of defeat in counter-attacking and routing an Austrian force in the Battle of Marengo in northern Italy. (He simultaneously provided the historical background for Victorien Sardou's play *La Tosca,* which Puccini later transformed into his glorious opera.)

In 1807 it was Napoleon's turn again, when he annihilated a Russian army at Friedland (then in Prussia, now in Russia) in a battle of about 60,000 troops on each side, which resulted in 19,000 Russian casualties.

Except for Turenne's brusque summary, even the French have now largely forgotten the Battle of the Dunes, but Marengo and Friedland are avenues in Paris, named in honour of the great Napoleonic victories. Apart from the street names, however, all three battles today conjure up little for most of us – just battles in which men died for questionable ends and the ego of nations. Marengo, however, leaves a somewhat better taste.

On the evening after the battle, Napoleon's chef Dunan sent out some soldiers to scavenge for food for his general. They returned with some tomatoes, onions, garlic, olives, some parsley and a chicken. Braising them skilfully with some white wine, Dunan then added some scrambled eggs on the side, creating Chicken Marengo, a dish still found today in good French restaurants, although most chefs now omit the scrambled eggs.

Also on this day
827: Arabs from North Africa first invade Sicily * 1645: Oliver Cromwell defeats royalist troops at the Battle of Naseby * **1801: American Revolutionary general and traitor Benedict Arnold dies in London**

15 June

The Duchess of Richmond's ball

1815 There was danger afoot on the Continent of Europe. Napoleon had recently escaped his exile on Elba, had returned to Paris, and this very day was at the head of an enormous army advancing on Belgium. In Vienna, news of these disturbing developments caused the Congress to give up its waltzing, but in Brussels this evening the Duchess of Richmond gave a ball, maybe the most famous ball in history, where the assembled company feasted and danced the night away, 'up to the very brink of battle'.

'There never was, since the days of Darius,' wrote Thackeray, 'such a brilliant train of camp followers as hung around the train of the Duke of Wellington's army in the Low Countries in 1815.' Chief among the attendees at this evening's ball was the cream of British and European military leadership, headed by the Prince of Orange, the Duke of Brunswick and the Duke of Wellington, now Commander-in-Chief of the Allied armies in Flanders. Ambassadors, military officers and aristocrats thronged the spacious rooms. Beautiful ladies abounded in a dazzling array of wives and daughters that included, in addition to the hostess herself, her daughter Lady Georgiana Lennox, Lady Charlotte Greville – a favourite of the Commander-in-Chief – and, if we wish to believe Thackeray's account in *Vanity Fair,* that arch-schemer Mrs Rawdon Crawley, better known as Becky Sharp.

The Duke of Wellington came late and left early. At midnight a rider arrived with a dispatch, and when he had finished reading it, the Duke began issuing orders to aides and conferring with senior officers. Later, at supper, where he sat next to Lady Charlotte, he was composed and attentive as always, but afterwards he asked the Duke of Richmond for a map, which he consulted in the privacy of the study.

Sometime after 2 am, with the festivities in full swing, Wellington left for his quarters. The French army was drawing very near now – had crossed the Sambre, in fact – and there was much to be done to prepare his own army for events. It was no longer the eve of battle, and the approaching dawn would see the commencement of a great military campaign that would culminate in three days' time at Waterloo.

Also on this day
1215: King John signs the Magna Carta * 1330: Edward, the Black Prince, is

born * **1381: Edward II crushes the Peasants' Revolt as its leader Wat Tyler is killed** * 1775: The Continental Congress makes George Washington Commander-in-Chief of the Continental army

> Events written in **boldface** are covered in full in
> *365: Great Stories from History for Every Day of the Year,*
> the first volume in this series.

16 June

The longest pontificate in history

1846 When wisps of white smoke drifted from the Vatican chimney on this sultry day in June, the waiting crowds knew that, through his cardinals, God had chosen another pope. The new pontiff was Giovanni Mastai-Ferretti, formerly Bishop of Imola and now enthroned with the name of Pius IX.

Pius was a sincere man of some sophistication, with a deep sense of humanity, a sharp intelligence and a disarming appearance of humility. (Despite his virtues, he was thought to have the 'evil eye', the power to injure people just by looking at them. In consequence villagers would hide their children when he rode through Italy.)

Initially somewhat of an ecclesiastical liberal, Pius became Pope at a time when the papacy was under sharp attack on both spiritual and temporal grounds.

The revolutions of 1848 across Europe terrified him, turning him ever more conservative in his views. Then came a direct threat to the temporal power of the papacy as Italy struggled to unify itself. The papal territories at its centre blocked the creation of a single Italian state.

Pius could not imagine the papacy depending on spiritual power alone and was aghast at the idea of the Church losing its lands and secular authority. Reacting against this threat, he turned his back on all progress and, in 1864, published his famous *Syllabus* listing 80 'principal errors of our times'. Of these, the 80th was the most doggedly reactionary, denying entirely the view that 'the Roman Pontiff can and should reconcile himself to and agree with progress, liberalism, and modern civilisation'. Such opinions earned Pius the (probably complimentary) nickname 'The Scourge of Liberalism' among the Catholic faithful.

Pius is also associated with two of Catholicism's most contentious doctrines, those of the Immaculate Conception and of papal infallibility, both of which were defined and accepted as Church doctrine during his pontificate.

In spite of his refusal to compromise (or perhaps because of it), in the end Pius lost everything he valued most when King Victor Emmanuel's troops marched into Rome in 1870. Church and state were finally separated.

194

Pius IX soldiered on until he died in 1878, still detested by many of his own countrymen. When his body was moved to the Basilica di San Lorenzo fuori le Mura, a gang of nationalists attempted to throw it into the Tiber.

Despite his reactionary record, Pius was beatified almost a century after his death. During the process his tomb was opened for inspection and his corpse was reported to be still in a state of perfect preservation, like medieval saints of old.

Pius's pontificate of 32 years is the longest in all the twenty centuries of Church history.

Also on this day

1487: King Henry VII crushes insurgent rebels at Stoke and captures twelve-year-old Lambert Simnel, who claimed to be the true heir to the throne * 1722: John Churchill, Duke of Marlborough, dies at Windsor * 1866: Prussian chancellor Bismarck launches an attack against Austria as the first step in the unification of Germany

17 June

The king who stole the Stone of Scone

1239 His grandfather, King John, had been treacherous and cruel, while his father Henry III was weak and vacillating. But Edward I, born this day at Westminster, was one of England's greatest kings.

Edward was a splendid athlete and horseman, blonde, handsome, regal and so tall (6 feet 2 inches) that he was known as Edward Longshanks. He was also highly intelligent and fluent in English, French and Latin. His main problem was his temper, which matched that of his legendary Plantagenet great-grandfather, Henry II. In his younger days he showed all the worst characteristics of a spoiled prince: cruelty, violence, intolerance and arrogance. But fortunately he did not inherit the throne until he was 33, by which time he had curbed his unpleasant excesses, except for the occasional terrifying rage.

Edward married twice and was a virile and faithful husband, a rarity for kings, especially in the Middle Ages. His two wives bore him at least twenty children, the last arriving when he was 67 years old.

Edward reformed the body of English law, moving the nation away from feudalism in the long, slow march towards democratic freedom. He was also a warrior of note and a superb general. His most famous victories were over the Welsh, whom he subdued to such a degree that they remained cowed for the best part of a century. He had less success with the Scottish, although he did manage to capture William Wallace, whom he had hanged, drawn and quartered: a punishment for treason that Edward was the first English king to use.

Edward's more lasting Scottish triumph concerned the Stone of Scone.

The Stone of Scone is a 350-pound block of pale yellow sandstone measuring 26 by 16 by 11 inches, decorated with a Latin cross. The Scots believed the patriarch Jacob had once used it as a pillow when he experienced visions of angels. The stone had somehow been taken from the Holy Land through North Africa and on through Sicily, Spain and Ireland before reaching Scotland, where it was taken to the village of Scone in the 9th century. There it was built into a throne on which Scottish kings sat during their coronation ceremonies for 400 years.

In 1296 Edward moved the stone to London and had a new coronation chair built with the stone fitted under it. It was to symbolise that kings of England were also kings of Scotland. The Stone of Scone remained in Westminster until the end of the 20th century when, in a gesture of political rapprochement, it was returned to Scotland.

Also on this day

1600: Spanish playwright Pedro Calderón de la Barca is born in Madrid * 1719: English writer Joseph Addison dies * **1775: American rebels prove their mettle while losing the Battle of Bunker Hill in the American War of Independence**

18 June

America declares war on Great Britain

1812 Caught in a trade vice between Great Britain's blockade of Napoleon's Europe and Napoleon's Continental System isolating Great Britain, today the United States Congress declared war on Great Britain to start the War of 1812.

'As for France and England,' wrote former president Thomas Jefferson, 'the one is a den of robbers, the other pirates.' The British, however, were considered worse, as they impressed American sailors to serve in their navy as well as seizing American ships.

To the British, on the other hand, America's belligerency was merely an annoying gnat to be batted aside compared with the true enemy, the eagle of Napoleon. Later generations of Americans also failed to understand why the US had gone to war. It was, according to another president, Harry S. Truman, 'the silliest damn war we ever had, made no sense at all'.

The War of 1812 is today principally remembered for the humiliation of British troops capturing Washington and putting the White House to the torch. But it also provided the inspiration for an American lawyer named Francis Scott Key to write 'The Star-Spangled Banner' and provided one further interesting historical footnote. During the conflict 63-year-old James Madison became the only US president to face enemy gunfire while in office, as he led an artillery battery during the attack on the capital.

The War of 1812 lasted until 1815, but in the end stalemate brought the belligerents to the peace table, with no territory acquired or lost by either side. The main beneficiary was the Amercian general Andrew Jackson, who gained national renown and ultimately the presidency for havign trounced the British at the Battle of New Orleans – even though, unbeknown to the comabatants, the peace treaty had been signed fifteen days before the battle.

Also on this day

1155: HRE Fredrick Barbarossa is crowned in Rome ∗ 1429: Joan of Arc leads the French army to victory over the English at the Battle of Patay ∗ **1815: Wellington and Blücher best Napoleon at the Battle of Waterloo** ∗ 1845: seventh American president Andrew Jackson dies in Nashville

19 June

The decapitation of Piers Gaveston

1312 Had Piers Gaveston been born a woman, he probably would be remembered as one of history's magnificent mistresses, like Nell Gwyn or Madame de Pompadour. Handsome, athletic, wickedly witty and vain, this Gascon-born Englishman was first brought to the English court by Edward I. It was the King's son, however, who was drawn to Gaveston, so much so that when the son was crowned as Edward II, his Gascon lover carried his crown in the ceremony.

In the years immediately following the coronation, Gaveston's power increased in tune to the King's infatuation – to the fury of the nation's earls, who saw regal offices and jewels squandered on the insolent favourite. Edward even made him regent of the realm when he journeyed to France in 1308.

Gaveston had already once been banished from England in 1307 on orders of Edward's father, and now the barons' wrath forced Edward to banish him once again, but this time he was sent to Ireland as lieutenant, where he remained for a year. But in 1309 Edward's obsession caused him to recall Gaveston to London, where he was as haughty and impertinent as ever, reigniting the barons' rage. Banished for a third time in 1311, he soon secretly came back to Edward's court, where the besotted king returned him to favour.

Finally the earls revolted, and despite the King's desperate attempts to hide him, they captured Gaveston at Scarborough and imprisoned him in the castle there.

On 19 June 1312 the earls took the once-proud favourite from his dungeon and marched him to Blacklow Hill, near the mighty castle of Warwick. There, despite his plea to his captor, Guy de Beauchamp, Earl of Warwick, 'O noble Earl, spare me!', Gaveston was rudely decapitated, and his head was presented to the vindictive king's cousin, the Earl of Lancaster.

To this day it is believed that Gaveston's malevolent ghost roams the ramparts of Scarborough Castle, hurling to their deaths any unwary enough to wander alone on the castle walls at night.

Also on this day

1623: French philosopher Blaise Pascal is born in Clermont-Ferrand * 1829: The House of Commons passes Robert Peel's law establishing a police force * **1867: Emperor Maximilian I is shot by a Mexican republican firing squad** * 1896: Wallis Simpson (née Bessie Wallis Warfield), Duchess of Windsor, is born in Blue Ridge Summit, Pennsylvania

20 June

The flight to Varennes

1791 Today Louis XVI, Marie Antoinette and their two children made a last desperate gamble to flee revolutionary Paris. Their attempted escape virtually guaranteed the end of the French monarchy and their own gruesome deaths on the guillotine.

By the beginning of the year Louis had already lost most of his power, and he and his family were virtual prisoners in the Tuileries. There they were both watched and protected by national guardsmen under the command of that revolutionary aristocrat, the marquis de Lafayette.

In mid-April the royal family had tried to leave for Saint-Cloud for Easter, but when Lafayette ordered his troops to clear a path through the rabble crowding around the palace gate, they refused to obey him, and after waiting in the carriage for almost two hours, the King was forced to make a humiliating return to the palace. It was then that he started to plan for a daring escape. Late in the evening on 20 June, he set his plan in action.

Marie Antoinette disguised herself as a governess, her daughter wore simple clothing, and the six-year-old Dauphin was dressed as a girl, wearing a curly wig. Louis took on the role of a valet, with a plain brown coat, a wig covered by a round hat, and a green overcoat. As the hour approached midnight, Louis and Marie Antoinette left separately, to rendezvous at a waiting carriage, while the real governess brought the children. The Queen almost ran into Lafayette and his guard doing their nightly rounds, and in avoiding them she lost herself in the gardens, incurring a vital half-hour's delay.

Finally they were off, reaching the Porte Saint-Martin at 2 am. Marie Antoinette had insisted that they all should ride together, so their carriage was a lumbering six-seater dark-green *berline* with lemon-yellow wheels. Even though pulled by six horses, it could make no more than ten miles an hour.

Their goal was Montmédy, 194 miles away on the frontier of the Austrian

Netherlands, where royalist troops waited. From there the King could either establish a headquarters or, in the worst case, flee to foreign territory.

At first all went well, as they made their way to Claye, where they were joined by Marie Antoinette's maid and hairdresser, without whom the frivolous Queen had insisted she could not travel. They drove on eastward past Meaux and Châlons, but at mid-morning the carriage hit a stone post crossing a bridge, breaking the traces and knocking down the horses. More time was lost. In the meantime, when the escape was discovered in Paris, enraged crowds rioted and smashed shops, and Lafayette sent couriers in every direction with a proclamation warning that 'the enemies of the Revolution have seized the person of the King' and ordering all good citizens to 'return him to the bosom of the Assembly'.

At six that evening the royal entourage arrived at Pont de Sommevelle, where Louis hoped to find an escort of 40 hussars, but, after waiting two hours, the soldiers had left, threatened by a suspicious mob of peasants; the King and Queen had missed them by half an hour. But news of the flight had preceded the royal carriage, and the local postmaster, a former dragoon called Jean Baptiste Drouet, recognised the Queen.

Dismayed by the failure of his escort to turn up, Louis continued to Varennes, only 30 miles from the border. But Drouet had arrived there before him and had persuaded the local mayor to sound the alert. As the royal carriage reached the town's gate, a group of armed men barred its way, shouting, 'If you go a step further, we fire!' The great escape was over.

The next day at dawn the National Guard arrived to command them back to Paris. Reading Lafayette's order, Louis spoke quietly in despair: 'There is no longer a king in France.' They departed Varennes surrounded by an escort of 6,000 armed citizens and National Guardsmen, and by 25 June were back in the Tuileries, which they had escaped so full of hope only five days before.

Before Louis and Marie Antoinette's flight most revolutionaries hoped that the National Constituent Assembly would rule with the monarchy, but now came calls for its abolition. '*L'individu royal ne peut plus être roi*' ('The royal creature can no longer be king'), declared the firebrand Jacques Danton, and he joined Jean-Paul Marat in publishing a petition to replace the King with a new form of executive.

The monarchy survived for only fifteen more months, abolished by the Convention on 21 September 1792, and Louis himself survived until he was guillotined in January of the next year. Marie Antoinette followed him nine months later.

Also on this day

AD 451: **Roman general Aetius defeats Attila the Hun at the Battle of Châlons** * 1756: Over 140 British subjects are imprisoned in the Black Hole of Calcutta in India * 1837: William IV dies, bringing Victoria to the British throne * 1923: Mexican revolutionary leader Pancho Villa is assassinated

21 June

Work starts on Sir Christopher Wren's St Paul's

1675 Although St Paul's Cathedral in London has stood for over 300 years, the current Baroque masterpiece is probably the fifth church to stand on that site, the first dating from the year 604.

In September 1666, the Great Fire of London destroyed the enormous Gothic St Paul's, which was by then already over 400 years old. Luckily there lived in London at that time one of history's greatest architects, Christopher Wren.

Only 34, Wren had already been a member of a commission studying ways to repair the old cathedral when the fire reduced it to rubble. Within a week of the disaster, he submitted preliminary plans for rebuilding the city of London, including St Paul's, but work was not started until 21 June 1675, when the foundation stone of the current church was laid.

St Paul's took 33 years to complete, although it was opened to the public on 2 December 1697. When Sir Christopher Wren finally died at the ripe age of 90 in 1723, he was buried within the walls of his greatest achievement. Today, if you enter St Paul's and stand beneath the great dome, you will see spelled out in Latin on the floor Wren's own epitaph: '*Lector, si monumentum requiris, circumspice.*' ('Reader, if you seek his monument, look around you.')

Also on this day

1377: Edward III dies of a stroke * 1521: Pope Leo X excommunicates Martin Luther * **1633: Pope Urban VIII condemns Galileo for claiming that the Earth moves around the Sun** * 1652: English architect Inigo Jones dies * 1813: The Duke of Wellington routs the French at the Battle of Vittoria in Spain * 1905: French existentialist and poseur Jean-Paul Sartre is born in Paris

22 June

Americans land on Daiquiri Beach

1898 Today should be observed as D-Day, and a generous-sized Daiquiri cocktail hoisted to honour the US forces that landed this morning on an enemy beach, the vanguard of a great invasion. It wasn't at Normandy or Iwo Jima or Inchon. It was at a remote spot on the long southern coastline of Cuba, where elements of the army's V Corps went ashore at Daiquiri Beach, some eighteen miles east of Santiago.

This was amphibious warfare with a distinctly holiday air about it. From the deck of a troopship the correspondent Richard Harding Davis described the first wave going in:

'Soon the sea was dotted with rows of white boats filled with men bound about with white blanket rolls and with muskets at all angles, and as they rose and fell on the water and the newspaper yachts and transports crept in closer and closer, the scene was strangely suggestive of a boat race, and one almost waited for the starting gun.'

A preliminary naval bombardment had evidently driven away any Spanish troops who might have been around to contest the landing site, which was just as well, for even a few hundred well-motivated defenders could have inflicted a terrible slaughter on the V Corps and changed the course of the war.

During this first day of invasion, 6,000 infantry, accompanied by a few reporters, got ashore in a continuous stream of launches and barges. Horses and mules for the artillery and pack trains were simply shoved out of cargo ports to swim ashore. Later, when cavalry dispatched by General 'Fighting Joe' Wheeler, who had once commanded troops of the Confederacy, raced up a hill behind the beach and raised their regimental flag, a reporter recorded that the entire invasion force, afloat and ashore, began cheering 'and every steam whistle on the ocean for miles about shrieked and tooted and roared in a pandemonium of delight and pride and triumph'.

With the advent of evening, the troops began pitching their tents above the beach. In the words of one historian: 'They were spending their first night in the field of war, in the near presence of the enemy. Whether or not they would even spend another they did not know.' So began the first ground operation of the Spanish–American War.

They don't make invasions like that any more. But you can make a Daiquiri by mixing four parts rum to one of lime juice, sugar to taste, and plenty of ice. Shake well before serving.

Also on this day

1527: Niccolò Machiavelli dies outside Florence * 1535: Cardinal Fisher is beheaded on the orders of Henry VIII * 1699: French painter Jean Chardin is born * 1815: Napoleon abdicates, proclaiming his four-year-old son Emperor of the French * 1941: The German army invades Russia

23 June

Mutineers set Henry Hudson adrift

1611 Henry Hudson was one of England's greatest explorers, but his obsession to find a north-west passage through the Americas to the Orient proved to be his undoing.

Hudson first sailed to the Americas in 1607, but three consecutive attempts to find his way through to the East ended in failure. In the meantime, however, he explored much of the north-east of what is now the United States, ascending the river named after him as far as present-day Albany.

In 1610 Hudson mounted a fourth expedition, and this time he headed north. Passing between Labrador and Greenland, he reached Hudson Bay where, stymied by snow and ice, he was forced to winter. By June of the following year his wretched and starving crew were driven to mutiny when Hudson refused to sail for home. On 23 June the great explorer, his son and seven loyal companions were set adrift in the bay named after him, without food or water. They were never seen again.

Four of the mutinous crew were subsequently killed by Eskimos, but eight returned to England on Hudson's ship. Although they were arrested, none was punished because they were considered too valuable a resource of knowledge about the New World.

Also on this day

AD 79: Roman emperor Vespasian dies * **1314: Scottish king Robert the Bruce defeats the English at the Battle of Bannockburn** * 1757: Clive of India wins the Battle of Plassey to take control of Bengal

24 June

Two emperors and a king slug it out at Solferino

1859 When a combined Piedmontese-French army met the forces of imperial Austria at Solferino near Italy's Lake Garda today, the troops were commanded by two emperors and a king: Napoleon III of France, Franz Joseph of Austria and Victor Emmanuel, already King of Sardinia-Piedmont and soon to be the first king of a united Italy.

The battle was fought in almost unendurable heat, as some 270,000 men met to kill each other. In the end, the Piedmontese-French army prevailed, but the cost was frightful. Each side lost some 15,000 men killed or wounded, and some 8,000 Austrians were captured or went missing. Even the victorious Victor Emmanuel recoiled at the slaughter, aware of how near he had come to losing. 'Luck plays too great a role,' was his view of war after this battle.

In addition to being a major step towards Italian reunification, the Battle of Solferino had other important effects. Because of French demands after the battle, Nice and Savoy were stripped from the Austrians and awarded to the French. One other result of Solferino was less apparent at the time. Among the appalled stretcher-bearers was a Swiss named Henri Dunant. So shocked was he by the savagery and suffering that he first wrote a book describing the horrors of Solferino and then went on to found the Red Cross.

Also on this day
1340: Edward III defeats the French at the naval battle of Sluys, the first real battle of the Hundred Years War * **1348: Edward III establishes the Order of the Garter at Windsor** * 1509: Henry VIII is crowned at Westminster * 1519: Lucrezia Borgia dies in Ferrara * 1812: Napoleon and the *Grande Armée* cross the River Nieman into Russia * 1894: An Italian anarchist assassinates French president Sadi Carnot at Lyon * 1911: Motor racing legend Juan Manuel Fangio is born in Balcarce, Argentina

25 June

Custer's last stand

1876 George Armstrong Custer was a tall, rangy man with a hard narrow face, a high forehead, flaxen hair worn long, and a droopy old-cowpoke moustache. Few remember today that he was also a noted soldier. In the American Civil War he was the youngest general in the Union army, and at the war's close it was he who received the Confederate flag of truce and was present at the South's surrender at Appomattox.

By 1876 Custer was 37 years old and now, instead of Southerners, he was fighting a coalition of Indian tribes, including Sioux, Cheyenne and Arapaho. Leading the Indians was the great chief Sitting Bull.

On 17 June the combined Indian forces had defeated American troops in the Battle of the Rosebud in the Montana territory. Shortly after this victory Sitting Bull had driven himself into a trance performing the Sun Dance, after which he reported having seen a vision of soldiers falling to earth like grasshoppers from the sky, accurately predicting the victory that was to follow in a few days.

Meanwhile, Custer was leading the US 7th Cavalry when on 25 June he came upon the Indian encampment by a river called the Little Bighorn. Not realising the number of enemy he faced, he rashly divided his force of some 600 troopers into three groups and attacked.

Custer was personally leading about 225 soldiers as the battle started. Of more than 1,000 waiting Indians was a 26-year-old chief named White Bull. Later, White Bull told his story: 'When I rushed him, he threw his rifle at me without shooting. I dodged it. We grabbed each other and wrestled there in the dust and smoke [. . .] He tried to wrench my rifle from me. I lashed him across the face with my quirt [. . .] He let go [. . .] But he fought hard. He was desperate. He hit me with his fists on my jaw and shoulders, then grabbed my long braids with both hands, pulled my face close and tried to bite my nose off [. . .] Finally I broke free. He drew his pistol. I wrenched it out of his hand and struck him with it three or four times on the head, knocked him over, shot him in the head, and fired at his heart.'

The general and his force were killed to the last man at Little Bighorn in a battle known as Custer's Last Stand. It was a fitting end for the man who coined the odious phrase: 'The only good Indians I ever saw were dead.'

After his victory at Little Bighorn, Sitting Bull continued to resist American attempts to capture him until 1883, when, his followers devastated by hunger and disease, he finally surrendered and was sent to the Standing Rock Agency to live. Two years later, however, he was given his freedom to join Buffalo Bill's Wild West show. In 1890, amid fears of further Indian uprisings, American troops were sent to arrest him but killed him while his warriors were trying to save him.

Also on this day

1279 BC: Pharaoh Ramses II becomes sole ruler of Egypt to start the longest reign in Egyptian history * 1646: The surrender of Oxford to the Roundheads signifies the end of the English Civil War * 1795: Tsar Nicholas I is born * 1950: At four o'clock on a Sunday morning, North Korea attacks South Korea

26 June

Did Peter the Great beat his son to death?

1718 The Tsarevich Aleksey was a weak and nervous young man of 28 who was terrified of his father Peter the Great – with good reason. For Aleksey wanted only peace and tranquillity, even offering to retreat to a monastery to get it, but Peter saw him as the inevitable inheritor of his realm, an inheritor who might undo the Westernisation that he had spent his life accomplishing.

So great was Aleksey's fear that eventually he fled in disguise, reappearing only in Vienna, begging the Austrian emperor for sanctuary. But Peter sent emissaries to Aleksey, promising a full pardon should he return to St Petersburg. Duped by his father's apparent forgiveness, Aleksey headed back to Russia.

Once back in Peter's control, Aleksey was told he would have to renounce the rights to the Russian throne and denounce those who had helped him escape. Although he accepted these harsh terms, still his father was not satisfied. He arrested and tortured Aleksey's friends and then turned to Aleksey himself.

Imprisoned and tortured, Aleksey received over 40 lashes and was reduced to gibbering fright, admitting every conspiracy his father could conceive of. He was then forced to admit all his supposed crimes before the Russian Senate before being speedily sentenced to death by a special court acting under orders from Peter.

Before the sentence could be carried out Aleksey died in prison on this day, possibly from the aftershock of torture or suffocated by the prison warders. Some historians believe his own father may have beaten him to death.

Whether Peter actually performed the deed is moot. He was certainly guilty of the murder of his son, which puts him in a class with his predecessor Ivan the Terrible, who killed his son with a poker.

Also on this day

AD 363: Roman emperor Julian the Apostate is killed in battle in Persia * **1284: 130 children disappear from the German town of Hameln, the foundation of the fairytale *The Pied Piper*** * 1541: Spanish conquistador Francisco Pizarro is assassinated in Lima * 1830: George IV dies at Windsor

27 June

Captain Joshua Slocum sails around the world alone

1898 In the midnight darkness a small vessel sailing close to shore made her cautious way towards the harbour of Newport, Rhode Island, recently mined against the possibility of a Spanish naval attack. 'It was close work,' wrote her captain, 'but it was safe enough so long as she hugged the rocks, and not the mines.' From a guard ship at the harbour entrance came a challenge. 'I threw up a light at once and heard the hail "*Spray*, ahoy." It was the voice of a friend, and I knew that a friend would not fire on the *Spray*. I eased off the mainsheet now, and the *Spray* swung off for the beacon-lights of the inner harbor. At last she reached port in safety, and there at 1 am on 28 June 1898, cast anchor . . . '

So ended one of the great sea voyages of history. Captain Joshua Slocum, aboard his 37-foot sloop the *Spray*, became the first man to sail around the world alone – a challenge he had undertaken simply because 'I was greatly amused [. . .] by the flat assertions of an expert that it could not be done.' Slocum cruised more than 46,000 miles in the course of three years, two months and two days, during which time his progress was closely reported to the world by newspapers in his ports of call and by ships he encountered at sea.

The *Spray*, with a single mast and a net tonnage of 9 tons, was 'an antiquated sloop which neighbors declared had been built in the year 1'. Slocum redesigned and rebuilt her for the long voyage at a cost of $553.62 for materials and thirteen months of his own labour. When the work was done, he was at once designer, owner, captain and ship's company. 'There never was a crew so well agreed,' he wrote.

Slocum, an experienced ocean mariner, began his great adventure intending to sail eastward from Boston, Massachusetts, across the Atlantic Ocean, into the Mediterranean and through the Suez Canal. But after a narrow escape from Moroccan pirates off Gibraltar, he reversed course, sailing back across the Atlantic, down the east coast of South America, and through the Magellan Strait. His first port of call in the Pacific was Juan Fernandez, Robinson Crusoe's island. Reaching Samoa, he was greeted by the widow of Robert Louis

Stevenson. At one stage in his long passage across the Pacific, he went 72 days without touching land.

Continuing westward through the Indian Ocean, he reached Cape Town, where the *Spray* spent three months refitting in dry dock. Slocum journeyed upcountry to Pretoria, where he was introduced to Paul Kruger, President of the Boer Republic of Transvaal, as someone who was 'sailing around the world'. The phrase offended Kruger, who knew from his Bible that the world was flat. 'You don't mean "*round* the world"', growled the old president. 'It is impossible. You mean *in* the world.' No one argued the point.

Leaving South Africa in March 1898, Slocum sailed north-west on the last leg of his voyage. Only when he reached the Caribbean did he learn that the United States was at war with Spain. His famous account of the voyage, *Sailing Around the World Alone,* was published in 1900 and became a best-seller through many editions. Slocum was as good a writer as he was a sailor, combining a natural style with a vivid eye for detail. Here is how he described the very beginning of his voyage leaving Boston harbour:

'The day was perfect, the sunlight clear and strong. Every particle of water thrown into the air became a gem, and the *Spray,* making good her name as she dashed ahead, snatched necklace after necklace from the sea and as often threw them away. We have all seen miniature rainbows about a ship's prow, but the *Spray* flung out a bow of her own that day, such as I had never seen before. Her good angel had embarked on the voyage; I so read it in the sea.'

Also on this day

1472: Jeanne Hachette saves Beauvais from the attacking army of Charles the Bold, Duke of Burgundy ∗ 1571: Italian painter and art historian Giorgio Vasari dies ∗ 1787: British historian Edward Gibbon completes *The History of the Decline and Fall of the Roman Empire*

28 June

Catherine the Great's coup in St Petersburg

1762 Tsar Peter III suffered three great misfortunes. First, he was a grandson of Peter the Great and thus heir to the throne of Russia. Second, he married a hard-headed German named Sophia, who changed her name to Catherine. Third, he was a fool.

Peter had become Tsar at the start of 1762 with the death of his aunt, Empress Elizabeth. He had married Sophia/Catherine as a teenager in 1744 but had never truly lived with her as man and wife. Physically he was short, thin and frail, but his greatest weakness was his character. He idolised Frederick the Great of Prussia and generally held his Russian courtiers in contempt. He paid scant attention to Catherine but doted on his mistress. There were rumours he would replace Catherine – or worse.

On the morning of 28 June, the 33-year-old Catherine and her lover Grigory Orlov staged one of history's most successful coups. At dawn Catherine was brought to the capital of St Petersburg, while her husband was away on military manoeuvres. Proclaimed Empress by Orlov and other powerful nobles, she almost instantly won over the army, the Church and the rest of the nobility. All were delighted to rid themselves of the weak and irresolute Peter. The coup was so fast and so complete that Peter could mount no resistance. Not a shot was fired. As Frederick the Great said of Peter: 'He let himself be driven from the throne as a child is sent to bed.'

The coup was all but bloodless – except for Peter himself, who was murdered in prison a week later. His reign had lasted 124 days. Catherine's would last 34 years. She is known to history as Catherine the Great.

Also on this day

1491: Henry VIII is born in Greenwich Palace * 1519: Charles I of Spain is elected Holy Roman Emperor as Charles V * 1712: French philosopher Jean-Jacques Rousseau is born * 1836: America's fourth president James Madison dies * 1838: Queen Victoria is crowned * **1914: Serbian revolutionary Gavrilo Princip shoots Archduke Franz Ferdinand and his wife Sophie at Sarajevo to trigger the First World War**

29 June

Birth of a pilot, an author, a patriot

1900 This is the birthday of Antoine de Saint-Exupéry, born in Lyon, France, to a well-connected family of the provincial nobility. He is remembered today chiefly as the author and illustrator of one of the great classics of children's literature, *The Little Prince,* written in New York City, where he had fled after the fall of France, and published in 1943.

American reviewers were surprised to see this gentle fairy tale issue from the pen of a man best known as a legendary aeroplane pilot, a Gallic Lindbergh, and a war hero for his recent combat service with the French air force. In the 1920s Saint-Exupéry had flown the mail routes for the airline company Aéropostale, first in North Africa, later in Latin America, where he pioneered the Buenos Aires–Patagonia run. Based on his experiences, he had written two highly acclaimed novels about flying that became international best-sellers. The second, *Vol de Nuit* (*Night Flight*), for which some critics likened his style to Joseph Conrad's, won the Prix Femina, became a movie, and inspired the French perfume company Guerlain to name a new fragrance Vol de Nuit.

By the time Aéropostale went out of business in 1931, Saint-Ex, as he had become known, was an established celebrity, an *homme de lettres,* and a symbol of French prowess in aviation. For a while, he worked as a test pilot for an aeroplane manufacturer; later, he took up public relations for the newly founded Air France. *France-Soir* sent him to Spain to write a series of articles on the Civil War. In 1935, taking up the challenge to break the speed record for the Paris-to-Saigon run, he crashed on the first leg of the trip and spent three days in the Libyan desert. On a visit to the United States in 1938, sponsored by the French air ministry, he crashed once again, this time in Guatemala while attempting a New York-to-Argentina run.

War was in the air when *Terre des Hommes* (*Wind, Sand and Stars*)*,* a collection of his writings, was published in Paris in 1939. A review in *Les Nouvelles Littéraires* said: 'The name "Saint-Exupéry" is one of the few that duchesses and café waiters pronounce with equal admiration.' Later that year, though over-age and still suffering from the effects of the Guatemala crash, he wangled a captain's commission in the French air force. When the German army invaded France in May 1940, he flew reconnaissance missions over enemy lines. On the day France fell, he escaped to Algeria, flying a plane crammed with passengers and military spare parts. In time, he managed to get to New York, where he spent the next two years and wrote *Flight to Arras* (*Pilot de Guerre*), an account of his wartime experiences.

Saint-Exupéry wrote *The Little Prince* in the summer and fall of 1942, as a distraction from problems of health and the boredom of exile. But by the time the book was published the following spring, he had left New York for North Africa, determined to take another whack at the Germans. For the next year, he flew P-38s for his old outfit, the 2/33rd Reconnaissance Group, now reactivated to fight with the Free French. For his service, Saint-Exupéry was scheduled to receive a Croix de Guerre. Unfortunately, the award was posthumous, for on 31 July 1944, he failed to return from a mission over southern France. Almost 60 years later, in 2003, a salvage team operating in the waters off Marseilles located the wreckage of a P-38, which was identified as his.

Also on this day

1577: Peter Paul Rubens is born * **1613: In London, Shakespeare's Globe Theatre burns down** * 1767: The British Parliament approves the Townshend Acts, imposing taxes and duties on American colonies * 1861: English poetess Elizabeth Barrett Browning dies in Florence * 1855: Trade unions are legalised in the United Kingdom

30 June

King Henri II ignores his wife's astrologer

1559 Queen Catherine begged her husband not to joust. In 1546 a seer named Gauric had warned her that the King 'should avoid all single combat around his forty-first year'. Three years later, her pet astrologer, Cosimo Ruggieri, had been more specific, predicting that the King would die in a duel, a prophecy repeated only a week before. And now the King had just turned 40.

But Henri II of France had never taken much notice of his wife's superstitions (or indeed of his wife). After all, she had been born in Italy with the name of Medici. So he ignored her pleas not to joust during the great 'Tournament of Queens' to be held at the Palais des Tournelles in Paris's Place des Vosges.

The tournament took place on a sunny Friday, 30 June. All had gone well, and the knights and spectators were on the point of leaving when Henri sent word to Catherine that he would try one more bout 'for the love of her' (in contrast to his earlier bouts, possibly fought for the love of his mistress Diane de Poitiers, who was watching with the Queen).

As Henri prepared for the final clash a boy in the crowd called out, 'Sire, do not tilt!' Feeling the tension, another knight offered to joust for the King. But Henri insisted and prepared to charge his opponent, Gabriel de Lorges, comte de Montgoméry, captain of his Scottish Guard.

The trumpet sounded and the armoured figures met with a mighty crash. The impact snapped Montgoméry's lance, and the sharp and shattered stump smashed into the King's face, penetrating his helmet and driving a splinter in over his right eye, coming out by his ear.

Rushed to bed, Henri endured the tortures of 16th-century medicine, as the splinter was painfully withdrawn. For ten days he struggled for life, repeatedly asking for his mistress Diane, but Queen Catherine barred her from the palace. Then, on 10 July, Henri died. Catherine's foreboding had been right.

Also on this day

1520: Spanish conquistadors murder Aztec chief Montezuma * 1934: Adolf Hitler orders the purge of his own party in the 'Night of the Long Knives' * **1908: In central Siberia the greatest cosmic explosion in the history of civilisation, equal to 1,000 Hiroshima bombs, flattens half a million acres of forest** * 1936: Margaret Mitchell's novel *Gone With the Wind* is published

1 July

Slaughter on the Somme

1916 At 7 am, as the sun pierced the morning mists, 100,000 British soldiers climbed out of their trenches and marched into no man's land, confident they would fulfil their commander-in-chief's plan. Before nightfall, God willing and with General Haig in command, they should have broken a large hole in the strongest, deepest and best-defended point in the entire German line.

But for these British soldiers along the Somme this day, most of them recent volunteers, it was not meant to be. Two years of war had given abundant proof that, in the absence of surprise, troops advancing against barbed wire, entrenchments in depth, machine guns and artillery had no chance of success. New technology was waiting in the wings in the form of the tank, but it was not ready to make its début. As for surprise, there could have been none after a week's preliminary artillery bombardment, which in any case failed to either cut the German barbed wire or destroy their front-line dugouts.

By nightfall, the British troops had advanced two miles but 20,000 of them lay dead, with another 40,000 wounded or captured, the greatest one-day loss ever sustained by an army in history. This was only the first day of an offensive that would last until mid-November. When it ended, both sides exhausted, the British had gained about seven miles. Tanks did make a brief appearance on 15 September and, before breaking down, achieved a spectacular local gain of some 3,500 yards – soon wiped out by strong German counter-attacks.

The rationale for the Somme offensive was to prevent the Germans from shifting troop strength away to fight in other sectors of the front. But Winston Churchill doubted that the strategic contribution of the battle was worth the cost: 'We could have held the Germans on our front just as well by threatening an offensive as by making one,' he advised the Cabinet on 1 August.

Total casualties for the battle were 420,000 for the British, 195,000 for the French, who fought alongside them south of the Somme, and a shocking 650,000 for the Germans, bled white by costly counter-attacks to regain lost ground.

Also on this day

AD 69: Vespasian becomes Roman emperor * 1646: German mathematician and philosopher Gottfried Leibniz is born in Leipzig * **1898: Teddy Roosevelt's Rough Riders storm San Juan Hill during the Spanish-American War**

> Events written in **boldface** are covered in full in
> *365: Great Stories from History for Every Day of the Year*,
> the first volume in this series.

2 July

'Strangulatus pro republica': *the murder of a president*

1881 Today America's twentieth president, James Garfield, became the second to be mortally wounded by an assassin.

Garfield had been a brave soldier, attaining the rank of major general and fighting at Shiloh and Chickamauga during the American Civil War. He was first elected to the House of Representatives at the end of 1863, resigning from the army to take his seat. He later became a senator and in March 1881 became President of the United States.

On 2 July, only four months after taking office, Garfield was waiting for a train in the Baltimore and Potomac railway station in Washington, when a disgruntled lawyer named Charles Guiteau shot him twice from behind at point-blank range. Guiteau was a religious fanatic who claimed that killing the president was an act of high morality that would 'save the Republic'. In reality it seems he was incensed because he had been refused the consular post he wanted.

Wounded in the arm and back, Garfield lay for weeks in the White House. By today's medical standards, his wounds would have been serious but not fatal, but in 1881 even surgeons had little idea of hygiene and Garfield contracted blood poisoning while doctors probed with unsterilised instruments.

By mid-July the President was clearly dying. Too weak to speak, he asked for pen and paper and scribbled, '*Strangulatus pro republica*' ('Tortured for the republic'). He never spoke or wrote again.

In early autumn Garfield was moved to the New Jersey seaside, to be with his family, but he died on 19 September, just two months before his 50th birthday. On 30 June the following year his assassin, Charles Guiteau, was hanged for the murder, his skeleton going to the Army Medical Museum.

Garfield was one of four American presidents who have been assassinated. The others were Abraham Lincoln in 1865, William McKinley in 1901 and John Kennedy in 1963. All were shot.

Also on this day

1566: Fortune-teller Nostradamus dies in Salon de Provence * 1644: The Roundheads defeat Prince Rupert and the Cavaliers at Marston Moor in the English Civil War * 1778: French philosopher Jean-Jacques Rousseau dies * 1850: British prime minister Robert Peel dies after being thrown from a horse * **1937: American aviatrix Amelia Earhart disappears in flight over the Pacific while trying to fly around the world** * 1961: American writer and Nobel Prize winner Ernest Hemingway blows his brains out with a shotgun in Ketchum, Idaho

3 July

Churchill wipes out the French fleet

1940 At 5.46 this evening, after a long day of unsuccessful negotiations, British Vice Admiral James Somerville gave his ships the order to open fire. Within ten minutes most of the powerful fleet anchored at the Algerian port of Mers-el-Kebir lay in ruins: one battleship blown up, two more beached, 1,250 sailors dead. Only a single battleship and a few destroyers managed to escape. What the British destroyed this day, however, was not the fleet of an enemy but that of their close ally, France.

Barely a month after Dunkirk, and facing the prospect of imminent German invasion, Great Britain had to ensure that the fleet of recently defeated France would never fall into the hands of their common enemies, Germany and Italy. Despite assurances from Marshal Pétain, who had led his nation into capitulation to Germany, Prime Minister Winston Churchill ordered his fleet to issue this ultimatum to the French admiral at Mers-el-Kebir: sail your ships to safety, in either England or the West Indies, or scuttle them. Or Great Britain will sink them for you. Elsewhere, British boarding parties seized French Navy vessels in Portsmouth and Plymouth and put their crews ashore. In Alexandria the French squadron disarmed itself under the orders of a British admiral.

Outraged by the humiliating loss of her fleet, France – now reduced by its armistice with Germany to the rump and puppet state of Vichy – broke off relations with Great Britain. Marshal Pétain complained to President Roosevelt of 'British aggression'. Many Frenchmen around the world now found themselves hating their former ally as much as they detested their conquerors. For General Charles de Gaulle, in London as the leader of the Free French, Mers-el-Kebir created a special problem. In the aftermath of Dunkirk there were thousands of French soldiers and sailors in England. From among these (and from among other Frenchmen in France's African colonies) he had been endeavouring to recruit a military force that would carry on France's fight alongside Great Britain. But after Mers-el-Kebir, could de Gaulle – could any Frenchman – remain on the side of his country's latest attacker?

De Gaulle was disheartened by the 'lamentable event', all the more so that the British treated it as a victory. Nevertheless, a few nights later, when he spoke to his countrymen over BBC radio, he told them this: 'Come what may, even if for a time one of them is bowed under the yoke of the common foe, our two peoples – our two *great* peoples – are still linked together. Either they will both succumb or they will triumph side by side.'

Vichy France sentenced de Gaulle to death for his 'refusals to obey orders in the presence of the enemy and inciting members of the armed forces to disobedience'. In the end, of course, it was a liberated France that sentenced Marshal Pétain to death for his role as a collaborator with Nazi Germany: a sentence commuted to life imprisonment by General de Gaulle.

Also on this day
1423: French King Louis XI (the Universal Spider) is born * 1853: Russia invades Moldavia to start the Crimean War * 1863: The North defeats the Confederates at Gettysburg, the bloodiest battle of the American Civil War * 1866: Venice becomes part of a united Kingdom of Italy

4 July

Saladin triumphs at the Horns of Hattin

1187 The two large hills known as the Horns of Hattin lie just a few miles west of the Sea of Galilee in northern Palestine, and it was there that, today, that most famous Saracen, Saladin, totally destroyed the power of the Christian Kingdom of Jerusalem.

Like all the Saracen leaders, Saladin was a Kurdish Turk. He had once served as a young officer under Nur ed-Din, the ruler of Syria, and on Nur ed-Din's death in 1174, Saladin became the leader of Muslim orthodoxy in the Middle East.

During the evening of 3 July 1187 Saladin's great army completely surrounded the smaller Christian force under the command of the King of Jerusalem, Guy de Lusignan. An eyewitness tells the tale: 'As soon as they [the Christian army] were encamped, Saladin ordered all his men to collect brushwood, dry grass, stubble and anything else with which they could light fires and make barriers, which he had made all round the Christians. They soon did this and the fires burned vigorously and the smoke from the fires was great; and this, together with the heat of the sun above them caused them discomfort and great harm. Saladin had commanded caravans of camels loaded with water from the Sea of Tiberias to be brought up and had water pots placed near the camp. The water pots were then emptied in view of the Christians so that they should have still greater anguish through thirst and their mounts too . . . When the fires were lit and the smoke was great, the Saracens surrounded the host and shot their darts through the smoke and so wounded and killed men and horses.'

By the next morning the Christians were dying and desperate. King Guy had no choice but to attack the larger enemy force. A division of knights 'charged at a large squadron of Saracens. The Saracens parted and made a way through and let them pass; then, when they were in the middle of them, they surrounded them. Only ten or twelve knights [. . .] escaped them [. . .] After this division had been defeated, the anger of God was so great against the Christian host, because of their sins, that Saladin vanquished them quickly; between the hours of tierce and nones [9 am and 3 pm] he had won almost all the field.'

Most of the European nobles who survived, including the King of Jerusalem, were captured and held to ransom. The Christian army was totally destroyed and 15,000 foot soldiers were sold into slavery. The Knights Templar and Hospitaller who were taken prisoner were given a grim choice: convert to Islam or face execution. Some 230 Templars and a smaller number of Hospitallers refused and were beheaded.

Three months later Jerusalem fell to Saladin after 88 years of Christian rule. When the news reached Europe, the Christian world went into shock. According to contemporary testimony: 'Pope Urban [III] who was at Ferrara died of grief when he heard the news. After him was Gregory VIII, who was of saintly life and only held the see for two months before he died and went to God.'

Also on this day

1190: English King Richard the Lionheart and French King Philip Augustus leave together on the Third Crusade * 1776: American leaders sign the Declaration of Independence, creating the United States and freeing its citizens from the yoke of British tyranny * 1807: Italian revolutionary Giuseppe Garibaldi is born in Nice * **1826: Former American Presidents John Adams and Thomas Jefferson die on the 50th anniversary of the signing of the Declaration of Independence**

5 July

The bikini is revealed

1946 Louis Réard had a problem. A former engineer with Renault, he had now turned to fashion and had drawn up plans for a new bathing suit that he thought would be just right for the liberated young women of post-war France. His design was a quantum leap from the Esther Williams one-piece that was the standard of the day: Réard had used a mere 30 square inches of fabric to provide a flimsy brassiere and two triangles of cloth held together by two strings. But just as he was preparing to go to market, a swimsuit designer from Cannes launched an almost identical item, christening it the Atome (French for atom, the smallest particle then known) and started a skywriting campaign trumpeting the Atome as 'the world's smallest bathing suit'. Clearly Réard was in danger of being left behind in his efforts to clothe (or, rather, unclothe) the women on France's beaches.

But then, on 1 July, four days before Réard was to unveil his new bathing suit in Paris, the United States dropped a 20-kiloton atomic bomb on the evacuated island of Bikini in the central Pacific, in its first peacetime atomic testing programme. Réard had found his inspiration and labelled his own swimsuit the bikini, a name with the not so subtle suggestion that it would hit the beach with explosive force. He immediately drew up his own advertising, calling it 'smaller than the world's smallest bathing suit'. He maintained that 'it's not a bikini unless it can be pulled through a wedding ring'.

Now Réard had the right product with the right name, but he ran into another problem when preparing for today's introductory show at the Piscine Molitor, a well-known Paris swimming pool – he couldn't find a model who would wear something so scandalously small on the catwalk. He solved it by hiring Micheline Bernardini, a nude dancer from the Casino de Paris. When newspaper coverage hit the streets, she received almost 50,000 letters.

The bikini instantly exploded across Europe and North America, while the Atome disappeared in the smoke. Although France took the new style in stride, it detonated high indignation in nations with sterner moral codes, which banned it from their beaches. In Franco's puritan Spain, daring young ladies who wore it were arrested by the Guardia Civil, while Americans (women, that is) were shocked, one women's magazine commenting that: 'It is hardly necessary to waste words over the so-called bikini, since it is inconceivable that any girl with tact and decency would ever wear such a thing.'

Today, of course, the bikini is de rigueur on beaches around the world. One wag has defined it: 'bikini: from the Latin *bi*, meaning "two" and *kini*, meaning "square inches of Lycra"', which in turn has spawned 'monokini' for the even briefer bottom-half-only version (the English tabloids instantly and predictably described the monokini as 'even more titillating'). But perhaps the bawdiest variety is just two Band-Aids and a cork.

Also on this day

1809: The first day of the Battle of Wagram, Napoleon's last major victory * 1810: American showman P.T. Barnum ('There's a sucker born every minute.') is born in Bethel, Connecticut * 1853: British empire builder Cecil Rhodes is born at Bishop's Stortford, Hertfordshire * 1943: 3,300 Russian tanks hold off 2,700 German tanks at the Battle of Kursk, the greatest tank battle in history * 1950: American forces engage the North Koreans for the first time at Osan, South Korea

6 July

The first Plantagenet king dies at Chinon

1189 The River Vienne runs just south of the Loire and on its north bank stand the grey and forbidding remains of the fortress of Chinon. No Renaissance jewel box this château, but 400 yards of impregnable defences from the Middle Ages, dominating the river below it. Although the site has been fortified since Roman times, the oldest part of the fortress yet standing is the Fort St Georges, built by that great English King, Henry II, who died there on this day over 800 years ago.

When Henry retreated to Chinon for the last time, he was an old man by the standards of the day (he was 56) and had just been humiliated by the young French King, Philip Augustus, who was allied with Henry's own son, Richard the Lionheart. Sick in body and spirit, Henry had to be carried to the fortress in a litter, and there he learned that among his enemies in league with the French was also his youngest son, the treacherous John.

Lying on a rude bed, Henry turned to face the wall. 'Shame, shame,' he muttered, 'shame on a conquered king.'

So died Henry, the king who had ruled England and virtually the whole of western France for 35 years and who had founded the Plantagenet dynasty, which was to last 332 years – longer than any other English dynasty before or since.

Also on this day

1415: In Konstantz, Czech religious reformer Jan Hus is burned at the stake for heresy * **1535: Sir Thomas More is beheaded for treason** * 1685: The army of James II defeats the rebel Duke of Monmouth at Sedgemoor in the last land battle ever fought on English soil

7 July

A tsar is strangled in his cell

1762 Only nine days earlier, Catherine the Great of Russia had orchestrated a bloodless *coup d'état* with the help of her lover, Grigory Orlov, to become Empress of Russia. Her hapless husband, Tsar Peter III, was sent under guard to a fortress prison at Ropsha, comforted only by his servants and his pet dog.

But Peter, although hopeless as a ruler, was deadly dangerous as a prisoner, an eternal threat to the usurper Catherine. So Orlov's brother Aleksei was sent to Ropsha.

Aleksei and two soldiers under his command entered the bedroom where Peter was held. The soldiers seized the Tsar and tried to smother him between two feather mattresses, but, although frail and small, the desperate Peter somehow threw them off and stood at bay, exhausted, in a corner of the room. Aleksei then threw himself on the royal prisoner and strangled him with his own huge hands.

The two soldiers who had been unable to smother Peter died the same day: not for their failure but to ensure secrecy of the deed. Both had been secretly poisoned just before they were ordered to execute the Tsar.

Catherine always claimed that she had no foreknowledge of this attack, but her plea of innocence, like that of Henry II about the murder of Thomas Becket, is disingenuous – the murder an expression of her will, without a direct order. She publicly attributed the death to 'haemorrhoidal colic', clearly a fabrication that was believed by almost no one.

Peter III has the distinction of being the first Russian tsar to be murdered – but not the last. Four more were to be assassinated, including his own son Paul I 39 years later.

Also on this day
1307: Edward I of England dies at Burgh by Sands, near Carlisle * 1860: Austrian composer Gustav Mahler is born in Kaliste, Czechoslovakia * 1887: Russian painter Marc Chagall is born in Vitebsk, Belorussia * **1937: A Japanese soldier is shot dead near Beijing, the first shot of the Second World War**

8 July

Peter the Great crushes the Swedes at Poltava

1709 This day brought mixed fortunes for Russia's Peter the Great. In 1695, when he was 23, Peter experienced his first real battle – and lost – against the Turks at Azov. In 1709 he was 37 and at war again, this time against one of the great soldier-kings of history, Charles XII of Sweden.

Charles had inherited Sweden's throne when he was just fifteen and ruled as an absolute monarch. By the time he was 27 in 1709 he had transformed Sweden into a great European power through a series of wars against Poland, Russia and various German states, which came to be known as the Great Northern War.

On 8 July 1709, Charles's small army of only 17,000 men attacked a Russian fortified camp under Peter's command at Poltava in the Ukraine. The Swedes had two distinct disadvantages. First, their army – already tired and battle-weary – was massively outnumbered by Peter's 80,000 troops and, second, Charles himself could not personally lead his army, as was his custom, because he had earlier sustained a wound in the left foot and had to be carried on a litter between two horses.

The Russians gave way before the initial Swedish assault, then launched 40,000 men in a devastating counter-attack that obliterated the Swedes. The shattered Swedish survivors retreated southwards and finally capitulated at the River Dnjestr, outside the village of Perevolotjna, four days later. Charles himself managed to escape with about 1,500 of his soldiers and took refuge in Turkey, where he was obliged to remain for the next six years.

Peter the Great's victory marked the start of Sweden's decline from being the dominant nation of northern Europe to the lesser nation that it has remained ever since. Poltava also marked Russia's ascendancy, one that it has never relinquished.

Also on this day
1521: Ferdinand von Habsburg marries Anne of Hungary, leading to the incorporation of Hungary into the Austrian Empire * 1606: The Pont-Neuf is finished in Paris * 1822: English poet Percy Bysshe Shelley drowns off Leghorn, Italy * 1839: American oil tycoon John D. Rockefeller is born * **1918: Ernest Hemingway is wounded by artillery fire on the Italian front, inspiring his novel *For Whom the***

Bell Tolls * 1943: After having been tortured by the Gestapo, French Resistance hero Jean Moulin dies in a train taking him to Germany

9 July

President Zach Taylor dies in office

1850 In 1849 Zachary Taylor became the first career soldier to be elected President of the United States. At 64, he had spent 40 years in the army fighting Indians and Mexicans, earning the nickname of 'Old Rough and Ready' for his informal ways and dishevelled appearance. Born in Virginia, he was the last American president to own slaves (he had about 100 of them) and was so apolitical that he had never in his life cast a vote before being elected.

Taylor battled the British in the War of 1812 and the Indians in the Black Hawk and Seminole Wars. But the conflict that propelled him to the presidency was the Mexican War, caused by the United States' annexation of Texas from Mexico.

Sent by President James Polk to disputed territory north of the Rio Grande, Taylor fought in the first battle of that war in April of 1846, a minor skirmish brought on by a Mexican attack before war had even been declared. But what made him a national hero was his great victory at Buena Vista in 1847. There he led a force of only 5,000 men to a stunning triumph over the Mexican dictator Santa Anna's army of over 20,000. (One of Taylor's wounded that day was Jefferson Davis, who would later marry Taylor's daughter and become president of the Confederacy.)

Scenting a chance of victory in the 1848 presidential elections, the American Whig party – a motley collection of Southerners, arch-conservatives and states-righters – persuaded Taylor to run as their candidate. Fortunately for him, incumbent president Polk was too ill to contest the election and Taylor easily defeated the lacklustre Democratic nominee, Lewis Cass, thus becoming America's twelfth president – and the seventh from Virginia.

Taylor took office in March of 1849, but he had little time to make his mark. On 4 July 1850 he attended Independence Day celebrations at the Washington Monument on a blisteringly hot day. In an effort to cool off he ate a large quantity of fruit, some of it unsanitary. By the end of the day he was ill with dysentery and five days later he was dead, after only sixteen months as president. Towards the end he realised his illness was fatal, commenting: 'I am about to die, I expect the summons soon.' His last recorded words were: 'I regret nothing, but I am sorry to leave my friends.'

Taylor was the second of seven American presidents to die in office and the second of only three to die of natural causes. The other four were assassinated.

10 July

The Battle of Britain

1940 On this morning 70 German bombers with fighter escorts took off from airfields in France and Belgium to attack a convoy in the English Channel. So began the contest of air forces known as the Battle of Britain. Hitler and his air force commander, Reichsmarschall Hermann Göring, thought it would be a quick and easy knockout punch: four days to destroy the Royal Air Force and then on to Act Two, Operation Sea Lion, the invasion of Great Britain. Invasion barges were being collected in the coastal ports of France and the Low Countries.

Indeed, the Germans had good reasons to be optimistic, for in the last ten months the Wehrmacht had conquered Poland, Denmark, Norway, Holland, Belgium and France. Only a month before, at Dunkirk, it had kicked the British army out of Europe. As for the Luftwaffe itself, while the toll on its resources from the French campaign had been heavy, it was well blooded, its morale was high and in fighter aircraft it outnumbered the RAF.

In this analysis, however, there were some factors the German high command did not – perhaps at the time could not – take into account. One was that the Luftwaffe's successes had been gained in support of ground operations and it had never carried out a strategic air campaign. Then there was the matter of British technology: outnumbered as it might be in planes and pilots, the RAF had developed a radar-based air defence system far more comprehensive than anything the Luftwaffe had ever encountered. Finally, there was the quality of the pilots of RAF Fighter Command, who would be scrambling in their Spitfires and Hurricanes to meet the invaders.

The German offensive began with daylight bomber attacks on coastal targets, such as ports, convoys and aircraft factories. The object was to lure the RAF fighters out over the Channel where German fighters could shoot them down in sufficient numbers to establish command of the air. When, in early August, it became clear that this strategy was not working, Göring gave new targeting orders: fly further inland to hit RAF airfields, radar stations, control centres and depots. This second phase, a battle of attrition fought between the two air forces at an absolutely furious pace, came near at times to putting the RAF out of business.

German losses, however, were also very heavy. In early September, just when it appeared that the Luftwaffe, if it persisted, might be close to achieving air superiority, Hitler gave orders to switch the main effort from airfields and radar stations to the city of London, as a quicker way of bringing the British to their knees. The destruction and loss of life from these city raids was frightful, but British morale did not crumble. Moreover, the new orders simplified Fighter Command's task by giving it a chance to concentrate its forces in the defence of the new German objective. When, on 15 September, a large German raid over London lost 56 aircraft, it was apparent that the RAF was still very much in business. There would be no knockout punch. Luftwaffe losses began to increase. By the end of the month it switched from daylight to night raids. On 12 October Operation Sea Lion, already postponed several times, was cancelled. Overall losses by the end of October were 1,733 German planes shot down against 915 British.

As the year drew to a close it became clear the battle was won. The invasion barges were put away. Hitler, defeated for the first time, turned his gaze eastward. And Churchill, addressing the House of Commons, said of RAF Fighter Command: 'Never, in the field of human conflict, was so much owed by so many to so few.'

Also on this day

AD 138: Roman Emperor Hadrian dies at Baiae (today's Baia) near Naples * **1099: Spanish national hero El Cid dies in Valencia, but his corpse leads his army to victory** * 1509: Founder of Calvinism John Calvin (Jean Cauvin) is born in Noyon * 1830: French painter Camille Pissarro is born in St Thomas, Danish West Indies * 1871: French novelist Marcel Proust is born in Auteuil

11 July

The Battle of the Golden Spurs

1302 The people of Flanders were in revolt against their overlord, King Philip the Fair of France. To teach the Flemings a lesson, Philip dispatched 2,000 armoured knights plus a large troop of infantry under the command of his uncle, Robert d'Artois, the greatest warrior in France.

Desperate, the Flemings formed a motley army of about 10,000 untrained workmen and artisans, mostly from the weavers' guild, armed with pikes and staves.

When the two forces met at Courtrai on this day, the Flemings, who knew the terrain far better than the French, took their stand on a patch of marshy ground surrounded by streams. The French cavalry tried to charge, but the horses could make no headway as their hooves sank into the soft ground. The Flemings then swarmed over the French knights before the French infantry could come forward.

The weavers and workmen had no use for the rules of chivalry: no prisoners were taken. At the end of the battle Robert d'Artois was knocked from his charger. Dropping his sword, he cried: '*Prenez, prenez le comte d'Artois, il vous fera riches!*' ('Take him, take the Count of Artois, he will make you rich!') But he was instantly pierced by Flemish pikes.

In all, some 1,200 French knights were slaughtered. At the end of the day the Flemings gathered over 700 'golden' spurs from the field of battle and hung them in the vault of Our Lady's Church in Courtrai. Ever since, this mighty victory by Flemish artisans over the flower of French knighthood has been known as the Battle of the Golden Spurs.

Also on this day

1274: Scottish King Robert the Bruce is born * 1754: Language bowdleriser Thomas Bowdler is born near Bath * **1804: American vice president Aaron Burr mortally wounds Alexander Hamilton in the most famous duel in American history**

12 July

Abraham Lincoln authorises the Medal of Honor

1862 Today, fifteen months to the day after the start of the Civil War, President Abraham Lincoln authorised 2,000 Medals of Honor for Union soldiers who 'shall most distinguish themselves by their gallantry in action and other soldier like qualities, during the present insurrection'. Following the establishment of a Navy medal eight months earlier, the Medal of Honor was now America's highest military decoration for valour in wartime for all Union combatants. (The Medal of Honor was not the first American medal, as George Washington had established the Purple Heart in 1782 for bravery in action. But only three Purple Hearts had been awarded and the medal was allowed to lapse until 1932, when it was revived as a decoration for having been wounded or killed in combat.)

Although the Medal of Honor was created during the Civil War, the very first action for which it was awarded took place even before the war had begun. On 13–14 February 1861 in what is now Arizona, Bernard Irwin, a 31-year-old army assistant surgeon, 'volunteered to go to the rescue of Second Lieutenant George N. Bascom, 7th Infantry, who with 60 men was trapped by Chiricahua Apaches under Cochise'. The citation for his MoH describes how 'Irwin and fourteen men, not having horses, began the 100-mile march riding mules. After fighting and capturing Indians, recovering stolen horses and cattle, he reached Bascom's column and helped break his siege.'

In the century and a half since its first award – a span in which American troops saw action in Cuba, Europe, Korea, Vietnam and the Persian Gulf – a total of 3,408 people have won the Medal of Honor. Almost one in five of these were killed during the action in which they earned it. Astonishingly, there have been fourteen men who have received two Medals of Honor. In all the Medal's history, however, only one was ever awarded to a woman – and that not without controversy.

Mary Walker was a 31-year-old doctor at the outbreak of the Civil War, when she volunteered as a nurse (the army hiring no female doctors). She served in army hospitals at the First Battle of Bull Run and later at Chickamauga and Chattanooga. Occasionally she would cross enemy lines to treat Confederate civilians. In April 1864 she accidentally wandered into a group of Rebel soldiers and was taken into captivity for four months, during which time she treated female prisoners. Eventually she was traded for a Confederate officer captured by the North.

At the war's conclusion she was awarded the Medal of Honor for having 'devoted herself with much patriotic zeal to the sick and wounded soldiers, both in the field and hospitals, to the detriment of her own health', but in 1917 Congress stripped her of her medal because she had been a civilian, albeit attached to the army. Furious, she refused to return it to the army and wore it proudly every evening until her death two years later. Finally, in 1977, the army ordered her medal restored.

There have been a few famous winners, such as Buffalo Bill Cody, Theodore Roosevelt, Douglas MacArthur and the future film star Audie Murphy, who was awarded the medal for action in France in January 1945. His medal citation gives some idea of the heroics demanded of winners.

'Second Lieutenant Murphy commanded Company B, which was attacked by six tanks and waves of infantry. Second Lieutenant Murphy ordered his men to withdraw to prepared positions in a woods, while he remained forward at his command post and continued to give fire directions to the artillery by telephone. Behind him, to his right, one of our tank destroyers received a direct hit and began to burn. Its crew withdrew to the woods. Second Lieutenant Murphy continued to direct artillery fire, which killed large numbers of the advancing enemy infantry. With the enemy tanks abreast of his position, Second Lieutenant Murphy climbed on the burning tank destroyer, which was in danger of blowing up at any moment and employed its .50 caliber machine gun against the enemy. He was alone and exposed to German fire from three sides, but his deadly fire killed dozens of Germans and caused their infantry attack to waver. The enemy tanks, losing infantry support, began to fall back. For an hour the Germans tried every available weapon to eliminate Second Lieutenant Murphy, but he continued to hold his position and wiped out a squad which was trying to creep up unnoticed on his right flank. Germans reached as close as 10 yards, only to be mowed down by his fire. He received a leg wound, but ignored it and continued the single-handed fight until his ammunition was exhausted. He then made his way to his company, refused medical attention and organised the company in a counter-attack which forced the Germans to withdraw. His directing of artillery fire wiped out many of the enemy; he killed or wounded about 50. Second Lieutenant Murphy's indomitable courage and his refusal to give an inch of ground saved his company from possible encirclement and destruction and enabled it to hold the woods which had been the enemy's objective.'

Also on this day

100 BC: Julius Caesar is born in Rome * 1536: Dutch humanist Desiderius Erasmus dies * 1730: American writer Henry David Thoreau is born in Concord, Massachusetts * 1884: Italian painter and sculptor Amadeo Modigliani is born in Livorno (Leghorn)

13 July

Bismarck starts a war with a telegram

1870 This is a day to be noted by all editors, speech-writers, spin-doctors and the like for the splendid – or cautionary, if you prefer – example it provides of what a few word changes can do to the fate of nations.

The editor in this case was Otto von Bismarck, Prime Minister of Prussia, a kingdom on the verge of becoming an empire but needing just that foreign threat that would induce the remaining German states to join it. As it happened, the throne of Spain was vacant and Bismarck had recently proposed a certain German prince, a cousin of King Wilhelm of Prussia, as a candidate. France, alarmed at the prospect of encirclement by Hohenzollerns, protested strongly. Wilhelm, having no wish for war – that would be a task for his grandson, he joked – instructed Bismarck to withdraw the candidate.

But bellicosity was in the Paris air and the Second Empire desired more than a withdrawal from its rival, Prussia. Napoleon III, believing in the invincibility of French arms, wanted a brilliant coup – diplomatic or military – that would show the world who was top dog in Europe, thereby restoring his regime's reputation at home and abroad. So the French ambassador to Prussia, Count Benedetti, was instructed to press King Wilhelm not only for confirmation of the withdrawal but also for 'assurance that he will never authorise a renewal of the candidacy'.

Benedetti went to Bad Ems, where Wilhelm was taking the waters. The King treated him with his customary courtesy, but declined to offer such a guarantee. He also refused the ambassador's request for a further audience with him on the subject. Afterwards, the King had a telegram sent to Bismarck in Berlin giving him an account of the meeting.

Bismarck read the message. Attuned to French sensibilities in the matter, he revised the account, eliminating any hint of the consideration with which the King had received Benedetti, thereby making it appear as if Wilhelm had delivered a humiliating snub. Then he released this edited version of the Ems telegram, as it is known to history, to the Berlin press and thence to the world. It was the Merlin touch.

The next day was the sacred Bastille Day in France. French papers emblazoned the now-insulting telegram on their front pages. *A Berlin! Vive la guerre!* And so, on this flimsy *casus belli*, France declared war against Prussia on the 19th.

France lost the war, an emperor and Alsace-Lorraine. What France lost, Prussia won and her king became Kaiser Wilhelm of Germany, crowned insultingly on French soil. A great editor, that Bismarck!

Also on this day

1585: Sponsored by Sir Walter Raleigh, 108 English colonists reach Roanoke Island, North Carolina, founding the first English settlement in North America * 1643: Lord Wilmot leads royalist troops to victory over the Roundheads in the Battle of Roundway Down in the English Civil War * **1793: Charlotte Corday stabs French revolutionary Jean-Paul Marat in his bath**

14 July

The reign of King Philip Augustus

1223 Although blind in one eye, Philip Augustus of France was a large and handsome man, once fair, who had become bald, it was said, from the heat of the sun encountered in the Holy Land when he was on crusade. His long reign of nearly 43 years was a great one in French history, as he more than doubled the size of his nation by conquering virtually all of the vast territories in France that had been under the control of the kings of England.

Beginning his rule in 1180 at the tender age of fifteen, Philip was a tough and intelligent realist. He played his rebellious barons off against each other to consolidate his own power and sent Simon de Montfort to crush the Albigensian heresy in the south of France.

Philip, however, spent most of his time fighting against the Plantagenet kings of England. First he fought Henry II for a period of about two years. Although the redoubtable Henry lost no territory, in the end he was forced to pay homage to Philip for his French lands only to die two days later.

Next, Philip took on Henry's son, Richard the Lionheart. (For those fans of historical minutiae, Richard was not the only Lionheart; Philip's son Louis VIII was also called Coeur de Lion.)

Philip's relationship with Richard began in apparent harmony, as they joined forces on the Third Crusade. During the journey, however, Philip fell ill and used his illness as an excuse to return to France, whereupon he immediately made war on Richard's French territories. Although Richard set sail for France the moment he heard the news, he was captured and imprisoned in Austria for a year, giving Philip that much more time to consolidate his gains.

From 1194 to 1198 Philip and Richard were almost constantly at war, with

Richard the predominant victor. Eventually, however, fortune favoured Philip when Richard was killed during an unimportant siege in 1199.

Philip's next opponent was Richard's brother, King John. Compared with Henry and Richard, John was militarily incompetent and Philip took virtually all the Plantagenet territories in France over a fourteen-year period.

Philip's other great victory was against the German Emperor Otto IV at the decisive battle of Bouvines, destroying Otto's plot to make France his fief and to dismember it for his vassals.

When Philip died on this day in 1223 he was a month short of his 60th birthday. Although remembered most for his military successes, he also left two other enduring monuments: he paved the streets of Paris and built a large palace there that today we know as the Louvre.

Also on this day

1789: In Paris, revolutionaries storm the Bastille * 1835: American painter James Abbott McNeil Whistler is born * 1881 American outlaw Billy the Kid is shot dead by Sheriff Pat Garrett * 1933: Germany passes the Law for the Protection of Hereditary Health, the beginning of the Nazi euthanasia programme

15 July

Monmouth faces the axe

1685 King Charles II of England had a lifelong passion for women. One of his mistresses, Lucy Walter, bore him a son named James while he was still a prince in exile in The Hague. After the Restoration, Charles brought the thirteen-year-old James back to England and made him Duke of Monmouth.

At 36, Monmouth was all a royal bastard should be: attractive, arrogant, ambitious and a trained soldier to boot. When Charles died, however, he explicitly left his throne to his brother, another James (II), rather than to his illegitimate son. King James immediately banished his nephew from England.

Monmouth understandably detested his uncle and was thirsting for power. Knowing King James's Catholicism to be highly unpopular with the English, he raised a small force to dethrone him.

With 82 followers, Monmouth landed at Lyme Regis in June 1685. Proclaiming his uncle a popish usurper, he announced that he was the rightful king. Marching north, he recruited an army of about 7,000 men, but on 6 July 1685 he was defeated and captured at Sedgemoor, near Taunton, by the royalist army under the command of John Churchill, later Duke of Marlborough. (This was the last battle ever fought on English soil, although they were still fighting in Scotland until 1746.)

Taken to the Tower of London, Monmouth was quickly convicted of treason and condemned to the block. At first he entreated his uncle James for mercy, but when his letters received no reply he stoically resigned himself to death.

Only nine days after his capture at Sedgemoor, Monmouth faced the axe. Retaining his bravado till the end, he turned to his executioner, Jack Ketch, and commanded: 'Do not hack at me as you did my Lord Russell.' He then gave Ketch six guineas and laid his head on the block. But still fearing a botched job, he asked to feel the edge of the axe with his thumb and complained that it was too dull. Ketch reassured him that the axe was sharp and heavy enough to perform its function.

Despite his guarantee, the nervous executioner failed three times to sever Monmouth's neck and finally threw down his axe in despair, crying: 'God damn me, I can do no more. My heart fails me.' But the onlooking crowd bayed for blood and once again Ketch lifted his axe to deliver the final terrible blow.

Also on this day

622: Muhammad flees from Mecca to Medina – the Hegira – the beginning of the Muslim era * **1099: Crusaders conquer Jerusalem during the First Crusade** * 1606: Rembrandt van Rijn is born in Leiden * 1808: Napoleon makes his marshal, Joachim Murat, King of Naples * 1834: The Decree of Suppression brings an end to the Spanish Inquisition after 342 years

> Events written in **boldface** are covered in full in
> *365: Great Stories from History for Every Day of the Year*,
> the first volume in this series.

16 July

The first fall of Rome

390 BC Today the city of Rome fell for the first time since its mythic founding by Romulus and Remus in 753 BC. Gallic barbarians had routed its legions in the field and now rampaged through the city, burning, looting and slaughtering thousands of Roman civilians. A few soldiers had retreated to the citadel on the Capitoline Hill, but could they save Rome from complete destruction?

Rome was still a fledgling power, a city state at uneasy peace with neighbouring Etruscan cities and now threatened by Gallic tribes that occupied much of northern Italy. Among the fiercest were the Senones from the Adriatic coast.

In early 390 BC the Senone chieftain Brennus had led his warriors to the outskirts of the Etruscan town of Clusium (today's Chiusi), some 100 miles north of Rome. Desperate, the Clusians turned to Rome for help.

Unwilling or unable to send an army, the Romans dispatched three envoys, who demanded by what right the Senones were threatening a Roman ally.

Brennus coldly responded: 'All things belong to the brave, who carry justice on the points of their swords.' After an exchange of insults, a fight broke out during which one of Brennus's lieutenants was killed and the envoys fled back to Rome, the Senones in hot pursuit. Brennus demanded that they be turned over to him but according to Livy, 'those who should have been punished were instead appointed military tribunes for the coming year'. Enraged, Brennus swore revenge, which was not long in coming.

By July Brennus's 40,000-strong army was marching through Roman territory. On this day six Roman legions, under the command of Quintus Sulpicius, met the Senones at the Allia river, about twelve miles north of the city. Accompanied by 'the dreadful din of fierce war-songs', the Senones smashed into the Roman right, then turned to flank the centre. The Romans panicked and fled, and only a handful made it back to Rome, where they took refuge in the citadel on the Capitoline Hill without even closing the city gates behind them. It was then that the Senones ran amok in the city.

For seven months the defenders on the Capitoline Hill held fast, despite repeated barbarian assaults. On one occasion the Senones tried a surprise attack at night, but the Romans were alerted by the cackling of the sacred geese of Juno and managed to throw back the invaders.

Now the Senones were struck by that curse of ancient armies, dysentery. Soon hundreds were dying and Brennus, despairing of conquering the citadel, called a brief truce and demanded that the Romans pay 1,000 pounds in gold as ransom. He then added insult to humiliation by weighing the gold using his own weights, which were heavier than standard. When the Roman commander objected, Brennus flung his sword onto the scale and disdainfully responded, '*Vae victis!*' ('Woe to the vanquished!')

What happened next is open to debate. Polybius maintains that the Senones 'withdrew unmolested with their booty, having voluntarily and on their own terms restored the city to the Romans'. But the patriotic Livy tells us that, just as the Romans were preparing to hand over the gold, their exiled dictator, Marcus Furius Camillus, arrived with a fresh army. Drawing his sword, he exclaimed: 'It is not gold but steel that redeems the homeland.' He then chased the Senones through the streets of Rome and out of the city. The following day he routed them in a battle outside the walls, personally dispatching Brennus and earning for himself the title of Second Founder of Rome.

From this time forth, Rome remained inviolate and unconquered for 800 years, until it fell to the Visigoth chief Alaric in AD 410.

Also on this day

1212: Alfonso VIII of Castile and Leon crushes the Moors at Las Navas de Tolosa, ending the threat of Muslim domination in Spain * 1796: French painter Camille Corot is born * 1918: Communist insurgents shoot Tsar Nicholas II, his wife Alexandra and their four children in a cellar at Ekaterinburg * 1945: The first atom bomb explodes at Alamogordo, New Mexico, at 5.24 am * 1951: American novelist J.D. Salinger publishes *The Catcher in the Rye*

17 July

Joan of Arc witnesses a coronation

1429 'And at the hour that the King was anointed and also when the crown was placed upon his head, all those assembled there cried out "Noël!" And trumpets sounded in so that it seemed the vaults of the church must be riven apart.' So reports an eyewitness to the coronation of Charles VII of France at Reims cathedral on Sunday 17 July 1429. Charles had already been King of France since his father's death in 1422, but insurrection at home and invasion by the English had prevented him from actually being crowned.

Coronations were long affairs in those days, this one lasting from nine in the morning until two in the afternoon. It was also a particularly poignant one. As the eyewitness testifies: 'During the said mystery the Pucelle was ever near the King, holding his standard in her hand. And it was a most fair thing to see.' The Pucelle, of course, was Joan of Arc, who only four months before had seen King Charles for the first time. In that short time she had forced the English to lift the siege of Orléans and had paved the way for the coronation.

In the few pictures we have of him, Charles looks rather like a tired and troubled monk, with his long nose, pessimistic mouth and wary, unblinking eyes. He was brought up in a court filled with passion and intrigue, with a mad father and a power- and sex-hungry mother, Queen Isabeau, who, under pressure from England's Henry V, agreed that Charles was a bastard and therefore not the true heir to the French throne. (Ironically, Charles's coronation took place on the anniversary of Isabeau's marriage to Charles's father.) But Charles was to be one of France's most successful kings, although he needed help. His famous mistress, Agnès Sorel, gave him wise counsel; Jacques Coeur gave him money and Joan of Arc started the defeat of the English. Yet Charles abandoned Joan to be burnt at the stake and he allowed jealous courtiers to drive Coeur away in disgrace.

Slowly and skilfully Charles overcame resistance from his Burgundian and Armagnac vassals, as well as a revolt largely orchestrated by his own son. He edged the English first out of Paris and at last out of France. It was on this same day in 1453 that Charles's army destroyed the English army at Castillon, the final battle of the Hundred Years War, which brought Bordeaux back under French control for the first time in 300 years.

As he grew older, Charles grew increasingly suspicious of those around him, particularly of his son Louis, whose deviousness would be a lifetime hallmark. In 1461 he found himself at Mehun-sur-Yèvre, where he started to suffer stomach pains. Convinced Louis was trying to poison him, he refused to take nourishment and died (of poison or illness, no one knows) on 22 July. He had reigned for 38 years and eight months.

Also on this day
1453: The French defeat the English at Castillon, the last battle of the Hundred Years War * 1674: The bones of two boys are found in the Tower of London, presumed to be the children of Edward IV * 1793: French patriot Charlotte Corday is guillotined * 1872: Mexican President Benito Juárez dies at his desk of a heart attack

18 July

The Spanish Civil War begins

1936 The Spanish Civil War began at 5.15 this Saturday morning, when, in a *pronunciamento* broadcast by radio from Las Palmas on Grand Canary Island, General Francisco Franco gave the order for the mainland garrisons of the Spanish army to rise against the republican government of Spain.

It was a rebellion in which an array of forces – landowners, monarchists, the Catholic Church, the army, the bourgeoisie, the fascist Falange party – sought to reclaim their country from an elected republican government they judged incapable of putting down the violent political disorder afflicting the nation. So it was that during the morning of 18 July, in city after city, garrisons seized public buildings, proclaimed a state of war, and arrested republican and left-wing leaders. In response, workers took to the streets, calling for a general strike and throwing up barricades.

The republican government of Spain faced a dilemma. It wished to put down the rebellion but found the institutions of law and order – the army and the civil guard – in the hands of the rebels. On the other hand, the forces remaining loyal to the republic were the unions and the left-wing parties – Socialists, Communists and Anarchists – whose victory, if it came, promised proletarian revolution. Late in the day, the government made its decision: arm the workers. As trucks sped through the streets of Madrid carrying rifles to the headquarters of the unions, German and Italian transport planes airlifted the Spanish army of Africa to mainland Spain. The fight was on.

At ten in the evening, in a radio broadcast, Dolores Ibarurri, the Communist leader known as La Pasionaria, told her listeners, 'It is better to die on your feet than to live on your knees!' then echoed the old phrase from Verdun, '*No pasarán!*' ('They shall not pass!'). It was to be the great rallying cry of republican Spain.

The war lasted almost three years, during which the world learned about such things as Guernica, the 'Fifth Column' and the Condor Legion. Nazi Germany and Fascist Italy supplied and reinforced Franco's Nationalists. Soviet Russia sent aid to the republican Loyalists. The democracies – France, Great Britain and the United States – practised non-intervention. When Madrid fell in March 1939, after 28 months of siege, and Nationalist forces marched into the city, the crowds shouted, '*Han pasado!*' ('They have passed!').

Franco was by now *El Caudillo* – The Leader – a designation he shared with *Der Führer* and *Il Duce*. Pope Pius XII cabled him: 'Lifting up our heart to God, we give sincere thanks with your Excellency for Spain's Catholic victory.' The Nationalist Government now aligned itself with the Axis powers by joining the Anti-Comintern Pact and signing a five-year treaty of friendship with Nazi Germany. Only Russia among the great powers refused to recognise the Nationalist regime.

No precise estimates of the losses in the Spanish Civil War exist, but Hugh Thomas offered this tentative assessment: a total of 500,000 people perished in the conflict, of which perhaps 300,000 died in action, 100,000 died of disease or malnutrition and 100,000 were executed or murdered. All in all, it was good practice for the Second World War, only five months away.

Also on this day

AD **64: Emperor Nero burns Rome** * 1610: Italian painter Caravaggio (Michelangelo Merisi) dies at Porto Ercole * 1811: William Makepeace Thackeray is born in Calcutta * 1817: Jane Austen dies in Winchester * 1869: Pope Pius IX proclaims the doctrine of papal infallibility * 1900: The first Métro line in Paris is inaugurated

19 July

The first Tour de France

1903 Today in Paris a small, wiry Frenchman named Maurice Garin flashed over the finish line to win the first ever Tour de France, the world's most testing and prestigious bicycle race.

At mid-afternoon on 1 July 60 riders had started near the Réveil Matin café in Paris – a mixture of professionals like Garin and amateur adventurers, including a butcher and a miner. Their route took them a gruelling 1,500 miles in six stages to Lyon, Marseilles, Toulouse, Bordeaux, Nantes and back to Paris. The 32-year-old Garin, only 5 feet 3 inches tall but with a bristling moustache, was dressed entirely in white. The crowd called him the 'White Bulldog' for taking the lead on the first stage and tenaciously holding it throughout the race. He averaged sixteen miles an hour and won by the greatest margin in the race's history.

The Tour de France was the brainchild of a French cycling reporter named Géorges Lefèvre, who suggested it to his boss Henri Desgrange at *L'Auto*, a paper that, despite its name, was devoted primarily to cycle racing. While discussing *L'Auto*'s circulation war with a rival paper, Lefèvre suggested sponsoring 'a race of several days [. . .] something like a six-day track race but on the open road', insisting that 'all the big towns are begging for cycle races'.

'You are suggesting, then,' another staffer asked, 'a cycling tour of France?' Desgrange, who himself had set the world's one-hour cycling record nine years earlier, was enthusiastic. Two months later *L'Auto* announced the Tour and after the first race its circulation rocketed from 25,000 to 65,000.

Another Desgrange innovation was the famous *maillot jaune* (yellow jersey), worn each day by the race's leader. He introduced it in 1919 so that spectators could distinguish the leader and picked yellow because *L'Auto* was printed on yellow paper.

Although the French have won 36 of the 92 Tours through 2007, the greatest champion was the American Lance Armstrong, victor seven consecutive times from 1999 through 2005. Other mythic racers with five wins apiece include Frenchmen Jacques Anquetil and Bernard Hinault, Eddy Merckx from Belgium and Miguel Induráin from Spain.

As well as heroes, the Tour has also produced scandal, tragedy and farce. In 1904, in a race marred by spectators attacking riders to help their favourites, Maurice Garin triumphed once again, only to be disqualified four months later for taking food during the race at an unauthorised time. The official winner was Henri Cornet, at twenty the Tour's youngest ever victor, who suffered a puncture on the first stage and rode 22 miles with a flat tyre.

In 1928 Nicolas Frantz did Cornet one better: when his racing bicycle broke down he borrowed a woman's bicycle and pedalled it for 60 miles, still maintaining the lead.

Tour organisers committed the ultimate faux pas in 1963 when the Irishman Seamus Elliott was on the award stand after winning a stage. Unaware that Elliott's father was a Sinn Fein revolutionary, the brass band struck up *God Save the Queen*.

The Tour has also witnessed three deaths on the road. In 1935 Francesco Cepeda plunged down a ravine and 60 years later Fabio Casartelli crashed at over 50 miles an hour during a descent. In 1967 the British cyclist Tom Simpson collapsed en route, his system weakened by amphetamines. As he lay dying on the roadside, he gained cycling immortality by pleading 'put me back on my bike'.

The greatest scandals came in 2006. Before the race even started 56 riders were suspended on suspicion of 'blood packing' – a banned process by which a cyclist's blood is drawn and spun in a centrifuge to separate oxygen-carrying red blood cells, which are later reinjected to give a performance boost. Then the winner, the American Floyd Landis, was disqualified when his post-race blood test showed he had taken illegal testosterone. And in 2007 the scandal continued, as prerace favourite Alexandre Vinokourov of Kazakhstan was expelled from the tour for blood doping.

With time trials and climbing stages, the Tour de France today is a far cry from the first race and Maurice Garin's victory in 1903. Instead of 60 competitors, there are now over 200, with teams of nine riders each. The race now covers around 2,200 miles in about twenty stages and includes either the Alps or the Pyrenees, so agonising a test that racers have been called *les forçats de la route* (the convicts of the road). No longer confined to France, the Tour sometimes wanders into Belgium, Switzerland, Italy, Germany or Spain and even

Ireland and Great Britain. Garin's victorious speed of sixteen miles an hour pales compared to Lance Armstrong's 26.

Nonetheless, despite the Tour's professionalism and sophistication, most of its riders concur with Maurice Garin, who, on the 50th anniversary of his great victory, recalled: '*Quelles routes impossibles, que de beaux souvenirs elles me laissent pourtant!*' ('What impossible roads, but what beautiful memories they leave me!')

Also on this day

1374: Italian poet Petrarch dies near Padua * 1799: The Rosetta Stone is found in Egypt * 1834: French painter and sculptor Edgar Degas is born * **1848: The first women's suffrage convention in America starts at Seneca Falls, New York**

20 July

The man who failed to save Russia

1917 Today, as a popular uprising against the Provisional Government fell apart and loyal troops took control of the capital, Alexander Kerensky, minister of war, became prime minister of Russia. The man of the hour, 34 years old and a fiery public speaker, carried the hopes of countless Russians, who saw him as the saviour of a nation facing military defeat abroad and political chaos at home.

Kerensky took the reins of a coalition government committed to keeping Russia in the First World War and to protecting its fledgling democracy, born only five months earlier with the abdication of the tsar. He might have been a uniting force – a 'human bridge between the socialist and liberal camps' – but he proved to be no more than an insecure opportunist without political principle, his talents as a leader more theatrical than real. And when he had the chance to save his nation, he made the wrong move and failed utterly.

Even as the Petrograd insurrection had been put down, the war news grew worse. The Russian army's June offensive against the Austrians and Germans, meant to demonstrate the nation's patriotic will, had collapsed, with the loss of thousands in the field and even greater numbers through desertion: a military failure that was turning much of the country against the war and playing to the advantage of the anti-war Bolsheviks.

To stabilise the military scene – at home and at the front – Kerensky appointed a new commander-in-chief, General Kornilov, a loyal and competent soldier, well thought of on the Right. But in August a new crisis arose: as German forces moved up the Baltic coast towards the capital, radicalised elements of the Petrograd garrison refused orders for the front and instead joined striking workers in the streets calling for 'All power to the Soviets' and threatening to overthrow the Provisional Government. From army headquarters at Mogilev, Kornilov sent a force of loyal units to put down the Leftist insurrection and protect Kerensky's regime.

But the Prime Minister – vain, ambitious and secretive as he was – misinterpreted the move as one through which Kornilov meant to become the dictator of Russia. Denouncing the general as a traitor, Kerensky made himself Commander-in-Chief. His cabinet ministers resigned to give him supreme power and in an ironic turnabout, Kerensky now called on the forces of the Left to defend the Provisional Government against 'counter-revolution' from the Right. Kornilov's columns were halted before they could reach the capital, but it was now clear that real power in Russia lay elsewhere than with the government.

Six weeks later, in early November, Vladimir Ilyich Lenin, a leader with a surer vision of what could be achieved, led a Bolshevik putsch that overthrew the Provisional Government virtually without opposition. Kerensky, so recently the saviour of Russia, had held the office of prime minister less than four months.

On the Bolshevik takeover, which inaugurated seven decades of Communist rule in Russia, Kerensky went into hiding and then escaped to Europe. In 1940, he fled further, to New York, where he died in 1970.

Also on this day

1402: Tamerlane (Timur) defeats the Ottoman sultan Bayezid I at the Battle of Ankara * 1881: Sioux chief Sitting Bull surrenders to the US Army * **1944: German staff officer Colonel Claus von Stauffenberg fails in his attempt to assassinate Hitler in his Wolfsshanze bunker**

21 July

The Battle of the Pyramids

1798 *'Soldats, songez que, du haut de ces pyramides, quarante siècles vous contemplent.'* ('Think of it, soldiers, from the top of these pyramids 40 centuries are looking down upon you.') So declaimed General Napoleon Bonaparte to inspire his troops just before they went into battle against a large Egyptian army, spearheaded by 8,000 ferocious Mameluke horsemen.

In fact, the French needed little inspiration, as Napoleon's cannon as well as his tactics destroyed virtually the entire Egyptian force of 24,000 men in less than two hours, with a loss of only 300 Frenchmen. The only real opposition came from the cavalry, superb riders and fanatic in their intent, who had come close to routing a section of his infantry. After the battle Napoleon expressed his admiration: 'If I could have united the Mameluke horse with the French infantry, I should have seen myself as master of the world.' Such was the Battle of the Pyramids, fought this day.

The political results of Napoleon's invasion of Egypt have long since vanished in the mists of time, but two souvenirs remain. The first is the Rosetta Stone, the key to deciphering hieroglyphic writing, which was discovered in

1799 in the town of Rosetta, near Alexandria, by a French officer named Bouchard. The second is the appearance of perhaps the world's most famous monument, the Sphinx. For 40 centuries the Sphinx had a prominent nose, but it is said that the flat-faced colossus we are all familiar with is the result of Napoleon's soldiers using it for target practice.

Also on this day

1403: Rebelling against King Henry IV, Henry Percy (Hotspur) is killed at the Battle of Shrewsbury * 1831: Leopold of Saxe-Coburg enters Belgium for the first time as Belgium's first king * 1861: The South defeats the North at Bull Run, the first major battle of the American Civil War * 1899: Ernest Hemingway is born in Cicero, Illinois * 1942: German general Erwin Rommel captures British-held Tobruk in North Africa

22 July

The end of the Little Eagle

1832 Today in the exquisite Schönbrunn Palace just outside Vienna died Napoleon François Charles Joseph, Duke of Reichstadt, only son of Napoleon and his empress Marie-Louise.

Franzl – as his mother called him – had been born in the Tuileries in Paris in March 1811, when Napoleon was at the height of his power. Initially entitled the 'King of Rome' and heir to Napoleon's throne, the French senate proclaimed him Emperor before it capitulated to the Allies after his father's first abdication in 1814. But although Tsar Alexander I preferred him to a restoration of the Bourbons, the other Allies would have no truck with further Bonapartes and saw to it that he was soon demoted and taken to Vienna. He never saw his father again.

Franzl then became the 'Prince of Parma' when his mother was made the ruling duchess there, but Metternich vetoed this title on the grounds that one day the son of Napoleon might have a territory to rule. Eventually, his grandfather, Emperor Franz of Austria, created him the Duke of Reichstadt – a Bohemian palatinate that he never ruled nor even visited. Many years after his death the romantic Victor Hugo christened him '*l'Aiglon*' ('the Little Eagle'), the name by which he is often referred to today.

From 1813 onwards Franzl remained in Austria, where he was held in a sort of luxurious captivity, with all communication in German. Nonetheless, he became a Bonapartist, once writing to his mother that he was trying to live up to his father, asking: 'Can there be a finer, more admirable model of constancy, endurance, manly gravity, valour and courage?'

By the time he was sixteen, Franzl was already showing signs of the tuberculosis that would kill him. Bravely he carried on, always hopeful that he would be cured, but by the time he was 21 it was clear that death was near. Installed in the Schönbrunn Palace, he waited for the end in the same bedroom in which his father had dictated peace terms to the Austrians after his victory at Wagram 23 years earlier.

On Sunday 22 July 1832 it was hot and humid in Vienna, with thunder in the air. In the early hours of the morning he murmured: 'I am going under. Call my mother.' He then quietly slipped away, Marie-Louise at his side.

Franzl was buried in the traditional Habsburg burial crypt in the Kapuzinerkirche in Vienna, where he lay for 108 years. Napoleon III tried to persuade Austrian Emperor Franz Joseph to allow the remains to be sent to Paris to lie beside his father in the Invalides, but his requests were ignored.

By 1940, however, Austria had been integrated into Hitler's German Reich and the Nazi government in Berlin wanted to persuade the Vichy French of Germany's goodwill. So on 12 December that year Franzl's coffin was shipped from Vienna to Paris, where he was buried near his father three days later.

Also on this day

1208: Troops of Simon de Montfort kill 15,000 men, women and children while sacking Béziers during the Albigensian Crusade * 1812: The Duke of Wellington defeats the French at Salamanca in the Peninsular War * 1943: American General George S. Patton's Seventh Army enters Palermo in Sicily.

23 July

Philippe Pétain – the hero who betrayed his country dies in prison

1951 Henri Philippe Benoni Omer Joseph Pétain, Marshal of France, died today at the age of 95, in prison on the lonely Ile d'Yeu. During the First World War he had been a great hero of his country. In 1916 he was the 'Saviour of Verdun' and the next year, as Commander-in-Chief, he had performed a true miracle: in the perilous military situation after the disastrous Nivelle offensives, he had restored the mutiny-ridden French army to discipline and battlefield efficiency, with the result that it fought valiantly and effectively through the remainder of the war. For these feats a grateful nation made him a marshal.

In the debacle of 1940, the hero of the last war was called upon once again to rescue his country from the Germans. This time, instead of rallying his forces, he negotiated the surrender of France, then ruled for the rest of the Second World War as the chief of the vassal state of Vichy. For these feats a dishonoured nation convicted the marshal of treason and sentenced him to death. Charles de Gaulle commuted the sentence to life imprisonment and later wrote of his old colonel: 'Monsieur le Maréchal! You who had always done such great honour to your arms, who were once my leader and my example, how had you come to this?'

Also on this day
1745: Bonnie Prince Charlie lands in Scotland in an abortive attempt to gain the throne of Great Britain * 1757: Italian composer Domenico Scarlatti dies * 1865: British revivalist preacher William Booth founds the Salvation Army * **1885: American General and President Ulysses S. Grant dies of throat cancer at Mount McGregor, N.Y.**

24 July

Nelson loses his right arm

1797 En route to proving himself Britain's greatest admiral, Horatio Nelson survived illness and injury that would have put a lesser man out of the running.

He nearly died while on duty in the Indian Ocean, through contracting malaria. He was so badly affected that the Navy sent him home to recover. Later, the British force he was part of was decimated by yellow fever while attacking San Juan in Puerto Rico and Nelson again was lucky to survive.

Nelson suffered his first serious battle wound in 1794 when his squadron was besieging Corsica, in the hope of using it as a new base in the war against France. Infantry led the attack, supported by naval guns brought ashore to pound the enemy fortress. Nelson, then a 35-year-old captain, was in charge of the naval unit.

During the morning of 12 July the British guns were battering the enemy's positions at Calvi when suddenly a French shell exploded, showering the attackers with sand and broken rock. Something struck Nelson in the right eye, permanently clouding his vision.

Three years later the fleet was on the attack again, this time against the Spanish at Tenerife. On this day Nelson – by then an admiral – was trying to land when a musket ball tore through his right elbow. Immediately brought back to his flagship, he greeted his officers with astonishing nonchalance, refusing help in climbing aboard with the comment: 'I have got my legs left and one arm.' He said he knew his arm must come off, so the sooner the better.

In these days before anaesthetics, the amputation must have been painful in the extreme, but Nelson bore it stoically. Half an hour later he was back in his cabin giving orders and writing dispatches with his left hand.

Although fighting the French almost continually for the next eight years, Nelson managed to avoid injury or illness until October 1805, when he received his final, fatal wound at Trafalgar.

Also on this day
1704: British Rear Admiral Sir George Rooke captures Gibraltar * 1783: South American liberator Simón Bolívar is born in Caracas, Venezuela * 1802: Birth of French writer Alexandre Dumas (père), author of *The Count of Monte Cristo*, *The Three Musketeers* and *The Man in the Iron Mask*

25 July

A neurotic spinster queen marries a cold-eyed prince

1554 It was a splendid wedding on this warm day at Winchester Cathedral, as Mary Tudor, Queen of England, married the future Philip II of Spain, the heir to the largest, richest and most powerful empire in history.

Philip, at 27, was already distant and austere – a bigoted Catholic who had been a widower for nine years. He would become King of Spain in 1556, to rule it for 42 years.

Mary was eleven years his senior, a neurotic virgin of 38 who looked even older than she was, having lost most of her teeth. Also an obsessive Catholic, she worshipped Philip as the man who would help her make Catholicism once more supreme in England, and at the same time sire the child she so desperately craved. The cold-eyed and tireless Philip, on the other hand, had agreed to marry Mary for the same reason he did everything else: duty to his country and to his religion.

In the end, of course, neither got what they wanted. Mary died childless and virtually abandoned by her prince, Protestantism remained England's state religion and Philip failed to bring England under Spanish domination, even when he sent his Armada against it 34 years later.

Also on this day

AD 44: St James's body arrives in Santiago de Compostela in north-west Spain, after his beheading in Jerusalem (according to Spanish tradition) * 1394: Charles VI expels all Jews from France * 1587: Chief Imperial Minister Hideyoshi bans Christianity and orders all Christians to leave Japan * **1593: To gain the confidence of his Catholic subjects, French king Henri IV abjures his Calvinism to join the Church of Rome, commenting 'Paris is well worth a mass'** * 1934: Nazis shoot and kill the Austrian chancellor Engelbert Dollfuss

26 July

The cheese of kings and popes

1926 The French have never been reticent about protecting their culinary superiority, as demonstrated today when the government established an *appellation d'origine* for Roquefort, the classic blue cheese made from ewes' milk. It was the first cheese ever so honoured. The effect of the new law was to ensure that only cheeses that have been aged in the limestone caves of Roquefort, a hamlet near Toulouse, may bear the name. But in truth the statute only confirmed what King Charles VI had already decreed in 1411, when he gave the Roquefort citizens the sole right to mature the cheese.

Roquefort is made by adding spores of the mould Penicillium roqueforti to the fresh cheese and then letting it mature for three months in damp caves, where the humid air encourages the development of the cheese's blue veins. The result is a crumbly cylinder about eight inches across and four inches high, which the French maintain should always be accompanied by other *appellation d'origine* products such as a good bottle of Châteauneuf-du-Pape (although in his *Mémoires*, the free-spending Casanova recommends Chambertin).

Roquefort was a worthy candidate for the esteemed *appellation*, for it is the oldest known French variety, mentioned by Pliny the Elder in the 1st century AD and later known as Charlemagne's favourite. Indeed, if legend is to be believed, Roquefort was first discovered in time immemorial. When a young shepherd who lived nearby was eating his lunch of bread and ewes' cheese, he suddenly spied a beautiful girl in the distance. Entranced, he ran after the girl, leaving his lunch untouched in a cave. A few months later he returned to the cave to find that the plain ewes' cheese had been transformed into Roquefort.

The French are so enthusiastic about their Roquefort that, not content with solely a royal pedigree, they call it *le fromage des rois et des papes* (the cheese of kings and popes).

Also on this day

1529: Holy Roman Emperor Charles V issues a royal warrant authorising Francisco Pizarro to explore and conquer Peru * **1826: In Rizaffa, Spain, the Spanish Inquisition executes its last victim** * 1847: Liberia becomes independent, the first African colony to do so * 1856: Irish playwright George Bernard Shaw is born in Dublin * 1947: President Harry Truman signs the National Security Act of 1947, establishing the United States Air Force as separate from the army

27 July

Philip Augustus triumphs at Bouvines

1214 Today, King Philip Augustus firmly established France as the predominant European power by defeating a formidable combination of enemies at the Battle of Bouvines.

Holy Roman Emperor Otto IV thought he had found the perfect way to reward his barons and keep them loyal. He would conquer France and distribute its territories piecemeal to those who helped him do it. Fearful that he alone could not defeat Philip, he formed an international coalition with King John of England and two rebellious French vassals, Ferrand, Count of Flanders and Reginald, Count of Boulogne.

Otto's plan called for John to land on the French coast and head for Paris, destroying as he went, while the two counts and the Emperor would descend on Paris from the north.

Things first went wrong when Philip met the incompetent John and his army near Angers on 2 July and completely defeated them. Philip then moved north, gathering reinforcements from the local populace as he went. By the time battle commenced, his force numbered some 7,000 cavalry and 30,000 infantry: somewhat less than the coalition ranged against him.

The armies met at Bouvines (near Lille). In the early stages of the battle it seemed that Otto and his allies would prevail, as imperial infantry drove back the French, but then King Philip boldly led his cavalry into a direct assault. Unhorsed and almost killed, he regained his mount and pushed on to rout the enemy through the brilliant use of his cavalry against the enemy's infantry.

Philip's victory was so decisive that Emperor Otto was deposed and replaced by Frederick II. Both Ferrand and Reginald were captured.

Bouvines was the first battle in which the French nobility and army were joined by the merchants and middle-class citizens, thus representing a milestone in the development of French nationalism.

Also on this day

1675: French Marshal Henri de La Tour d'Auvergne, vicomte de Turenne is killed by a cannonball near Sasbach * 1694: The British Parliament founds the Bank of England * 1809: The start of the Battle of Talavera, in which the Duke of Wellington defeats the French in the Peninsular War * 1946: American expatriate writer Gertrude Stein dies in Neuilly-sur-Seine * 1953: The Korean War comes to an end

28 July

A wedding and a beheading in the reign of Henry VIII

1540 It was a May–December wedding when, on this day, 49-year-old King Henry VIII took to the altar in a private ceremony his fifth wife, nineteen-year-old Catherine Howard. Henry was enamoured, calling her his 'rose without a thorn', although looking at her portrait today we see a large-featured, coarse and rather dim-looking woman. Catherine had first come to his notice when she was a maid of honour for Henry's previous wife, Anne of Cleves, when they had married only six months earlier. Henry divorced Anne on 9 July (it was rumoured that the marriage had never been consummated) and dashed off to marry Catherine nineteen days later.

History does not state if Henry's wedding to Catherine was a festive occasion, but perhaps a few spirits were dampened by the fact that Thomas Cromwell, for nine years Henry's closest adviser, was beheaded on the very same day. Cromwell had served Henry loyally and well. He had largely emasculated the Church's power in favour of the King and had overseen the destruction of the monasteries, bringing the treasury (i.e. Henry) enormous wealth.

But Cromwell had made a principal error. Mistakenly thinking that England needed alliances with German principalities, he had persuaded the King to marry Anne of Cleves, to whom Henry took an immediate and visceral dislike. Within a month of their marriage it became clear that Henry had no need of German allies and that the marriage to Anne had not been necessary after all.

Cromwell had inevitably made enemies during his years of power and they quickly circled like vultures on seeing his position weaken, persuading Henry that he was in truth a traitor and a heretic. Henry condemned him to the block without a hearing.

Cromwell's execution that day turned out to be an omen for those who cared to read it. Although Henry at first seemed enamoured with his new bride, Catherine found the fat old man repulsive. She made a cardinal error in inviting a previous lover, Francis Dereham, to court and a worse one in embarking on affair with the dashing Thomas Culpepper of the King's Privy Chamber (although historians debate if Catherine and Culpepper actually consummated the affair). Inevitably, rumours of these liaisons reached the ear of the King, who was initially incredulous. But investigation, including the torture of Dereham and Culpepper, soon corroborated the allegations. Catherine was arrested and both men were executed as traitors.

By now Henry had resolved to get rid of Catherine and, since adultery was difficult to prove (Catherine insisted she was innocent), two months after the putative lovers had been executed, Parliament passed a bill making it treason for an unchaste woman to marry the King. Consequently, even Catherine's affairs before she met Henry would be enough to send her to the block. Two days later, on 13 February, Catherine was beheaded in the Tower of London, only nineteen months after her wedding day.

Also on this day

1794: French Revolutionary fanatic Maximilien Robespierre is guillotined
* 1741: Antonio Vivaldi dies in Venice * 1750: Johann Sebastian Bach dies in Leipzig
* 1914: Austria declares war on Serbia, starting the First World War * 1920: Mexican outlaw and revolutionary Pancho Villa surrenders to the Mexican government

29 July

The birth of Benito Mussolini

1883 Predappio – a small town just a few miles from Ravenna, once the proud capital of the Western Roman Empire – perhaps a fitting place for the birth today of Benito Mussolini, the last Italian leader to try to build an empire of his own.

Mussolini was the son of a poor blacksmith, who doubled as a socialist journalist, and a schoolteacher mother. He inherited his parents' brains and perhaps the violence of the forge, as bullying his classmates marked his school years and he twice assaulted other pupils with a knife.

As a young man he became a violent socialist, spending some time in prison in Switzerland, where he was a full-time journalist and part-time rabble-rouser. He later started an affair with Rachele Guidi, the daughter of his father's mistress (but not of his father). The couple eventually married shortly before Mussolini was sent to prison for the fifth time.

In his twenties Mussolini had been a dedicated Socialist Party member, opposed to all wars, and a committed internationalist. But slowly his views became narrower and by the time he was 30 he had become a xenophobic warmonger, strongly backing Italy's entry into the First World War. Joining the Italian Bersaglieri, during the war he was wounded in a training accident, although later the incident was blown up into a heroic action on the front line. Imagining himself to be the great leader he believed Italy so desperately needed, Mussolini returned home totally opposed to the Socialist Party that had, by then, expelled him.

In 1919 Mussolini formed a new party in Milan, christening it the Fasci de Combattimento, harking back to the glories of ancient Rome with reference to the 'fasces' or wooden staves carried by Roman lictors as symbols of authority as they guarded Rome's magistrates. Soon his followers were wearing the famous black shirts to distinguish them from the crowd – no doubt inspired by Garibaldi's Red Shirts of the Risorgimento.

By 1920 Italy was becoming increasingly chaotic and Mussolini's posturing as a man of destiny, coupled with his open call for authoritarian leadership, had strong appeal for a populace fed up with riots in the streets and the unceasing strikes paralysing the nation. At a Fascist rally in Naples, on 24 October 1922, he openly threatened the government: 'Either the government will be given to us or we shall seize it by marching on Rome.' A week later the King appointed him Prime Minister – at 39, the youngest in Italy's short history.

Once in power, Mussolini did not make the trains run on time, although he made the world think he did. A neurotic who wouldn't shake hands because he thought it unhygienic, he did build the first *autostrada*, temporarily crush the Mafia, and excavate the Roman Forum. He also took complete dictatorial control of his country.

Mussolini considered Adolf Hitler 'a terrible sexual degenerate' (presumably because of Hitler's apparent lack of sex life) and Germany 'a racist insane asylum'. But when Hitler invaded Poland and then rolled up the rest of Europe, Mussolini was consumed by jealousy of his military success after Italy's costly failure in Ethiopia. And so, half for reasons of envy, half to protect Italy from German aggression, Mussolini committed himself to the Axis and declared war on an already defeated France. In explanation, he portentously announced: 'One moment on the battlefield is worth a thousand years of peace.'

The rest, as they say, is history – Italy's catastrophic defeat in the war and Mussolini's ignominious end. He was executed with his mistress by his own people.

Also on this day
1588: The English first sight the Spanish Armada off Lizard Point, in Cornwall
* 1830: The 'Citizen King' Louis-Philippe usurps the French throne * 1890: Vincent van Gogh fatally shoots himself * 1900: King Humbert of Italy is assassinated by anarchists at Monza

30 July

The First Defenestration of Prague

1419 We've all heard of the 'Defenestration of Prague', such a bizarre title for a historical event, but how many of us know what it really was? Well, there were actually two events; the first happened today.

The early 15th century was a period of religious turmoil. Two popes reigned during the Great Schism (sometimes three) and the Catholic world was already pregnant with the Protestantism, to be born in the next century. There was no place of greater ferment than Bohemia, where the well-meaning but weak King Wenceslas IV ruled from Prague, headquarters of the Bohemian Reformed Church, which was considered heretical by most of Christendom.

One of the great proto-Protestant reformers of the time was the Czech religious thinker Jan Hus, but Wenceslas failed in his efforts to save him and in 1415, in Konstanz, the Church had him burnt at the stake. Now Wenceslas himself was caught between two fires, as the Bohemian nobility cursed him for not saving Hus while Rome pressured him to suppress the Protestant heresy and return his people to unsullied Catholicism. A weak and vacillating man, Wenceslas turned to drink.

Then, on 17 November 1417, one Oddone Colonna was elected Pope as Martin V. Within months he had forbidden all contact between Christendom and the heretical Bohemian lands – an act that succeeded only in enraging Prague's reformers still further. At last Wenceslas had to act to defuse the situation, but his decision to replace all of Prague's councillors was calamitous. Religious unrest now turned into full-scale rebellion: rioting broke out in Prague and on this hot and humid 30 July, a mob led by the priest Jan Zelivsky broke into the Old Town Hall and hurled several of the new councillors out the window to their deaths. It was the beginning of the Hussite revolution in Bohemia, a precursor to the rise of Protestantism.

Luckily for King Wenceslas, he wasn't in the town hall to be thrown out. In panic he fled to Kunratice castle, where, only seventeen days later, the shock of it all did him in, as he died of chagrin (more probably a stroke), letting out a terrible roar.

Such was the first Defenestration of Prague. The second came 199 years later on 23 May, when Bohemian Protestants once more threw unwanted officials (this time agents of Holy Roman Emperor Matthias) out the window.

31 July

Etienne Marcel is hacked down

1358 Beside the Hôtel de Ville in Paris stands a great equestrian statue of Etienne Marcel, honoured for trying to make the King accountable to his citizens but murdered while betraying his own city.

The mid-14th century was a time of calamity in France. 1337 had seen the start of the Hundred Years War with England, and a decade later the Black Death had devastated the population. The country was ruled by King Jean (II) le Bon, aided by his famously rapacious officials. The Estates General (roughly, a parliament, with representatives of the clergy, the nobility and commoners) served only as a forum to hear the King's decisions, without legislative power.

In 1355 King Jean came to the Estates General to impose taxes to finance the war. The leading commoner representative was the provost of Paris's merchants, Etienne Marcel, a man determined to strike out against a corrupt monarchy and gain some authority for the Estates General over the affairs of the country. When King Jean announced his new taxes, Marcel daringly proposed that the tax money should be controlled by the assembly rather than the crown.

Marcel failed at this first attempt, but soon found a better opportunity. A year later the English captured King Jean at the Battle of Poitiers and carted him off to London, leaving France under the rule of his 18-year-old son, the Dauphin Charles (the future Charles V).

Desperate to ransom his father, the young Dauphin summoned the Estates General to initiate a new tax levy. Now Etienne Marcel had a new demand: if Charles wanted money, he must remove King Jean's more corrupt officials and place himself under the assembly's control.

Charles reacted by proroguing the assembly, but a year later, still without funds, he was compelled to recall it. Now Marcel was able to force through a great edict of reform: the royal administration would be supervised by a *conseil de tutelle* (guardianship council) of twelve leading citizens, the King (or regent, in this case) would not be able to impose new taxes without the agreement of the Estates General, and nobles would no longer be exempt from taxes. It looked to be the first step in making the monarchy answerable to the nation's people.

Unhappily, however, Marcel had forgotten King Jean, who, from luxurious captivity in London, declared the edict null and void, a veto welcomed by the Dauphin.

Now Marcel determined to intimidate Dauphin Charles into sharing his authority, and in February 1358 led an insurrection of the people of Paris. With Marcel at its head, the mob charged into the royal palace and murdered two of Charles's marshals before the Dauphin's eyes.

But even then Dauphin Charles was not so easily cowed. Leaving Paris in Marcel's control, he fled the city to raise an army and re-establish his authority.

Then in May, the peasant revolt called the Jacquerie exploded in north-eastern France; some 100,000 rampaging peasants destroyed 150 castles, torturing and killing scores of nobles. Unwisely, Marcel allied himself with the uprising, but the Jacquerie was short-lived; in only a month it had been brutally suppressed. Now Marcel's last hope was to back the King of Navarre, Charles the Bad, even though this king had earned his nickname through treachery and double-dealing with principalities all over Spain and France. As grandson of Louis X, Charles the Bad asserted that he was the rightful heir to the French throne. Furthermore, his armed bands roamed throughout the countryside around Paris. In desperation, Marcel schemed to let Charles and his men into the walled city.

At midnight on this day Marcel crept secretly to the Porte Saint-Antoine to open the city gates. But there he was caught with the keys in his hand by one of his oldest supporters, Jean Maillart. Maillart, however, had resolved to stand by Dauphin Charles, realising that Marcel was now acting more from his own ambition than to help his fellow Parisians. Seeing Marcel about to open the gates, Maillart challenged him, to which Marcel coolly answered: 'Jean, I am here to take care of the city of which I have charge.'

But Maillart, sensing that Marcel was about to betray the city, instantly felled his old friend with an axe. So ended the life of Etienne Marcel at the age of 40, the first Parisian who had successfully (for a while) stood up to royal power and forced through changes to help the common man.

Also on this day

1556: St Ignatius of Loyola dies in Rome * 1886: Hungarian composer and piano virtuoso Franz Liszt dies in Bayreuth * **1914: French Socialist leader Juan Jaurès is assassinated**

1 August

Hindenburg's departure clears the path for Hitler

1934 Today Paul von Hindenburg, President of Germany and the nation's enduring hero for his great 1914 victories at Tannenberg and the Masurian Lakes, died at the age of 87 at Neudeck, Germany. It is ironic that this old *Junker* (nobleman), anti-democratic and monarchist to the end, was the last best hope of the liberal Weimar Republic. In the final months of his life, he was all that stood between Adolf Hitler and total power in Germany.

As Supreme Commander during the last two years of the First World War, Hindenburg, aided by his Quartermaster-General, Erich Ludendorff, had been virtual ruler of Germany, and in that capacity had led his nation to defeat and revolution. Mainly as a dignified symbol of the nation's former stability, of its better days and past glories, the old soldier was called from retirement and elected President of the German republic in 1925. 'Better a zero than a Nero', one observer wrote.

When his five-year term was up he was re-elected. But despite the enormous respect and admiration in which he was held in Germany, Hindenburg was no bulwark against the ominous trend of events. He loathed Hitler and the Nazis – '*That* man a chancellor? I'll make him a postmaster and he can lick stamps with my head on them' – but the army chiefs finally prevailed upon the President to send for Hitler because they thought they could do business with him if they brought him to power. Hitler took office as Chancellor on 30 January 1933.

The next year, when it was clear that Hindenburg was dying and that a successor as President would have to be found, the army leaders once more chose Hitler, in the mistaken belief that they could control him. Within hours of Hindenburg's death, Hitler announced that the functions of President would be combined with those of Chancellor, and that from now on he would be '*Führer und Reichskanzler*'.

The very next day, anxious to cement the bargain with their new leader, the German armed forces, from the highest commanders to the newest recruit, swore their unconditional obedience to the Führer, their supreme commander, as once they had done to the Kaiser. It would prove a tragically misplaced act of fealty.

At Hindenburg's funeral service on 6 August, his coffin was borne down the aisle to the strains of the funeral march from *Götterdämmerung*. It was appropriate music with which to mark the death of a field marshal – and that of the German republic.

Also on this day

10 BC: Roman Emperor Claudius is born * 527: Justinian takes power as Roman Emperor * 1498: Christopher Columbus discovers South America * 1714: Queen

Anne dies, bringing George I and the Hanoverian dynasty to the English throne * **1798: Admiral Nelson destroys Napoleon's fleet at the Battle of the Nile**

> Events written in **boldface** are covered in full in
> *365: Great Stories from History for Every Day of the Year*,
> the first volume in this series.

2 August

King William Rufus is slain in the New Forest

1100 Today, Walter Tirel was riding with his king, William Rufus, through the New Forest in the south of England, enjoying a day's deer hunting. Suddenly a stag bounded between them. 'Shoot, Walter, shoot, as if it were the devil', cried the King. Tirel loosed an arrow, but, glancing off the stag's back, it impaled the King, who tumbled from his horse and lay dead in the silent forest. Aghast at the accident and fearful of its consequences, Tirel galloped from the scene and fled across the Channel.

When other nobles who had been part of the hunt found William's body, they left it where it had fallen and rode hard for their own estates, in a kingdom now without the authority of a king. A local charcoal-burner loaded the corpse onto his cart and hauled it to Winchester. Such at least is the tale related by contemporary historians such as William of Malmesbury, but rumours persist that the King was murdered.

William II was a blonde, heavy-set man with sharp eyes, an occasional stammer and a fiery red complexion, from which he gained his nickname of Rufus. Second son of William the Conqueror, he inherited his father's ruthlessness but added to it an opportunism and brutality of his own. He succeeded to the English throne on his father's death in September 1087, while his elder brother received the preferable inheritance, the Duchy of Normandy. In his thirteen years as king, William Rufus maintained order in troubled times, further consolidating his father's conquest, but never shrank from cruelty or bloodshed to achieve his ends. The English clergy hated him because of his open contempt for the Church – when he needed money, he raided monasteries. Another issue was his probable homosexuality, one historian recording that his court was rife with 'fornicators and sodomites'. He never married.

Despite William's many bitter enemies, chroniclers of the time maintained that the King's death was an accident and that Walter Tirel fled only from fear that he would be blamed. Some even denied that Tirel had shot the fatal arrow. The French abbot Suger, who sheltered Tirel in France, wrote: 'I have often heard [Tirel], when he had nothing to fear nor to hope, solemnly swear that on the day in question he was not in the part of the forest where the king was hunting, nor ever saw him in the forest at all.'

But ever since that fatal day people have whispered that the King's death was no accident but a foul murder orchestrated by his younger brother Henry, who was also hunting in the forest that day.

Although the legitimate heir to the throne was William's elder brother Robert, he was on Crusade in the Holy Land. The day after William's death Henry rode to Winchester and seized the royal treasury. Then, just two days after that, he was crowned as Henry I in Westminster Abbey.

Cut down by deadly plot or pure mischance, William Rufus was interred in the cathedral tower at Winchester but was refused religious rites by the clergy there because of his bloody career. A year later the cathedral tower collapsed, a sure sign of God's rejection of this irascible king.

Also on this day

216 BC: Carthaginian general Hannibal annihilates the Romans at the Battle of Cannae * 1589: King Henri III of France dies of a stab wound dealt the previous day by the fanatical Dominican friar Jacques Clément, who hated him for naming Henri of Navarre (Henri IV), a Protestant, as his heir * 1788: British portrait and landscape painter Thomas Gainsborough dies of cancer * 1876: American frontiersman and lawman Wild Bill Hickok is shot dead at a poker table in the Number Ten Saloon, Deadwood, South Dakota

3 August

Jesse Owens humiliates the Nazis at the Olympic Games

1936 So far it had been a good year for the Third Reich. In February Germany hosted the fourth winter Olympic games at Garmisch-Partenkirchen, where her athletes finished a highly creditable second behind the Norwegians. In March German troops reoccupied the Rhineland unopposed. And in June, in New York City, Max Schmeling knocked out Joe Louis in the twelfth round at Yankee Stadium.

This morning, however, in a Berlin made resplendent for the summer Olympics, something occurred to take the edge off the notion of Aryan invincibility. Before 110,000 spectators jam-packed into the new Olympic Stadium, with Adolf Hitler and the Nazi brass in attendance and Leni Riefenstahl's camera crews set to film the scenes of German triumph, an American sprinter burst from the starting line like a rocket and streaked down the cinder track to win the finals of the 100-metre dash in a world record time of 10.2 seconds. For the victor – a tall, graceful black man named J.C. Owens (hence 'Jesse') – this victory would be the first of four he would accomplish at the Berlin games.

In a towering performance, acclaimed even by the German crowds, Owens in the next six days went on to win gold medals for the United States in the 220-metre dash, the 400-metre relay and the long jump, setting or equalling Olympic records in each event. The Führer was disgruntled. He told Baldur von Schirach, the Hitler Youth leader: 'The Americans ought to be ashamed of themselves for letting their medals be won by Negroes. I myself would never even shake hands with one of them.'

In the end, however, despite American domination of the track and field events, Germany 'won' the 1936 Olympics with 181 points, the United States coming second with 124 points and Italy third with 47 points. Some 4 million spectators, including thousands of visitors from overseas eager to see the 'New Germany', witnessed the Berlin games. Both as mass pageantry and sports triumph, the eleventh Olympiad proved an extraordinary propaganda victory for Hitler and the Nazi leadership. 'The generous congratulations he and his lieutenants received for their Olympic successes,' wrote the historian of *The Nazi Olympics*, Richard D. Mandell, 'were both emboldening to them and deceiving to their opponents'. Indeed, even as the games got under way, Hitler had begun his fateful meddling in the Spanish Civil War. In the aftermath, with the world's attention still held by the glamour of Olympic feats, he turned his eyes towards Austria.

Also on this day

1492: Christopher Columbus sets sail from Palos de la Frontera in Andalusia with the *Niña*, the *Pinta* and the *Santa Maria* * 1876: British prime minister Stanley Baldwin is born * 1914: Germany declares war on France

4 August

German cavalry invade Belgium to start the First World War

1914 Today at 5 am, just 35 days after Austrian Archduke Franz Ferdinand had been assassinated at Sarajevo, German cavalry units swept over the frontier into neutral Belgium, in the first fighting of the First World War, ending 43 years of peace among the Great Powers of Europe.

Although the great Bismarck had completed the unification of Germany in 1870, the country, in truth, was an amplified Prussia: the Kaiser was the Prussian king and the German army was loyal to him alone. The prime minister, too, was responsible only to him, not to the Reichstag. Furthermore, the country had a three-tier voting system giving disproportionate weight to the rich and powerful. The most populous European nation, this military autocracy was determined to be reckoned among the greatest of powers and alarmed its neighbours by its military and naval build-up. Yet Germany felt itself a victim, encircled by France on the west and Russia on the east: two countries that had allied themselves solely from fear of German might. When Germany launched its attack, most of her citizens felt they were only defending themselves.

Germany's northern sweep through Belgium was a central element in the 1905 plan developed by the Prussian General Alfred von Schlieffen. His aim was to destroy the French with a massive attack while fighting a holding action against Russia. But heavy fortifications on the German–French border precluded direct assault, so von Schlieffen advocated sending a massive army on a quick enveloping dash through neutral Belgium. The Germans would storm past Brussels and down into France at Lille and along the coast, then swing around below Paris to catch the main French army from the rear. He thought France would be defeated in 40 days – too short a time for backward Russia to get more than a few token troops to the eastern front, or for Great Britain, tied by treaty to Belgium, to get its troops across the Channel. Once the French had been defeated, the German army would swing east to crush the Russians.

But nothing went according to plan. The Germans met fierce Belgian resistance at Liège, which slowed down their attack, and when they reached France in early September they found themselves facing the French army and the British Expeditionary Force. In the opening clashes of the war, at the Ardennes, the Sambre, Mons, Le Cateau and Guise, the Germans continued their inexorable advance. But at the Marne, in early September, the Allies managed to hold the line and mount a counter-attack, stalling the German onslaught and forcing them back into positions that would not change much over the next four years. In like manner, war against Russia proved far more difficult than anticipated. Despite early German victories at Tannenberg and the Masurian Lakes, by the autumn the two sides were stalemated in the horrors of trench warfare on both the eastern and western fronts. Instead of 40 days, the war had another four years to run.

By the time the conflict finally ground to a halt, Germany had committed some 11 million men, of whom 1,774,000 had been killed and an additional 4 million had been wounded. Perhaps luckily for General von Schlieffen, he died in January 1913, too early to see how disastrous his great plan would turn out to be.

Also on this day

1347: English King Edward III spares the Burghers of Calais * 1265: The future Edward I wins the Battle of Evesham, in which the usurper Simon de Monfort is killed * 1792: British poet Percy Shelley is born at Horsham, Sussex * 1901: Jazz trumpeter and singer Louis Armstrong is born in New Orleans

5 August

The first American income tax

1861 To fight a war you need money: a principle well understood by Salmon P. Chase, Secretary of the Treasury for the North during America's Civil War. With that same principle in mind, and with the encouragement of Chase and other Republican leaders, the 37th Congress today enacted the very first federal income tax in American history: a 3 per cent levy on incomes over $800, thus exempting most wage earners. (Chase's innovation was, in fact, no innovation at all, for Great Britain had introduced the world's first income tax in 1799 to finance the Napoleonic wars.)

One reason an income tax was needed was to pay the interest on the war bonds the federal government was now so actively selling, not just in large denominations to bankers, but for as little as $50 to ordinary people – another Chase innovation.

There was, of course, opposition to the new income tax, as the US Constitution prohibited a direct tax on American citizens, but Chase easily persuaded the Supreme Court to OK the idea.

Although Chase's income tax was repealed in 1872, future generations of Americans have suffered more than Northerners did in 1861. On 3 February 1913 the states ratified the 16th Amendment to the US Constitution, authorising the collection of income tax broadly in its current form, but even then the maximum rate reached only 7 per cent. During the Second World War the top bracket was set at 94 per cent and although rates have declined ever since, by the 21st century the revenue raised by the tax exceeded a trillion dollars a year.

Also on this day

1850: French writer Guy de Maupassant is born near Dieppe * 1858: Queen Victoria exchanges greetings with US President James Buchanan when the first transatlantic cable is opened * **1864: Union Admiral David Farragut damns the torpedoes and goes full speed ahead in defeating the Confederates at Mobile Bay**

6 August

The first coronation in Reims's new cathedral sets a six-century trend

1223 Today, when Louis VIII and his wife Blanche of Castile were crowned in the new cathedral of Notre-Dame in Reims, they set a precedent that was to last for 602 years.

Thirteen years before, an earlier church had burnt down, but in less than a year work was begun on the new cathedral. The site was a particularly holy one to the French, for it contained (and indeed still contains) the remains of Saint Remi, the bishop of Reims who converted France's first king, Clovis, to Christianity in AD 496. It was to honour this event that King Louis had chosen Reims for his coronation. Fortunately, the new building had reached a suitable state of glory to justify its choice, although it required over 80 years to be finished.

Reims Cathedral is often compared to two contemporary Gothic cathedrals, also both named after Our Lady, Notre-Dame de Chartres and Notre-Dame de Paris. Like the church at Reims, Chartres Cathedral was destroyed by fire (in 1194), but the new (current) building was started only in 1260, half a century after work began at Reims. Construction on Notre-Dame de Paris started in 1163 and, escaping the ravages of fire, the cathedral was consecrated in 1189, making it older than either Reims or Chartres. (Identifying the first Gothic church is a contentious undertaking, as the evolution from Romanesque was not sudden or precise, but the abbey of Saint-Denis north of Paris, rebuilt about 1135, is often cited.)

Reims is larger than either Chartres or Notre-Dame, with an interior length of 496 feet, with two glorious towers soaring to a height of 270 feet. Although the cathedral's stained-glass windows are perhaps marginally inferior to those of Chartres (and to those in Sainte-Chapelle in Paris), it remains one of the architectural and artistic gems of the French High Gothic.

Over the centuries Reims Cathedral was the site of 25 French coronations, including Charles VII's in 1429, witnessed by Joan of Arc. The last French king to be crowned there was the 68-year-old reactionary Charles X, who was booted into exile five years later by the Revolution of 1830.

Also on this day

1623: Shakespeare's wife Anne Hathaway dies * 1637: English dramatist Ben Jonson dies in London * 1680: Diego Velázquez dies in Madrid * **1806: The Holy Roman Empire comes to an end when, under pressure from Napoleon, Holy Roman Emperor Franz II renounces the title, becoming Franz I, Emperor of Austria** * 1809: Alfred, Lord Tennyson is born * 1945: The US drops an atomic bomb on Hiroshima, killing 70,000

7 August

A papal candidate fakes his way to election

1316 For over two years there had been no pope, as the cardinals grappled for power and fought either to keep the papacy in Avignon or to return it to Rome. In June the cardinals met in Lyon but still failed to agree, so Prince Philip of Poitiers (later King Philip V of France) invited them to meet in the Church of the Jacobins for one more deliberation. But as soon as the cardinals were inside, Philip's men slammed the doors and bricked up all the entrances except for one narrow doorway. A pope must be elected, declared Philip and no one would leave until one was. And so the days started to pass.

Among the horrified holy men was a small, slight cardinal with a pallid complexion and a large store of hidden ambition. He was Jacques Duèse, son of a cobbler from Cahors, now 72 years of age. Seeing his chance, Duèse feigned increasing weakness and ill health, planting the idea that if he were elected, his reign would be a short one. Finally, after more than a month incarcerated in the church, the 24 cardinals came to an agreement. The feeble and ancient Duèse would be their choice. On 7 August 1316 he was duly elected and at last the imprisoned conclave was released.

How the rival cardinals would regret their choice! John XXII (as he was subsequently called) was both dictatorial and pigheaded. His unceasing conflict with Holy Roman Emperor Louis IV provoked the Emperor into establishing an antipope and having John briefly deposed. He was also accused of heresy for the abominable sin of preaching that saints do not go straight to heaven at their deaths but must wait for the Last Judgement.

John was also a world-beater in the art of cronyism: twenty of the 28 cardinals he created were, like him, from southern France and three were his own nephews, thus denying most of the other cardinals a chance to promote their own favourites. Worse, the crafty Duèse outlived almost all his rivals, reigning for eighteen years and dying at the ripe age of 90.

Also on this day

1485: Henry Tudor (the future Henry VII) lands at Milford Haven to challenge Richard III for the throne of England * 1815: Napoleon is exiled to St Helena * 1819: The Spanish surrender to revolutionary Simón Bolívar at Boyaca, Colombia * **1942: US Marines storm ashore to begin the Battle of Guadalcanal**

8 August

A fly in amber

1827 Today, at Chiswick, died British prime minister George Canning, the astute, witty and acerbic politician whose liberal policies infuriated many members of his own party but opened a path towards a more forward-thinking Britain.

In the minds of England's ruling classes of the time, Canning's antecedents were dubious. When he was only a year old, his barrister and sometime-wine-merchant father had died broke, disinherited for having married a ravishing but penniless girl. With no resources to fall back on, his mother had become an actress, and then the mistress of an actor, and young Canning was whisked away by a wealthy uncle for a 'proper upbringing' at Eton and Oxford. Such an unseemly background made Canning suspect for the rest of his life among the aristocrats who dominated Britain.

Canning early decided on a life in politics and was duly elected to Parliament when he was just 23. He soon became a protégé of William Pitt the Younger, occupying increasingly important offices as he 'climbed the greasy pole': under-secretary of state for foreign affairs at 26 and joint paymaster and privy councillor at 30, the same year he put his financial worries behind him by marrying an heiress. Canning's formidable debating skills earned him the nickname of 'The Cicero of the British Senate'.

In March of 1807 Canning was promoted to Foreign Secretary, where he gained much credit for outmanoeuvring Napoleon by dispatching the British naval expedition that destroyed the Danish fleet at Copenhagen, and for preparing the way for Britain's critical role in the Peninsular War. But his bitter criticism of Secretary of War Viscount Castlereagh became so hostile that Castlereagh challenged him to a duel. Canning, who had never before fired a pistol, left Castlereagh unscathed, but his opponent's ball caught him in the thigh. In the wake of the scandal, both men resigned from the Cabinet.

Canning remained out of office for seven years, while his rival Castlereagh returned to become a distinguished foreign secretary and a major player at the Congress of Vienna. Gloomy about his prospects of again gaining an important Cabinet post, in 1822 Canning became Governor-General of Bengal, but, just before his ship was to sail, Castlereagh committed suicide. Canning was asked to take his job as Foreign Secretary and become Leader of the House of Commons – effectively the most influential man in Britain after the Prime Minister.

Now Canning could act on his forward-looking beliefs, taking Britain out of the repressive Holy Alliance led by Russia, Austria and Prussia. He then recognised the independence of the rebellious Spanish colonies in Latin America, memorably claiming that he had 'called the New World into existence to redress the balance of the Old'. He also supported Greece in its fight for independence from Turkey. Domestically, he was the government's leading proponent of Catholic Emancipation. (The fat and feckless George IV opposed all of these measures, but Canning cheerily ignored him, causing the King to splutter that 'he is a plebeian and has no manners'.)

While Foreign Secretary, Canning consolidated his reputation for wit by sending the British ambassador to The Hague a dispatch in cipher that read:

> In matters of commerce the fault of the Dutch
> Is offering too little and asking too much.
> The French are with equal advantage content,
> So we clap on Dutch bottoms, just 20 per cent.

Finally, when Lord Liverpool stepped down in 1827, Canning was asked to lead the government. Conservatives and aristocrats were distressed, one witty preacher claiming that Canning was like a fly in amber. 'Nobody cares about the fly', he cracked. 'The only question is, how the devil did it get there?'

Disdainful of Canning's pedestrian beginnings, resentful of his liberalism and dismayed by his support for Catholic emancipation, half the Cabinet walked out, including the Duke of Wellington and Sir Robert Peel. More than 40 other Tory ministers and appointees also resigned. After only 119 days as Prime Minister, Canning's health collapsed and he died of pneumonia, having held the office for the shortest period in British history. Perhaps wistful for triumphs of earlier years, his last words were 'Spain and Portugal'.

But Canning had not laboured in vain. Two years after his death Parliament passed the Emancipation Act allowing Catholics in Parliament and most public offices, and Palmerston followed his international policies when he became Foreign Secretary. Younger MPs, who had admired Canning's liberal spirit, passed the Reform Bill in 1832, which greatly increased the number of MPs from heavily populated urban areas at the expense of 'pocket boroughs' controlled by the nobility.

Also on this day

AD 117: **Hadrian becomes Roman Emperor following the death of his adoptive father Trajan** * 1786: Jacques Balmat and Michel-Gabriel Paccard reach the summit of Mont Blanc, the first ever to do so * 1883: Mexican revolutionary leader Emiliano Zapata is born

9 August

The French and Indians conquer Fort William Henry

1757 On this late summer morning, Fort William Henry, the British bastion at the head of Lake George, fell after six days of siege in which 'the cannon thundered all day and from a hundred peaks and crags the astonished wilderness roared back the sound'.

The attackers, a mixed force of 8,000 French regulars, Canadian militia and their Indian allies, were commanded by the marquis de Montcalm. They had sailed up the lake from their stronghold at Fort Ticonderoga with the aim of driving the British military forces out of central New York.

A drum was beaten, a white flag was raised above the fort, and a mounted officer rode out towards Montcalm's tent. There it was agreed that under the civilised custom of European warfare the British garrison, consisting of regulars and colonial militiamen, after swearing to be non-combatants for eighteen months, would march out with the honours of war for their brave defence, leaving their dead and wounded behind, and receive safe passage under guard to Fort Edward, on the Hudson River fourteen miles distant.

Montcalm's Indian allies, however, did not care for such a settlement, preferring to plunder their defeated foe. The next day, as the British column, which included many wives and children of militiamen, began the march to Fort Edward, the Indians struck, demanding rum, baggage, clothing, money and weapons. Anyone who resisted or ran was tomahawked. Children and women were seized and dragged into the forest. When the French finally restored order, 185 people had been killed and some 500 or 600 wounded, mistreated, or dragged away, although of this last category Montcalm's men eventually recovered 400 from the forest.

Now, the Indians cleared out for Montreal, taking with them their plunder and some 200 captives. The following day, the French successfully escorted the survivors of the British column to Fort Edward.

The French withdrew down the lake to Fort Ticonderoga on 16 August, leaving Fort William Henry a smoking ruin in the wilderness. Then, as Francis Parkman wrote: 'The din of 10,000 combatants, the rage, the terror, the agony, were gone; and no living thing was left but the wolves that gathered from the mountains to feast upon the dead.'

The fall of Fort William Henry, described by James Fenimore Cooper in *The Last of the Mohicans*, was not the last French victory in the bloody conflict called the French and Indian War. The very next year the French under Montcalm inflicted an even greater defeat on a British force at Fort Ticonderoga. At the same time, however, the British strategy began to prevail with the capture, first of the French fortress at Louisbourg and then of Fort Duquesne at the forks of the Ohio river. Finally, in the culminating effort of the war, General Wolfe took the great French stronghold at Quebec in 1759 and North America was fairly won to British arms.

Also on this day

48 BC: Julius Caesar defeats Pompey the Great at the Battle of Pharsalus, becoming master of the Roman Empire * AD 378: The Visigoths defeat and kill Roman Emperor Valens at Adrianople * 1595: Izaak Walton, author of *The Compleat Angler*, is born * 1945: Americans drop an atomic bomb on Nagasaki, forcing the Japanese to surrender * 1974: Richard Nixon becomes the first and only US president to resign

10 August

The mob butchers Louis XVI's Swiss Guard

1792 The Bastille had fallen three years earlier and France was in turmoil as revolutionaries tried to extend the Revolution, while émigrés abroad did everything to stop it. King Louis XVI was virtually a prisoner in the Tuileries, but retained some royal powers. In April the government had declared war on Prussia and Austria, who insisted on the full restoration of the monarchy, but

French forces had suffered ignominious defeats as the Austro-Prussian army crossed the French border and advanced on Paris.

Believing that King Louis was behind the foreign intervention, revolutionary fanatics in the Paris Commune ordered the Legislative Assembly to bring the monarchy to an end by depriving the King of his few remaining powers. When the Assembly dithered, on 10 August 1792 militants recruited a huge crowd of 20,000 marching and chanting peasants. Threats exploded into violence.

The gigantic crowd approached the Tuileries, defended only by Louis's Swiss Guard, the last troops loyal to the King. Suddenly, shouts became rocks and small-arms fire and the mob swept through the buildings, massacring all 800 Guards. Louis looked on helplessly, finally saving himself by fleeing to the Assembly and pleading for protection. The monarchy was doomed and the King had only five months to live.

Most historians see poor Louis as a hapless and powerless victim of an unstoppable revolutionary explosion. But one observer of the massacre of 10 August did not agree. In the crowd watching the assault on the Tuileries was another absolute ruler-in-waiting, a 23-year-old soldier named Napoleon Bonaparte. Shortly after the event he expressed his own ideas about leadership in a letter to his brother. 'If Louis had mounted his horse,' he wrote, 'the victory would have been his.'

Also on this day

AD 258: During the persecution under Roman emperor Valerian, Roman deacon St Lawrence is roasted on a gridiron, remarking to his executioners: 'I am cooked on that side; turn me over and eat.' * **1557: Philip II's victory at the Battle of St Quentin on the Feast of St Lawrence inspires the building of El Escorial** * 1810: Italian patriot and unifier Camillo Benso, conte di Cavour, is born * 1874: US President Herbert Hoover is born

11 August

A Borgia becomes Pope

1492 This was a watershed year for Europe: King Ferdinand and Queen Isabella finally conquered the last Moorish stronghold in Spain (and three months later expelled the Jews) to unite the country under Christian rule, Christopher Columbus discovered America, and Lorenzo the Magnificent died after 23 years of leading Florence, Europe's most civilised city state. It was also the year that the papacy moved into its most worldly, cynical and corrupt period, with the election of Roderigo Borgia, who on this day became Pope Alexander VI.

Roderigo was 61 at his elevation and had long been a highly capable vice chancellor of the Church. Nonetheless, he assured his election by appropriate bribes, including four mule-loads of silver to one of the more influential cardinals.

Even at his election there were many who feared what was to come. 'Now we are in the power of the wolf', said the young Cardinal de' Medici (later Pope Leo X). 'The most rapacious perhaps that this world has ever seen; and if we do not escape, he will inevitably devour us.'

Indeed, the Borgia legend is stuffed with tales of corruption, treachery and murder by poison, many of them probably true. But what is absolutely certain is that Alexander was one of the most venal of all popes. During the course of his eleven-year pontificate he appointed 47 cardinals primarily for their political support and willingness to turn a blind eye to his depredations. He also schemed with his three sons and his daughter to create a Borgia dynasty with enormous temporal power in Italy, making Juan a duke and Cesare a cardinal, although still a teenager. But he spent most of his reign ministering to his mistresses and patronising the arts. Among other achievements, he persuaded Michelangelo to draw up plans for the rebuilding of St Peter's Cathedral.

Also on this day

1239: Christ's Crown of Thorns is brought to France, inspiring Louis XI (St Louis) to build Sainte-Chapelle in Paris to house it * 1297: Pope Boniface VIII canonises French King Louis IX as Saint Louis * 1495: Flemish painter Hans Memling dies in Bruges * 1890: English Roman Catholic theologian John Henry Newman dies

12 August

The building of the Berlin Wall

1961 At 4 pm today, a Saturday, Walter Ulbricht, Stalinist dictator of the Deutsche Demokratische Republik, signed Operation 'Wall of China' to construct the infamous Berlin Wall. At midnight, 25,000 militiamen and Vopos (*Volkspolizei,* i.e. People's Police) armed with Kalashnikov machine guns were posted at six-foot intervals along the border between East Germany and West Berlin, and 25 miles of barbed wire was unloaded from warehouses. Then, at 1.11 am Sunday morning, while Berlin slept, the Communist government – claiming that Warsaw Pact countries had demanded 'effective controls' – placed barbed wire barriers across 74 of the city's 81 crossing points, stopped all traffic to West Berlin, and closed down the sections of the *S-Bahn* linking the two sections of the city.

From now on the citizens of the German Democratic Republic could no longer seek freedom and a better life in the West, but would remain incarcerated in the totalitarian East.

Ever since Russia had established the GDR in 1949, people had fled to the West, some 2.5 million of them by the time the Wall was built. Still worse, most of these were educated professionals and skilled workers and their loss jeopardised the economic viability of the country. Even with the border between East and West Germany effectively closed, thousands continued to flee through Berlin, where a simple subway ride could bring escapees to West Berlin for a quick flight to freedom. Hence the Wall: in effect a prison door clanging shut, and almost instantly a global symbol of repression and Communist failure.

Initially the Wall consisted of concrete slabs and barbed wire, watched by 116 guard towers. Almost 200 streets were abruptly terminated when they reached the border and submerged railings were implanted in lakes and rivers, constantly patrolled by armed police boats. But even this failed to stop all traffic, so the Wall was constantly strengthened, guarded by soldiers with machine guns and German Shepherds. Even the soldiers were in two echelons: the first to guard the Wall, the second to guard the first. Eventually the Wall and its fortifications extended for a total of 103 miles, dividing the two Berlins and separating West Berlin from the rest of East Germany. British thriller writer John Le Carre memorably describes it in his spy novel, *The Spy Who Came in from the Cold* as 'a dirty, ugly thing of breeze blocks and strands of barbed wire, lit with cheap yellow light, like the backdrop for a concentration camp'.

Even these draconian measures failed to stop East Germans from fleeing to the West. Some 5,000 people went over, under and around the Wall, while the Vopos captured an equal number attempting to break out. Some 191 people were killed, gunned down while escaping.

But the story, as we all know, has a happy ending. Starting in 1987, Russian General Secretary Mikhail Gorbachev initiated the processes of *Glasnost* (openness) and *Perestroika* (restructuring), which hugely speeded up the collapse of Communist totalitarian regimes throughout Eastern Europe. In October 1989 the East German government fell, its hated leader Erich Honecker deposed. Finally, on 9 November, the sinister Wall was opened amid the frantic cheers of onlookers from both sides and Berlin – and East Germany – were free at last. Soon the Wall itself was demolished and the concrete blocks were crushed and used to make roads. In good capitalist fashion, 250 sections of the Wall were auctioned off at prices from 10,000 to 150,000 deutschmarks.

Also on this day

1624: Cardinal Richelieu is named first minister by King Louis XIII * **1822: British foreign secretary Robert Stewart, Lord Castlereagh cuts his throat** * 1827: English poet and painter William Blake dies * 1896: Gold is discovered near Dawson City, Yukon Territory, Canada * 1898: Hawaii is annexed by the United States

13 August

The Edict of Nantes establishes freedom of religion in France

1598 Ever since the Protestant Jean Vallière was burned at the stake in Paris in 1523, France's Protestants, or Huguenots, had suffered from the most calamitous religious persecution as Catholics and Protestants alike resorted to murder and mayhem in defence of God's true faith, as they saw it. The persecution of the Huguenots had reached its deadly zenith during the Massacre of St Bartholomew in 1572, when 2,000 were murdered in Paris and perhaps as many as 70,000 in France as a whole. But then in 1589 Henri of Navarre, the nation's first Bourbon monarch, came to the throne as Henri IV, a nominal Protestant who outwardly turned Catholic to consolidate his power.

On this date, nine years after assuming the throne, Henri signed the Edict of Nantes in the ducal château in the city of that name in Brittany. The Edict's 92 articles gave France's Protestants the religious freedom that had been denied them so long, including the right to worship openly, except in Paris, where Catholic feeling was still too strong. Protestant pastors, along with Catholic priests, would be paid by the state. The Religious Wars that had torn the nation apart for 36 years had come to an end at last.

Sadly for the nation, Henri's great edict would stay in force for less than a century. On 18 October 1685 his grandson Louis XIV revoked it, once more denying the Huguenots both religious and civil rights. In the years that followed almost half a million of them left the country for the more welcoming Protestant regimes in Holland, England and Prussia, where their talent, wealth and industry helped their new homelands to the detriment of France.

Also on this day

1521: Spanish conquistador Hernán Cortés recaptures Tenochtitlán (Mexico City) and overthrows the Aztec empire * **1704: The Duke of Marlborough and Prince Eugene of Savoy defeat the French at the Battle of Blenheim** * 1863: French painter Eugène Delacroix dies * 1899: English director of thrillers Alfred Hitchcock is born * 1923: Kemal Atatürk is elected the first President of Turkey

14 August

The most cultivated pope

1464 Although not a patron of the arts, Enea Silvio Piccolomini, who died today, was perhaps history's most cultivated pope. Early in his career, Holy Roman Emperor Frederick III made him poet to the court in Vienna and later Piccolomini became acknowledged throughout Europe as a diplomat, historian, geographer, propagandist and orator. He also wrote at least one scandalous novel, entitled *The Tale of Two Lovers*, and was the father of several bastard children.

During his early career Piccolomini served as secretary to several ecclesiastical figures, including the antipope Felix V, but then Emperor Frederick took him under his wing, moving him to Vienna. There, frightened by a serious illness, he abandoned his dissolute life, disavowed the antipope and received sacred orders at the advanced age of 41. Only a year later he was made a bishop.

At 53 Piccolomini was elected Pope as Pius II. It was said that he selected his papal name because his own was Enea (Aeneas) and one of his favourite heroes, Virgil, had made reference to 'pious Aeneas'.

The great issue of the day was the conquest of Constantinople, which had fallen to the infidel Turks just five years before the start of his pontificate. Pius spent most of his six papal years trying to persuade the princes of Europe to launch a crusade to recapture the city. By June 1464 he was ailing but nonetheless left Rome for the Adriatic port of Ancona, personally to lead the campaign. To his chagrin, he arrived to find no one to lead, as Europe's Christian princes refused his call. After two months of anxious waiting, on the evening of 14 August Pius took to his bed and succumbed to his illness. His heart was left in Ancona for burial, a symbol of the crusade he had hoped to lead. His other remains were transported back to Rome for interment in St Peter's.

Although he failed in his struggle to launch a crusade, if Pius looked down on us today he would still no doubt feel satisfied that his literary pre-eminence remains intact. In the 2,000 years of the papacy, he is the only pope to write his autobiography.

Also on this day

1385: João o Bastardo defeats John of Castile at the Battle of Aljubarrota, guaranteeing Portugal's independence * 1900: A British-led international military force captures Peking to put down the Boxer Rebellion * 1945: Emperor Hirohito announces Japan's unconditional surrender to the Japanese people (the official surrender takes place on 2 September)

15 August

Loyola founds the Jesuits

1534 Today a lame, middle-aged Spanish soldier named Ignacio de Loyola led a small band of six followers to the Chapel of the Auxiliatrices in the Rue Yvonne-Le-Tac on the Left Bank in Paris. There they formally swore to serve the Catholic Church with vows of chastity, poverty and obedience. In time this new organisation would become the Jesuits.

It had started three years earlier at the University of Paris, where Loyola was studying. He had been crippled by a cannonball thirteen years before and now, unable further to serve his king, he had decided to dedicate himself to God. He soon recruited two younger disciples, a Frenchman named Pierre Lefèvre and another Spaniard and future saint, Francisco Javier. As a mark of their devotion, they fixed a picture of Jesus on the door to their room. On seeing this ostentatious display of piety, other students derisively called the three the *Societas Jesu* and the name stuck – and has now for almost 500 years.

Loyola was the driving force behind the new organisation and within three years he had enlisted four more followers. The members continued to proselytise new converts and six years later Pope Paul III recognised the order. The Jesuits were well on their way to becoming the spearhead of militant intellectual Catholicism combating the Protestant Reformation.

Although Loyola died 22 years after founding his order, the Jesuits grew in number and influence over the following centuries. But the society has always provoked controversy, especially in Catholic countries, where it was strongest.

The Jesuits' devotion to the Pope sometimes ran counter to the absolutist ambitions of kings and queens, while their passion for ecclesiastical reform infuriated Church leaders. The order has been expelled by virtually every European country and came close to extinction in 1773, when Pope Clement XIV suppressed it. It was saved only by the intervention of Frederick the Great of Prussia and Catherine the Great of Russia, admirers of the society's erudition and educational zeal, who refused to publish the Pope's ban.

Pius VII, who had himself been educated by Jesuits, finally re-established the society in 1814. Since that time the order has generally flourished, combative, intellectual, proselytising – just like its founder Ignacio de Loyola.

Also on this day

778: Charlemagne loses the Battle of Roncesvalles, inspiring the legend of *La Chanson de Roland* (*The Song of Roland*), the oldest major work of French literature * 1057: (The real) King Macbeth is killed in battle by Malcolm III Canmore near Lumphanan, Aberdeen, Scotland * **1769: Napoleone Buonaparte is born in Ajaccio, Corsica** * 1771: Scottish writer Walter Scott is born

> Events written in **boldface** are covered in full in
> *365: Great Stories from History for Every Day of the Year*,
> the first volume in this series.

16 August

A bad day at Bennington

1777 Today's nasty encounter with rebel militia near Bennington, Vermont, marked a break in General John Burgoyne's invasion of New York, heretofore a most successful – and possibly war-winning – campaign.

Things had begun so well. Barely six weeks earlier, Burgoyne's army had sailed into Lake Champlain from Canada and captured the American stronghold at Fort Ticonderoga without a shot being fired, an event that prompted King George, when news of it reached London, to exult to his queen:

'I have beat all the Americans!'

Since then, his army's southward progress had been marked by further successes against the Americans, at Hubbardton, Skenesborough and Fort Anne – small victories to be sure (and won by narrower margins than he cared to admit), but ones he could well crow about in despatches to London. Rebel resistance was proving slight at best.

Now camped at Fort Edward, Burgoyne's British and German regiments were within striking distance of their strategic objective, Albany, New York. But what they needed to sustain the momentum of their advance was horses, not just to mount the horseless German dragoons (whose pace afoot was greatly impeded by their heavy cavalry boots and cumbersome broadswords) but more importantly to keep the army's supplies moving over frontier trails that were proving too rough and narrow for the heavy wagons of his train. Then came intelligence to the effect that the rebels had a supply depot at Bennington – only 30 miles to the south-east and lightly guarded – where horses, draught animals and other supplies were available in suitable quantities.

So Burgoyne sent off a column of raiders, a mixed force of 800, composed mainly of the unmounted German dragoons fleshed out with grenadiers, British sharpshooters, Canadian and Tory volunteers, Indian scouts and a few pieces of artillery. To command this mission into hostile territory, he selected Lieutenant-Colonel Friedrich Baum, a Brunswick officer with no experience in frontier warfare, not a word of English and orders from Burgoyne that included the phrase, 'always bearing in mind that your corps is too valuable to let any considerable loss be hazarded'.

Three days later, on the 14th, Baum's column was within five miles of Bennington. By now there were indications that the rebels were gathering in larger numbers than had been reckoned. He sent word back to Burgoyne for reinforcements, then hunkered down in a defensive deployment that spread his forces in non-supporting detachments along both sides of the Walloomsac river and up a hillside. It rained heavily on the 15th, postponing action from either side and Baum put the lull to use by constructing redoubts and entrenchments.

On the 16th it cleared by noon. At 3 pm the American assault began. Devised by New Hampshire Brigadier General John Stark, who now had 2,000 militia at his disposal, it was a three-pronged attack against the rear and flanks of Baum's position, followed by a main thrust down the Bennington Road. Retreat was quickly cut off and the action was over by 5 pm, a complete victory for the rebels. Shortly thereafter, the reinforcement column numbering 600 soldiers arrived on the scene, surprising the Americans with a strong attack, but held off with help of newly arrived militia. By nightfall, after fierce fighting, the relief column, low on ammunition, was in full retreat towards the Hudson.

The British losses sustained by both columns at Bennington totalled well over 900 killed, wounded or captured – some 15 per cent of Burgoyne's entire force. Among the slain was Baum himself.

For the Americans, Bennington was a rousing success, greatly heartening a local population so recently cowed by what seemed an inexorable British advance through their countryside. It gave the rebels a hint of what they might achieve. One of their number jubilantly declared it: 'The compleatest Victory gain'd this war.' George Washington, defending Philadelphia against another British army, expressed his elation at 'the great stroke struck by Stark at Bennington'.

For 'Gentleman Johnny' Burgoyne, the playwright–warrior, Bennington was a severe shock and an embarrassing turn of events, but he probably did not recognise it as a sign of things to come. No doubt he assumed that even in their reduced circumstances, his army would soon be in Albany, 'masters of the Hudson'. But a true assessment of his defeat would have been along the lines of Winston Churchill's famous formulation after El Alamein: that it was not the end, or even the beginning of the end, but perhaps it was the end of the beginning.

Also on this day

1717: Austrian general Prince Eugene of Savoy crushes the Turks at the Battle of Belgrade * 1819: In St Peter's Fields in Manchester, untrained yeomanry, the 15th Hussars and the Cheshire Volunteers attack a crowd demanding suffrage at the so-called Peterloo Massacre, wounding about 500 and killing eleven * 1948: American baseball icon Babe Ruth dies * 1977: Rock and roller Elvis Presley dies of a heart attack at Graceland, his mansion in Memphis

17 August

A magnificent château dooms a French minister

1661 Today, Nicolas Fouquet thought to impress the young King Louis XIV with a magnificent house-warming at his extraordinary new château of Vaux-le-Vicomte, some 35 miles south-west of Paris. But instead of the glory he sought, he found life imprisonment.

The son of a wealthy shipowner, Fouquet had been appointed *surintendant des finances* (finance minister) under Cardinal Mazarin in 1653. There he had helped both the government and himself, as he became excessively wealthy. On Mazarin's death he hoped to climb even higher in the King's service, in keeping with his family motto: *'Quo non ascendet'* ('What heights will he not scale?').

Hence the lavish fête. Apart from the King, Fouquet invited some 6,000 guests, to whom he distributed favours such as diamond brooches and thoroughbred horses. He arranged a spectacular display of fireworks that dazzled his visitors as they wandered through almost 100 acres of manicured gardens studded by 250 fountains and he even commissioned Molière to write a ballet-comedy, *Les Fâcheux*, for the occasion.

What Fouquet did not know was that Mazarin's confidant, Jean-Baptiste Colbert, was determined to discredit him and place himself at the King's right hand – and thanks to Colbert's secret briefings, King Louis now believed that Fouquet had enriched himself through misappropriation of royal funds. The spectacular house-warming at Vaux-le-Vicomte was the last straw: appalled by his minister's '*luxe insolent et audacieux*', Louis then and there decided that no man should surpass the King. As Voltaire later wrote: '*Le 17 août à 6 heures du soir, Fouquet était le roi de France: à 2 heures du matin, il n'était plus rien.*' ('On 17 August at 6 in the evening, Fouquet was King of France; at 2 in the morning, he was nobody.')

Only weeks after the fête Fouquet was accused of embezzlement (he was arrested by a commander of Musketeers named d'Artagnan) and brought to trial. The case continued for almost three years; Louis hoped for the death penalty, but most of the judges wanted only to banish the former minister. Then, for the first and last time in French history, the head of state overruled the court's decision, not to lighten the sentence, but to increase it. Fouquet was imprisoned in the château-fort of Pigneroles, from which he never emerged. There he died after sixteen years of captivity.

King Louis would never again see one of his subjects outshine him. From this evening sprang his determination to build the greatest of all royal châteaux, Versailles. He even engaged Fouquet's architect, landscaper and decorator to work on it.

Also on this day

1786: Frederick the Great of Prussia dies at Sans Souci, Potsdam * 1786: Legendary American frontiersman Davy Crockett is born in Tennessee * 1850: French novelist Honoré de Balzac dies * 1876: The first performance of Wagner's *Götterdämmerung* is given in Bayreuth * 1896: Gold is first discovered near the Klondike River in the Yukon Territory of Canada, igniting the Klondike Gold Rush

18 August

A Borgia pope dies addressing God

1503 On this day died Roderigo Borgia after 72 years on this earth, eleven of them as Pope under the papal name of Alexander VI. Apparently addressing the God he had so often ignored during his pursuit of secular power, his final words are reported to have been: 'I come. It is right. Wait a minute.'

Alexander had been born Spanish in the town of Játiva but had easily progressed through the ranks of the Church through the patronage of his uncle, Pope Calixtus III, who created him a cardinal when he was still only 25.

Alexander's career was famous for ambition, treachery, simony, nepotism and lust for power and the number of his mistresses (three) and illegitimate children (nine) was high, even for a priest. But he also had his accomplishments, embellishing much of the Vatican. One of his decisions left a lasting mark on history when, in 1494, he negotiated the Treaty of Tordesillas that divided South America into Spanish and Portuguese zones of influence.

In August of 1503 both Alexander and his son Cesare fell ill with fever, prompting the rumour that they had accidentally ingested white arsenic that Cesare carried with him to use on others. Cesare recovered, but Alexander suffered from severe bleeding dysentery, his skin began to peel off and his face turned puce. After a week of fever and pain, he accepted the last rites and passed into history.

It is likely that Alexander died of what the Italians called *mal aria* (bad air – they had no idea the disease was borne by mosquitoes), a constant menace of Roman summers 500 years ago. But such was the ruthlessness of the age and the reputation of the man that there are still suspicions that he may have been poisoned. The most dramatic (and improbable) account is that Catarina Sforza, whom Alexander had imprisoned, sent him a bamboo cane, inside which was a secret letter that had been rubbed with the shirt of a man who had died of plague, leading to Alexander's grisly death.

Also on this day

1227: Mongolian conqueror Genghis Khan dies in Mongolia * 1587: Virginia Dare, the first English child born in what would become the United States, is born in the Roanoke Island colony * 1830: Austrian Emperor Franz Joseph I is born

19 August

Allied disaster at Dieppe

1942 This morning at 4.45 Operation Jubilee commenced: Allied troops landed at the French port of Dieppe to launch a daring attack on Nazi-held Europe, the first such operation since the all-triumphant Wehrmacht had kicked the British Army off the Continent at Dunkirk two years earlier. By early afternoon it was all over, a terrible disaster in which of the 5,100 men who went ashore – two brigades of the Canadian Division supported by British commando units – 3,684 did not make it back, either killed or captured. Among those killed was Lieutenant Edwin Loustalot, one of 50 US Rangers taking part in the attack. He was the war's first American battle death in the European theatre.

Operation Jubilee suffered from inadequacies in almost every aspect: objective, planning, intelligence, communications, tactics and strategy. Loss of surprise also contributed to the mission's failure. Only courage among the attackers was not in short supply, but alone it could not prevail. The Royal Navy lost a destroyer and 33 landing craft, while the RAF lost 106 planes to the Germans' 46.

The raid at Dieppe was meant to be a practice run for the great cross-Channel attack that would establish the Second Front and reclaim Europe from German occupation. In its two strategic purposes, however, the raid failed either to draw off German units from the Eastern Front, where Soviet Russia was reeling under Operation Barbarossa, or to inflict heavy losses on the Luftwaffe units sent to defend the port. Finally, the utter failure of the raid went a long way to bring US war planners around to the British contention that the time was not yet right for a full-scale invasion of the Continent.

The German High Command described the Dieppe raid as 'an amateur undertaking', but Winston Churchill was also right when he called it a 'mine of experience'. Among the valuable lessons the Allies learned this day was that for such an operation air dominance is vital; another was that the initial landings should be made not at a port, where urban warfare would be the order of the day, but on a long stretch of open beaches providing adequate room for the fast build-up of an invasion-sized force. Like Normandy, for instance.

Also on this day

AD 14: First Roman emperor Caesar Augustus dies (perhaps murdered) in Nola, near Naples * 1662: French mathematician, philosopher and writer Blaise Pascal dies in Paris * 1692: Six 'witches' are executed during the Salem witch trials in Massachusetts * 1871: Aviation pioneer Orville Wright is born in Dayton, Ohio

20 August

Richard the Lionheart slaughters his prisoners

1191 Over the centuries England's King Richard the Lionheart has come to symbolise the virtues of knightly valour and chivalry. His reputation is based largely on his famous adventures during the Third Crusade, when he matched armies and wills with that pinnacle of Saracen honour and courage, Saladin. Nothing displays Richard's true character better than the story of his triumph at Acre.

Saladin had been supreme in the Holy Land since the destruction of the main Christian army in 1187. But in the fiery summer of 1189 the King of Jerusalem, Guy de Lusignan, gathered his small remaining forces to lay siege to Acre, a key Saracen fortress and seaport. Saladin soon arrived with his army to relieve the siege but was unable to dislodge King Guy before Christian reinforcements arrived. First came the French, under King Philip Augustus, then the remains of the army of German Emperor Frederick Barbarossa (Barbarossa himself had drowned while bathing in a river). Then came the Austrians under Duke Leopold and finally the English commanded by Richard.

The siege, which lasted for two years, was fierce, with casualties high on both sides. Eventually Saladin's commanders inside the fortress could see that their lord could not relieve them and they surrendered on 12 July 1191.

When the crusaders took possession of the fortress they captured some 3,000 surrendering Saracens, including women and children, whom Richard was anxious to barter for Saladin's Christian prisoners and the True Cross that Saladin was reputed to have in his possession. But the days passed and no agreement could be reached.

On 20 August Richard's patience came to an end. All 3,000 Saracens, bound with ropes, were marched outside the city walls so that they would be well in view of Saladin's nearby army. Then Richard ordered one of history's most barbarous slaughters. All the prisoners were to have been beheaded, but, finding this method too slow, Richard ordered his soldiers in with lance, sword and mace. To a man the Saracens were murdered where they stood.

The conquest of Acre was the crusaders' only important victory during the Third Crusade: they never reached Jerusalem. But in 1192 Richard concluded a treaty with Saladin that guaranteed the rights of Christian pilgrims in Jerusalem.

Also on this day

480 BC: The Persians under Xerxes kill the last of the Spartans at their heroic defence at the Battle of Thermopylae * 1625: French playwright Pierre Corneille is born * 1940: In Coyoacán, Mexico, on orders from Stalin, Russian NKVD assassin Ramon Mercader stabs Russian Bolshevik Leon Trotsky with an ice pick, who dies the next day

21 August

Catherine the Great marries the heir to the throne of Russia

1745 The groom was sixteen, the bride a year younger. Both had been born and raised in Germany, but now, in St Petersburg, he was heir to the throne of Russia and she was his loving wife, mother of future Romanov tsars.

The bride and groom who married today would each rule Russia, he as Peter III for a scant six months, she as Catherine the Great for 34 years.

According to her autobiography, Catherine was such an ignorant bride that, until her mother informed her on the day before the wedding, she had no concept of her expected wifely duties. Not that it mattered much – Peter was also a virgin and made no demands on their wedding night.

In fact, we know that the marriage was still unconsummated seven years later, perhaps never consummated, although by then Catherine was far from the fifteen-year-old virgin she had been. She had already started on her string of lovers, one of whom was probably the father of her son, the future tzar Paul.

Perhaps Peter should have been more passionate. Seventeen years after their wedding, he finally inherited the crown, but only six months later Catherine staged her famous *coup d'état* and had her husband strangled in his prison cell.

Also on this day
1165: French king Philip Augustus (Philip II) is born in Paris ∗ **1810: Napoleon's marshal Jean-Baptiste Bernadotte becomes Crown Prince of Sweden, founding the dynasty that still reigns** ∗ 1872: English illustrator Aubrey Beardsley is born

22 August

Why the French heir to the throne is called a dolphin

1350 Although he is little known today, Philip VI, who died on this date at the age of 57, established some landmarks in the history of France.

First, he was France's first Valois king (he had inherited the throne from the last of the Capetians, his first cousin Charles IV) and the Valois would rule the nation for 261 years.

Second, he (along with England's Edward III) started the longest war in history, the Hundred Years War, pitting France against England, which began in 1337 and actually lasted 115 years.

Third, he instituted the most hated tax, the *gabelle*, which eventually became a tax on salt but in Philip's time was the first sales tax on consumer goods.

Fourth, he created the title of Dauphin for the heir to the French throne. The Dauphiné was an area of France near Lyon. It was thus called because its sovereign lords wore a dolphin (*dauphin* in French) on their coats of arms. When the Dauphiné became an integral part of the King's territory in 1349, Philip agreed that from that time forward the eldest son of the King would bear the title Dauphin.

These accomplishments apart, Philip's reign was notably unsuccessful, as he suffered catastrophic defeat by the English at the Battle of Crécy and later the Black Death killed perhaps a third of his people, including his queen, Jeanne. Philip himself met his maker after 22 years, six months and 21 days as King.

Also on this day
1485: Henry Tudor defeats and kills Richard III at Bosworth Field to become King of England as Henry VII ∗ 1642: The English Civil War begins when Charles I raises his standard at Nottingham ∗ 1806: French painter Jean-Honoré Fragonard dies in Paris ∗ 1864: The International Red Cross is founded by the Geneva Convention

23 August

William Wallace pays the price for treason

1305 For the crime of treason there was only one penalty in England. First the traitor was hanged but cut down while still alive. He was then emasculated and disembowelled and his entrails were burned before his eyes. Finally, he was decapitated and his body cut into four parts, to be hung in public places as a reminder of the fearsome wrath of the King. On this day in London the Scottish patriot William Wallace suffered such a death. His left leg was displayed in Aberdeen, his right one in Perth and his left arm in Berwick, his right one in Newcastle. His head was impaled on a spike and put on view at London Bridge.

In the late 13th century, Scotland was in leaderless turmoil. When eight-year-old Queen Margaret died, there were thirteen claimants to the throne and competing Scottish lords ravaged the country. At length the Scottish leaders asked England's King Edward I to arbitrate and the Scottish crown finally went to John de Balliol, who promptly swore fealty to Edward. For this act, John earned from his subjects the name 'Toom Tabard' – 'Empty Coat'. But then John refused to send troops for Edward's wars in France, rejected his demand to cede three border castles and renounced his homage to England. This provided all the excuse Edward needed to invade the country.

Into this confusion stepped a member of the lesser Scottish gentry, William Wallace, a giant of a man (about 6 feet 6 inches), who, according to a near-contemporary historian/hagiographer, was 'all-powerful as a swordsman and unrivalled as an archer'. Furthermore, 'his blows were fatal and his shafts unerring; as an equestrian, he was a model of dexterity and grace; while the hardships he experienced in his youth made him view with indifference the severest privations incident to a military life'.

By 1296, when Wallace was about 27, he was leading what amounted to a guerrilla band against the invading English. Initially successful, he was once captured and left to starve in a dungeon but subsequently rescued by local villagers. After recovering his strength, he recruited another band of about 30 rebels and continued his attacks. Drawing ever more Scots to his banner, in 1297 he became the scourge of the English and scored a major victory at Stirling Bridge where, although heavily outnumbered, he slaughtered some 5,000 English as they crossed the river. For this triumph Wallace was knighted, probably by Scotland's future king, Robert the Bruce.

But Wallace's great triumph had been against Edward I's lieutenants rather than against the redoubtable English king. The following year Edward himself led an army of 25,000 deep into Scotland and annihilated Wallace's force at Falkirk. Wallace escaped the rout and spent the next few years alternately hiding from the English and keeping his revolt alive, at one point slipping off to France to seek aid.

Edward never relented in his search for Wallace, whom he regarded as a traitor for his resistance to his feudal overlord, which Edward considered himself to be. In August 1305 Wallace was captured near Glasgow and brought to London, where he was tried for treason and the murder of civilians (the indictment claimed he spared 'neither age nor sex, monk nor nun'). Although Wallace claimed that he was wrongly accused because he had never sworn fealty to Edward, under Edward's vengeful eye only one verdict was possible.

The man the English considered a treacherous outlaw and the Scottish a national hero was condemned to be hanged, drawn and quartered.

With Wallace dead, Edward believed he had cowed the Scots, but in fact, by his barbarous method of execution he had turned Wallace into a martyr. By the time of his own death in 1307 Edward was already facing a new and far more dangerous enemy, Robert the Bruce. By 1314 Robert had reasserted Scottish independence by totally destroying the army of Edward's son Edward II at the Battle of Bannockburn, only two miles from Wallace's great triumph at Stirling Bridge seventeen years before.

Scotland retained its autonomy for centuries to come, although in 1603 its king, James VI, became James I of England, thus uniting the crowns if not the two countries. Finally in 1707 England and Scotland were formally brought together under the name of Great Britain.

Also on this day

1244: Jerusalem is sacked by the Khwarezmian Turks * 1839: The British capture Hong Kong to use as a base to fight against China, effectively starting the First Opium War * **1939: Dictators Adolf Hitler and Joseph Stalin sign a non-aggression pact**

24 August

Rome falls to 'the licentious fury of the tribes of Germany and Scythia'

AD 410 Today the city of Rome, inviolate and unconquered for 800 years, fell to the troops of the Visigoth leader Alaric.

Alaric was a Visigoth nobleman by birth who had once commanded the Gothic troops in the Roman army, but when he was 25 he left the Romans and was elected chief of the Visigoths. From the moment he took power he was constantly at war with his former masters, first in Turkey, then in Greece and ultimately in Italy itself.

Twice he tried and failed to conquer Rome, still a great city even though the Emperor of the Western Roman Empire had moved his capital north to Ravenna in 402. In 410 he tried once more, demanding land and gold from Emperor Honorius in return for leaving the city in peace. The Emperor unwisely refused and in August Alaric besieged the city. The defiant Romans threatened to send their army out to fight him, to which Alaric made the famous reply: 'The thicker the hay, the easier it is mowed.'

At first it seemed that Alaric would be stymied by the city's monumental walls, but the Romans had forgotten their own slave population that was ready to welcome Alaric as liberator. Edward Gibbon describes the scene: 'At the hour of midnight, the Salarian gate was silently opened [by disaffected slaves] and the inhabitants were awakened by the tremendous sound of the Gothic trumpet. Eleven hundred and 63 years after the foundation of Rome, the Imperial city, which had subdued and civilised so considerable a part of mankind, was delivered to the licentious fury of the tribes of Germany and Scythia.'

In fact, Alaric, a Christian, spared the city's churches and, by the standards of the time, restrained his soldiers from mass murder, although Saint Augustine tells us of some killing and arson. Gibbon informs us that 'the matrons and virgins of Rome were exposed to injuries more dreadful, in the apprehension of chastity, than death itself'. After having occupied the city for six days, Alaric and his army marched away laden with plunder, leaving Rome poorer but intact. He died in Cosenza in Calabria just a few months later at the age of 40 and was buried, together with his looted treasure, in the riverbed of the Busento near Cosentia (today's Cosenza).

Also on this day

1572: On St Bartholomew's Day, the massacre of French Protestants begins, ordered by King Charles IX and his mother, Catherine de' Medici * 1724: English horse painter George Stubbs is born in Liverpool * 1812: The British burn Washington during the War of 1812

25 August

St Louis dies of plague

1270 Louis IX was one of France's good kings and great men. Born in 1214, he inherited the throne at the age of twelve and was initially guided by his formidable mother, Blanche of Castile. Although Blanche remained regent until he was twenty, Louis was an assiduous student of kingship and at the age of fifteen he personally commanded his army in the field.

France was largely prosperous and at peace during Louis's reign, but his real fame comes not from the excellence of his governance but from the quality of his character. He was highly religious, purchasing the Holy Lance, parts of the True Cross and the Crown of Thorns to enshrine them in his greatest monument, the breathtaking Sainte-Chapelle in Paris. He heard Mass twice a day, often fasted and surrounded himself with priests chanting the hours even when he was on horseback. His piety notwithstanding, Louis was also a courageous knight, undaunted by adversity and (between prayers, at any rate) a good companion, the ideal king of the Middle Ages. (On one occasion, however, he must have left his courtiers somewhat bemused when he gave each a present of a hair shirt.)

On a more practical level, Louis had hospitals built, including the 'Quinze-Vingts' for 300 knights who had been blinded by the Saracens. Sometimes he cared for the sick himself and he felt strong responsibility for the poor of his realm. By his order, 100 beggars were given food or alms from royal provisions every day.

In August 1248 Louis embarked on his first crusade, setting sail for Egypt with his wife Marguerite and 35,000 soldiers. Unfortunately, it was a disastrous adventure. Louis's brother was killed and plague struck the army. Louis almost died of dysentery and was captured by the Saracens. He returned to France only four years later.

On 1 July 1270 Louis once more set out on crusade, leaving France from a Mediterranean port he had ordered built some 30 years before, the small walled town with the ominous name of Aigues-Mortes, derived from *aquae mortuae* (dead waters), after the surrounding saline marshland.

Seventeen days later Louis landed in Tunis, near the ruins of ancient Carthage. Initially his army gained some painless victories, but the summer heat was frightful and soon plague appeared, first ravaging the army and then striking the King himself. Knowing he was dying, Louis instructed his son and successor Philip (III) to take special care of the poor.

Louis died on 25 August 1270 at the age of 56, having reigned for 43 years. His entrails were buried on the spot where he died (you can still visit the Tomb of St Louis there today), but his body was brought back to France in one long funeral procession, with mourners lining the roads as it passed through Italy, over the Alps and on to Paris. This great king was entombed in the Abbey of St Denis just north of Paris, historic last resting place of the kings of France. (Bizarrely, tradition among the local Tunisians denies Louis's death, claiming that he converted to Islam under the name of Sidi Bou Said and lived on for another quarter century, to die as a saint of Islam.)

From the moment of his burial Louis was thought a saint and people prayed for miracles at his tomb. He was canonised in 1297, only 27 years after his death, by Pope Boniface VIII. He is the only French king ever declared a saint.

Also on this day

AD **79: 20,000 people are killed when Vesuvius erupts during the last day of Pompeii** * 1530: Ivan IV (the Terrible) is born * 1688: Welsh buccaneer Sir Henry Morgan dies in Jamaica * 1830: The Belgian revolution starts, resulting in modern Belgium * 1900: In Weimar, Friedrich Nietzsche dies after contracting pneumonia after eleven years insane * 1944: Free French units under General Jacques Leclerc enter Paris during the Second World War

26 August

Catherine the Great gives Poland to her lover – and then takes it back

1764 Catherine the Great of Russia was famous for her lovers – she had at least sixteen of them, perhaps modest by today's standards but scandalous for a woman in the 18th century. She also rewarded her lovers generously, none more so than an ineffectual but handsome and intelligent Pole named Stanisław Poniatowski, who had struck the Empress's fancy in the mid-1750s.

When the Polish king died in 1763, Catherine wanted a weak and pliant successor. Under enormous pressure from Catherine's troops (sent to Poland to 'ensure stability'), the Polish Sejm (parliament) today unanimously pronounced in favour of none other than Stanisław, who became the new king under the grand name of Stanisław Augustus. It was Catherine's greatest gift to a lover – an entire country.

Stanisław turned out to be a thoughtful and progressive ruler, although he lacked the grit and determination the job required. During his eleven years on the throne he introduced a remarkably forward-looking and democratic constitution, but Russia and Prussia both backed Poland's enraged nobility in crushing his reforms and twice partitioned the country.

In 1795 Poland was once again split up, this time by Austria, Prussia and Russia, where an ageing Catherine the Great was still Empress. But this time the entire country was annexed and Stanisław was forced to abdicate on 25 November 1795. Brought back to Russia by Catherine, who died the following year, Stanisław lived as a quasi-prisoner in St Petersburg until his death in 1798.

Poland remained the pawn of other nations, frequently reshaped and repartitioned, until the restoration of the Polish Republic in the aftermath of the First World War in November 1918.

Also on this day

55 BC: Julius Caesar lands in Britain * 1278: HRE Rudolf I von Habsburg defeats King Otakar Przemysl of Bohemia at Dürnkrut, taking control of Austria, which the Habsburgs will rule for the next 640 years * **1346: Edward III and his son the Black Prince defeat the French at the Battle of Crécy** * 1676: First English Prime Minister Robert Walpole is born * 1819: Prince Albert, Consort to Queen Victoria, is born in Coburg, Germany * 1850: Louis-Philippe, the last king of France, dies in exile in England * 1920: In the United States, the 19th Amendment is proclaimed by the secretary of state, enfranchising women on an equal basis with men

27 August

Lope de Vega, the Spaniard who wrote 1,500 plays

1635 Lope de Vega was not only Spain's greatest playwright and the founder of modern Spanish drama, he was also one of the most prolific writers to put pen to paper. He wrote lyric poetry, some prose (including his autobiography) and more than 1,500 plays (some 100 of which, he boasted, were composed and staged in 24 hours). Almost 500 of his works are still extant.

Given his incredible output, it is a wonder he had time for anything else, but Vega also led a tempestuous life, enlivened by two wives and innumerable mistresses.

At fifteen he entered the university at Alcalá de Henares outside Madrid to study for the priesthood, but soon left to pursue a married mistress. In need of work, he established himself as secretary to various Spanish nobles, with the essential role of finding women for them. All the while he continued his adventures with the fair sex, but at one point ended up in prison for issuing libels against a mistress who had deserted him for another man.

On top of these entertaining activities, Vega was also a fighting man. At 21 he participated in an expedition against the Azores and five years later sailed with the Spanish Armada.

When not fighting or seducing, Vega was busy writing plays. His work revolutionised Spanish theatre, abandoning the classical 'rules' of place and time and introducing the real life of ordinary people as fit subject matter for drama. The public flocked to his work and he became a national hero. Because of his extraordinary output his contemporary, Cervantes, called him a 'prodigy of nature'.

In his early 50s Vega suffered terrible tragedy when, in a few short years his wife, his son and his favourite mistress all died. Understandably depressed, in 1614 he entered the priesthood, although continuing to provide young women for his patron, the Duke of Sessa. Fearing that Vega's religion might interfere with his services as procurer, the Duke persuaded one of Vega's former mistresses to seduce him, thereby forcing Vega to return to the secular world.

But Vega's final years were unhappy ones. His last mistress went blind and then insane, finally dying in 1632. Two years later his youngest daughter was seduced and abandoned and his son was lost at sea. Vega entered a quiet monastery in Madrid, dying on this day in 1635 at the age of 72. His death evoked mourning throughout the nation he had entertained so well for so long.

Also on this day

551 BC: Chinese philosopher Confucius is born * 1576: Titian (Tiziano Vecellio) dies in Venice * 1770: German philosopher Georg Wilhelm Hegel is born in Stuttgart * **1883: A colossal volcanic eruption destroys the island of Krakatoa**

28 August

Wagner the revolutionary misses the premiere of Lohengrin

1850 Today in Weimar Franz Liszt conducted the first performance of his friend Richard Wagner's opera *Lohengrin*, although Wagner himself had fled Germany under threat of arrest the previous year.

1848 was the 'Year of Revolution' all over Europe. Louis-Philippe had been chased from the throne of France, Metternich had been forced to flee from Austria and riots had broken out in the German principalities. Wagner had been working on *Lohengrin*, which he completed in 1849. But when he submitted it to the Dresden court for production, the court authorities turned it down. The rejection was not for musical but for political reasons, for Wagner had recently proposed the creation of a national theatre with productions chosen by composers and dramatists, an arrangement that would have taken all control from the court.

Furious at being rejected, Wagner joined the uprising in Dresden, manning the barricades with his close friend, the Russian anarchist Mikhail Bakunin. When order was restored, a warrant was issued for his arrest and he fled to Zurich disguised as a coachman.

In April 1850 Wagner wrote to Liszt: 'Bring out my *Lohengrin*! You are the only one to whom I would put this request; to no one but you would I entrust the production of this opera; but to you I surrender it with the fullest, most joyous confidence.' And so it was that Liszt organised *Lohengrin*'s premiere without its composer. Eleven years later Wagner was finally permitted to return to the Germanic states and on 15 May in Vienna he heard his opera for the first time.

Lohengrin is based on a German folk tale about a knight – Lohengrin – who arrives wearing silver armour in a boat drawn by a swan to rescue a princess. He defeats her persecutor in single combat, becomes betrothed to her, slays her treacherous persecutor and then leaves her when she breaks her promise never to ask him who he is (in fact, the son of Parsifal, Knight of the Holy Grail). In other words, a perfect story for an opera.

Although *Lohengrin* initially received a lukewarm reception, one who loved it was Mad King Ludwig of Bavaria, who nineteen years later built his own fairy-tale castle and called it Neuschwanstein (New Swan Stone) after the Swan Knight. Indeed, even non-opera lovers among us have all heard at least part of *Lohengrin*, the Bridal Chorus, generally referred to as 'Here Comes the Bride'.

As Wagner grew older, his operas grew longer, culminating in *Der Ring des Nibelungen*, composed of four separate operas taking some sixteen hours to perform. For all its enduring popularity, his work has also drawn some inspired criticism. One composer complained that a Wagner opera 'starts at six o'clock and, after it has been going three hours, you look at your watch and it says 6.20', while Friedrich Nietzsche derided *Die Meistersinger* as 'German beer music'. Here are some other choice critiques:

- Gioacchino Rossini: 'Wagner has beautiful moments but awful quarter hours.'
- Oscar Wilde: 'I like Wagner's music better than any other music. It's so loud that one can talk the whole time without people hearing what one says.'
- Charles Baudelaire: 'I love Wagner, but the music I prefer is that of a cat hung up by its tail outside a window and trying to stick to the panes of glass with its claws.'

The gentlest of the barbs came from Mark Twain, who helpfully proclaimed that: 'Wagner's music is better than it sounds.'

Also on this day

AD 475: Roman general Flavius Orestes appoints his son, the eleven-year-old Romulus Augustus, as the last Roman Emperor after chasing Emperor Julius Nepos out of Ravenna * **1749: Johann Wolfgang von Goethe is born in Frankfurt** * 1808: Leo Tolstoy is born * 1862: General Robert E. Lee's Confederates overwhelm the Northern forces at the Second Battle of Bull Run

29 August

Suleiman the Magnificent conquers Hungary

1526 Mohács lies on the west bank of the Danube, straight south from Budapest. It was there on this day that the great battle took place that was to change Hungary's history for over a century.

The Turkish sultan Suleiman the Magnificent had been demanding tribute from the Hungarians and when they foolishly refused to pay, he invaded with an enormous army of 100,000 men.

Hungary's 20-year-old king Louis II hastily gathered whatever troops he had at hand and, without waiting for reinforcements from other parts of his kingdom, marched down from Buda to engage the Turks.

When he reached Mohács, Louis found Suleiman's vast army waiting for him and immediately ordered his 4,000 cavalry to charge. Briefly it appeared that the Hungarians' insane attack might rock the invaders into panic as the Turkish line buckled under the weight of so many tons of armour plate. Immediately the Hungarian infantry, another 21,000 men, followed the mounted knights into the assault.

But not even mad courage could defeat odds of four-to-one and the Turkish counter-attack produced an appalling slaughter. Hungarians fell and died, as the Turks gave no quarter, routinely massacring their prisoners. Seeing that catastrophic defeat was inevitable, King Louis tried to escape but was crushed by his own warhorse when it fell on him. (Poor Louis had inherited the throne at ten and married at fifteen. Later Hungarians wisecracked: born too soon, king too soon, married too soon, died too soon.)

In all some 24,000 Hungarians died on the plain of Mohács. After the battle, Suleiman marched up river to Buda and razed it to the ground and then withdrew from the country, taking 100,000 Hungarian captives with him. Hungary was finished as a fighting force and twenty years later the nation was formally absorbed into the Turkish Empire, where it would remain for a century and a half.

Also on this day
1789: French painter Jean-Auguste Ingres is born in Montauban * 1835: The city of Melbourne is founded in Australia * **1842: By the Treaty of Nanking the British force China to cede Hong Kong at the close of the First Opium War**

30 August

The king who brought France out of the Middle Ages

1483 When Louis XI was born 60 years earlier, France was still a medieval country, a feudal nation of semi-independent and warring baronies, where the English ruled large chunks of its territory. Louis himself, at the age of eight, had actually met that final glory of medieval French mysticism, Joan of Arc.

But during Louis's lifetime the world changed. When he was thirteen, Gutenberg invented mobile type. In Italy the Renaissance, although not yet at high noon, was in the ascendant (Leonardo was born when Louis was 29). The classic symbol of the end of the Middle Ages, the fall of Constantinople to the Turks, had occurred when he was 30. The Hundred Years War ended the same year. Martin Luther was born in the year that Louis died.

Louis also changed his world. Known as the Universal Spider because of his incessant machinations and deceptions, he broke forever the feudal power of his barons, manoeuvring Charles the Bold of Burgundy to destruction. Perhaps more than any other king, he brought France into the modern era, as a Frenchman's primary loyalty was now to the crown rather than to the local feudal lord.

Oddly, in temperament, Louis remained medieval. Fat, ugly and suspicious in the extreme, he spent his last years in his fortress of Plessis-les-Tours in Touraine, guarded by 40 crossbowmen day and night on the castle towers, plus 400 archers on patrol. Highly superstitious as well, Louis collected religious icons and relics, endowed churches and seemed to think he could bargain with God.

Louis died at eight in the evening on this day, a Saturday, at Plessis-les-Tours at the age of 60, probably of a cerebral haemorrhage.

Also on this day
30 BC: Egyptian Queen Cleopatra commits suicide by clasping an asp to her breast * 526: Theodoric, King of the Ostrogoths and of Italy, dies in Ravenna * 1748: French Neoclassical painter Jacques-Louis David is born in Paris * 1797: *Frankenstein* author Mary Wollstonecraft Shelley is born

31 August

Henry V dies at Vincennes

1422 One of the few extant portraits of England's Henry V now hangs in London's National Portrait Gallery. It shows the King in profile, at first glance looking somewhat monkish, as the hat that conceals his blonde hair gives him the air of a medieval canon. His face is strong, long and bony, with a large straight nose and contemplative brown eyes that would offer more justice than mercy. The anonymous artist read his subject well.

Stern Henry, England's last great warrior monarch, victor of Agincourt and de facto ruler of France, died today, less than a month after his 35th birthday. He was, according to his brother, 'too famous to live long'. Although the cause is uncertain, it seems likely that he died of dysentery, the scourge of medieval soldiers.

Henry had been ill for some months and was forced to leave his final campaign on a litter, returning to his headquarters at the château of Vincennes, just east of Paris. There he spent his last three weeks putting his dominions in order and securing the royal inheritance for his infant son (the future Henry VI), whom he had never seen.

In his day, Henry was seen as a hero, who, as a youth, had been a boisterous scapegrace but as king became renowned for his determination, bravery and justice. He could also be brutal, contemptuous of men's lives and piously priggish as well. He spent most of his nine years as king in a largely successful attempt to crush a France already riven by civil war and saddled with a lunatic monarch. But within seven years of Henry's death, France's Charles VII was crowned at Reims with the help of Joan of Arc and the claims of Henry's son were discarded.

When Henry died, his flesh was boiled from his bones to preserve it and both flesh and bones were placed in his casket, which made a stately return to London over the next two months. There Henry enjoyed a great pageant of a funeral, when even his horses were led to the altar in Westminster Abbey for a final farewell to their illustrious master.

Also on this day

AD **12: Roman Emperor Caligula is born in Latium (Anzio)** * 1688: English preacher and writer John Bunyan dies in London * 1867: French writer Charles Baudelaire dies in Paris * 1888: Polly Nichols, the first victim of Jack the Ripper, is found dead and mutilated in Buck's Row, London

1 September

The Napoleonic dreams are crushed forever at Sedan

1870 The 1st of September marks the beginning and the end of Napoleonic glory. It was on that date in 1785 that Napoleon Bonaparte first received his commission as an artillery officer, the true start of his military success and the Napoleonic saga. Exactly 85 years later to the day came the battle that ended the Napoleonic story, as the army of his nephew, Emperor Napoleon III, crashed to defeat at the hands of Prussia at Sedan.

For 22 years Napoleon III had been the master of France, first as President of the Second Republic, then as Emperor. During that time he had helped his country to prosper, but now France's position in Europe was threatened by the potential unification of the German states under Prussia's Iron Chancellor, Otto von Bismarck. In July 1870 the crafty Bismarck, who wanted the conflict as a means of drawing together some reluctant German principalities, cunningly manoeuvred Napoleon into war.

After some early French successes, the larger and better-trained Prussian army quickly got the measure of the French, culminating on 31 August in the surrounding of a French army of 130,000 men in Sedan, where Prussian artillery mercilessly pounded the city. Leading the beleaguered French was Napoleon himself, the last emperor ever to command in the field. Accompanying the Prussian army was Crown Prince Wilhelm Friedrich, soon to become Emperor of the combined German states as Kaiser Wilhelm I.

By 1 September Napoleon could see that the situation was desperate. The Prussians had completely encircled Sedan, cutting off all hope of reinforcements, and the most senior French general, Marshal Mac-Mahon, had been seriously wounded. Knowing that he could never continue as Emperor after such a disastrous loss, Napoleon spent the day riding where the action was hottest, apparently hoping for a stray shell to end his reign in dignity. He survived unscathed, but his army was completely shattered, with 17,000 dead or wounded against half that number of Prussian casualties. On the afternoon of the following day he sent this message to Crown Prince Wilhelm: 'Monsieur mon frère; Not having succeeded in dying in the midst of my troops, nothing remains for me but to deliver my sword into your majesty's hands.' He thus became one of almost 100,000 French prisoners of war.

On 3 September, his captors took Napoleon to Prussia, never to see France again. After a few months in regal confinement with Crown Prince Wilhelm Friedrich, he went into exile in England where he died in January two years later at the age of 64.

Also on this day

AD 70: Roman Emperor Titus orders the destruction of Jerusalem * **1281: The 'Divine Wind' (Kamikaze) destroys the fleet of Kublai Khan at Hakata Bay,**

Japan * 1339: England's King Edward III declares war on France to start the Hundred Years War * 1715: Louis XIV dies * 1939: Germany invades Poland and captures Danzig, starting the Second World War in Europe

---

Events written in **boldface** are covered in full in
365: Great Stories from History for Every Day of the Year,
the first volume in this series.

---

2 September

The Battle of Omdurman and the last cavalry charge in British history

1898 The colonel 'ordered "Right wheel into line" to be sounded. The trumpet jerked out a shrill note, heard faintly above the trampling of the horses and the noise of the riders. On the instant all the sixteen troops swung round and locked up into a long galloping line …

'Two hundred and fifty yards away the dark-blue [Dervish soldiers] were firing madly in a thin film of light-blue smoke. Their bullets struck the hard gravel into the air, and the troopers, to shield their faces from the stinging dust, bowed their helmets forward … The pace was fast and the distance short. Yet, before it was half covered, the whole aspect of the affair changed. A deep crease in the ground … appeared where all had seemed smooth, level plain; and from it there sprang … a dense white mass of men nearly as long as our front and about twelve deep … Eager warriors sprang forward to anticipate the shock. The rest stood firm to meet it. The Lancers acknowledged the apparition only by an increase of pace. Each man wanted sufficient momentum to drive through such a solid line … the whole event was a matter of seconds. The riflemen, firing bravely to the last, were swept head over heels … and … at full gallop and in the closest order, the British squadrons struck the fierce brigade with one loud furious shout. The collision was prodigious. Nearly thirty Lancers, men and horses, and at least two hundred Arabs were overthrown. The shock was stunning to both sides, and for perhaps ten wonderful seconds no man heeded his enemy. Terrified horses wedged in the crowd; bruised and shaken men, sprawling in heaps, struggled, dazed and stupid, to their feet, panted, and looked about them …

'Meanwhile the impetus of the cavalry carried them on … They shattered the Dervish array, and, their pace reduced to a walk, scrambled out of the [crease] on the further side, leaving a score of troopers behind them, and dragging on with the charge more than a thousand Arabs. Then, and not till then, the killing began; and thereafter each man saw the world along his lance, under his guard, or through the back-sight of his pistol; and each had his own strange tale to tell …'

This last-ever British cavalry charge took place on this day, during the battle of Omdurman. The stirring account quoted above was written by a 25-year-old Lancer officer who, armed with a Mauser automatic pistol, shot three Dervishes himself. His name was Winston Churchill.

The British had occupied Egypt in 1882, seven years after having purchased the Suez Canal. Three years later, a certain Abd Allah took control of neighbouring Sudan, then a Muslim theocracy. He resolved further to expand the Islamic state, first through conquest in Ethiopia and then by invading Egypt. Feeling their interests threatened, the British dispatched Major General Sir Herbert Kitchener with an Anglo-Egyptian army of 26,000 men to bring Abd Allah and his Dervish army to heel.

On 1 September, Kitchener reached Abd Allah's capital at Omdurman, across the White Nile from Khartoum. Opposing him was a vast Dervish force of some 40,000 men, equipped with rifles. The following day Abd Allah launched successive attacks, but, armed with artillery and Maxim guns, the Anglo-Egyptians scythed down the advancing Dervishes in swathes. At the climax of the battle, Kitchener ordered the famous last cavalry charge, which had little real effect on the Dervish army, although five of its officers, 66 men, and 119 horses out of fewer than 400 were killed or wounded. But Kitchener's heavy guns and a subsequent assault on Omdurman itself soon obliterated all resistance.

The battle was a catastrophe for Abd Allah, who lost 20,000 men killed and wounded plus another 5,000 taken prisoner. He managed to escape the slaughter, but a year later he encountered another British force and was killed in the battle. As for the British, they stayed in Egypt one way or another until Gamal Abdel Nasser kicked them out for good in 1956.

Also on this day

31 BC: Octavian (the future emperor Augustus) defeats Marc Antony at the Battle of Actium * 1666: The Great Fire of London starts in a baker's shop in Pudding Lane * 1752: Britain and its colonies change from the Julian to the Gregorian calendar; the following day becomes 14 September * 1910: French painter Henri Rousseau dies in Paris * 1945: Japan surrenders, ending the Second World War

3 September

The crowning of the Lionheart

1189 On this date, just five days short of his 32nd birthday, Richard I, the Lionheart, was crowned in Westminster Abbey. But the ceremony was ill-omened, marred by the presence of a black bat that swooped about the church. Indeed, although Richard was one of England's most storied kings, in truth he was a disaster for the country.

Richard's interests included war, glory, France and England, in that order.

He considered his new kingdom as nothing more than a milch cow to finance his dreams of crusade, selling numerous titles and positions to raise money. He claimed: 'I would sell London if I could find a bidder', a sentiment uttered in French, as he never learned to speak English. In less than a year after his coronation, he was off to the Holy Land.

En route to Palestine, Richard dropped by Cyprus to wed a princess from the Kingdom of Navarre named Berengaria, to whom he brought no more luck than he did to England. Once married, he left his wife to join the crusade, was captured in Austria returning home and didn't see Berengaria again for over four years. The couple had no children, and when Richard was killed in 1199, Berengaria retired to her own convent in Le Mans, where she lived for 30 more secluded years. She was the only English queen who never set foot in England.

While on crusade, Richard failed to achieve his acclaimed objective, the liberation of Jerusalem from the Saracens. Worse, the ransom paid to free him from his Austrian captors virtually bankrupted England.

Richard spent the last few years of his life fighting in France, until his death from gangrene caused by a wound from a crossbow bolt during the siege of Châlus. Although his reign lasted for nine years and nine months, he spent only 179 days of it in England.

Also on this day

1650: Oliver Cromwell defeats the Scots at the second Battle of Dunbar * 1651: Oliver Cromwell defeats Charles I's troops at Worcester, ending the English Civil War * 1658: Oliver Cromwell dies * **1886: Apache Indian Chief Geronimo surrenders to the US Army** * 1939: Great Britain declares war on Germany

4 September

Queen Elizabeth's favourite dies

1588 At ten o'clock on this Wednesday morning Queen Elizabeth's favourite, Robert Dudley, Earl of Leicester, died peacefully near Oxford at the age of 55.

Although Leicester came from England's highest aristocracy, the fifth son of the Duke of Northumberland, he was thrown into the Tower of London at 22 when his father was executed for attempting to place his daughter-in-law Lady Jane Grey on the throne of England. Leicester's grandfather had also previously been beheaded for treason.

Leicester was twice lucky in his time in the Tower; first that he survived, second that a fellow prisoner at the time was the future Queen Elizabeth, who was just a few months younger than he. (Her sister Queen Mary had dispatched Elizabeth to the Tower in 1554 after Thomas Wyatt's abortive rebellion, wrongly suspecting her of treason.)

Leicester was a bold and handsome man, an exceptional horseman and so dark that he was mockingly referred to as 'the gypsy'. After Elizabeth's ascension in 1558, he soon became a court favourite. She affectionately called him Robin, and if she was not the Virgin Queen of common legend, he would certainly have been the reason why. She made him Master of the Horse, and later a Privy Councillor, Knight of the Garter and Constable of Windsor Castle.

Then, in 1560, when Leicester was 27, his wife Amy was found lying dead at the foot of her grand staircase, her neck broken. The Earl was widely rumoured to have given her a push to clear the way for marriage to the Queen, and scandal tore across Europe. 'The Queen of England', said Elizabeth's deadly enemy Mary, Queen of Scots, 'is going to marry her horse keeper who has killed his wife to make room for her.'

Despite the malicious gossip, Leicester entreated Elizabeth to marry him, but she steadfastly refused, although they remained close friends until the end of his life.

Even after Leicester's death, two family traditions were maintained. His stepson Robert Devereaux, Earl of Essex, replaced him as Queen Elizabeth's favourite – and was executed for treason in his turn, just as Leicester's father and grandfather had been.

Also on this day

AD 476: **The last Roman emperor Romulus Augustolus resigns** * 1781: Forty-four Spanish settlers found Los Angeles as El Pueblo de Nuestra Señora La Reina de los Ángeles de Porciúncula (the City of Our Lady, the Queen of the Angels of the Porziuncola (the church where St Francis died)) * 1870: Léon Gambetta, Jules Favre and Jules Ferry proclaim the Third Republic from the Hôtel de Ville in Paris * 1907: Norwegian composer Edvard Grieg dies

5 September

Suleiman the Magnificent dies in the field

1566 Suleiman the Magnificent, greatest of all Turkish sultans, died today while attempting to put down a revolt in one of his many conquered territories.

Suleiman ruled Turkey and its empire with an iron hand for 46 years. He added Hungary to his domains and twice nearly conquered Austria. Domestically he was known as a great law-giver, and he ordered built many of the finest buildings in Constantinople, Baghdad and Damascus. But as he grew older he became increasingly megalomaniac, perhaps even paranoid, to the point that (on separate occasions) he ordered two of his three sons strangled for imagined treason, as well as a number of their children.

Even at 71, sick and ageing, Suleiman thought primarily of consolidating his power. When revolt broke out in Hungary he personally led the avenging army.

Setting out from Constantinople, this formidable despot marched with his army for 97 days to mount his attack on Hungary. But he was already so ill that he could not ride; he had to be taken in a carriage all the way from his capitol.

By mid-summer of 1566, Suleiman was camped outside the castle of Sziget, his enemies under siege within. Eventually Turkish sappers would blow a fatal gap in the castle's walls, but the great sultan was not there to see his final triumph. On the night of 5 September he was stricken by either a heart attack or a stroke, dying in his tent. His Grand Vizier embalmed his body and dressed it in the sultan's finest clothes, leaving it sitting up in a litter to make his troops believe he was still alive until the siege had been successfully completed.

Suleiman's body was brought back to Constantinople where he was buried outside the great mosque he had built, known as the Suleiman Mosque, one of the largest and most beautiful in the world.

Also on this day

1569: Flemish painter Pieter Bruegel the Elder dies in Antwerp * **1638: Louis XIV is born at Saint-Germain-en-Laye** * 1857: French philosopher and founder of sociology Auguste Comte dies in Paris * 1877: American Indian Chief Crazy Horse is killed in a scuffle with his prison guards in Fort Robinson, Nebraska

6 September

François I orders the building of the Château de Chambord

1519 On this day 25-year-old King François I gave orders for work to begin on 'a beautiful and sumptuous edifice' in the valley of the Loire. Some historians believe that Leonardo da Vinci, who at the time was François's guest at Amboise, created the original design. The result was France's most grandiose Renaissance building, the Château de Chambord, a grand palace 170 yards long with 440 rooms, 84 staircases and 356 sculpted chimneys. This breathtakingly beautiful building also contains a magnificent double staircase built of two superimposed spirals, so constructed that people ascending one spiral can see the people descending the other but never meet them. Such playful architecture perfectly suited this rakish king who kept a number of mistresses and welcomed high-class prostitutes at his dissolute court.

François was as passionate about Chambord as he was about women, committing funds for its construction even when he himself was a prisoner, captured at the Battle of Pavia by Holy Roman Emperor Charles V. Later, however, François invited Charles to Chambord as his guest, suitably impressing the Emperor with the château's lavishness and taste.

On François's death, the château was passed on to his son Henri II and subsequently down the line of French kings. But no other owner quite shared François's enthusiasm for Chambord. Louis XIV visited it only nine times during his reign of 72 years (although during one visit Molière staged the first performance of *Le Bourgeois Gentilhomme*). Eventually it was plundered during the Revolution and finally bought by the state.

Chambord today stands virtually empty, a colossal and beautiful monument for wide-eyed tourists, brought to wonderful false life only by the *son et lumière* on summer evenings. Inside is François's study, where a brief verse is engraved on a window, purportedly cut by the King himself with his diamond ring:

> *Souvent femme varie,*
> *Bien fol qui s'y fie.*
> (A woman is very fickle; he who trusts her is a fool.)

Also on this day

1522: Ferdinand Magellan's seventeen surviving crew members reach Spain for completion of the first round-the-world voyage * 1664: The British take over New Amsterdam (New York) from the Dutch * **1862: 'Barbara Frietchie' defies Confederate general Robert E. Lee by waving an American flag from her window as his army marches through Frederick, Maryland** * 1901: Anarchist Leon Czolgosz shoots and fatally wounds American President William McKinley * 1914: General Joseph-Simon Gallieni uses Paris taxis to move French troops to the front to defend Paris during the start of the Battle of the Marne

7 September

Queen Elizabeth is born

1533 She said of herself: 'I am more afraid of making a fault in my Latin than of the kings of Spain, France, Scotland and the House of Guise and all their confederates.' Her chief minister Robert Cecil said of her: 'More than a man but sometimes (by troth) less than a woman.'

She was Queen Elizabeth I, born this Sunday morning at Greenwich Palace just outside London, exactly seven months and thirteen days after the hasty and secret marriage of her parents, Henry VIII and Anne Boleyn.

Elizabeth's start in life was a dismal one. Just four months before her third birthday, her mother was convicted of adultery (and therefore guilty of treason, in the eyes of Henry) and beheaded on her father's orders. Henry also directed Parliament to void his marriage with Anne from the beginning, making Elizabeth a bastard, while blithely ignoring the fact that if Anne had never been married to him, she could not have committed adultery.

Henry died when Elizabeth was just thirteen, and she managed to survive the reigns of her half-brother Edward VI (who was fond of her) and half-sister

Mary (who mistrusted her). Elizabeth finally inherited the throne when she was 25, beginning one of the greatest reigns in British history, and one of the longest – 44 years, four months and eleven days. Of Britain's 41 monarchs since the Norman Conquest of England, only three kings and two queens reigned longer, and many believe that none ruled better.

Also on this day

1191: Richard the Lionheart's heavy cavalry routs Saladin and his army at the Battle of Arsuf * 1651: Thirteen-year-old Louis XIV is proclaimed of age and takes full powers in France * **1812: The Russian army holds Napoleon to a bloody draw at the Battle of Borodino** * 1901: The Boxer Rebellion in China ends with the signing of the Peace of Peking

8 September

The slap at Anagni

1303 King Philip the Fair of France was young, blonde and handsome, while Pope Boniface VIII was over 60, with a pinched, suffering face that reflected both his character and the torments of gallstones. Like Philip, he was cunning, ruthless and arrogant, with a strong will to power. 'It is necessary to salvation', he said, 'that every human creature be subject to the Roman pontiff.' Boniface's ambitions had been clearly revealed when still a cardinal. Then he had manoeuvred Pope Celestine V into an unprecedented resignation that allowed for his own elevation to the papacy, and he then imprisoned his predecessor until he died.

Conflict between King and Pope was inevitable, especially since Philip greedily eyed the riches of the Church in France and decided to tax the clergy. Later he even imprisoned a French bishop on patently trumped-up charges in an attempt to gain secular control of the clergy. Boniface's response was to draw up a bull excommunicating the French king.

Reacting with cold fury, Philip dispatched his Keeper of Seals, Guillaume de Nogaret, with a small army to seek out the Pope and formally charge him with papal misconduct. Nogaret headed for the Pope's summer residence in Anagni, 45 miles south-east of Rome. Along the way he picked up an ally in Sciarra Colonna, leader of the pope-producing family that had largely been disenfranchised by Boniface.

On the night of 7 September, Nogaret and Colonna attacked Anagni and quickly overcame all resistance. Boniface had barricaded himself in his palace, but Colonna smashed down the doors the following morning. The Pope was now the prisoner of the King. Fearing assassination, he boldly if somewhat melodramatically declared: 'Here is my neck, and here is my head. Betrayed like Jesus Christ, if I must die like him, at least I will die a pope.'

But Nogaret was intent on inflicting humiliation rather than death. First he and his lieutenants openly discussed in front of Boniface whether or not to execute him on the spot, without trial. Then he presented the frail old man with a list of charges: heresy, idolatry, nepotism, simony, sorcery and sodomy. The recitation of accusations was accompanied by a ringing slap across the face.

It mattered little that the next day the loyal citizens of Anagni finally rescued their pontiff. Boniface was a broken man, mortified and treated with contempt by his enemies. A few days after his humiliation he seemed to forget the excommunication of Philip and returned to Rome in a daze. Only a month later, on 11 October, Boniface expired in the Vatican. Tradition says he died of shame and rage.

Also on this day

1157: Richard the Lionheart is born in Oxford * 1886: After gold is discovered nearby, the city of Johannesburg is founded * **1935: American politician and demagogue Huey Long is shot and killed in Baton Rouge, Louisiana**

9 September

Captain Bligh and the other mutinies

1754 In 1932, Charles Nordhoff and James Norman Hall published a spectacularly successful novel entitled *Mutiny on the Bounty* that was shortly followed by an Academy Award-winning film starring Clark Gable. Between them, the book and the movie created the image we have today of British Captain William Bligh as the cruel and tyrannical bully who drove his men to history's most famous mutiny on HMS *Bounty*.

Bligh, who was born today, was a disciplined master who had gone to sea at the age of seven and who had later sailed with Captain Cook. Cook had been so impressed by Bligh's seamanship that he named an island after him. Although not the tyrant of legend, Bligh undeniably was intolerant of error and gave vent to his anger in abusive terms. In his career he managed to play a role in no fewer than three mutinies.

The first and best known was in 1789 aboard the *Bounty*, when he was 35 years old, having already been a ship's officer for thirteen years. His magnificent seamanship was put to the test when he and eighteen others were cast adrift in an open longboat. Some 41 days later, Bligh brought them to a safe landing near Java.

When Bligh returned to England, the Admiralty treated him as hero and victim rather than villain, and soon gave him a new command. But in 1797 once again he was involved in a mutiny. The ship he commanded was anchored with the rest of the British fleet at the Nore, off the coast of Kent. His crew joined a fleet-wide mutiny of sailors, and Bligh was put ashore.

Once more the Admiralty found no fault with the captain and in 1805 sent him to New South Wales as Governor. Three years later came the third mutiny, this time led by an English major who put Bligh under arrest, but again the captain escaped with honour when a court found the mutineers guilty of conspiracy.

In Great Britain's long naval war with Napoleonic France, Bligh distinguished himself at the battles of Camperdown and Copenhagen. The Admiralty clearly considered his fighting record more important than his involvement in three mutinies, for it promoted him to Rear Admiral in 1811 and to Vice Admiral in 1814. Bligh died in London in 1817 at the age of 63.

Also on this day

1087: Near Rouen, William the Conqueror dies from internal injuries received when his horse stumbled and he fell forward onto his saddle's iron pommel * 1585: French 'Eminence Rouge' Armand-Jean du Plessis, Cardinal Richelieu, is born in Paris * 1828: Leo Tolstoy is born * 1901: Henri de Toulouse-Lautrec dies in Malromé

10 September

Commandant Perry defeats the British on Lake Erie

1813 The War of 1812 was not going well for the Americans – the British had burned Washington and the governor of Detroit had surrendered the town – but today Master Commandant Oliver Hazard Perry struck a blow for his country when he attacked the British fleet on Lake Erie.

Perry, a young (28) and courageous officer who had joined the navy at fourteen, was determined to regain not only the lake but Detroit as well from the conquering British. His fleet of ten vessels outnumbered the enemy almost two to one, and his firepower was greater. Hostilities began at noon. At first the battle went badly, as the American flagship, the brig *Lawrence*, was severely hit, but Perry quickly transferred to the *Niagara* and led his fleet directly into the British line so that his short-range firepower could take full effect.

By three o'clock the British had surrendered, and Perry was able to earn his place in the American book of famous quotations by sending a message to the future president, General William Henry Harrison, that: 'We have met the enemy and they are ours.' The British suffered 40 dead with another 94 wounded, while of Perry's force 27 were killed and 96 wounded.

With the British fleet out of the way, American ships controlled Lake Erie, and Harrison was able to take the offensive, soon retaking Detroit. Perry became something of a national hero in America for his exploits and was soon promoted to Captain. Sadly, only five years later he died from yellow fever contracted on a voyage to South America.

As for the war, with neither side able to achieve a decisive victory, it ended docilely with the Treaty of Ghent, signed in December 1814.

Also on this day

1419: The Duke of Burgundy Jean Sans Peur is assassinated by the Armagnac faction, leading to a Burgundian alliance with England's Henry V and his takeover of France * 1823: Simon Bolívar is named president (read dictator) of Peru * 1898: On a quay in Geneva, an Italian anarchist stabs to death Elisabeth of Bavaria (Sisi), the estranged wife of Austrian Emperor Franz Joseph

11 September

The British trounce George Washington at the Battle of Brandywine

1777 Today was a bad day for George Washington and the Continental army, and the result came close to destroying the main American fighting force and with it, perhaps, the cause of American independence.

A British army, 13,000-strong, led by Generals Howe and Cornwallis, had sailed from New York, landed in Delaware, and was now marching eastward on Philadelphia, the rebel capital, whose capture the generals hoped would end the war in America. But George Washington, with 8,000 regulars and 3,000 militia, decided to contest the issue by holding the fords along some five miles of Brandywine Creek, thereby blocking the British route of advance.

The day before the battle, when the Americans took up their positions along the east bank of the creek, they unaccountably neglected the job of reconnoitring the terrain, roads and landmarks across the creek from which the British would advance. Therefore, commanders were largely unacquainted with what lay beyond their immediate front, including the existence of fords further upstream and roads leading to them.

At 5.00 am, Howe set his army in motion from Kennett Square, seven miles west of the Brandywine, sending a force of 5,000 troops straight down the main road to make a show at Chadd's Ford, and the balance of his command, 7,500 men under Cornwallis, marching north on a wide flanking manoeuvre designed to cross the creek undetected at a ford well above the American right.

Reaching Chadd's Ford at 10.00 am, the smaller force opened up with artillery fire on the American positions but made no attempt to cross. Presently, a rider brought Washington news that a cavalry patrol had spotted a British column marching north along a road that paralleled the creek. The commander-in-chief's first reaction was to send forces immediately across the Brandywine to destroy the column, then prepare for a later attack from another quarter. But soon a second dispatch arrived reporting that militia sent to verify the earlier sighting had found no sign of enemy on that road. Which report was correct? Where were the enemy? No one at headquarters could say. Only much later was it discovered that the militia unknowingly were watching a different road from the one the cavalry had reported on. In any event, confused and wary, Washington called off his attack to await developments. At 2.00 am a local farmer rode in to say that the British had crossed the creek, were coming down the east bank of the creek, and would soon surround Washington's army.

Washington realigned his forces to meet the threat from the north, which began at 4.00 pm. Cued by the noise of Cornwallis's cannon, the British also attacked across Chadd's Ford. In a two-front battle, the fighting was fierce, and Washington rode up and down the line exhorting his men to stem the British tide. But as the action continued, the line began to sag, artillery pieces were abandoned, the militia withdrew, and as darkness fell the Americans were beaten and in full retreat. Their losses for the day reached almost 1,300, including 400 captured, and eleven guns.

Fortunately, the Continental army managed to elude what might have been a greater disaster, for Cornwallis's troops, having marched over seventeen miles since dawn, were in no shape to pursue them further. The Americans regrouped at Chester. Late that night, Washington sent news of the battle to the President of Congress in a masterpiece of understatement that began: 'Sir: I am sorry to inform you, that in this day's engagement, we have been obliged to leave the enemy masters of the field.'

So it was luck, not intelligence, that saved the Continental army this day. But outgeneralled by Howe though he was, Washington quickly reorganised his army and kept it active in the field. Philadelphia fell two weeks later, but the event did not have the significance the British generals had hoped for. The rebels did not lay down their arms, the war continued, and the Americans spent a bitter winter at Valley Forge keeping a watchful eye on the enemy occupying their capital. In the spring, the British army evacuated Philadelphia and marched all the way back to New York City, from which it had first sailed the autumn before.

Also on this day

1297: Scottish rebel William Wallace defeats the English at the Battle of Stirling Bridge * **1697: Prince Eugene of Savoy defeats the Turks at the Battle of Zenta and in 1709 he and the Duke of Marlborough defeat the French at Malplaquet** * 1855: During the Crimean War the Russian city of Sevastopol falls to British, French and Piedmontese forces after a siege of almost a year * 1885: English writer D.H. Lawrence is born

12 September

Peter the Great starts to transform Russia

1689 Today seventeen-year-old Peter the Great took personal control of his country to start Russia's momentous transformation from a priest-ridden Byzantine backwater to a formidable European power.

Peter had been Russia's anointed co-Tsar in 1682 along with his weak-minded brother Ivan, but the country had in fact been ruled by his older half-sister Sophia, who was technically regent but who was determined never to relinquish her power. By the time he reached seventeen, Peter felt himself ready to supplant Sophia but feared that if he failed, she and her lover Fedor Shaklovity would put him to death.

When Sophia tried to take advantage of a revolt by the palace guard to consolidate her position, Peter fled the Kremlin to hole up in a monastery outside Moscow and commanded his army generals to come to him, the legal ruler of the country. The generals vacillated between brother and sister. Sophia tried everything from bribes to threats to keep them on her side, while Peter attempted to persuade them to support their tsar. When he succeeded, Sophia was instantly entombed in a local nunnery, but she fared far better than her lover, who received sixteen lashes of the knout and was subjected to the strappado before being decapitated.

Peter allowed his half-brother to remain as nominal co-Tsar, but Ivan's health, never strong, deteriorated further until he became partially paralysed and died. Peter continued to rule for 35 dictatorial years until his death in 1725.

Peter was a man of immense contradictions. In turning his country westward he established it as a military power and largely broke the traditionalist stranglehold of the Orthodox Church. He forced his nobles and churchmen to adopt the European custom of shaving (which many considered a mortal sin), and founded the first hospital in all of Russia, as well as the Russian navy. But his rule was both despotic and capricious, and Peter himself was one of history's most cruel and violent monarchs. He often executed his enemies personally and not only approved of judicial torture but supervised it in person.

Yet this same man created a European Russia. He fought Turkey to gain access to the Baltic and Black Seas, defeated Persia to secure the southern and western shores of the Caspian Sea, and moved the capital to St Petersburg.

Also on this day

1683: Christian forces destroy the Turkish army of Kara Mustapha outside Vienna (leading to the invention of the cappuccino and the croissant) * 1830: Belgium becomes an independent country * 1846: English poet Robert Browning secretly marries poetess Elizabeth Barrett * 1852: British prime minister Henry Herbert Asquith is born * 1943: Italian dictator Benito Mussolini is rescued by German glider troops from a hotel high on the Gran Sasso d'Italia

13 September

A brave defence against a British attack inspires 'The Star-Spangled Banner'

1814 Today an unsuccessful British attack on an American fort gave birth to the country's national anthem, 'The Star-Spangled Banner'.

In 1814 Baltimore was America's third largest city, with a population of some 45,000. It had been a particular thorn in the side of the British, as privateers based there had seized or sunk over 500 British ships. Now Britain was at war with the United States, and the British fleet was determined to pound it into submission.

The plan was to sail into Baltimore harbour and attack the city with cannon fire, but a star-shaped fortress named Fort McHenry protected the entrance to the harbour, so the first assault came against the fort.

At 6.30 am, the schooner *Cockchafer* opened fire, and during the next 24 hours British warships and bomb vessels fired about 2,000 shells and 800 rockets at Fort McHenry, which was defended by only 1,000 men and 57 guns, commanded by Major George Armistead. Over the fort flew an enormous American flag measuring 42 feet by 30 feet, hand made by Mary Pickersgill, whose mother had made flags for George Washington.

From eight miles away an American lawyer named Francis Scott Key observed the firing from the deck of a British flag-of-truce ship, where he was negotiating the exchange of an American prisoner. As he watched the battle and the flag, Key rejoiced when the British finally pulled back at dawn the next day, the Americans undefeated. Based on what he saw, he wrote the words to 'The Star-Spangled Banner', scanned to go to an old English drinking song called 'To Anacreon in Heaven'.

'The Star-Spangled Banner' was immediately published in newspapers around the United States, an instant success. But even its popularity couldn't rush the American Congress, which waited until 1931 before declaring it the American national anthem.

Also on this day

1506: Italian painter Andrea Mantegna dies * 1592: French essayist Michel de Montaigne dies in Bordeaux * **1759: General James Wolfe is killed as the British defeat the French at the Battle of Quebec; French General Louis-Joseph de Montcalm is mortally wounded and dies the next day**

14 September

Douglas MacArthur lands at Inchon

1950 Early this morning, in darkness off the Korean coast, the United States X Corps, 40,000 strong, prepared to launch one of the boldest amphibious assaults in all military history. Its purpose was to reverse an impending military disaster at Pusan, where United Nations forces defending the Republic of Korea were facing almost certain annihilation by the Communist North Korean Army.

With X Corps and directing the entire operation was General Douglas

MacArthur, Commander-in-Chief of United Nations forces, whose intention it was to land his force behind enemy lines at the port of Inchon, cut the North Korean army's supply line, and strangle the invasion that the Communists had launched so savagely on 25 June.

MacArthur's plan was extremely hazardous. It required complete surprise, and in addition the enormous tides at Inchon would allow only two hours for the initial landings. When he first proposed the operation, the Joint Chiefs of Staff opposed it as too hazardous. But at a strategic conference in Tokyo, MacArthur countered Washington's assessment with a forceful argument in which he incorporated this history lesson:

'Surprise is the most vital element for success in war. ... On the Plains of Abraham [in 1759], Wolfe won a stunning victory that was made possible almost entirely by surprise. Thus he captured Quebec and in effect ended the French and Indian War. Like Montcalm, the North Koreans would regard an Inchon landing as impossible. Like Wolfe, I could take them by surprise.'

On 29 August the Joint Chiefs cabled their approval.

In the tense pre-landing atmosphere, MacArthur, aboard his command ship *Mount McKinley*, stared into the darkness. 'Then I noticed a flash', he wrote, 'a light that winked on and off across the water. The channel navigation lights were on. We were taking the enemy by surprise.' By 8.00 am, the Marines carrying out the first wave of the assault had secured a beachhead without losing a man. With the evening's tide most of X Corps was ashore, moving inland.

As their author predicted, the Inchon landings forced the Communist invaders out of South Korea. The military scene in Korea went from almost certain disaster to what seemed like war-ending victory. But MacArthur's feat, unlike Wolfe's, did not end the war. When United Nations forces moved north to destroy what was left of the retreating North Korean army, they suddenly encountered half a million Chinese Communist 'volunteers'. A new phase of the war began in which the front line see-sawed back and forth for another eighteen months. In the end, the invasion of South Korea was decisively defeated, but that success was obscured by military stalemate, endless armistice negotiations, and the heavy cost in lives: 142,000 deaths in the UN forces (including over 33,000 Americans), 415,000 in the South Korean army, and perhaps 1,500,000 Chinese and North Koreans.

Also on this day

1321: Dante Alighieri dies in exile in Ravenna * 1516: French King François I defeats Swiss mercenaries in the Battle of Marignano (Melegnano) to regain control of Milan * 1598: Spanish King Philip II dies at El Escorial of gangrene caused by gout * 1812: Napoleon enters Moscow * 1847: General Winfield Scott enters Mexico City to bring America victory in the Mexican War * 1852: The Duke of Wellington dies at Walmer Castle in Kent * 1901: Theodore Roosevelt becomes the 26th president of the United States on the assassination of President William McKinley

15 September

Tanks are used in warfare for the first time

1916 Today, in a sector of the Western Front between the French villages of Courcelette and Flers, on the 76th day of that endless carnage called the Battle of the Somme, a secret weapon was unveiled. Its appearance was brief and the results inconclusive. But the event itself was electrifying and, literally, earth-shaking.

Thirty-two armoured caterpillar vehicles – code-named 'tanks' to preserve secrecy during their development – rumbled heavily out of the British lines heading towards the German entrenchments. Most of the machines broke down before reaching the objective, but thirteen of them, with British infantry close behind, managed to advance some 3,500 yards, punching a gaping hole in the enemy line, whose defenders – taking one look at the monstrous machines moving inexorably towards them, invulnerable to machine gun fire – fled to the rear. From above, a French aeroplane observer described one segment of the action in a message that was translated for an eager British press as: 'Tank walking up High Street of Flers with British Army cheering behind.'

The triumph was momentary, for there was no way for the British to exploit the sudden breakthrough, so the long tragedy of the Somme resumed, unaffected by the brief intrusion of technology. The Germans regained the lost territory through stubborn counter-attacks, and their high command failed to perceive the value of the phenomenon that had breached their line. On the British side, some called the attack a failure, while others pronounced it as merely unconvincing or a premature disclosure of a secret weapon. There were those, however, including the British commander-in-chief General Haig, who saw a weapon that could win the war.

The development of the tank began in early 1915, based on the success of armoured car squadrons against German infantry attacks and on the increasingly obvious need for a cross-country vehicle that could break the stalemate of trench warfare. The project attracted the attention and enthusiasm of the First Lord of the Admiralty, Winston Churchill, who described its promise to the Prime Minister. 'The caterpillar system would enable trenches to be crossed easily and the weight of the machine would destroy all wire entanglements. Forty or fifty of these machines prepared secretly and brought into position at nightfall could advance quite certainly into the enemy's trenches, smashing away all the obstructions and sweeping the trenches with their machine gun fire and with grenades thrown out of the tops.'

The tanks at the Somme were designated the Mark I. They were some seven feet high and 32 feet long, with a crew of eight, a Daimler engine, and a rarely achievable top speed of 3.7 miles per hour. The Mark I came in two versions distinguished by size of armament and inevitably nicknamed 'male', with two six-pounders, and 'female', with two machine guns.

After their Somme début, tanks with improved designs made appearances in several battles on the Western Front – Arras, Chemin des Dames, the third battle of Ypres, and St Julien. But it was at Cambrai in November 1917 that 300 Mark IV tanks, leading eight infantry divisions against the Hindenburg Line, fulfilled Churchill's promise by achieving a victory whose scope, even amid tactical failures, was sufficient to convince the doubters that the future was at hand. Like the stirrup, the bow, and gunpowder, the tank had transformed the practice of warfare.

Also on this day

1613: French aphorist François, duc de La Rochefoucauld is born in Paris * **1814: The Congress of Vienna begins** * 1935: The Nürnberg Laws deprive Jews of their citizenship and make the Swastika the official emblem of Nazi Germany * 1949: The German Bundestag confirms Konrad Adenauer as Chancellor by one vote

---

Events written in **boldface** are covered in full in
365: Great Stories from History for Every Day of the Year,
the first volume in this series.

---

16 September

'A king of France may die, but he is never ill'

1824 Fat King Louis XVIII was in agony. Paris was choking in a heatwave that lasted three interminable days, and in the streets near the palace straw had been thrown over the cobblestones to dull the noise of horses' hoofs. A crowd had gathered to pray.

The dying king's legs were mottled by gangrene. He lay propped up in bed, eyes closed, mouth half open, his face suffused with blood. In spite of the pain, he made light of his symptoms, telling his hovering courtiers: 'A king of France may die, but he is never ill.' Finally, at four in the morning of 16 September, the 68-year-old monarch tried to rise from his bed, whispering: 'A king should die standing up.' Falling back, his breathing weakened and then stopped.

Louis-Stanislas-Xavier, as he had been christened, had been born at Versailles on 17 November 1755, son of the Dauphin Louis and grandson of the reigning Louis XV. Few thought that he would ever mount the throne of France, since he was the third son still living and his father was still alive. When he was five he moved up a place on the waiting list on the death of his ten-year-old brother, and five years later another place when his father died of tuberculosis. In 1774 his grandfather Louis XV died of smallpox and his remaining elder brother became King as Louis XVI. The younger Louis's chances of the crown seemed to grow dimmer with the birth of his brother's two sons. Then, when he was 37, the French Republic abolished the monarchy, and suddenly there was no throne to inherit. A less determined royalist might have abandoned all hope.

By this time, however, Louis XVI was virtually under house arrest, and Louis had fled the country for Koblenz, before moving on to Italy, Russia and England. Safely abroad, he devoted his energies to raising the royalist banner and issuing counter-revolutionary manifestos. When the King was guillotined in 1793, Louis instantly proclaimed himself regent for his remaining nephew, the imprisoned Dauphin (Louis XVII), and when he, too, died in 1795 Louis announced that he was now Louis XVIII.

Through the remaining years of the Republic, and through Napoleon's reign as well, Louis continued to assert his right to the throne, and, perhaps to his own astonishment, in June 1814 he finally became the king he had long claimed to be. In truth, however, he owed his success not to his own efforts but to the wily diplomat Talleyrand, who at the Congress of Vienna successfully persuaded the other European powers on his restoration. In less than a year, however, on Napoleon's escape from Elba, Louis had to flee to Ghent, returning only after Waterloo. One of his first acts was to order the execution of Napoleon's Marshal Michel Ney, who had promised to support the King but then had abandoned him for Napoleon during the 100 Days.

During the ten years that remained to him, Louis steered a moderately con-servative course between restored reactionaries and discontented republicans. When he died, another brother inherited the monarchy, the truly reactionary Charles X, whose extremist views caused Talleyrand to voice his famous maxim that the Bourbons 'have learned nothing and forgotten nothing'.

Also on this day

1387: Henry of Monmouth (Henry V of England) is born at Monmouth Castle, Wales * **1498: The first Grand Inquisitor of the Spanish Inquisition, Tomás Torquemada, dies in the Monastery of Santo Tomás in Avila** * 1701: British King James II dies in exile at Saint-Germain in France

17 September

The king who discovered Velázquez

1665 Today in Madrid, Philip IV of Spain died at the age of 60, one of history's most feckless monarchs.

In his 44 years as King, Philip's only lasting accomplishments were in the arts. He encouraged Lope de Vega, brought Calderón to his court as official playwright and even wrote some plays himself. He collected many of the paintings for the royal collection that later became the basis for the Prado Museum, and he appointed Diego Velázquez as court painter in 1623. Ironically, it is thanks to Velázquez that we have such a complete and accurate record of what Philip looked like. Through the great artist's work we can see the arrogant face with a petulant, full-lipped mouth, the high, intellectual forehead, the jutting Habsburg jaw, the silly upturned moustache and the baggy, debauched eyes.

In life, Philip was just as Velázquez presented him in art – intellectual but weak, a tall, indolent man of great place and little consequence. Historian Philippe Erlanger memorably describes him as 'a hot-house plant rooted in solitude and boredom'. At court he conducted himself with imperious gravity and was seen to laugh only three times during his entire public life. Meanwhile, his nation slid steadily downhill.

During the first half of his reign, Philip left the running of the country to his ambitious and greedy minister, the Conde de Olivares, who attempted to regain Spain's supremacy in Europe during the Thirty Years War. Meanwhile, Philip devoted himself to his mistresses, by whom he had over 30 bastard children.

Eventually Philip felt compelled to dismiss Olivares. France had declared war in 1635, and in 1640, Portugal, ruled by Spain since the time of Philip's grandfather Philip II, revolted and won its independence.

Philip replaced Olivares with Luis Méndez de Haro, who remained his first minister until he died eighteen years later. Now, without a first minister, Philip still felt the need for guidance, and turned to a mystical nun named Sor María de Agreda, with whom he regularly corresponded, seeking her advice on critical matters of state.

Sor María's counsel was as unproductive as Olivares's. By the time of her death in 1665, Spain, once the greatest power in Europe, had become a second-class power both economically and militarily. Just four months later Philip followed the mystical nun to the grave.

Also on this day

1630: John Winthrop founds the town of Boston * 1787: The Constitution of the United States of America is signed * 1796: President George Washington delivers his 'Farewell Address' to Congress * 1862: The Battle of Antietam begins during the American Civil War, the bloodiest single day in US history with over 26,000 casualties * 1916: German fighter pilot Manfred von Richthofen ('The Red Baron') wins his first aerial combat near Cambrai, France * **1944: British airborne troops parachute into Holland near Arnhem in a disastrous attack on German positions**

18 September

Two royal dynasties get started

1517, 1714 The 18th of September seems to be a day of dynastic arrivals, as it marked the start of two great royal families, the Habsburgs in Spain and the House of Hanover in England.

On this day in 1517 a blonde, strapping seventeen-year-old named Charles von Habsburg landed at a point called Tazones in Asturias on the north coast of Spain. Charles's father was dead and his mother Juana was morbidly and incurably insane. Since his maternal grandfather King Ferdinand had died the previous year, Charles arrived as King Charles I on this, his first visit to Spain. (Two years later he would be chosen Holy Roman Emperor as well, becoming Charles V for the Empire while confusingly remaining Charles I for Spain.) As well as being Spain's first Charles he was also the country's first Habsburg monarch, and the House of Habsburg would rule the country until the death of his imbecilic great-great-grandson, the hapless Charles II, on 1 November 1700, some 183 years later.

Just fourteen years after the Spanish Habsburgs died out, 18 September once again became a day of dynastic arrival, as towards evening on that date in 1714 a fat, 54-year-old German prince landed in the fog at Greenwich on the Thames. Named George Louis of Brunswick-Lüneburg, he was the Elector of Hanover, but he arrived in England as King George I, the first Hanoverian king, having inherited the throne on the death of Queen Anne the previous 1 August.

George had a difficult life in England, as his total lack of the language forced him to communicate with his ministers in French. Moreover, he was widely mistrusted by the public for having imprisoned his wife for adultery and replacing her with two grasping German mistresses. (His wife died in the castle of Ahlden in 1726, incarcerated for 32 years.)

Nonetheless, George's line in Britain proved even more durable than Charles's in Spain, as the House of Hanover held the throne until 1901, a run of 187 years. It was then succeeded by the house of Saxe-Coburg-Gotha (the family name of Queen Victoria's consort Prince Albert). In 1917 George's great-great-great-great-great-grandson, George V, rechristened the family Windsor in a fit of patriotic fervour during the First World War. The same sentiment also caused all the wicked German shepherds in England to be renamed Alsatians.

Also on this day

AD **96: Roman emperor Domitian is murdered by his wife** * 324: Roman emperor Constantine defeats Licinius at Chrysopolis, becoming the sole emperor of the whole Roman Empire, east and west * 1709: Samuel Johnson is born in Lichfield, Staffordshire * 1851: The first issue of the *New York Times* appears

19 September

A bad day for Burgoyne

1777 This afternoon, a remote clearing called Freeman's Farm, on a forested bluff above the Hudson River, was the scene of a remarkable display of fighting spirit that proved to be a major turning point in the American Revolution, now well into its third year.

In four hours of raging combat, marked by thrusts and counter-thrusts, General John Burgoyne's British and German regulars were fought to a bloody standstill by Horatio Gates's ragtag collection of American troops fleshed out with militia. With timely reinforcement, which their over-cautious commander refused to send, the Americans, on the point of breaking through the centre, could have sent the entire British line into retreat. As it was, darkness and the arrival of a German regiment prevented such an outcome.

Not that Burgoyne recognised the result of the battle for what it was. After all, the rebels had finally withdrawn to their lines, leaving the field to him. Surely, that meant a victory. 'A smart and very honourable action', was how he chose to describe it to a colleague.

But the general's brave words concealed a different reality: his losses for the day neared 600, a serious diminution of his force; his path to Albany, the strategic target of his campaign, remained blocked; and his army was running out of food. But most central to his situation was what one observer in his camp wrote about the Americans' behaviour that day: 'The thought of fighting for their country and for freedom made them braver than ever.'

Freeman's Farm, or the first battle of Saratoga, led to a second confrontation, for Burgoyne now had little choice but to defeat – or find a way around – the American forces, which, with a steady influx of regional militia, now greatly outnumbered him. On 7 October he sent a reconnaissance in force to outflank the Americans on the bluff called Bemis Heights. But the wooded terrain favoured American musketry over British bayonets, and the tables were quickly turned, as American regiments came around the British flank to halt the advance. Then, as the British right withdrew in some disorder, General Benedict Arnold rode onto the field, and in a memorable feat led two American brigades in a savage counter-attack that took the British redoubts and turned the enemy's withdrawal into a battle-ending rout.

The second battle of Saratoga sealed the fate of the British army, now trapped along the Hudson. On 17 October, Burgoyne surrendered to General Gates, giving up almost 6,000 officers and men, as well as guns, small arms, ammunition, and military stores. At the surrender ceremony, an American band played 'Yankee Doodle', and a German soldier observing the American troops wrote: 'Not one of them was properly uniformed, but each man had on the clothes in which he goes to the field, to church or to the tavern. But they stood like soldiers, erect, with a military bearing which was subject to little criticism.'

Aside from the psychological benefits to the Patriot cause, the British surrender at Saratoga – the first in the war – persuaded King Louis XVI that it was time to formalise his country's relationship with the Americans, whose rebellion France had been secretly subsidising for a year. On 6 February 1778, in Paris, representatives of both countries signed a treaty that would make France an ally of America in the war against Great Britain. France would join the war the following June.

Also on this day

1356: The Black Prince defeats the French and captures King Jean II at the Battle of Poitiers * 1812: Founder of the House of Rothschild, Mayer Amschel Rothschild, dies in Frankfurt * 1881: American President James Garfield dies of blood poisoning, having been shot on 2 July by a deluded and disappointed office-seeker, Charles Guiteau * 1955: President Juan Perón of Argentina is deposed and exiled after a military coup

20 September

'Duke by the grace of God'

1455 Today Philip the Good of Burgundy achieved his lifetime's ambition of becoming independent from his suzerain, King Charles VII of France, by virtue of a treaty that granted him the title of Grand Duc d'Occident. From this day forward, Philip styled himself 'Duke by the grace of God' rather than by the grace of the King of France.

Philip's territory consisted not only of the wine-growing Burgundy around Beaune and Dijon that is now part of France, but also most of what today is Belgium, Holland and Luxembourg. Philip himself had added much of this area through wars, diplomacy and marriage. The great cities of Brussels, Ghent and Bruges were among the richest in the world, and Philip's court promoted a civilisation of sophistication, taste and high artistic merit.

The Duke was a great patron of the arts, a highly cultured man with a narrow but strong and intellectual face. In his youth he had been an exceptional athlete, not only a fine horseman and jouster but also a talented archer and tennis player. His other sporting interest was women, and he fathered so many illegitimate children that he was publicly criticised by the Bishop of Tournai.

In 1429, when Philip was 32, he founded the famous chivalric Ordre de la Toison d'Or (Order of the Golden Fleece) to rival England's Order of the Garter that had been created almost a century before. He named his order after the heroic quest of Jason and his Argonauts, but by using the word 'fleece' he also made a complimentary reference to the flourishing wool industry of his duchy. The order was originally restricted to 24 noblemen but was later enlarged.

After Philip died, the Ordre de la Toison d'Or's leadership was inherited by his son and then descended to the Habsburgs (Philip's granddaughter married the Holy Roman Emperor Maximilian von Habsburg). It became predominantly a Spanish order when Philip II of Spain inherited it, but when the Spanish Habsburgs petered out in 1700, both the Spanish Bourbons and the Austrian Habsburgs claimed the order, and so two branches continued to exist.

In Austria the Ordre de la Toison d'Or disappeared with the Habsburgs in 1918, but it continued in Spain until the Spanish Republic abolished it in 1930 after a run of 501 years.

Sadly for Philip the Good, his great Duchy of Burgundy proved far less durable, once again becoming part of France when Philip's son, Charles the Bold, was killed in battle on 5 January 1477.

Also on this day

356 BC: Alexander the Great is born * **1378: Robert of Geneva is elected Pope 'Urban VIII' to start the Great Papal Schism** * 1519: Ferdinand Magellan starts his round-the-world voyage with five ships and 280 men * 1857: The siege of Delhi ends, leading to the collapse of the Indian Mutiny * 1946: The first Cannes Film Festival opens

21 September

The French abolish the monarchy and replace the calendar

1792 The Bastille had fallen three years earlier, but Louis XVI still lived, a captive king restricted to the Temple in Paris, a 12th-century construction once the headquarters of the Templars.

But the members of the National Convention were becoming daily more revolutionary, and on this day they formally abolished the monarchy in France, marking the start of the First Republic.

Not content with initiating a new political era, the representatives decided to get a truly fresh start – by abolishing the Gregorian calendar altogether and starting anew. So the following day, 22 September, became Day One of Year I. The new calendar still contained twelve months but specified that each would have 30 days, with five days left over for Republican holidays. The seven-day week was also gone, replaced by one of ten days with the sensible but boring names of Primidi, Duodi, Tridi, Quartidi, Quintidi, Sextidi, Septidi, Octidi, Nonidi and Décadi.

Even the months of the year gained a more rational nomenclature, with names based on the weather thought to be characteristic of the season. For example, winter months were called Nivôse (snowy), Pluviôse (rainy) and Ventôse (windy). Other months included Germinal (in the spring) and Thermidor (indicating the heat of late July and August).

Having abolished the monarchy and the calendar, the Convention rested for precisely four (old-fashioned) months and then abolished poor Louis XVI with the guillotine.

It's probably a good thing that today the Revolutionary calendar is long forgotten. How would we feel about Bastille Day were it on 26 Messidor? About the only legacy that remains from this great French calendarial innovation is Lobster Thermidor, said to have been named by Napoleon after the month in which he first tasted it, and Emile Zola's novel *Germinal*, the title of which echoes the hopes of the republican Revolution, suggesting that mankind is on the verge of a new spring.

301

Also on this day
490 BC: Greeks annihilate the Persians at the Battle of Marathon * 19 BC: Roman poet Virgil dies * 1452: Fanatical preacher Girolamo Savonarola is born in Ferrara * 1832: British writer Sir Walter Scott dies

22 September

'I only regret that I have but one life to lose for my country'

1776 Next time you are in New York, go to the corner of 63rd Street and 3rd Avenue. You will be standing on the spot where Nathan Hale, one of America's greatest Revolutionary heroes, was hanged.

Hale was born in Connecticut in 1755 and, after attending Yale, became a schoolmaster. When the American Revolution broke out, he joined his state militia and soon rose to the rank of captain.

In the autumn of 1776 General George Washington's troops were sparring with the British around New York. On 21 September young Hale volunteered for the dangerous mission of going behind enemy lines to learn the British strength and position. Once his assignment had been accomplished, Hale intended to return to the American lines, but fires started by Washington's soldiers blocked his route. Unable to rejoin his own forces, he took refuge in a local tavern, where British soldiers picked him up during a routine sweep.

Hale openly admitted his mission, and a British officer sentenced him to hang the next day, without further trial. Remarkably composed throughout, just before his execution he pronounced his famous words: 'I only regret that I have but one life to lose for my country.' He then climbed the ladder that would be pulled from beneath his feet.

Hale became much more famous after the Revolution than he ever was during it, so it is possible that his celebrated words have been embellished by history. They bear a remarkable resemblance to the hero's speech in Joseph Addison's play *Cato*: 'What a pity is it that we can die but once to serve our country!'

Also on this day
1327: Edward II of England is murdered in prison on orders of his wife Isabella and her lover Roger de Mortimer * 1692: Six women and two men are hanged during the Salem witch trials in America * 1862: US president Abraham Lincoln frees America's 4 million slaves by issuing the Emancipation Proclamation, which comes into force the following 1 January

23 September

The first and greatest of all Roman emperors

63 BC Just before sunrise on this day was born the first and greatest of all Roman emperors, Gaius Octavius Caesar, later known as Augustus. He grew to be a handsome man with light brown hair and blue eyes, although slight in stature, only 5 feet 7 inches tall.

Octavian, as he was known before becoming Emperor, had the great good fortune to be the child of Julius Caesar's niece, and that relationship, together with Caesar's high regard for his abilities, caused Caesar to adopt him as his son when Octavian was eighteen. When Caesar was assassinated, Octavian inherited not only his colossal wealth but also the fidelity of some of his legions.

For the next thirteen years, Octavian shared power in uneasy alliance with Lepidus and Mark Antony. Lepidus was the first to be sidelined, and after Mark Antony was finally defeated at the Battle of Actium in 31 BC, Octavian ruled alone for the next 44 years. From 27 BC he began to style himself 'Augustus'.

Augustus could be utterly ruthless to achieve his ends. He once starved the town of Perusia – today's Perugia – into submission, executing 300 prisoners of equestrian rank, and after the downfall of Antony and Cleopatra he had Caesarion, Cleopatra's son by Julius Caesar, executed even though he was Augustus's brother by adoption. But generally he ruled by clever compromise, careful to give the appearance that Rome was still a republic governed by the Senate when in fact he had total autocratic power.

Augustus added huge areas to his empire, including Egypt, northern Spain, Switzerland, Austria, Hungary, and parts of Yugoslavia. He completely changed the empire's administrative systems and gave it over 40 years of uninterrupted peace and prosperity. He established Rome's first standing army and then set up armed camps throughout the empire that subsequently became some of Europe's greatest cities. In Rome itself he made vast improvements. As Augustus himself accurately boasted: 'I found Rome built of bricks; I leave her clothed in marble.'

In his private life Augustus was devoted to his wife Livia. In order to marry her he had compelled her to divorce her first husband while still pregnant by him. He passed rather puritanical laws against adultery and banished his own daughter for scandalous conduct, although he kept a string of mistresses himself.

Although essentially a simple man with little regard for his own appearance, Augustus did have one slightly narcissistic moment of which the effects are with us still. Because, according to Suetonius, 'in the month of Sextilis he won his first consulship and his most decisive victories', Augustus renamed Sextilis 'August' after himself.

Also on this day
480 BC: Themisticles leads the Greeks to victory over Persian King Xerxes at the Battle of Salamis * 1779: American captain John Paul Jones loses the *Bon Homme Richard* but still defeats the British at Flamborough Head * 1938: British premier Neville Chamberlain flies to Munich to meet Hitler * 1939: Austrian founder of psychoanalysis Sigmund Freud dies

24 September

The second conquest of England?

1326 It is common knowledge that no one since William the Conqueror has ever successfully invaded England – but is it really true?

Take the case of Queen Isabella, wife of England's Edward II. Bored, insulted and generally fed up with her feckless and homosexual husband, Isabella manoeuvred herself into a diplomatic mission to the court of France. Once there, she openly lived with her paramour, one Roger de Mortimer, an English baron whom she had helped to escape from the Tower of London.

With great energy and resource, Isabella and Mortimer moved on to Holland where they raised an army and borrowed a Dutch nobleman, John of Hainault, to share command of the troops.

On this day the invasion force landed on the Suffolk coast and within four months had captured poor, pathetic Edward, forced his abdication and imprisoned him. Nine months later Mortimer, with Isabella's knowledge, had Edward hideously murdered in his cell, a red-hot iron rod thrust into his anus. Isabella then took power as regent for her teenage son with Mortimer at her side.

Does this constitute a conquest? The army was Dutch, as was one of its two commanders. And the driving force of the invasion was Isabella, who, although Queen of England, was in fact French, the daughter of King Philip the Fair. So French was she that she was known then and since as the She-Wolf of France.

Also on this day
1435: Death of lubricious Queen Isabeau of France, who disinherited her own son and signed the notorious Treaty of Troyes, making Henry V of England heir to the French throne * 1541: Swiss physician and alchemist Paracelsus dies * 1667: John Churchill, the future Duke of Marlborough, is gazetted as Ensign in Charles II's Foot Guards, his first military assignment * 1789: President George Washington signs the Judiciary Act of 1789 to establish the United States Supreme Court * 1896: American novelist F. Scott Fitzgerald is born in St Paul, Minnesota

25 September

One victory too few for King Harold

1066 At Stamford Bridge today, England's King Harold, leading an out-numbered army, won a crushing victory over Viking invaders. It should have been enough to ensure his reign. Instead, Harold would soon learn that one victory was not enough.

Only nine months earlier, on his deathbed, King Edward the Confessor had left his realm to Harold, the country's most powerful noble – or at least so Harold earnestly insisted. But across the Channel another pretender staked his claim: the powerful Duke of Normandy, Guillaume le Bâtard, William the Bastard.

Learning that William was preparing to invade, Harold gathered his forces near London, only to hear that a more immediate danger came from the north. The legendary Viking warrior, King Harald Hardrada of Norway – called Harald the Ruthless by his fellow Norsemen – had landed at Riccall, near York, with a force numbering some 10,000 men. Supporting him was King Harold's exiled brother Tostig.

To meet the invaders, Harold now led his army of some 5,000 mounted infantrymen out of London, heading north along Watling Street, the old Roman road. Spurring his men on at top speed, he arrived at Tadcaster on Sunday, 24 September, having covered an astounding 200 miles in only four days.

The next morning was warm and sunny. Harold led his army to Stamford Bridge, which crosses the River Derwent some eight miles to the east of York. There he caught Harald Hardrada's soldiers completely by surprise, most without their chain mail, as they relaxed by the river. The first the Vikings saw of the approaching force was a huge dust cloud churned up by the horses. One Nordic source relates: 'And the closer the army came, the greater it [the column of dust] grew, and their glittering weapons sparkled like a field of broken ice.'

Harold called out to his brother Tostig, offering him an earldom if he would change sides. Hesitant, Tostig asked what reward would be offered to Harald Hardrada if he pulled back his army. 'He shall have seven feet of good English soil, or a little more perhaps, as he is so much taller than other men', responded the English king. Rebuffed, Tostig turned back to rejoin the Vikings, who were urgently preparing for battle.

To attack the invaders, Harold first needed to cross the Derwent, but a single armoured Viking desperately defended the bridge, defeating all comers. Finally a resourceful English warrior commandeered a boat and rowed beneath the bridge. There he plunged his spear through a gap in the planks, impaling the frenzied defender.

As the English poured over the bridge, the Vikings formed a triangular shield wall, awaiting the enemy onslaught. Bloody hand-to-hand fighting lasted throughout the day, the English attacking from all sides, raining down spears and arrows. Then, according to a Norse saga, an enraged Harald Hardrada suddenly charged out in front of his men, 'hewing with both hands. Neither helmet nor armour could withstand him, and everyone in his path gave way before him.' But, just when the English line started to waver, an arrow caught him in the throat, and his life bled away on the grass.

Now Tostig rallied the demoralised Norse and reorganised the defence. Reluctant to spill yet more blood, King Harold offered a truce, but the invaders responded that they would 'rather fall, one across the other, than accept quarter from the Englishmen'. Once again the two sides hurled themselves at each other, the invaders reinforced by more Vikings from their ships, but the hammering of English swords and battleaxes forced them back, and Tostig was slain. At the end of the day, the Vikings fled back to their ships at Riccall. Of the 300 ships that had brought the invaders to England, only 24 returned to Norway.

King Harold's victory was monumental; he had so completely defeated the Vikings that they never again attacked England. But within a week he learned that two days after his triumph at Stamford Bridge, William of Normandy had landed at Pevensey in Sussex. Once again, Harold set his troops on a forced march, this time headed south, but on 14 October he was defeated and killed at Hastings, England's last Anglo-Saxon king.

Also on this day

1396: The Turks defeat French and Hungarian armies at Nicopolis, the last battle of the last Crusade * 1534: Medici pope Clement VII dies * 1780: American general and traitor Benedict Arnold flees to the British after spying for them for over a year * 1897: American novelist and Nobel Prize winner William Faulkner is born in New Albany, Mississippi

26 September

Death of a backwoods legend

1820 One of the legendary figures in American history died this day in Missouri. He was the original man in the coonskin cap, the quintessential frontiersman who came to exemplify the restless vitality of American life moving ever westward across the continent. He was Daniel Boone, dead at the age of 85.

Born and raised in a blacksmith's family, living first in Pennsylvania, then in a remote area of North Carolina, Boone learned early the survival skills of the hunter, the trapper, and the explorer. Even though at times in his life he was a farmer and even a storekeeper, he found that prowling the wilderness held greater rewards than living in civilisation. In time, he became famous and influential not only for his prowess in the back country – pioneering trails, guiding settlers, and fighting Indians – but for the inspiration these celebrated deeds gave to others. His greatest achievement was to explore the unknown territory beyond the Cumberland Gap that is now Kentucky. In 1775 he took a team of 30 axemen and cut a 250-mile route, the Wilderness Road, across the mountains into the new and fertile land, then led one of the first group of settlers (including his own family), who founded a settlement and named it Boonesborough in his honour. In the next twenty years, over 100,000 settlers followed the path he blazed through the mountain passes into Kentucky.

During the American Revolution, Boone spent much of his time protecting the Kentucky frontier settlements against attacks by Indian tribes allied with the British. In one particularly dramatic event, he rescued his daughter and two other girls who had been kidnapped by Indian raiders. In another famous episode, he was captured by a party of Shawnee Indians but escaped after five months of captivity, walking 160 miles in four days, and reaching Boonesborough in time to warn the settlement of an impending Indian attack. Subsequently, he led the successful defence of the fort against a siege in which the settlers were outnumbered by the attackers ten to one.

After the war came the 1784 publication of *The Adventures of Col. Daniel Boone*, purporting to be a first-person account by Boone but actually written by John Filson. It proved immensely popular and was soon translated for publication in France and Germany. Now Boone became more than locally celebrated for his deeds as a hunter and Indian-fighter. He was the model for James Fenimore Cooper's character in the 'Leatherstocking' tales, Natty Bumppo; and the rescue of the young girls was retold as an episode in *The Last of the Mohicans*.

Through much of his adult life, Boone was usually land-rich and cash-poor. But most of his land holdings – at one point he had 100,000 acres under claim in Kentucky – were later lost in legal challenges to his often carelessly filed titles or sold to pay taxes and other debts. Happier and more successful as a hunter and backswoodsman than as a land speculator or merchant, Boone always said he needed 'more elbow room'. In 1799 he left Kentucky, now filling up with farmers and with game becoming scarce, and headed off with his large family for Missouri, then part of the Spanish province of Louisiana, lured by the promise of territory largely untouched by European settlement. Active into his final years, he went on his last hunting and trapping trip in November 1817, at the age of 82.

After his funeral, he was buried next to his wife in a plot near the Missouri River. There was no monument, a fact addressed in the Kentucky poet Thomas O'Hara's poem 'The Old Pioneer Daniel Boone':

> A dirge for the brave old pioneer.
> The patriarch of his tribe.
> He sleeps, no pompous pile marks where,
> No line his deeds describe.
> They raised no stone above him here
> Nor carved his deathless name.
> An empire is his sepulcher,
> His epitaph is fame.

Also on this day
1513: Conquistador Vasco Núñez de Balboa reaches the Pacific Ocean and claims it for Spain * 1791: French painter Théodore Géricault is born in Rouen * 1888: American (later British) poet T.S. Eliot is born in St Louis * 1898: American composer George Gershwin is born in Brooklyn

27 September

The age of the train begins

1825 Today the world's first steam-powered passenger train pulled out of Darlington bound for Stockton-on-Tees, nine miles away. Carrying 500 passengers, all in coal wagons except for a few dignitaries in a wooden coach, the train was led by a man on horseback carrying a flag reading *Periculum privatum utilitas publica* (The private danger is the public good). The engine, christened *Locomotion*, looked rather like a brown barrel laid sideways on four large black spoked wheels, with a huge black smokestack up front.

Soon the horseman moved aside, and George Stephenson, the engine's driver and designer, opened the throttle and the train raced forward at fifteen miles an hour. The age of the train was born.

The age of the train, however, had been a long time in gestation, since the beginning of the 18th century. The earliest trains were horse-drawn goods wagons that ran on wooden rails. Most were used to haul coal to the nearest waterway, but in 1758 the Middleton Railway near Leeds became the first line authorised by Parliament to go beyond the colliery's boundaries – although the government demanded fences built to protect the public.

In 1803 iron rails for the first time replaced the unstable wooden ones, but the horse remained the only power unit. That was soon to change; in the same year a Cornishman named Richard Trevithick built the world's first steam locomotive, based on the stationary steam engines of Thomas Newcomen and James Watt. (Trevithick later cheekily named one of his locomotives *Catch Me Who Can*.)

1807 saw two steps forward and one step back as the world's first railway carrying fare-paying passengers was opened – but horses once again pulled the carriages.

At the end of the Napoleonic wars, however, the advantages of steam power were becoming evident. Horse fodder had become costly, and the growth of coal mining brought a demand for more transportation. Although the first steam locomotives were unreliable and expensive, they could haul more wagons, faster, than horses and slowly started to replace them on the rails.

Locomotive pioneer George Stephenson was the son of a mechanic and was completely uneducated, learning to read and write only when he went to night school at nineteen. He then earned a living fixing clocks, repairing shoes and making clothes for coal-miners' wives. Eventually he became an engine-wright at the Killingworth colliery near Newcastle-upon-Tyne, and came to Leeds to see some of the early steam engine experiments. Soon he was developing his own engines.

In 1814, when he was 33, Stephenson designed his first locomotive. Named *Blücher* after the Prussian general who had helped defeat Napoleon at Waterloo, it could haul 30 tons of coal. In 1821 he became engineer of the Stockton & Darlington Railway, and two years later opened the world's first locomotive construction company, which he turned over to his son Robert to run. Stephenson not only designed *Locomotion* for the historic first steam-operated passenger line, he also invented the first train whistle after an engine had collided with a horse-drawn cart that was travelling on the same tracks. For this he has been called the 'Father of Railways'.

Even after Stephenson's groundbreaking trip from Darlington to Stockton, there was still plenty of confusion to come. Both horse- and steam-powered trains used the same tracks, and the railway line owned only the tracks, not the trains. Anyone could 'hire' the rails, and there was no timetable, so rival drivers often fought each other for right-of-way.

Such was the beginning of the railroad, which soon became the most important form of transportation, until the advent of the automobile and then the aeroplane. Today the train seems to be making a comeback, and now high-speed lines are beginning to vie with planes and cars. Indeed, France's TGV (Train Grande Vitesse) regularly runs at 185 miles an hour and has set the most recent world record at 317 miles an hour, more than twenty times as fast as Stephenson's *Locomotion*. But Stephenson brought us not only the train but also its tracks: the rail gauge he used of 4 feet 8½ inches is still the world's standard gauge.

Also on this day

1389: Florentine leader and patron of the arts Cosimo de' Medici is born * 1917: French painter Edgar Degas dies * 1940: Japan agrees a pact with Hitler and Mussolini to form the Axis * 1944: French sculptor Aristide Maillol dies

28 September

Clemenceau le Tigre *is born*

1841 This should be an occasion worth celebrating for all small-d democrats and small-r republicans, wherever they may be, for on this day was born Georges Clemenceau, a member of both species. Known and feared as *le Tigre* for the Jacobin ferocity he brought to the arena of French politics, Clemenceau defended the Third Republic for almost half a century against all threats, whether launched by the Catholic Church, royalist plotters, Bonapartists, the army, anti-Dreyfusards, defeatists of every persuasion, or foreign enemies.

Early on, Clemenceau studied medicine. He had strong intellectual interests – he translated John Stuart Mill into French – and a special fascination with ancient Greece, which he called 'a republic of islands'. During the Paris Commune of 1871, he was mayor of Montmartre. Later, as a journalist and newspaper-owner, he championed the cause of Captain Dreyfus. His marriage to a young woman from America failed, in part no doubt because she was out of her depth in his surroundings, but mostly because, as Clemenceau himself admitted, his only true love was *la belle France*.

A loner at heart and opposed to the elitist nature of French politics, Clemenceau understood the fragility of the Third Republic's parliamentary system, which produced a seemingly endless stream of governments, one of which he had headed as premier early in the new century. But in his unremitting pursuit of the causes he believed in, he became known as a wrecker of governments, and accordingly his enemies far outnumbered his supporters.

On 17 November 1917, with France reeling from the blows of war and with the voices of defeat and despair growing louder, President Poincaré asked Clemenceau, now 76, to form a government. Winston Churchill was in Paris at the time and described the dire situation: 'The last desperate stake had to be played. France had resolved to unbar the cage and let her tiger loose upon all foes, beyond the trenches or in her midst. With snarls and growls, the ferocious, aged beast of prey went into action.'

Clemenceau's policy was: 'I wage war!' While the French armies confronted the Germans in the field, his government rallied the nation at home and crushed every form of opposition. His end was victory, not surrender, and every means was justified: civil liberties were curtailed, secret dossiers consulted, dissidents arrested.

Victory came in November 1918. Afterwards, Clemenceau presided over the Versailles Peace Conference, but a France at peace no longer needed her great war leader, and his government fell in 1920. He died on 24 November 1929. He is in the pantheon with Lincoln, Churchill, and Roosevelt.

Also on this day

48 BC: Roman general Pompey the Great is assassinated on orders from the Egyptian Pharaoh Ptolemy * AD 929: (The real) Good King Wenceslas is murdered by his brother at Stara Boleslav, Czechoslovakia * 1215: Mongol Emperor of China Kublai Khan is born * 1573: Italian painter Caravaggio (Michelangelo Merisi) is born * 1864: Karl Marx founds the First International in London * 1895: French scientist Louis Pasteur dies

29 September

Darius the Great is chosen King by his horse

522 BC Ever since Cyrus the Great had completed his conquests, the Persian Achaemenian empire had been the greatest the world had known, encompassing the Near East from the Aegean to the Indus River. When Cyrus died, his son Cambyses claimed the throne, but now Cambyses had succumbed to the horrors of gangrene after having stabbed himself in the thigh with his own sword while mounting his horse in Syria. This left the empire to his ambitious brother Bardiya, whom many believed had stage-managed Cambyses' death.

Not everyone welcomed Bardiya as the new king, especially a group of seven of Cambyses' officers, headed by a distant cousin named Darius, who was only 28 but carried the high title of Cambyses' 'lance-bearer', as befitting a member of the Achaemenian clan. Now this cabal resolved to do away with Bardiya and replace him on the throne.

To escape the heat of the summer, Bardiya had retreated to Ecbatana, the Achaemenian kings' summer residence (now Hamadān in Iran). But the conspirators knew he must soon leave the safety of the city to return to the Persian capital at Susa, and they waited for news of his departure.

By the end of September, Bardiya was headed home but he stopped en route at the stronghold of Sikayauvatiš, near Nisaea. On the evening of this day, the seven plotters also arrived at the fortress, and, by virtue of their high rank, easily talked their way past the guards. Then, drawing their daggers, they surged into Bardiya's bedroom, where he was diverting himself with one of his concubines. Caught unawares, Bardiya desperately grabbed a broken footstool to ward off the assailants, but Darius's brother Artaphernes drove his blade home.

So yet another Persian ruler was dead, but apparently the regicides had not determined who would take his place. They settled on a novel way of selecting the new king.

The assassins mounted their horses and rode out onto the plain beyond the fortress, there to await a sign from Ahura Mazdā, the great god who ruled the world. They agreed that when the sun rose, whoever's horse would neigh first should be King; when the dawn broke, Darius's horse shook its head and whinnied.

As a signal from Ahura Mazdā, it was beyond dispute – Darius had been chosen. But afterwards a rumour began to circulate: during the night, Darius's groom Oebares had rubbed the genitals of a tethered mare with his hand, and when the sun rose he had held his fingers beneath the nose of Darius's stallion, causing it to neigh. The almost contemporary Greek historian Herodotus tells us that the first thing Darius did after winning the throne was to order built a monument of himself on horseback with the inscription: 'Darius, son of Hystapes, by virtue of his horse and of his groom Oebares, won the throne of Persia.'

Now Darius was king, thanks to his co-conspirators, who had probably stage-managed the selection in order to give it the imprimatur of the god. For good measure, Darius now revealed that the cabal had not killed a king after all but only an impostor. The murdered man, he informed his subjects, was not Bardiya but a sorcerer named Gaumâta, who had impersonated Bardiya after the real Bardiya had been secretly put to death by Cambyses. As Darius ordered graven on a rock face: 'By the grace of Ahura Mazdā I became king; Ahura Mazdā granted me the kingdom.' All in all, as good a piece of political flummery as ever has been disseminated to a credulous public.

Although the beginning of Darius's reign was troubled by internal revolt, he soon stamped out all resistance, fighting nineteen battles against rebels in his first year in power. He conquered Babylon, then Sindh in India and the Punjab while extending the Persian empire to its greatest extent. He built the great city of Persepolis and even a 52-mile canal connecting the Red Sea with the Nile. One of his few failures came in 490 BC, when he tried to invade Greece but was famously defeated at the Battle of Marathon.

Darius the Great died in his bed in 486 BC at the age of 64, King of Kings for 37 years, thanks to the great god Ahura Mazdā – and his horse.

Also on this day

1273: Rudolph von Habsburg becomes the first Habsburg Holy Roman Emperor * 1758: Admiral Horatio Nelson is born in Norfolk * 1902: French writer Emile Zola dies in Paris * 1910: American painter Winslow Homer dies

30 September

Birth of a great editor

1884 This should be an important day of observance for writers – especially for novelists – because the great book editor Maxwell Perkins, of Charles Scribner's Sons, was born this day in Windsor, Vermont. When we think of Perkins, the names of F. Scott Fitzgerald, Ernest Hemingway and Thomas Wolfe come to mind. But we forget that there were so many other distinguished writers for whom he was editor, among them Ring Lardner, Marcia Davenport, Douglas Southall Freeman, John P. Marquand, S.S. Van Dine, Allen Tate, Edmund Wilson, Dawn Powell, Erskine Caldwell, Marjorie Kinnan Rawlings, Alan Paton and James Jones.

What was it his authors thought Perkins did for them? Well, among other things he urged every one of them to read – and reread – *War and Peace*, his favourite book. He was also a good listener and, perhaps because of a reticent manner face-to-face, a remarkable letter-writer.

He was a creature of habit. When the Western writer Will James (*Smoky, Lone Cowboy*) came to New York, Perkins admired his ten-gallon hat. James sent him one, and after that Perkins was rarely seen without some sort of hat on his head, indoors or out.

He always drank a martini or two at lunch, usually at Cherio's on 53rd Street between Fifth and Madison. The drinks were invariably followed by roast breast of guinea hen. How many aspiring authors have dreamed of lunching over martinis and guinea hens and hearing Perkins say: 'Go ahead and write it. We will publish it.' That's what he told Marcia Davenport before she had written a word of her Mozart biography.

After Cherio's it was back to the office. For many years Perkins lived in New Canaan, Connecticut, so his evening procedure was to leave Scribner's before five, stop off for 'tea' at the Ritz bar (46th and Madison), and then on to Grand Central, just in time for the 6.02.

With a routine like that, who wouldn't want to be an editor?

Also on this day

1399: Richard II abdicates as King of England * 1520: The rule of Suleiman the Magnificent in the Ottoman Empire begins * 1791: The first performance of Mozart's *The Magic Flute* takes place in Vienna * 1900: Winston Churchill is elected to Parliament for the first time for the constituency of Oldham * 1955: Screen icon James Dean is killed when he crashes his Porsche

1 October

Henry III – the king who reigned for 56 years but ruled for only 24

1207 Today Henry Plantagenet was born at Winchester, first son of John of England and his queen Isabella. Only nine years later King John would be carried off by dysentery and his young son would become Henry III, a weak and vacillating monarch who would reign for 56 years, a period exceeded among English sovereigns only by Queen Victoria (64 years) and George III (60 years). (Queen Elizabeth II, who inherited the throne in 1952, is closing fast.)

Although Henry reigned long, he often did not rule. For his first thirteen years as King a council of barons ran the country, led by the venerable knight William Marshal. But even when Henry came of age, powerful nobles continued to rule until 1234 when the King was 27.

When Henry finally took charge of the government himself, he ruled capriciously and badly, spending outrageous sums in unsuccessful efforts to reclaim English territories in France and gain the Kingdom of Sicily for his infant son. So unhappy did these expensive failures make his barons that in 1258 they forced on him what are called the Provisions of Oxford, which effectively allowed the barons to oversee (and overrule) all of Henry's decisions. Three years later Henry reasserted himself, only to face another baronial uprising under the leadership of the powerful Simon de Montfort in 1264. Montfort easily captured Henry at the Battle of Lewes and controlled England for the next fifteen months.

Luckily for Henry, his son Edward (later Edward I), now 26, defeated and killed Montfort at the Battle of Evesham in August 1265. Even then, however, poor Henry had no opportunity to regain personal command, as his son took charge of the government while the King relapsed into senility, dying seven years later.

In all, poor Henry ruled for only 24 of the 56 years of his reign. His accomplishments as monarch were less than nothing, but he did leave one great memorial, Westminster Abbey, which he transformed from the Romanesque church of Edward the Confessor to the Gothic masterpiece we know today.

Also on this day

331 BC: Alexander the Great defeats the Persian emperor Darius III at Gaugamela * 1066: William the Conqueror lands at Pevensey in Sussex * 1684: French playwright Pierre Corneille dies * 1856: Flaubert publishes the first instalment of *Madame Bovary* in the *Revue de Paris* * 1936: Francisco Franco becomes Head of State (read dictator) in Spain

> Events written in **boldface** are covered in full in
> *365: Great Stories from History for Every Day of the Year*,
> the first volume in this series.

2 October

Birth of the Mahatma

1869 Today at Porbandar, the capital of a small principality in Gujarat in western India, was born one of the greatest men that India has ever produced – Mohandas Gandhi.

Although educated as a lawyer in London, Gandhi became to Western eyes the archetypal Indian. Gnome-like and bespectacled, he was a fervent Hindu dressed in a loincloth who ate no meat. He became the most important person in India's battle for independence from Great Britain and was so greatly admired by his fellow Indians that he was called 'Mahatma', or 'great-souled'.

Gandhi grew up in a strongly religious Hindu family, whose beliefs included commitment to non-violence and vegetarianism, but despite their religious zeal, Gandhi and his family were equally tolerant of other faiths if sincerely held.

Gandhi virtually invented passive resistance as a political tool and used his moral pre-eminence to great effect, both in persuading the British to free India and in quelling the Muslim–Hindu riots that followed the partition (which he opposed) of India and Pakistan. He became famous for his principled fasting, used to put unbearable pressure on both the British and varying factions within India.

Gandhi was, by Western standards, something of a religious mystic. He believed Western medicine was evil, since it healed bodies sick from wrong living, and considered hospitals as institutions for propagating sin. At age 36 he renounced sex, observing the Hindu practice of *Brahmacharya* (celibacy). He sorely tested his commitment (successfully, by all reports) by sleeping naked in the same bed as young women. He lived in poverty and, some believe, retarded India's ability to escape it by the example he set.

Despite his ascetic lifestyle, Gandhi could occasionally share a joke. Once, when asked his opinion of Western civilisation, he responded: 'I think it would be a very good idea.'

On 30 January 1948 a disgruntled fellow Hindu, who blamed Gandhi for the partition, shot him to death at a prayer meeting in New Delhi. He was 78.

Also on this day

632: The Prophet Mohammed ascends to heaven from Jerusalem * **1187: Saladin reconquers Jerusalem** * 1452: Richard III of England is born at Fotheringhay Castle, Northamptonshire * 1851: French Field Marshal Ferdinand Foch is born at Tarbes

3 October

The battles of Philippi and the deaths of Brutus and Cassius

42 BC Ever since Caesar had crossed the Rubicon with a legion behind him in 49 BC, the Roman nobility had suspected he was intent on making himself king. When he defeated the official government forces of Pompey and two years later made himself dictator-for-life, they had plotted his murder, determined to restore the republican government – which would have equally restored the power of the nobles themselves. But instead of bringing back the republic, the assassination triggered civil war.

On this day, just twenty months later, the armies of Caesar's principal murderers – Marcus Junius Brutus and Gaius Cassius Longinus – met those of his avengers, his adopted son Octavian (the future emperor Augustus) and his one-time general Mark Antony, at Philippi on the Macedonian coast of Greece. It was the first of two battles that would forever change the Roman Empire from a mildly democratic oligarchy to fully-fledged dictatorship.

In the months leading up to the battles there were omens aplenty. According to 2nd-century historian Cassius Dio, in Rome 'meteors darted here and there; blaring of trumpets, clashing of arms and shouts of armies were heard at night from the gardens both of [Octavian] and of Antony [. . .] A child was born with ten fingers on each hand, a statue of Jupiter sent forth blood from its right shoulder; there were also rivers that began to flow backward [. . .] But [in Greece] the thing which most of all portended the destruction that was to come upon [Brutus and Cassius] [. . .] was that many vultures and also many other birds that devour corpses gathered above the conspirators' heads and gazed down on them, screaming and screeching in a ghastly and frightful manner.'

On the day of the first battle the two armies faced each other across the Philippi plain. 'Then one trumpeter on each side sounded the first challenge, after which all the trumpeters joined in [. . .] to rouse the spirit of the soldiers. Then there was suddenly a great silence and after waiting a little the leaders uttered a piercing shout and [. . .] the heavy-armed troops gave the war cry, beat their shields with their spears and then hurled their spears, while the slingers and the archers flung their stones and missiles. Then the two bodies of cavalry charged out against each other.'

Brutus's army soon had the better of Octavian's, killing many and burning the enemy camp, but, after a stand-off, Mark Anthony suddenly ordered his men to storm Cassius's camp. Unaware of Brutus's triumph and believing all was lost, Cassius withdrew to his tent with his freedman Pindarus. Drawing his robes up over his face and laying bare his neck, he ordered Pindarus to kill him. After the battle his head was found severed from his body.

The armies separated, each one part-victorious, part-defeated. For twenty days the generals eyed each other nervously, until on the afternoon of 23 October Brutus lined up his forces, once again preparing for battle. But in reviewing his troops he noticed their hesitation, especially his cavalry, which seemed to be waiting for the infantry to attack. Then, suddenly, one of his bravest soldiers dashed from his lines to desert to the enemy. Fearful that more would follow, Brutus ordered an instant assault.

This time Octavian's and Mark Antony's forces quickly overwhelmed Brutus's uncertain troops. Retreating from the field, Brutus grasped his sword with both hands and fell upon it, killing himself instantly. When Mark Antony found Brutus lying dead, he ordered him clothed in the best of his own robes, intent on honouring his dead opponent with a ritual cremation, but the unforgiving Octavian insisted that Brutus's head be sent to Rome for display in the Forum.

Brutus's corpse was decapitated and the head pickled in brine to be shipped to Rome. During the voyage, however, a hurricane threatened to wreck the ship and the crew, convinced that the severed head displeased the gods, threw it overboard. Back in Rome Brutus's wife Porcia killed herself by swallowing burning coals.

The Roman Republic was now dead forever and eleven years later Octavian destroyed Mark Antony's forces at Actium, to become Rome's first emperor and sole ruler of the Roman world.

Also on this day

1226: St Francis dies at the Porziuncola just outside Assisi * 1656: Myles Standish, leader of the Plymouth Colony (the first permanent settlement in New England), dies in Duxbury, Massachusetts * 1867: French painter Pierre Bonnard is born in Fontenay-aux-Roses * 1896: English artist William Morris dies * 1910: Leading republican Miguel Bombarda is murdered by a maniac, igniting the Portuguese revolution that ended the monarchy

4 October

'Thy necessity is yet greater than mine'

1586 Today died Sir Philip Sidney at the age of 31, knight, courtier, poet, soldier, diplomat, scholar, friend and supporter of artists and scientists, a man widely admired in his time, not so much for any particular accomplishment but as the quintessence of what an Elizabethan gentleman should be.

Sidney was one of the best-connected young men in England. His grandfather was the Duke of Northumberland, one uncle was the Earl of Warwick and another was Queen Elizabeth's favourite, Robert Dudley, the Earl of Leicester. He was godson to King Philip II of Spain and son-in-law to Sir Francis Walsingham, Queen Elizabeth's Secretary of State.

In spite of these spectacular relations, Sidney failed to get the state appointments he wanted after he had shown poor judgement in an early ambassadorial assignment. Fortunately for posterity, this gave him the time to pursue his literary career and other intellectual interests.

Sidney's chance to serve the Queen came in 1585 when Elizabeth decided to come to the aid of Dutch Protestants in their struggle with Catholic Spain. She sent a small force under the command of Sidney's uncle, Leicester, and Sidney was put in charge of a company of cavalry.

By the autumn of 1586 the rebellious Dutch and their English allies were besieging the town of Zutphen, trying to prevent the Spanish resupplying the small garrison within. Suddenly an enemy supply train was spotted. Sidney was about to lead his cavalry into attack when he noticed that one of his men had been caught without full armour. The gallant commander threw across his own thigh piece and then thundered off into the assault.

Three times Sidney charged the enemy, but on his last attack a musket ball smashed into his leg just above the knee, shattering the bone. Seriously wounded, he managed to retain his mount and escape from the battle to a nearby field filled with English casualties. As he lay injured, he saw a common soldier stretched out near him, clearly on the point of death. In a moment of conspicuous gallantry, Sidney handed the soldier his own cup of water, saying, 'Thy necessity is yet greater than mine.'

Sidney's men then carried their stricken leader to nearby Arnhem, his wound already showing signs of infection. Eleven days later, on 4 October, he died. Subsequently he was given a state funeral in St Paul's Cathedral in London, the last to be so honoured until Nelson over two centuries later.

Also on this day

1582: Pope Gregory XIII replaces the Julian calendar with the Gregorian calendar; the following day becomes 15 October (Great Britain waits until 1752 to make the change) * 1669: Rembrandt van Rijn dies in Amsterdam * 1720: Italian artist Giambattista Piranesi is born * 1814: French painter Jean François Millet is born * **1853: The Crimean War begins**

5 October

Grigory Potemkin – larger than life

1791 Today died the most influential minister in Russia's history, Prince Grigory Potemkin, the manic and sybaritic genius who was the lover and possibly the husband of Catherine the Great.

Potemkin was larger than life both literally and figuratively. He stood well over six feet tall and, after his more athletic youth was past, was gigantic in girth as well. He was also endowed with a mountainous flow of energy, with ambition to match. Given incomprehensible sums by the Empress – some say over 9 million roubles at a time when a field marshal earned about 1,000 roubles a year

– he spent all of this and more, making no distinction between his own almost unlimited funds and those of the government.

Potemkin helped Catherine greatly enlarge her empire, adding Lithuania, Belorussia and the Ukraine through conquest and treaty. He was also responsible for Russia's takeover of the Crimea from Turkey, but in this project he failed in his even more ambitious goal of restoring the Byzantine Empire under one of Catherine's grandsons. He also built innumerable splendid palaces for himself and lived in a more regal fashion than any monarch.

Born at a time when Russia boasted only about 20 million inhabitants, of whom almost half were serfs, Potemkin came from a family of minor nobility. At sixteen he joined the horseguards in Moscow and played a minor role in Catherine's *coup d'état* seven years later. But his participation gave the voracious Empress the chance to notice the then handsome soldier ten years her junior and he was rewarded with a small estate. For the next twelve years he served Catherine in various ways and was finally taken on as the Empress's official lover. The affair lasted for two years, during which time he and Catherine may have been secretly married. The relationship was too stormy to last – both he and Catherine probably had other lovers during the affair – but Potemkin probably continued intermittently to sleep with Catherine for the rest of his life.

Potemkin was an insatiable seducer of women, with an endless string of mistresses, including three of his own nieces. He was reputed to be so robustly endowed that Catherine ordered a mould taken of his powerful appendage and cast a copy in porcelain.

Also on this day

1713: French writer and philosopher Denis Diderot is born * **1795: Napoleon Bonaparte's 'Whiff of Grape': he disperses the Paris mob with grapeshot and saves the nascent French Republic** * 1910: Portugal is proclaimed a republic as King Manuel II is driven from the country

6 October

The Moulin Rouge and the cancan

1889 When you reach the boulevard de Clichy, seek out number 82 at the foot of the Butte Montmartre. There you will find, in all its garish opulence, a large red windmill with four blades ablaze with lights. You have found the famous cabaret and nightclub, the Moulin Rouge, which first opened on this day.

It was an exciting time for Parisians: the Eiffel Tower had been inaugurated at the end of March and, just a stone's throw from the Moulin Rouge, the Basilica of Notre-Dame du Sacré-Coeur would open just two years later.

Montmartre was a raffish area, where working men, louche aristocrats, criminals and girls of easy virtue all came to spend an evening of uninhibited fun.

From the very beginning, what set the Moulin Rouge alight was the boisterous cancan, featuring *Chahuteuses* (high-kicking girls) in frilly underskirts, black stockings and garters. Mildly shocking at the time, the cancan gained its name from the French word *cancan*, scandal. The undisputed queen of the dance was La Goulue, who was immortalised by Toulouse-Lautrec. (His painting of her is only one of seventeen of his works directly inspired by the Moulin Rouge.) Another cancaner he made famous was a prostitute's daughter named Jane Avril. Other noted *Chahuteuses* earned bizarre nicknames from the Paris crowd, such as Nini Pattes-en-l'Air (Paws-in-the-Air) and La Môme Fromage (the Cheese Urchin).

But the cancan wasn't the only entertainment on offer at the Moulin Rouge. One of its early attractions was le Pétomane (the Farting Man) and no doubt even more popular were the ladies in the buff. Four men carrying a nude Cleopatra, surrounded by other naked girls who lay languidly on flower beds, enlivened the evenings. So enticing were its attractions that in 1893 the Société générale de protestation contre la licence des rues (General Society of Protest against Public Licentiousness) thundered that the show was '*un fait d'une gravité extrême et d'une inadmissible impudeur*' ('an event of extreme gravity and unacceptable indecency').

By the end of the century, however, Parisians were turning to other amusements and the Moulin Rouge was briefly turned into a concert hall. But soon it was back to more raucous entertainment and courting scandal. In 1906 a newly divorced Colette, not yet known as a writer, diverted the audience in a play in which she dreamily kissed a woman dressed as a man.

A year later the comedienne and singer Mistinguett appeared on stage: she remained a Moulin Rouge stalwart for 22 years. All the while, of course, the cabaret continued to feature dancers and semi-nude chorus girls.

Between wars the Moulin Rouge declined because of the popularity of films and when Paris was occupied, it was frequented by German soldiers. But at war's end, Edith Piaf, who had only entertained French prisoners during the war, at last appeared on stage, bringing her protégé Yves Montand.

And so the Moulin Rouge has continued to this day, presenting famous performers, such as singers Charles Trenet, Frank Sinatra, Elton John, Liza Minnelli, Maurice Chevalier and Charles Aznavour. To keep audiences titillated, it has brought back a giant aquarium, originally installed in the 1960s, where nude mermaids frolic. Recently it lent its name to the celebrated film and it still provides spectacular entertainment with '60 Dancing Girls!'. But the Moulin Rouge has never forgotten the cancan, although it is now performed bare-breasted.

AD 105: At Arausio (now Orange in Provence) the German Cimbri and Teutoni tribes rout the Roman armies of Caepio and Mallius, killing 80,000 (an awful lot, anyway) * **1536: English biblical translator, humanist, and Protestant martyr William Tyndal is burned at the stake** * 1887: Swiss architect Charles-Edouard Le Corbusier is born, La Chaux-de-Fonds * 1891: Irish nationalist Charles Stewart Parnell dies at Brighton * 1892: Alfred, Lord Tennyson dies

7 October

The mystifying death of Edgar Allan Poe

1849 At 5 am this Sunday morning Edgar Allan Poe died in the Washington Medical College Hospital in Baltimore. Four days earlier he had been found in the gutter outside a saloon that had been used as a voting place. According to the man who found him, he was 'a gentleman rather the worse for wear' who was delirious and 'in great distress and [. . .] in need of immediate assistance'. Rushed to the hospital, the confused Poe could explain neither where he had been nor why he was dressed in someone else's clothing. He then relapsed into a coma from which he never emerged. One of the hospital doctors wrote, in a soothing letter to Poe's aunt, that the writer's last words were a pious (and unlikely): 'Lord help my poor soul.'

Although the *Baltimore Clipper* reported that Poe had died of 'congestion of the brain', the exact cause of his death has been debated ever since. Most credit it to alcoholism, but other candidate killers are diabetes, syphilis, cholera, some form of brain disease and even rabies. Because the bar where he was found doubled as a polling station, it has also been suggested that he was shanghaied, drugged and taken from station to station in a ballot-stuffing fraud.

Poe's life was a mixture of literary success and idiosyncratic personal failure. He was born in Boston in 1809, but his father abandoned the family when he was three weeks old and his mother died a year later. He was raised in Virginia by a foster father, who forced him to drop out of the University of Virginia after eleven months for piling up $2,500 in gambling debts.

A year later Poe enlisted in the army under the name of Edgar A. Perry and served for two years, but his foster father purchased his release and helped him win a place at West Point, where he was expelled in his first year for deliberately neglecting his classes and drills. At 26 he married his cousin Virginia, who was only thirteen years old, although the marriage certificate stated she was 21. Employed as a magazine editor in Richmond, Poe was fired for drinking and wandered to New York, then Philadelphia, then back to New York. Although his erratic behaviour and his frequent bouts with the bottle gave rise to the rumour that he was a drug addict, he continued to write successfully. He entered into the odd affair, which his wife seemed to tolerate, but she died of tuberculosis in 1847, still only 25.

Despite his outlandish life, Poe was one of America's foremost men of letters. He was a poet of distinction ('Annabel Lee', 'The Raven'), an acclaimed writer of macabre short stories ('The Fall of the House of Usher', 'The Cask of Amontillado', 'The Pit and the Pendulum') and the father of the modern detective story ('The Murders in the Rue Morgue', featuring the sleuth Arsene Dupin). His impact on later writers was significant.

Baudelaire mentions him in the preface to *Les Fleurs du mal*, as do Nabokov in *Lolita* and Nietzsche in *Beyond Good and Evil*. Dostoyevsky called him 'a hugely talented writer' and refers to 'The Raven' in *The Brothers Karamazov*. Others who admired him include Franz Kafka, Jules Verne, Thomas Mann and Jorge Luis Borges. George Bernard Shaw thought he was 'the greatest journalistic critic of his time', while Oscar Wilde called him 'this marvellous lord of rhythmic expression'. Algernon Swinburne, Paul Valéry, Stéphane Mallarmé and Marcel Proust all regarded him highly. The director Alfred Hitchcock confessed that 'It's because I liked Edgar Allan Poe's stories so much that I began to make suspense films', and no less an authority than Sir Arthur Conan Doyle mused: 'Where was the detective story until Poe breathed the breath of life into it?' (One of his few critics was T. S. Eliot, who claimed he had 'the intellect of a highly gifted person before puberty'.)

Only 40 when he died, Poe was buried in the Westminster Hall and Burying Grounds, which is now part of the University of Maryland School of Law in Baltimore. The epitaph on his tombstone is the refrain from his own poem:

Quoth the Raven, 'Nevermore'.

Also on this day

1571: The fleet of the Holy League (Spain, Venice and the papacy) defeats the Turks at the Battle of Lepanto * 1769: Captain Cook discovers New Zealand * 1777: American revolutionaries defeat the British at the Second Battle of Saratoga

8 October

Napoleon's last trip to Paris

1840 On this day the Emperor Napoleon entered Paris for the first time since his famous Hundred Days 25 years before, but this time he came in a coffin.

In an attempt to curry popular favour, French King Louis-Philippe had laboured for seven long years to gain British agreement to allow the return of Napoleon's body to France. It was only now, some nineteen years after the Emperor's death, that the corpse was brought back from St Helena aboard a frigate with the glorious name of *La Belle Poule*. Accompanying the dead emperor was Louis-Philippe's son, the Prince de Joinville.

When the Prince and the defunct Emperor arrived in Paris, the coffin was opened for two minutes. All those present testified that, like some medieval saint, Napoleon had remained in a state of perfect preservation.

Louis-Philippe ordered that Napoleon's remains be transferred to the Hôtel des Invalides, the beautiful building founded by Louis XIV to house old or infirm veterans. But the former emperor had to wait another 21 years to reach his final resting place, for it took until 1861 for Visconti's great marble tomb in the Invalides to be completed.

Also on this day

1085: St Mark's Cathedral in Venice is consecrated * 1754: British novelist Henry Fielding dies in Lisbon * 1871: The Great Chicago Fire starts in Patrick O'Leary's cowshed, killing over 250 people and making 95,000 homeless * **1918: American Corporal Alvin York single-handedly puts 35 German machine guns out of action, kills over twenty machine-gunners and captures 132 enemy soldiers in a single morning**

9 October

The Lionheart heads for home

1192 On this day King Richard the Lionheart sailed for home from Acre on the Palestinian coast, after sixteen months of bloody but profitless fighting during the Third Crusade.

In the beginning the Crusade had been full of promise. Pope Gregory VIII had called for action, offering absolution to the warriors of Christianity who would fight for the reconquest of Jerusalem, fallen to the Saracens of Saladin at the end of 1187. Europe's most powerful monarchs agreed to join forces and preparations were soon under way. From France came the scheming but intelligent Philip Augustus, from Germany the Emperor Frederick Barbarossa, now almost 70, from England the redoubtable Richard the Lionheart and from Sicily Richard's brother-in-law, King William the Good. A massive force was gathered to crush the Saracens and return the Holy Land to the control of Christians.

But all had not gone according to plan. William of Sicily, still only 35, died even before setting off and Barbarossa was tragically drowned bathing in a river in Turkey. Richard and Philip succeeded in conquering Acre, but the victory was sullied by Richard's brutal slaughter of several thousand Saracen prisoners, men, women and children.

After Acre, on the excuse of illness, Philip returned to France to plot with Richard's brother John in dismembering Richard's French possessions. Richard continued southward towards Jaffa and finally met Saladin in battle at Arsuf in 1191, where his heavy cavalry drove Saladin's lighter horse into panicky retreat. Then the English King took Daron and led his army to within twelve miles of Jerusalem.

But there Richard had to stop. His force was so depleted that he had little chance of taking the city and even if he had succeeded, he could not have garrisoned it sufficiently to keep it.

Reluctantly, Richard turned back for Acre. On 2 September 1192 he and Saladin finally agreed a five-year peace treaty that gave Christian pilgrims free access to Jerusalem. But the only territory now in Christian hands was a thin strip of coastline 100 miles long, from Acre to Jaffa. Saladin controlled everything else.

So, a month after peace had been agreed, Richard boarded ship. The Third Crusade was over, with little achieved and much lost. Richard found only further disaster on his route home, captured and held for ransom in Austria.

Also on this day

1000: According to legend, Scandinavian explorer Leif Erikson lands in North America * **1547: Miguel de Cervantes is baptised** * 1835: French composer Charles Camille Saint-Saëns is born in Paris

10 October

The scandalous death of Fra Filippo Lippi

1469 Today, in Spoleto, died one of the greatest painters of the Renaissance, Filippo di Tommaso di Lippo, known to art history as Fra Filippo Lippi. Even now, art critics and the public revere his serene and unworldly Madonnas and saints. It may come as a surprise, then, that this great artist died in the midst of scandal, probably poisoned by the family of a woman he had seduced.

Lippi was born in Florence in 1406, the son of a butcher. Both his parents died when he was a child and he lived with his aunt until he was fourteen, when she placed him in the monastery of Santa Maria del Carmine. A year later he took religious vows as a monk.

As good luck would have it, at the time Masaccio was working in the Carmine church and Lippi was inspired by his painting. According to the art biographer Giorgio Vasari, 'instead of studying, [Lippi] spent all his time scrawling pictures on his own books and those of others and so eventually the prior decided to give him every chance and opportunity of learning to paint'.

Finally, after twelve years in the monastery it became clear to both Lippi and the monks at Santa Maria del Carmine that his future was in art rather than the church and he left the monastery, even though he continued to sign himself 'Frater Philippus'. The next few years of his life are largely undocumented, although Vasari claims that at one point he was captured and enslaved for eighteen months by Barbary pirates, eventually earning his release through his skill as a portraitist.

In about 1439 Lippi returned to Florence, where Cosimo de' Medici commissioned him to create several works for churches and convents. But vying with Lippi's love of art was his love of the women and taverns of Florence.

'Fra Filippo was so full of lust that he would give anything to enjoy a woman he wanted', Vasari reports. 'His lust was so violent that when it seized him he could never give full attention to his work. Because of this, when he was working for Cosimo de' Medici, Cosimo had him locked in so he wouldn't wander off.

'After he had been locked up for a few days, one night Fra Filippo's amorous, or rather animal, instincts drove him to take a pair of scissors, make a rope from his own bed sheets and escape through a window to pursue his own pleasures.'

After fifteen years spent mostly in Florence, Lippi was nominated chaplain in the nunnery of Santa Margherita in Prato, about fifteen miles north-west of the city. There he bought a house – and caused the biggest scandal of his scandalous life.

One of the novices in the convent was Lucrezia Buti, the beautiful daughter of a Florentine aristocrat. Asked to produce a painting of Santa Margherita, Lippi chose Lucrezia for his model and quickly seduced her. He then moved her into his own house and resisted all the nuns' efforts to get her back. A year later Lucrezia gave birth to a son, who would one day be a great painter in his own right, Filippino Lippi. The couple subsequently produced a daughter, Alessandra.

But even the ties of family were not enough to put Lippi on the straight and narrow, as he continued to philander. Vasari relates that 'the Pope wanted to give him a dispensation so that he could make Lucrezia [. . .] his legitimate wife, but as he wanted to stay free and give full rein to his desires, Fra Filippo refused the offer'.

Towards the end of his life Lippi moved to Spoleto to paint scenes from the life of the Virgin for the apse of the cathedral, but before he had completed the work, he died. Vasari informs us that, 'in one of those sublime love affairs he was always having, the relations of the woman concerned had him poisoned'.

Many doubt that a 63-year-old painter could still arouse the passion to provoke a murder and Vasari's account is the only evidence. Nonetheless, such a death seems fully in keeping with Lippi's tempestuous life.

The great painter is buried in the Duomo of Spoleto, in a tomb designed by his son Filippino, erected by order of Lorenzo the Magnificent.

Also on this day

732: Charles Martel leads the Franks to victory over Muslim invaders from Spain at the Battle of Tours * 1684: French painter Jean-Antoine Watteau is born in Valenciennes * 1813: Giuseppe Verdi is born in Le Roncole * 1886: The dinner jacket makes its début at a ball in Tuxedo Park, New York * 1911: China's imperial dynasty abdicates and Sun Yat-Sen proclaims a republic

11 October

The Boer War begins

1899 War in South Africa began today, to no one's surprise. Two days earlier, the Boer leader, Paul Kruger, president of the Transvaal, had sent a message to the British Cabinet demanding arbitration on 'all points of mutual difference' between the two nations and an immediate halt to the British military build-up in South Africa. Unless his terms were met within 48 hours, Kruger's ultimatum read, his government would 'with great regret be compelled to regard the action as a formal declaration of war'. There was no response from London.

No shots were fired this first day, or the next, although this was a condition soon to be corrected, but Boer commandos rode south to launch a series of pre-emptive, over-the-border attacks before the British could begin their invasion. A participant, seventeen-year-old Deneys Reitz, who would write a classic account of the war, remembered the opening scene: 'As far as the eye could see the plain was alive with horsemen, guns and cattle, all steadily going forward to the frontier.'

For the British, whose geopolitical goal was to bring the gold-rich Boer republics – Transvaal and the Orange Free State – under direct imperial rule, the prospect of war was welcome, particularly if it was the Boers who made the first move. Moreover, a recent report from military intelligence in London gave this assessment of the Boers' military capability: 'It appears certain that after [one] serious defeat, they would be too deficient in discipline and organisation to make any further real stand.'

Like so many other military adventures in history, this one was predicted to be over by Christmas. At the outset, however, the war seemed a disaster for British arms. Badly underestimating the mobility, field skills and firepower of the Boer forces, the British Army soon found its border garrisons bottled up at places like Kimberley, Ladysmith and Mafeking. Then came a string of major defeats at Modder river, Magersfontein and Colenso, which provided the period 10–15 December with the name of 'Black Week'. In the midst of it all, a young correspondent for the *Morning Post*, Winston Churchill, was captured by the Boers and spent almost a month in a Pretoria jail before escaping.

Suddenly, it was a serious war. Now, the British field commander was replaced with Lord Roberts, large-scale reinforcements were ordered in to South Africa and Her Majesty's forces reorganised with a stress on mounted infantry. Embarrassing defeats and surrenders continued, but in the new year, the tide of war began to change. The sieges were lifted and British armies advanced onto Boer soil, occupying and annexing both republics. In October President Kruger fled to the safety of Europe. At the end of 1900, Roberts pronounced the war 'practically over' and headed home to England, leaving his chief of staff, General Kitchener, to clean up. By now, there were now almost half a million troops fighting for the British, facing a Boer force that never exceeded 50,000 in the field.

With their homelands largely in enemy hands, the Boers now turned to a guerrilla war, directed against the enemy's vulnerable lines of communications, which stretched far inland from the seaports. Their far-ranging commandos raided within 50 miles of Capetown. In response, the British adopted harsh tactics, which would become all-too-familiar features of modern wars: they erected lines of blockhouses – 8,000 of them, built and manned mainly by black African troops – with barbed-wire fences criss-crossing the countryside; they burned the Boer farmlands on which the commandos relied for supplies; and they herded much of the civilian population – including women and children – into concentration camps, where 25,000 of them died of disease and unhygienic conditions.

In this way, resistance was at last worn down and the Boer leadership came to realise that, in order to preserve any control over their homelands in the future, the only hope lay in ending the fighting. In May of 1902 General Kitchener called a peace conference, held at the village of Vereeniging, on the Vaal river. The resulting treaty, signed at Pretoria on 31 May, brought the two former republics into the British Empire as colonies, with King Edward VII as their sovereign; provided amnesty to all those who agreed to disarm; granted the two colonies internal self-government; and offered financial assistance for rebuilding the devastated countryside.

The historian Thomas Pakenham gave this assessment of the war: 'It proved to be the longest (two and three-quarter years), the costliest (over £200 million), the bloodiest (at least 22,000 British, 25,000 Boer and 12,000 African lives) and the most humiliating war for the British between 1815 and 1914.'

Also on this day

1521: The Medici pope Clement VII gives Henry VIII the title 'Defender of the Faith', which every English sovereign has held ever since * **1531: Swiss Protestant reformer Ulrich Zwingli is killed in the Battle of Kappel** * 1932: President Franklin D. Roosevelt receives a letter from Albert Einstein suggesting the possibility of an atomic bomb

12 October

The first Oktoberfest

1810 Today in Munich, Crown Prince Ludwig of Bavaria invited all the citizens of the city to join festivities held on the fields in front of the city gates to celebrate his marriage to Princess Therese von Saxe-Hildburghausen. The celebration proved such a success that it became an annual event, soon to be known as the Oktoberfest, and in time, the world's largest festival. Now, every year over 7 million people flock there to quaff the world's best beer and munch on Bavarian specialities such as *bratwurst*, *sauerkraut*, roast ox tail, *backhendl* (roast chicken) and *käsespätzle* (cheese dumplings).

In 1810 the royal couple also staged a horse race five days after the wedding, a tradition that was part of the Oktoberfest until 1961. Then, in 1816, carnival booths were erected. By 1819 the festival had grown so large that the city fathers of Munich took over its management and decided that it should be held every year, although it has been cancelled 24 times, mostly because of wars and twice for outbreaks of cholera.

To take advantage of better weather, in 1872 the festival's start date was moved forward into September. Today it lasts about sixteen days, traditionally ending on the first Sunday in October.

Each year the Oktoberfest is opened at noon by a twelve-gun salute. Then the mayor of Munich taps the first keg of beer, declaring '*O'zapft is!*' ('It's tapped!' in Bavarian). A strong, dark beer called *Wiesnbier* is brewed specially for the festival, although traditional Bavarian beers, such as Löwenbräu, Augustiner, Paulaner and Hofbräu are also on tap.

Then comes the Oktoberfest parade, an institution that goes back to 1835. Some 8,000 people, accompanied by elaborately decorated beer wagons and floats, march from Maximilianstraße through the centre of Munich. Men sport traditional Bavarian lederhosen, while women wear dirndls (the historical costume of Alpine peasants). Leading the parade is the *Münchner Kindl* ('Munich child' in Bavarian), the symbol on the coat-of-arms of the city. (Over the centuries the *Münchner Kindl* has experienced a pleasing metamorphosis. Originally, in the 13th century a hooded monk holding a Bible, it evolved into a child holding a radish and a beer mug.) Nowadays the *Münchner Kindl* is played by a young woman.

The parade ends at the Theresienwiese, the 64-acre field where the first and every subsequent Oktoberfest has been held, named in honour of Princess Therese. There the crowd can enjoy music, dancing and a roller coaster and other rides, while downing a beer or something to eat in any of several tents, such as the Hofbräu-Festhalle, which can accommodate 10,000 people. During the festival, beer consumption is now over 5 million litres. The Oktoberfest authorities have helpfully erected large tents for the drunks, referred to by the locals as *Bierleichen* (beer corpses), mostly young foreigners who swallow a litre too many.

Now the whole world knows the Oktoberfest, but probably only Bavarians recollect that it was all started at the wedding of Crown Prince Ludwig and Princess Therese. Sadly for the princess, if her husband is remembered at all today, it is not for their marriage but for his celebrated liaison with that scandalous courtesan, Lola Montez, which made him so unpopular with his subjects that he was forced to abdicate in 1848.

1492: Columbus sights land in the New World, calling it San Salvador * 1809: American explorer Meriwether Lewis, of the Lewis and Clark expedition, commits suicide * 1822: Brazil gains independence from Portugal * 1870: Confederate general Robert E. Lee dies in Lexington, Virginia * **1915: British nurse Edith Cavell is executed by a German firing squad in Brussels for helping British and French prisoners of war escape to Holland**

13 October

A usurper is crowned King

1399 Today Henry Bolingbroke, so-called because of his birth in Bolingbroke Castle, was crowned in Westminster Abbey to become King Henry IV.

Henry was the son of John of Gaunt and grandson of King Henry III, but in spite of his royal antecedents he had not inherited the throne – he had usurped it from his cousin, the egotistical and feckless Richard II.

In 1398 Henry became embroiled in a bitter quarrel with the Duke of Norfolk and denounced him to King Richard as a traitor. When Henry and Norfolk were on the point of fighting a duel, Richard intervened and exiled both of them for five years, promising to protect their estates until their return. But in February 1399 Richard confiscated Henry's inheritance while he was still abroad. Bent on revenge, Henry wasted no time in collecting an army and invaded England in July, just when Richard was on a punitive operation in Ireland. Richard hurried back to meet the invader, but soon found that most of his support had melted away. By August he had surrendered and then was forced to abdicate on the last day of September. Henry then confined the ex-king to a cell in Pontefract Castle in Yorkshire (where eventually he was murdered).

Henry has three unrelated distinctions. He was the first king since the Conquest to have been born on English soil of an English father and English mother. He was England's first king from the Lancaster branch of the royal family, so his usurpation of the crown was a root cause of the Wars of the Roses, which started under the reign of his grandson, Henry VI. He also passed the law that permitted the Church to burn heretics and sanctioned the first such execution in English history.

As he grew older, Henry began to suffer from some disfiguring disease, which his contemporaries thought to be leprosy but which may well have been syphilis. Too incapacitated to rule, he finally died on 20 March 1413 at the age of 47.

Also on this day
AD 54: Roman emperor Claudius dies, poisoned by his wife Agrippina * 1775: The United States Navy is founded * 1792: President George Washington lays the cornerstone of the White House * 1815: King and Napoleonic marshal Joachim Murat is executed trying to regain his Kingdom of Naples * 1925: Britain's only woman prime minister Margaret Thatcher (née Margaret Hilda Roberts) is born in Grantham, Lincolnshire

14 October

How William the Conqueror won at Hastings

1066 In January, King Edward the Confessor died childless and the throne of England was up for grabs. First came Edward's brother-in-law, Harold Godwinson, who asserted that Edward had named him on his deathbed. But the English barons had no sooner agreed to Harold's suzerainty than the Norwegian King Harald Hardrada claimed the crown, supported by Harold Godwinson's exiled brother Tostig. And of course there was a third claimant, a certain Norman duke called Guillaume le Bâtard because of his illegitimate birth. Guillaume, or William, swore that Edward the Confessor had promised the throne to him.

The first invasion of England came in September, launched by Tostig and Harald Hardrada, who landed in Scotland and came down over the border. On hearing of the incursion, King Harold marched his men almost 200 miles in five days and crushed the intruders at Stamford Bridge (near York), killing both his brother and the Norwegian King. But just as his soldiers were recovering from this hard-fought battle, Harold heard that William had landed with another invading force at Pevensey on the Sussex coast. Desperately he turned his army south for another forced march.

On the evening of 13 October Harold caught William by surprise six miles from the coast, near the town of Hastings, but it was already growing late and too dark to fight.

The following morning the two armies faced each other, Harold's soldiers protected by great war shields and armed with axes, William's infantry better armoured and equipped with swords and crossbows. But William's trump was his cavalry, some 2,000 strong.

At first, William's assaults made little progress against Harold's wall of shields and William himself was nearly slain, with three of his horses killed under him. After repeated failure to break the enemy line he finally resorted to ruse, ordering his men to pretend to panic and break to the rear. In spite of Harold's efforts to restrain his troops, the English line broke in triumph, eager to pursue what they saw as a defeated enemy.

With the English were streaming towards his retreating men in a chaotic charge, William unleashed his cavalry, which ploughed into the disorganised enemy, cutting them down in hundreds.

Harold still held part of his original line, but many of the English were dead or dying. Resolutely he pulled his men behind their wall of shields, but now Norman arrows constantly bombarded them and they could not return fire as the English archers had all been routed. Before the battle could reach a conclusion, a Norman arrow struck Harold in the eye and killed him.

William the Bastard had vanquished the English and in the years ahead he would subjugate the Welsh and Scots too. Enthroned in Westminster Abbey on Christmas Day 1066, he was known henceforward as William the Conqueror.

Also on this day

1633: King James II is born in London * 1806: Napoleon defeats the Prussians at the Battle of Jena * 1890: General and president Dwight D. Eisenhower is born * **1944: The Desert Fox, German Field Marshal Erwin Rommel, is forced to commit suicide for his knowledge of the plot to assassinate Hitler** * 1947: American pilot Chuck Yeager becomes the first man to break the sound barrier

15 October

The tale of Madame Tussaud

1795 Today in Paris a 34-year-old sculptress named Marie Groshlotz married a young Frenchman eight years her junior named François Tussaud, thus gaining the name that she would make world-famous.

Marie was born in Strasbourg, where her mother was a domestic servant and her father apparently came from a long line of public executioners. When she was still a child she moved first to Bern and later to Paris, where she learned the art of wax modelling from her uncle, who owned two wax museums. When she was sixteen she sculpted her first wax figure, that of Voltaire. So talented was she that, by the time she was twenty, she had already been engaged by King Louis XVI's sister to teach her the art.

When revolution exploded in France in 1789, Marie was accused of royalist sympathies and flung into prison. Fortunately, she convinced the authorities of her republicanism, but she was nonetheless given the macabre job of moulding death masks from newly severed heads. She often found herself working on the heads of friends.

Just before the end of the Revolution Marie's uncle died and she inherited his wax museums. One of the more popular displays she created was a scene showing Charlotte Corday stabbing Jean-Paul Marat in his bath, a figure that some think was the model for David's famous painting.

The following year she married François Tussaud, an engineer from Mâcon, by whom she had two sons. Ultimately, however, the marriage failed, so Marie left France for England, bringing her sons and wax models with her.

For 27 years Marie – or Madame Tussaud as she now was – travelled around England to local fairs and fêtes, displaying her wares and creating new models. Finally, at the grand old age of 72 she established her own museum in Baker Street in London and continued to work there until she died seventeen years later. In 1884 – 34 years after her death – her museum, now world-famous, was moved to the Marylebone Road, where it has remained until this day.

Also on this day

202 BC: Roman general Scipio Africanus defeats Hannibal's Carthaginians at the Battle of Zama * 70 BC: Roman poet Virgil is born * 1839: Queen Victoria proposes marriage to Prince Albert * 1844: Friedrich Nietzsche is born in Röcken, Saxony, Prussia * 1917: Dutch courtesan and spy Mata Hari is shot by a French firing squad after being convicted of passing military secrets to the Germans * 1946: Nazi leader Hermann Göring takes cyanide in his Nürnberg prison cell the day before his execution

> Events written in **boldface** are covered in full in
> *365: Great Stories from History for Every Day of the Year*,
> the first volume in this series.

16 October

The walls of Vienna

1809 As if to add a spiteful exclamation point to the humiliating treaty he had forced Austria to sign two days earlier, the Emperor Napoleon had ordered the walls of Vienna to be demolished. At four this afternoon great explosions shook the city, as commanding gates and high ramparts were blown up. The Viennese were appalled, for these walls – or their predecessors – had protected them and their city since time immemorial, although now they no longer possessed real military value.

Celts had originally founded Vienna in about 500 BC, but it fell to the Romans during the reign of Augustus in 15 BC. They turned it into one of a number of military installations on the Danube guarding the Roman Empire against marauding Germanic tribes and called it Vindobona, Celtic for 'White Field' – possibly in reference to the severe winter snows. Although not walled in stone, the entire site was a sturdy fortress constructed of wood.

At the beginning of the 2nd century these wooden fortifications were replaced by the first stone walls, but even these could not save Vindobona when a Germanic tribe named the Marcomanni sacked it sometime after 166 AD.

Emperor Marcus Aurelius later rebuilt the walls but died there of the plague in 180 AD.

Somewhere around 250 AD Vindobona's fortifications were once again strengthened, as the city had progressed from fortified military camp to a city of about 20,000. For well over a century the walls kept out intruders, but in about 395 AD another German tribe pillaged the city. The walls were shortly rebuilt, but during the first decade of the 5th century, a fire levelled most of the fortress.

In 433, during the Roman Empire's final decline, the East-Roman Emperor Theodosius II relinquished Vindobona altogether, allowing the Huns to take over. (According to the *Niebelungenlied*, Attila was married there.) By now the name 'Vindobona' was evolving to Wenia, which in turn became Wienis and eventually today's Wien (Vienna).

During the Dark Ages Vienna was overrun several times; in 1251 by Ottocar II of Bohemia, who was the first to construct truly massive stone walls around the city. These resisted all attacks, even in 1485, when Matthias I Corvinus of Hungary occupied Vienna. To avoid a long siege, the city fathers surrendered, but the walls were never breached.

The walls' biggest test came in 1529 when Suleiman the Magnificent laid siege to Vienna with a vast Turkish army. The fortifications held firm and the Turks were forced to retreat precisely 270 years to the day before Napoleon pulled the walls down. In 1555 these medieval walls were reinforced and largely replaced by new fortifications, which protected the city for centuries, even during the summer of 1683, when once again they stymied a massive Turkish attack.

Then came Napoleon. He first occupied Vienna in 1805 but left the walls intact. On his return four years later, however, he ordered their destruction. Even then, remnants of the walls and their moats remained and as the city grew, they became a severe impediment to traffic.

Finally, in 1857 Austrian Emperor Franz Joseph issued his famous decree *Es ist Mein Wille* (It is My Will), which ordered the walls' final demolition. He had been swept to power during the Revolution of 1848 and, mindful of a restless public, wanted a broad street that made the erection of revolutionary barricades impossible. But he also wanted a new boulevard as a showplace for grand imperial buildings, so the beautiful Ringstraße, the most spectacular street in what remains one of Europe's most enchanting cities, finally replaced the last vestiges of the ancient city walls.

Also on this day

1555: English Protestant bishops Hugh Latimer and Nicholas Ridley are burned at the stake for treason * **1793: Marie Antoinette is guillotined** * 1854: Irish playwright Oscar Wilde is born in Dublin * 1946: Eleven Nazi war criminals are hanged after the Nürnberg trials

333

17 October

Chopin's finale

1849 If you step out of the front door of the Ritz Hotel in Paris and look diagonally across Place Vendôme, you will see number 12, where Frédéric François Chopin coughed himself to death of tuberculosis on the morning of 17 October 1849. Mozart's Requiem was played at his funeral, as Chopin had requested.

Chopin was just 39 when he died, yet his life had been an extraordinarily full one: first concert at eight, fame in his native Warsaw by nineteen, Paris by 21, where he was quickly recognised as the musical genius he was. In all, he wrote some 200 pieces and during his lifetime his audience and patrons were of the highest French society. In fact, even his mistress of eight years was a baroness named Aurore Dudevant, although her readers knew her better as the writer George Sand.

In the autumn of 1848 Chopin visited London on a playing tour and it was in the Guildhall there that he played his last concert. He had already been ill for some time and after the exertions of foreign travel he returned to Paris. Fearing the worst, he wrote in his last letter: 'The earth is suffocating. Swear to make them cut me open, so I won't be buried alive.'

He died a few weeks later, on 17 October. On the morning of his death a doctor asked him if he was in pain, to which Chopin replied '*Plus*' ('No more'), his last word. Although buried in Paris's Père-Lachaise cemetery, he is interred in Polish soil, scattered over his coffin from a supply the far-sighted composer had brought with him from his native country twenty years before.

Today Chopin is still considered one of history's greatest composers and pianists. In fact, his music is still with us on a more pedestrian level than he would ever have dreamed. Apart from classical concerts, it endures in debased form in songs like 'I'm Always Chasing Rainbows'.

Also on this day

1483: The Spanish Inquisition is established and Dominican priest Tomás de Torquemada is named as the first Grand Inquisitor * 1651: England's Charles II flees to France * 1777: The British under General John Burgoyne surrender to American forces at the Battle of Saratoga, causing France to recognise the new nation and openly give military aid * 1941: Japanese Prime Minister Konoye's government falls, bringing army minister Hideki Tojo to power

18 October

Farewell to Lord Cupid

1865 Harry Temple was born to the richest and proudest in England, succeeding his father as Viscount Palmerston when only eighteen years old. From then on this brash, calculating, jingoistic and somewhat mediocre man devoted his life to politics. He won a seat in the House of Commons when he was 23 and retained it with one break of a few months until he died today of fever, just two days before his 81st birthday. He had served as Secretary of War, Foreign Minister, Home Secretary and for nine years as Prime Minister, an office he held at his death. (In spite of his success in politics, Palmerston had his violent critics. When he attained the premiership at the age of 71, Disraeli described him as 'utterly exhausted and at best only ginger beer and not champagne, an old painted pantaloon, very deaf and short-sighted, with dyed hair and false teeth which would fall out of his mouth when speaking if he did not hesitate and halt so much in his talk.')

After politics, Palmerston's overriding interest was women, whom he pursued with insatiable appetite throughout his long life, earning the sobriquet 'Lord Cupid'. Among his conquests were Lady Jersey, the Princess Lieven and Lady Cowper, the last of whom he finally married at the age of 55 when she was widowed, after years of scandalous affair. At the time a contemporary wrote: 'There will be nothing new about it except the marriage vow which they both know does not bind them.'

By 1865 Pam, as he was universally known, had attained the great age of 80 and his energies both political and sexual were spent. On 18 October he lay frail and feeble on his sumptuous bed at Brocket Hall in Hertfordshire, clearly approaching the end.

But even then his brashness and wit did not desert him. Gravely his doctor told him that he must die. 'Die, my dear doctor', Pam whispered. 'That's the last thing I shall do!' He then closed his eyes – and did.

Also on this day

1520: Portuguese explorer Ferdinand Magellan finds a route to the Pacific – now called the Straits of Magellan * 1663: Prince Eugene of Savoy is born in Paris * 1685: Louis XIV revokes the Edict of Nantes, effectively banning Protestantism in France * 1697: Italian topographical painter Canaletto (Giovanni Antonio Canal) is born in Venice * **1812: Napoleon begins his retreat from Moscow** * 1931: American inventor Thomas Edison dies

19 October

King John loses his treasure and then his life

1216 King John of England quarrelled with everyone – his father, Henry II, his brother, Richard the Lionheart, the kings of France, the Pope and most of all his own barons. He was cunning, vengeful and vicious; he had murdered his nephew, Arthur of Brittany (some say with his own hand) and once starved to death the wife and son of a mutinous baron.

The autumn of 1216 found him in an ever-worsening position. The French had been conquering John's once vast Angevin territories for over a decade and Normandy, the traditional 'home' fief of all British kings since William the Conqueror, was now gone as well. Only the previous year his rebellious barons in England had forced him to sign the humiliating Magna Carta that restricted his power to tax or seize property and ended with the mortifying provision that a council of 25 barons would have the right to make war on him if he failed to follow the agreement.

Now John was marching with his army across England, revenging himself on his barons one by one. Because he trusted no one, he carried with him the great royal treasure, a vast hoard of gold and precious jewels, including the crown and sceptre of England.

John and his forces were about 85 miles north of London, near the part of the North Sea known as the Wash. Here there was a small river to be forded, but it was running fast with the autumn floods. With typical rashness, the king ordered his men forward. Suddenly the current gripped the treasure wagons. In a flash they were overturned and England's invaluable treasure was lost forever to the waters, swept down into the sea.

Thunderstruck by this disaster, John pushed on to the nearby abbey at Swineshead, where he feasted in despair, consuming a heavy meal followed by peaches mulled in wine. Immediately severe dysentery struck, but still he pushed on the same night, carried on a litter to the palace of the Bishop of Lincoln in Newark.

The next day John collapsed completely and in a few hours lay dead, tradition has it in the midst of a howling gale. On 19 October 1216 England's worst king was no more. Treacherous, lecherous, murderous and cruel, John had ruled for seventeen years, dying at only 48.

Also on this day

1330: Edward III breaks into Nottingham Castle to remove his mother Queen Isabella, arrest her lover Mortimer and seize power * 1469: Ferdinand of Aragon marries Isabella of Castile * 1745: Irish satirical writer Jonathan Swift dies in Dublin * **1781: British General Cornwallis surrenders to George Washington at the Battle of Yorktown, the last battle of the American Revolution** * 1813: Austrian, Prussian, Russian and Swedish forces defeat Napoleon at the three-day Battle of Leipzig *

1872: The Holtermann Nugget, weighing 630 pounds, is mined at Hill End, Australia, the largest gold-bearing nugget ever found

20 October

Eddie Rickenbacker gets his last kill

1918 Today, with the First World War drawing to a close, Captain Eddie Rickenbacker, commander of the 94th Aero Pursuit Squadron, flew his Spad high above the trenches of the Western Front and shot down his 26th – and final – German aircraft of the war. Over the past six months, he had become America's best combat pilot, her 'ace of aces'.

Rickenbacker was a natural in the air. Before the war, he had won fame – as well as money and influence – as one of the world's top racing-car drivers, but he had never flown a plane. When the United States entered the war in March 1917 he joined the army with the hope of organising a flying squadron of former racing drivers, counting on their experience operating powerful engines at high speeds to make them first-rate pilots. When the War Department proved resistant, he managed to get to France as a driver, first for General John J. Pershing, then for Colonel 'Billy' Mitchell, head of the recently formed American Air Service. Eventually, with Mitchell's help, Rickenbacker got assigned to a flying unit as an engineer, then to pilot training and an officer's commission and finally, in March 1918, to the 94th Squadron, the famous 'Hat-in-the-Ring' Squadron. He took his first combat flight on 25 April and four days later, piloting a Nieuport, downed his first enemy plane. At the end of May, Rickenbacker was a five-victory ace.

In the course of the long war, there were plenty of aces who had more kills than Rickenbacker – Billy Bishop, the Canadian ace flying for the British, had 72, for instance, and on the other side Manfred von Richthofen had 80 – but no other pilot ever matched Rickenbacker's rate of 26 in just six months. For his feats he received the Croix de Guerre, the US Distinguished Flying Cross and the Congressional Medal of Honor.

Three weeks later, on 11 November 1918, Rickenbacker took his plane out over the front lines to see the war end. 'It was a foggy morning at the base,' he wrote years later, 'and I wriggled my way out just a half minute before eleven o'clock. I was flying down no-man's land, between the trenches of the opposing forces and they were shooting at each other just as madly as they could. And then the hour of eleven struck. The shooting stopped and gradually men from both sides came out into no-man's land and threw their guns and helmets into the air. They kept talking to each other and shaking hands and doing something for the men who had been hit … I was only about 100 feet over no-man's land. I got out to see what I went out to see and went back home and that was it.'

337

1632: English architect Sir Christopher Wren is born ∗ 1818: Britain and the United States agree on the 49th parallel as the boundary between Canada and the USA ∗ 1784: British prime minister Lord Palmerston is born in Broadlands, Hampshire ∗ 1854: French poet Arthur Rimbaud is born ∗ **1935: Mao Zedong's Long March ends in Yenan, north China**

21 October

An author in search of a title

1940 He had started writing the novel in Cuba the year before and was up to Chapter 35 in April 1940 when he decided he needed a title. He came up with many possibilities – *The Undiscovered Country* was the best of them, he thought – before turning to Shakespeare and the Bible. Searching further, he consulted *The Oxford Book of English Prose*, where at last he found just what he was looking for. He sent his editor the first draft of the manuscript with his proposed title and got this cable in reply: ALL KNOCKED OUT. THINK ABSOLUTELY MAGNIFICENT. TITLE BEAUTIFUL. CONGRATULATIONS.

When the final longhand draft was completed in July, he took it up to New York for typing before handing it over to his editor. All signs were favourable. The publisher had set an October publication date and a first printing of 100,000 copies. In August the Book of the Month Club made the novel its main selection for November. From Hollywood came the news that Paramount Pictures wanted the film rights.

And so it was that on this date Charles Scribner's Sons published Ernest Hemingway's fifth novel, a story of the recently concluded Spanish Civil War. It bore the title *For Whom the Bell Tolls*, drawn from one of John Donne's *Devotions* that begins, 'No man is an Island, entire of itself …' and ends with: 'And therefore never send to know for whom the bell tolls; it tolls for thee.'

The critical reception seemed to bear out what his editor Max Perkins had written to him in April: 'I think this book has greater power and larger dimensions, greater emotional force, than anything you have done …' In the *Atlantic*, Robert Sherwood called the book 'rare and beautiful'. Clifton Fadiman in the *New Yorker* said: 'I do not much care whether or not this is a "great" book. I feel that it is what Hemingway wanted it to be: a true book.' Edmund Wilson in the *New Republic*, J. Donald Adams in the *New York Times Book Review* and Lionel Trilling in the *Partisan Review* all followed suit. Only on the Left were there voices of dissent complaining of a misportrayal of the war in Spain and of the Loyalist leaders. Among them was Alvah C. Bessie, writing in the *New Masses*, who objected that Hemingway was concerned only with the fate of his characters and that 'the cause of Spain does not, in any *essential* way, figure as a motivating power, a driving, emotional, passional force in this story'.

At least as good as the critical reception were the sales. By the end of 1940 Scribner's had sold 189,000 copies. Three years after publication 785,000 copies of all editions had been sold in the United States, not far below the sales of *Gone With the Wind*. The only sour note came when the judges of the Pulitzer Advisory Board unanimously chose *For Whom the Bell Tolls* as the best novel of 1940 but were overruled by the conservative President of Columbia University on the grounds that the university would not wish to be associated with 'an award for a work of this nature'. There was no Pulitzer award for fiction that year.

Hemingway dedicated *For Whom the Bell Tolls* to Martha Gellhorn with whom he had been living for three years in what she described as 'contented sin'. Learning just two weeks after publication that his divorce from Pauline Pfeiffer had come through, he married Gellhorn in late November in Cheyenne, Wyoming.

Also on this day

1680: Louis XIV signs a decree establishing the Comédie Française 1760: Japanese printmaker Katsushika Hokusai is born * 1772: English poet Samuel Taylor Coleridge is born * **1805: British Admiral Horatio Nelson is killed destroying French Admiral Villeneuve's fleet off Cape Trafalgar** * 1918: The Great Influenza Epidemic, which will kill 30 million people, begins at an American army base at Camp Funston, Kansas

22 October

A Frenchman makes the first parachute jump

1797 The first balloon flight had taken place only fourteen years earlier, when two French brothers, the Montgolfiers, launched an unmanned hot-air balloon that reached a height of just 90 feet. Later the same year two other Frenchmen, Jean-François Pilâtre de Rozier and his aristocratic friend François Laurent, marquis d'Arlandes, achieved the first manned flight when they soared over Paris in a Montgolfier balloon, staying aloft for almost half an hour. Now, however, the challenge was not so much how to go up but how to come down.

The idea of the parachute may have originated in the 1100s in China and it had certainly been explored as early as the 15th century, when Leonardo da Vinci experimented on paper with the idea. But it was three centuries later, in 1783, when yet another Frenchman, Louis-Sebastian Lenormand, became the first man ever to descend with something like a parachute. Holding two parasols, he climbed a tall tree and jumped – and made it safely to the ground. Lenormand made several other experimental jumps, envisaging the contrivance as a safety apparatus with which to escape from burning buildings. Two years later yet another Frenchman, Jean Pierre Blanchard, dropped a terrified dog with a parachute on its back from a hot-air balloon.

Finally, on this day in 1797, the first true parachute came into being, once more with a Frenchman in the lead. The 28-year-old Jacques Garnerin took off from Paris in a hot-air balloon, rose to 3,200 feet and then leaped into space. His parachute opened and he landed safely in the Parc Monceau. Man's first parachute jump had been accomplished and its French origins remain in the word itself. Pierre Blanchard (the man who dropped the dog) coined it from *para* (preventing), plus *chute* (fall).

Also on this day
180: The mad Roman emperor Commodus takes power in Rome * 1746: Princeton University receives its charter * 1811: Hungarian composer and pianist Franz Liszt is born * 1906: Paul Cézanne dies in Aix-en-Provence

23 October

When the world began

4004 BC That's when it all began – the entire Universe, that is – according to the elaborate calculations of the Anglo-Irish prelate James Ussher who, in 1650, published the conclusions of a lifetime's work with biblical and Semitic texts, *The Annals of the Old Testament*. (He also revealed that Noah's ark had touched down on Mount Ararat on 5 May 2348 BC 'on a Wednesday'.)

Ussher was not the first to identify the date of creation, or *Annus Mundi*. The Byzantine Church had declared it to be 5509 BC, the Jewish calendar fixed it at 3760 BC and in the 8th century the English monk and historian, the Venerable Bede, had calculated 3952 BC.

But Ussher's reckoning was so persuasive that much of the Christian world came to accept it as accurate, concurring as it did with the widely believed biblical assertion that God had created Heaven and Earth in a mere six days. And Ussher was no minor priest: he had risen from professor and then vice-chancellor of Trinity College, Dublin, to Archbishop of Armagh by the time he was 44. He later moved to England, where he advised King Charles I and, after Charles's execution, continued as a noted preacher at Lincoln's Inn in London. He collected such a fine library that it is now in the University of Dublin.

Ussher died an admired figure six years after the publication of his definitive findings, so respected that Oliver Cromwell gave him a state funeral and a tomb in Westminster Abbey.

Ussher's chronology of the Creation was largely accepted until the 19th century. Although he had established the dates of Creation, one of his contemporaries, Dr John Lightfoot, Vice-Chancellor of the University of Cambridge, was even more precise, authoritatively demonstrating that God had created Adam at nine in the morning. Amen.

Also on this day

1642: Charles I defeats the Roundheads at Edgehill in the first battle of the English Civil War * **1917: American soldiers go into combat against the Germans for the first time in the First World War** * 1940: Brazilian football (soccer) superstar Pele (Edson Arantes do Nascimento) is born in Três Corações, Brazil

24 October

Catastrophe at Caporetto

1917 Between 1915 and 1917, on the Italian front, there were eleven battles of the Isonzo: a series of costly and mostly inconclusive assaults by the Italian army on Austrian positions north of Trieste. The twelfth battle began on 24 October 1917 and it is usually called the Battle of Caporetto, after the place where the breakthrough occurred, 'a little white town with a campanile in a valley'. The battle was anything but inconclusive, but this time it was the Austrians who launched the assault and it proved to be a disaster for Italy.

The attacking forces, greatly bolstered by the presence of German divisions, knocked a fifteen-mile hole in the Italian line and then kept moving, infiltrating their forces into the rear of the Italian strong points. 'The further we penetrated into the hostile positions, the less prepared were the garrisons for our arrival and the easier the fighting', wrote a young German infantry leader named Erwin Rommel, whose exploits during the offensive won him the Pour le Mérite.

The Italian Second Army crumbled in panic, forcing the armies on either side to pull back. When the Italians finally stopped retreating eleven days later at the Piave river, they were some 80 miles to the rear of their former line on the Isonzo. The Austrians were now in a position to threaten Venice but, mercifully, had outrun their supplies. The Piave line held. In the retreat, the Italians had lost some 40,000 men killed and wounded and another 275,000 taken prisoner.

A few good things came out of the catastrophe at Caporetto. General Count Luigi Cadorna, an unimaginative martinet, was sacked as the Italian Commander-in-Chief. Then, Great Britain and France, at long last recognising that the informal and haphazard direction of the Allied war effort was proving inadequate to the task of defeating the Central Powers, called a meeting of the Allies in Locarno on 5 November, at which the parties agreed to establish a Supreme War Council.

Finally, a man who wasn't even in Italy at the time of Caporetto left a vivid account of the retreat that ranks with the very best war fiction: he was Ernest Hemingway, who wrote of it in *A Farewell to Arms*.

Also on this day

1273: The first Habsburg Holy Roman Emperor Rudolf von Habsburg is crowned at Aachen * 1537: English Queen Jane Seymour dies twelve days after the birth of the future Edward VI * **1648: The Treaty of Westphalia ends the Thirty Years War, the most destructive in European history until 1914** * 1725: Italian composer Alessandro Scarlatti dies in Naples * 1929: Share values on the Wall Street stock market crash on 'Black Thursday', starting the Great Depression

25 October

The Charge of the Light Brigade

1853   Theirs not to reason why,
Theirs but to do or die,
Into the valley of death
Rode the six hundred.

So wrote Alfred, Lord Tennyson of the famous Charge of the Light Brigade, which took place today during the Battle of Balaclava in the Crimean War.

Early in the battle the British commander Lord Raglan sent orders to the Light Brigade to attack an isolated Russian outpost on the Vorontsov Heights. In transmission to the Brigade's commander, General James Cardigan, the message became muddled. Cardigan was a wealthy earl, a quarrelsome martinet of an officer just a few days short of his 56th birthday. At first he tried to question the confused order, but then commanded his cavalry to charge down the valley between the heights rather than towards the enemy outpost.

Some 673 British horsemen swept forward over a mile of open ground, but a battery of 30 Russian guns opened fire, scything down the attackers. Nevertheless, the British managed to reach the Russian guns and temporarily put them out of action. They then galloped back down the same valley, always under fire. Only 198 survived.

The Charge of the Light Brigade remains one of the most senseless and horrifying displays of proud courage in all of military history. Nothing sums it up better than the comment of the French general Pierre Bosquet, who witnessed the heroic debacle: '*C'est magnifique, mais ce n'est pas la guerre.*' ('It's magnificent, but it's no way to fight a war.')

Also on this day

1400: Geoffrey Chaucer dies * **1415: The English under Henry V defeat the French at the Battle of Agincourt** * 1510: Italian painter Giorgione (Giorgio Barbarelli) dies in Venice * 1825: Johann Strauss the Younger (The Blue Danube) is born in Vienna * 1838: Composer Georges Bizet is born in Paris * 1881: Pablo Picasso is born in Malaga

26 October

Alfred the Great, the king who saved Anglo-Saxon England

899 Today, at Winchester, died Alfred the Great, the first King of England, who against all odds saved his country from Viking conquest and unified the Anglo-Saxon kingdoms into a single nation.

The son of King Aethelwulf of Wessex, Alfred was born in the royal palace at Wantage in one of the most calamitous periods of English history. Since the end of the 8th century, savage pagan Danes had raided and plundered, searching for slaves and occupying much of the country.

When King Aethelwulf died in 1858, two of Alfred's older brothers took the throne of Wessex in brief succession; the second, Aethelred, in 865. The Danes had seized York and set up their own kingdom in Northumbria, while subjugating East Anglia and Mercia and torturing to death their conquered kings. Now the Great Heathen Army advanced on Wessex, the only remaining independent Anglo-Saxon kingdom.

After capturing the royal palace at Reading, in January 871 the Danes met the Anglo-Saxons at Ashdown. It was now that Alfred first showed his prowess in war. As the two sides faced each other, King Aethelred abruptly left the field to pray for victory in a nearby church. Impatient for battle and judging that he must strike immediately, Alfred ordered his men to charge. The result was victory – a pyrrhic one with great slaughter on both sides – but at least the Danes were temporarily halted. One of the casualties was Aethelred, who later died of his wounds. Now Alfred, still just 22, was King of Wessex, but his troubles were only beginning.

Temporarily beaten but far from subdued, the Danes resumed their raids. Early in 878 Alfred narrowly escaped a surprise attack and fled to Somerset. There, according to legend, the disguised king lodged in the rude hut of a peasant woman. Asked to keep an eye on some cakes cooking on the fire, he was so preoccupied by his predicament that he allowed them to burn. Scolded by the peasant woman, the hapless Alfred could only apologise, reproached by the lowliest of his subjects.

Despite the seeming hopelessness of Alfred's cause, recruits flocked to his banner of the golden dragon. For months he waged hit-and-run warfare before being reinforced by the militia from Hampshire and Wiltshire. Now with an army at his command, he defeated the Danes at Countisbury Hill. Afterwards the King himself slipped into the enemy camp in the guise of a minstrel to learn their plans.

Next came the critical Battle of Edingham. According to his contemporary, Bishop Asser: 'Alfred attacked the whole pagan army, fighting ferociously in dense order and by divine will eventually won the victory, made great slaughter among them and pursued them to their fortress [at Chippingham].' After a two-week siege, the Danes 'were brought to the extreme depths of despair by hunger, cold and fear and they sought peace'. Their king, Guthrum, and his top lieutenants agreed to be baptised and Alfred and the Anglo-Saxons took control of the south-western half of England. So great was his triumph that the Vikings claimed he must be descended from Odin, the Nordic god of war.

A year later the Vikings were chased from Mercia and in 886 Alfred reconquered London. He had stopped the Danes from conquering the whole of England and was recognised as monarch by all Anglo-Saxons not living in Danish-controlled territory. By the early 890s his coinage pictured him as King of England, rather than of Wessex.

In addition to routing the Vikings, Alfred made major contributions to English culture. A fervent believer in learning, both for his people and for himself, he mastered Latin in his late thirties and arranged the translation into Anglo-Saxon of books he considered 'most needful for men to know'. Alfred himself translated Boëthius, Bede and St Gregory. He also put in motion the compilation of the Anglo-Saxon Chronicle.

Influenced by Christian kingship ideals, Alfred was also a far-sighted lawgiver, combining what he thought were the best laws of Mercia and Kent with his own. Alfred's Code, expanded by his successors over the centuries, finally became the basis for English law and the principles of the Magna Carta. Some historians believe he also established trial by jury.

Alfred had ordered the construction of a New Minster in Winchester, to serve as a final resting place for English kings, but when he died at 50, it was still under construction, so he was buried in the Old Minster. The monks there, however, were much alarmed when his ghost walked in the cloister at night and transferred his remains to the New Minster as soon as it was ready. Later his sepulchre was relocated to Hyde Abbey, but the tombs of the Anglo-Saxon kings were destroyed when Henry VIII dissolved the monasteries in the 16th century. Pious monks collected some of the royal bones and put them willy-nilly into caskets that are now above the chancel in Winchester Cathedral.

Also on this day

1764: English caricaturist William Hogarth dies in London * **1759, 1879, 1916, 1947: A date with a political orientation? French revolutionary Georges Danton, Russian Bolshevik Leon Trotsky, French socialist François Mitterrand, American Democrat Hillary Rodham (Clinton) are born** * 1860: Italian unification leader Giuseppe Garibaldi proclaims Victor Emmanuel King of Italy * 1881: Wyatt Earp, Doc Holliday and Earp's brothers defeat the Clanton gang at the 'Gunfight at the OK Corral' at Tombstone, Arizona * 1905: Norway and Sweden sign a treaty of separation, making Norway an independent nation

27 October

Michael Servetus goes to the stake

1553 The fact that bigotry knows no borders was perfectly demonstrated today when the unorthodox Christian theologian Michael Servetus was burned at the stake, not by the Catholic fanatics of his native Spain but by the obsessive Calvinists of Switzerland.

Servetus (Miguel Servet in Spanish) had been born in Villanueva but as a young man had studied medicine at the University of Paris, the university where both John Calvin and Ignatius Loyola had studied only a few years before. Loyola went on to found the Jesuits, to spearhead the Counter-Reformation, while Calvin launched the joyless, militant brand of Protestantism that eventually would bear his name.

Servetus was in theory a Catholic, but at nineteen he attended the coronation of Emperor Charles V at Bologna, where he was deeply shocked by the worldly ostentation of the Pope and his retinue. This led him to doubt the whole faith in which he was raised and two years later he published his own views, denying the Trinity and the concept of original sin.

Later Servetus became a physician and found a position in the French town of Vienne, near Lyon, where he published his discovery of the pulmonary circulation of the blood. Here he continued his religious explorations and wrote several books stating his convictions. He then began writing to Calvin, perhaps hoping for a kindred spirit who challenged the established beliefs of the Catholic Church.

Calvin took no notice of Servetus's correspondence, but, unfortunately for the Spaniard, some of his letters were sent to the inquisitor-general of Lyon, who immediately imprisoned both Servetus and the printers of his books on charges of heresy.

Terrified of what penalty the French inquisitors might impose, Servetus managed to escape, leaving the ecclesiastical authorities with the small satisfaction of burning him in effigy. Fearing recapture, he fled across the border to Calvin's City of God in Geneva, under the delusion that Calvinist Puritanism would be more understanding than inquisitorial Catholicism.

Upon his arrival in Geneva, one of Servetus's first acts was to go to church. During the service he was seized once more, this time by uncompromising Calvinists. Once again he was tried for heresy, with John Calvin himself playing a prominent role in the prosecution. When Servetus was convicted, Calvin urged his execution but displayed his moderation by suggesting decapitation. His sterner co-religionists, however, demanded a more draconian end and Servetus was led to the stake.

Also on this day

AD 312: Inspired by a cross in the sky, Emperor Constantine defeats Maxentius

at **Milvian Bridge near Rome to gain sole control of the Roman Empire** * 1466: Dutch humanist Erasmus is born in Rotterdam * 1728: English explorer Captain James Cook is born * 1782: Italian composer and violin virtuoso Niccolò Paganini is born in Geneva * 1858: America's 26th President Theodore Roosevelt is born in New York

28 October

The story of the Statue of Liberty

1886 For millions of immigrants arriving by ship at New York's Ellis Island, the first sight of their new country was a colossal statue on a nearby island of a woman holding a 29-foot torch in her raised right hand and a tablet bearing the date of their new nation's birth (4 July 1776) in her left. The seven spikes in her crown symbolised the seven seas and seven continents from which the immigrants came.

Originally called 'Liberty Enlightening the World', this giant figure was conceived to commemorate the French and American Revolutions and the friendship between the peoples of France and America. Eventually it was rechristened the Statue of Liberty and was officially dedicated by American President Grover Cleveland on this day in 1886.

The idea was French, dreamed up by the historian Edouard de Laboulage and financed by a French organisation called the Franco-American Union. The sculptor, an Alsatian named Frédéric-Auguste Bartholdi, modelled the face on his mother's. His original working model reached a height of nine feet, but the lady who welcomes visitors to New York today is 151 feet tall, standing on a 150-foot pedestal.

Formed of hammered copper sheets, the Statue of Liberty requires an enormous underpinning to support the weight. The ingenious engineer who designed the internal steel framework was Gustave Eiffel, the man who gained the nickname 'magician of iron' when he later built the eponymous tower in Paris.

The Statue of Liberty was constructed entirely in France, taking twenty years to complete. Then the enormous figure, weighing 225 tons, was disassembled and shipped to New York in 1885.

At the statue's entrance a plaque is inscribed with the sonnet of a 37-year-old American poet named Emma Lazarus. It concludes with the ringing words:

> Give me your tired, your poor,
> Your huddled masses yearning to breathe free,
> The wretched refuse of your teeming shore.
> Send these, the homeless, tempest-tost to me,
> I lift my lamp beside the golden door!

When the Statue of Liberty was dedicated in 1886, the population of the United States was just under 60 million people. Today it has risen to 300 million, as millions more have accepted the Statue of Liberty's bold invitation.

Also on this day

1533: The future Henri II of France marries Catherine de' Medici at Marseilles
* 1636: Harvard University is founded * 1828: Victor Hugo is born in Besançon
* 1704: English philosopher John Locke dies, Oates, Essex

29 October

Birth of the greatest biographer

1740 Born in Edinburgh today was James Boswell, one of history's most convivial, entertaining and amiable characters, who would leave his mark on English literature with his *The Life of Samuel Johnson, LL.D.*

Son of a Scottish lord, Boswell was a well-meaning but feckless man with a passionate interest in women. His first known conquest was when he was an eighteen-year-old student at Edinburgh University. His paramour had three scandalous defects in the eyes of Boswell's father: she was married, a Roman Catholic and an actress. His father quickly slipped him off to the University of Glasgow to end the liaison. By the time he was twenty he had already tasted the fleshpots of London and contracted gonorrhoea for the first, but hardly the last, time in his adventurous life. He also managed two illegitimate children by two different mistresses before he finally married at 29.

A genial man with a taste for a good drink, Boswell was fascinated by people of all sorts, including himself, but particularly by famous ones. He met Samuel Johnson for the first time in 1763 when he was 22 and the good doctor already 54. At the first encounter he found the great man 'of a most dreadful appearance', 'slovenly in his dress', with 'a most uncouth voice' and a 'dogmatical roughness of manner'. But the two men got on famously and in time, as Christopher Morley observed: 'Each became, for the other, the son or father he had never had.' Boswell soon knew Johnson's associates, such as Sir Joshua Reynolds and Oliver Goldsmith. He was also on familiar terms with Hume, Voltaire and Benjamin Franklin and once shared a mistress with Jean-Jacques Rousseau.

Johnson died at the end of 1784, but it was almost seven years before Boswell published his great biography on 16 May 1791, 28 years to the day after he first met the great doctor. With typical insouciant self-assurance, Boswell described his work as 'without exception, the most entertaining book you ever read'.

Boswell himself died at the age of 54 on 19 May 1795 at his house in Great Portland Street in London.

Also on this day
1618: Sir Walter Raleigh is beheaded in Old Palace Yard, Westminster * 1628: Cardinal Richelieu conquers La Rochelle, ending Protestant independence in France * 1787: In Prague, Mozart's opera *Don Giovanni* is performed for the first time * 1863: Swiss philanthropist Henri Dunant founds the International Committee for the Relief of the Wounded, forerunner of the International Red Cross * 1923: The Turkish Republic is proclaimed after the fall of the Ottoman Empire

30 October

The last Muslim invasion of Spain

1340 What chance did a poor sultan of Morocco have against two Alfonsos – Alfonso XI from Castile, called the Just, and Alfonso IV from Portugal, called the Brave? As it turned out, not much.

When he succeeded to the Moroccan sultanate in 1331, Abu al-Hasan dedicated himself to a familiar Muslim goal, to cleanse all Spain of Christian infidels. To that end he crossed from North Africa (present-day Morocco) with a vast army, captured Gibraltar and Algeciras and then utterly destroyed the Castilian fleet in the Strait of Gibraltar when the Spaniards tried to reclaim the Rock. The entire Iberian Peninsula looked ripe for the picking, for its two principal Christian states, Castile and Portugal, were enmeshed in deadly rivalry. The sultan marched his divisions north, towards Seville.

Abu al-Hasan's mistake was to forget that the Christian powers hated the Muslims even more than they hated each other. Although the two Alfonsos had long been at loggerheads about disputed territory, Abu al-Hasan's victory at Gibraltar inspired them to forge an alliance to combat the Moorish threat.

And so it was that on this day the combined forces of Alfonso the Just and Alfonso the Brave met Abu al-Hasan's Saracen army at Rio Salado just outside Seville. During the battle the Castilian Alfonso came under severe attack and was saved only by the timely intervention of the fighting Archbishop of Toledo, Alvarez Carillo Gil de Albornoz. But the Christian forces rallied for a quick, complete and merciless victory. It was such a disastrous defeat for Abu al-Hasan that he was forced to flee for North Africa, never to return. This was the last Moorish attempt to conquer Spain. The Muslim *jihad* was over and, little by little, the forces of Christianity would reconquer all of Spain until that day in 1492 when Granada, the last Moorish stronghold, would open its gates to the army of Ferdinand and Isabella.

Also on this day
1485: Henry Tudor is crowned as Henry VII of England, starting the Tudor dynasty * **1735: America's second president John Adams is born in Braintree (now Quincy), Massachusetts** * 1821: Fyodor Dostoyevsky is born in Moscow

31 October

Jan Vermeer

1632 On this day in the Nieuwe Kerk (Reformed Church) in Delft a baby boy was baptised, who one day would become one of history's greatest painters – Jan Vermeer. He had been born in his family's tavern in the Delft marketplace a day or two before.

We know very little about this quiet genius, who painted simple Dutch household interiors with timeless and exquisite beauty, presented in 'frozen silence'. Son of an innkeeper/art dealer father, he married Catharina Bolnes at 21 and fathered eleven children who survived, four others dying in infancy. Earning his living primarily as an art dealer, he remained in Delft all his life and his paintings consist almost entirely of beautifully constructed interiors. Even his two known landscapes were painted from a window. (The skewed perspective in some of his paintings has caused critics to speculate that he may have used a camera obscura to project the image of the scene he was painting onto a screen.) Only 35 paintings are unquestionably attributed to him and only three of these are reliably dated.

There is considerable scholarly debate concerning Vermeer's success in selling his own work. Some experts believe that his few paintings were acquired by a small number of local patrons, while others maintain that he never sold a single one of his own paintings. What is certain is that when Vermeer died at 43 he left his wife and family bankrupt. According to his wife, 'as a result and owing to the great burden of his children, having no means of his own, he had lapsed into such decay and decadence, which he had so taken to heart that, as if he had fallen into a frenzy, in a day or day and a half had gone from being healthy to being dead.'

Also on this day

1517: The 'first day of the Reformation': Martin Luther nails his 95 theses to the Schlosskirche door in Wittenberg * 1795: English poet John Keats is born * 1902: The first telegraph cable across the Pacific Ocean is laid * 1940: The Battle of Britain ends * 1952: The United States detonates the first hydrogen bomb at Eniwetok Atoll in the Pacific

1 November

The death of Spain's last Habsburg king leads to war

1700 Carlos el Hechizado they called him, Charles the Bewitched. Weak-brained and slightly deformed, he had been carried around like an infant until the age of ten – but had inherited the throne of Spain as Charles II when he was only four. He died today in Madrid, just five days short of his 40th birthday, the last king of the Habsburg dynasty that had ruled Spain for 196 years. His last (and perhaps only) significant act as King was to leave his throne to a new dynasty, which would be even more durable than the Habsburgs.

Charles was rational, if dim, but his prognathous Habsburg jaw made his speech almost unintelligible and prevented him from chewing, so he subsisted on soups and slops. And if that were not enough, he was also impotent, which may have been a blessing for his two wives.

During the last years of his 35-year reign, he was constantly in ill health and Spain was impoverished and depopulated during a period of constant minor warfare and emigration to Spanish colonies abroad. Since the King had no heirs, competing European powers jockeyed to put forward their favourites to inherit the throne on his death or to dismantle his empire by depriving Spain of its possessions in the Netherlands and Italy.

Even Charles was aware of the problems likely to follow on his death and became determined to settle his inheritance while he was still alive. Desperate to make the right choice but confused as to whom to choose, the befuddled king descended to the funeral vaults of the Escorial and opened the tombs of his father, his mother and his first wife, kissed their mouldering faces and begged them for guidance. Finding no inspiration among the dead, he then turned to his ministers and court theologians, who persuaded him that only France would leave Spain and its possessions intact. Convinced at last, he willed his throne to a Frenchman, Philippe, duc d'Anjou, grandson of France's Louis XIV.

In his determination to put things right, the unfortunate Charles succeeded in putting things wrong, as his testament ignited the bloody fourteen-year War of the Spanish Succession. Louis XIV clearly favoured Charles's choice, but other European powers feared it would lead to a union of Spain and France under a single king.

Despite the victories of Prince Eugene of Savoy and the Duke of Marlborough over the French, in the end Charles's will was honoured and Philippe became and remained Spain's king as Philip V, founding Spain's Bourbon line, which still holds the crown today, over three centuries later.

Also on this day

1500: Italian sculptor and jeweller Benvenuto Cellini is born * **1503: Giuliano della Rovere is elected pope as Julius II, who asked Michelangelo to paint the Sistine**

Chapel * 1757: Italian sculptor Antonio Canova is born * 1800: The White House becomes the residence of American presidents as John Adams spends the first night there * 1858: Queen Victoria is proclaimed sovereign of India, ending the rule of the East India Company

> Events written in **boldface** are covered in full in
> *365: Great Stories from History for Every Day of the Year,*
> the first volume in this series.

2 November

Which American president gained the most territory for his country?

1795 These days few people remember much about America's eleventh president, James Polk, who was born today. Austere and distant, he served only one term in the White House, leaving office a sick man with only three months to live. But in that single term, he gained more territory for the United States than any other American president before or since, increasing the size of the country by two-thirds.

Even in 1844, when Polk ran as the Democratic Party's candidate for the presidency, he was a colourless and anonymous character. Despite having served fourteen years in Congress, he was so obscure a figure on the political scene that his Whig opponents thought they could beat him by raising the derisive cry: 'Who is James Polk?'

But in his campaign Polk adopted the alliterative slogan of 'Fifty-four Forty or Fight', a reference to his determination to seize disputed territory from the British even if it meant a war.

'Fifty-four Forty' referred to the northern boundary of an enormous parcel of land on the west coast of North America between the Mexican territory of California and Russian-held Alaska. Known as the Oregon country, this land had been occupied jointly by the United States and Great Britain for the last 35 years. But American settlers were streaming into it and many believed in their country's 'Manifest Destiny', the supposedly inevitable march of the nation westward to the Pacific. American annexationists wanted the entire Oregon territory, right up to its border with Alaska at 54 degrees, 40 minutes north latitude. Great Britain, however, wanted the line drawn at the 47th parallel, along the Columbia river. Such was the appeal of Polk's bellicose slogan that it overcame his previous obscurity and he won the election.

Once in office, however, Polk renounced war for negotiation and offered a compromise line at the 49th parallel, accepted by Great Britain in June 1846. With that agreement, the United States took sole possession of land that would eventually comprise the states of Washington, Oregon, Idaho and parts of

Wyoming and Montana. Great Britain received what is now the Canadian province of British Columbia and Vancouver Island.

That was only part of Polk's enlargement of his country. In May 1846 he brought on war with Mexico over Texas, already annexed to the United States, which resulted not only in military victory but also in the addition of territory that would eventually become the states of California, Nevada, Utah, most of Arizona and parts of New Mexico, Colorado and the remaining part of Wyoming. In all, Polk gained over 1 million square miles for the United States, easily surpassing the 833,000 square miles of Thomas Jefferson's Louisiana Purchase in 1803.

When he wasn't busy expanding the United States, Polk managed to create the Department of the Interior, establish the Naval Academy at Annapolis and authorise the founding of the Smithsonian Institution. All in all, a very creditable performance for a one-term president no one much remembers.

Also on this day

82 BC: Roman general Lucius Cornelius Sulla marches on Rome, forcing the Senate to make him dictator * **1470: Birth of Edward V of England, who was murdered by his uncle Richard III in the Tower of London after 79 days as king, the shortest reign in British history** * 1699: French painter Jean-Baptiste Chardin is born in Paris * 1755: Marie Antoinette is born in Vienna * 1950: Irish playwright George Bernard Shaw dies

3 November

Stanley finds Dr Livingstone

1871 'I noticed that he was pale, looked worried, had a grey beard, wore a bluish cap with a faded gold band round it, had on a red-sleeved waistcoat and a pair of grey tweed trousers . . . I did not know how he would receive me, so [. . .] I walked deliberately up to him, took off my hat and said, "Dr Livingstone, I presume." "Yes," he said, with a kind smile. Lifting his cap slightly . . . and we both grasped hands.'

So wrote Henry Stanley, intrepid reporter sent out by the *New York Herald* to find Africa's most famous explorer, Dr David Livingstone, who had seemingly vanished into the Dark Continent. Leading a small caravan of native guides and bearers, Stanley tramped through the African bush for over six months, encountering disease and hostile tribes along the way, eventually making his way to Ujiji, on Lake Tanganyika, where on this day he found Livingstone living among the natives. The doctor had seen no other white man for five and a half years – and after meeting Stanley, would never see another.

For the next four months the two men together explored parts of Lake Tanganyika, but, despite Stanley's urgings, Livingstone resolutely refused to return to England.

For the next year and a half after this famous encounter, Livingstone continued to wander through the heart of Africa, eventually almost penniless and virtually deserted by his guides and bearers, sick and feeble from dysentery, malaria and skin ulcers. Finally, unable to walk and in too much pain to be carried, he camped at a place called Chitambo on Lake Bangweulu (now in Zambia). On 1 May 1873, in the hope of clearing his system he asked his servant Susi for a dose of calomel and then told her: 'All right, you can go out now.' Those were his last words. When Susi returned a few hours later, she found him kneeling as if in prayer, dead at the age of 60. It seems likely that severe bleeding from haemorrhoids caused his demise.

Even in death Livingstone's wanderings were not over. Two of his native followers buried his heart and viscera beneath a tree, on which they carved his name and then carried his corpse out to civilisation. Eventually it was shipped back to England, where it was interred with great ceremony beneath the floor of Westminster Abbey on 18 April 1874.

David Livingstone had spent 33 years in Africa and was widely recognised as its greatest explorer. Yet he had failed in the three tasks he had set himself: to find the source of the Nile, to stop the slave trade and to convert to Christianity black Africans whom he called 'these sad captives of Sin and Satan'.

Also on this day

BC: **The Hilaria, Rome's April Fools' Day** * 1870: The Reunification of Italy is completed * 1903: Panama declares independence from Colombia * 1957: Russia launches Sputnik 2 carrying a dog named Laika, the first living passenger in space

4 November

Howard Carter finds the tomb of Tutankhamen

1922 Today a 49-year-old Englishman named Howard Carter made the most spectacular archaeological discovery in history, when he and his excavating team found the nearly intact tomb of the 14th-century-BC Egyptian pharaoh Tutankhamen.

Carter had been digging in Egypt off and on since he was seventeen, at one time serving as inspector general of the Egyptian antiquities department. When he was 24 he was contacted by the noted Egyptologist Lord Carnarvon, who wanted him to supervise further excavations in the Valley of the Kings. From that time forward the two men worked in close collaboration.

In late October 1922 Carter was once again in the field, exploring an area near the tomb of Ramses VI, where he had found a large number of ancient workman's huts. Suspecting something might lie beneath, he decided to have his workers clear away some of the huts. Then, in Carter's own words: 'Hardly had I arrived at work next morning (4 November) than the unusual silence, due to the stoppage of the work, made me realise that something out of the ordinary had happened and I was greeted by the announcement that a step cut in the rock had been discovered underneath the very first hut to be attacked.' It was the first sighting of the entrance to Tutankhamen's tomb.

Working 'feverishly' for all that day and the next, Carter and his team soon were certain that what they had found was indeed the tomb entrance, with its seals intact. Although they continued to clear away rubble, since Carnarvon was away, they waited until his return on 26 November to open the tomb itself. Then, Carter reports: 'With trembling hands I made a tiny breach in the upper left-hand corner [of the door] [. . .] I inserted a candle and peered in [. . .] At first I could see nothing, the hot air escaping from the chamber causing the candle flame to flicker, but presently [. . .] details of the room within emerged slowly from the mist, strange animals, statues and gold – everywhere the glint of gold.'

When Carter's team finally entered the tomb, they found Tutankhamen's mummy encased in three coffins, the innermost one of solid gold. Covering the king's face was the now world-famous inlaid gold funerary mask. The burial chambers were stuffed with beautiful statuary and furniture, the king's weapons and a magnificent gold chariot.

Carter's find ignited a Tutankhamen mania throughout Europe and America – there was even a brand of cigarette called King Tut. Eventually most of the tomb's contents were transferred to the Cairo Museum, where today you can gaze with awe at the large and exquisite collection of artefacts that lay buried with the young king for almost three and a half thousand years.

Also on this day

1791: Having infiltrated the sleeping camp of General Arthur St Clair the previous night, Indian warriors kill 600 militiamen in a dawn surprise attack south of the Maumee River in America's Northwest Territory * 1847: German composer Felix Mendelssohn dies in Leipzig * **1942: The British under General Montgomery defeat the Germans at El Alamein**

5 November

The general who wouldn't fight

1862 The war changed, but General McClellan didn't. So on this date President Abraham Lincoln signed General Order No. 182, which began: 'By direction of the President, it is ordered that Major General McClellan be relieved from command of the Army of the Potomac . . . ' George Brinton McClellan received the news two evenings later, sitting in a tent at his headquarters in Rectortown, Virginia.

McClellan had arrived in Washington, DC, some sixteen months earlier, right after the Union army's shocking defeat at Bull Run in July of 1861.

Splendidly uniformed, a well-connected professional soldier and only 35 years old, he looked every inch the successful military leader. Lincoln picked him to command the shattered Army of the Potomac, restore it to fighting trim and lead it to some badly needed Union victories against the Confederates.

McClellan quickly rebuilt and reinvigorated the demoralised army. He proved popular with the troops, who cheered him at every opportunity. He was promoted to General-in-Chief of all the Union armies. In the autumn a series of stirring military reviews took place in the capital. But parades were no substitute for success in the field and as the campaigning months passed, the President, his Cabinet and the Republicans in Congress grew frustrated by the chief general's reluctance to engage in offensive operations against the enemy, whose picket lines after Bull Run were visible from the Union capital. At one point, an exasperated Lincoln asked whether he might 'borrow' the army if the general had no plans to use it.

McClellan countered the pressures on him to get moving with demands for more troops, citing intelligence estimates of enemy strength that were soon found to be highly inflated. As more government officials and committees called for action, he met them with active hostility, for he considered the war and its conduct matters to be dealt with solely by professional soldiers. He referred to politicians as the 'incapables' and Lincoln as the 'gorilla'.

The heart of the problem was McClellan's fear of risking his considerable reputation by engaging in actual combat, where defeat was always a possibility. The historian Bruce Catton summed up the general this way: 'McClellan had nearly all the gifts: youth, energy, charm, intelligence, sound professional training. But the fates who gave him these gifts left out the one that a general must have before all others – the hard, instinctive fondness for fighting.'

Finally, in April of 1862, after eight months as commander, 'Little Mac' took the Army of the Potomac towards the enemy capital at Richmond. It was a campaign that, had he pressed it, might have ended the war that year. Instead, he dawdled away all the Union's considerable advantages of numbers and initiative in an effort that ended in stalemate and withdrawal five months later. In self-defence, he cited the enemy's superior strength – which he managed to double – and the lack of support from the 'incapables', whom he accused of 'sacrificing' his army.

With his Richmond campaign a failure, it looked as if his days as commander were numbered, but after General Pope's 29 August disaster at Second Bull Run, there was simply no other senior officer deemed capable of putting the battered army back into working order. So McClellan got a second chance.

Again, he rose to the occasion, quickly refitting the army, this time setting it in motion to intercept Lee's invading army at Antietam. There, on 17 September, the two armies fought to a bloody tactical draw. A more vigorous and better coordinated push might have won a war-ending battle for the Union, but McClellan, in an excess of caution, never committed his reserve against an outnumbered enemy. And on the second day he avoided combat all together, allowing Lee's battered army to slip away.

In any event, Antietam went down as a strategic victory for the Union, for it not only repelled the Confederate invasion of Maryland, but also gave Lincoln the platform of success he needed to issue the Emancipation Proclamation freeing the Southern slaves, which he did on 22 September.

And there was still a chance to secure a Union victory in the field. In early October Lincoln ordered McClellan to send his forces across the Potomac and pursue the retreating enemy. The general, however, pleading the necessity of visiting Mrs McClellan in Philadelphia, kept his army idle for three weeks before sending it south, a delay that allowed the Confederates to reach safety east of the Blue Ridge mountains.

Now, Lincoln had had enough and issued today's order relieving McClellan of command. 'Little Mac' never held another military command. His immediate successors – Burnside and Hooker – were, in turn, notably unsuccessful in attaining Union victories, but in time Lincoln found what he was looking for – a general who fights – in the slightly dishevelled figure of Ulysses S. Grant, in every way the antithesis of McClellan.

'Little Mac' ran against Lincoln in the presidential election of 1864, on the Northern Democrats' peace platform, but in the face of timely Union victories at Atlanta and Cedar Ridge – of the sort he himself had never been able to achieve – he lost in a landslide. He retired to New Jersey, where in 1877 he was elected Governor and served a single term.

Also on this day

1556: Indian emperor Akbar defeats the Hindus at Panipat and secures control of the Mughal Empire * **1605: Guy Fawkes fails to blow up the Houses of Parliament** * 1955: French painter Maurice Utrillo dies

6 November

Philippe Égalité to the guillotine

1793 Philippe, duc d'Orléans carried royal blood in his veins; he was the great-great-great-grandson of Louis XIII. Nonetheless, he professed to be a democrat and had once been exiled from Paris for challenging the king's authority.

Although he was probably the richest man in the country, as France came ever closer to revolution he consistently backed the Left, joining the Third Estate (bourgeoisie), which turned into the National Assembly. His splendid Parisian palace became a meeting point for militants and he joined the extremist Jacobin Club. After he gave up his title in August 1792, the Paris Commune awarded him with a new one, Philippe Égalité. By January of the next year he even felt radical enough to vote for the execution of his cousin, Louis XVI.

Philippe Égalité may have been sorely disappointed, then, when in November the same year he himself was tried by the Revolutionary Tribunal, largely because his son had fled to the safety of Vienna and the Habsburg court, accompanied by Charles-François du Périer Dumouriez, the revolutionary French general who also had deserted to the Austrians.

Convicted of treason, he went to the guillotine on this day at the age of 46. Apparently, he was unmoved by the proceedings and died calmly, with a smile on his lips. Could he have guessed that one of his descendents would rule France again one day? Thirty-seven years later the son who had fled to Austria would become King Louis-Philippe.

Also on this day

1796: Catherine the Great of Russia dies of a stroke * 1860: Abraham Lincoln is elected 16th President of the United States * 1893: Russian composer Peter Ilyich Tchaikovsky dies of cholera, possibly self-induced * 1924: British Tory leader Stanley Baldwin is elected Prime Minister

7 November

The last man hanged at Tyburn

1783 Today a convicted forger named John Austin gained unfortunate fame by becoming the last man ever to be publicly hanged at Tyburn Tree, the famous London gallows that stood at the north-east corner of what is now Hyde Park, near Speaker's Corner.

The first execution at Tyburn may have taken place as early as 1196 and the Scottish rebel William Wallace may have met his end there in 1305. What is certain is that Roger de Mortimer, the lover of Queen Isabella who arranged the murder of her husband Edward II, was hanged, drawn and quartered at Tyburn in 1330.

It was in 1571, however, that Tyburn became the official venue of choice for execution, its first client being a certain Dr John Story. By now, though, the method had, except for treason, been reduced to simple hanging. In the intervening years thousands went to the gallows there: in the 18th century alone about 1,300 died on the Tyburn gibbet, including at least four children under fourteen.

Most criminals condemned to death were held in Newgate Prison. On the day of their execution they were carried by open horse-drawn carts along a three-mile westward trek, which ended with a long pull down today's Oxford Street to the gallows at Tyburn. Some of the more flamboyant convicts wore their wedding suits, in order to leave the world with a splash. Along the way spectators cheered and jeered and prisoners were much admired if they could banter with the crowd as they headed for their deaths. The carts would usually stop so that the criminals could enjoy one last drink of ale at the Bowl Inn at St Giles in the Fields.

At Tyburn huge throngs would wait in holiday mood, including anatomists, who would fight for the dead bodies at the execution's end. Normally some 10,000 people would attend, but for a particularly famous execution – like the Cato Street conspirators' in 1820 – approximately 100,000 watched. Among those who enjoyed a good hanging were the diarist Samuel Pepys and the biographer James Boswell. William Hogarth even painted the scene.

The condemned men (and 90 per cent of those executed were men under 21) were either hooded or blindfolded and their wrists tied behind their backs before the noose was placed around their necks. Some died quickly with broken necks, but others dangled, choking, until a friend or relative hurried forward to pull on their legs to bring their suffering to an end.

It is no surprise that the rowdy crowds, fuelled by drink, often erupted in riot. Therefore, after John Austin's hanging in 1783, Tyburn was never used again for executions. The venue was moved to Newgate Prison, where (for a fee) the public could still watch men being put to death, but in 1868 public executions were ended forever in Great Britain. Finally, on 9 November 1965, capital punishment was abolished altogether.

Also on this day

1805: Explorers Meriwether Lewis and William Clark become the first Americans to travel across North America and reach the west coast * 1867: Polish scientist Marie Curie (née Sklodowska) is born in Warsaw * 1913: French philosopher, novelist and Nobel Prize winner Albert Camus is born in Mondovi, Algeria * **1917: Bolsheviks in Russia ignite the October Revolution**

8 November

The Battle of the White Mountain

1620 It all started on 23 May 1618 with that famous farce, the Second Defenestration of Prague, during which Bohemian Protestants tossed three agents of the Holy Roman Emperor out of the first-floor window of the Hradčany Palace in protest against the Catholic Habsburgs. No one was hurt, but imperial dignity was badly bruised and Catholics and Protestants were further polarised.

Sixteen months later, the Habsburg Ferdinand II, who had been elected King of Bohemia in 1617 only to be deposed by the largely Protestant Bohemian Diet (parliament) a year later, became the new Holy Roman Emperor. Educated by Jesuits, he was a fervent Catholic and determined to restore the true faith – by force if necessary.

Then some Protestant Bohemian nobles rose in revolt, under the leadership of the 24-year-old Frederick V, the very man who had replaced Ferdinand as King of Bohemia. This gave the Emperor all the excuse he needed to send in his army. It was the beginning of the Thirty Years War.

On this day in 1620 imperial troops under the command of Johann Tserclaes, Graf von Tilly met the rebel Bohemians on the outskirts of Prague in what is known as the Battle of the White Mountain. The Bohemian commander, Christian Anhalt, endeavouring to block the road to Prague, deployed his troops on the side of a hill called the *Bílá Hora* (White Mountain). His position looked impregnable, with his left flank protected by a stream and his right flank by a hunting lodge, while between him and the advancing imperial army was a small brook to slow their charge.

What Anhalt had not counted on, however, was the power of faith – or at least of anger. A monk with Tilly's soldiers suddenly displayed a picture of St Mary that, he said, had been defaced by Protestants. Incensed, the Catholic troops charged across a small bridge crossing the brook and, in less than two hours, annihilated the Bohemians.

Tilly now entered Prague and hanged 27 noble leaders of the insurrection in the Old Town Square, while King Frederick and his wife fled to Holland.

Although the Thirty Years War would continue to drench Europe in blood for another 28 years, in Bohemia the Counter-Reformation was victorious as Protestantism was crushed under the heel of Rome. Prior to the battle, the Bohemians had been semi-independent. When it was over they had become an integral part of the Holy Roman, and later the Austrian, Empire, not to regain their independence for three centuries until the creation of Czechoslovakia in the aftermath of the First World War.

Also on this day

1656: English astronomer Edmond Halley is born * 1674: John Milton dies * **1793: The Girondist Madame Roland is guillotined in Paris** * 1895: William Röntgen discovers X-rays at the University of Wurzburg * 1923: Adolf Hitler leads the unsuccessful Beer Hall Putsch in Munich, resulting in his imprisonment for eight months * 1942: British and American forces commanded by General Dwight Eisenhower invade North Africa

9 November

Piero de' Medici flees Florence

1494 The first Medici to gain official power in Florence was a certain Ardingo, who in 1296 became *Gonfaloniere* (standard-bearer) of the Florentine Republic. Two centuries later the family was by far the dominant force in the state. Thus, today was a black and shocking day for the Medici, when 22-year-old Piero de' Medici was forced to flee the city, never to return.

Only two years earlier he had assumed the leadership of his family (and of Florence) on the death of his father, Lorenzo the Magnificent. But from the first his arrogance had annoyed his fellow citizens and then he found himself caught between the messianic zeal of the fanatical prelate Savonarola and the threat of invasion by Charles VIII of France. Hoping to placate the French king, he hurried to meet him as he descended on Italy with his army. The Florentines saw this attempt at diplomacy as abject capitulation, giving them all the excuse they needed to revolt. They sacked the Medici palace and drove a desperate Piero from the city. From then on Piero was known as *lo Sfortunato* (the Unfortunate) by his supporters and *Il Fatuo* (the Fatuous) by his enemies.

Now Piero had no recourse but to join the forces of King Charles and later those of his cousin Louis XII, but after nine years of service as courtier and soldier, on 28 December 1503 he was drowned in the Garigliano river while attempting to flee during a battle near Naples. Even his corpse didn't make it back to Tuscany: it was interred in the cloister of the monastery at Monte Cassino. It looked as if Medici power in Florence was gone for good.

Fortunately for the family, however, Piero's brother Giovanni had all the guile and toughness that Piero lacked. A cardinal by the age of thirteen, with the tacit backing of Rome he re-established Medici ascendancy by 1512 and a year later was elected Pope as Leo X. The family reigned supreme until the Medici magic was stilled forever in 1737.

Also on this day

1799: Napoleon stages a *coup d'état* to become First Consul of France * 1918: Germany's Kaiser Wilhelm II abdicates and flees to Holland * 1925: Adolf Hitler establishes the SS (*Schutzstaffel* or 'Protection Squad') as his personal bodyguard * 1938: Nazis attack Jewish property throughout Germany during *Kristallnacht* * 1965 Capital punishment is abolished in Great Britain

10 November

Draconian persuasion leads to the second shortest reign in papal history

1241 When Pope Gregory IX was felled by the August heat, there was an urgent need to replace him. The short-tempered, headstrong Gregory had led the Church for fourteen years, during which time he had proved to be one of the strongest (and perhaps most misguided) popes in history, famous for his turf battles with Holy Roman Emperor Frederick II and for establishing the Papal Inquisition. The Church sought an equally dynamic successor.

As always, the election of a new pope was fraught with politics. In Rome the Orsini and Colonna families were fighting desperately for their candidates, while Emperor Frederick had actually captured two cardinals en route to the papal conclave, in the hope of influencing the outcome. The result was a sharply divided group of prelates – and no conclusion. And so the weeks went by.

Growing impatient, Matteo Orsini (a powerful senator from Rome) had the assembled cardinals locked into the ancient and decrepit Septizonium Palace, where guards were instructed to use the leaky roof as a lavatory. Occasionally the electors were even shackled together and conditions were so terrible that the English cardinal fell ill and died. In fury at the continued indecision, Orsini threatened to dig up the decomposing corpse of Pope Gregory and lock it in with the bickering churchmen.

Finally, on 25 October the cardinals chose a compromise candidate, Goffredo da Castiglione, who was cardinal bishop of Sabina and came from a powerful Church family (his uncle had been Urban III). Castiglione selected the papal name of Celestine IV.

Sadly, Celestine did not turn out to be the forceful successor to Pope Gregory that the Church so desired. His only noteworthy act was to excommunicate Matteo Orsini, the man who had imprisoned the conclave. On 10 November, just sixteen days after his election, he died before he could even be consecrated. For 349 years Celestine held the record for the briefest reign in papal history, to be bested in 1590 when Urban VII succumbed to malaria after only thirteen days as pope.

Also on this day

1483: Martin Luther is born in Eisleben, Saxony * 1683: Louis XIV secretly marries his mistress, Madame de Maintenon * 1697: English painter and caricaturist William Hogarth is born * 1759: German poet and dramatist Friedrich Schiller is born in Marbach * **1775: Birth of the Continental Marines, now the US Marine Corps** * 1793: The French republican government abolishes the worship of God

11 November

Louis XIII fools his mother on the Day of Dupes

1630 Today is known in French history as the Day of Dupes, for on this date King Louis XIII fooled everybody in his court by doing what no one – especially his mother – expected him to do and thereby changed the course of history.

France stood at a crossroads, having to choose between reverting to the spirit of pre-Reformation Europe (allied to the Church and the reactionary Holy Roman Empire) and thrusting forward as an independent nation that would lead the world rather than follow.

Urging consolidation with the forces of Catholicism and the powers of the Habsburgs in Spain and Germany was Louis's mother, Marie de' Medici, backed by a restless nobility itching for a return to a feudal society in which their ancient privileges would be restored.

Opposing her was the great cardinal Armand-Jean du Plessis de Richelieu, a playwright and musician of some ability, who contended that France's natural role was to lead the world, not only politically but also in the arts, firmly believing that the cultural shape of civilisation should be defined and moulded by France.

In previous years, Marie's incessant scheming had earned her repeated exile from court, but in the end she always managed to re-ingratiate herself, thanks largely to the intercession of her chief adviser Richelieu, then still a bishop. She later rewarded Richelieu by using her influence to gain for him a cardinal's hat and persuaded young Louis to make him his first minister.

Shallow, selfish and stupid, Marie never understood that Richelieu would always put the *gloire* (glory) of France ahead of any lingering gratitude to her. As the years passed, the astute cardinal increasingly dominated King Louis, while progressively pushing the Queen Mother even further from the centre of power. By 1630 Richelieu had been first minister for six years and Marie, now hating the cardinal whom once she had befriended, resolved to act.

On 11 November, bidden by his mother to the Palais de Luxembourg, Louis heard yet another venomous attack on Richelieu. But the cardinal, hearing of the meeting, boldly broke into their private conversation by slipping in through a side door. Exploding in hysterical rage, Marie demanded that Louis choose between the cardinal and herself and Richelieu, for once abashed, left the room in tears.

Almost instantly the whole court buzzed with rumours as to what had happened, fully convinced that Richelieu's ascendancy was over, the cardinal disgraced and perhaps even in mortal danger. Richelieu himself seems to have believed that all was lost and planned to flee from Paris as his enemies prepared to take over the reins of government.

But Louis wanted above all else to be a great king. It took him only a few hours to decide that only Richelieu could give him the canny advice he so urgently needed to guide him through the labyrinth of European politics. That evening he commanded the cardinal to his hunting lodge in Versailles and there informed him he would keep his post as first minister.

Aghast at her son's incomprehensible decision, Marie de' Medici fled first the court and then France, never to return. The courtiers allied to her were disgraced and in one case executed. In the twelve years left to him before he died, Richelieu became the architect of French national glory. He set France on the path to political and cultural pre-eminence to which it has aspired ever since, from the time of Louis's son, Louis XIV, to the 20th century and Charles de Gaulle.

Also on this day

1417: The Great Papal Schism comes to an end after 39 years when Martin V is elected sole Pope * 1855: Danish philosopher Søren Kierkegaard dies in Copenhagen * 1868: French Intimist painter Edouard Vuillard is born in Cuiseaux * **1918: On the eleventh hour of the eleventh day of the eleventh month, the Allies and Germany sign an armistice in Compiègne, France, ending the First World War** * 1918: French poet Guillaume Appolinaire dies in Saint-Germain-des-Prés

12 November

An army major general publishes Ben-Hur

1880 Today Harper & Brothers published a historical novel set in the time of Christ. The plot concerned a young Jew falsely accused of plotting to kill the Roman governor of Palestine, who escapes his imprisonment, becomes a Roman officer, avenges himself on his betrayer in a climactic chariot race and at the end, with the aid of Jesus, is converted to Christianity. The novel, titled *Ben-Hur: A Tale of the Christ*, became the greatest American best-seller of the 19th century.

Printed through the years in countless editions and translations, *Ben-Hur* also spawned many versions in other media: an 1899 play ran for some 6,000 performances in New York and on tour around the world; a 1907 one-reeler featured only the spectacular chariot race; a 1925 film, starring Roman Novarro as Ben-Hur and Francis X. Bushman as his nemesis Messala, cost $4 million but helped establish MGM as a major studio; and the 1959 version starring Charlton Heston in the title role won eleven of the twelve Academy awards for which it was nominated.

The author of the best-seller that spawned this string of box-office successes wrote his novel while resident in the Governor's Palace in Santa Fe, serving as governor of the lawless frontier territory of New Mexico. He was Lew Wallace, Indiana native, sometime lawyer, newspaper reporter, artist, veteran of the Mexican War and, in the Civil War, a major general in the Union army. At war's end he was a member of the court martial that convicted the conspirators in the assassination of President Lincoln. He also presided over the military trial of Henry Wirz, commandant of the notorious Confederate prison camp at Andersonville, Georgia.

Wallace had written an earlier novel, *The Fair God: A Story of the Conquest of Mexico*, published in 1873, which enjoyed a substantial sale. In 1875 he began to 'shape the Jewish story', as he called it, which he originally intended as an illustrated serial for magazine publication on the subject of the journey of the Three Wise Men to Bethlehem. After he began writing, he seems to have undergone a religious conversion and the work turned into a fully-fledged biblical epic.

Shortly after publication, Wallace sent a copy of *Ben-Hur* to President James Garfield, a fellow Union army veteran, who read it and replied: 'With this beautiful and reverent book you have lightened the burden of my daily life and renewed our acquaintance which began at Shiloh.' When, a few weeks later, Garfield named Wallace Minister Resident of the United States to the Ottoman Empire, it was widely assumed that the appointment was made on the strength of the President's enthusiasm for the novel.

For all Wallace's popularity as a novelist in an earlier era, his novels – a third one, *A Prince of India*, was published in 1893 – inevitably lost their appeal to more modern tastes. Edmund Wilson, commenting on the 'romantic trappings' of Wallace's style, concluded that: 'In the novels of Lew Wallace . . . we usually find Walter Scott at his worst.'

Also on this day

1035: English and Danish king Canute dies at Shaftesbury in Dorset * **1611: Gustavus Adolphus, Protestant warrior in the Thirty Years War, is enthroned as King of Sweden** * 1840: French sculptor Auguste Rodin is born * 1866: The 'father of modern China' Sun Yat-Sen is born in Hsingshan, Kwongtung Province

13 November

The king who started the Hundred Years War

1312 On this day at the great medieval fortress of Windsor was born a baby boy who one day would become the seventh king in the Plantagenet line, the future Edward III of England. His parents were the inept and homosexual Edward II and his implacably ambitious queen, Isabella of France (who eventually acquiesced to the murder of her husband).

Tall, blonde and handsome, young Edward was crowned in the January before his fifteenth birthday, while his mother's lover, Roger de Mortimer, held his father in prison. Eight months later his father was brutally murdered in his cell.

In 1330, when Edward was king in fact as well as name, he avenged his father by executing Mortimer as a traitor and sending his mother into permanent retirement, eventually to join the Poor Clares order of nuns.

Edward is known as one of England's great warrior kings, with famous victories over the French at Sluys and Crécy. His contemporaries considered him an exemplary knight – chivalrous, good-tempered and brave in battle. Even his extravagance and taste for the ladies endeared him to his court and his people. Today he is perhaps best remembered as the founder of England's highest chivalric honour, the Order of the Garter.

Unfortunately, Edward's most important legacy was his obsessive claim to the throne of France, based on historic Plantagenet holdings in Gascony and his insistence on the rights of his mother, despite France's Salic law, which excluded females from the throne. Edward made his first claim when he was still only sixteen and a dozen years later in January 1340 he added the title of King of France to his own. He repeatedly tried to invade France, igniting the Hundred Years War. So persistent was Edward's belief in his right to the French crown that his successors continued the claim for half a millennium. Every English sovereign called himself King of France until George III finally abandoned the claim in 1801.

Also on this day

AD 354: St Augustine is born in Tagaste, Numidia (now Souk Ahras, Algeria) * **1834: Talleyrand resigns his last diplomatic post as ambassador to Great Britain at age 80, ending the most spectacular and the most successful career of all of history's diplomats** * 1850: Robert Louis Stevenson is born in Edinburgh * 1868: Italian composer Gioacchino Rossini dies in Passy * 1903: French Impressionist Camille Pissarro dies in Paris

14 November

Emperor Justinian dies after 38 years in power

565 Today, in Constantinople, the Byzantine Emperor Justinian died at the age of 82. He had ruled for 38 years in a time of unusual turmoil, as during his reign the bubonic plague killed perhaps two-fifths of the population of his empire.

Justinian was an unusual man by any measure. Historian Joan Mervyn Hussey describes him as 'a man of large views and great ambitions, of wonderful activity of mind, tireless energy and an unusual grasp of detail'. But he could also be petty and vindictive, as witnessed by his shameful treatment of his great general Belisarius, whom he continually (and unfoundedly) suspected of treason and whom, according to some accounts, he eventually blinded.

Justinian also had the courage and the judgement to marry an actress named Theodora at a time when actresses and prostitutes were virtually synonymous and the Church denied them the sacraments. Theodora eventually shared Justinian's rule and saved his throne, if not his life, when the Nika insurrection in Constantinople threatened to overturn the government.

Although Justinian successfully defended his empire against the Persians in the east and conquered parts of North Africa, his attempts to reunite the eastern and western parts of the old Roman Empire were doomed to failure. Those against whom he battled make a list of long-vanished tribes, including the Vandals, the Ostrogoths, the Bulgars, the Slavs, the Kotrigur Huns and the Avars.

Some historians believe that, in spite of his generally laudable ambitions, Justinian set the stage for the turmoil of the Middle Ages. They maintain that his attempt to reconquer the Western Empire only ensured its final and irrevocable split, a division made worse when he abandoned Latin as the language of government in Constantinople. They also claim that his failure to defeat the Persians – decisively – left them in a position to weaken the Byzantine Empire so much after his death that the eventual triumph of Islam became inevitable.

Whatever your judgement on Justinian, he left two enduring monuments. The first is the Great Church, today called the Hagia Sophia, in what is now Istanbul. The second is his contribution to Europe's fashion industry. During his time China carefully guarded its lucrative monopoly on the production of silk. Justinian bribed two monks who had lived there to return and steal silkworm eggs. These they secreted in hollow bamboo canes and brought back to Constantinople, allowing the Emperor to develop a thriving silk industry. Today, all of Europe's silk-producing caterpillars descend from those smuggled worms.

Also on this day
1650: William of Orange, the future William III of England, is born in The Hague & 1677 William marries Mary, daughter of the future James II * 1687: Charles II's mistress Nell Gwyn dies at 37 * 1840: French Impressionist Claude Monet is born in Paris * 1862: Lewis Carroll begins writing *Alice's Adventures in Wonderland* * 1916: Scottish writer Saki (H.H. Munro) is shot dead by a German sniper instantly after telling a fellow soldier: 'Put that bloody cigarette out.' * 1940: German bombers devastate Coventry, killing 568

15 November

Sherman's march through Georgia

1864 This morning advance units of the Union army began moving out of Atlanta, heading south-east in two columns. Behind them the city lay 'smouldering and in ruins', as their commander, General William Tecumseh Sherman, later described the destruction he had ordered. Grown tired of chasing his Confederate opponent, General Hood, and of having to protect a supply line stretching all the way back to Louisville, 'Uncle Billy' Sherman had decided to cut his force loose against the heartland of the Confederacy. For over a month the North would have no news of Sherman and his troops. 'I know the hole he went in at,' said his brother, the senator from Ohio, 'but I can't tell you what hole he will come out of.'

The hole he came out of was Savannah, Georgia, on 22 December. In the intervening weeks his two columns, with a combined strength of 62,000 and for the most part unopposed by rebel forces, destroyed much of what the Confederacy needed to keep fighting: crops, industry, transportation, infrastructure and morale. Sending their foragers ('bummers' in Union army parlance) far and wide, Union soldiers stripped Georgia bare, helped immensely in their task by thousands of runaway slaves who accompanied the invading forces. No army on either side had eaten so well. And what the troops didn't take, they let rot or they burned.

Sherman's march could not have been a pretty sight, but as military strategy it worked by shortening the war. It also produced one of the greatest marching songs of this or any war, 'Marching through Georgia':

Hurrah, hurrah, we bring the jubilee.
Hurrah, hurrah, the flag that makes you free.
So we sang this chorus from Atlanta to the sea,
As we went marchin' through Georgia.

Also on this day

1684: The Galarie des Glaces at Versailles is first opened to the French court * 1708: British statesman William Pitt the Elder is born * 1787: Austrian composer Christopher Gluck dies in Vienna * 1802: English painter George Romney dies * 1908: Chinese dowager empress Tz'u-hsi dies

---

Events written in **boldface** are covered in full in
365: Great Stories from History for Every Day of the Year,
the first volume in this series.

---

16 November

The battle that saved the German Protestants

1632 Today Europe's two greatest generals, King Gustavus Adolphus of Sweden and Prince Albrecht von Wallenstein, met near the Saxon town of Lützen in a battle of which the outcome prevented the destruction of Protestantism in Germany. The victor died on the field.

Gustavus Adolphus's portraits show a man of high and noble brow, calm, speculative eyes and a long, strong nose above his moustache and narrow, pointed goatee. He was intelligent and enlightened, an inspiring leader and brilliant commander.

He had inherited the Swedish throne in 1611, seven years before the outbreak of the terrible Thirty Years War between Germany's Protestant principalities and the reactionary Catholic Holy Roman Emperor Ferdinand II of the House of Habsburg.

Wallenstein was an altogether different animal. Eleven years Gustavus Adolphus's senior, he was born in Bohemia, orphaned at thirteen and raised a Protestant by his uncle. But at 23 he cynically converted to Catholicism to strengthen his position with the emperor of the day and three years later married an elderly but fabulously rich widow, whose money he inherited five years later. His wealth enabled him to provide an army at his own expense in the service of the Emperor and by 1625 he had become the head of all imperial forces, while grabbing for himself enormous swathes of Germany and Denmark. As his power grew, so did his ambitions, as he then started to trade alliances like any unscrupulous king, negotiating for advantage with Protestants and Catholics alike, finally causing Emperor Ferdinand to sack him in August 1630.

But only weeks later, seeing the cause of Protestantism in danger of collapse, Gustavus Adolphus joined the German principalities in their conflict against the Emperor. Supported financially by France's crafty Cardinal Richelieu, the 34-year-old king swept across northern Germany, utterly crushing the imperial forces under the command of Wallenstein's replacement, Johann von Tilly, at Breitenfeld, earning himself the sobriquet of the 'Lion of the North'. Desperate, Emperor Ferdinand was now forced to recall the arrogant, ambitious – but supremely talented – Wallenstein.

The morning of 16 November 1632 was cold and misty as Gustavus Adolphus launched his assault against Wallenstein's army at Lützen. His Swedish soldiers rushed to the attack singing Martin Luther's hymn *'Eine feste Burg ist unser Gott'* ('A Mighty Fortress is Our God') and another hymn composed by the King himself. The fate of Protestant Germany rested on the outcome.

All day long the two forces battled, with the Swedish King leading his own cavalry. But in one fierce charge Gustavus Adolphus became separated from his men and was cut down by encircling imperial horsemen. According to the mythmakers, his last words were a noble: 'I seal with my blood my religion and the liberties of Germany.'

In spite of his death, Gustavus Adolphus's army continued to batter Wallenstein's, capturing the enemy artillery and forcing Wallenstein to retreat in defeat. At the close of battle the King's body was found on the field and the spot was marked with a stone. Later the German people raised a monument there.

In bringing about the death of the Empire's most capable enemy, Wallenstein performed a great service for the Emperor, but it also meant he was no longer vital to the Emperor's cause. Unwisely, he kept his army at the ready but failed to bring it to Ferdinand's support. Now considering his one-time favourite a traitor, the Emperor ordered his assassination two years later.

Also on this day

42 BC: Roman Emperor Tiberius is born * **1272: Henry III dies incarcerated in the Tower of London after 56 years as king** * 1913: Marcel Proust publishes *Du côté de chez Swann (Swann's Way)*, the first volume of *À la recherche du temps perdu* (*Remembrance of Things Past*)

17 November

Bloody Mary is gone at last

1558 At seven o'clock this morning Bloody Mary, one of the saddest and most disastrous monarchs in all of England's history, died of influenza at the age of 42.

Mary lived a miserable and unrewarding life from the age of seventeen, when her father, Henry VIII, after six years of effort, finally forced through the annulment of his marriage to her mother, Catherine of Aragon, so that he could marry Anne Boleyn. The annulment made Mary a bastard, a status with which her father concurred.

With Anne as Queen, Mary's life became even worse, for she lost her title of Princess and was forced to defer to her newly born half-sister, Elizabeth. Moreover, Henry sent Catherine into retirement and Mary was never allowed to see her mother again.

Over the years Mary was a pawn to Henry's political ambitions, betrothed to a long list of European royalty, ranging from her cousin, Holy Roman Emperor Charles V, fifteen years her senior, to Charles's son, Philip II, eleven years her junior, whom she finally married in a loveless and childless union.

Finally, on the death of her teenage half-brother, Edward VI, Mary became England's first queen regnant at the age of 37. During the five and a half years of her reign, her Catholic fanaticism made her one of her country's most hated monarchs, as she had over 300 Protestants burnt at the stake, including her father's chief adviser, Archbishop Thomas Cranmer, and Bishops Ridley and Latimer. About 60 of her Protestant victims were women. While Mary was Queen, France wrenched back Calais, the last scrap of territory England possessed in continental Europe.

On Mary's death, several of her courtiers rode out to Hatfield House just north of London to announce the news to Elizabeth. They found the new queen contemplating the Bible beneath an oak tree in the garden, in spite of the damp chill of the season. She is said to have responded to the courtiers' news with a quotation from the 118th psalm: 'This is the Lord's doing; it is marvellous in our eyes.'

Indeed, the day of Mary's death was a day of celebration for the English and in a sense it has remained so ever since, as it was the first day of that glorious period that we now call the Elizabethan Age.

Also on this day

8 BC: Roman poet Horace dies * AD 284: Diocletian is proclaimed Roman Emperor * 1800: The US Congress meets for the first time * **1869: After ten years of construction, the Suez Canal opens for business** * 1922: Kemal Atatürk deposes the last sultan of Turkey

18 November

Nathaniel Palmer discovers a new continent

1820 Further and further south the seal hunters sailed, as each successive breeding ground was discovered – and depleted – in the unending search for profitable pelts.

In October 1820 American Captain Nathaniel Palmer headed south from the Falkland Islands in command of the tiny sloop *Hero*, just 45 tons and only 47 feet long. Palmer was still only 21 but had already made his mark, first as a blockade-runner during the War of 1812, then as an outstanding navigator in southern waters.

Palmer's course first took him to the South Shetland Islands, but once again he found few seals, so he determined to probe yet further south.

Sailing past immense icebergs, *Hero* continued through uncharted waters. Early on the morning of 18 November Palmer came to inhospitable land, a shore of massive icy cliffs dropping straight to the sea. After following the coast for some hours and finding neither landing place nor sight of seals, the captain finally turned his ship north. Only later would he come to realise that he had discovered a vast continent of over 5 million square miles, for which explorers had been searching for 200 years. He had discovered Antarctica.

Also on this day

1095: At the Council of Clermont, Pope Urban II launches the First Crusade * 1626: St Peter's Cathedral in Rome is consecrated * 1789: French photography pioneer Louis Daguerre is born * 1922: French novelist Marcel Proust dies

19 November

The Man in the Iron Mask

1703 Today in the Bastille in Paris, death came to a mysterious prisoner who had been held in French prisons for almost 34 years. He had two distinctions: no one knew who he was and he was wearing a mask.

For three centuries historians have laboured without success to identify this masked prisoner, but most agree that:

On 24 August 1669 one of Louis XIV's ministers sent a prisoner to the prison of Pignerol, putting him under the direct care of the governor, with the instructions: 'It is of extreme importance that [the prisoner] be closely guarded and that he is unable to communicate by letter or any other means [. . .] He must be kept in a completely isolated place, so that his guards cannot hear him [. . .] and you will never listen to anything he wishes to tell you, threatening to put him to death if he ever opens his mouth to speak to you of anything other than his needs.'

Twelve years later the prisoner was transferred to the prison at Exiles and then in 1687 to the prison on the Ile de Sainte-Marguerite, carried there in a sealed sedan chair, his face covered by a mask – although the mask was not iron but of black velvet.

Finally, in 1698, the prisoner was taken to the Bastille under orders that included 'taking all precautions to prevent that he is seen or recognised by anyone'. The Bastille's second in command noted that the prisoner was 'always kept masked and whose name has not been given to me, nor recorded'. In the meantime Louis XIV's sister-in-law, the Princess Palatine, wrote to her aunt that, according to court gossip, two musketeers were ready at all times to kill the prisoner if he took off his mask, even when eating or sleeping. Five years later the prison log records the death of the 'unknown prisoner, who has worn a black velvet mask since his arrival here'.

These are the known facts. Then in 1717 the French writer Voltaire was held in the Bastille for almost a year, where he learned from his jailors that the prisoner, when he was on the Ile de Sainte-Marguerite, was finely dressed and accomplished on the guitar. But Voltaire maintained that the man's mask was iron, riveted on and featuring a 'movable, hinged lower jaw held in place by springs that made it possible to eat wearing it.'

Then in 1789 the journalist Frederic-Melchior Grimm claimed that a royal valet had told him that Louis XIV had had an identical twin brother. Fearful that his two sons would fight each other for the throne, their father Louis XIII had sent the younger to be raised incognito by a French noble, but later the boy had seen a picture of his brother, who by now was King Louis XIV and had guessed his own identity. Louis had immediately condemned his brother to prison wearing a mask.

This was the tale that Alexandre Dumas told in 1850 with the publication of *The Man in the Iron Mask*, a sensational best-seller around the world. Since then there have been innumerable books and articles speculating on the identity of the man in the mask, and in the 20th century there have been at least five films, all based largely on Dumas's novel.

Although the existence of a masked prisoner is irrefutable, most historians agree that there is no evidence that he was Louis XIV's twin brother. But there is no consensus regarding who he might have been. The most famous candidates include the playwright Molière, Louis XIV's Minister of Finance, Nicolas Fouquet, British King Charles II's bastard son, the Duke of Monmouth, the duc de Beaufort (the Austrian lover of Louis XIII's wife Anne of Austria) and Louis XIV's bastard son, the comte de Vermandois. But although there are reasons why each of them might have been imprisoned, they all suffer from the same defect: their actual deaths are well attested and therefore would have had to have been faked.

There are also over 60 more obscure possibilities, including an Italian count, a French valet and a French army officer, but there seems to be no convincing reason why any of them should have worn a mask.

So the mystery continues of, as Victor Hugo put it, *'un prisonnier dont nul ne sait le nom, dont nul n'a vu le front, un mystère vivant, ombre, énigme, problème'* ('a prisoner of whom no one knows the name or has seen the face, a living mystery, shadow, enigma, problem').

If you want to do some investigating of your own, try visiting the prison on the Ile de Sainte-Marguerite – it's a ten-minute boat ride from Cannes – where you can inspect the cell where the masked prisoner was held.

Also on this day
1523: Giulio de' Medici becomes Pope Clement VII * 1600: British king Charles I is born in Dunfermline Castle, Scotland * 1828: Viennese composer Franz Schubert dies of syphilis at the age of 31 * 1863: American President Abraham Lincoln gives the Gettysburg Address

20 November

Judgement at Nürnberg

1945 The Nürnberg trials opened today, with the top brass of Hitler's Nazi Germany in the dock, accused of the most heinous war crimes of the 20th century. The 21 defendants sat in two rows, white-helmeted American military police stationed behind them. At precisely 10 am the four judges from Russia, Great Britain, France and the United States took their seats.

Before the German collapse, Winston Churchill had suggested the summary execution of Nazi government leaders, while Stalin had proposed shooting '50,000 to 100,000' German staff officers, but in late 1943 the Allies agreed to bring the Germans to trial. Nürnberg, the scene of massive Nazi rallies before the war, seemed a fitting place to determine their fate.

The defendants uniformly claimed innocence of the charges against them: either they had never done the deeds described, or, if they had, it was only to follow someone else's orders. Reichsmarschall Hermann Göring set the tone. Relaxed and confident (and 80 pounds lighter owing to the prison diet), he explained: 'We had orders to obey the head of state. We weren't a band of criminals meeting in the woods in the dead of night to plan mass murders. The four real conspirators are missing: the Führer, Himmler, Bormann and Goebbels.'

Following suit, High Command Chief of Staff Wilhelm Keitel offered: 'We all believed so much in him [Hitler] and now we take all the blame – and the shame! He gave us the orders. He kept saying that it was all his responsibility.'

Interior Minister Wilhelm Frick, who had promulgated the Nürnberg laws, abolished opposition parties and looked on complacently as 'useless eaters' such as the insane and disabled were put to death, defended himself: 'Hitler didn't want to do things my way. I wanted things done legally. After all, I am a lawyer.'

Fritz Sauckel, Hitler's Chief of Slave Labour, who had deported 5 million labourers to work in conditions so desperate that many of them died, testified that: 'I did everything possible to treat them well.'

The pornographer, sadist and Jew-baiter Julius Streicher, organiser of boycotts against Jewish businesses, helpfully explained, according to Prosecutor

Jackson, that his program for the destruction of synagogues was 'only because they were architecturally offensive'.

The other most vicious criminals in the dock were as follows:

- Ernst Kaltenbrunner, top man in the organisation controlling the Gestapo, the SD and the Criminal Police, had been the chief organiser of the 'Final Solution'. He had also ordered prisoners in Dachau and other camps liquidated just before the Allies would have liberated them.
- Alfred Rosenberg, the Nazi 'philosopher', had developed Germanisation policies that led to the extermination of Nazi opponents and to segregation of Jews into ghettos, facilitating their mass murder.
- Albert Speer, Hitler's architect and head of armaments and munitions, had used slave labour to boost Germany's war output.
- Arthur Seyss-Inquart had been in charge of the Netherlands when over 50,000 Dutch starved to death and another 40,000 were shot as hostages.
- Hans Frank, called the 'Jew butcher of Kraków' for atrocities he organised while governor-general of Poland, had unwisely noted in his diary: 'The Jews must be eradicated. Whenever we catch one, it is his end.'
- The once arrogant Foreign Minister Joachim von Ribbentrop, now grey and bewildered, had helped plan invasions of Czechoslovakia, Poland and Russia.
- Hitler's deputy, Rudolf Hess, who in 1941 had secretly flown to England to try to negotiate a peace treaty, had previously participated in the takeovers of Austria, Czechoslovakia and Poland. Emaciated and broken in spirit, he pretended not to remember his Nazi role.

The trial lasted eleven months, with 216 sessions in court. Then, on 1 October 1946, came the verdicts: three defendants were acquitted, seven, including Hess and Speer, drew prison sentences and the other eleven were sentenced to hang.

The executions were set for 16 October, but Göring cheated the hangman by swallowing a cyanide capsule hidden in a container of pomade the night before. After the hangings, the condemned men's bodies were incinerated in a Munich crematorium and their ashes were consigned to oblivion in the Isar river.

Also on this day

1700: Sweden's 17-year-old King Charles XII defeats the Russians at Narva * 1818: Simón Bolívar declares Venezuela to be independent of Spain * **1910: Russian novelist Leo Tolstoy dies of heart failure at a railway station in Astapovo** * 1943: US Marines storm ashore on Japanese-occupied Tarawa in the Gilbert Islands

21 November

Louis Napoleon gains a dictator's majority – 97 per cent of the vote

1852 Dictators love elections. Hitler was appointed German Chancellor after his Nazi party gained 37 per cent of the popular vote, thus setting the stage for his eventual dictatorship and later was supported by over 90 per cent of the electorate in a plebiscite. Franco conducted a referendum in 1947 that confirmed his lifetime dictatorial powers in Spain and Fidel Castro regularly stages elections in his one-party Cuban state. Even Louis Napoleon Bonaparte, in the middle of the 19th century, felt the need for a popular mandate.

In 1848 Louis Napoleon had been elected President of France, but the law decreed that he could not succeed himself at the end of his four-year term. The result was his successful *coup d'état* of 2 December 1851, which made him effectively the nation's dictator. Having not only a taste for power but also a grasp of popular politics, he decided to put the final choice to the French people.

Thus, on this day in 1852, the French went to the polls. The results were overwhelming. Some 97 per cent of the voters – 7,824,189 to 253,145 – voted Louis Napoleon Emperor, a title that he took officially on 2 December that year, the anniversary of his own coup and of the crowning in Notre-Dame of his uncle, Napoleon I, in 1804.

Also on this day

570: The Prophet Muhammad is born * 1694: Voltaire is born in Paris * **1783: Pilâtre de Rozier and the marquis d'Arlands make man's first aerial voyage in a hot-air balloon over Paris** * 1898: Belgian surrealist painter René Magritte is born * 1916: Austrian Emperor Franz Joseph I dies after 68 years on the throne

22 November

Frederick II, a most unusual Holy Roman Emperor

1220 Today in Rome, a month before his 26th birthday, Pope Honorius III crowned Frederick II Holy Roman Emperor, thus confirming another Hohenstaufen in an office the family had held (with one four-year interruption) since 1138. Short, stout, bald and, according to a contemporary, not worth 200 dirhams on a Muslim slave market, he was nevertheless the most remarkable monarch of the Middle Ages.

Insatiably curious, Frederick learned to speak seven languages, including Arabic, and was both a patron of the arts and a scientist. In his most famed experiment he ordered some nurses to raise a group of foundlings without talking to them, to discover what language they would 'naturally' speak. Sadly, according to a chronicle of the time, 'he laboured in vain, for the children all died, unable to live without the loving words of their mothers'.

On another occasion Frederick had two criminals fed identical large meals and sent one to run in the woods while the other slept. He then ordered both cut open to see which had better digested his food (the sleeper).

Frederick was a strong believer in education and founded the University of Naples. He was an expert on falconry and wrote a book on it and was the father of Italian poetry, being the first to write love songs in the vernacular. His fondness for words extended even to spelling – so much so that, when a notary misspelled his name, Frederick had his thumb cut off.

Because Frederick was already King of Sicily (which included most of southern Italy as well as the island), the territory he gained by becoming Holy Roman Emperor virtually encircled the Church's lands, keeping the Emperor and the papacy in conflict for 30 years.

Frederick hardly improved relationships with the Pope by his unorthodox behaviour. He kept Jewish and Muslim scholars at his court, maintained a harem and corresponded with non-Christian rulers in Egypt. (He even sent one a polar bear as a present.) But his greatest sin was in denying papal suzerainty over temporal rulers. He claimed to believe that the Church should return to the conditions of poverty and prayer of the first Christians. The Church's response was to excommunicate him, comparing him to the Antichrist.

Frederick did go on crusade, but he did it while excommunicated and kept his harem with him on campaign. Worse, he managed to negotiate the rights to Jerusalem, Bethlehem and Nazareth without spilling a drop of Saracen blood and then arranged for his own coronation as King of Jerusalem in the Church of the Holy Sepulchre. This so enraged Pope Gregory IX that thereafter he referred to Frederick as 'Christ's foe, the serpent'.

In fact, Frederick set a record of sorts for Holy Roman emperors in that he was excommunicated three times in all, twice by Gregory IX and once by Innocent IV. Innocent even declared a crusade against Frederick, the first time any pope had used this device against a political enemy rather than an enemy of the faith.

Frederick died thirteen days short of his 56th birthday. Although excommunicated at the time, on his deathbed he had himself dressed in the robes of a Cistercian monk, symbolising the relinquishment of all worldly goods. This final show of piety failed to placate Pope Innocent, whose comment on hearing of Frederick's death was: 'Let Heaven and Earth rejoice.' Soon rumours arose that the Emperor was not really dead but entombed alive in a volcano, waiting to return to Earth to scourge the worldly Church.

Also on this day

1428: Warwick the Kingmaker is born * 1774: Robert Clive of India commits suicide * 1819: English novelist George Eliot (Mary Ann Evans) is born * 1869:

French author André Gide is born * 1890: French General and President Charles de Gaulle is born in Lille * 1963: American President John F. Kennedy is shot dead by a sniper in Dallas

23 November

A bright victory at Missionary Ridge

1863 Today, a Monday, Ulysses S. Grant, commander of all Union armies in the Western Theater, began the battle to lift the Confederate siege of Chattanooga. For that purpose, he had brought along the Army of the Tennessee, the very force he had led to the great victory at Vicksburg last summer and now commanded by his favourite comrade-in-arms, General William Tecumseh Sherman.

The war was in its third year and it had become clear to President Lincoln and his army planners that the path to a Union victory lay in an invasion of the Southern heartland. The possibility of such a move had been opened when Vicksburg, on the Mississippi, fell to Grant. But the next step required control of Chattanooga, a key railway junction at the eastern end of Tennessee and the strategic gateway into the Deep South.

Grant had concluded that the Union force actually holding Chattanooga, the Army of the Cumberland, was too battered and demoralised by its recent defeat at the battle of Chickamauga to be of much use in the effort to raise the siege. Even with a newly promoted commanding general, George H. Thomas, who had won the epithet 'Rock of Chickamauga' for his sterling performance in an otherwise disastrous engagement, the Army of the Cumberland, in Grant's plan, was to be used only in support. The main effort would be Sherman's Army of the Tennessee.

On this first day of battle, however, Sherman, commanding the Union left, was unable to get sufficient forces across the Tennessee in time to mount the scheduled attack against the northern end of Missionary Ridge, the main Confederate position around Chattanooga. In contrast, Thomas, sending in two divisions of the Army of the Cumberland against the centre, managed to turn a reconnaissance in force into a rousing, full-blown attack that pushed the Union line a full mile closer to the ridge. It was a hint of things to come.

On Tuesday, Sherman got his troops up to the high ground for an attack on what he supposed was Missionary Ridge, only to discover that through a failure of intelligence the Confederate positions lay on the far side of yet another valley. The day's only excitement was far down on the Union right, where 'Fighting Joe' Hooker led two brigades up the steep slopes of Lookout Mountain, 1,200 feet above the city and chased the Confederate defenders off the mist-shrouded summit, a showy action that became famous as the 'Battle above the Clouds'.

At dawn, on Wednesday, Sherman finally attacked. But by now, an enemy well alerted to his intentions had strongly reinforced the northern end of the ridge. By 3 pm the Army of the Tennessee had made little headway at a cost of 1,500 casualties. A Confederate counter-attack seemed imminent. A worried Grant asked General Thomas for a diversionary attack against the Confederate lines at the base of Missionary Ridge. Thomas gave the order: at the firing of a signal gun four divisions of the Army of the Cumberland started across the plain. As Confederate artillery on the crest of the ridge opened up, the advancing infantry quickened their pace, then broke into a run. As they did, they began yelling, 'Chickamauga! Chickamauga!' It was a day for revenge and redemption.

The Union attack carried the first line of Confederate rifle pits, but now came under heavy musketry from a second line halfway up the ridge. It was retreat or keep on going. There was no hesitation. From his command post, Grant was stunned at the improbable spectacle of regiments clawing their way up the steep slope, flags waving, troops shouting, officers as well as men caught up in the spirit of the moment. Passing through the second line, the attackers pounded for the crest. Suddenly, blue-clad figures filled the ridge-line, firing their muskets, cheering, clapping each other on the back and pointing jubilantly at the sight of the enemy in full flight down the other side of the ridge.

Grant was always disappointed that it was the Army of the Cumberland, under Thomas, rather than his own Army of the Tennessee, under Sherman, that played the major role in the notable victory at Chattanooga. But there was glory enough to go around. Soon, Grant would become general-in-chief of all the Union armies; Sherman, succeeding him as commander in the Western Theater, would, in the following year, lead a Union army from Chattanooga to capture Atlanta and make the famous march through Georgia to the sea; and the redoubtable Thomas would be confirmed as the commander of a redeemed army that would perform with distinction throughout the rest of the war.

News of the victory at Chattanooga reached much of the North the next day, which was, appropriately, the last Thursday of the month – a date President Lincoln had recently proclaimed Thanksgiving Day.

Also on this day

1407: Queen Isabeau sends her lover Louis, duc d'Orléans to his death * 1804: 14th American president Franklin Pierce is born in New Haven, Connecticut * 1874: Thomas Hardy publishes *Far from the Madding Crowd* * 1876: Spanish composer Manuel de Falla is born in Cádiz

24 November

The king who never joined a battle

1542 The most famed English kings gained their renown primarily on the field of battle – witness William the Conqueror, Richard the Lionheart, Edward III, Henry V and Henry VII to name but a few. But the exception to the rule is perhaps the most famous of them all, King Henry VIII.

The English fought only two serious battles during Henry's reign. Both were against Scotland, both were victories, both resulted in the death of a Scottish king and both left an infant behind to inherit the Scottish throne. And Henry was at neither of them.

The first, the Battle of Flodden, was fought on 9 September 1513. During the fighting Scotland's King James IV was killed on the field. But the victory was due to the generalship of Thomas Howard, Earl of Surrey, as Henry was in France at the time. On James's death his son of just seventeen months inherited the crown as James V.

On this day, 29 years after Flodden, came the second major battle, at Solway Moss, fought while Henry was in London, once again leaving the combat to his barons. Here a small force of only 3,000 Englishmen met a Scottish army of 15,000, but most of the Scots turned and ran without a fight. The victors captured 1,200 prisoners, including 500 gentlemen, five barons and two earls, thus eliminating Scotland as a military threat for the remainder of Henry's reign.

This time the Scottish king, the same James V who had inherited the crown on his father's death after the Battle of Flodden, survived the battle – just. But although he escaped the English, the defeat brought on a mental breakdown and just twenty days later he died, it is said, of shame. Six days before his death, his wife Mary of Guise gave birth to a daughter, named Mary after her mother, who on her father's death became Mary, Queen of Scots.

Henry lived on for another five years, never imagining that his then thirteen-year-old daughter Elizabeth and five-year-old Mary would never meet but would in their turn become mortal enemies.

Also on this day

1713: Novelist Laurence Sterne is born in Clonmel, Ireland * **1859: Charles Darwin publishes *On the Origin of Species by Means of Natural Selection*** * 1864: Henri de Toulouse-Lautrec is born in Albi * 1929: French statesman and journalist Georges (Le Tigre) Clemenceau dies in Paris

25 November

Disraeli buys the Suez Canal

1875 Isma'il Pasha, Khedive of Egypt, was one of history's great government spenders. When the Turkish sultan placed him in the job in 1863, Egypt's national debt stood at a modest £7 million. Twelve years later it had ballooned to a gargantuan £1 billion – hence the need for cash.

The Suez Canal had finally been completed in 1869, after ten years of labour, its ownership split between the Egyptians and the French, who had engineered its construction. But by 1875 Isma'il was desperate for money and so offered Egypt's shares for sale. News of Isma'il's plight was picked up by a British newspaperman, who immediately sent it on to the British Foreign Office.

In a moment of myopia, the Foreign Office recommended against the acquisition, but Britain's prime minister, Benjamin Disraeli, had a broader understanding of the canal's strategic value and the remarkable opportunity it offered for shipping and trade, especially with the jewel of the Empire, India. But where to get the money? He could probably persuade Parliament to go along with the deal, but that would take time and in the interim some other foreign power might snatch up the shares.

Without a word to Parliament, Disraeli went straight to the richest man in the country, Lionel Rothschild, who coughed up the then-staggering sum of £4 million within a few hours. On this day the Prime Minister quietly purchased the shares, later persuading Parliament to ratify the transaction.

This was Great Britain's first step into Egypt, a step that led inexorably to the British occupation of the country in 1882. In 1922 an Egyptian monarchy was established, still largely under British control, but 30 years later Egypt finally freed itself from British domination when Gamal Abdel Nasser ousted the last Egyptian king, the fat and licentious King Farouk.

Also on this day
1562: Spanish dramatist Lope de Vega is born in Madrid * 1616: Cardinal Richelieu joins the French government for the first time * **1741: Peter the Great's daughter Elizabeth stages a *coup d'état* to become Tsarina of Russia**

26 November

Death of the formidable Blanche of Castile

1252 Today died Blanche of Castile, one of history's most forceful characters, if not the most appealing. She was born in Spain in 1188, but at the age of eleven was taken to France by her grandmother, Eleanor of Aquitaine, to marry the future Louis VIII. Tradition has it that Blanche kept such a sharp eye on her husband that he remained impeccably faithful for their 26 years of marriage – something of a miracle for a king in an arranged marriage in the Middle Ages (or perhaps in any age).

Blanche was twice regent of France, the first time on her husband's death, when their son, Louis IX, was only twelve. Sensing weakness with a boy king on the throne, France's barons rose in revolt, with clandestine support from England. The barons had sadly underestimated the indomitable Blanche, who, dressed entirely in white, personally led her armies to eventual victory.

Blanche attempted to dominate her son even more than she had his father, particularly in his private conduct. When Louis reached maturity and married, court gossip had it that her attempts to regulate his sex life forced the young King to meet his wife in secret on the staircase between their rooms.

By the time Blanche reached 60, she had developed a worrying heart condition, but nonetheless agreed to take charge of the country once again when Louis and his wife embarked on a crusade to the Holy Land. Four years later she was struck down by a fatal heart attack when Louis was still in Jaffa.

There is some debate about the exact place she died. One source claims that she expired at an abbey in Melun, just south of Paris, having intended to renounce the world. Another contends that she suffered a heart attack en route to the abbey but was brought back to the Louvre in Paris, where she was improbably laid on a bed of straw to repent her sins and receive the last rites. A third maintains that she breathed her last in a palace located on the current site of Paris's Bourse de Commerce, in the area of Les Halles.

Also on this day

1504: Queen of Castile and Aragon Isabella I dies at Medina del Campo in Spain * 1607: Founder of Harvard University John Harvard is born * **1789: George Washington proclaims this day Thanksgiving Day**

27 November

Roger de Mortimer establishes a grisly tradition at Tyburn

1330 Stroll through London and stop at Marble Arch, at the north-east corner of Hyde Park. Where now stand the handsome houses of Connaught Square and the shops of the Edgware Road once was England's most famous place of execution – Tyburn. Its name derives from the Tyburn river, a small tributary of the Thames, which formerly went through London's West End before it was culverted.

There is some evidence that Tyburn's first gallows was erected as early as 1190, but most historians believe that the execution of Roger de Mortimer on this day in 1330 was the start of a grisly tradition (although some maintain that the Scottish rebel William Wallace, who was hanged, drawn and quartered in 1305, was executed at Tyburn).

The darkly handsome, arrogant Mortimer was one of England's premier villains. A powerful baron who joined a minor rebellion against King Edward II, he was imprisoned in the Tower of London but shortly escaped and fled to France. There he seduced Queen Isabella, Edward's French wife, who was home for a visit to escape the humiliation of her husband's homosexual lovers.

Queen and paramour soon returned to England, but this time leading an army. They captured and foully murdered the King and ruled the country for three years until the King's son, Edward III, escaped from their care and captured them in turn.

Although shielding his adulterous and murderous mother, young Edward had no qualms about her lover and ordered the once supreme Mortimer to be hanged, drawn and quartered at Tyburn before an assembled multitude of ghoulish onlookers.

From that day Tyburn became England's location of choice for executions, which it remained until 1783.

Also on this day

43 BC: Octavian (the future Augustus), Lepidus and Mark Antony form the Second Triumvirate * AD **511: Clovis, the first French king, dies in Paris** * 1770: Twelve-year-old Horatio Nelson enters the British Navy * 1953: American playwright and Nobel Prize winner Eugene O'Neill dies in Boston

28 November

Bernini, the man who created the Baroque

1680 Today died the man who more than any other created the Baroque style and transformed 17th-century Rome, Gian Lorenzo Bernini. Sculptor and architect extraordinaire, he was also a stage-set designer, painter, playwright and creator of fireworks displays.

Although born in Naples, Bernini spent almost his entire life in the Eternal City. Learning his trade from his sculptor father, he was a child prodigy who was already working in marble at the age of twelve.

A fervent Catholic who went to church every day, Bernini served eight popes during the 50-odd years that he dominated the artistic life of the city. His work represents his own strong religious views and reflects the triumphant militancy of the Church during the Counter-Reformation. Of all his work his sculpture is the most distinctive, characterised by a feeling of movement and strong emotion.

Bernini's first commission was remodelling the Church of Santa Bibiana, but he was simultaneously appointed to design the enormous baldachin, a giant bronze canopy supported by columns, standing over the tomb of St Peter in St Peter's Cathedral, which took almost ten years to complete.

Other Roman landmarks created by the great sculptor include the fountain in the Piazza Barberini, with its four dolphins supporting a giant seashell holding Triton, and two magnificent fountains in Rome's Piazza Navona, the Fountain of the Moor and the Fountain of the Four Rivers.

The Fountain of the Four Rivers includes four huge human figures, one of which has his right hand raised as if to ward off a blow. Legend has it that this was Bernini's comment on the work of the rival architect Francesco Borromini, who created the façade of the church opposite. The figure raises his hand to protect himself not from a blow but from falling masonry from the church, which Bernini was sure would collapse.

Of all of Bernini's works, his greatest masterpiece is undoubtedly the giant encircling colonnade of 96 columns in the Piazza San Pietro before St Peter's, designed to accommodate the large crowds that gather before the cathedral to receive the Pope's blessing on special religious occasions.

When Bernini died today in Rome, shortly before his 82nd birthday, he was recognised as the greatest artist of his time.

Also on this day

1290: Edward I's wife Eleanor dies, inspiring him to construct eleven 'Eleanor Crosses' across England * 1582: William Shakespeare marries Anne Hathaway * 1820: Communist philosopher Friedrich Engels is born in Barmen, Prussia * 1757: English poet and painter William Blake is born

29 November

A future saint is crowned in France

1226 It was St Andrew's Eve on this day in 1226 when Louis Capet was crowned King of France at Reims, three weeks to the day after the death of his father, King Louis VIII. Only twelve years old, he was blonde and handsome but with a delicate and sensitive face. He would grow up to become one of Europe's very greatest kings and the only king of France ever to be judged a saint by the Roman Catholic Church.

At first Louis was carefully guided by his formidable mother, Blanche of Castile, who brought him up to be strongly but tolerantly religious. But by the time he was fifteen, although constantly and sometimes well advised by his mother, he was largely taking his own decisions and personally led his troops in the field. Fortunately, the enemy (the perfidious English, as usual) fled before battle was joined and the young King saw no combat.

Indeed, during the 44 years of Louis's reign, he won no great wars, conquered no territory and twice led disastrous crusades to the Holy Land. During the first he commanded a force of 35,000 men, but after attaining a victory at al-Mansurah, plague struck his army and he was forced to retreat. Thousands died and the expedition ended in ruinous failure, as Louis and his chief barons were captured and had to be ransomed. Louis's second crusade was even less successful, as plague struck once again, this time killing the King (although some scholars believe he died of dysentery).

Unlike other famous medieval kings, Louis earned his enduring fame through his character rather than conquest. He was known for the justice of his decisions, which he often handed down personally, gathering his subjects at the foot of an oak tree in the grounds of his palace in Vincennes. But Louis was not simply 'good'. He was a cheerful, affable man who talked easily and frequently with those around him.

One of Louis's lasting marks on history came through his firm religious beliefs. His private confessor was a priest named Robert de Sorbon, a man of poor family who had made his own way through devoutness and hard work.

By 1253 Sorbon had started instructing students as well as the King. Four years later he bought some land and, with the King's backing, founded a seminary for impoverished students called the Maison de Sorbonne. The Maison de Sorbonne soon grew into the core of the University of Paris, which to this day bears his name.

Immediately upon Louis's death his subjects took to considering him a saint, a judgement confirmed by the Church only 27 years later.

Also on this day

1530: Cardinal Thomas Wolsey dies at Leicester while travelling under arrest to face trial * 1780: Austrian empress Maria Theresa dies * 1797: Italian composer Domenico Donizetti is born * 1864: American cavalry units kill over 150 disarmed Cheyenne and Arapaho Indians during the Sand Creek massacre * 1924: Opera composer Giacomo Puccini dies of throat cancer in Brussels

30 November

The apex and nadir of Sweden's Charles XII

1700, 1718 On this date, eighteen years apart, occurred both the greatest triumph and the untimely end of Sweden's warrior king, Charles XII. In between these events fell a far-ranging conflict known to history as the Great Northern War.

When his father died of stomach cancer on 5 April 1697, Charles became an absolute monarch at the age of fourteen. Despite his youth, he was exceptionally strong willed, not to say obstinate, with a fervid belief in his country's destiny and his own moral duty to serve it. Fearless in the face of danger, he shot his first bear at eleven and became an outstanding horseman. Later in life he developed an interest in painting and architecture, could quote Swedish poetry and relished philosophical arguments. But his real genius was war.

In February 1700, when Charles was still seventeen, Denmark, Poland and Russia launched an attack against Sweden to start the Great Northern War, which was to last for 21 years. First turning his attention to the Russians, Charles led his army into what today is Estonia, where on this day he annihilated the army of Peter the Great at the Battle of Narva.

Rain was pouring down when Charles's army reached the battlefield, but it shortly turned to snow. Although the 40,000 Russians far outnumbered the 10,000 Swedes, Charles managed to split the enemy's forces and destroy them piecemeal.

Charles himself was always where the action was hottest. When his fifth horse was shot under him, he laconically commented: 'These people seem disposed to give me exercise.' At one point he fell into a swamp and lost his boots and sword when his men pulled him free. Cheerfully he continued to fight in his socks.

Soon the Russians were fleeing in panic, thousands surrendering while others threw themselves in the Narva river in an attempt to escape. In all, some 15,000 Russians perished against only 667 Swedes. So many Russians were captured that the Swedes couldn't guard them and had to let them go, after confiscating their guns and equipment. The high point for many Swedish soldiers came after the battle, when they celebrated their extraordinary triumph with a huge store of captured Russian vodka.

Charles continued to crush his enemies for the next nine years. He defeated the Danes, the Saxons and the Poles, capturing Kraków. Convinced of his righteous cause, he had little mercy for his defeated enemies, commenting: 'Rather let the innocent suffer than the guilty escape.' He instructed his troops to 'ravage, singe and burn all about! Make the whole district a wilderness!'

But in 1709 Charles made the mistake of attacking a vastly superior Russian force at Poltava and his army was obliterated. Charles escaped and fled to Turkey, where he remained for the next six years.

By the time Charles finally returned to Sweden in 1715 he had been away for fifteen years, either fighting his enemies on foreign battlefields or fleeing from them in Turkey and Poland. Extraordinarily, during all of this time he had continued to rule his kingdom *in absentia*. And the Great Northern War ground on without result.

In 1718 Charles launched a new campaign to conquer Norway (then a Danish province) to force the Danes to sue for peace. In November he brought his army before the enemy fortress at Fredrikshald (today's Halden) and surrounded the town with trenches. On this day Charles entered the trenches to get a better look at the enemy's positions. As he peeped over the parapet a bullet suddenly smashed into his head, killing him instantly.

Almost immediately rumours began to spread that someone from his own side had shot him – anyone who had kept his country in a state of war for eighteen years was bound to have enemies. The question will never be definitively answered, but most historians now believe he was killed by a lucky shot from the enemy.

The Great Northern War continued for another three years, reducing Sweden to the minor power that it still is today. Charles remains a contentious character. Some blame him for Sweden's precipitous decline from major power status, but many celebrate him as a great general and leader. More ominously, both Napoleon and Hitler looked to his example as a guide for their own invasions of Eastern Europe, and even now he is extolled by Sweden's right-wing extremists for his chauvinism.

Also on this day

1508: Italian architect Andrea Palladio is born in Padua * 1667: Irish writer Jonathan Swift is born in Dublin * 1835: American writer Mark Twain (Samuel Clemens) is born in Florida, Missouri * 1874: British statesman and author Winston Churchill is born at Blenheim Palace * **1900: Oscar Wilde dies at a hotel in the rue des Beaux Arts in Paris** * 1939: Russia invades Finland

1 December

King Henry I dies of a surfeit of lampreys

1135 Today King Henry I, William the Conqueror's youngest son, died at Lyon-la-Forêt in eastern Normandy, the French duchy he ruled along with England. The legend is that his cook served him a dish of lampreys beyond their sell-by date and the King expired of food poisoning. His body was returned in state to England, where it was buried in Reading Abbey, which Henry had founded.

Most contemporaries were not sad to see Henry go. As one of them wrote, 'God endowed him with three gifts, wisdom, victory and riches, but these were offset by three vices, avarice, cruelty and lust.'

Henry certainly had the last-named vice, as he fathered over twenty bastard children. As for avarice and cruelty, the case is proved by his treatment of his two brothers.

In 1100 Henry had inherited the throne of England from his elder brother William II (Rufus), who had been killed in a mysterious hunting accident that many believe Henry instigated in order to gain the crown.

Later he invaded his brother Robert Curthose's duchy of Normandy, captured Robert in battle, imprisoned him for the last 28 years of his life and took over the duchy for himself.

Of Henry's many children, the only legitimate one surviving at the time of his death was a daughter named Matilda, to whom he left the throne of England. But Henry's favourite nephew, Stephen of Blois, was just as ruthless as his uncle. He ignored Matilda's rights and seized power. This usurpation eventually led to a mini civil war, when Matilda unsuccessfully invaded the country. Stephen finally died in 1154 and England returned to Henry's direct bloodline in the person of his grandson, Matilda's son Henry Plantagenet, who founded the Plantagenet line as King Henry II.

Also on this day

1455: Death of Lorenzo Ghiberti, the sculptor who created the 'Gates of Paradise' bronze doors for the baptistery of the cathedral of Florence ∗ 1521: Medici pope Leo X dies ∗ 1800: The American government is transferred from Philadelphia to Washington, DC ∗ **1919: US-born Lady Nancy Astor becomes the first woman to take her seat in the House of Commons, as MP for the Sutton division of Plymouth**

Events written in **boldface** are covered in full in
365: Great Stories from History for Every Day of the Year,
the first volume in this series.

---

2 December

Napoleon Day

1804, 1805, 1851, 1852 Today should be called Napoleon Day, as it commemorates the greatest triumphs of the Napoleons, uncle and nephew.

The first notable 2 December was a Sunday in 1804 when Napoleon Bonaparte, once Napoleone Buonaparte, shed his last name altogether to become Emperor Napoleon I. A crowd of 8,000 jammed Notre-Dame to witness the coronation. There Pope Pius VII officiated but did not crown, as Napoleon reserved that honour for himself, famously placing the iron crown of Charlemagne and the old Lombard kings on his own head, then solemnly repeating their challenge: *'Dio me la diedes, guai a chi la tocca!'* ('God gave it to me; woe to him who touches it!') He then crowned his wife Joséphine Empress of France.

Precisely one year later, on 2 December 1805, 62,000 Frenchmen under Emperor Napoleon utterly routed a combined Russian–Austrian army of 80,000 commanded by Alexander I of Russia and Franz I of Austria. Fought near a Moravian town called Austerlitz (now Slavkov u Brna in the Czech Republic), this seismic victory was called the Battle of the Three Emperors.

Napoleon split the enemy force with a determined assault by Marshal Soult against the centre and then vigorously pursued both enemy halves. Allied losses came to 15,000 killed and wounded and 11,000 captured, compared with Napoleon's loss of only 9,000 men. Because of the unusually bright sunshine on this winter day, the battle is remembered as 'the sun of Austerlitz'. It was Napoleon's greatest military victory, and France now became the dominant power in Europe.

By 1851 the first Emperor Napoleon was long in his grave, but his nephew Louis Napoleon added to the Napoleonic mythology of 2 December.

When Louis Napoleon had been elected President of France in 1848, his term of office had been limited to four years and the constitution forbade him from succeeding himself. In July 1851 he tried and failed to persuade the Assembly to revise the constitution and this failure had set his resolve to seize by force what he could not gain by persuasion.

Working closely with his half-brother the duc de Morny, Louis Napoleon chose 2 December for his *coup d'état*. On the previous evening his men placed posters throughout Paris proclaiming him Emperor and his confederate Maupas, the Prefect of Police, secretly arrested 78 troublemakers at dawn on 2 December. (Ironically, one of those taken into custody was Adolphe Thiers, who nineteen years later would become the president of France on Napoleon's downfall.)

Later in the day Louis Napoleon rode through the streets of Paris accompanied by a glittering troop of splendid soldiers, including most of France's generals. And so it was done. There was no bloodshed that day and little resistance. Louis Napoleon was now the nation's dictator, although his imperial position had been gained by force and had yet to be endorsed by the French Senate. (Karl Marx's reaction to Louis's coup was his famous dictum: 'Hegel says somewhere that all great events and personalities in world history reappear in one fashion or another. He forgot to add: the first time as tragedy, the second as farce.')

The final 2 December in the Napoleonic legend occurred one year later, in 1852. On that day the Senate passed a resolution confirming that the French Empire was restored and Louis Napoleon its emperor, with the title of Napoleon III.

Also on this day

1547: Spanish conquistador Hernán Cortés dies in Seville * 1697: The newly rebuilt St Paul's Cathedral in London reopens * 1814: French writer, philosopher and pornographer the Marquis de Sade dies in the insane asylum at Charenton * 1823: American President James Monroe issues the Monroe Doctrine, banning more European colonies in the Western hemisphere * 1848: Austrian Emperor Ferdinand abdicates, Archduke Franz Karl renounces his rights of succession and Franz Joseph begins his reign of 68 years * **1859: American abolitionist John Brown is hanged for insurrection**

3 December

The Council of Trent sets Church doctrine for centuries to come

1545 Today in the northern Italian town of Trent the 19th Ecumenical Council of the Roman Catholic Church began its deliberations. Known for ever after by the name of the town in which it was convened, the Council of Trent met on and off for eighteen years and defined Church dogma and doctrine for centuries to come.

In the 16th century Christianity was in turmoil. Luther had posted his theses on a church door in 1517, Calvin fled to Basel in 1533, the same year Henry VIII effectively took England out of the Church of Rome and trouble was brewing throughout Germany and Holland. In response, Pope Paul III, still vigorous at 78, issued a bill proclaiming the Council.

Among the issues decided, confirmed or set in motion at Trent were: only Catholics could enter heaven; Latin should be the only language of prayer; priests should be celibate; the plan for drawing up an Index of Forbidden Books was agreed; faith and good works plus the seven sacraments were proclaimed as the sole means to salvation (thus repudiating Luther's doctrine of salvation through faith alone); the nature and consequence of original sin were defined. Some of the Church practices that were most controversial – indulgences, the veneration of relics and saints and the veneration of the Virgin Mary – were strongly reaffirmed.

On 4 December 1563, eighteen years and one day after the Council had begun, the final session closed with the ringing denunciation: 'Anathema to all heretics, anathema, anathema.' A year later Pope Pius IV published a summary of the great issues that had been resolved. The Council both shaped the future Church and created some much-needed reforms. But it failed in its original purpose – to bring all of Christianity into one Church.

Also on this day

1368: The future Charles VI of France is born and is given the Dauphiné as his apanage, thus becoming the first Dauphin, a title given to all subsequent heirs to the French throne * 1469: Leading Florentine citizens call on Lorenzo de' Medici to take over the rule of Florence * 1533: Ivan IV (the Terrible) becomes grand prince of Moscow at the age of three * 1552: St Francis Xavier dies of fever on the island of Sancian (now Shang-ch'uan Tao) off the coast of China * 1857: Polish-born English writer Joseph Conrad is born in what is now Berdichev, Russia * 1894: In Samoa, Robert Louis Stevenson dies of a stroke going to the cellar for a bottle of wine

4 December

The first Spanish Bourbon king

1700 Charles II, the last Spanish Habsburg, had died two months earlier, deranged and childless, finally leaving his great empire to his first Bourbon cousin twice removed, Philippe, duc d'Anjou, grandson of Louis XIV of France and great-grandson of Philip IV of Spain.

Louis emphatically agreed that Philippe was the man for the job, hoping to turn mighty Spain into a docile appendage of France. To the French court he grandly announced: 'It was the command of Heaven and I have granted it with pleasure.'

On 4 December the seventeen-year-old Philippe set off from France for his new kingdom. Asking his grandfather for a final word of advice, he may have been somewhat dampened in spirit to receive the reply: 'Never form an attachment for anyone.'

Philip V of Spain, as he now was, remained King for 46 years until his death, in spite of the fourteen-year War of the Spanish Succession fought by Austria, England and France, disputing his right to wear the crown. (Philip abdicated the throne in favour of his son Luis in January of 1724 but resumed it eight months later when Luis died of smallpox.)

In his artistic tastes, Philip remained resolutely French, building the beautiful La Granja palace near Madrid in French architectural style. During his last years he suffered fits of insanity, leaving control of the state largely to his wife. He was the first Spanish Bourbon, the royal house that has reigned on and off to this day, for over three centuries.

5 December

Frederick the Great's greatest victory

1757 During the Seven Years War Prussia's population totalled only 4.5 million, while the opposing alliance of Austria, France and Russia could draw their armies from over 100 million inhabitants. But Prussia had Frederick the Great.

Frederick was the greatest general of the 18th century, perhaps the greatest of any century. On this day he proved it and saved his nation from extinction.

The town of Leuthen lies just west of the Oder in land that Frederick had seized from Austria only a few years before. Here his force of just 36,000 men would face an Austrian army of 60,000–80,000. Aware of the enormous odds against his success, Frederick offered his officers the chance to leave before the battle, but none defected. The evening before the battle he laconically remarked: 'Shortly we shall either have beaten the enemy, or we will never see one another again.'

The next day, through a brilliant flanking manoeuvre, Frederick utterly routed the Austrians. Although Prussia lost some 6,000 killed and wounded, the enemy lost 10,000 killed, plus another 21,000 captured. And within two weeks another 17,000 dispirited Austrian soldiers surrendered almost without a fight at Breslau.

The war dragged on until 1763, sometimes favouring Frederick's enemies, but the great general always managed to extricate himself from disaster with a timely victory. As Napoleon remarked in the following century: 'It is not the Prussian army which for seven years defended Prussia against the three most powerful nations in Europe, but Frederick the Great.'

In the years ahead, the Battle of Leuthen became a totemic victory for the German people, a symbol of German superiority that would play its role in the eventual unification of the country, reverberating through the centuries to the First World War and culminating in the militarism of the Third Reich. As Frederick's contemporary, the comte de Mirabeau, commented: '*La guerre est l'industrie nationale de la Prusse.*' ('War is the national industry of Prussia.')

6 December

Napoleon meets Talleyrand

1797 Napoleon was still only General Buonaparte, defender of the Republic and servant of the French Revolutionary government called the Directory. On this day he came to the Hôtel de Galliffet on Paris's rue de Grenelle to be presented to the newly nominated Foreign Minister, the 43-year-old Charles-Maurice de Talleyrand.

It was the first time they had met, but clearly Napoleon must have been impressed, for two years later, just eleven days after staging a *coup d'état* to take control of the French government, he appointed Talleyrand as his foreign minister. He knew exactly what he was looking for. 'I needed', he later wrote, 'an aristocrat and an aristocrat who knew how to handle things with an entirely princely insolence.' Talleyrand fitted the bill perfectly: both his parents came from old, patrician families (his father was a count) and at 21 he had entered the Church largely because he envied the luxurious life led by its princes. (Although Talleyrand became a bishop, eventually this opportunistic aristocrat had been excommunicated for subordinating the interests of Rome to those of the French Revolution.)

For his part, Talleyrand entirely agreed with Napoleon's assessment of the sort of man the new government required. 'A monarchy', he wrote, 'should be governed by democrats and a republic by aristocrats.'

Talleyrand served Napoleon skilfully, helping him establish himself as 'Consul for life'. Less honourably, he advised the illegal abduction from Germany of the duc d'Enghien, an aristocratic émigré who could have a claim to the French throne. Enghien was brought to Paris and shot, a crime that later Talleyrand tried to expunge from government records. Such services brought him the title of Grand Chamberlain with a salary of half a million francs a year.

Despite his success, Talleyrand slowly began to detach himself from the Emperor, finally resigning his office in 1807, even though Napoleon continued to consult him periodically. But now the wily diplomat began to play both ends against the middle. In 1808 he secretly advised the Russian tsar Alexander I not to ally himself with France, with the oily compliment: '*Le peuple français est civilisé, son souverain ne l'est pas; le souverain de la Russie est civilisé, son peuple ne l'est pas.*' ('The French people are civilised, their sovereign is not; the Russian sovereign is civilised, his people are not.') When Napoleon learned of Talleyrand's duplicity, he raged at him: '*Vous êtes de la merde dans un bas de soie.*' ('You are a shit in silk stockings.')

Even then, Talleyrand had one more important service to perform for the Emperor: in 1810 he helped to arrange his marriage to the Austrian Emperor's daughter Marie-Louise. Two years later, however, when Napoleon lost most of his *Grande Armée* on the retreat from Moscow, Talleyrand connived with the Russians for the restoration of Louis XVIII.

After Napoleon's fall and exile, Talleyrand continued to serve the French government, becoming Foreign Minister once again in the reign of Louis XVIII. In exile on St Helena, the former emperor reflected: 'I have two faults with which to reproach myself regarding Talleyrand. The first was not to have followed the wise advice he gave me; the second was not to have hanged him.'

Also on this day

AD **343: St Nicholas, the bishop who became Santa Claus, dies in Myra, Turkey** * 1882: British novelist Anthony Trollope dies * 1916: David Lloyd George becomes British prime minister * 1917: Finland declares independence from Russia * 1926: French Impressionist Claude Monet dies of lung cancer in Giverny

7 December

Marshal Ney is executed in the gardens of the Palais Luxembourg

1815 Today Michel Ney, one of Napoleon's most illustrious marshals, was shot by firing squad in the gardens of the Palais Luxembourg in Paris.

Ney was a beefy, red-haired, tobacco-chewing man of the people. Although his mother tongue was German (he was of Alsatian origin), he was exactly the kind of soldier Napoleon most valued: brave under fire to the point of recklessness, intimate with his troops and intensely loyal.

Ney's blacksmith father had hoped for a genteel future for his son and had found him a position as apprentice to a lawyer, but at nineteen the adventurous young man ran away to join a regiment of hussars. He had already risen to the rank of general by the time he was 32, when he first met Napoleon.

Promoted to marshal three years later, Ney served the Emperor loyally, participating in the great victories at Jena, Eylau and Friedland and heroically commanding the rearguard in Napoleon's retreat from Moscow, for which the Emperor created him Prince de la Moskowa. He also fought courageously in the crucial defeat at Leipzig, where he was wounded.

When Napoleon was packed off to Elba, Ney allowed fat King Louis XVIII to persuade him to remain a marshal of France and when the ex-emperor escaped, Ney vowed to 'bring him back in a cage'. But on seeing Napoleon again, he returned to his original loyalties, rejoined him for his 100 Days and commanded the left wing at Waterloo. There he had five horses shot from under him and at the battle's end tried to stop the rout, crying to his soldiers: '*Venez voir comment meurt un maréchal de France!*' ('Come and see how a marshal of France can die!')

This reversal of loyalties engendered the special hatred of King Louis. Soon after Waterloo Ney attempted to escape from France but was captured and returned to Paris in chains.

Tried for treason, he was sentenced to death and on the cold, clear morning of 7 December, the bold marshal bravely faced the firing squad. Refusing a bandage over his eyes, he addressed his executioners and gave the order to fire: 'Don't you know that for 25 years I have learned to face both cannonballs and bullets? Come on, soldiers, straight to the heart . . . I have fought a hundred battles for France and not one against her . . . Soldiers Fire!'

Ney died a criminal in the eyes of his government but a hero in the eyes of the French people. In 1853 sculptor François Rude's vigorous statue of the great marshal was placed around the corner from the Luxembourg Gardens in the Avenue de l'Observatoire in front of what today is the Closerie des Lilas, the café so beloved by Ernest Hemingway.

Also on this day

43 BC: Roman statesman Cicero is executed on orders of the triumvirate of Octavian, Mark Antony and Lepidus * 1709: Dutch landscape painter Meindert Hobbema dies in Amsterdam * 1837: Benjamin Disraeli makes his maiden speech in the House of Commons * 1941: Japanese warplanes launch a surprise attack on the American base at Pearl Harbor

8 December

Pius IX promulgates the first new dogma in 291 years

1854 In 1846 the College of Cardinals had elected 54-year-old Giovanni Mastai-Ferretti as Pope, in the hope that his liberalism would be more in tune with realities of the 19th century than the hard conservative beliefs of the other leading contender, Luigi Lambruschini. Selecting the papal name of Pius IX, the new pope turned out to be quite the opposite of what his supporters had anticipated. Shaken by the revolutions around Europe of 1848, when he was chased from Rome for two years, Pius returned an uncompromising reactionary.

Pius made his first controversial decision on this day in 1854, when he promulgated the first new Catholic dogma since the Council of Trent in 1563. In the bull *Ineffabilis Deus* he declared the dogma of the Immaculate Conception of the Virgin, which holds that the Virgin Mary was free from original sin, making this long-held Catholic belief an article of faith.

Christians had celebrated the Immaculate Conception as early as the 5th century and although opposed by luminaries such as St Bernard of Clairvaux and St Thomas Aquinas, by the mid-19th century it had become a widely accepted belief. Now it was confirmed, straight from the throne of St Peter.

Ten years later Pius issued the far more contentious *Syllabus of Errors*, which censured a raft of social trends and movements then developing across Europe. Pius's list of errors included civil marriage, socialism and even non-Catholic education for children. In the words of historian Ivor Burton: 'By thus appearing to put the Church on the side of reaction against the forces of liberalism, science, democracy and tolerance, the *Syllabus* seemed to be part of the retreat of Roman Catholicism from the modern world.' For his reactionary pronouncements Pius became known as 'the scourge of liberalism'.

But just in case any believer should have doubts about his pronouncements, during the first Vatican Council of 1869–70 Pius promulgated yet another new dogma, that of papal infallibility.

Also on this day

65 BC: Roman poet Horace is born * 1542: Mary, Queen of Scots is born at Linlithgow Palace, Scotland * 1793: Louis XV's mistress Madame du Barry is beheaded by French revolutionaries * 1813: Beethoven's Seventh Symphony is performed for the first time, with Beethoven as conductor * 1914: A British force sinks the German cruisers Scharnhorst, Gneisenau, Nürnberg and Leipzig in the Battle of the Falkland Islands * 1941: The US and Great Britain declare war on Japan

9 December

The Index of Forbidden Books

1565 Today died Pius IV, who had served as Pope for just under six years, since his election on Christmas Day 1559. He was a good but unexceptional pope and a cultured one, a patron of Michelangelo. Today he would probably be little remembered except for one action – the creation of a register of books forbidden by the Church, considered necessary to fight emergent Protestantism.

In 1545 a beleaguered Church convened the Council of Trent to map plans for Church reform and the counter-attack against Protestantism. The Council continued intermittently until 1563, but at its conclusion not all the agreed tasks had yet been carried out. Pope Pius was given several assignments for completion, including drafting the catalogue of banned books.

Since at least AD 496, when Pope Gelasius I issued a list of both prohibited and recommended reading, the Church had been periodically proscribing books deemed inimical to the faith or morals of believers. Pius's list, christened *Index Librorum Prohibitorum* (Index of Forbidden Books), was more permanent. It would stay in force, continually amended, for the next 400 years.

The Index came to include works by a virtual Hall of Honour of distinguished writers. Included were obvious opponents of Catholicism such as Calvin, Luther, Erasmus and Descartes. Sexually explicit books also fared badly, ranging from Boccaccio's *Decameron* to Casanova's *Memoirs* to the notorious *Justine* by the Marquis de Sade.

Not too surprisingly, freethinkers such as Montaigne, Voltaire, Rousseau and Thomas Paine were added to the list, and 19th-century French writers seemed to be there en masse with the prohibition of novels by Hugo, Balzac, Dumas, Flaubert and Stendhal.

It took the Vatican only seven years after publication to ban Gibbon's *Decline and Fall of the Roman Empire*, in which the decline of Rome is largely attributed to the enfeebling influence of the Church. (Instead of supporting the army, the Church, claimed Gibbon, caused emperors to 'lavish' funds on priests and nuns, 'useless multitudes of both sexes, who could only plead the merits of abstinence and chastity'.) Other writings took longer to be outlawed: Charles Darwin's great work *On the Origin of Species* was not banned until 1937 – some 78 years after it first appeared.

Not that the Catholic Church had a monopoly on banning books; virtually every country in the world has at some point prohibited works that were deemed too radical, too irreligious or too sexy. D.H. Lawrence's *Lady Chatterley's Lover*, which seems virtually prudish by today's standards, was banned in Great Britain until 1960, but on its first day of sale on 10 November, over 200,000 copies – the entire paperback print-run – were sold in one day, demonstrating the appeal generated by the prohibition.

As so often happens, however, totalitarian states suppress things better than democracies. Nazi Germany and Soviet Russia took the censorship of books to the logical extreme: all books were outlawed unless specifically approved.

In 1948 the Vatican published the final edition of the *Index Librorum Prohibitorum*, prohibiting over 4,000 titles. This list of suppressed books was itself suppressed in June 1966.

Also on this day

1608: John Milton is born * 1641: Flemish portrait painter Anthony Van Dyck dies * 1854: Alfred, Lord Tennyson publishes his poem 'The Charge of the Light Brigade' * **1868: William Gladstone is elected Prime Minister, beginning the first of his four terms**

10 December

Death of the man who gave birth to the world's greatest prize

1896 Aged 63 years, one month and nineteen days, the Swedish scientist Alfred Nobel this day quietly passed away in the beautiful resort of San Remo on the Ligurian coast of Italy. Five years later, the anniversary of his death would be turned into a celebration of excellence.

Nobel had studied chemistry in St Petersburg and had been further educated in Paris and the United States. His family's company in Heleneborg manufactured explosives for use in torpedoes and mines, but when Nobel was 31 his younger brother was killed in an accidental nitroglycerine explosion that destroyed the factory. When the Swedish government refused the company permission to rebuild, Nobel set up a laboratory on a barge, where he started searching for a way to make explosives safer to handle.

At length Nobel discovered that nitroglycerine combined with a chalk-like material called kieselguhr would form a stable substance that could be safely handled until its intended detonation. His invention, which was patented in 1867 as 'Dynamite, or Nobel's Safety Blasting Powder', promptly established his fame and fortune. In the years that followed, he set up factories throughout Europe and his invention was used in the construction of canals, tunnels and railways around the world.

When Nobel died he left $9 million – an enormous sum at the time, to be invested in a fund from which the interest would be 'annually distributed in the form of prizes to those who, during the preceding year, shall have conferred the greatest benefit on mankind'. There were to be awards in chemistry, literature, peace, physics and physiology or medicine. A sixth discipline, economic sciences, was added in 1969.

The first Nobel Prizes were awarded exactly five years after the day Nobel died and to this day are given on the anniversary of his death. Two each of the first year's winners came from Germany and France and one each from Holland and Switzerland. They ranged from still famous men, such as Henri Dunant, who founded the Red Cross and Wilhelm Röntgen, the discoverer of the X-ray, to a now obscure French poet named Sully Prudhomme. Now, over a century later, the Nobel Prize has been awarded to almost 800 people, of whom four have won it twice. Linus Pauling, with the Chemistry Prize in 1954 and the Peace Prize in 1962, is the only person to win in two different categories. Of all prizewinners, a mere 34 have been women. Perhaps the most unfortunate candidate was the Indian statesman Mohandas Gandhi, who was nominated for the Peace Prize five times but never selected.

The United States has dominated the awards, with almost 300 winners, but Great Britain ranks second with almost 100 since Sir Ronald Ross won in 1902 for his work on malaria. The first American winner was President Theodore Roosevelt, who received the Peace Prize in 1906 for his help in settling the Russo–Japanese War. (Other US Presidents honoured with the prize were Woodrow Wilson in 1919 and Jimmy Carter in 2002, for humanitarian rather than presidential achievements.)

In the field of literature, the Nobel Foundation has recognised many outstanding authors but also managed to ignore some of the best. In early 2001 literary critics around the world opined about the finest writers of the 20th century. Almost all agreed that the two greatest were James Joyce and Marcel Proust, neither of whom received a Nobel Prize.

Britain has produced seven prizewinners for literature. The first was Rudyard Kipling in 1907, followed by John Galsworthy (1932), the American-born T.S. Eliot (1948), Bertrand Russell (1950), Sir Winston Churchill (1953), William Golding (1983) and Harold Pinter in 2005 (although many believe Pinter's simian rages against America rather than his literary talents were the primary reason he was chosen by Left-leaning Swedish judges).

In 1930 Sinclair Lewis became the first American to win the Prize for Literature, to be followed by Eugene O'Neill, Pearl Buck, William Faulkner, Ernest Hemingway, John Steinbeck, Saul Bellow (a transplanted Canadian), Isaac Singer (a transplanted Pole), Joseph Brodsky (a transplanted Russian), Czezlaw Miłosz (another transplanted Pole) and Toni Morrison.

Although the Nobel Prize committee has made occasional bizarre choices, perhaps the greatest accolade the organisation itself ever received was in 1937, when Adolf Hitler forbade German citizens to accept Nobel awards.

Also on this day

1475: Florentine painter Paolo Uccello dies * 1848: Louis Napoleon is elected President of France * 1898: Spain and the United States sign a peace treaty to end the Spanish–American War * **1936: Edward VIII abdicates in order to marry the twice-divorced American Wallace Simpson**

11 December

Leo X, the first Medici pope

1475 The expectant mother's dream had been wild and unnerving. She dreamt that she was giving birth not at home but in Florence's great red-domed cathedral and when the baby arrived, it was not in human form but a large and powerful lion. It was a prophetic vision because the child born today was to become master of the Church of Rome and the most powerful man in Italy. He was Giovanni de' Medici, son of the great Lorenzo the Magnificent.

Second son in the family, from birth Giovanni was earmarked for the Church. Through his father's influence he became a cardinal at only sixteen and his family's position and his own hard work enabled him to become Pope as Leo X at only 37.

Short, round-faced and corpulent, Leo ruled well as pontiff, but his foremost interests were temporal. As he commented to his brother Giuliano on his elevation: 'God has given us the papacy. Let's enjoy it.' (Another notable quotation attributed to Leo – *'Quantum nobis nostrique que ea de Christo fabula profuerit, satis est omnibus seculis notum.'* ['All ages can well testify how profitable that fable of Christ has been to us and our company.'] – was probably written by a Protestant satirist.)

Leo became the most powerful man in Italy. As Pope he was ruler of both the Church and the Papal States and, as head of the Medici family after the deaths of his father and brother, he was also de facto ruler of Florence.

Powerful as he was, Leo dreamt of elevating his family yet higher and planned to create a kingdom in central Italy for his younger brother, who unfortunately died before Leo's ideas could be put into effect.

Like many men in command, Leo could be ruthless. When he was 42 and had been Pope for five years, an attempt was made to assassinate him. Discovering several cardinals among the plotters, he had some tried and executed for their crime and one strangled in his prison cell.

Leo spent extravagantly of both his own and the Church's treasures as a great patron of the arts. He was instrumental in furthering the construction of the new St Peter's Basilica, which his predecessor Julius II had started, and commissioned Raphael to create the magnificent series of tapestries that today hang in the Vatican.

Leo died of malaria just ten days before his 46th birthday. In his role as leader of the Catholic faithful, Leo utterly failed in his attempts to stem the Protestant Reformation, but from a cultural viewpoint, he was one of the better Renaissance popes. In commenting on Leo's secular reign, Alexandre Dumas (père) commented: 'Under his pontificate [. . .] crimes temporarily disappeared, replaced by vices; but charming vices, vices in good taste, such as those indulged in by Alcibiades and sung by Catullus.' Sadly for Leo's reputation, today he is best remembered for having excommunicated Martin Luther.

Also on this day

1688: James II flees England for France, never to return * 1803: French composer Hector Berlioz is born * 1941: Adolf Hitler declares war on the United States

12 December

The crusaders' most barbarous victory

1098 For three years since Pope Urban II had urged the faithful to deliver Jerusalem from the Saracens, crusader armies from Europe had trudged towards the Holy Land, killing and dying in equal number. Now two of their leaders were commanding the assault on Ma'arat al-Numan, a fortified town now in Syria, a few miles south of Antioch. One was one-eyed Raimond de Saint-Gilles, comte de Toulouse and marquis de Provence, at 55 the oldest and richest leader among the Christians and the first to heed the Pope's summons.

The second was Bohemond of Otranto, a blue-eyed Norman from southern Italy who was christened 'Mark' but nicknamed 'Bohemund' after a legendary giant because of his height – a contemporary recorded that 'he was so tall in stature that he overtopped the tallest by nearly a cubit [eighteen inches] [. . .] narrow in the waist and loins, with broad shoulders and a deep chest and powerful arms'.

On 3 June 1098 Raimond and Bohemond had conquered the great walled city of Antioch after a difficult siege of 21 months, the city finally falling only when a traitorous Saracen commander allowed Bohemond and his soldiers over a section of the city's walls. The crusaders' triumphant entry was followed by the customary Christian slaughter of its Muslim inhabitants. Even then the citadel held out until, three weeks later, the crusaders annihilated a Muslim relief force outside the city.

Although successful, the siege of Antioch had drained Christian resources. Little food was left; inside the fallen city there was none and crusader raids on the surrounding countryside failed to produce an adequate supply, especially when summer turned to autumn and autumn to winter. Leaving Antioch garrisoned with Christian reserves, Bohemond and Raimond now marched onward to Ma'arat al-Numan, still in enemy hands. By this time many of the invaders were sufffering from starvation, with scant prospect of finding supplies in winter.

Inspired by visions of food, loot and Christian conquest, on this day the crusaders breached Ma'arat's walls and slaughtered some 20,000 Saracens, mostly civilians, even those who had paid Bohemond to spare them. Many of the children were sold to the slave market at Antioch. But at Ma'arat al-Numan, even now no provisions could be found.

What followed was the most barbarous act in all the barbarous crusades. Frantic with hunger, Christian troops turned to cannibalism. One commander reported to Pope Urban: 'A dreadful famine tormented the army in Ma'arat and placed it in the cruel necessity of feeding on the bodies of the Saracens.' Another chronicler wrote (one hopes with some hyperbole), 'our soldiers boiled pagan adults alive in cooking-pots; they impaled children on spits and devoured them grilled'.

These monstrous acts left an indelible stain on the reputation of the crusaders. In some Arabic dialects crusaders are still called 'cannibals' and many Muslim writers have claimed that their heinous behaviour was driven not by starvation but by their belief that Muslims were lower than animals. Even today the shadow of the crusaders' bestial deeds distorts the Muslim view of the Christian West.

Also on this day

1821: Gustave Flaubert is born in Rouen * 1863: Norwegian painter Edvard Munch is born * **1889: English poet Robert Browning dies in Venice** * 1915: Crooner Frank Sinatra is born in Hoboken, New Jersey

13 December

The birth of France's first Bourbon king

1553 The town of Pau lies on the south-western edge of France, practically in Spain, and there, on this cold December morning, a baby boy was born to Jeanne d'Albret and her husband, Antoine de Bourbon. Christened Henri, one day he would become one of his nation's greatest kings.

When Henri was born, he neither cried nor wailed – a sure sign that he was determined to enjoy life in spite of its occasional harshness. The infant's grandfather, Henri d'Albret, King of Navarre, attended the birth and the moment young Henri saw the light of day the elder Henri seized him and rushed to the next room. There he held a cup of Jurançon wine under the baby's nose and rubbed his lips with garlic to give him strength and vitality. Henri clearly seemed to like both, accurately foretelling his love of food and drink throughout his life. Outside, bells pealed and all of Pau rejoiced at Henri's birth, for he was expected one day to become King of Navarre.

But fate had an even greater kingdom in store, for during the next 36 years France would be riven by religious wars as the Valois line of kings came to an end during the successive reigns of three weak, neurotic and childless brothers: François II, Charles IX and Henri III. When a deranged monk stabbed the last of these to death in 1589, the boy born in Pau came to the throne as Henri IV, the first of France's Bourbon kings.

Henri was an exemplary monarch, perhaps France's greatest. He ended the religious wars that had torn the country apart for almost half a century and issued the Edict of Nantes, which effectively gave Protestants freedom of worship. He was famously lenient with the opponents he subdued, commenting: '*La satisfaction qu'on tire de la vengeance ne dure qu'un moment: celle que nous donne la clémence est éternelle.*' ('The satisfaction you get from revenge lasts only a moment; that which we get from being merciful is eternal.')

Henri also did his utmost to help the lot of ordinary Frenchmen, famously declaring: '*Je veux qu'il n'y ait si pauvre paysan en mon royaume qu'il n'ait tous les dimanches sa poule au pot.*' ('I wish that there should not be a peasant in my kingdom so poor that he can't have a chicken in his pot every Sunday.') He renewed a rundown Paris, constructing the Pont Neuf (near which his statue still stands) and building the beautiful Place des Vosges.

Henri's other passion was passion: he had at least eight mistresses and eleven illegitimate children (along with six legitimate ones) and was nicknamed the *Vert Galant* (the Green Galant, i.e. evergreen playboy). No wonder the French have always called him *le bon roi Henri* (the good King Henry).

Also on this day

1466: Florentine sculptor Donatello dies * 1642: Abel Tasman discovers New Zealand * **1784: Dr Samuel Johnson dies in London** * 1937: Nanking falls to the Japanese and the six-week 'Rape of Nanking' begins * 1961: American primitive painter Grandma Moses dies at age 101

14 December

'I have no tenacity for life'

1861 An indefatigable worker, Queen Victoria's consort Prince Albert journeyed to Sandhurst to inspect some new buildings at the Military Academy there, in spite of the chill November damp. This was in character for the man who had created the Great Exhibition ten years before and who had become the Queen's chief adviser, obsessed with doing his duty.

Already feeling ill, Albert insisted on continuing his work and travelled on to Cambridge. Only then did he agree to return to Windsor Castle, tired and feverish.

Although Albert's condition worsened, the royal doctor, one James Clark, assured the Queen that he would soon be well. Albert himself was less sanguine, but had no fear of death. 'I have no tenacity for life', he told the doctor. At 10.45 on the evening of 14 December he murmured, 'Good little woman' to an inconsolable Victoria at his bedside and died holding her hand. He had succumbed to typhoid fever, probably contracted from the faulty drains at Windsor and totally undetected by Dr Clark. He was still only 42.

Victoria was prostrate with grief. 'My life as a happy one is ended!' she wrote to her uncle Leopold, King of Belgium. She never relinquished her widow's weeds in the 40 years that remained to her. In remembrance of her husband she ordered the construction in London of the Albert Memorial in Kensington Gardens, a 175-foot neo-Gothic spire decorated with mosaics and pinnacles. At its centre is a fourteen-foot gilded bronze statue of a seated Albert, looking rather like a deified Egyptian pharaoh. One guidebook today succinctly describes the memorial as 'the epitome of Victorian taste and sentiment'.

Now that Albert was dead, the British public, which for years had scorned him as a 'foreigner', also began to appreciate his many contributions to the nation. As the great British prime minister Benjamin Disraeli wrote: 'With Prince Albert, we have buried our sovereign. This German prince has governed England for 21 years with a wisdom and energy such as none of our kings have ever shown.'

Also on this day

1503: French astrologer Nostradamus is born in Saint-Rémy de Provence * **1799: George Washington dies at Mount Vernon at 67** * 1911: Norwegian Roald Amundsen and his expedition become the first to reach the South Pole, 35 days before Captain Scott

15 December

The world's most successful movie opens in Atlanta

1939 You were lucky in your connections if you had secured one of the 2,500 tickets for this evening's event at the Loew's Grand Theatre. Luckier still if you could afford to pay the $10 price at a time when movie tickets usually went for 50 cents. Most likely, though, you weren't so lucky, so you stood outside on Atlanta's Peachtree Street, along with thousands of others, gazing up at the theatre's facade. There, above a spotlit marquee, a huge medallion enclosed the faces of Vivien Leigh and Clark Gable kissing. And to the left, a sign running down the theatre's front bore these already immortal words: GONE WITH THE WIND.

The scale of the celebration was breathtaking: three days of parties, benefits, parades and balls, culminating in tonight's world premiere. As a U.P. correspondent, Henry McLemore wrote: 'I've covered many a spectacle in many a country – the Olympic Games in Berlin and the Grand Prix in Paris . . . but I have never seen a city give itself so completely to one thing as Atlanta has to the movie premiere of . . . *Gone With the Wind*.'

The movie had been three years in preparation after producer David O. Selznick's prepublication purchase of the film rights to a 1936 novel of the same name. But the novel, over 1,000 pages and written by Margaret Mitchell, an unknown author, soon turned out to be a phenomenal success in its own right, selling a record million copies in its first year and winning the Pulitzer Prize for fiction in 1937. The British critic Gavin Lambert noted the novel's extraordinary impact on women readers and compared it with the 'deep emotional chords' set off by the publication of *Jane Eyre* in England a century earlier.

But if the novel was a success, it was only a prelude to the film's. Selznick, who had already produced movie adaptations of famous novels – *David Copperfield*, *A Tale of Two Cities* and *The Prisoner of Zenda* – now set about casting the new venture. Thousands of letters poured into the studio from the readers around the country with their suggestions of which actors would be perfect for the lead roles of Scarlett, Rhett, Ashley and Melanie. Clark Gable, the overwhelming favourite for Rhett, was available, so Gary Cooper and Ronald Colman were set aside. The search for the right Scarlett was more difficult. Bette Davis, Katherine Hepburn, Norma Shearer, Paulette Goddard and Joan Crawford were among those considered, but the role remained unfilled – even as the burning of Atlanta was being filmed – until Vivien Leigh came to Hollywood determined to have it. She signed with Selznick International on 13 January 1939, the same day two other English actors signed for the remaining leads, Olivia de Havilland as Melanie and Leslie Howard as Ashley.

On MGM's back lot, where all the filming took place, Tara and the neighbouring plantation Twelve Oaks had been built, landscaped and decorated; the city of Atlanta created (for burning); and over 4,000 costumes completed (including 1,200 Confederate uniforms). With producer Selznick taking charge of virtually every detail of the film ('There's only room for one prima donna on this lot and that's me', he said), one director (George Cukor) quit over 'artistic differences'; a second director (Victor Fleming) was hired to replace him; and at one point a third was required to relieve an overworked Fleming.

Filming was set to begin on 26 January. But there was a problem: the dialogue for many key scenes remained unfinished. An army of writers – among them John Van Druten and F. Scott Fitzgerald – had worked to finish the screenplay, but now, with cast, cameras and crews standing idle at a huge daily cost, Selznick paid the veteran writer Ben Hecht $10,000 for two weeks' heavy rewriting. Filming resumed on 1 March and was completed five months later. The total footage ran to some six hours; over the next few months, Selznick and his team whittled it down to a final length of three hours and 45 minutes. Max Steiner was hired to write the score.

And so to Atlanta for this world premiere came many of the film's stars and featured players, including three of the four leads (with the war against Germany declared on 1 September, Leslie Howard had returned to England). They were joined for the occasion by the Hollywood pantheon. In the motorcade that took some of the arriving stars from the airport to their downtown hotel, through streets lined with cheering fans, Vivienne Leigh heard a local band playing 'Dixie': 'They're playing the song from the picture', she exclaimed.

In the new year of 1940, *Gone With the Wind* went into general release around the country, then won a record ten Oscars. The movie was banned in Nazi Germany but played to big crowds in bomb-ravaged London. In the following decades, the film remained as popular as ever with movie-goers. Today, it is estimated to be the biggest box office success in all film history.

And tonight in Atlanta, as the film began and the titles rolled over shots of a gentle Southern landscape, these words flowed onto the screen: 'There was a land of Cavaliers and Cotton fields called the Old South. Look for it only in books, for it is no more than a dream remembered, a Civilisation gone with the wind.'

Also on this day

AD 37: Roman emperor Nero is born * 1675: Dutch painter Jan Vermeer dies * 1734: English painter George Romney is born * 1791: The Bill of Rights' ten amendments become part of the US Constitution * **1809: Napoleon divorces Joséphine because she failed to produce an heir**

> Events written in **boldface** are covered in full in
> *365: Great Stories from History for Every Day of the Year*,
> the first volume in this series.

16 December

The Battle of the Bulge – Hitler's last gamble

1944 At 5.30 this morning Operation *Wacht am Rhein* began its short but violent life with an intense artillery barrage. The German surprise attack, formally the Ardennes campaign but better known as the Battle of the Bulge, would last for six weeks of savage warfare.

For Hitler it was a last-ditch chance to turn the war around. He planned to send his Panzer armies crashing through the weakest point in the Allied line, across the Meuse, on to Brussels and thence Antwerp, the Allies' key supply point. Then, with the British–American coalition thoroughly disrupted, he could face eastward to concentrate his forces against the advancing Russians. His generals said the plan could never succeed, but they had told him exactly the same thing in 1940 and look what had happened then.

The surprise was, of course, an intelligence failure of the first magnitude. Viewed from Allied headquarters in Versailles, the war had looked close to being won. There were some indications of a build-up in the Ardennes, but few people read the signs to mean significant trouble. Code-breaking ULTRA gave no such warnings. No one among the top commanders – not Ike, not Monty, not Brad – believed that Hitler would mount such a desperate attempt to seize the initiative in the west. So, when it began this morning, they were caught flat-footed.

Remarkably, however, as the rampaging Panzers broke through the line and two US divisions crumbled, the Allied commanders regrouped their forces and improvised to meet the threat. They threw reserve units into the line on either side of the Bulge and, with the help of courageous stands at places like St-Vith and Bastogne, slowed and constricted the German attack. When the weather mercifully cleared, Allied airpower joined the fray. By the 25th – Patton described it as 'a clear cold Christmas, lovely weather for killing Germans' – the offensive had been corralled, short of the Meuse.

Even so, much heavy fighting remained and the cost was horrendous all around. By late January, when the Germans had been thrust back and the line restored, the Allies had lost an estimated 81,000 soldiers, killed, wounded or captured. For the Germans the comparable figure was well over 100,000, but, worse, they sustained absolutely crucial losses in tanks, planes and equipment. Now the war would resume its course, once again on Allied terms.

'It is not a disgrace to be defeated', Frederick the Great is supposed to have said. 'It is a disgrace to be surprised.' But the maxim doesn't fit the case of the Battle of the Bulge. Badly surprised though they were, the battlewise Allied forces recovered, fought back and prevailed. At this stage in the war, defeat would have been the real disgrace.

Also on this day

1653: Oliver Cromwell is declared Lord Protector of England * 1770: Ludwig van Beethoven is born in Bonn * **1773: American rebels throw tea carried by English ships into Boston Harbor in what is known as the Boston Tea Party** * 1946: On the Avenue Montaigne in Paris, Christian Dior opens his first showroom

17 December

Death of El Libertador

1830 When he died today at only 47, the great liberator of South America, Simón Bolívar, must have wondered where it had all gone wrong. For 22 years he had fought to free South America from the dead hand of Spain and how he had succeeded! But now, rejected by the very nations he had brought into being, penniless and dying of tuberculosis, he would meet his end not even in his own native Venezuela but in Colombia, in the house of a Spaniard.

Bolívar had been born in Caracas, the scion of a wealthy Creole family. When he was 21 he moved to Paris for three years, where he encountered the enlightened ideas of Europe's great liberal thinkers such as Locke, d'Alembert, Voltaire, Montesquieu and Rousseau. On a trip to Rome he vowed that he would return to liberate his own country.

From the age of 25 Bolívar fought for Venezuela's freedom, leading an expeditionary force that defeated the Spaniards in six pitched battles in what is called the *Campaña Admirable*. In 1813 he entered Caracas and was proclaimed *El Libertador*.

Although Spain retook Caracas and Bolívar had to escape to Jamaica, his vision was always grand: to establish something like a United States of Hispanic America, from Chile and Argentina to Mexico. Returning from exile in 1816, his first point of attack was the Spanish viceroyalty of New Granada (a federation covering most of today's Venezuela, Colombia, Panama and Ecuador). He led a group of only 2,500 men (including a small contingent of British and Irish mercenaries) through impossible terrain to surprise the Spanish expeditionary force, defeating them first at Gámeza and then at the Vargas River, culminating in the Battle of Boyacá, where his soldiers captured 1,800 prisoners, including the Spanish commander. On 17 December 1819, eleven years to the day before his death, Bolívar proclaimed the Republic of Gran Colombia, with himself as president.

Now victory followed victory. In mid-1821 he led a force of 6,500 men in the attack against a Spanish/royalist army at Carabobo on the plains near Caracas. Breaking the enemy line, Bolívar's troops sparked a Spanish panic. At the battle's end there were fifteen Spanish/royalist dead for each of Bolívar's losses. Venezuela was free at last.

Then, in May 1822, a victory at Pichincha secured the liberation of Ecuador. Two years later he marched on Peru, where the Argentinian revolutionary José de San Martín had already chased the Spaniards into the highlands east of Lima. Realising that only Bolívar had the ability and the men to free all of Peru, San Martín left the country and the Peruvian congress elected Bolívar dictator. By December he had crushed all Spanish opposition, his able lieutenant, Antonio José de Sucre, smashing the last Spanish army on the American mainland at

Ayacucho. In August 1825 Bolívar received the ultimate accolade: the Republic of Bolivia, in what had been upper Peru, was created in his honour.

Now that Spain had been comprehensively defeated, Bolívar devoted himself to his grandest dream, that of establishing a pan-Hispanic American confederation of nations, with similar political institutions and perhaps a shared army. But although a revolutionary, Bolívar was at heart dictatorial. While his ideal government was based on an elected assembly, it also included a hereditary upper house and a president for life. His elitist and autocratic policies rubbed other leaders the wrong way – especially since many of them harboured their own ambitions. Venezuelans, Colombians, Ecuadorians and Peruvians vied for power and Peru even invaded Ecuador, while other leaders staged periodic revolts. When Bolívar assumed dictatorial powers to quell the insurrections, mutinous officers tried to assassinate him. He only survived thanks to the quick thinking of his mistress, who convinced him to flee by his bedroom window while she stalled the attackers. (For this she was called *La Libertadora del Libertador*.)

Bolívar could now see that his presence was creating more problems than it was solving and in 1828 he resigned all his offices. Bitter, tubercular and broke (he had used all his wealth to support the revolutions) he left public life. Intending to return to Europe, he stopped with a Spanish friend in La Quinta de San Pedro Alejandrino in Santa Marta, Colombia, where he became too ill to travel. Shortly before he died he commented somewhat histrionically: 'The people send me to the tomb, but I forgive them.' His mortal remains were brought back to Venezuela with great pomp in 1942, to be interred in the National Pantheon in Caracas.

Also on this day

1599: French king Henri IV divorces the notorious Reine Margot after 27 years of marriage, for failing to provide him with an heir * 1843: Charles Dickens's *A Christmas Carol* is published * 1903: At Kitty Hawk, South Carolina, Wilbur Wright takes man's first aeroplane flight, lasting 59 seconds

18 December

The original Éminence Grise

1638 Today in the small town of Rueil about twelve miles west of Paris died 61-year-old Père Joseph, a Capuchin monk who, as secretary to Cardinal Richelieu, was the original 'Grey Eminence' and one of the most powerful – and hated – men in France.

François-Joseph le Clerc du Tremblay was born in Paris to an aristocratic family, inheriting the title of baron de Maffliers. He joined the Capuchin order at 22 and was assigned to the court of Henri IV, where he soon became known for his brilliance and his rhetoric. The king's mistress Gabrielle d'Estrées called him 'the Cicero of France and of our time'. When he was ordained in 1604 he became known simply as Père Joseph, devoting himself to the Church and especially to the conversion of heretics.

A decade later, however, Père Joseph reached the true turning point in his life. Asked to reform a nunnery at Fontevrault, he called on the help of the young Bishop of Luçon, Armand du Plessis de Richelieu. There the two men established a friendship and alliance that would last until Père Joseph's death.

In 1628, Richelieu, by now a cardinal, became first minister of France and at his side as confidant and adviser was Père Joseph. In a country where Louis XIII was an absolute monarch, even Richelieu's power came 'by the grace of the King' and he was known as *L'Éminence Rouge* (The Red Eminence) due to the colour of his robes. Père Joseph had even less official power than Richelieu but became notorious as a shadowy figure behind the cardinal, dressed in Capuchin grey, thereby earning for himself the sobriquet of *L'Éminence Grise* (The Grey Eminence), a phrase still with us today denoting hidden and unaccountable power behind the scenes.

While Richelieu's goal was to gain European supremacy for France (that is, principally over the Habsburgs of the Holy Roman Empire), Père Joseph's great ambitions were to crush Protestant heresy at home and to organise a European crusade against the Turks.

What suited the aspirations of both Richelieu and Père Joseph was to place France at the centre of the Thirty Years War. The cardinal wanted the Habsburgs brought to heel so that France could dominate Europe, while the monk wanted them subservient because, unless forced, they would never join France on crusade. Thus Catholic France supported the Protestant nations against the Catholic Habsburgs.

The Thirty Years War was the most destructive in European history prior to the First World War and many thought Père Joseph had intentionally prolonged it in his efforts to bring the Habsburgs to their knees. France did emerge as Europe's strongest nation, but no crusade against the Turks ever took place – and in any case, by the war's end, both Richelieu and Père Joseph were long dead.

While prosecuting the war, Père Joseph had negotiated an alliance with Bernard of Wiemar, who, in 1638, was besieging the enemy fortress of Brisach on the upper Rhine. But in December of that year the monk was struck down by 'apoplexy' – i.e. probably a stroke. The (probably apocryphal) story goes that Richelieu was determined to give his fading friend a boost in morale. Entering Père Joseph's bedroom waving a letter, he leaned over the dying man and whispered: '*Père Joseph, Père Joseph, Brisach est à nous!*' ('Père Joseph, Père Joseph, Brisach is ours!') even though Richelieu himself was still unaware that Brisach had indeed fallen the previous day.

So died the *Éminence Grise*. Because of the horrors of the war in which he involved his country, and his draconian attitude towards Protestants, he had lived feared by his countrymen and died despised by them.

Also on this day

1737: Violin maker Antonio Stradivari dies in Cremona * 1892: In St Petersburg, the Russian Imperial Ballet performs Tchaikovsky's *The Nutcracker* for the first time * 1916: The Battle of Verdun ends with the French and Germans each having suffered more than 330,000 killed and wounded in ten months of fighting * **1915: American president Woodrow Wilson marries Edith Galt, who will cover up his incapacity to govern when he suffers a stroke** * 1941: 610 American defenders surrender to 5,000 attacking Japanese on the island of Guam after a three-hour battle

19 December

Poor Richard's Almanac *first appears*

1732 That almanacs have existed for centuries is shown by the origins of the word, which derives from *al manâkh*, meaning 'calendar of the heavens' in Spanish Arabic, probably coined before 1492, when the Spaniards completed their conquest of the Moors. But for most Americans the most famous almanac is *Poor Richard's*, which first appeared on this day, written, published and printed by that unique American polymath, Benjamin Franklin.

Franklin first published his famous almanac under the pen-name of Richard Saunders. In it, the eponymous Poor Richard was portrayed as an earnest and somewhat pious farmer who spouts a seemingly unending stream of trenchant and witty aphorisms, to many of which we have become so accustomed that we no longer remember they were originally Franklin's. Many were wise and rather worthy, such as:

> Early to bed and early to rise, makes a man healthy, wealthy and wise.
> God helps those who help themselves.
> Little strokes fell great oaks.

Occasionally Franklin penned a maxim that reflected his belief in America's principles of equality, such as: 'A ploughman on his legs is higher than a gentleman on his knees.' But *Poor Richard's* was also peppered with more irreverent observations such as:

> There's more old drunkards than old doctors.
> A countryman between two lawyers is like a fish between two cats.
> Neither a fortress nor a maid will hold out long after they begin to
>   parley.
> Three removes is as bad as a fire.
> He's a fool that makes his doctor his heir.

Occasionally, Franklin would include an aphoristic couplet:

You cannot pluck roses without fear of thorns
Nor enjoy a fair wife without danger of horns.

Some seem remarkably up to date, none more than: 'There are no gains, without pains.'
Franklin published *Poor Richard's Almanac* until 1757.

Also on this day

1154: Henry II is crowned King of England, founding the Plantagenet dynasty that ruled for over 300 years * 1562: Huguenots and the Catholics fight the first battle of the French Wars of Religion at the Battle of Dreux * 1783: William Pitt becomes Britain's youngest prime minister at age 24 * 1848: English novelist Emily Brontë dies * 1851: English Romantic landscape painter J.M.W. Turner dies * 1915: French *chanteuse* Edith Piaf ('*Non, je ne regrette rien*') is born in Paris

20 December

The Bonapartes are back

1848 Today, in the 'Year of Revolution' in Europe, Prince Louis Napoleon took his oath as President of France, restoring the Bonapartes to power after a hiatus of 33 years.

Louis had been born to the purple, son of Napoleon's brother, also named Louis, who at the time was King of Holland. But Napoleon's fall in 1815 had driven the family into exile and young Louis had spent most of the next 30 years wandering around Europe, with periodic attempts to return to France.

At the beginning of 1848 Louis was a 39-year-old bachelor, a man of only medium height but with an imposing appearance: high, intellectual forehead, piercing eyes, a twirled and waxed moustache and a four-inch goatee. Something of a *roué* (a rake or debauchee), he was highly intelligent and an accomplished linguist, speaking German, Spanish, English and Italian, as well as the French which he pronounced with a slight German accent due to his early schooling in Augsberg. He was living in exile in England, as King Louis-Philippe wanted no Bonaparte threat in France.

But on 24 February a popular uprising forced Louis-Philippe to flee the country, bringing the monarchy to an end. Three days later Louis Napoleon made a brief foray to Paris, but the provisional government peremptorily ordered him to leave the country within 24 hours, so he scuttled back to London to wait for the next opportunity.

At the end of June Paris exploded into mayhem, as unemployed workers set up stone barricades in the streets and for four days fired on all who opposed them. Troops were soon in position, returning fire. Then an army general was shot and killed trying to negotiate with the workers, soon to be followed by the

Archbishop of Paris. Finally the rebellion was brutally suppressed by General Louis-Eugène Cavaignac, for which act he became known as 'the butcher of June'.

By-elections were scheduled for September and Louis Napoleon, scenting new opportunity, put his name forward from his exile in England. Elected in five departments, he once again embarked for France, the government no longer able to force him to remain abroad. He immediately started campaigning for the presidential election scheduled for 10 December.

Louis was fortunate in that, while Louis-Philippe had permitted only a token 200,000 people to vote, the government that replaced him extended the franchise to some 8 million citizens. Most of these knew little about politics and less about most of the candidates, but the one thing they recognised was the name Napoleon. Louis swept to victory with 5.5 million votes versus 1.5 million for his closest competitor. On this day ten days later he was sworn in as President of France.

Most men would see such an overwhelming triumph as the apogee of their careers. Not Louis Napoleon. Three years later he violated his presidential oath by staging a *coup d'état* and making himself dictator.

Also on this day

AD 69: **Roman Emperor Vitellius is murdered by supporters of Vespasian, who becomes Emperor** * 1860: South Carolina is the first Southern state to secede from the United States, the first step towards civil war * 1894: Australian prime minister Sir Robert Menzies is born in Jeporet, Victoria * 1915: The ANZACS, Australian and New Zealand forces with British troops, are evacuated from Gallipoli

21 December

'So we beat on, boats against the current, borne back ceaselessly into the past'

1940 It is an irony of literary history that an author whose works are now regarded among the very best that America has ever produced, and have become staples of the English curriculum in high schools and colleges, died a failure, not only as a man, a husband and a father but also, it seemed, as a writer. This was the fate of F. Scott Fitzgerald, who suffered a fatal heart attack on this date, in the Hollywood apartment of the gossip columnist Sheilah Graham, the solace of his final years. He was only 44 years old – an alcoholic and virtually forgotten. His royalty statement for the previous year had amounted to $33.

Yet this was the very same man who had burst upon the American scene in 1920 with the publication of *This Side of Paradise*, a novel that ushered in the Jazz Age and captured the imagination of a generation seeking liberation from the mores of its elders. Fitzgerald was, as an observer put it, 'a kind of king of

American youth'. And his wife Zelda, once described as 'a young goddess of spring', became its flapper-queen.

Their hedonistic, fast-living lifestyle was glamorous: an endless round of 'gleaming, dazzling parties' held in fashionable spots along the East Coast, or abroad in places like Paris, Rome, Capri and the French Riviera, and always in the company of the social and artistic avant-garde of two continents. In his novels and short stories, Fitzgerald faithfully recounted the life he and Zelda led, for he was the chronicler, as well as the symbol, of his age. Ultimately, their life proved destructive of them both. 'First you take a drink,' he wrote, 'then the drink takes a drink, then the drink takes you.'

It was also very expensive. Even in his heyday, the 1920s, the sales of Fitzgerald's novels never came close to producing for him the income needed to support their desperate extravagances. The work for which he is best remembered, *The Great Gatsby*, published in 1925, sold fewer than 23,000 copies in his lifetime. So to pay the bills, he produced a steady stream of short stories and novellas for publication in the mass-circulation magazines of the day, like the *Saturday Evening Post*, which for a while paid him $4,000 a story. The titles suggest the spirit of the times: 'Bernice Bobs Her Hair', 'The Diamond as Big as the Ritz' and 'The Rich Boy'.

But the 1929 Crash and the depression that followed put an end to the Jazz Age and with it everything Fitzgerald had hoped to achieve. His generation – the 'Lost Generation' as Gertrude Stein christened it – had grown up: the new one had very different tastes. The last book to come out in his lifetime was *Taps at Reveille*, a collection of stories, published in 1935. Meanwhile, as early as 1930, Zelda had begun to suffer nervous breakdowns, the cause of which was eventually diagnosed as schizophrenia. Now, much of her time was spent in sanatoriums and the cost almost bankrupted Fitzgerald. In debt to his publisher and his literary agent, he left the East Coast for Hollywood in 1937 to try his hand at screen writing for MGM. In three years of work, his lone credit, shared with another writer, was for the script of the 1938 film *Three Comrades*. After his first heart attack, in November, 1940, Sheilah Graham installed him in her apartment.

Immediately after his death, his body was laid out for viewing in a Hollywood funeral parlour. Among the few who came by was his friend, the tart-tongued writer and critic Dorothy Parker, who said, 'The poor son of a bitch', echoing words uttered at Jay Gatsby's funeral in *The Great Gatsby*.

Fitzgerald died a writer without an audience, but there were a few – friends, admirers, fellow writers – who discerned what was of value behind the sad waste of a once-promising life. The eventual recognition of his place in American literature began slowly, starting in 1941 with Scribner's' publication of his half-finished novel, *The Last Tycoon*, issued in a volume that also contained some short stories and, in a second effort, *The Great Gatsby*.

By the 1950s, a gathering force of critics, editors and biographers – among them, Edmund Wilson, Arthur Mizener and Dorothy Parker – had succeeded in awakening widespread public interest in Fitzgerald and his writing.

And so it was that the success of these efforts bore out the vision the author himself had once expressed, with the airy confidence of a young man at the very beginning of his career: 'An author ought to write for the youth of his own generation, the critics of the next and the schoolmasters of ever afterwards.'

Also on this day

1192: While returning from crusade in the Holy Land, Richard the Lionheart is captured near Vienna by Austrian Duke Leopold * 1375: Italian writer Giovanni Boccaccio dies in Certaldo * 1804: Benjamin Disraeli is born in London * 1879: Joseph Stalin (Ioseb Dzhugashvili) is born in Gori, Georgia * 1958: Charles de Gaulle is elected President of the French Fifth Republic

22 December

At the Tsar's mercy

1849 The scene is Semenovsky Square in St Petersburg, a bitterly cold morning, fresh snow on the ground, the sun just up, troops formed in the centre of the square, a crowd of civilians gathering farther off. Presently, fifteen men are brought into the square in carriages. Soldiers herd them to a raised stand. The prisoners do not know why they are here, only that they have been held in prison since the spring on suspicion of their involvement and perhaps conspiracy in 'an overall movement for change and destruction'. Now, at last, they may learn how long each will have to serve at hard labour.

An official begins reading the sentences. But, to the growing consternation of all, each sentence is the same: death by firing squad, to be carried out this morning, by the approval of Tsar Nicholas.

While peasant blouses and caps are handed out as death shrouds to the stunned prisoners, a priest addresses them: 'Brothers! Before dying one must confess [. . .] I call you to confession.' Only one man comes forward. A firing squad is drawn up, ready for duty. Guards tie the first three men to stakes, pulling the prisoners' caps down over their eyes. The firing squad takes aim.

Suddenly a drum roll signals retreat. The rifles are lowered. A horseman rides into the square. He announces the Tsar's pardon for the condemned men, then proceeds to read their revised sentences, now commuted from death to penal servitude.

The prisoners are thunderstruck, confused, astonished, joyful; one of the three men at the stakes goes irretrievably insane. Now they are led back to the carriages for return to prison and the preparations for their exile and the beginning of their true sentences.

What the prisoners never knew is that the Tsar's commutation of their sentences was not an act of mercy but one of careful calculation. Their crimes involved membership of a political group, the Petrashevsky circle, which discussed and espoused – and, according to some, meant to bring about – a variety of radical solutions to issues like government censorship, individual rights, serfdom and the monarchy. At a time when similar issues had already convulsed Europe in the bloody revolutions of the year just past, 1848, these matters were far too dangerous for circulation within autocratic Russia. So Nicholas ordered the mock executions carried out for the shock they would produce in the victims and then the dramatic reprieves as a sign of imperial clemency, for which each man would stand humbly, eternally grateful.

One of those saved was a 28-year-old writer, Fyodor Dostoyevsky. Years later, his second wife Anna recorded the description he gave her of this fateful day: 'I remember standing on Semenovsky Square among my condemned comrades. As I watched the preparations taking place, I knew that I had no more than five minutes left to live. But those minutes seemed years – decades – so much time, it seemed still lay ahead of me! They had already dressed us in our death robes and divided us into groups of three, I was number eight in the third row. The first three had been tied to the execution posts. In two or three minutes both rows would be shot and then it would be our turn.

'My God, my God, how I wanted to live. How precious my life seemed to me, how much that was fine and good I might have accomplished. My whole past life came back to me then and the way I had sometimes misused it; and I so longed to experience it all over again and live for a long, long time. Suddenly I heard the drums sounding retreat and I took heart.'

For his crimes – they included reading aloud material that was critical of Russia's social-political structure and being insufficiently repentant of his radical views – Dostoyevsky spent ten years in Siberian exile, four of them at hard labour in a remote prison camp, another six in compulsory military service. Only in 1859 was he permitted to return to European Russia, regain his rights as a citizen and begin his life anew as a writer. Behind him lay a decade of life- and mind-altering punishment. Ahead were his greatest novels, *Crime and Punishment, The Idiot, The Possessed* and *The Brothers Karamazov*. And for most of his remaining years – he died in 1881 – Dostoyevsky remained under the surveillance of the Tsar's secret police.

Also on this day

1135: Stephen of Blois is crowned King of England * 1858: Giacomo Puccini is born in Lucca * **1793: Napoleon Bonaparte becomes a general after directing the artillery at the Siege of Toulon** * 1894: French officer Alfred Dreyfus is convicted of espionage and sent to Devil's Island * 1895: German physicist Wilhelm Röntgen makes the first X-ray, of his wife's hand

23 December

Henri III murders the duc de Guise

1588 Cultivated and intelligent – but weak, neurotic and effeminate – France's Henri III had spent most of his fourteen-year reign dominated by his appalling mother, Catherine de' Medici. The great issue of the day was France's Wars of Religion, which had festered since 1562 as fervent Catholics of the so-called Holy League had endeavoured to repress all Protestantism, while French Huguenots bitterly fought back with no holds barred. Heading the Holy League was the country's most powerful noble, the muscular and athletic Henri, duc de Guise, called *Le Balafré* – The Scarred – because his face had been distinctively scarred by a war wound.

More interested in his *mignons* than in the subtleties of religious difference, the King had tried to soothe Catholics by cracking down on Protestantism, but his ineffectual efforts were taken by the Holy League to signify a lack of proper zeal and in May 1588 they had tried to depose him, instigating an uprising in Paris that chased him from the city.

For Henri the situation was intolerable. He resolved to rid himself of the Holy League's leader, the duc de Guise, but Guise's position was so strong that he could not be arrested. The only solution was assassination.

In December the court was at the beautiful château of Blois on the Loire river, the meeting place for the Estates-General, the assembly of representatives of the French nobility, clergy and the so-called Third Estate – the ordinary people. The King knew the hated Guise was sure to attend. On the morning of the 23rd Henri summoned twenty hirelings to his bedroom, accompanied by two priests who were to pray for a successful murder. The King then sent word for Guise to join him and hid behind a curtain. When the duc entered the room, eight of the murderers threw themselves at him, swords drawn.

The immensely strong Guise threw off several assailants but at length fell to the floor, pierced by a dozen sword strokes. King Henri then stepped out from behind the curtain and kicked the dead man in the face, exclaiming: 'My God, he's big! He looks even bigger dead than alive.'

Henri then rushed downstairs proudly to announce his deed to his mother, but she, only too conscious of her son's precarious hold on power, replied: 'God grant you have not made yourself king of nothing.' Ignoring her concern and untroubled by conscience, Henri left her to go to the Chapel of St Calais to hear Mass.

The following day Henri ordered the assassination of Guise's brother Louis, the Cardinal of Lorraine and had their bodies burnt and the ashes thrown into the Loire.

Also on this day

1790: Decipherer of the Rosetta Stone Jean-François Champollion is born in Figeac * 1823: 'A Visit from Saint Nicholas' (''Twas the night before Christmas . . . ')

by Prof. Clement Clark Moore is first published in the *Troy Sentinel* * 1834: English economist and demographer Robert Malthus dies * 1948: Japanese general and prime minister Hideki Tojo and six other military leaders are hanged for crimes against humanity * 1953: Soviet secret police chief Lavrenti Beria is shot for treason

24 December

The birth of England's worst king

1167 Today at Beaumont near Oxford was born John Plantagenet, son of England's King Henry II and his remarkable Queen, Eleanor of Aquitaine, who was 45 at John's birth. Although born in England, his first language was French. He grew up to be plump but strong, 5 feet 6 inches tall. While he was young he had curly dark hair, but later he went partially bald.

John was the fourth of four royal sons, the only one without an *apanage* (a prerogative or grant of land from the King) in his parents' extensive territories in France. Hence he was dubbed *Jean Sans Terre* (John Lackland) by his father.

In 1199 John succeeded to the throne of England on the death of his brother Richard the Lionheart, but within seven years he lost Normandy, Maine, Anjou and parts of Poitou to Philip Augustus of France.

John's rule in England was no more successful than that in his French possessions, and still today he is considered England's worst king. 'Selfish, cruel, shameless, cynical, lustful, dishonourable and utterly false', is the way Thomas Costain describes him. J.C. Holt calls him 'suspicious, vengeful and treacherous'.

He betrayed his father when Richard the Lionheart rose against him, then conspired with Philip Augustus to keep Richard in prison when Richard had been captured in Austria, returning from crusade. He murdered his nephew Arthur. He came into such bitter conflict with the Pope that all of England was placed under interdict for over five years. He is also notorious for plundering the Jews for their money, ordering their teeth extracted one by one until they revealed where they had hidden their hoarded gold.

Every cloud must have a silver lining and in the case of John it was the Magna Carta, the great charter of civil liberties that John's rebellious barons forced him to sign in 1215.

John ruled England for seventeen years and died of dysentery at the age of 48.

Also on this day

1524: Portuguese navigator Vasco da Gama dies in Cochin, Kerala, India * 1822: English poet Matthew Arnold is born * 1865: The original Ku Klux Klan is formed in Pulaski, Tennessee * **1888: At Arles in Provence, Vincent van Gogh cuts off his own earlobe to give to a prostitute**

25 December

The origins of some good old Christmas traditions

AD **336 (or thereabouts)** There seems to be some considerable doubt concerning when Christmas was first celebrated on 25 December. Some sources put it at 336, others at 354 and yet others contend that the pope and saint-to-be Julius I fixed the date, but his pontificate lasted from 337 to 352.

What all agree on is that the Church selected 25 December because, not knowing Jesus' actual birthday, it was canny enough to choose a time when pagans had traditionally celebrated the winter solstice.

In pagan Rome this meant the Saturnalia, a seven-day holiday starting on 17 December, when all business was suspended, executions postponed and gifts exchanged. During this *natalis solis invicti* (birthday of the unconquered sun) slaves were given temporary freedom and were served by their masters.

In Scotland, on the shortest day of the year, the Druids worshipped the Sun god, hoping to ensure his return, and used holly as a symbol of eternal life. Meanwhile, in Scandinavia, the *midvinterblot* (midwinter blood) was a bit more grisly, as it featured animal and human sacrifices. (The Scandinavians, however, originated one of Christmas's more pleasurable customs, kissing under the mistletoe, a plant that Norsemen thought special to Freya, the goddess of love.)

Early Germanic tribes went one better than the Scandinavians by celebrating the winter solstice by butchering slaves and male animals and hanging them (or parts of them) on the branches of trees, thus anticipating the Christmas tree ornaments of today. At the beginning of the 8th century, St Boniface (actually an Englishman named Winfrid) went to Germany to convert the pagan tribes there. According to legend, one day he came upon a group about to slaughter a child to adorn an oak tree in honour of the god Donner. Enraged, he chopped it down (or, alternatively, knocked it down with a single punch), only to have a pine tree spring from its roots, which he took to be a sign from God. Along with Christianising the Germans, St Boniface urged them to continue the ritual embellishment of trees at Christmas, but with fruit and nuts rather than body parts and to use cone-shaped pine trees because their triangular shape represented the Trinity.

The earliest certain references to the modern Christmas tree come from Riga, in Latvia, in 1510, and Alsace in 1521 (although hagiographers credit it to Martin Luther, who on a Christmas Eve at about the same time decorated a fir tree with candles to simulate the stars in God's Heaven). On the night before Christmas Germans would set up a 'Tree of Paradise' (Genesis 2:9), an evergreen festooned with apples representing the Garden of Eden. Then nuts, dates, pretzels and paper flowers were added, which children were allowed to collect the following morning. It is primarily to the Germans that we owe the spread of the Christmas tree.

German settlers probably introduced the Christmas tree to America as early as the 17th century, although some claim that Hessian mercenaries in the pay of the English brought it with them during the American Revolution. (There is even a tale that in 1776 these soldiers, far from home, abandoned their posts on Christmas night to celebrate around a candlelit tree, only to be surprised and routed at dawn the next morning when George Washington crossed the Delaware and attacked Trenton.)

It wasn't until 1837 that the Christmas tree was introduced into France, but once again credit goes to the Germans. The German princess Hélène de Mecklembourg-Schwerin brought the custom with her when she married Ferdinand-Philippe d'Orléans, duc d'Orléans, the son of King Louis-Philippe. (The French already enjoyed another Christmas institution, the *bûche de Noël* [Yule log]. Originally this was literally a log burned in the village church at Christmas, so that the poor could warm themselves. It was supposed to be a reminder that baby Jesus had only the 'breath of mules' to keep him warm when he was born in a stable. Now a chocolate-and-chestnut cake shaped like a log has replaced the real thing. The English phrase 'Yule log' derives from *giuli*, the Anglo-Saxon name for a two-month period roughly corresponding to January and February when important feasts were held.)

Great Britain, too, owes its tradition of Christmas trees to Germany. They first appeared there under George I, who came from Hanover, but the convention failed to catch on because of his unpopularity. But at Christmas in 1841 another German, Prince Albert, gave one to Queen Victoria and the Christmas tree became a national institution.

Also on this day

AD 496: French King Clovis is converted to Christianity * **800: Charlemagne is crowned in St Peter's in Rome** * 1066: William the Conqueror is crowned in Westminster Abbey * 1642: Sir Isaac Newton is born in Woolsthorpe near Grantham * 1883: Maurice Utrillo is born in Paris * 1899: Screen icon Humphrey Bogart is born in New York

26 December

The Battered Bastards of Bastogne

1944 Just before 5 pm, with night fallen, five American tanks reached the outskirts of the French town of Bastogne. Their timely arrival, at the head of a relief column bringing supplies and reinforcements to the town's beleaguered defenders, meant that Bastogne would continue the vital role it had played over the past week: clogging the throat of the great German counter-attack known as the Battle of the Bulge.

Ten days earlier the Germans had smashed through the Allied line in the

Ardennes to begin Hitler's last-ditch effort to avoid defeat in Western Europe. Three Panzer armies were poised to pour through the gap, heading for Antwerp and a stalemate of the Allies. But at the shoulders of the gap, the Allied lines held, thus limiting the space through which the Germans could rush their armour westward.

And in the middle of that space lay Bastogne, the principal road junction in the Ardennes region. As long as it remained in Allied hands, Bastogne forced the Germans to move around it on a circuitous set of secondary, often unpaved roads, while denying them all but one of the main east–west routes so crucial for the support of their fast-moving offensive.

In their eagerness to press on towards the Meuse, the German Panzer divisions left Bastogne behind for the infantry divisions to take care of. Surrounded, supplied by airdrops and under heavy attack were some 18,000 American troops, mostly of the 101st Airborne Division, brought up to help defend the position after the German offensive commenced. On the 22nd the Germans sent in a team under a white flag bearing a message: 'There is only one possibility of saving the encircled USA troops from annihilation. That is the honourable surrender of the encircled town.' This occasioned the famous reply from the 101st's commander, 'Nuts!' a term for which the German party required clarification.

By now, elements of General George Patton's Third Army were making headway towards Bastogne. And so it was that by the 26th, tanks of the 4th Armored Division pushed through a corridor to reach the town.

Meanwhile, the German offensive had been stopped short of the Meuse, brought to a halt by stiff Allied resistance, aided by snow, fog, challenging terrain and the lack of supplies needed to sustain the advance. Frustrated with the results and furious with the 'incompetence' of his commanders, *der Führer* ordered Bastogne taken. For Hitler, as one historian observed: 'The capture of Bastogne provided a convenient replacement for the lost grail of Antwerp.' Now the heaviest fighting began, as some 100,000 German troops were concentrated around the town. Moving against them, Patton's divisions pressed northward, widening the Bastogne corridor into a salient, a bulge into the Bulge. By 4 January it was evident to all that Bastogne would hold and the great Ardennes battle would end as an Allied victory.

On 19 January, with the battle well over, General Patton and his staff visited the scene of the airborne division's heroic stand. There they encountered a large sign that read: 'Bastogne: the Bastion of the Battered Bastards of the 101st.'

Also on this day

1776: Having secretly crossed the Delaware River on Christmas night, George Washington defeats Hessian mercenaries fighting for the English at the Battle of Trenton * 1890: German archaeologist and finder of 'Troy' Heinrich Schliemann dies * 1891: American expatriate novelist Henry Miller is born * 1893: Dictator, mass murderer and founding father of the People's Republic of China Mao Tse-tung is born

27 December

An attempt to kill a king

1594 Today King Henri IV's love of women almost cost him his life.

A seducer of accomplishment, Henri had numerous mistresses, but his favourite was the ravishing 21-year-old Gabrielle d'Estrées, celebrated in French history and song as *La Belle Gabrielle*. Of noble birth, she had first been kept by Roger de Saint-Lary, who introduced her to the King. She became his paramour in 1591 when she was just nineteen. Henri fell deeply in love, but Gabrielle used her position to amass a fortune, while occasionally taking less royal, if younger, lovers (Henri was twenty years her senior).

Returning to Paris from a royal tour of Normandy, today the King hurried impatiently to visit his beloved Gabrielle at her *hôtel particulier* in the rue Saint-Honoré. He found her surrounded by a large group of courtiers, among whom was a 19-year-old Catholic extremist named Jean Chastel, a teacher at the Jesuit college at Clermont. There other fanatical monks had persuaded him that, since the Pope had not yet recognised Henri's abjuration of Protestantism made seventeen months before, killing the King would be a service to God.

As the King bent down to raise up two courtiers on their knees before him, Chastel struck at him with a knife, missing his throat but wounding him in the lip and knocking out a tooth. Henri leapt back, bleeding, and his bodyguards instantly dragged his assailant to the ground.

Henri soon recovered from the attack and Gabrielle remained his adored mistress. The scheming Jesuits, however, fared less well, as Henri banished the entire order from France. A sterner fate awaited Jean Chastel, who was taken to the place de Grève (now the place de l'Hôtel-de-Ville) and torn apart by four wild horses for his attempt to kill the King.

Also on this day

1822: French chemist and microbiologist Louis Pasteur is born * **1831: HMS *Beagle*, with Charles Darwin on board, departs from Plymouth** * 1901: Singer and actress Marlene Dietrich is born in Berlin * 1927: Leon Trotsky is expelled from the Communist Party in Russia

28 December

The death of an ill-starred queen

1694 Today died one of history's most ill-starred queens, Mary II of Great Britain.

The daughter of James II, Mary had been bundled off to Holland at fifteen to marry her cousin, the Dutch *Stadtholder* (roughly, head of state) William of Orange, who was twelve years her senior and whom she found repulsive. Reportedly she wept throughout the ceremony.

Although, over time, Mary came to love him, William soon publicly took a mistress, Elizabeth Villiers, who had been one of Mary's own ladies-in-waiting and whose mother had been her governess. This liaison, which the subservient Mary was powerless to stop, continued until Mary's death.

Unable to hold the affection of her husband, Mary hoped for children, but her unhappiness was only compounded by three pregnancies ending in miscarriage or stillbirth. (England's Stuart sovereigns had problems producing heirs; three of the six – Mary, her sister Anne I and her grandfather Charles II – had no legitimate children.)

Brought up a Protestant at the insistence of her grandfather, when she was 27 Mary was forced to choose between her very Catholic father and her Protestant husband during the so-called 'Glorious Revolution' (really a *coup d'état*) of 1688. Protestant rebels chased James into exile abroad and invited Mary and William to become Queen and King. Torn between loyalty to her father, devotion to her husband and a sincere belief in the Protestant faith, Mary agreed, but when some argued that only she should become monarch, she steadfastly refused, insisting that she 'would be no more but [William's] wife' and that she and William would share power. Although Mary was still upset by her father's predicament, when the new sovereigns made their triumphant entry into London, William ordered her to greet the crowds with a cheerful face, something that caused her father to damn her for disloyalty, further distressing the well-meaning new queen.

During her five and a half years as Queen of England Mary found she really preferred her smaller life in Holland and continued to be troubled by her estrangement from her father, now living in exile in France. She left the ruling to William, except when he was away on the Continent fighting Catholics. During those periods, however, she was a conscientious monarch. Once again, however, she came into conflict with her own family. First she imprisoned her uncle for scheming to restore James to the throne, and then, in 1692, she virtually broke with her sister Anne when she disgraced the future Duke of Marlborough for secretly corresponding with James. (Anne was totally in thrall to Marlborough's wife Sarah.)

Then, at the end of 1694, this luckless queen contracted smallpox and died at only 32. During their seventeen years of marriage William had often paid scant attention to his wife, but now he realised he had come to love her and was overwhelmed by her death. Now that she was gone, he at last ended his liaison with Elizabeth Villiers and, too late for Mary to hear, mourned that 'from being the happiest' he was 'now going to be the miserablest creature on earth'.

29 December

The Jameson raid on Johannesburg

1895 Towards sunset on this Sunday evening, Dr Leander Starr Jameson, right-hand man of the great British empire builder Cecil Rhodes, led 600 armed and mounted men on a daring raid. Their destination was Johannesburg, 200 miles away in the Boer republic of Transvaal, their mission – a wild imperial gamble in the spirit of Wolfe, Clive or Gordon – to make Britain supreme in all of South Africa.

The Jameson raid was a disaster and failed utterly in its purpose of over-throwing the anti-British Boer government of President Paul Kruger. Jameson and his men were captured miles short of Johannesburg and carted away to jail. Found on them were incriminating copies of telegrams that linked the raiders with Rhodes, the Prime Minister of the Cape Colony, and with his superiors at the Colonial Office in London.

It was a terrible foreign policy embarrassment for Great Britain. In another age, CNN would have had a field day. In London and Cape Town, there were official investigations and public trials. The involvement of unnamed higher-ups was suspected. It was the Iran–Contra affair of its day: there was a cover-up and deals were made. A Colonel North figure in the Colonial Office was found, who testified that he had never informed his chiefs of his dealings with the now thoroughly discredited Rhodes and the plotters of the raid. Rhodes was forced to resign.

Like John Brown's abortive 1859 raid on Harper's Ferry before the American Civil War, the Jameson raid succeeded in hastening conflict. Winston Churchill called it 'the herald, if not indeed the progenitor of the South African War'. War came in 1899 and lasted two and a half years at a frightful cost to Boers and Britons. It resulted in the Boer Republic's incorporation into the British Empire, Rhodes's intention from the beginning. Jameson spent fifteen months in a British jail for leading the raid, but after the war he got Rhodes's old job as Prime Minister of the Cape Colony. Cecil Rhodes died in 1902, reputation in ruins, but wealth intact. He is remembered today not for his imperial mischief in South Africa but for the scholarships that bear his name.

Also on this day

1170: The 'turbulent priest' Archbishop Thomas Becket is murdered in Canterbury Cathedral * 1721: Louis XV's mistress Madame de Pompadour (née Jeanne-Antoinette Poisson) is born in Paris * 1809: William Gladstone is born in London * 1825: French painter Jacques-Louis David dies * 1890: At Wounded Knee, South Dakota, while losing 30 dead, American soldiers massacre more than 200 Sioux men, women and children during the last major conflict between American Indians and US troops

30 December

The House of Savoy takes the throne of Spain

1870 Spain had the Habsburgs for 184 years and then came the Bourbons, who have now held the throne off and on for three centuries and still counting with the current reign of Juan Carlos. But in these 500 years there have also been two republics, the Nationalist regime of Francisco Franco and, less well known, two periods of monarchy neither Hapsburg nor Bourbon. The first, from 1808 to 1813, was that of Joseph Bonaparte, the puppet-king of his brother Napoleon. The second was that of Amadeo of the House of Savoy, who arrived in Spain today to take up his kingly duties.

In 1868 Queen Isabella II (a Bourbon, or Borbòn, as the Spanish would say) was chased into exile for her political incompetence, reactionary rule and scandalous private life. The key architect in her ouster was General Juan Prim, who now headed the hunt for a royal replacement, grumbling that searching for a king for a democracy was like looking for an atheist in heaven.

Prim's first choice was Prussia's Prince Leopold of Hohenzollern-Sigmaringen, but when his nomination helped spark off the Franco-Prussian War, Prim settled on a less contentious candidate, Amadeo, the 25-year-old Duke of Aosta, son of Victor Emmanuel, King of Sardinia–Piedmont (and future King of Italy). On 16 November 1870 the Spanish Cortes affirmed Prim's preference and the following month the new king came to his new country.

Unfortunately for Amadeo, on 27 December, just three days before his arrival in Madrid, Prim was mortally wounded by an assassin and died on the same day that Amadeo entered the city.

Amadeo took up his duties, then, with good intentions, no patron and a heavy heart. Speaking no Spanish, he was treated as the foreigner that he was and totally isolated, the target of repeated assassination attempts. Worse, rebellion was everywhere. In Cuba, nationalists revolted against Spanish rule and Spain itself was in chaos. Republicans and Carlists (an extreme reactionary and clerical political movement) both staged uprisings, and even the Spanish artillery went on strike.

Disgusted, on 12 February 1873 Amadeo declared to the Cortes that Spain was ungovernable and abdicated the throne to return to Italy for the remaining seventeen years of his life. At ten o'clock that same night Spain was declared a republic (but only nineteen months later the Bourbons were returned to power).

With the exception of poor King Luis in the 18th century, who had died of smallpox after a reign of only seven months, Amadeo holds the Spanish record for short spells in power – King of Spain for just two years and 88 days.

It seems that Amadeo's family may have had abdication it its genes: 68 years later his grandson, Tomislav II of Croatia, abdicated after 29 months of powerless kingship, and his distant cousin, Victor Emmanuel III of Italy, abdicated in 1946.

Also on this day

1865: British writer Rudyard Kipling is born in Bombay * **1916: Prince Feliks Yussoupov assassinates Grigori Rasputin in St Petersburg** * 1922: The USSR is established * 1924: American astronomer Edwin Hubble announces the existence of other galactic systems

31 December

The birth of the first papal Borgia

1378 His father Domingo was a prosperous landholder and gentleman farmer who lived in the small town of Játiva, near Valencia in Catalonian Spain. It was there that Alfonso de Borja was born on the last day of 1378. Who would have predicted that he would be the first luminary in a famous dynasty of the Church?

In Spain Alfonso rose to the rank of Bishop of Valencia, hoping but not expecting to go further. But in 1455, when he was 77, the rivalry between the Orsini and Colonna families in Rome reached such a pitch that the College of Cardinals elected him Pope, expecting a short reign that could serve as a cooling-off period between the two Roman factions.

Indeed, Alfonso, or Pope Calixtus III as he now was, lived only another three years, his pontificate noted only for proclaiming the innocence of Joan of Arc, who had been burnt at the stake in 1431. But during his stay in the Vatican he brought large numbers of his Catalan relations to Rome, among whom was his nephew Roderigo, whom he created cardinal and named as generalissimo of the papal army.

Roderigo, who Italianised the family name to Borgia, rose to the papal throne in 1492. During his eleven years as pontiff he supported a series of mistresses, fathered the notorious Cesare and Lucrezia and set new standards for nepotism.

Despite the corruption of Roderigo and his offspring, the Borgias continued to play a leading role in the Church. Roderigo's great-grandson Francisco de Borja became the third general of the Jesuits and eventually was canonised, while his great-great-grandson, Giovanni Panfili, became Pope Innocent X in 1644.

After Innocent, the Borgia religious bloodline seemed to be wearing thin, but in 1799 there was one last family thrust for Church prominence when Cardinal Stefano Borgia was very nearly elected Pope.

Also on this day

AD 192: The mad Roman emperor Commodus is assassinated * 1384: English theologian and promoter of the first translation of the Bible into English John Wycliffe dies of a stroke * **1720: Bonnie Prince Charlie is born in Rome** * 1869: Henri Matisse is born in Le Cateau, Picardy * 1877: French painter Gustave Courbet dies at La Tour de Péliz, Switzerland * 1880: American general and father of the Marshall Plan George Marshall is born

Index

1812, War of 18 June 1812; 10 September 1813; 13 September 1814

Abu al-Hasan, Sultan of Morocco 30 October 1340

Acre, Fall of 20 August 1191; 9 October 1192

Actium, Battle of 23 September 63 BC

Adams, President John Quincy 29 March 1790; 22 March 1820

Adams, Samuel 19 April 1775

Addison, Joseph 22 September 1776

Adrian IV, Pope (Nicholas Breakspeare) 18 June 1155

Adwa, Battle of 1 March 1896

Aeneas 21 April 753 BC

Agincourt, Battle of 23 April 303

Alaric 24 August 410

Alaska, US purchase from Russia 30 March 1867

Albert III of Monaco 8 January 1297

Albert, Prince of Saxe-Coburg-Gotha (consort of Queen Victoria) 22 January 1901; 14 December 1861

Albigensian Crusade 14 July 1208

Alexander I of Russia 6 December 1797; 12 January 1833

Alexander II of Russia 2 December 1805; 22 July 1832; 3 March 1861

Alexander VI, Pope (Roderigo Borgia) (Borja) 31 December 1378; 29 February 1468; 11 August 1492; 18 August 1503; 11 March 1507; 23 June 1519

Alfonso III of Portugal 16 February 1279

Alfonso IV of Portugal (the Brave) 30 October 1340

Alfonso XI of Castile and Leon (the Just) 30 October 1340

Alfonso XIII of Spain 14 January 1858; 31 May 1906

Alfred the Great, King of Wessex, then of England 26 October 899

Allen, Ethen 10 January 1738

Allia River, Battle of 16 July 390 BC

Almayer's Folly 25 April 1895

Amadeo I of Spain 30 December 1870

Amaterasu 11 February 660 BC; 29 April 1901

Ambrose, Saint 4 April 397

American Civil War 29 March 1790; 16 March 1802; 12 February 1809; 5 August 1861; 9 March 1862; 12 June 1862; 12 July 1862; 5 November 1862; 1 January 1863; 23 November 1863; 18 May 1864; 15 November 1864: 9 April 1865; 25 June 1876; 12 November 1880; 2 July 1881

American Revolution 10 January 1738: 18 April 1775; 19 April 1775; 27 February 1776; 22 September 1776; 16 August 1777; 11 September 1777; 19 September 1777; 26 September 1820; 20 May 1834

Anafesto, Doge Paolo Lucio 1 May 1797

Anglo-Saxon Chronicle 26 October 899

Anne I of Great Britain (Stuart) 19 June 1566; 6 February 1665; 28 December 1694; 10 June 1704

Anne of Austria (wife of Louis XIII of France) 29 January 1630; 19 November 1703

Antarctica 18 November 1820

Antietam, Battle of 5 November 1862; 1 January 1863

Apollinaire, Guillaume 2 June 1740

Appomattox Courthouse 9 April 1865; 25 June 1876; 7 January 1942

Aquinas, Saint Thomas 8 December 1854

Arbroath, Declaration of 6 April 1320

Armada, Spanish 27 August 1635

Armstrong, Lance 19 July 1903

Arnold, General Benedict 10 January 1738; 19 September 1777; 16 March 1802

425

Louis XV of France 16 September 1824;
16 May 1770
Louis XVI of France 16 May 1770;
19 September 1777; 4 June 1783;
20 June 1791; 10 August 1792;
21 September 1792; 6 November 1793;
15 October 1795; 14 May 1796;
16 September 1824; 20 May 1834
Louis XVII of France 16 September 1824
Louis XVIII of France 17 March 1787;
6 December 1797; 7 December 1815;
16 September 1824; 17 May 1838
Louis, Joe 3 August 1936
Louisiana Purchase 30 April 1803;
2 November 1795
Louis-Philippe of France 6 November
1793; 20 May 1834; 17 May 1838;
8 October 1840; 24 February 1848;
13 March 1848; 20 December 1848;
28 August 1850
Loyola, St Ignatius (Ignacio de Loyola)
15 August 1534; 27 October 1553
Ludendorff, General Erich 1 August
1934
Lunéville, Treaty of 2 March 1835
Lupercalia 2 February AD 1; 14 February
270
Luther, Martin 25 December 366;
30 August 1483; 24 May 1543;
3 December 1545; 18 February 1546;
24 April 1547; 9 December 1565
Lützen Battle of 16 November 1632

Ma'arat al-Numan, conquest of
12 December 1098
MacArthur, General Douglas 12 July
1862; 14 September 1950; 7 January
1942
Macdonald, Flora 27 February 1776
MacDonald, General Jacques 11 April
1814
**Mac-Mahon, Marshal Marie-Edme-
Patrice-Maurice, duc de Magenta**
1 September 1870; 18 March 1871
**Macrinus (Caesar Marcus Opellius
Severus Macrinus Augustus),
Roman emperor** 8 April 217
Madison, President James 18 June 1812;
20 May 1834

Magna Carta 26 October 899;
24 December 1167; 19 October 1216
Maillart, Jean 31 July 1358
**Maintenon, Mme Françoise de,
mistress then wife of Louis XIV**
9 June 1660
Malenkov, Georgy 5 March 1953
Mallarmé, Stéphane 7 October 1849
Malory, Sir Thomas 14 March 1471
Malplaquet, Battle of 10 June 1704
Mancini, Olympia 22 February 1680
Mandell, Richard D. 3 August 1936
Manet, Edouard 23 January 1832
Manin, Lodovico, Doge of Venice
1 May 1797
Mann, Thomas 7 October 1849
Mantuan Succession, War of the
29 January 1630
Manuel II of Portugal 1 February 1908
Marat, Jean Paul 20 June 1791;
15 October 1795
Marcel, Etienne 31 July 1358
Marcus Aurelius, Roman emperor
16 October 1809
Marcus Furius Camillus 16 July 390 BC
Marengo, Battle of 14 June 1800;
2 March 1835
**Margaret of Anjou, Queen of England
(wife of Henry VI)** 22 May 1455;
4 March 1461
Margot, Queen (wife of Henri IV) See
Marguerite de Valois
**Marguerite of Provence, wife of Louis
IX** 25 August 1270
Marguerite de Valois, wife of Henri IV
17 December 1599; 27 March 1615
**Maria Theresa, Archduchess of Austria
and Queen of Hungary and Bohemia**
10 February 1741; 20 February 1790
Marie Antoinette, Queen of France
16 May 1770; 4 June 1783; 20 June 1791;
2 March 1835
**Marie-Louise (wife of Napoleon I)
(Maria Louise Leopoldina Franziska
Theresia Josepha Luzia von
Habsburg-Lothringen, Duchess of
Parma, Piacenza and Guastalla)**
6 December 1797; 1 April 1810; 22 July
1832; 2 March 1835

Montaigne, Michel Eyquem, seigneur de 28 February 1533; 9 December 1565
Montand, Yves 6 October 1889
Montcalm, General Louis Joseph 14 September 1950
Monte Carlo 8 January 1297
Monte Cassino monastery 9 November 1494
Montespan, Mme Françoise-Athénaïs de (mistress of Louis XIV) 9 June 1660; 22 February 1680; 9 August 1757
Montez, Lola 12 October 1810
Montfaucon gallows 30 January 1278
Montfort, Simon de 14 July 1223
Montfort, Simon de, Earl of Leicester 1 October 1207
Montgolfier, Jacques-Étienne & Joseph-Michel 4 June 1783
Montgomery, General Bernard Law 16 December 1944
Moore's Creek, Battle of 27 February 1776
Morgan, Captain Henry 2 January 1669
Morley, Christopher 29 October 1740
Morrison, Toni 10 December 1896
Morte d'Arthur, Le 14 March 1471
Mortimer, Roger de 13 November 1312; 24 September 1326; 27 November 1330; 7 November 1783
Moscow, Napoleon's retreat from 6 December 1797; 7 December 1815
Moulin Rouge 6 October 1889
Mozart, Wolfgang Amadeus 17 October 1849
Mühlberg, Battle of 24 April 1547
Murat, Joachim, Marshal and King of Naples 11 April 1814
Murphy, Audie 12 July 1862
Mussolini, Benito 2 June 1740; 1 May 1797; 29 July 1883
Mussorgsky, Modest 21 February 1598
Mutiny on the Bounty 9 September 1754

Nagumo, Admiral 3 June 1942
Nantes, Edict of 13 December 1553; 13 August 1598; 14 May 1643
Napier, Sir Charles 17 February 1843
Napoleon I of France (Napoleon Bonaparte) 9 May 1386; 8 January 1297; 30 November 1700; 5 December 1757; 22 April 1766; 1 September 1785; 10 August 1792; 1 May 1797; 6 December 1797; 21 July 1798; 21 November 1799; 7 February 1800; 14 June 1800; 4 January 1802; 30 April 1803; 21 March 1804; 2 December 1804; 20 April 1808; 16 October 1809; 1 April 1810; 18 June 1812; 11 April 1814; 7 March 1815; 7 December 1815; 16 September 1824; 8 August 1827; 22 July 1832; 12 January 1833; 2 March 1835; 17 May 1838; 8 October 1840; 2 December 1851
Napoleon III of France (Louis Napoleon Bonaparte) 4 January 1802; 20 April 1808; 23 January 1832; 22 July 1832; 25 May 1846; 20 December 1848; 2 December 1851; 21 November 1852; 14 January 1858; 14 January 1858; 24 June 1859; 20 January 1860; 13 July 1870; 1 September 1870; 19 January 1927
Napoleon, Joseph (brother of Napoleon I), King of Spain 11 April 1814
Napoleon, Louis (brother of Napoleon I), King of Holland 4 January 1802
Narva, Battle of 30 November 1700
Nasser, Gamal Abdel 25 November 1875; 2 September 1898
Naval Academy, US 2 November 1795; 1 June 1813
Necker, Jacques 27 April 1737
Neipperg, Adam Adalbert, Count von 1 April 1810
Neipperg, Field Marshal Phillip von 10 February 1741
Nelson, Admiral Horatio 4 October 1586; 24 July 1797
Ney, Marshal Michel 11 April 1814; 7 December 1815; 16 September 1824
Nice, integration into France 24 June 1859; 20 January 1860
Nicholas I of Russia 22 December 1849
Nietzsche, Friedrich 7 October 1849; 28 August 1850; 3 January 1889
Nika Revolt 14 November 565
Nimitz, Admiral Chester 4 May 1942; 3 June 1942

440